Herring Girl

A Oneworld Book

First published in North America, Great Britain &
Australia by Oneworld Publications, 2014

A CIP record for this title is available from the British Library

Hardback ISBN 978-1-78074-492-6
Paperback (Export Edition) ISBN 978-1-78074-538-1
ebook ISBN 978-1-78074-493-3

Text designed and typeset by Tetragon, London
Printed and bound by CPI Group (UK) Ltd, Croydon CR0 4YY

Oneworld Publications
10 Bloomsbury Street
London WC1B 3SR
England

In memory of my father,
Roy Picton Taylor (1926–2012)

PROLOGUE

1898

I'm on the high bank, staring out to the Tyne's mouth, where the slow brown river meets the hickety sea – for it's canny breezy today, with white spume blowing off the tops of the waves. And from every direction, here come the luggers racing home, red sails bellying with the gold of the sun and their holds brimming with silver fish. And that's just how I feel: full of gold and silver and racingness.

For he's out there somewhere, on his way home. And when they've moored up and cranned out, and he's lain down for his bit sleep in the afternoon, that's where I'm going straight after work's finished. Never mind my tea, never mind folk talking, today all I'm doing is throwing off my oilies and running to my lad.

I mean to kiss him awake and I don't care who sees me opening his door. For aren't we promised now, and can't a promised lass kiss her lad awake from his bit sleep? And later – oh, later! – we'll go wandering out to where the wyn's thick and tight-knit, and the sun's warmed the long grass, and find a hollow to lay out my shawl. There's a fluttering in my innards just to think of it.

And all the while I'm checking the sails as they swoop in, for the *Osprey*'s dark mizzen. Oh, and there she is! Tacking out along the far shore, swift as a bird, for if there's a breeze Da likes to ride it in, and save on tug fees, and scoff at the crews being towed home, tame as lapdogs on a lead. She's too far off for me to make out the lads on deck or what they're about, but if she's the *Osprey* – and she is, she is! – then my lad's aboard somewhere, feeling this same sun on his face, this same breeze that's whipping my skirt round my ankles.

So now I'm walking along the top bank, to Nater's Stairs, with my eyes fixed on that dark mizzen, watching her sails fold like a butterfly's wings as she comes about, then belly out again till she's aiming straight as a red arrow for the quay. And I'm thinking, if I run I can meet her, and watch her tie up, and who cares if I'm late to the farlane for once? For this is the first day of my life as his promised lass, and I want to taste every last bit of it.

I'm running now, and my shawl's coming adrift, and my scarf loosening so my hair's fairly whipping round my face. And here's Nater's Stairs thronging with folk, so I must dodge round them, and grab at my scarf to stop it falling, and unhook my shawl where it's snagged on a cran, here, and again here, and say sorry, sorry, as I gallop past, taking one step, two steps at a time, and trying not to look down, for I'll lose my balance if I do, and stumble, and be delayed and I mustn't be delayed for I've a boat to meet…

CHAPTER ONE

2007

Ben stares at his face in the mirror, just stares, trying to see who's in there. He feels like his body's a coat that belongs to someone else. He's put it on by mistake and now he can't get it off. It feels like at school when you write down the wrong answer in pencil, then rub it out and write over it, but the dent of the old writing's still there underneath – and it was *right all along*.

He's been awake for hours waiting for Dad to leave, listening to him moving around the big open-plan flat: boiling the kettle, slamming the fridge, the dishwasher, the tumble dryer. Then finally, finally, the clomp of his boots down the hall to Ben's room, and the slap of his hand on the door: 'Hey, lazybones! That's me off now. I've left a couple of twenties on the table. Remember and call Nana if you need anything.'

The front door bangs shut and Ben waits a minute before unlocking his door. Still in pyjamas, he pads around the flat in bare feet to check Dad's really gone – which is daft, because of course he has. Plus Dad couldn't lurk quietly if he tried. Still, Ben checks every room just to make sure, then puts the chain on the front door in case he pops back for something or the cleaners turn up on the wrong day.

Dad's away on the boat all this week, which means Ben's got loads of time to do what he's decided. Nana's supposed to drop in later with his tea, but that still leaves the whole day.

He goes back into his room and locks the door again. It's second nature now: push it shut, lean on it a moment with his eyes closed, turn the key, then drape his dressing-gown over the keyhole. Not that Dad would ever crouch down to peer through, plus the key's in the way, but it makes Ben feel safer.

After burrowing to the back of his wardrobe, he tugs out the old sports bag he had in Year 5. He keeps it hidden under a load of other stuff: his new sports bag, all his trainers and flip-flops, odd bits of diving gear. He heaves it onto the bed and unzips it. There's a couple of old Newcastle shirts on top, in case Dad breaks in to his room – he never would, but still. Underneath the shirts are all his private things, in separate washbags: his make-up and nail varnishes, his jewellery, all his hair stuff. Poor old Lily the Pink's squashed in there too, during the day. Dad stuffed her in a bin liner for Oxfam four years ago, but Ben swapped her for a cushion at the last minute.

He tugs Lily out and sits her on his pillow. Then he takes a deep breath and starts pulling out the clothes he's going to wear.

'Nothing too feminine for your first outing,' it said on the website. 'You want to blend in, not draw attention to yourself.' So he's got a pair of denim cut-offs and one of those pink peaked caps that show your hair, like a baseball cap with the top missing; and a short-sleeved stripy pink T-shirt. He was going to wear one of the little strappy tops he's bought, but he was worried people would be able to tell, somehow, just by looking at his shoulders, that he was a boy.

He's been buying clothes for months now, from that big all-night supermarket on the Coast Road: just one or two things at a time, making sure he always goes to a different checkout girl. And he always buys a girl's birthday card too, so it looks like he's getting pressies, plus normal boy's socks or something, and crisps and that, so the checkout girls never batted an eyelid.

He thought for ages about shoes, because trainers always make his feet look enormous, even though they're still only a five. In the end he got some of those open-toed sandals with Velcro fastenings, that could be for a boy or a girl. He was going to get the pink, but then he remembered what the website said and got the blue instead.

When everything's ready he goes into his en-suite and has a shower to wash away being a boy – at least that's what it feels like. He uses one of the fruit shampoos he keeps hidden in the sports bag, with the matching conditioner and shower gel; then blow-dries his hair with styling mousse, so it's a bit feathery in the front where he put in some blonde streaks last week.

Dad's always trying to get Ben's hair clipped short like his, but Ben can't stand the macho Bruce Willis look he goes in for. What he really wants is hair long enough to do in different styles, but Dad would never go for that. Plus he'd get serious grief at school if he started turning up with long hair. So in the end they compromised. Dad says he can have it long as he likes at the front, provided there's what he calls 'a proper barber job' at the back.

Ben's practised this feathery style loads of times – it's the one that makes him look most like a girl – but he's always had to brush it out before anyone sees it. And wipe off his mascara and his careful layer of glittery eyeshadow. But this time he leaves it all on, then goes back into the bedroom where his outfit is laid out neatly on the bed.

He unfolds some new cotton knickers and pulls them on. He's been planning this for months, but now he's actually doing it, he feels sick and a bit shivery. The knickers are covered with tiny pink hearts. Standing sideways, he checks out his reflection in the mirror. Do they hold him flat enough? He's not sure. Maybe. But what if someone looks closely? Shivering properly now, and feeling like he might actually throw up, he grabs his old grey hoodie and trackie bottoms off the floor. He'll wait till he feels better, he decides. Have some breakfast first, maybe; see what's on TV. Be a normal boy for a bit longer.

Except he's not a normal boy, is he? Not inside, not deep down. And he can't put it off any longer. Dropping the hoodie back on the floor, he reaches for the stripy pink T-shirt.

When he's ready, he opens the front door a crack, and listens for the chuntering of the lift, or footsteps tramping up the stairwell. The flat's on the top floor, and the last thing he wants is to bump into one of the neighbours. He's decided to go down by the stairs so he can nip back up and hide if he has to, because with the lift there's always a risk of the door sliding open and coming face to face with someone he knows.

He goes down one flight at a time, peering nervously along each landing. By the time he reaches the bottom his heart's thudding so hard he feels sick again. Tilting the cap down a bit more over his face, he pushes out through the big security door then walks quickly along the street – not looking left or right, hardly daring to breathe – until he rounds the corner, when he starts to relax a bit. Away from the flat it's less likely that someone will connect the little blonde girl in the stripy T-shirt with 'Big Paul's lad from Collingwood Mansions'. But now there's another problem. What do girls do with their hands? It feels awkward to leave them just hanging by his side. And his feet seem all wrong walking along, too big and clumsy – do girls take smaller steps? – so he's sure anyone looking properly will realize straight away.

The website said for your first time out you should go where nobody knows you, so he's off to this mega shopping centre on the other side of the river, which people flock to from all over and there's loads of Norwegian-looking couples and crowds of women with Scots accents trailing round with bulging carrier bags. He goes the back way to the station, where it's mostly boarded-up pubs and charity shops and he's less likely to meet someone from school – though all his friends are off on holiday now, which is why he decided on this week in the first place.

They won't let you go in for the operation unless you've been 'passing' as a girl for up to two years, which means he's got to start now, before puberty sets in. Well, he should have started ages ago, really, because he's finished Year 7 and some of the lads in Year 9 have already got spots and smudges of dark hair round their mouths. But he's read there are some hormones you can get that stop puberty from happening – which is something else he's got to worry about, because how is he ever going to get hold of those without Dad finding out? Plus they stunt your growth, and probably have all other kinds of side effects, but that has to be better than a hairy chest and Adam's apple.

On the train he grabs a corner seat. His palms are sweating; he wishes he had a magazine or sunglasses to hide behind. He'd forgotten how everyone always stares at you on the train, because there's nothing else to do. He's the only young girl on her own, which makes it worse somehow. There's a gang of noisy girls down the carriage a bit, who keep glancing over at him; and an old bloke opposite grinning over the top of his newspaper. What are they looking at?

Ben gets out his phone, for something to do, and switches it on. It beeps straight away. There's a message from Nana asking if he's fine with a fish supper for his tea, which is weird because she never usually bothers what he wants; and another one from Dad just saying hi, which means he's probably been on to Nana.

Seeing the girls giggling together gives Ben a real yearning to be in a gang like that, and go for sleepovers and nail parties, and try out all the milkshakes and fancy lattes in different coffee shops. And he starts wondering where he could meet some girls to hang out with who don't already know him from school. But everywhere he thinks of – like a girls' footie team, or dance lessons, or swimming – means going in changing rooms. Which means sharing cubicles and stripping off, which he'll never get away with. Which brings him back to the operation. Everything he thinks of always brings him back to the operation.

He's been to this shopping centre loads of times with Nana, so he knows where all the different shops are – she's always dragging him around, buying him puffa jackets he never wears and boring jumpers and navy slippers.

He goes to an accessories boutique first to try on the sunglasses, and chooses some big ones with pinky-brown glass and gold frames, and a little gold heart on a chain. There are loads of girls his age wandering around, rotating the stands of earrings and hair stuff. Nobody stares at him, which is a relief, and the assistant's really friendly and pops a free watch ring in his bag when he goes to pay.

On his way out, he catches sight of this young blonde girl coming out of the shop opposite: petite and pretty in denim cut-offs and a pink visor just like his. When he realizes he's looking at his own reflection, a fantastic buzzy feeling zips straight through him, from his toes to his throat, that makes him want to laugh out loud. He's doing it! He's really doing it!

The buzzy feeling takes him into Markie's, past the men's and the children's bits, and up the escalator to the lingerie department. He's seen it in the distance, when Nana's been getting her pop socks: a massive maze of underwear stands, with flesh-coloured models in coloured tights or matching bra-and-panty sets on stands towering above the displays. Now he's going to see it close up. He wants to buy a bra to stuff with cotton wool: one of those little skimpy ones he's glimpsed through the tops of the girls at school.

At the teen bras bit it's mostly mams flicking through the bras, and their daughters lurking behind them looking embarrassed. Ben starts to feel sort of yearning again, because this is another girlie thing he's never done: going shopping with your mam for your first bra. He leafs through the little packets, trying to make sense of the labels. What does 30AA mean? Is it bigger or smaller than 32A? He takes a 30AA out of its packet and opens it out like he's seen one of the mams doing. Would it fit him? He has no idea.

There's another girl, about his age, looking at the bras on a neighbouring stand. She's scowling like she hates the sight of them, and she's on her own so Ben thinks maybe her mam's forced her go and buy a bra by herself, or maybe her mam's dead, or divorced, so she's got no option. Which makes him feel sorry for her, like they're both in the same boat, so when she looks up he forgets about not drawing attention and smiles at her.

She sighs. 'God, I hate this. How are you supposed to choose?'

'Do you understand the sizes?' Ben asks, then worries that he sounds stupid – *then* worries that his voice sounds like a boy's.

'The numbers are for your chest and the letters are the cup size.' She glances at Ben's front. 'You'll be an AA like me,' she says. 'I was going to leave it, but everyone else in my class has started, so—'

Ben can hardly believe it: he's talking to a girl who thinks he's a girl! 'I don't know if I'm a 32 or a 30,' he says. Most of the bras seem to be 30 or 32, so he feels on pretty safe ground.

'Do you need some help there?' An old lady in a Markie's uniform comes up behind them. 'We've got a free measuring service if you want.' She beams down at them.

'No, I'm all right,' Ben mutters, backing away.

'Go on,' urges the girl. 'Mam says they're brilliant. They find out what size you need, then bring you loads of different styles to try on.'

'I was only looking,' says Ben.

'Why don't you both come with me?' suggests the old lady. 'I'll see if there's a fitter free.'

Ben looks at the girl. She's smiling and turning, expecting him to follow her. And he can see it all suddenly, how it could be. The two of them in the same cubicle, snaking their arms through the lacy straps and adjusting them. Trying all the different styles and comparing them. Then maybe going for a milkshake at McDonald's.

The Markie's lady puts her hand on his shoulder to steer him towards the changing rooms, which is the one place he can't ever go – *ever* – and it hits him like a punch to the stomach, how fucking impossible this is, trying to 'pass as a girl', when he can't even manage it for two hours, let alone two years.

'Sorry,' he says. 'I can't—I mean, it's not—' And he turns away, his eyes stinging with tears, and rushes off, then breaks into a run, and doesn't stop running till he's out of the shop.

CHAPTER TWO

2007

Mary is smoking a Gitanes – a pungent French 'gypsy lady' – her chosen brand of cigarettes for over two decades, though she suspects she'd smoke grass-cuttings if nothing else was available. She often jokes that she took up psychotherapy because the analytic hour only lasts fifty minutes, which is the exact limit of her nicotine withdrawal period.

She smokes outside – she's punctilious about that – so the ashtray is a large flower pot of sand beside the garden bench. When it rains she shelters in the porch, blowing fragrant smoke out through the open door. But she feels foolish and undignified doing this, like some callow clerk shivering in the lee of his office block, urgently sucking in and flicking ash in his tea break. (Do people still have tea breaks? She has no idea. Is 'clerk' still a viable job description?) So as soon as the rain ceases, she returns to the wet bench, on a blue towel she keeps precisely for this purpose.

She fears she may smell of smoke – how can she not? – but she hopes that this airing to which she subjects herself forty times a day ameliorates the worst of it. It helps that the house is situated in a bracing position overlooking the mouth of the Tyne, where on a rough day you can literally taste the salt spray on the wind. Which brings its own set of problems, of course – because Mary is deeply afraid of the sea. So every time she opens her front door to light up, and spies the enormous grey expanse of the North Sea in the distance, she comes face to face with her phobia. The karmic irony of the situation is not lost on her.

It's her own fault, of course: for choosing a house with a sea view. But she was unaccountably drawn to the building despite her better judgement as soon as she saw it – and she's learnt in her fifty years not to argue with unaccountable impulses.

She stubs out her cigarette and returns indoors to her consulting room. She was due to see Mrs Hargreaves at eleven and Mr Barnard at two, but she's just cancelled them both, claiming a sudden migraine: which is a blatant lie, and something she heartily disapproves of. But how can she concentrate on clients with this occupying her mind? 'This' being the two envelopes that came in the post this morning: one a much-recycled brown Jiffy bag addressed in shaky biro capitals; the other slim and white, professionally typed.

She extracts a single folded sheet from the white envelope and rereads it, though she already knows every word by heart. It's from the editors of the *British Journal of Clinical Psychology* rejecting a paper she's submitted for publication.

> We have now received the peer reviews of your manuscript, 'Past Life Experience as an Heuristic Principle in Psychopathology', and we are sorry to tell you that, on balance, they are not favourable. We therefore have no choice but to decline publication.

The fact that it's a pro forma letter makes it more humiliating, somehow. But it's the contents of the jiffy bag that have really destabilized her: three closely typed pages – plus a copy of her own manuscript, liberally underlined and annotated in bold spiky writing. The package has been sent to her by Karleen Bryce – Mary's old supervisor and one of her staunchest academic supporters – who was on the committee that rejected the paper.

'Mary dear, I'm so sorry about this,' wrote Karleen in her covering note. 'I argued till I was blue in the face, but the others wouldn't be swayed. Anyway, I'm enclosing a copy of Hester's report. Totally against the rules, of course, but I thought you ought to see what you're up against. I'm here, as ever, if you want a chat. *A lutta continua!* K.'

Sighing, Mary sits down at her desk and leafs through her rejected manuscript again. She knew she was going out on a limb with this paper – about how certain clinical phenomena, such as phobias, false memory syndrome and schizophrenic hallucinations, might be the result of past life memories intruding. But she had been so tentative in her conclusions – *some* instances in *some* patients was all she was suggesting. And she had supported every hypothesis with reputable experimental research, along with evidence she herself had painstakingly amassed during twenty-five years of helping clients access memories of their past lives as a way of resolving their current neuroses. Her plan had been to use the paper to spark a debate in the literature, which she would then incorporate into an introduction to the four-hundred-page book about past life regression she's been working on for the last three years. The book would then be published to resounding critical acclaim and her reputation secured. Spit, spat, spot, as Mary Poppins would have said. How could she have been so naive?

Mary leans back in her chair. It never occurred to her that others might find her latest hypotheses preposterous. Challenging, certainly, and unorthodox – but derisive? Dangerous? Why, Hester's report practically accuses her of malpractice: 'How many schizophrenics are walking around without medication because Dr Mary Charlton has convinced them that their hallucinated voices are simply emanations from a prior incarnation?' she had written. 'How many sex abusers have escaped prosecution because Dr Charlton has persuaded the victims that the molestations they remember occurred in a previous life?'

Unable to settle, Mary gets up and wanders into her tiny back kitchen where she enacts the comforting ritual of grinding fresh coffee beans and loading up the two espresso attachments of the Gaggia. The bulky chrome-and-black contraption dominates the gloomy little room. Like almost everything she owns, this machine has a previous incarnation – in this case, donated by Laura when she was renovating the café.

Setting out a cup and saucer, she thinks she really ought to eat something: boil an egg, perhaps; put some toast in the toaster. But her appetite's vanished – not that she ever had much of one. The kitchen is rather dank and unfrequented as a result. Investigating an intermittent smell here a few years back, the plumber had lifted a floorboard and discovered a puddle of water glinting far below in the foundations. On closer examination, it turned out to be a small sluggish spring that rose briefly beneath the kitchen, then seeped back underground to meander its way down to the river.

'You should have the whole place tanked,' the plumber had said. 'Your walls are wringing wet.'

But when he outlined the process – replacing the wooden floor with layers of polythene and concrete – Mary couldn't face it. It seemed like an insult to a building that had been standing unmolested for nearly three centuries. And she found she quite liked the idea of the spring being there, a relic of the site as it once was. Did someone dig a hole there once to create a small pool, she wondered, and line it with pebbles until the water welled up clear? And scoop it up with a tin jug and set it to boil on a cooking fire? She envisaged a barefoot woman squatting down to tend the fire, feeding twigs of kindling into its hot yellow mouth.

That would have been long before her house was built, of course – at least in its current form. But old maps reveal that there has been a dwelling on this site for over five hundred years: first an unremarkable two-room cottage (beside, it would seem, a small spring); then an irregular five-storey tower made of ships' timbers and sandstone blocks pilfered from Hadrian's Wall. When Mary considers those sandstone blocks, how they were hewn and by whom – and how very *very* long ago – she feels something akin to awe at the Heath Robinson structure in which she lives.

The tower was built to house the light-keeper, who tended a candle beacon in the cupola above the fifth floor to guide vessels navigating through the sandbanks at the mouth of the Tyne. In 1808 an elegant new bespoke Georgian lighthouse was constructed further along the bank, and the light in Mary's tower was snuffed out for good. The building was then pressed into service as an almshouse for the wives and children of fishermen lost at sea. She pictures them crowded into her rooms, these family groups, with their pathetic bundles of worldly goods – the women perhaps stoical and in shock, the children whimpering or whingeing. She pictures them laying out their blankets, their one suitcase, their few tin cups and spoons.

Occasionally Mary finds herself drawn to the window of her bedroom and transfixed for one, two, hours at a time, gazing down at the river. Why she chose that particular room, of four bedrooms, she can't explain. It's up three flights, which is a damn nuisance; but there's something familiar about the view from just that height that tugs at a memory at the back of her mind. For Mary the past is a series of chambers, along a corridor lined with doors that can be opened at any time. One day, she promises herself, she will investigate that part of her past that once looked down from her bedroom window at the river viewed from exactly that height.

CHAPTER THREE

2007

Ben's not sure what he was expecting: an anonymous door, maybe, with a subtle little sign and one of those buzzers that let you in and straight up the stairs. Not this noisy brightly-lit caff, with 'Café Laura' in big curly pink writing above the window, and lace netting half way up like at Nana's so you can't see inside. Hanging inside the netting on the door there's a smaller sign saying, 'When café closed, please ring bell for Salon Laura', with the cross-dressing website address underneath, so he knows he's come to the right place.

But the caff's obviously not closed. The windows are all steamed up and the door's got one of those old-fashioned bells, which keeps dinging as old ladies and mams with prams keep shuffling in and out, nattering away like they all know each other. Ben hovers about vaguely outside, trying to pluck up the courage to go in. There's obviously no kids his age, so he's going to stand out like a sore thumb. Maybe he should come back later, when it's less crowded – but then he'll stand out even more.

He edges nearer, trying to see inside. It looks cosy, more like someone's house than a caff; with cakes and sandwiches on a pine table instead of a counter. There are two women serving: a young waitress in a black skirt and white pinny, and an oldish lady in one of those big flowery aprons with a frilly top bit that goes round the neck and a big bow tied at the back.

It's her, Ben realizes, that Laura from the website; he'd know her face anywhere. He takes a step closer – next thing he knows he's been jostled inside by a fresh surge of old ladies and steered towards a small table by the young waitress, who thrusts a menu at him and swoops crumbs away briskly with a J-Cloth.

Ben asks for hot chocolate and picks up a newspaper someone's left on the chair beside him so he doesn't have to look at anyone. The table's a bit rickety, so he keeps one elbow on it, but once his drink's arrived and he's found the Sudoku page, he feels a bit less like a sore thumb and his heart settles back down in his chest. If anyone asks, he'll say he's waiting for Nana, but no one does – they're all spreading jam on scones and fiddling with baby bottles – and at five-thirty the waitress takes off her pinny and there's just him left, and Laura helping the last two old ladies into their coats.

He's been sneaking looks at her, to see if you can tell. The feet are the hardest to disguise, but she's in ankle boots with heels, so you can't work out how big they are. And men's necks are thicker, but she's a bit jowly and old so it doesn't really show there either. And if that hair's a wig, it's a good one: reddish brownish curls heaped up on top with some kind of clip. If anything, she looks like a thinner version of Nana, if Nana was a bit more colourful and arty, because she'd never wear those big dangly earrings and magenta tights; she's more of a fleece and leggings type.

'Want a top-up, pet?' Laura's shut the door after the old ladies and she's standing right there by his table.

'I'm all right.' Ben's heart starts going nineteen to the dozen again and his chest aches, like it's filling with concrete. He's scared to look up in case she thinks he's staring. Her hands are all freckly and covered with rings and her nail varnish matches the roses on the apron, which match the tights.

'Go on, no charge. I'm making a fresh pot anyway.'

'OK, thanks,' he says, then wants to kick himself because that means he's got to stay.

She bustles off on her high heels round the tables, straightening doilies and cruet sets, then turns her back and gets busy with cups and saucers. She's got a bit of a waist – not much, but old ladies never do really – and the high heels make her bum stick out, which helps the overall shape of her.

'There you go,' she says, setting down a tray. 'Hot chocolate with whipped cream and a couple of chocolate digestives for luck.'

'I saw you on that website,' Ben blurts out before he can stop himself.

'Well now you can see me in the flesh.' She does a little twirl and stands there, with her knee cocked and sort of swaying, one hand on her hip and the other behind her head. 'All me own riah, touch wood, in case you were wondering,' she says. 'Though it's getting a bit thin on the top now. Hence *la bouffant* styling.'

She turns the sign on the door to 'Closed' and plonks herself down opposite with one of those little sighs old people do when their feet are killing them. 'No one will come in now,' she says, 'but it's not locked, so you can leave any time.'

She's smiling at him. Waiting.

She knows why he's there.

As soon as he realizes, all the concrete that's been building in Ben's chest dissolves and there's a sudden embarrassing hot prickle of tears at the back of his eyes.

'You look like your photo,' he says, 'only different.'

'What, fatter? Uglier?'

'Not as pink,' he says, then wants to kick himself again. Why did he say that?

She laughs. 'It's because of the green background. I keep meaning to get that photo changed.'

'Does it cost a lot?' Somehow she's made it OK to ask. 'The operation, I mean.'

'Depends what you want to have done.' She looks at him closer, more seriously. 'It's for you, is it?'

He nods. 'I tried to do it myself when I was little, but I made a mess of it. So I've been saving up to get it done properly.' He sees her flinch and the table rocks suddenly, slopping hot chocolate into his saucer. Why did he tell her about that? He never talks about it to anyone, not even Dad.

'What did you do to yourself?' she asks – of *course* she asks; he's mentioned it so she has to ask.

Ben can hear the blood pumping in his ears. He can't look at her. 'I tried to cut everything off,' he says quietly, almost whispering. 'I got a knife and just sort of sawed, but I passed out before I could finish.'

'How long ago was this, pet?'

'When I was seven. Dad says I could have died. I was in hospital for ages.'

'Did you realize you were risking your life?'

'I didn't care. I just wanted it all off.' He looks up. 'I still want it all off.'

'You do know that's not what happens at Salon Laura, don't you?' she says carefully. 'I just make clothes for men who want to look like women. And do depilation and make-up and that; a bit of voice coaching and deportment. Advice and support, that sort of thing.'

'I've been trying to, like, pass as a girl,' he explains. 'But there's no way I can turn up at school like that. But they say I've to pass for up to two years before I can even go on a waiting list, and I'm twelve already.'

She nods. 'So you're worried about puberty.'

'I thought if I could get some hormones, it would give me a bit more time.'

'And what does your mam think about all this?'

'There's only my dad,' he says. 'He's at a meeting today.'

'You mean he doesn't know you're here.'

'Your website said "strictly confidential",' he says, begging her to understand.

Laura sighs, as though she's heard it all before. 'Look, I won't tell your father, and that's a solemn cross-your-heart-and-hope-to-die promise. But even if I had them, I couldn't just hand over hormones to an underage—Hey, wait a sec—'

Ben's scraping back his chair, slopping more hot chocolate. He was mad to think someone he's never met before would help him get hormones without telling his dad.

Laura puts a hand on his arm. 'Don't run off yet. I know what it's like, being in the wrong body, with everyone treating you as a lad.' Ben hesitates and sits down again on the edge of his chair, half turned to the door ready to leg it. 'That was me for years,' she's saying. 'I kept thinking I'd grow out of it—'

'I'll *never* grow out of it,' he says, and the tears are back, but spilling out this time. 'And it's just going to get worse and worse. I'll have, like, hair growing everywhere and my voice will break. I can't wait two years. That's all the time I've got before I start turning into a man.'

Her lipsticked mouth goes soft and sort of sags, so he knows she understands. 'So let's work out how I can help.'

Ben wipes his eyes with the serviette. 'There's loads of sites selling hormones, but they're all big drug companies, or for body builders, or sort of mixed up with porno.'

Laura pulls a face. 'I can imagine.'

'I think I've got the right name of the puberty drug, but—'

'Hey, hold on, hinny! Do you realize how dangerous it is ordering drugs off the internet? You've no idea what they're putting in them packets.'

'But it's got to be better than being in a panic the whole time about leaving it too late, and growing into totally the wrong shape, with a beard and big feet like Dad's.'

She hands him a fresh serviette. 'Have you talked to anyone else about this?'

Ben shakes his head.

'Look, I'll tell you what I'll do,' she says. 'But you've got to promise not to run away again, OK? I'm going to send you to a doctor I know. Now she's not a surgeon—'

'Is she a hormone expert?' he asks hopefully.

'No, she's a psychoanalyst.'

'Oh, a therapist,' he slumps again. 'Dad's taken me to therapists. They're useless. All they do is talk about getting me to feel "comfortable in my own body".'

Laura smiles, as if to say 'tell me about it'. 'Mary's not a normal kind of therapist. She won't try to stop you wanting a remould. She's more about trying to work out why you want it so much.'

Ben eyes her doubtfully.

'You'll need a report from someone like her anyway,' she adds. 'You need someone to declare you're in your right mind before they'll accept you for surgery. I had to go six rounds with a shrink before my op.'

Alarm sweeps through him. How could he have forgotten that? It's on every website he's ever looked at: the need for some kind of 'psychological assessment'. He's been so worried about 'passing' and getting hold of the right hormones that he must have pushed it to the back of his mind.

'So what do you think?' Laura asks.

'OK,' he says, weak with relief. Maybe if this Mary's a doctor, she can get him a prescription for the puberty hormones too.

'*Bona.* At least that's one thing sorted,' she says, tearing a page off her order pad and scribbling down an address and phone number. 'Here's her details. Say Laura sent you.' She glances at her watch, and Ben starts to get up.

'No, you're all right,' she says. 'I was just seeing if I had time to take you upstairs for a tour of La Salon. Try on a few wigs maybe, show you a few tricks of the trade.' She winks at him. 'If you like, that is. No obligation.'

Yes he would like, more than anything. He tries to smile and say so, but the tears are there again, clogging his throat so he can't speak.

'Go on, you daft filly,' says Laura, handing him a whole wodge of serviettes. 'You'll start me off.' And sure enough she's dabbing away under her mascara. Then they're both laughing and blowing their noses and Ben feels himself relaxing for the first time since he got there.

'Oh dearie mearie,' sighs Laura at last, pouring more tea. 'Let me gather my strength.'

'When did you have your op?' Ben asks, watching her fishing in her apron for a compact and sponging some fresh face powder under her eyes.

'Only fifteen years back, but I always knew I was a lass. I had this vision of Sophia Loren in my mind, probably because I was a bit plump and my lips have always been pouty, so I thought right that's me – hence the Laura, savvy? Loren, Laura?' She shrugs. 'Well it made sense to me at the time.

'So anyway, there I was obsessed with *la Loren*, and I found this waspie in me nana's drawer from when she was young, and I started wearing it at night to pull my waist in. Some hope, eh? And Veet had just been invented, so I went to town with that, because I was right hairy in them days, before I started on the hormones. And I was sneaking off to the cottages every Saturday to get changed, then on to La Continental to ogle up the sea-food and fruit. Then blow me, didn't I go and fall for a lass?'

Ben's been checking out Laura's chin while she's been speaking: there's no trace of stubble now. And her arms are just like Nana's: a bit freckly, and wrinkly at the elbows, typical old lady arms.

'It was before the op, so I sashayed straight into the closet and went back to being a lad. Anyway, we got married and had two lovely girls, then one day Jen comes home to find me prancing around in her baby-dolls. Give her credit, she tried to cope. And we went to Marriage Guidance and all that. But it was hopeless really. There was no way I was going to stop. And she was a Presbyterian, which put paid to any role-play hanky panky. So we staggered on for a few years, me trying to cut back, her turning a blind eye, till she took up with Harry the Crab and went off with the bairns.'

Ben dunks a digestive in his tepid hot choc and sucks the soggy end while Laura ferrets in her apron again for a pack of Nicorettes and pops one into her mouth.

'That's why I started the business really. Because back then there was no one to go through the options with. I mean, are you gay or straight?'

Ben sits up. He's never thought.

'See? You're so caught up with getting the op, you haven't thought about what it means for the future. Like, do you want to marry an adam or an eve? A molly or a dolly? At your age neither, most likely. Or maybe both, who knows?'

Ben takes a bite of the digestive and tries to get his head round what she's saying.

'Sorry, duckie. Am I embarrassing you? I forget that people aren't usually as forthright as *moi*. You will say if I'm going a bit OTT, won't you?'

'No, you're all right,' he says. Though she is *totally* embarrassing him, especially as she looks vaguely like his nana. Plus it's hard to keep track, with all the weird words she keeps using.

'I mean, what if you go ahead with the op and it turns out you're a lesbian? You know about lezzies, I assume? Right, then, so what if you go to all that trouble only to find out that your meat and two veg would have come in quite handy after all?' Laura tops up her cup and clicks in another sweetener. 'Doesn't mean you have to give up your *maquillage* and frocks. You can still slip in your falsies and mince up the Bigg Market of a Saturday night. Or get implants if you want to go the full dowry and live as your actual zelda. What I'm saying is, there's different options. Right, where was I?'

'Harry the Crab,' Ben says. 'Is he a big bloke with a beard; smokes a pipe? I think I met him once down the Seamen's Mission with my dad.'

'That's the lad. Tell you the truth, it was a relief when Jenny left. I sold the house, spent a thousand smackers on zjoush and cossies, went on the hormones, got the riah sorted, and never looked back. Then I had the op and it all went horribly wrong. Not the op, that was textbook remould. But suddenly there I was cut like a lady, dressed like a lady, out on the town with lads like bees round a honeypot – I was still fairly young at that point, remember. But when it came to a clinch I wasn't interested. What, rub that bristly chin against my *ecaff? Excusez-moi*, I'd say, I'm off home to the cat.

'Don't get me wrong. I'm not saying I shouldn't have gone ahead with the op. There's nothing like slipping on a Lycra one-piece in Lanzarote and not worrying about your lunchbox. Though talking of Lycra, you'd be amazed what they've come up with in the way of underwear these days, so you can hang onto your giblets and no one's any the wiser.'

'But I hate them.' Ben bursts out. 'I hate everything about being a boy. It's not just what it looks like, it's what it feels like inside. I'd just be pretending to be a girl if I had Lycra squashing everything flat.'

'So, go and see Mary and get your assessment. Then—'

This time it's Ben who looks at his watch and jumps up in a panic. 'I've got to go,' he says. 'Nana'll be going nuts.' He opens the door, then stops. 'Can I – I mean, about them wigs and that…' He feels his ears going red.

'What about tomorrow? The caff's shut all day and my first client's not till three, so we won't be rushed. How does ten o'clock sound? Right, I'll be expecting you.'

CHAPTER FOUR

2007

Ben always looks forward to Dad coming home off the boat, and it's always great for the first six minutes. But then the pressure will start up, all the macho stuff Dad goes in for, and Ben will start half wishing he'd go away again.

So he'll breeze in smelling of the sea, with this great gust of wind behind him. Because he's a big bloke – not fat, because he's always on and off that Atkins diet, and not exactly tall. But he takes up a lot of space, with beefy shoulders and tattoos, and a belly you can punch hard as you can and he doesn't even flinch. And his sea boots are enormous, with thick socks folded over the top, and his jerkin's thick as a bullet-proof vest, all zips and pockets for his gipping knife and tools and that. And he's always carrying a load of creaky yellow oilskins and his 'sea bag', he calls it, packed with gloves and socks and weird long underwear – though they hardly ever change when they're out, so he always niffs when you get up close.

'If you think I'm bad, son, you should stick your nose down the cabin after a few days,' Dad says, almost bragging. 'Minging's not the word for it.'

It's great to see him, though. And his first night back they always have an Indian and get out a DVD, it's a sort of tradition; and sit on the sofa digging into greasy cartons, side by side, though it's usually explosions and car chases, but sometimes Dad gets out something funny and they have a laugh together. Then later Dad goes out and gets hammered with the lads from the boat and Ben goes to his room and locks his door, gets out his nightie and Lily the Pink and goes to bed.

This time, though, feels different. Ben's always had his secret life, but since he's met Laura he doesn't feel so sad about it. It's more a proper quest now;

and even though he doesn't know how it will turn out, he feels like he's on the road to somewhere.

This morning she showed him how to pluck his eyebrows – not so they were obvious, not so anyone would notice, but definitely more like a girl's. She said there are loads of 'tricks of the trade', as she calls them, to make you look more feminine without people putting their finger on quite why. Like dyeing his eyelashes; they're doing that next time.

Tomorrow Dad's borrowing a motor launch from Harry the Crab and they're going diving, Ben and Dad and two of the lads from Deep Blue who taught them to dive. The visibility's usually rubbish this time of year, with all the summer plankton, and the wind churning everything up, but it's been calm all week so Dad reckons it's worth a go.

Ben's always in two minds about diving. He loves being under water, the quivery green light, the dreamy way the weed sways; and he likes being with Dad, up to a point – but he hates all the macho talk about the gear and the wrecks and that. To Ben, a wreck's just a place for fish to shelter from predators and storms; but to Dad it's the HMS whatever, with X tonnage, sunk on X date with the loss of X men. Ben wonders sometimes about all those lost men. Can ghosts haunt under water? Does it bother them being forever dived on and rummaged through by lads in wetsuits with metal detectors?

They set off first thing and the water is flat as a mirror, and clear to ten fathoms, which is really unusual for the North Sea. They take it in turns going down, and the two Deep Blue lads go first – because you've always got to go down with a buddy, that's the first rule of diving: in case something happens, like running out of air or your line breaking. Then it's just Ben and Dad waiting on the boat, all togged up except for masks and fins, just rocking gently in the sunshine and sipping tomato soup from the Thermos.

Dad throws him a smile that says, clear as you could write it, 'Love you, son,' and Ben's just basking in it, and flashing the same message back, when the thought sneaks in like a shadow: 'What if you'd seen what I was doing yesterday, Dad? Would you still love me then?' And it dims everything a bit.

When it's their turn, Dad takes ages checking Ben's gear – is the tank strapped on properly, are the pressures OK? When he checks his mask he's right up close, so Ben's looking up at his big white teeth, with the vampire incisors; and the scar on his lower lip from that bottle fight at the New Dolphin pub years ago. Ben remembers Dad kissing him when he was little – even more often than

Mam did – and cuddling him on his lap when they were watching telly; but that all stopped when he came back from the hospital.

When they go down everything seems to be in slow motion, because the gear's so bulky you can't turn quickly, and the fins make it feel like you're kicking through treacle. And there's always that moment when he panics at bit, when he puts in the mouthpiece – because it's different from normal breathing; you have to pull the air in, like sucking on a baby's bottle. However many times he's done it, it freaks him out to have to suck in air all the time. And sounds are really weird under water too, so it's like you're deaf, and have to use a special sign language with your buddy; and if the boat engine's going there's a faint throbbing sound, but at the same time there's this really loud roaring and hissing noise, which is the air from your tank.

Once he's got over that though, it's brilliant, with the sunlight dappling down through the water near the surface. Then deeper down, once he's switched his torch on, there's loads of starfish, and crabs bumbling along through the weed; and it totally takes over his brain, so he doesn't have to think about footie or school or pretending to be what he's not. Then suddenly there's this humongous blue lobster peering out from a cranny. This whole bit of sea is protected, so there's always loads of shellfish, because they stick around where they're spawned, mainly. But there's hardly any proper fish, because they get caught as soon as they swim away – just a few little sand gobies darting about near the bottom.

Afterwards Dad's in one of his high-five moods, because they've done this 'father-and-son activity', like when he comes to watch footie practice and Ben's done some really quick moves – which he's practised over and over, because he knows Dad will worry that he'll be 'failing as a father' if his son's not interested in sports.

And that's the trouble really. The times that should be the best times, when they're off with a bunch of lads to the match, or getting on their gear for a big dive, that's when Ben feels saddest. Because Dad's in his element, and full of pride, grinning at Ben. And you can tell he's just praying that everything's OK, and Ben's got over what Dad always calls his 'accident' and is a normal boy after all.

Ben wonders sometimes if his mam left because of him; because he didn't know to hide it when he was little, and was always nagging at her to buy him Barbies and Polly Pockets.

After she left, the flat looked pretty much the same, which was weird – even in Dad's en-suite, because he didn't dump her old moisturizers and shower gels for ages. It was only when Ben opened her side of the wardrobe that it really hit him. And there was just this one pair of beige pop socks balled together, all dusty in a back corner; and that floaty black negligee Dad gave her for their anniversary, on the matching padded hanger. Then one day they disappeared too.

'It's just you and me now, buddy,' Dad says. 'And buddies always stick together, right?'

CHAPTER FIVE

2007

Mary's phone rings deafeningly in the hall. It's a wall-mounted seventies contraption installed by the previous owners in a vain attempt to hear it from the fifth floor. It's Laura, ebullient as ever: '*Bonjour*, duckie! How's it diddling?'

'Actually I've hit a bit of a setback,' Mary says. 'So I've been drifting about rather pathetically wondering what to do about it. You remember that paper I sent off to the *BJCP*? The one I was planning to use as an introduction to my book? Well they sent it out for peer review and one of my peers has reviewed it rather badly.'

'Does that mean it won't be published?'

'She's suggested I send it to the *TPR* instead – that's the *Transpersonal Psychology Review* – because, and I quote, "this is exactly the kind of pseudo-scientific mumbo-jumbo they like to publish". Sorry, Laura, you've probably no idea what I'm talking about.'

'*Excusez-moi.* I can speaka da English. You've sent a chunk of your *magnum opus* to a pukkah scientific journal and some miserable bint's said it's only fit for the cat's litter tray.'

'She's accused me of endangering my clients too.'

'Well there was that rampaging nutter last year,' Laura reminds her, referring to a client who'd torn up his prescription – with rather florid results.

'But that happens all the time. A client starts to improve then discontinues their medication. It's a perennial problem, regardless of the type of therapy.' Mary extends the telephone cord to its limit out into the porch and reaches for her Gitanes.

'So why has this peer review bint—'

'Professor Hester Griffin is a highly articulate, formidably intelligent—'

'OK, this *brainy* peer review bint – why has she got it in for you?'

Mary sighs. 'It's not me she has a problem with – it's anything that smacks even vaguely of the paranormal. It's a bit of a crusade for her. She assumes that because I can't cite a physical mechanism for the transfer of memories from a past life, then that transfer can't possibly occur – even though the documented evidence is overwhelming.'

'So why is she still banging on about it?'

'It's so frustrating! In any other scientific field, if you encounter some evidence that doesn't fit your current theory, you question the theory – not the evidence. It's as though the whole quantum revolution never happened. I've had run-ins with her before, at various conferences. Cryptoamnesia's her specialism, so I suppose I should have expected something like this.'

'*Pardonez?*'

'Cryptoamnesia. False memory. Where people remember things that didn't happen. Hester's published quite widely on the subject.' Cleverly argued papers, Mary recalls, with a hint of rhetorical flourish.

'So she reckons people who remember their past lives are making it all up.'

'Yes, in a nutshell.'

'But why would they? Why would I invent a toerag like Tom to explain why I wanted a sex change?'

'She'd argue that there are alternative explanations that don't involve reincarnation.'

Laura snorts scornfully. 'Hormones in the womb, you mean? They don't explain all them nightmares though, do they? It was finding out about Tom that got rid of them.'

'Hester would argue that you created your Tom persona as a *post hoc* rationalization – a way of making sense of the nightmares – and that I colluded with you.' Is that what she's been doing all these years, Mary wonders, constructing elaborate castles in the air with her clients?

'Hey, you're not taking this seriously, are you?'

'Perhaps I've been working on my own for too long,' muses Mary, cradling the phone under her chin to light her cigarette. 'Most of my clients these days come fully expecting me to regress them to a past life. It's not exactly an uncontaminated sample. Whereas if I was in some sort of group practice, or attached to a university, rubbing up against other opinions—'

'You'd still be seeing the same clients,' Laura reasons.

'Yes, but perhaps I wouldn't be so ready to look for a past-life explanation.'

'Actually I've just found you a *bona* new one – totally uncontaminated too.'

'Oh no,' Mary says in dismay. 'I'm sorry, Laura. I can't face taking on anyone new at the moment – not with all this hanging over me. It wouldn't be fair.'

'Oh, go on,' Laura puts on a wheedling voice. 'He's only little.'

'What do you mean?' Despite herself, Mary's curious.

'I mean he's only twelve years old and if ever a lad needed your help it's this one.'

The boy sits on the very edge of the red sofa, trying not to sink into it. He's jiggling his bony knees, rubbing a finger over a scab on his arm, obviously just dying to pick at it.

Mary inherited this sofa from her aunt, but it's served her unexpectedly well over the years, being unusually yielding and womb-like; even the most resistant of clients usually succumbs to its embrace eventually. In fact it's such an effective way of inducing relaxation, that when it wears out she will immediately search for an identical replacement. She settles into her own chair, a far more upright and utilitarian item from the local Oxfam shop – known technically as a 'cottage chair', apparently – and adjusts her old cashmere cardigan around her shoulders. 'So what can I do for you?' she asks.

'I want to be a girl,' the boy blurts out. 'I mean, I think I *am* a girl. I mean like deep down.'

'Do you? How intriguing. Tell me a bit more about that.' He's a pretty boy; rather girlish in fact, so that's interesting. Small, blonde, skinny, intelligent-looking. How *does* one look intelligent? It's a quality of watchfulness, Mary muses, of attention. Many children seem so vacant.

The boy stops jiggling and moves on to wiping his palms on his jeans. 'Ever since I can remember I've felt like a girl, even though I've been to doctors and that, and they said I've got, like, male chromosomes and male "secondary characteristics".' He pauses, obviously embarrassed.

'Go on.' She smiles encouragement and reaches for her double espresso. Caffeine at the start of each session, to get her neurons firing, nicotine at the end, to top up her endorphins; though at her level of addiction it's more to fend off withdrawal symptoms than for additional stimulation per se.

'When I was little I thought I was a girl called Annie.'

Something tightens in Mary's chest when she hears this: a held breath, a surge of adrenaline. 'I don't remember it very clearly now,' the boy is saying, 'but I used to know loads about her, like where she lived and what her mam looked like and that. Dad says I kept crying and pushing my real mam away, saying I wanted to go home.'

Mary quells an impulse to lean forwards. If she's right, this is a classic spontaneous past-life manifestation; the clearest she's ever encountered.

'Dad says that I made her up,' the boy continues, 'like she was an invisible friend, but it didn't feel like that. It felt more like she was inside me, like she *was* me, and I was born into the wrong body.'

'And do you still have Annie inside you?' Mary asks neutrally, controlling her excitement.

'Not really. I can sort of feel her sometimes, like when you see something out of the corner of your eye. But I don't really *know* about her any more – except what I can remember from when I was little. But even that's faded now – it's like being Ben has taken over. Except I still feel like I'm really a girl.'

The sun's in his eyes through the window – nice bright blue eyes – so he has to squint at her. Excellent, Mary thinks automatically. When her clients' vision is compromised, they ease into the trance more completely. 'Laura tells me you want gender reassignment surgery, and that you tried to mutilate yourself a few years ago.'

'Dad thinks that was because Mam left and I was upset and trying to get her to come back. But it wasn't that. I mean I *was* still upset about her going, but I was even more upset about being a boy.'

'You did say that your father was going come with you,' Mary chides mildly.

'He was going to, but he was called to a meeting.'

She hides a smile. 'Well we can talk for a while today, but if we're going to see each other properly I will have to meet your father.'

'I've brought the money,' he volunteers, worming a hand into his back pocket and tugging out four £20 notes.

'It's not because of the fee, Ben. It's because you're under sixteen. He has to sign a form to say he agrees for me to see you.'

The boy's narrow shoulders sag when he hears this, and he closes his eyes for a moment. Mary's aware, then, in a way she hasn't been before, of how very young he is to be doing all this – going to see Laura, setting up this consultation – and what a very heavy, lonely burden it is that he's carrying.

And she has a sudden visceral and utterly uncharacteristic impulse to gather him onto her lap and rock him against her, with his fair head tucked snugly beneath her chin.

'Look, don't worry about your father now,' she says. 'I'll give him a ring later and sort it out with him.'

The boy looks up in alarm. 'Can't you just write that report? Laura said I need an assessment before—'

'I'm sorry Ben. It's illegal to assess you without parental consent.'

He hangs his head. 'I never actually told him I was coming,' he confesses.

'I'll talk to him and explain, if that would help,' she offers. 'You'd be surprised how persuasive I can be.'

'*No!*' he bursts out, almost shouting. 'No,' he repeats, more quietly. 'Please don't say anything.'

'Don't you think perhaps it's time he knew? If you're really set on surgery, you'll need parental consent for every stage of the process.'

'But I can't tell him,' he says miserably, close to tears. 'It would totally freak him out.'

Mary watches him stuff the money back in his pocket. 'You know where I am if you change your mind,' she says opening the door for him. Then, touching him gently on the shoulder: 'You don't have to do this on your own, you know.'

As she watches him walk down the street, a small dejected boy in jeans and trainers, she experiences a wrench that's almost physical in its intensity. Observing it in herself, she muses that this must be what's referred to by the expression 'her heart went out to him'.

She returns to her consulting room and starts writing up her notes on the aborted session. 'Client reported spontaneous regression in early childhood, similar to cases reported by Stevenson, Weiss, Shroder, etc. Client subsequently declined treatment due to…' How ironic that the one case that might have supported her thesis, the only case of spontaneous regression she's ever seen, has been both proffered then withdrawn on the same day. Perhaps it's karma, she thinks wanly, a sign that it's time to rethink her approach.

She's just tidying away her case notes when the front doorbell rings. It's the boy: pink-cheeked and out of breath, as though he's been running. 'Dad's off on the boat now,' he says. 'But he'll be back tomorrow if you want to meet him. Or I could let you have his satellite number.'

Mary feels like cheering, but satisfies herself with a broad smile. 'I think I could probably wait until then,' she says. 'It would be better to explain things face to face, anyway.' She conducts him back into her consulting room and he sits down on the sofa again.

'And you can do that report, can you?' he asks. 'So I can go on the list for the operation and hormones and that?'

'Of course – if and when it's called for. But I will have to spend some time talking to you first.'

Mary pauses, deliberating. Now he's agreed to let her meet his father, perhaps it wouldn't be entirely unethical to check whether her suspicions are confirmed? 'We could make a start now, if you like,' she suggests. 'I could introduce you to the way I work, and perhaps we could talk a bit more about Annie.' Just a few minutes, she promises herself, just to see… 'You know, I see quite a few clients like you,' she goes on. 'People who feel they may be carrying someone else's memories as well as their own.'

The blue eyes widen. 'Other children?'

'Yes, children especially.' Mary notices with satisfaction that he's begun to sink back into the red sofa. 'I suspect everyone has these feelings sometimes, but most people in our society ignore them or push them away. But I think some children may have a special gift for tuning in to other memories.'

She's always careful, at this stage, not to say 'past lives'. 'Now I want you to lie down with your head on the cushion – that's right, good, don't worry about your shoes. I'm going to help you relax and see what we can find out about Annie.'

The words she uses to induce the trance are so familiar, she could repeat them in her sleep. 'Keep breathing slowly and deeply. Think of a place you know where you feel happy and relaxed…' The boy's under in just a few minutes, his limbs loose and unguarded, like a cat splayed in front of a fire.

'There's a door in front of you. Can you see it? Good. Stand up and touch it. Think what it feels like under your hand. The door leads to a place in your past. Push it open. What can you see?'

'I'm outside the smokehouse on the quayside, and the lumper's upending another cran of herring into the farlane. And here's the fish tumbling in, all silver and a-slither, hitting the farlane like water and splashing up the sides – and right out, some of them, so you have to scoop them off the ground before some daftie kicks them.'

Mary lets her breath out in a long silent whistle. She's listening to a herring girl! Annie must have been a herring girl! It's all there: the accent, the vocabulary, the historic detail – material no boy of Ben's age could possibly know.

'Good, very good,' she says, controlling her excitement. 'What else can you see?'

'I'm looking down at my hands, and Flo's beside me, shovelling salt on the fish so's we can hold them, because they're that slippy, you can't get a grip without a roughening of salt. A Shields herrings is that full of oil this time of year, all you've to do is squeeze it and the oil's slipping through your fingers like dripping.

'So now we're back to gipping again, getting up a rhythm, the dip and slit and flick of it. You've to let your hands do the thinking, and keep only half an eye on them, because if you pay too much mind, that's the best way I know to a sliced finger. Flo picked it up quicker than me, because she was less hasty. But that's Flo, isn't it? She likes to be sure what she's about, but I'm like a sand-flea on a hot dune.

'It's hard on the hands mind, this job; what with the salt pining them, and the skin cracking, and the salt nipping in the cracks. Then there's the gipping knife to watch out for, because the edge must be sharp as lightning or you can't keep up your speed. We bind up our fingers and thumbs with flour sacking to be safe, and that's a right canny job of itself when you're dim and bleary of a misty morning.

'They're alive, some of the herring, when you gip them. They look dead, but when the warmth of your hand gets to them, they start moving: like you're a saint, bringing them back to life, except the blade's going in like the very Devil himself, to scoop out the slither, the teeny heart, the wee sliver of its soul.'

CHAPTER SIX

2007

Best fucking time of the day, Paul reckons, striding along the top bank above the Fish Quay. Not quite light yet, couple of boats steaming home with a wake of offal and mewling gulls. Can't beat it. Smell of bacon frying at the Seamen's Mission. Further along the bank, Charlie and Jimbo are sitting hunched on their bench as usual, seventy if they're a day, with their tabs and a six-pack of Stella between them, watching the boats come in.

'All right?' says Paul as he passes.

'Right y'are, Paul,' says Charlie, and Jimbo grunts, never much of a one for conversation. Worked the same boat all their lives and still in each others' pockets. Fishing does that for you.

Paul takes a deep breath, sucks down the cold brown river smell, along with the chugging diesel from the two boats mooring up and a whiff of seaweed from the Black Middens. And the fish smells, a nebfull like nothing else: the silver smell of fresh-caught, the sharp yellow stink of the scaggy old skeletons in the gutter that even the rats won't touch.

Nessa never could stand the smell of fish. The old man said that should've ruled her out from the start. She said she could always smell it on Paul's hands, even after he'd scrubbed them. Reckoned it got under his skin, even though he'd made skipper the year after they got together and hardly gipped a fish since. That was Nessa for you, though: finicky, with all her lotions; squeamish. They all are these days, mind. Herbal this, herbal that. Not that he minds a bit of nicey-nice. It's just tiring to keep it up all the time.

Paul's off down the fish market to meet Dougie, his Shields agent, to go through the boat's gear: what needs getting, what needs mending. Old Dougie's all right, if a bit of a stickler for his to-do lists. But you need a lad like that on shore when you're off on a trip, keeping in with the buyers, the trades; pricing up diesel from different suppliers. The cost of diesel's wicked these days, and the boat just drinks it on a trawl: with the twin rig you can literally watch the fuel gauge dropping. Still, it scoops the fish up no bother, that rig – nearly three hundred boxes this last trip: cod, haddock and whiting; plaice and lemons; hake, turbot, dabs; couple of halibut, the odd few Dovers. That's over eight grand for the five days, though there's fuck-all left once you've deducted the diesel and the lads' shares.

Dougie likes his tabs, so they're sat on a bench outside the Mission: Paul sucking on an Extra Strong mint while Dougie puffs away on a Marlboro, ticking things off on his clipboard. Typical Dougie: must be the only lad in Shields taking any notice of that new No Smoking sign they've put up in the Mission.

By the time they're done, the boats are unloaded and the market's well under way, with Big Bill Palmer and Weasel Willie clomping through the melt in their Timberlands, working their way round the catches with their chitty books, rattling out bids to the buyers. And forklifts zooming up and down, loading boxes on to the vans backed up outside.

Paul checks out a couple of 'sold' boxes before the market lads shovel the ice on. A few decent halibut and monk; but the haddock are all under a kilo as usual – you never see a decent haddock these days.

There's a couple of younger lads hanging about down the far end of the shed, squatting and peering in the boxes: student types, by the looks of it; hoodies and trainers. Weird hair. They've got a clipboard each, and a cool box.

'They've been here since Monday,' Dougie tells him. 'From that lab place along by Cullercoats, that Dove place. They're saying there might be something up with the fish, so they're checking.'

Paul wanders over. 'Howay,' he says. 'What's going on?'

'We're taking samples,' says the taller one, straightening up and pushing a pansy flop of hair off his face with the back of his hand. 'Just a routine survey. Nothing to worry about.'

'You from DEFRA then?' Paul asks.

'They've provided some of the funding, but we're nothing to do with them really. We're marine biologists, from the university. Part of a team investigating the effects of water-borne pollutants.'

'What, from that chemical plant in Blythe? I thought they sorted that out years ago.'

'It's more general trends we're looking at. Mutation rates, abnormalities, that sort of thing.' He's from down south; London by the sound of it. A bit posh, a bit fake cockney like that Jamie Oliver.

'They've found some flatties with dodgy innards,' says one of the market lads, jumping down off his forklift. 'Males loaded with roe instead of milt.'

'Who told you that?' asks the tall lad sharply – and he seems pissed off. 'Look, I promise there's nothing to worry about. A certain number of anomalies are to be expected in any natural population.'

'How many of these "anomalies" are there, then?' asks Paul. He'll have to ask the deckies if they've noticed anything.

The other lad drops a plaice into his cool box and stands up. He's chubbier than his mate, a pale couch potato with spiky dyed-black hair. 'It's too early to say,' he says, not meeting Paul's eye. 'We're still collating the samples.'

It's obvious the lad's lying through his teeth, but there's no point trying to push it. He'll get nothing out of these two. Still, fish with dodgy innards – that's the last thing Paul needs, the state the business is in right now.

Nana's in the flat when Paul gets home, stuffing Yorkshires and profiteroles in the freezer. Paul swallows a sigh. Why doesn't she keep this stuff at her place? She knows he's trying to cut back on the carbs. She'll say they're for Ben – 'He's a growing lad,' she'll go – but it's because she's narked at how Paul's shifted the weight, when she's still Michelin Woman in her red trackie bottoms.

'Howay, Mam,' he says, filling the kettle. 'Where's the bairn?'

'I shouted when I came in, but there's no sign and his door's locked.'

'It's always locked, even when he's in. Fuck knows what he gets up to in there.'

'Lad his age needs his privacy,' says Nana, piercing the film on an individual syrup pudding and putting it in the microwave. 'Shall I do you one, son?'

'No!' he says, sharper than he means to. Then, 'I'm all right, thanks.' There's a freckled banana in the fruit bowl and an unopened four-pack of red apples he bought before he went away. So much for the lad's five a day. 'You've not been feeding the bairn puddings for his breakfast, have you?'

'He says he'll get his own, so I leave him to it.'

He shoots her a look. She's supposed to do Ben's meals when he's off on the boat, but he wouldn't put it past her to skip the breakfast shift altogether. Roll up later with some baps for dinner instead. Still, it's the school holidays so he doesn't say anything.

He watches her upend the pudding into a bowl and slather cream over it, then take it through the arch to the open-plan lounge. Cost a fucking fortune, this flat: big bay windows right along the far wall looking out on the river. The wow factor they call it. Nessa was on at him night and day till he put in an offer. He's glad he did though, now she's gone. It's safer for the bairn on his own on the fifth floor, behind all them security doors. And Paul likes to think of the lad looking out these windows when he's away on the boat, and him looking back, like they can see each other, though that's daft when he's three hundred and fifty fucking miles northeast, off Aberdeen, trawling for whitefish.

'Bring us a cup of tea, will you, son?' Nana says, kicking off her sandals and reaching for the remote.

'How you getting on with them books?' he asks. She's always done the boat's books: back when Da was skipper, and before that even, when it was old Skip in charge and Da was third man.

'Nearly done. Them DEFRA forms are still giving me gyp, mind. I were here till past eight Friday getting them sorted.' (Good, Paul's thinking. At least the bairn had some company.) 'Then I had one of them dreams where you go on working. Except I had to take all the papers to Portugal for some reason, and fit them in under my twenty-two kilo limit.' She chuckles, and it turns into a juicy cough. 'Had to take out all me party shoes.'

'Monk's going for a good price at the moment,' Paul says as some chat show appears on the telly. 'But you've to go through that much by-catch to get them, it's hardly worth it.' Nana nods vaguely, eyes on the screen. She's always yammering on about how he never talks to her, but look what happens when he does.

Standing, sipping tea, he feels his mobile buzz in his pocket and takes it out. 'This is Dr Charlton,' says some woman in a posh raspy voice – and his heart does that thing: stops for a second, then dunts against his ribs like it's been kick-started.

'Is it Ben?'

'He's fine, Mr Dixon,' says the woman. 'He's not ill and there hasn't been an accident. But he came to see me yesterday requesting therapy. So I thought I should discuss it with you before proceeding.'

Paul slides the phone shut, then strides over and grabs the remote to switch off the telly. 'Did Ben say anything to you about going to a therapist?'

Nana shrugs. 'Never tells us a thing. But he's at that age, isn't he? What kind of therapist?'

'Analytic psycho something. She wants to see me. "In her consulting room", for fuck's sake.'

Paul feels a slight pressure building in his chest, like there's too much air in there, like when you've been diving and come up a bit fast. He feels stupid, embarrassed. What's going on with the bairn? He seemed fine last night. Tucking into his tikka marsala; jabbering away after the dive.

'I doubt it's owt to worry about,' says Nana, licking sweet gunk from the back of her spoon. 'Audrey Robson's going to a therapist for her spider phobia. It got so she couldn't go in the bathroom without Terry hoovering the Venetians and pouring boiling water down the plugholes.'

'He could be up to all sorts on that computer,' he says. 'Locked inside that room.'

She's sneaked back the remote and put the chat show on mute. Paul wants to shake her; make her focus on what's happening with her fucking grandson. 'It'll just be some hoo-hah with the school,' she says. 'That Gifted and Talented nonsense. That new Head's always sending them on trips and that.'

It's not that, Paul knows. But it's hopeless talking to his mam. She's already distracted, flicking through channels with the sound off.

'It's because he's an only child,' she says – her pat answer for everything. 'If he'd had a little brother to play with, maybes he wouldn't be on the computer all hours.' As if Paul and Nessa hadn't spent five fucking years trying for another baby.

'How's Nessa getting on with that new wean?' Nana asks: not to wind him up – she's not that devious – more because what's on her mind just pops out of her mouth without her thinking what effect it'll have.

Paul breathes out slowly. 'Canny,' he says. 'Just started nursery.'

When Nessa wrote that she was pregnant with the first one, Paul's knees went weak, literally, just like they say when you get a shock.

He hadn't been that bothered when she buggered off, not really. Just bloody fuming that she'd upset the bairn – and pissed off that she'd made him look a prat in front of the lads. And her new bloke whisked her straight off to New Zealand, so at least they weren't rubbing his nose in it.

Then he got this letter out of the blue saying she was expecting, and giving the date. So he did his sums and worked out – surprise, surprise – that she was already three months gone when she moved out. And it just got to him, didn't it? The idea of her bloke's sperm doing their thing while she was sleeping right next to him in the fucking bed.

It was like a double whammy, because Paul has a problem with *his* sperm. When Nessa couldn't fall pregnant again after Ben, they went for tests; her first, then him when they couldn't find anything. And it turned out his lads were slow swimmers and pegging out before they got to the egg. Plus they were deformed, loads of them – they showed him a photo they'd taken – with big heads, or bits missing. It was just as well she hadn't fallen pregnant, they said, because there might have been a problem with the baby. So that was that.

Then he got her letter from New Zealand. And it started him thinking about Ben. Because she'd fallen pregnant slap-bang no problem with her new bloke (Paul refuses to use his name, even to himself). But it took three years of trying before they had Ben. And it got him thinking, what if he'd always had this problem with his sperm, like from way back when he was a nipper? What if Nessa had been having it away with some other bloke behind his back, and kept quiet about it when she fell pregnant with Ben?

He couldn't get the thought out of his head. What if he wasn't Ben's real dad? He phoned Ness up in a lather, and she denied it of course. Still, it was all he could think of for ages; getting out all the old holiday snaps to see which bits of Ben looked like Nessa and which like him. He even got Nana to fetch round some photos of himself as a bairn to do a comparison. It was driving him nuts.

Then Ben had his accident and it all kind of slotted into place. Like maybe this stuff about wanting to be a girl was something Ben had inherited from this other bloke? And it was a relief in a way, to think it wasn't Paul's fault, for having dud sperm or not being a proper role model or whatever. Then he read about DNA testing and decided to go for it to find out for sure.

The results came back when he was off on the boat, so it was in a stack of post piled up on the hall table when he got home. He recognized the logo on the envelope straight away, but Ben was there just in from school and nattering on about something, so he shoved it in the drawer under the *Yellow Pages*. Then when he came to get it out later, he couldn't bring himself to open it – even though it cost a packet to get the test done.

The envelope's still there where he left it, like a tab smouldering under a blanket. All he has to do is hoy off the blanket and the flame will leap out. He doesn't know what he'll feel when he opens it, one way or the other, but he knows there'll be no going back.

CHAPTER SEVEN

2007

Paul recognizes Dr Charlton's house. He must have seen it a million times from the boat: the cream tower at the end of that row of old houses on the top bank, with that weird thing on the roof. When he gets there, he sees it's got one of them blue plaques on the wall, dated 1727, and he's just started reading when this little bird of a woman pops out from behind a bush, puffing on a French ciggie.

'They painted the whole building black at one point,' she's saying. 'So it wouldn't distract from the new lighthouse further along.' She sticks out a hand for him to shake, and she's in gloves, even though it's the middle of summer. Funny, that. 'May I offer you an espresso?' she goes. 'Or would you prefer a gin and tonic at this time of day? I'm afraid I don't keep beer.'

He follows her inside, to a room that's like a cross between a posh antiques shop and one of them old railway waiting rooms. So the window and skirtings are dark maroon and there's one of them fancy Axminster squares on the floor, like his great granny used to have. There's a big scuffed leather-topped desk in one corner with one of them old captain's chairs, and the mantelpiece is crowded with elephant ornaments, all sizes – from India by the looks of it, somewhere foreign anyway.

Paul sits down on a big soft sofa and she perches in an armchair opposite with her gloved hands resting in her lap like she's about to play the piano. The gloves are those fingerless jobs, the same dark green as her Doc Marten boots and that fringed paisley shawl. She's got style, he's got to hand it her – though God knows what century it's from.

The cream walls are jam-packed with books, with more piled up on the floor, and there's a squashed-looking leather pouffe by the fireplace, where there's one of those ancient coal-effect electric fires Paul thought didn't exist anymore.

'Before you ask,' she's saying, 'Ben's told me all about his gender dysphoria. That's why he came to see me.'

Paul takes a breath. Shit. So that's what this is about. 'But that was years ago,' he says. 'He's into sports and that now. Computers and diving and what have you.'

'I'm afraid not, Mr Dixon. Your son's simply learnt to hide his feelings and "gone underground" as it were. But from what he tells me, they're as strong as ever – though it seems they've lost the hallucinatory features that must have been so alarming for you and your wife when he was younger.'

'That Annie business, you mean.' Christ, he'd nearly forgotten about that. Bairn bawling in his buggy down on Bell Street because there was a tyre factory where 'Annie's house' should have been.

'We talked quite a bit about Annie,' she's saying. 'Your son's a very unusual child, Mr Dixon. He displays a great deal of self-awareness, but I have to tell you that he has been extremely distressed for a very long time.' And now she's looking straight at him, a look with a weight behind it, for all that she's hardly up to his oxter.

'I can't believe he came to see you without telling me.'

'Ben's afraid you'll reject him.' The look's still there, pinning him down so he couldn't get up off the sofa if he tried.

'But I've never given him any reason—'

'Children pick up nuances, Mr Dixon. Far more than we realize. Not just from what we tell them, but from how we react to things. And as I say, Ben's an unusually perceptive child who's desperate to gain your approval.'

Paul shakes his head, to clear it. He keeps getting this picture of Ben at St James in his Toon Army gear, sat beside him and shouting for Shearer. 'So he's still on about all that stuff, about being a girl?'

'Very much so,' she says. 'But if you are agreeable, I think I may be able to help him. Do you believe in the soul, Mr Dixon?'

'*What?*' Is she some kind of religious nut?

She laughs then: a proper wide laugh with her head back. 'Oh dear, I can see how that must sound. Don't worry, Mr Dixon. I'm not planning to reclaim your son for Jesus.' She looks younger when her solemn look goes, and quite attractive if you like the type – long skirt, amber brooch, and one of those heavy buns that's really a thick plait wound round and round. But those green gloves – what's that about?

'To reassure you on that count, I am not affiliated to any kind of religious group, Christian or otherwise. I am a fully qualified Jungian therapist, with a doctorate in neuropsychology and over twenty-five years' experience in the NHS and private practice.' She waves vaguely in the direction of a load of framed certificates on the wall over the mantelpiece. 'I lecture at universities up and down the country, and I've published three books and numerous papers in reputable journals.'

She sounds almost bored as she recites all this; it's obviously something she's said over and over. But it helps to know she's got a decent brain in there.

'Ben tells me he has been to therapists in the past?'

'Fat lot of good they did.'

'Well, that's why I'm hoping my approach might prove more helpful. In recent years I've found myself concentrating on my clients' recall of what appear to be previous incarnations – past lives if you like – hence my rather inopportune mention of the soul. So it would help me to know whether this is an approach you'd find acceptable.'

'Now just hold on there—' Paul's not sure he finds this acceptable at all.

'I know it may sound rather far-fetched—'

'Damn right.' He should have known when he clapped eyes on those elephants that there was something off about the whole set up.

'—but please bear with me a moment.'

'Go on then,' he says grudgingly. He'll give her three minutes, he decides, and if she hasn't convinced him by then, he's off out of it.

'Thank you. And I appreciate your candour. Believe me, you're not the first person to find my approach somewhat unusual. But before I say anything else, I should stress that I've had a great deal of success with my clinical method. It enables me to achieve catharsis – that is, get to the heart of a client's problem – far more rapidly than other methods I've used over the years.'

'Go on,' he says again, crossing his arms. If she's trying to impress him, she's got a long way to go.

'Right, let's start with the soul. Have you ever heard of a phenomenon called near-death experience?'

'You mean all that seeing a white light, and going towards it?'

'That's part of it, yes. But I'm talking about the many reported cases of people on the point of dying – from a heart attack, perhaps – who are subsequently revived and recall floating above their bodies and seeing things they couldn't possibly have seen from their hospital beds. There are even cases of blind people who were able to describe the clothing of the people who revived them.'

'And you think it's the person's soul seeing those things.'

'That's not the only explanation, of course. It could be some kind of telepathic knowledge, for example, that's only available to the unconscious brain. But the existence of something we might call a soul seems as good an explanation as any. And it's the one I base my clinical practice on.'

That's when it starts to go really weird: when she starts talking about people dying and their souls lurking about, like at a bus stop, waiting to jump aboard the next baby to be born. Though she doesn't put it like that, of course, because it's all spouted in her posh boarding-school voice like it's some *Open University* lecture on the telly. Anyway, it turns out that scientists have been studying this reincarnation business for years and, if she's telling the truth, it looks like there could be something in it.

'It's worth reflecting,' she's saying now, 'that ours is the first era in which humans have not simply *assumed* the existence of past lives, ancestor spirits and spirit possession – the latter of which I suspect is actually a manifestation of a past life intruding into the current one—'

'So what's all this got to do with Ben?' Paul cuts her off mid-sentence. She might have persuaded him she's not a nutter, but he can do without the lecture, thank you very much.

'I believe your son may be the reincarnation of this girl he calls Annie. I think that may be why he has become obsessed with procuring gender reassignment surgery—'

'Did you say *surgery*?' Paul's mind tilts dizzily for a second, and he's back in the flat six years ago, pulling Ben's blood-soaked pyjamas back up and wrapping his limp little body in his duvet, then charging down four flights of stairs with him in his arms, and the lad weighs nothing, nothing.

'You're not aware that Ben's been investigating the possibility of surgery?' Her voice has gone soft, so he knows it must be all over his face: the knife, all that blood, the shock of it. Bairn almost *died*, for fuck's sake.

Paul shakes his head dumbly.

'One thing transsexuals complain of prior to surgery is a profound sense of having been born into the wrong body. Well I hypothesize that in some cases – Ben's included – that may be exactly what's happened.' That weighted look is back on her face, making him focus on what she's saying. But her brown eyes are kinder now, like they can see what he's going through.

'The doctors said it was hormones in the womb made him like that,' he says. 'Or something about how we were bringing him up – but he started on about Annie pretty much as soon as he could talk.'

She nods, like this is par for the course. 'All I can say is that I've treated several cases of gender dysphoria, and in my experience there can sometimes be powerful reasons in a past life that prevent a soul embracing its current physiological gender.'

He takes a deep breath. 'So how can you help Ben?'

'Well, there are no guarantees, but with the majority of cases I've treated, I've found that once the precipitating past-life trauma has been identified – and recalled in full – many of the neurotic symptoms in the current life resolve.'

Paul tries to weigh it all up. If you think about what she's saying logically, it's completely barmy. Investigating someone who's been dead for years as a way of curing someone who's alive today. But the way she puts it, in her la-di-dah professor voice, makes it seem almost reasonable. Like it's the obvious explanation for what's been happening with the bairn.

'So how does it work?' he asks guardedly.

'I put the client into a light trance, and follow his or her associations back into the relevant past life. In some cases the memories are very close to the surface, and only one or two sessions are required to access them. Sometimes it takes many sessions – if there's more than one past life to explore, or if for some reason I meet resistance.'

'So you could end up going right back to the Stone Age.' He's half joking, but she doesn't take it like that.

'Theoretically, yes, but that's extremely rare. Statistically speaking there were relatively few humans alive during the Stone Age, so the odds of a soul today tracing its provenance back to a member of a Stone Age population would be many millions to one.'

They're starting to talk as though he's agreed to the therapy, Paul realizes. 'So what's the down side?' he asks bluntly, back-tracking a bit. 'Isn't it dangerous, hypnotizing a twelve-year-old?'

'I am a highly qualified and experienced practitioner,' she says, 'and what I do is perfectly legal, but the client is vulnerable in any therapy. Having said that, it is my judgement that without help Ben could be in an even more vulnerable situation—'

'What do you mean "vulnerable"?'

She fixes her eyes on him again. 'Mr Dixon, I believe your son has been very lonely and unhappy for a very long time. We know he's tried to mutilate himself in the past, so there's every reason to fear he might try to force the issue again – and of course he's older now.'

'So he'd make a better job of it, is that what you're saying?' Paul feels light-headed, like he's going to faint. His kitchen at home's full of fucking knives.

'I think he's unlikely to attempt another mutilation, but I can't be sure. What I do know is that there are documented cases of children committing suicide when their desires for a sex change are thwarted.' She leans forward. 'Mr Dixon, I believe I can help Ben, but I can't predict the outcome. Whether you let me try or not is completely up to you.'

CHAPTER EIGHT

2007

Ben's dad always carries a wad of cash in his back pocket. Where most men have wallets, he always has this folded sheaf of tens and twenties. Ben used to get a buzz when he'd bring it out to buy just a burger and Coke, peeling a twenty off the outside, and the girl behind the counter with her eyes popping. But these days it's a bit embarrassing, like boasting he's OK, even though everyone knows the fishing's crap and lads are selling up right, left and centre. That's just Dad though: he never thinks, just barges in with a big grin and orders drinks all round.

Ben's dad's almost famous in North Shields; he can't walk down the street without someone saying howay or tooting their horn. That's just the way he is: fingers in lots of pies. The boat's the main thing, of course. But he's got all these other deals going on too, that he calls his nice little earners. It's like when anyone in Shields gets an idea for making a bit on the side, the first thing they do is call Dad. It got so bad that he had to stop giving out his number because the home phone never stopped ringing. And it would either be someone calling about trawling gear – Dad once bought a load of second-hand rigs from somewhere – or rough blokes with Scottish accents on about cheap diesel. Then there was some DEFRA training thing, then the lads with the fishcakes. Eventually he got two separate mobiles: one for business and one just for Ben and Nana, so they can always get through. Plus the satellite phone on the boat, which is a different number again.

Today Ben's tagging along to the ships' chandlers where Dad's checking out some new shackles or something, but they're stopping off for breakfast at the Seaman's Mission first.

Dad's really quiet, which is weird because he's usually chatting away about the footie or diving or something. Ben sneaks a look at his face, but he's just staring out towards the Black Middens. Maybe that doctor's phoned, Ben thinks, then pushes the thought right down to his feet and concentrates on the pavement instead, trying to match his pace to Dad's, just the two pairs of black trainers walking along, sizes five and ten.

The canteen at the Seamen's Mission smells of tabs and chips and the air's blue with smoke, even though there are big new No Smoking signs everywhere because the ban's just come in. It's full of blokes in woolly hats, with big jackets on the backs of their chairs and newspapers spread out, like they've got no homes to go to. Dad says that's because they haven't really, because when you're at sea all you want is to get home, but when you're home you can't wait to get back on the boat. Dad says the canteen is like half way between the two: with the river just outside and lads packed in all round eating fry-ups, which is just like on the boat.

Dad does his usual howays to everyone and loads up a tray. When they're settled at a table, Ben opens his sausage bap like a book and squirts brown sauce in a careful squiggle; and Dad rips open a mustard sachet with his teeth and reaches over to the next table for the ketchup.

'I went to see your doctor friend yesterday evening,' he says in a bit, quietly, so no one can earwig.

Ben closes his bap carefully and sits back. 'I was going to tell you,' he says. 'But I didn't know where to start.'

'She says she can help you,' Dad says, cutting up bacon then lifting fried eggs onto his toast. The smoke's making Ben's eyes sting. He feels sick.

'Look, I know I've not been much of a dad—' Dad goes on in this same quiet voice.

'No, you have!' Ben says. 'Don't say that. It's got nothing to do with—'

'Nay lad, hear me out. I'm away most the time and fucking shattered when I'm back, or off out somewhere. I just wanted to make some dosh so I could give you the best, try to make up for losing your mam. I didn't realize you still—' He pauses, glances round, clicks two sweeteners into his mug. 'And then you got in the under thirteens and, well, I just didn't realize. I should have asked, I suppose. Truth is, I didn't want to know.'

They both look at his plate, where he's getting his next mouthful organized, a bit of each thing on his fork.

'Are you cross?' Ben asks.

'Shit, Ben,' says his dad, like a sigh. 'I wish you'd said something.'

'I thought you'd hate me.' It comes out in a whisper.

'I ought to batter you within an inch of your life.' Ben looks up. He's been bracing himself for a telling off, but Dad just sounds weary. 'I mean, think what it's like being told by some shrink that your son wants – what does she call it?'

'Gender reassignment.'

The words sound so daft, hanging there in the blue air of the canteen. Ben feels a giggle starting, from nowhere, and checks out Dad, who's half smiling too.

'She's quite something, that doctor,' Dad says, shaking his head. 'Like, what's with all those elephants, for fuck's sake?'

'Did she have her gloves on?'

'She said there's this disease she's got in her hands, where they go all white and numb if they get cold. If it's severe, she says it can turn into frostbite or gangrene or something and they have to cut bits off.' He winces, and Ben winces back.

'But she's written loads of books and stuff,' Ben adds quickly, in case she's sounding too weird. 'I looked her up on Google.'

'It's OK, son.' That tired voice again. 'There's no need to argue the toss. I signed you up for six sessions, starting tomorrow. Then we'll take it from there.'

Ben doesn't say and Dad doesn't ask about the rest of it: his visits to Laura and his bleaching kit; checking out those puberty-delaying hormones; his M&S nighties and still sleeping with Lily the Pink. They just sit opposite each other munching away like nothing's happened.

And a minute later, two young blokes with trays of All Day Breakfast come and sit at the same table, so they have to budge over a bit to make room; and the young blokes start going on about DEFRA this, DEFRA that, with Dad. And Ben just sits quietly munching on his bap, breathing in the smoke and the chip smell, and feeling his tummy slowly fill up like a smile.

'Do you know how gurnards sleep?' Ben asks, like the start of a joke, not expecting an answer. 'They wriggle into a rock crevice and wedge themselves in with their front fins, so the sea can't wash them out.'

They're strolling along the Fish Quay to the chandlers, checking the moorings to see who's in and who's out. Ben wants to run and shout – because Dad *knows* and it's OK! The thing he was most dreading in the *world* and it's OK! – but they're just walking, sizes five and ten, not touching, just like normal.

'And herring and cod sink down to the sea bed and lie totally still. But they have to separate from each other a bit, because if they slept in a shoal, they'd be found by predators. So they just hang in the water by themselves, or find somewhere to hide.' Ben likes the idea of the sea bed as an actual bed. He likes to think of the fish sleeping there, and the sand rucked up like a blanket, with seaweed duvets draped over the rocks and silver bodies tucked snugly inside – though it's fucking freezing in the North Sea, even in the middle of summer, because of the currents from the Arctic.

'So what do they dream about?' Dad asks, teasing. But it's actually something Ben's thought about.

'I think you probably need eyelids to dream,' he says, 'so you can shut out the real world. And fish don't have eyelids.'

He's tried not blinking, to see what it would be like to have eyes like a fish: flat and round and always open. First they felt cold and dry, then they sort of ached and he *really* wanted to close them. It must be weird not to have the choice, to just stare out even if it's pitch black in the middle of the night, or you're half dead in the hold waiting to be gutted, with your eye right up against another fish's eye.

'Most of our catches are at night,' says Dad. 'So we're probably scooping them up when they're napping.'

He's joking, but Ben doesn't think it's very funny. That's the weird thing about Dad. He can go diving with Ben, into that echoey green world, that's all swooshy water noises and bubbles, and little shrimps pootling about, and weed waving like brown ribbon, then put on his leather jacket and stride into the chandlers and buy a mile of new tickler chain for the trawl gear to go crashing through the lot of it.

Afterwards they climb the Ropery Stairs up to the top bank. Ben counts the 119 steps, like he always does, feeling his heart pumping, but Dad refuses to stop for a breather till they're at the top; then they hold on to the railings and look out across the river to South Shields and wait until their chests stop burning.

There's an old artist bloke setting up an easel along the road, stretching bungee straps around the painting to stop the wind catching it. Ben's noticed him before – same place, same painting gear, same four tins of Stella – but it turns out Dad knows him from way back.

'That's old Skip,' he says. 'Owned the first boat I ever went on. Bloody brilliant skipper but daft as a brush – in and out the loony bin, but always held it together on the boat. Then something happened, his auntie or his mam died or something, and he finally lost it.'

'Cheers, Skip,' he goes as they get nearer. 'How's it going?'

'Not too bad,' grunts the old bloke, mixing paint on an enamel plate.

Looking at the painting, Ben feels the breath catch in his chest. It's a view of the Fish Quay from where they're standing, but it's as though he's seeing through Annie's eyes again. The 119 steps are there still, going down to the quayside; but instead of bushes and grass, the old bloke's painted tall houses either side, with dirty brick chimneys and great billows of grey smoke. And down on the Fish Quay, instead of just five trawlers tied up, there's a zillion masts with reddish brown sails furled around them, and the boats all moored so close together you can't see the water.

'I should take you to his stall down Tynemouth Market,' says Dad, looking over Ben's shoulder. 'He's done views of Shields going right back to the year dot.'

There are people on the steps in the painting, faces Ben thinks he half recognizes: that scowling woman with the basket and a shawl criss-crossed over her chest; those two lads hanging nets on a wall. And they're all wearing hats, even the two grubby bairns squatting together in the shadows halfway down, on a front step that Ben knows has a slight dip in it from being scrubbed so often.

He looks from the painting to the real Ropery Stairs – litter snagged on the bushes, crumpled tin of Stella on its side, KFC bag mashed in a corner – then back again. The old bloke's painting the weather now: thick grey storm clouds over South Shields in the distance and scrappy specks of white foam on the water. In the middle of the river two small boats are tilted over sideways, as if their sails are full of fish instead of wind. And Ben can almost hear the snap of the rigging in that forest of boats moored in the harbour, feel the sting of the salt on Annie's bandaged hands.

CHAPTER NINE

1898

It's the middle of June, I don't know the exact date, but I do know it's a Friday, around six o'clock. The sun's sailing upriver toward Newcastle and the home lums are trickling smoke for folks' tea.

We're walking home together, Flo and me, because she's shifting to our house today. We've a crew of Scots lasses coming to lodge with us tomorrow, and another lot's arriving at Flo's place any day, so we've all to squash in a bit tighter, like wrens in a nest, till the herring season's done.

It's a right puffing climb up the bank to the house, specially when you've been on your feet all day. My boots are Jimmy's old uns, padded with layers of socks, so they weigh a ton. On the way up, we keep having to press back against the wall to let the Scots lasses pass by with their kists on their heads. It's like swallows in April. One day the skies are empty, next they're full of swooping and chattering. Just last week there was only us local lasses gipping and a couple or three drift boats down from Grimsby. Now suddenly the quay's fairly bristling with masts and our lanes jostling with lasses lumping kists to their lodgings.

Climbing the stairs, Flo's full of daffy blether, saying she'll be out on the gin every night now she's stopping at ours. She doesn't even like gin, the daftie! She's just that giddy to be out from under the thumb. I've told her Da drives a harder cart any day of the week than her folks, but she won't have it.

She thinks being at ours will make it easier for her to see Tom, but how can it? Less she's planning to winch him up on the pulleys to the net loft of a Saturday night, for that's where we're sleeping – up in the loft with Mam's lints.

Tom's a lad off Da's boat; Flo's been walking out with him this past month, ever since she turned sixteen and was allowed. It's early days yet, but she likes him a deal more than the others who've come knocking. They're all after her, mind, all the lads. Because she's canny bonny, is Flo, all yellow-haired, sweet and pillowy, like a cream cake from the Howard Street Bakery. And Tom's a fine-looking lad, right enough, though a bit of a rogue for the lasses. But he'll have his own boat one day soon, no bother, for Da says he's forever on about the gear and the way things are going, and nagging Da to get shot of the long lines come winter and go over to the otter trawl – though he'll have a job shifting Da over to that monster load of metal gear.

I turned sixteen back in March, but I've never walked out with a lad yet, so I've been bursting to ask Flo how it is with Tom, where they go and that, what it's like being kissed. But I've been shy till now, because these are not things a nice lassie speaks about, and Flo's never been a one for smutty talk. But maybes now we're in the loft together she'll let on a bit.

Speak of the Devil, here's the lad himself, broad and dark, gallumphing down the steps towards us, hoying a rolled sail on his shoulders – fresh from the cutch tank, russet and reefed like a giant's tab – and our Jimmy's got the other end of it, clomping along behind like a shadow.

'Why aren't yous at home?' says I, for this is normally the time for the lads to catch up on their sleep after a night out chasing the shoals.

'Your da's sent us to fix this afore we set out,' says Tom – and he's not looking best pleased. 'The old un ripped in that squall last night. And a couple of lints were holed, so he's wanting them switched too.'

He sets the sail down and fetches out his bakkie tin. 'Why it couldn't wait till Saturday, I don't know,' he grumbles, leaning against the wall and rolling a tab.

'Da said we can sleep on the boat later, going out,' says our Jimmy. 'But I don't see him missing his precious lie down.'

Now here's Flo giving Tom her sideways look. 'I'm shifting to Annie's today,' she says. 'So that's where I'll be if you want to find me.' She's pulling her scarf off and shaking out her hair, which I'd do too if I'd hair like that to show off.

'And why would I want to do that?' says Tom, teasing like and leaning in.

'I don't know,' says she, teasing back. 'Maybes go for a bit walk?'

'And where were you thinking we could walk to?'

And they're off on one of those flirty blethers that go nowhere and are just a sort of daylight canoodling, so I leave them to it and turn to our Jimmy.

He's taken a pinched out tab-end from behind his ear and is lighting up. 'Mam's on about me shifting to Nana's today,' he's saying, 'but I won't have time now.'

He's looking tired, but handsome enough, I suppose, in his tidy way, though you hardly notice when Tom's about. And I'm thinking it must be rough being on Da's boat, soft lad like him, with Da on at him the whole time.

'I'll hoy your stuff over if you like,' says I. 'I've to take the bairns along later anyway, most likely, as I can't see Mam finding the time.'

'What's that?' says Tom, coming over.

'I'm hoying Jimmy's shiftenings over to Nana's,' says I.

'Well, mind you don't leave it too late coming back,' says Tom. 'Bonnie lass like you, on her own, could be asking for it.' And he leans a hand on the wall over my head, so it's almost like he's got his arm around me, and it's me who's his lass instead of Flo.

I feel like ducking away, but don't want to make a fuss – because it's just Tom, isn't it, and means nowt. Still it's a mite too bold, the way he's leaning over, looking in my eyes, then down at my mouth, then lower, to where my boobies are pushing at my blouse, smiling and checking me over, like a ransacker at a net, like he's never seen me before.

I glance round for Flo, but she's nipped into the sweetie shop along the lane. Which means he's waited till her back's turned, hasn't he? And I'm just building up to asking what he's about, when the dinger on the shop door goes and he straightens up, all casual, like nothing's happened.

There's a sort of awkwardness between me and Flo after the lads have gone, which starts me wondering, did she see? Even though I know fine well that she couldn't of. But the thought that she *might* of is making it so's I can't think of anything to say, which is not like me at all.

So now she's looking suspicious at me, and asking am I jealous of her walking out with Tom. Which gets me into a right flummox, gabbling no no, don't be daft, and he'd never look at me anyway. Which is a barefaced lie, because that's exactly what he *was* just doing, which is why I'm flummoxing in the first place.

So now she's on about that time, when we were bairns, when Tom told everyone that him and me were promised. Which I'm amazed she's even remembered, for it was years ago, but just goes to show how much she thinks about him, I suppose.

It was just after his mam passed, and his da was tooken off to jail for drunk and disorderly. Tom was staying over at ours and started on about us getting married, and taking over the boat and the nets, once Da had retired to his coble. But it was all just bairns' blether, and to tell the truth, I think it was the boat he was mostly interested in, because the *Osprey* belongs to Da, see, so I was just a prize that went with her.

Anyway, I say all this to Flo, but she's only half mollified, for I was right soft on Tom back then, and she knows it. I thought him canny brave and funny: always first to test the ice on the boating lake come winter, and fiercest with his fists in a scrap – not like our Jimmy, who'd never say boo to a goose. Nowadays, though, I'm not so sure; for what's brave in a lad can turn hard in a man, and that's the way it's seeming with Tom.

'Honest to God, cross my heart, I don't mind you walking out with him,' I say now. 'The only thing I *would* mind about is if he were to come between you and me.' So now Flo's saying, over her dead body, and smiling, and we start on up the steps again, but side by side this time, and linked in, so folk have to edge round us.

Which is how it's always been with Flo and me – like sisters, though there's no blood tie between us. But Da says when you've been on a boat with a body for as long as him and Flo's da, you become closer than blood kin. And Mam says she can't count the number of times she passed me as a wean for a suckle with Flo's mam, if she'd her round to do, or took Flo under her blouse for a feed. So we were raised on the milk of both our mams, and if that doesn't make us sisters, I don't know what does.

But I can't help worrying about Tom, and thinking if he carries on with his nonsense, I don't know how Flo'd take it. She can spit nails when she's riled, for all her placid ways, and you don't want to be nearby.

When we get home Mam's got the rooms ready for the Scots lasses and pinned brown paper to the walls to save the plaster from the herring oil, because it stinks to high heaven if it soaks in. See, even if you take off your boots and oilies before you come in, you've still to hoy them through the house to the yard. Then there's our skirts to think of, and shawls. However hard you try, there's always some splatter, and you can't be washing your clothes every day, even if you'd that many spares to change into.

The bairns are in the kitchen munching on jammy pieces, and our Emily's whingeing on that she doesn't want to shift to Nana's and Mam's shushing her because Da's asleep. I've never known him wake before his time, but that doesn't stop Mam shushing and tiptoeing round, like he's royalty, which he is to her, I suppose.

She's got a brew on, and fresh rolls in for Flo, but says our tea'll be late because she's still her round to do. She's sweating and a bit breathless, like she's been running, and her ankles are swollen again, and her varicoses bulging, which is a worry after what happened with our Emily. So I try to get her to sit down a spell before setting off, but I might be talking to the wall for all the notice she's taking.

Mam's one of those folk that takes on too much, then wonders why she's still on the go when everyone else has their feet up. With the fish round, see, she could easy leave off during the summer and stick to the smoked fish come winter when the boats are stuck in dock. But she's got her regulars up the High Town and doesn't like to disappoint them.

So here's her cutting board ready, and her weighing scales, and her slabs of halibut and cod under a clean cloth. I help lift the board onto her head and off she goes, plodding up the stairs to Saville Street and Dockwray Square where the cooks of the rich folk are waiting on her.

Now it's after tea and I've taken the two bairns along to Nana's, and I'm wishing I'd not stayed to help settle them in, nor sat for cocoa on the step after, listening to Nana mythering on about poor old Mrs Carlton, who's opened up her front room to sell bacon buns in the wee hours to the night crews – for if there's a shilling to be made in this town, now's the time to make it.

Nana's offered to walk me home, but that's daft, for who'd walk her back? So I've pulled my scarf low on my forehead and set off, keeping close to the walls, for the lanes are thronging with rowdy lads, what with the late crews setting off, and the morning crews out for a quick bevvy, or a slow one and stotting home, and some of them never even getting there.

The lamp-lighter's done his rounds, but them are just puddles of light really, and leave a thousand and odd nooks for a lad to unbutton and do his business, or linger with a lassie of a certain kind; and he'll have his long coat on, even though the night's warm, and his back to the lane, and I don't want to think what's going on behind that coat.

Now here's a big beardy lad stotting out of the darkness, stinking of whisky, and asking my name, then lunging at me before I can answer. He's grabbed my arm, his fingers are digging in. I'm twisting around and trying to wriggle free, but he's so strong I've to kick him before he leaves go.

So now I'm fairly running, and faces and bodies are blurring past in the dark between the lamp posts, and here's two more rowdy sailors piling out of the Black Swan and one's got ahold of my skirt and the other's tugging at my shawl, so I'm scared they're about to strip me off there and then – and they're laughing fit to burst, the both of them, that wild sort of laughing lads do when they've had a skinful, stotting against the wall.

I can see their eyes gleaming in the lamplight, and the wet on their teeth. They're so far gone they don't care if I'm a decent lass or a loose one, and they're trying to push me down an alley, so I'm screaming and kicking out, and I can see one's got his gipping knife in the brim of him cap, so I'm thinking no, please God—

Oh – there's wet on my cami, my blouse – it's blood, my hand's covered. Where's it coming from? I never felt the knife go in—

CHAPTER TEN

2007

Ben sits up and hugs his knees. He can't stop shivering, violent shudders that shake his whole body. The doctor takes off her cardigan and drapes it round his shoulders, then heaves the pouffe closer and squats down next to him on it. Her cardie smells of tabs and coffee, which is comforting, as though she has her arms around him, because no one ever puts their arms round him these days, not ever.

'Scary stuff, eh?' she says.

'I forgot to do my emergency sign.' They'd agreed that he'd wiggle the fingers of his right hand if he wanted to stop.

'Sometimes it happens like that, Ben. You can jump forwards without warning to a different episode in someone's life. That's why you came out of the trance so suddenly. There's probably something there that you're not ready to look at quite yet.'

'Something really bad happened to Annie, didn't it?' he asks in a small voice.

'Yes, I think so.' Her eyes are on him, warm and brown, *really* on him, like she really cares.

'Something to do with one of those men – God, there were so many rough men around, like everywhere, all over the girls.'

'So you remember all that. Good.'

'And everyone's got a knife, like *everyone*. And they're so sharp, like you wouldn't believe.' He's still shivering, teeth clattering together.

'Are you all right? Shall I turn on the fire?' She does it anyway and a smell of burning dust starts to waft through the room, as if the fire hasn't been on for years. 'Don't try to get up yet. One shouldn't underestimate the power of these experiences.'

Ben closes his eyes and sinks back against the cushions. He can hear the doctor bustling around, clomping upstairs in her green boots, then down again a bit later with a blanket, which she tucks around him like his mam did when he was little. The blanket's got little mirrors sewn on it and smells of that perfume you get in Indian shops.

'When she'd stuck me full of needles,' the doctor's saying, 'my acupuncturist always used to wrap me in warm towels, then turn up the heater and leave me to cook like a joint of lamb. Which is precisely what I plan to do with you.'

Ben tries a smile. He can't imagine her with needles sticking out of her. He can't imagine her without her boots and gloves on either. He opens his eyes, then closes them again. She's moving around as though he's not there: shuffling papers together, writing something, rewinding the tape. Then he hears the front door opening and the outside noises get clearer: the seagulls squabbling and that ice-cream van in the distance, some little birds twittering in the bushes. Then there's a faint smell of French cigarettes.

He wakes to find her back on the pouffe. His forehead feels chilly, as though she's had a hand there stroking his hair back, but they're both folded in her lap when he opens his eyes. There are two glasses of Coke on the table.

'It's one-thirty,' she says. 'Do you think you should contact your father to let him know you'll be late?'

'He's off on the boat till Thursday. So it's only Nana and she won't be bothered.' He pushes the blanket off and sits up. Her cardie's still round him, which is embarrassing, so he takes it off and folds it. There's a man's white hanky poking out of the pocket. The other glass of Coke is for her. It's really cold, enough to hurt your teeth, and they both sip for a bit, looking at the red lights flickering on the fake coal of the electric fire.

'Annie really likes that Flo,' he says. 'I hope nothing happens to her.' His finger draws a zigzag in the condensation on his glass. 'But that's daft, because she's probably dead now anyway, isn't she? So something must have happened to her, even if it's only dying of old age.' He pictures Flo's face, her pink cheeks, the dusting of freckles on her nose. 'Do you think she's still alive?'

The doctor smiles sadly. 'It's extremely unlikely. From what you were saying, I'd estimate that we entered Annie's life, as it were, at around the turn of the century. Which would make Flo well over 100 today – around 125 in fact, assuming she was in her late teens when we met her.'

'So they're all dead. Annie and Flo, Jimmy, that Tom bloke.'

'I'm afraid so.'

'God, that's so weird,' he says. 'To be there with them, talking to them, *smelling* them, even though they're all dead.'

'The process is not unlike time travel, I always think, though without the trouble of constructing a Tardis.'

He can't imagine her watching *Dr Who*, but there's a telly on a carved table in the corner: a clumpy black cube that must be a hundred years old, probably only gets one channel.

There's a quiet knock on the door, three quick raps like a code.

'It's OK, Laura,' the doctor calls out. 'We're finished in here.'

Laura bursts in like a holiday ad, with red strappy high-heels and matching capris, Gucci sunglasses pushed up on her head. 'Hey, what have you been doing to my pal?' she says, frowning at the blanket, the pouffe, the fire flickering away.

'It was rather a powerful session, wasn't it Ben?'

'Threw a wobbly did you?' Laura plumps down two carrier bags. 'Well I've got just the thing to set you right. Oxtail soup from your *bona fide* oxen – bet you've never had that before. And my famous walnut bread made with real walls.'

'Laura!' hisses the doctor through her teeth. 'I'm sorry Ben,' she says. 'I can't let you stay to lunch. It's not considered ethical for a therapist to socialize with her clients.'

Laura turns on her. 'You can't turf the lad out in the street.'

'He's a client, Laura, not an asylum seeker.'

'Client schmient. I'm doing the cooking, so he's my guest *por manjare.* If it makes you feel better, you can stop in here with yours. Come on Ben, let's get this lot into that kitchen.'

'No, I'll go. It's all right,' he says, getting up and edging towards the door.

'Mary?' Laura squares up to the doctor until she's towering over her, all high heels and big hair, and the doctor just caves in, just like that, as though she knows it's hopeless.

'It would be good to keep an eye on him for a bit longer,' she goes.

'*Bene!*' Laura hands Ben a carrier and heads for the hall. 'Follow me, duckie, but avert your eyes from the avocado suite in that bathroom.' She gives a fake shudder. 'It's like a shrine to the seventies in there. Mirror tiles, Ascot heater, the lot. She should charge an entry fee and open it as a heritage site.'

The kitchen's really dim, because it's at the back of the house, with wood-effect lino on the floor, and a set of heavy brown spotlights that light up different parts of the room when Laura switches them on. One is pointing at a massive chrome coffee machine and another at an ancient little gas cooker on legs.

'She never chucks anything out, that's the trouble,' Laura's saying. 'If something works, she'll hang on to it until it conks out. Place is like a museum, but what can you do? I took her to Ikea once and she came away with a bag of tea lights and a paperweight.'

She's bustling round the kitchen as though she knows it inside out: lighting the oven, emptying the rubbish and shaking out a new bin liner. 'Someone gave her a huge roll of that parquet lino, so that's this room frozen in time for the foreseeable future. And don't get me started on all those tins of maroon paint she's got stashed in the attic.'

There's a cat flap in the maroon door, but no sign of a cat, and the maroon window looks out on a concrete yard with an old bike propped against the wheelie bin, a carrier bag tied over the saddle.

'I swear she'd live on boiled eggs if I wasn't here,' says Laura. 'She gets so caught up in her work she forgets to shop. Or if she shops, she forgets to cook. I'm forever finding mince past its sell-by at the bottom of the fridge. Be a love and fill the kettle, will you? Now where's that broom? I can't stand a crumb underfoot when I'm cooking.'

'Do you come in every day?' Ben asks.

Laura chuckles. 'Like Meals on Wheels you mean? No, I just like to visit, and a boiled egg with a Ryvita's not my idea of *bona manjare*.' She's opening Tupperware and tipping soup into a pan. 'It started when she got pneumonia – years back when I was still having sessions. I turned up for my appointment on the Monday and she was in a right state: hacking cough, dressing-gown over her clobber, didn't know what day it was. So I got the doctor round and slept on the sofa till she was back on her batts.

'Why didn't she call someone?'

'Kept thinking it would get better, I suppose – and when you spend your life helping other people, you get out of the habit of asking for yourself.'

Ben switches on the kettle and looks around for tea bags. 'It must have been weird being the one looking after her, like swapping places.'

'Weird wasn't the word, duckie. She was that red hot with fever she got delirious. So she'd be half asleep but with her eyes open and shouting her head off. What with me and my nightmares, we were a right pair.'

'What was she shouting?'

'I couldn't make out all of it. You know what it's like when someone's talking in their sleep and it's mostly mumbles and grunts? But then she'd sort of focus, like when you find a channel on the radio in the middle of a load of interference. And she was on a boat, in a storm it seemed like, shouting instructions about nets and ropes. Though what do I know? Never set so much as a toe on a boat in my life, unless you count that pedalo in Benidorm.'

'Was it another life coming through?'

'Well that was her first thought, obviously – once she'd recovered, I mean. Especially seeing as she's so scared of the sea. She thought maybe she'd been a fisherman who'd drowned. Scads of lads were lost at sea in the old days, see. It was even more dangerous than mining, and that's saying something.' She peers through the window up at the sky. 'There's quite a bit of blue up there. So you choose: shall we eat outside or in?'

'Out, please,' says Ben.

'Put some crocks on that tray then,' she says, checking the bread warming in the oven. 'So then we thought maybe she'd just been dreaming. Because it was smack bang in the middle of my therapy that she fell sick, so she'd been hearing about my past life traumas on and off for weeks.'

Ben opens a cupboard. 'What shall I get out?' he asks, eyeing the uneven stacks doubtfully.

'Three of everything – cups, saucers, bowls, plates. Don't worry about matching. She's been collecting odds and sods of that willow pattern from antique shops for years, so it's all from different sets. And it's proper tea she likes, not tea bags: a spoon each and one for the pot. The caddy's over there by the tea pot and there's a strainer in the drawer.'

'Were you a fisherman too?' Ben asks.

'Born and bred, and a right moody bastard I was too – *he* was, I should say. Me, I'm pure as the driven snow.' She winks at him. 'He was in that many scrapes. Drinking, brawling, going on the pull; battering that poor old wife of his. He should have croaked long before he did, but he had nine lives, that Tom. Eventually died inhaling vomit after a drinking binge – at least that's what we think. Because of course he wouldn't have been conscious when it happened. Last thing he remembered was slapping some poor lass round the head – see, I told you he was a mean bastard – and slumping on the bedroom floor.'

'Wow,' is all Ben can think of to say to that. And he hopes, really hopes, that his Annie – because that's how he thinks of her now, as *his Annie*, not him but part of him – won't have ended up with someone like that.

There's a folding table in the porch and they set it up in front of the bench. The doctor's already out there, in her gloves in the blazing sunshine, sucking on one of her weird-smelling French tabs and talking to that old artist bloke Dad knows, who's hovering by the gate.

'Don't be silly,' she's saying. 'Laura always makes far too much.'

So in he comes with his tin of Stella, and fetches a plastic Coke crate from around the side of the house, as though this is a regular arrangement, and sets it up a bit away from the table, and creaks down onto it as though he's a leper trying not to infect anyone.

'Howay, Paul's lad,' he says to Ben. 'Your da all right?' Then nods nervously, sort of sideways, to Laura as she passes him a hunk of warm bread and bustles off for more crocks.

Ben sits on the bench next to the doctor then shuffles along so Laura can fit on the end, so they're all in a row with Ben in the middle and the folding table in front of them loaded with soup bowls, so he has to serve everyone. And even though it's really weird having lunch with an old artist bloke he hardly knows and two old ladies – though the doctor's not that old really – he doesn't feel like he has to be polite all the time. It just feels sort of normal and cosy, and the soup's really good, though he hopes no one from school sees him or he'll never live it down.

The old bloke finishes his really fast, slurping up his soup and mopping bread round his empty bowl almost before the others have started. Two minutes later he scuttles off back to his painting.

'Is he really a loony?' Ben asks when he's gone. He doesn't seem like a loony, just a bit scruffy around the edges, though he's obviously an alky so it's hard to tell.

'If by "loony" you mean schizophrenic, then yes, that has been his clinical diagnosis over the years,' says the doctor. 'Though I gather he's always coped exceptionally well with his illness. But more recently it's become overlaid with a touch of Korsakoff's psychosis, which rather complicates the picture.'

'What she's trying to say is he is a loony, but his memory's a bit shot these days because of the booze,' explains Laura, 'so it's hard to tell what's going on with the poor old fungus.'

'Actually it's only his memory for recent events that's impaired,' says the doc. 'He has very clear and vivid recall of events in his past.' She's spooning her soup in a really weird way, tipping the bowl away from her and scooping it up from the far side.

'What is schizophrenia?' It's a word Ben's heard before and he's always wondered.

'It's a mental illness where the person loses touch with reality and believes things to be different from how you or I would see them,' says the doc. 'So the schizophrenic might think his thoughts are being controlled by invisible rays emanating from the TV, or he might hear voices in his head that stop him from concentrating, or that berate him for what he's doing. With Mr Skipper, auditory hallucinations – hearing voices – are the main symptom, though he does appear to experience visual hallucinations too, which he incorporates into his paintings. That's rare in schizophrenia, but it can be associated with alcoholic brain damage. As I say, the picture is complicated.'

It's tricky to follow when she talks like a textbook, but Ben thinks he's understood most of it.

'Aren't you going to tell Ben about your theory?' Laura asks, slicing more bread.

The doc sighs and puts down her spoon. 'Given the current situation, I hardly think that's appropriate,' she says.

'What theory?' Ben asks.

'Mary thinks that schizophrenics aren't imagining the voices they hear,' says Laura, butting in again as usual. 'She reckons they're hearing real voices from their past lives.'

'Laura, please! That is exactly the sort of thing that gets me into trouble: people turning a purely speculative academic hypothesis into a tabloid headline.' The doc jabs a crust into her soup; she seems really annoyed. 'All I've ever suggested is that *some* instances of auditory hallucination *may* have their provenance in a previous incarnation – please note the caveats – and that once the habit of hearing voices is established this *may* burgeon, as it were, into a more pervasive hallucinatory condition.'

Ben's not sure he likes the idea of loonies being people who can't block out their past lives. Does that make him a loony too? 'Have you hypnotized him?' he asks.

'Has she ever!' says Laura. 'Poor old Skip was sat outside in the freezing cold crying his eyes out one day. Guy Fawkes night it was, or going to be later. Anyway, I was here doing the lunch and she invited him in to get warm. That was the first time we'd ever spoken to him, wasn't it, Mary? Anyway, before you know it, he's lying down on the sofa spilling the beans – and five minutes later he's shrieking fit to blow the roof off.'

'Laura, I've told you before. You mustn't give out that kind of information. It's a violation of client confidentiality.'

'Well it wasn't very confidential at the time. You could hear him in South Shields, for God's sake.' She turns to Ben. 'People were knocking on the door to see if she was being attacked. Someone even called the police!'

'Nevertheless, it's up to Mr Skipper to decide who else knows about his illness,' says the doc crossly. 'Suffice it to say, that was the one and only time I attempted any regression therapy with him. But since then, well, he's become rather a fixture.'

'You encourage him,' says Laura. 'She says she just wants to make sure he eats properly, takes his vitamins and that, to stop the Korsakoff's getting any worse. But you can see how she is with him, soft as putty.'

'He remembered me from yesterday,' says Ben. 'So his memory can't be that bad.'

The doc smiles. 'It's a funny thing, memory,' she says, rooting about in her cardigan for her tabs. 'Some things pass through with barely a trace, but others leave a mark so deep we can't forget them however much we try.'

CHAPTER ELEVEN

2007

Nana's supposed to come round to make Ben's breakfast when Dad's away, but she stopped ages ago and told him to keep quiet about it, which was fine with Ben because she's always going on at him about why doesn't he wear the latest puffa jacket she's bought him, and has he got any homework, and who his best friend is at school. Plus it means he can visit Laura without anyone knowing, because even though Dad's found out about him wanting the sex change, he's not exactly over the moon about it, so he might not be too chuffed about Ben practising walking in high heels at Salon Laura on a Friday morning.

Laura says Ben's got the knack. 'Naturally graceful,' she called him, which is not like most boys, apparently. She says that walking in heels is a dead giveaway if you're a man trying to pass. You need to bend at the knees and ankles, and let your hips go loose, otherwise you get that stiff look, like a dog on its hind legs. Then there's that other thing men do in high heels, which she calls mincing, which is basically the same as the dog look, but with shorter steps and flappy hands.

Once she's explained it, Ben can see what she means. Men move their legs completely differently. Either they're striding along with their hips locked in position and their arms swinging, or they're standing still, or sitting with their knees wide apart, which women never do, even if they're wearing jeans. Women do more of a wander, as though their legs are made of rubber, or wiggle along quickly. It's like dancing, Laura says. That's how she teaches men to get into it. You've got to forget walking and think dancing instead.

At Salon Laura there's a whole room just for shoes, including an entire wall of stilettos, in boxes with a picture of the shoe on the end, because that's what most TVs want: stilettos, to go with their evening dresses. TV is short for transvestite, which is a man who wants to dress up as a woman. But someone who wants an actual sex change is called a TS or transsexual, which are divided into MtFs (male to female), like Ben and Laura, and FtMs, who don't need special shops because they can buy ordinary men's clothes anywhere.

The shoe room is off a long hallway Laura's had fitted with a red carpet and a full-length mirror, 'for those filmstar fantasies'. But the main room is a proper beauty salon, with a massage table and machines for electrolysis and waxing and laser-zapping, plus a hair salon area with a proper hairdresser's sink and dryer, and a manicure table and foot spa with a million different varnishes. Then there's the sewing room with two sewing machines and an adjustable dummy; and a utility with washer and dry-cleaner. The other four rooms, on the floor above, are filled with racks and racks of clothes, mostly evening and fancy-dress, on two lots of rails right up to the ceiling, so you have to hook the top ones down with a special pole.

But one of the rooms is just underwear. Most of it's just things you might find in any shop: bras and panties and corsets and that, except in men's sizes; but there's a whole load of other stuff that looks like something you'd need a prescription for, with pads and buckles and elastic bits – Ben's not even sure which parts of the body they're meant for – which is really interesting but also a bit gross.

They have a routine now, every time he visits. First they have a snack – tea and toast for Laura, hot chocolate and a KitKat for Ben – then he does his chores, like mopping the floor and topping up the bottles in the salon, while she does invoices and that on the computer. Then if there's time before her first client, he'll get a lesson, but if not he'll check the returned stock to see if anything needs mending or stain-removing, or he'll just hang out in the store rooms tidying the clothes and trying things on.

Today he's had a walking lesson, and he's practising up and down the red carpet in some high heels he's found in his size, when Laura gets a call on her mobile. It's another client cancelling: the third in a row that morning.

'"Oh, Laura, I'm coming down with the flu and I'd hate to give you my germs,"' says Laura, imitating them in a fake squealy voice. '"Oh Laura, I have to wait in for the plumber." Pull the other one, duckie, it plays *I Believe.* They've seen the weather forecast, haven't they? And booked a session at the stand'n'tan for a top-up before the weekend.'

Hands on hips, she turns to Ben. 'Looks like I've got the rest of the day off. What say we drag Mary down to the Long Sands for a picnic?'

* * *

The doc doesn't want to go, of course – Ben could have predicted that. But Laura can be quite a bully when she sets her mind to it, and she marches straight up the stairs to the doc's bedroom, something Ben would never dare to do, and clatters back down with a towel and one of those boring navy Speedo swimsuits, which seems a bit hopeful as the doc's supposed to be scared of the sea.

So off they go, down the ninety-five steps of High Beacon Stairs and across the Fish Quay to the sea wall that stretches from North Shields all the way along beside the river to Tynemouth. And the doc starts off complaining about how she hates sand and she'll freeze to death on the beach. But soon even she has to admit that it's a totally brilliant day, with the sun glittering on the river, which is just lapping gently around the Black Middens, making the seaweed shine, so it's hard to believe how many boats have been wrecked on those rocks – so many, there's a special plaque to commemorate them – because today they're just basking quietly in the sunshine, with turnstones and oyster-catchers scampering over them, flicking bits of weed aside with their beaks, and cormorants sitting like statues staring into the bright water.

And it's as though the whole of Shields has taken the afternoon off and put on a T-shirt and flip-flops, and got out a stripy towel and baby buggy and is heading to the beach. And there's a smell of summer in the air, of chips and suntan lotion and seaweed, and radios blaring and little kids zooming past on their bikes, and heat shimmering above the concrete of the sea wall, so the feet of people in the distance are transparent, as though they're walking on a cloud.

Laura's evil plan is to get the doc in the sea. She explained it to Ben when they were getting the picnic ready; how she wants to start her off just sitting on the beach, then next time maybe paddling in the rock pools.

'What about her hands and feet getting cold?' Ben asks. He's looked up gangrene on Google and it's like something out of a zombie movie. Plus smoking makes it worse, so she should definitely give that up.

'We've not got her on the beach yet,' says Laura. 'First things first.'

The tide's right out when they get to the Long Sands, which is a mile of yellow sand with clumps of people dotted about and vans parked along the road selling ice-cream and burgers. Laura spreads out a pink blanket near the rocks and they sit down; though Ben's up again in a trice with his shoes off, racing down towards the sea and swerving side to side with arms out like an aeroplane, clearing the gulls off the beach and splashing though the shallows – then charging back again with his wet jeans rolled up to his knees.

'Is it OK to swim in my boxers?' he asks, peeling off his jeans and thanking God he's not put on his lacy knickers. His boxers are plain grey, so that's OK. Though who's going to look at him when there's Laura stripped off in her red and purple jungle-print tankini? She's taken out a bottle of that fake-tanning suntan lotion and the doc's smearing it on her back as though they're an old married couple, which they are in a way.

Seeing Laura lying in the sun, you'd never know she was a man. Even up close she just looks like anyone's nana sunbathing on the beach. She's doing that trick she taught him for bare feet, pointing them so they arch and it's harder to see what size they are. Ben tries it with his feet and it really works, though it would be better if his toenails were painted.

Looking at the doc's thin white feet, those gangrene photos flash across his mind again, which makes him wish he'd never done that Google search. Somehow Laura's managed to bully her into the navy swimsuit and she's sitting with her knees up like a nerdy kid, all stiff and pale and shivery, smoking a tab really fast and sucking the smoke right down.

'Do you want a towel round you?' he asks, though it's really hot in the sun.

'I'll warm up in a minute,' she says. Then: 'Pathetic, isn't it? This is the first time I've been on a beach since I was a girl.'

'Is it the waves that freak you out? Because they're really tiny today.'

'It's more the size of the sea itself,' she says, taking a last suck on her tab and stubbing it out in a little ashtray hole she's dug in the sand. 'Your "tiny waves" don't seem tiny at all to me, because I know they're part of an absolutely monstrous mass of water that stretches to the horizon and beyond, right around the planet.' Her hands are shaking as she lights up again. 'When I was a child I used to think the sea was actually higher at the horizon, because that's what it looks like, doesn't it? A towering wall of water. I was terrified it would come crashing down on me like a tidal wave.'

'Dad says he's been in seas where the waves are higher than a house, higher even than our flat. But the boat just sort of bobs over them.'

He's trying to cheer her up, but she winces. 'I can't help thinking of the sheer weight of all that water. Apparently there's a part of the Pacific that's over seven miles deep.'

'It's called the Marianas Trench,' he says, and this is something he really knows about. 'There are mud volcanoes down there, and loads of weird microbes that actually need the pressure and low temperature to survive. But no actual fish because under water the pressure increases one atmosphere for every ten metres you go down, so at the bottom of the Marianas Trench it's well over a thousand atmospheres, which would crush you flat as a pancake.'

She forces a thin smile. 'I suspected as much.'

'But you'd never get down that far,' he adds quickly. 'You need a really heavy weight-belt to make you sink even fifty metres. In normal sea water you just float on the surface like a boat.'

'I know it's irrational. That's why it's a phobia – thalassaphobia is the correct technical term, if you're interested.'

'Laura said it might be because you drowned in another life.'

'Did she now?' The doc sighs. 'Oh well, I suppose therapeutic opacity was a bit much to hope for with her involved.'

'Is it true?' he asks, ignoring the last bit because he has no idea what it means.

'It's possible, yes. Though I have only fragmentary recollections to go on. In my training we tended to concentrate on my most recent incarnation, a rather colourful character called Peggy, who died in unfortunate circumstances when she was in her thirties. But before Peggy it seems there was at least one fisherman – as you might expect, living where we do.' She nods sideways towards the distant waves, as though she can hardly bear to look. 'Before the First World War over ninety percent of boys in North Shields went to sea straight from school, either as fishermen or keelmen ferrying coal to the collier ships.'

'Do you remember him drowning then?'

'No, thankfully, though I have had some suggestive dreams. As with your Annie, the exact circumstances of his death are obscure, partly because my supervisor didn't focus on that particular incarnation. As I say, we were more interested in Peggy at the time.'

'But if you found out, maybe you'd be cured.' It pains him to see her sitting there all hunched up and nervy, puffing away.

'You're right, of course.' She sighs again. 'And I've been intending for years to make the trip to deepest Dorset where my supervisor lives and ask her to hypnotize me again. But it's such a terribly long way to go, and the trains don't link up easily. And apart from situations like this, which are obviously ridiculous, my phobia's not especially disabling.'

'Do you remember anything else about him?'

'I'm not sure. That's why I suspect there may have been more than one fisherman. Because the details didn't seem to cohere properly at the time. So I recalled one episode in a bar where a man was blowing smoke in my face, obviously taunting me for not being a smoker and trying to pick a fight. But in another episode I was fashioning tobacco into a roll-up cigarette, enjoying the sweet smell of it and really relishing the ritual. And I remember a tobacco tin with a sailor painted on it – I can see it so clearly – and the initials "T.H." scratched on the side.'

While they've been talking, Laura must have nodded off, because now her mouth's hanging open a bit and she's started snoring. Ben catches the doc's eye and they share a grin. 'Is that why you smoke now?' he asks. 'Because you liked it so much before?'

'Perhaps. But nicotine addiction would also have something to do with it. As Freud said once when quizzed on his fondness for Havana cigars, "The cigar is indeed a phallic symbol, my friend – but it is also a *cigar*." But I'd also be tempted to blame a certain Jane Hill, who smuggled ten packs of Number Six into my boarding school when I was fourteen – "numbies" we used to call them. One cough and I was hooked for life.' When she inhales her lips go all puckered. She's still sucking in and blowing out like she can't get the smoke down fast enough. 'However, your question has touched on an important principle. Have I mentioned the concept of "scarring"?'

'I don't think so.' Ben settles back on his elbows, stretching his legs out in the sun and pointing his toes.

'About forty years ago a psychologist called Ian Stevenson decided to make a scientific study of reincarnation. He travelled to the Indian subcontinent, where such cases abound. Hindus believe that a soul may occupy many bodies during its journey – Buddhists do too, though in a slightly different way. Of course that doesn't mean reincarnation is limited to Hindu and Buddhist societies, but it does mean that it was relatively easy for Dr Stevenson to find cases to investigate. To cut a long story short, he did indeed find a number of children—'

'Children?' Ben sits up.

'Where a person does have some conscious awareness of a past life – and that is rather rare – it tends to surface as the child learns to speak, then fades away by the age of eight or nine. Thereafter the fine details of that person's past-life memories can only be accessed via the unconscious, in dream states and hypnosis for instance.'

'Like me.'

'Precisely.' She smiles at him. 'Which is one reason I'm so glad you decided to visit me. Anyway, what Professor Stevenson subsequently discovered, which is germane to our discussion, was that if a person had died violently in a previous incarnation, this was sometimes reflected in the form of unusual birthmarks or disabilities – "scars" I call them – in the subsequent reincarnation. In one case, a boy had a series of birthmarks on his chest and back exactly where a volley of bullets had passed through the torso of his previous incarnation.'

Ben whistles: how weird is that? Then he thinks about it a bit more: 'But he could have seen the pattern the scars made and just made up the story of the bullets,' he says.

'Well spotted. Which was why Stevenson only reported cases where he was able to find objective evidence to verify the child's story. In this particular case, the child remembered the name of the village where the shooting had taken place and Stevenson was able to access an autopsy report detailing the dead man's injuries.'

'And they matched.'

'Like a glove, as they say. As did the birthmarks or disabilities of hundreds of other children he investigated. The phenomenon is so pervasive that one community has developed a custom of marking a dead body with charcoal so that they can look out for a birthmark in the same place on babies born afterwards and identify where the dead person's soul has migrated for its next incarnation.'

'So what's that got to do with you smoking?'

'Well it seems that it's not only physical injuries that can leave a mark, so to speak, on a subsequent incarnation. Intense fears and passions may also be passed on in this way – though of course there's no scientific explanation at present for exactly how any of this might occur.'

'I've got a weird mark here,' Ben says, showing her a pinkish line at the base of his neck. 'It's faded now, but Dad says it was bright red when I was born. He thought it might be because they had to use forceps to get me out.'

'That's a possible explanation, of course. But it could also be a clue to what happened to Annie.'

'So why don't you do the same as that professor?'

'What do you mean?'

'Look up old police reports and that from that time. Nana says you can find out all sorts. Dad got her this book with a DVD about tracing your ancestors and she got really into it for about two weeks, which is ages for her.'

Laura snuffles a bit and rolls onto her side.

'I did travel some way down that road with Peggy's life,' says the doc, 'though this was before the advent of the Internet, so my investigations were somewhat limited. But I have always considered the facts surrounding my clients' previous incarnations to be outside my remit. My role, as I see it, is to help the client access unconscious material for therapeutic purposes. If they wish to investigate further, that's up to them.'

'But the answer could be right there, just waiting to be found out.' Ben kneels up, thinking how cool it would be to do some proper detecting, to find clues and follow them.

'Theoretically, yes,' says the doc cautiously. 'But discovering something in a police report is unlikely to have the same therapeutic benefit as remembering it as it happened in a previous life.'

'But what if you're like me and you can't remember what happened? There might be an old newspaper story or something that would jog my memory.'

'Sounds like a great idea to me,' says Laura, opening her eyes and heaving up on one elbow.

The doc scowls. 'Thank you, Laura,' she says through gritted teeth.

'Oh, come on. It's not as if you're overwhelmed with work at the moment. Half your clients are off on their hols and after all that hoo-ha with Hester thingummy I can't see you writing any more papers for a while.'

'If it's any of your business, which it isn't, I have to produce a chapter for a psychosynthesis textbook before the end of September, and I need to update my religion and therapy book for the new edition—'

'Think how much fun we could have fossicking around the local history section in the library.'

'And a two-thousand-word review for the *TLS* of three books I haven't even opened yet.'

'I'll help.'

'That's supposed to persuade me, is it?'

While they bicker away, Ben lies down and closes his eyes, as though he's ducking underwater away from it. But it's not like when Mam and Dad used to fight, in quiet low voices, with the door shut so he couldn't hear them, but he could really. When Laura and the doc argue, Ben just wants to giggle. Laura's going to win this one, he reckons, because the doc's stopped chain-smoking, which means she must be interested.

The blanket's prickling the backs of his legs and the sun's glowing through his eyelids. It feels like he's floating in a warm red sea.

CHAPTER TWELVE

1898

It's early morning and I'm waiting for Flo. She was wanting to go to the nettie on her own, so I'm guessing it's maybe her time – though she'd never say – because I've just come on and we're usually on our rags together.

It's just after six, a bonny morning, with a soft wispy fret crawling upriver and the water smooth as a mirror. There's an elbow bend in the stairs a nip up from our house, with a bit wall where I like to sit, that catches the rising sun through a gap in the roofs this time of day. So I'm closing my eyes, and feeling the warmth on my face, and just listening to the day waking up.

I can hear the lumpers yelling for landing lines down on the quayside and the capstans chugging away to winch the crans ashore – and the gulls of course, always the gulls, bickering over fish innards.

Now here comes Flo, frowning and blushing a bit, but she doesn't look at me so I can't tell if she's come on or not. So off we set down the bank, and I swear this town's filling up more every day. There's nets all over, like brown spiders' webs: hanging from the walls, draped over every bush and washing line; or spread out for the ransackers on the grass in the distance like a brown mist. And standing at every window in every loft, caught like flies, you can see the beatsters at work mending them.

Flo's dragging her feet so I'm worried we'll be late. She's still not letting on, but she's looking pained, so I think maybes her belly's nipping her. But when we get there the work's never even started, because the lasses are all crowded round fat Sally, and I can see straight away that she's not right.

She looks pale – and Sal's normally ruddy as an apple – and there's fresh blood seeping through her bindings where she cut herself a few days back. She's making out she's fine to gip, but Mrs Gibson's taking her knife away, and folding it, and pulling up the sleeve to see if there's poison in the wound. And I can tell by Mrs Gibson's face that it's not good. See, when a wound goes bad, and the poison starts to spread, there's a red line appears under the skin, going from the wound up the arm, taking the badness into the body. They say if that line reaches your heart, it'll kill you stone dead, so Mrs Gibson's giving Sal a sixpence and sending her off to the doctor.

Once she's gone and we've set to gipping, we none of us feels much like talking, because it can get you just like that, the blood poisoning. One minute you're laughing and full of blether, next your hand's swelled up and leaking pus and there's a rash starting, and the doctor's there with his bone saw. And if you're lucky, you'll lose a hand, and if not – well, that's you poisoned to death.

When we get in, the Scots lasses have arrived and are crowded into the kitchen with their kists open on the floor, unloading things they've brought for Mam – tin cups and raisins, bags of tea and sugar, a big roll of leaf lard for their late suppers. And if words were smoke, you'd not be able to see across the room, there's that much blether going on.

We've the same crew as always lodging with us: two gippers and a packer – Ellie, Mags and Sue. We've known them since we were wee, when they'd bring a string of broken herring home for tea and show us how to gip them. It always seemed a grand way of life, following the herring round the coast, from Shetland to Peterhead to Shields, and on up to Yarmouth and Grimsby. Then, come winter, boarding the train to Plymouth for the mackerel, then on across to Ireland to gip in the snow.

I asked Ellie once, don't your hands freeze? For we've the lums at the smokehouse to take the chill off. But she just laughed, no, it's your feet that suffer, even when you've four layers of socks and newspaper in your boots. Mam says it's the same in the net loft. Your legs can be numb as wood and your neb dripping with cold, but the busyness of your needles keeps your hands pink.

So now Mam's poured the tea and Ellie and them are telling how they'd got in a right barny down Eyemouth, and would've been driven out except the herring shoals had shifted anyway, so it was time for them to leave. They'd got up a protest for a better rate for their night barrels, because it's harder to keep up your speed under the lamps.

For us smokehouse gippers it's different. Once the lums are loaded and the rousing floors heaped high, there's no point gipping more fish. But the Scots lasses are gipping for the coopers' barrels, and so long as there's herring to gip, they have to keep going – right into the night if needs be. See, once a herring's out of the water it won't wait. If you don't get the innards out and the salt on, or the pickle, or get it on the baulks in the lum, it'll go rotten in the blink of an eye, specially in the warm weather.

So anyway, that's Ellie for you: always on about how the gippers get tret. And now she's asking about our pay in the smokehouse, if it's by the hour or the cran, and have we got a union organizer yet. Which is another of her bugbears, how the lasses hereabouts just take what they're given and never think to complain.

Then here comes Da's voice from upstairs, roaring for his water, which puts Mam in a canny dither, for she's forgotten to heat him a kettle, hasn't she? And Ellie and them are laughing at him roaring and her scurrying and I'm trying to shush them, even though they're guests, for it seems disrespectful to laugh at a man in his own house.

After tea, as it's a Friday, Flo and me set off up the bank to the High Town to look at the shops – though looking is all we *can* do, as our pay goes straight to our mams and what's left is barely enough for a hair ribbon. By, but it's grand to be linked in and strolling along in the late sunshine, with our oilies off and our hands washed, and our feet light in clogs for a change, instead of slurruping along in heavy lads' boots.

Some of the Scots lasses are out strolling too, blethering and knitting away at socks and ganseys to keep their lads warm under their oilies. Never mind your diamond rings, among fishing folk there's no surer sign a lass is promised than when she's knitted her lad's initials into the hem of a gansey. That's how I know Flo's really hooked on Tom, for she's brought a skein of new wool to our place so she can work a gansey without her mam mythering on about it. Flo's mam and da are canny tidy folk, see, so a rough lad like Tom's not exactly what they're wanting for a son-in-law.

So now we're back home and up in the loft with the candle lit, and Flo's sorting through her shiftenings and hanging up her good clothes. I've rinsed out my day rags and hung them to dry, and set a fresh pail ready for my night ones – not saying anything to Flo, mind, but not hiding what I'm doing neither. For I want her to feel at ease and not need to ask what to do with hers. But she's never lifted her pettie nor unpinned any rags, so it seems I'm wrong about her coming on.

So anyway, we're laying out the bedding and settling down all cosy, with Mam's nets hanging up like curtains all around, for she was beating today, while we were gipping – Da doesn't trust the big beating lofts and keeps his lint-work in the family, so it's hard on Mam and Nana this time of year.

Now Flo's asking have I ever been kissed, though she knows the answer well enough, and it's just her way of talking about Tom. For he has kissed her, of course, and once you're used to it, she says, you can even get to like it. Though his tongue coming in was a bit of a shock, what with the taste of the bakkie on it. Which is a shock to me too, for I'd never thought there might be a tongue involved, so we're giggling, pulling our blankets up to hide our faces.

And when she catches her breath, Flo says that she daresn't relax into liking the kissing part anyway, for that would distract from where his hands are going – which sets us off again. So now I'm asking where *are* they going, but she won't tell, so I'm guessing at some places, at cami-buttons and boobies, and she's never saying no, which is another shock, though I never let on. So now I'm wondering about other places a lad's hands could go, which makes me shiver at the thought, and I can't even find the words to ask, but try anyway, so we're giggling into the small hours.

Now it's Sunday, and we've had our dinner and done the pots and Da's sat outside on the bench with his pipe and bakkie tin, and the Scots lasses are off in the yard rinsing out their shiftenings for tomorrow, so there's enough chairs for a change. Flo's helped wash my hair, so it's smelling of sea wind and sunshine, instead of oak-smoke and herring; and we've kicked off our clogs so we're barefoot as bairns, and leaning back with a brew and a sweet biscuit.

And I can hear Da's speaking to someone outside, and calling for a chair, so I carry mine out and his visitor steps forward to take it off me. But in that daft way that happens sometimes, I can't let it go neatly into his hands, so we're stood there for a long blushing moment, tussling politely over this chair.

He's younger than I guessed from his voice, with pale eyes and pale skin and a tangle of black curls – Celt colouring, Mam would say. And when he looks at me with my hair loose, I'm all of a fluster suddenly, though it's only my feet that's bare.

So anyway, I let go the chair at last, and he gives a little bow before setting it down, and there's the shadow of a smile in his eyes that says he's seen me, and maybes likes what he's seen, before he straightens his shoulders and turns back to Da and the business he was minded to do.

So what do I do then? Well, I go back through to the front room, where Mam and Flo have taken out their knitting, but I can't settle. So I wander about a bit with a cloth, wiping the mantle, for there's always a need for that, even in summer. And I think of that soft noticing look that lad's given me, and hold on to it like a curl in a locket. For I know fine well that once he's seen Flo, that's the last time he'll pay me any mind.

CHAPTER THIRTEEN

1898

If you're a lass in Shields, you're forever watching the horizon and waiting for news of your lads. Even in summer, when the winds are kind, a squall can blow up from nowt. Or you'll get a calm, with a thick white fret, that has the herring drifters rocking blind on a flat sea, till some massive collier heaves up out of the fog and bears down on them blaring its horn. Two colliers collided in a fret just last week and six men drowned before the lifeboat could get to them.

Of course when you're gipping, or beating, you can't keep a look out, but the bairns know all our boats by the patches on their sails, and scoot off to the Priory to see who's coming in, and earn a ha'penny for their pains. So there's a deal of running off and reporting back this morning, for all the crews who set out in that high wind last night.

See, you can't go for the herring in the daytime, for fear of netting up a batch of gurnards, which spoil the herring with their spines. That's why you'll see the drifters setting out with the setting sun on their backs, and plying home with the sun rising behind them.

I often think of Da and Jimmy out there on the night sea, bucking though a ghostie world of black waves and stars and bobbing lights. That dark world is nearly all our lads know, for their time ashore is spent mostly asleep, or sleep-walking as it seems to me, stotting home after a night's hauling followed by a morning's cranning and sluicing out. You can be five hours hauling a big catch, Da says, and that's heavy going, even with the capstan to help.

So this evening, here's Da sat at the table, and since I last seen him he's been out all night and had his bit sleep, and now he's getting ready to set off again. But just now his hands are trembling that much from fatigue that Mam's insisting on giving him his shave, which is serious, for he normally likes to do it himself, even though it's cheap enough to go to the barber. But Da complains the barbers never make the water hot enough, and the soap's wrong, and the cloths minging – though I can't see a barber staying in business long with minging cloths.

But that's Da all over. If a thing's worth doing, he says, it's worth doing right. So he's got his own strop and razor, and good lathering soap, and gives himself a proper shave – like a prayer, almost – last thing before he goes to sea.

Though this evening it's Mam doing it, and he's growling like a tetchy dog, but sitting obedient even so, and tipping his head back so she can lather his throat. And I'm thinking this must be the lovingest thing I ever did see: my soft mam standing her ground, and my hard da offering his throat to her.

For Da can be that fierce when he's crossed, so there's many that fear him – though respect and fear are close cousins round these parts, as they must be when a lad's life can depend on him minding his skipper.

Most evenings after tea, Mam gives Flo and me a dish of something to take over to Nana's, to help out with our Jimmy and the bairns, for she's *six* Scots lasses lodging at hers, and that's a deal to be cooking for.

And every day, for the fun of it, we take a different way home: now up along the top bank, past the New High Light and the mansions in Dockwray Square; now down the Low Town, along Union Street and Bell Street; or wandering along all the little quays, watching the tugs chugging at anchor, coaling up, and smacks taking on ice for another trip to the cod grounds – for this town's that jumping we can't take to our beds without tasting a bit of that jumpingness first.

Tonight Flo's wanting to linger at the bottom of our stairs, waiting on Tom on his way to the boat. But soon as I spy him a-lolloping down, with his crotch-boots and oilies under his arm, I slip away because I'm chary of him looking at me again in that bold way, and Flo seeing him looking and taking it amiss.

It must be nineish now and the lamplighter's making his way along the street with his taper; and on the boats, too, lights are winking on all along the little quays, with the dusky water rocking and winking back.

Then here he is, that curly-haired lad from last Sunday, quiet as a cat at my elbow, saying, 'Good evening, Miss Anne', and making me jump out of my skin. Which puts me in a fluster, so he's saying sorry for surprising me, and I'm saying sorry for squealing, then blurting out about how the lights blinking on in the gloaming make the river a magical place. And he's smiling down at me, still with that noticing look, and telling how this is the best time of day for a fisherman, because you're fresh from your bit sleep, and there's that buzzing always, about what you'll haul, how much and how soon, and whether you'll catch a fair wind.

And I see he's carrying his oilies and boots, too, and ask what boat he's on. Why, the *Osprey*, says he, which is Da's boat. And it turns out that's why he came visiting – though Da's never said – for he's been hoping for a place in Da's crew for more than half a year, after he went out as a nightman on the long lines before Christmas when Tom was took bad with his chest. And he liked the way the boat worked, and the craik, and our Jimmy's cooking. But mostly, he says, it's Da he wants to work under. For Da's what they call a 'don' skipper, which means he can fairly smell the shoals and read the sea bed, and always brings the boat in safe with a canny catch.

And before you know it, I'm telling about how Da is with his razor, because that's the same strictness he brings to his fishing. Then the lad's saying his name, which is Sam, and I'm saying pleased to meet you, like we're being introduced for the first time, which we are, I suppose, except for my feeling that I've known this lad Sam for as long as I've lived, and longer yet than that. And that this talk is but a continuing of a talk we left off long ago.

Does he feel the same? I can't tell, for he's stopped talking now, though he's never left neither, but has set down his oilies and is standing beside me – just standing quiet, as if this were his rightful place – looking out over the river, to where the tugs are tying on the tow warps to pull the luggers out to sea. Then after a bit, he turns and looks at me again, then hoists up his gear and he's gone.

Next time we meet is on the Saturday, on the monkey run – that's the strolling young folk do at the week's end, when we've sluiced down our oilies and had our baths, and put on our good clothes. It's a time for the lads to look at the lasses, and for the lasses to look back, and for the old folk to make sure all our dealings stay decent – but if two sweethearts meet, who's to say where they might sneak off to?

So here's Flo and me in our summer blouses, and the sun's dipping low towards Newcastle so the light's spilling like honey on the cobbles and stairs. And we're that giddy, the two of us, for she's promised to meet her Tom, and I'm hoping to meet my Sam – though I can't really think he's mine, for nowt binding's been said, and I've never even seen him this past week, for all my lingering where we stood that one time.

I tell you, there's a feeling you can get in your chest, a sort of burstingness, like a mattie herring, full of roe and oil, who's as ripe and sleek as she'll ever be. So I find I'm squeezing Flo's arm as we're strolling along, and she's squeezing back, and we're thinking we must be the bonniest two lasses in Shields. And here's the strangest thing, for though I'm linked in with Flo, and her cheeks are pink as ever, and her hair glinting just as yellow under her scarf, here's lads' eyes roving over the two of us and resting on me for a change.

Can love turn a lass into a woman? Or is it being a woman that calls out to love? I can't tell, but I'm fairly bubbling with something, like the tickle of ginger beer on your nose.

And now, like a spell's been cast, here he is! Standing alone, outside Fraser's Cocoa House, with a proper jacket and shined shoes, and his hair still damp under his cap. And we're stopping, Flo and me, for he's stepped forwards and raised his cap, and's wishing us good evening, like it were the simplest thing in the world.

Which it is, of course, except my cheeks are blazing and my heart thudding, so I fear he must hear it. And there's another fear, for this is the first time he's seen Flo close up, and I'm waiting for his noticing look to fall on her, and wondering how I'll manage if it does.

But she could be a duff pudden for all the noticing he's giving her, though he's civil enough when she greets him. Which fills me with that much joy, I can't stop from laughing, so now he's asking why, but I can't make a sensible answer. But it doesn't matter one ticky-bit, for Flo's taken herself off to give us our privacy, and he's asking me to walk out with him tomorrow after dinner, along to St Edward's Bay for an ice cream at Watt's Refreshment Rooms.

And I suppose I'm saying yes – though I'm that flummoxed I can't tell – for then he's asking would I take it bad if he doesn't ask Da for his permission just at the minute, on account of him being new on the boat and not wanting Da to think he's taking advantage. Leastways I think that's what he's saying, for to tell the truth, it's all I can do not to kiss him right there in the street, for he has the kissingest mouth I ever saw, and I find I'm watching for his tongue as he's speaking, and wondering about it, then blushing again at the wondering.

Once it's settled where we're meeting, it's just as it was that other evening, and a calm comes over the two of us, like the sigh of an old nana easing down on to a chair, and my heart quietens a mite, so I can look around and see that Flo's calling out to Tom and our Jimmy, and they're grinning and striding over.

But now something's awry, for Tom's seen Sam, and come up short, like a dog when it spies another dog in the distance. 'So, *Wellesley* lad,' he says with a smile, 'what you doing with one of my lasses?'

It's a joke, of course, and we're all of us laughing, but there's something sharp there too – like I said before about Tom – that reminds me how quick he can be with his fists.

A minute later Sam's gone and Tom's staring after him and asking if we're walking out. So I say, no, we're just blethering, for I'm wary of Da hearing about it before Sam makes his proper visit. And Tom says, good, because he doesn't want any of his lasses going with a *Wellesley* boy. Which has us laughing again, Flo and me, and protesting that one lass should be enough for any lad, and him declaring he's not 'any lad', with a swagger that's half a joke and half serious.

Then he's linking in with Flo and they're off down the street, and I'm looking round for our Jimmy to walk us home, but he's disappeared off God knows where. So I wander along the quayside instead, gazing out at the lofty lamps on the *Wellesley*, which is a towering great ship – big as the Grand Hotel almost – anchored in the middle of the river. And I'm wondering was Sam really a bairn on that ship? For the *Wellesley*'s a floating prison for the roughest lads in Shields, where they teach them seamanship and try to set them on the right path.

And what with the gazing and the wondering, I suppose I've been lingering nigh on an hour, when I should have been hitching my skirts and hastening up the stairs home. Because there's rowdy lads gathering outside all the pubs already, so I've to edge past them and pretend I don't notice them looking or hear what they're saying; and loose lasses are gathering too, with their blouses unbuttoned, so I wrap my shawl tighter over my chest and duck my head and walk faster, and chide myself for forgetting the time, and vow this is the very very last time I'll be out on my own after sunset.

Now all at once here's a strong hand grabbing my arm and swinging me round, and I'm just about to kick out when I see that it's Tom, appeared out of nowhere. At which I'm that relieved, almost to tears, so I'm thanking him and wiping my eyes, while he links in and starts walking me home.

'When you never came back, I was worried that *Wellesley* lad might be bothering you,' he says. So I say, no no, I just forgot the time. And what with the relief of being saved, and them stotting lads in the lanes, I'm not minding that he's pressing closer as we start up the stairs. It seems a caring, protecting sort of thing, for a lad to lean in to a lass when she's upset. So I'm paying no heed, neither, when he's pulling me into a doorway to let some rowdies pass by. But now he's facing me, looking down in the darkness, and his hands are on my shoulders, and his face is bending towards me. There's a smell of beer and tabs and red herring on his breath, and too late I understand that he's – he's about to—

CHAPTER FOURTEEN

2007

The boy's asleep now, curled foetus-fashion on the red sofa, beneath the rug Mary wrapped around him last time, the one she wore as a poncho in India all those years ago, that's been on her bed, or whichever horizontal surface has been serving as her bed, ever since.

She stands in the doorway, fingering the Bic lighter in her skirt pocket, its warm blue plastic cylinder, its little ridged trigger. His eyelids seem translucent: delicately veined, flickering, chasing some occipital image. His cheeks are streaked with tears.

Usually the children are so easy – embarrassingly so, given the size of her fee – slipping effortlessly into their trances like seagulls launching from a cliff face, then soaring weightlessly for fifty minutes, before alighting gently again at the end of each session with the burden of their symptoms lightened. But with Ben, almost every time, there's been a crash landing, and he's lurched back into consciousness with staring eyes and flailing arms, gulping down ragged lungfuls of air.

This last time, she'd held him. Though it goes against every tenet of her professional code, what else could she do? Though God knows she wasn't much good at it: hardly knew where to put her arms, they were so rusty from disuse. She was all elbows, whereas what was required, she suspects, was a wide lap and a decent bosom, and one of those floral talcs the National Trust used to sell.

The boy was as bad. He's not used to this cuddling lark either, so it was rather akin to comforting an armful of twigs. They managed though, the pair of them, easing their awkward bones under and over somehow, finding a way to hold and be held, and mop tears with her perennial clean hanky, and rock back against the cushions until his sobbing abated and he started to drowse and Mary, too, closed her eyes and felt his meagre warmth – his skinny shoulder, his hair that smells of apples – seep into her for a few minutes before she settled him down under her Indian rug.

Does he have friends, she wonders? She's heard his mobile phone burping on occasion, and seen him seen him tapping away at the buttons; but with so much to conceal, she guesses he'd probably steer clear of close friendships. He'd tend to gravitate towards the girls anyway, but would need to keep a safe distance for fear of a ragging from the boys – though Mary doubts that's the correct term for it these days. Being good at sports would help avert suspicion, however, and get them 'off his case' as he might put it. Still, it must be lonely living in Ben's skin, with that unreconstructed father and a grandmother who seems adequate at best. No wonder he's round at Laura's all the time.

Pulling the door closed, she moves outside, absently lighting a Gitanes and exhaling on a sigh as she lowers herself onto her bench. It's chilly today: grey and windy with a touch of drizzle in the air. Hunching her shoulders, she pulls her cardie across her chest and squints through smoke at that seagull on its nest on the chimney of the fish and chip shop down on the Fish Quay. It's been sitting for months, but there's been no sign of a chick.

Mary flicks ash and scuffs it away with her foot. One advantage of turning fifty is that people stop asking questions about one's private life; they assume that one's situation is a fait accompli.

Mary doesn't mourn the lack of what her mother would have referred to as 'the physical side'. From her perspective, it's simply the logical consequence of events that took place long ago: at Oxford, in India, in that grim mental hospital on the outskirts of London – Shenley, that was it. And before that, of course, of events in Mary's most recent past life – Peggy the washerwoman, Peggy the whore – and other past lives she has yet to revisit.

Peggy never could stand being touched – and who could blame her? She said her body was her work, and when she stopped working she put her tools away. She had a clever way with words, that woman, and a sharp brain when it wasn't addled with cheap whisky. It was hard on her little boy, though, when she'd slap him away like a stray dog.

The truth was, the boy irritated Peggy intensely. She considered him her 'mistake', conceived before she knew how babies were made, let alone prevented, when girls grew up being told about the midwife's 'magic golden scissors' – for God's sake! – that were reputedly used to deliver babies without scar from their mothers' bellies. Hard to credit such ignorance existed, given the cheek-by-jowl conditions in which Peggy and her ilk lived. But she'd been right about one thing: it was the disgrace of that boy's birth that set her on the inexorable road to the Push and Pull Inn, and that squalid single room where she lived and conducted her business, and eventually died.

Peggy would have adored Mary's house: all this space to roam about in, and a double bed, blessedly all to herself. Mary had felt much the same herself when she bought the place, pacing from room to room, with the sun blazing in through the front windows. But as she grows older, and her flesh starts to shrink back from her bones, she can't help thinking about her double bed, the only stick of new furniture she has ever purchased, and wondering whether she is fated to sleep alone for the rest of her life.

It's the following day and, against her better judgement, Mary's on her way to the library in North Shields to meet Laura and Ben. It's one of those ghastly concrete and glass blocks they were so fond of building in the sixties that seem perpetually shrouded in scaffolding to address some basic design fault in the roof. Inside, typically for July, the central heating's on and it's sweltering. The heat intensifies as she trudges up stairs splodged with chewing gum to the local history section, where all the windows are open – at least they *can* open – and desk fans are whirring, lifting the edges of every paper not anchored by a hand or pile of books.

Laura's sitting before a desk in a garish peasant skirt, legs crossed sideways, secretarial style, chatting up a surprisingly grizzled male librarian. Ben's perched on the edge of a chair beside her; even from this distance Mary can sense his excitement.

He jumps up when he sees her. 'They've got a list of who lived in every house in Shields, going right back to 1841!' he exclaims. 'And everyone who got married. And when they were born and when they died. You just need a password to get on the website.'

Laura turns round, beaming. 'Fantabulosa, *n'est ce pas*? And Pete says we can check for murders and missing persons and that in the *Shields Daily News*. It's all on microfilm, isn't it, Pete? In that cabinet over there, right back to the year dot.'

Mary suppresses a sigh. She'd hoped to conduct this investigation in a rather more systematic manner. 'I've brought three notebooks, one for each of us,' she begins, 'so I suggest—'

'Why don't you and Ben go on the computers to see if you can find Annie,' interrupts Laura, 'and I'll start going through the *Daily News* to see if there's anything about how she died.'

'But we don't know *when* she died,' Mary objects. 'We don't even know for sure that she *did* die when we think. There could be any number of explanations for why Ben's memories appear to stop where they do.'

'Oh, buff-puff! You said he seems to be stuck in that one year when she was a teenager. We've got to start somewhere. It was during the herring season, right? Which Pete says was June to September back then, so I thought I'd start looking around June 1895 and work forwards for the next ten summers, to be sure of covering the right period.'

'Wouldn't it be easier to wait until we know the actual year?'

But Laura's already turned back to Pete. 'Right, lead on McDuff,' she declaims. 'Where's that microfilm machine?'

Shrugging helplessly, Mary looks at Ben. 'Shall we get started? You'd better do the driving, assuming you know how to operate these contraptions.'

They settle at a computer, Ben at the keyboard tapping instructions; but it soon becomes obvious that without a surname it will be impossible to track down the right Annie. Typing in just 'Anne' and 'North Shields', with a likely date range, brings up hundreds of possibilities.

'I don't even know if it's spelt with an 'e',' Ben says. 'Or if the Annie's short for Mary-Anne. That's so weird. Why can't I remember?'

'In my experience, people often have trouble recalling the surnames of a previous incarnation. I think it's probably because the nature of this type of recall is via the unconscious – which has a tendency to elide facts it doesn't consider important. If you think about it, how often do you dwell on your own surname? Or even your official Christian name, assuming you are actually a Benjamin rather than a Ben.'

'So what can we do?'

'Can you remember the address? Your father mentioned you became very upset once because there was a tyre factory where Annie's house used to be.'

He shakes his head. 'I can remember the stairs down to the house from the top bank. There were loads of stone steps going down to the river, in alleys between the houses on the bank, loads more than today, so you were always climbing up or down somewhere. It was right knackering. And really dark, because the houses towered up either side, so you'd just get these little glimpses of the river as you were going down.'

'So let's see if we can work with that. Can you remember anything particular, something on the opposite bank, perhaps, that Annie might have noticed on her way down her particular flight of stairs?'

He shakes his head again, then: 'Yes!' he says excitedly. 'The *Wellesley*! Do you remember? That ship Sam was on. It was like a boarding school for these really rough lads, like proper thieves, and orphans and lads with crap parents who beat them up and that. Anyway, it was moored in the middle of the river, right near where we lived – I mean where Annie lived. You could see it, just the stern of it, from the top of the steps.

'If you saw a photo of the river bank, with the ship on it, do you think you might be able to estimate the position of Annie's house? Good. Let's ask the obliging Pete if he can direct us to his image archives – always assuming such things exist.'

The picture archive, such as it is, is housed in a bank of ancient green filing cabinets. Trundling open a drawer, Mary feels the tug of her nicotine leash and ignores it. When it comes again, as she's flicking through dog-eared files of old photos, she realizes she's enjoying herself.

The *Wellesley*'s easy to find – it was clearly something of a landmark at the time – and they spread out a range of misty photos, taken from various angles, at high and low tide, from the north and south banks of the river – including several from 1914 surrounded by tugs spraying water to douse the fire that destroyed it. The vessel's gigantic, an enormous floating hostel, four storeys above the water and probably a further one or two below, with three elaborately rigged masts.

'How cool was that?' Ben's saying. 'Living on a ship with a load of other kids.' Then he thinks again. 'Except the food was probably crap, wasn't it? And there'd be really hard blokes in charge, to stop them fighting and that. So it was probably more like a prison.'

He pauses, dredging up another memory. 'Annie used to stare at the ship. There was a sort of bend in the steps near the top, and a bit of broken down wall she used to sit on.'

Mary peers at the rows of windows on the ship's flank, and a little shudder of something – empathy? recognition? – goes through her. 'Look at the buildings on the bank,' she tells Ben. 'Imagine Annie sitting on that wall. Can you work out where she might have been?'

'About here,' he says, confidently pointing. 'I remember the bottom of those stairs. She lived about half way up the bank.' Then: 'Oh no, hang on. There's another set of stairs, just along a bit. I think it might have been that one. Sorry.'

'They knocked the whole lot down in the thirties,' says a gruff voice as Pete materializes behind them. 'After the Housing Act the whole area was condemned. But they documented everything before the bulldozers went in.' He tugs open a drawer. 'The photos are in here – what's left of them. That's the trouble with public-access archives,' he remarks without rancour. 'Things tend to disappear.'

He heaves out a sheaf of buff folders and Mary and Ben start to leaf through the photos inside: scene after scene of brick walls and grimy windows, a haphazard zigzag landscape of tiled roofs and lofty chimneys. And steps everywhere, like an Escher painting: stone stairs down to the river with open sewage channels running alongside; wooden flights to first and second floor flats, some with tin canopies; rickety wooden bridges between buildings; shared yards with a single tap and toilet; buckets and coal bunkers, patched lean-tos and crumbling brick buttresses – and washing lines, like ships' rigging, strung across every meagre open space.

'Where are the people?' Ben wants to know. Save for a scattering of bedraggled hens, the buildings and alleys are empty.

'They moved them out, onto the Ridges Estate, what they call the Meadowell now. All the keelmen and deckies, shipyard workers, fishwives, all decanted into little modern semis miles from the river.'

'Meadowell – that was the scene of those riots, wasn't it?' Mary asks. 'I didn't realize all those families came from the quayside.' She recalls the shock of it on the news in 1991: all that tangible anger, so close to her home; the sealed-off roads and police sirens; the stench of burning plastic, the pall of smoke hanging over the town.

'They never settled, is what I think,' says Pete. 'Uproot a man from his home, his livelihood, it's bound to cause trouble down the line. I mean, what did they have? Inside toilets, fair enough, but no jobs after the fish disappeared, and the mines had closed down, then Swan Hunters went belly-up, no community, nothing to take pride in. It was a no-go area for years. Police didn't dare put a nose in.'

'So the people who rioted were the children and grandchildren of the people who were displaced from these houses.'

'They thought changing the name to Meadowell would make a difference, but it was still the same folk living there.'

Mary taps Ben on the shoulder. 'Where's that photo you found?' She shows it to Pete. 'We're looking for a particular house on this bit of the bank,' she explains. 'We think it's near where the *Wellesley*'s moored, but we don't know the address.'

'Looks like the Liddell Street, Bell Street area, what they used to call the Low Town,' says Pete. 'What year are you after? Eighteen nineties? Nineteen hundred? What you need is a map.'

They follow him to a large cupboard with old maps swinging gently like coats on metal hangers inside. He extracts three large sheets and lays them out on a table. 'Will this do you – 1896? Forty feet to the inch, so you can see the different buildings. The *Wellesley* was moored about here, so you'd probably be looking around the Ropery Stairs.'

'Wow, there's all the alleys I told you about, going down from the top bank to the river,' says Ben. 'But they're all called "stairs" and "bank" instead of "road". I remember that; people going, "Oh he bides on the Ropery Stairs." Weird. It's all just bushes now, apart from them posh flats down by the ferry.'

'Presumably there was a rope-maker, or a clutch of rope-makers, plying their trade on Ropery Stairs,' says Mary. 'What amazes me is the number of public houses – though I suppose I shouldn't be surprised, given the provenance of the area.'

'There were more pubs in Shields per square mile than anywhere else in the whole country,' says Pete with a note of pride in his voice. 'At one time pretty much every other building was some kind of pub or hotel. They needed them too, to house all the men from outside, all the seasonal fishermen and traders and that.'

Ben starts reading out the names: 'Highlander Inn, Lord Collingwood, Newcastle Arms, Bluebell Inn, Edinburgh Castle. I like this one, look: Push and Pull Inn. Probably because it was so hard to get up all them stairs when you were drunk.'

'Look at the alleys leading down to this bit of the river,' Mary tells him. 'Tully's Bank, Dale's Bank, Lighthouse Stairs – are they familiar names? What about Coble Entry, Turpin's Bank, King George Stairs?'

'I don't know,' Ben says uncertainly, running his finger down the alleys, one after another. Then: 'Hang on. Here – this little alley leading up to Turpin's Bank. It's not labelled but I think it's called Lamb's Quay Stairs, because – can you see? – it goes straight out onto Lamb's Quay, on the river.'

'Are you sure?' Mary looks at his face. The blue eyes are narrowed, concentrating on another shadowy memory.

'I think the lads moored the boat at Lamb's Quay sometimes, when they were unloading the nets for Mam and Nana to mend. Do you remember me saying we had to stop inside when they were putting to sea? Because it was bad luck to wave them off? That was because we lived just up the bank from where the boat was, so we couldn't help seeing it if we went outside.'

Mary smiles to hear him saying 'we' instead of 'they'. 'So you think Annie lived on Lamb's Quay Stairs.' She turns to Pete, who's listening, rather bemused, to their conversation. 'Is there any way of finding the names of people at a particular address? Assuming Lamb's Quay Stairs even existed, of course.'

'You'd have to go to the census data,' he says. 'There was a census done every ten years, starting 1841. So 1891 and 1901 would bracket the years you're interested in. Most people start with a name, but if we go back to the old index, we can work through the streets no bother.'

CHAPTER FIFTEEN

2007

There's an old pork butcher's in the shopping arcade beside the library. It sells flanks and shanks and suchlike; trotters and pease pudding; various indigenous pies. In the back room, Mary has no doubt, entire heads and curly tails are stockpiled, waiting to be minced into unspeakable pâtés. Laura and Ben order hot bacon baps; Mary opts for a 'jumbo' sausage roll, rendered damp and flabby by the microwave. She eats it outside, in a scabby little park, while Ben and Laura examine the life-size statue of a fishwife that adorns a low plinth in the centre. There are benches in the park, but none of them sits; they're fired up to continue their research.

Inevitably perhaps, Laura has deviated from her stated mission and is burbling on about irrelevant items from the *Shields Daily News*. 'I came across a report of this earl in London,' she's saying, 'who was fined fifteen guineas for speeding. D'you remember guineas, Mary? Posh folk's money. Anyway the earl was arrested for, and I quote, "driving furiously" in his car at – listen to this – twenty miles an hour!'

'I can run faster than that,' laughs Ben.

'The car must just have been invented,' Laura goes on. 'People were still using horses and carts, or steam engines – and boats called "steam packets" to get to London and Edinburgh. There were loads of ads for stable boys and that in the paper. And 'strong daily girls', whatever they were. Cleaners, I suppose. Twelve shillings a week. Eighteen shillings for a cook.'

'What's a shilling?' Ben wants to know.

'Five p. in today's money,' Laura says. 'Hardly bears thinking about, does it?'

'Did you find anything about Annie?' Mary asks, screwing up greasy paper.

'Not yet, but I'm only up to September 1896. The Tynemouth Ladies Temperance Society has just held its AGM, and there's been a big church do for a couple of reverends setting off as missionaries to Africa. Then of course there's Veronica Chisholm's classes in dancing, elocution and deportment. All very hoity-toity, until you get to the Police Court reports on page three.

'That's where to go for your local colour. It's like two different worlds in Shields: one up round Dockwray Square, buying pianos and that, lace for their ruffled camisas, and patterns for the latest "cycling costumes for ladies", if you don't mind. Then the riff-raff in the Low Town, picking pockets and scrapping, then getting stotting drunk and passing out on the quayside. Talk about upstairs downstairs.'

'Annie and them lot were definitely in the Low Town,' Ben says. 'And we think we've found where she lived, so we're going to check with the census.' He turns his gaze hopefully in Mary's direction as she grinds out a Gitanes with her boot and reaches into her pocket for another. 'Can we go back in now?' he asks.

After the circumnavigations of the morning, Mary had envisaged further detours en route to their goal in the afternoon. But in the event, matters proceeded smoothly. Pete had the 1891 census microfiche loaded in the viewer, and had already scrolled through to the relevant section.

'The streets are in the order the enumerator would have walked, so you have to think of him on your map, working his way along Bell Street at the bottom of the bank, and turning off to climb up and down all the different stairs and banks, and out along all the quays, knocking at doors.'

The data's all hand-written, in an untidy copperplate that invites speculation about the personality of the enumerator in a way no databank these days ever could. Is it Mary's imagination, or does the writing waver rather more following his visit to the Black Swan Inn?

'People are recorded where they sleep on the night of the census,' Pete's saying. 'So if a lassie's stopping over with her nana when the enumerator knocks, she'd be recorded at her nana's house, not at her mam's.'

'What about men out fishing?' Mary asks.

'You'd have to go to the boat logs for them. All the boats operating out of Shields had to fill in a log twice a year to say what they're doing and who's on board. But I expect quite a few men were left out – if they were just out on a coble, crabbing for the night.'

Pete shows them how to scroll through the hand-written sheets – Ropery Stairs, Miller's Bank, Turpin's Bank – until, there it is: Lamb's Quay Stairs, just where Ben said it was. And there, at number 23, is Dorothy Milburn, aged twenty-seven, housewife; her three sons: James, aged eleven, Frank, aged four, Richard aged six months – and one daughter, Anne with an 'e', aged nine.

'There she is.' Mary puts a finger on the screen and tears sting her eyes: the girl actually existed. After Hester's damning review, it's more than she dared hope. And the thought occurs to her that she should write up Ben's case, along with as much supporting evidence as she can find – and see what Professor Hester Griffin makes of that.

'So that's where she lived in 1891. Now we have to find out if she's still there ten years later,' she says.

Pete retrieves the 1901 census microfiche and loads it onto the machine. There's a different enumerator, with smaller hand-writing, walking a slightly different route, but eventually they find number 23 Lamb's Quay Stairs. And there the family is again, ten years older, with the head of household at home this time: Henry Milburn, aged forty-two, Master Mariner.

Mary scans down the list of inhabitants. There's James again, aged twenty-one now, working as a mariner; and Frank, aged fourteen, just a few years out of school, also down as 'mariner' – and a new name, Emily, aged seven, the little girl Ben remembers, who has presumably been born in the intervening years.

Ben grips her arm. 'Annie's missing,' he says.

'So is Dorothy, the mother,' says Mary. 'And that baby boy, Richard, from 1891. He'd have been ten in 1901.'

She's been sitting braced forwards in her chair. Now she leans back to digest the information. Annie being absent is expected. But the mother too? And the youngest brother? 'So where are they?' she says.

'If someone's missing, there are three possibilities,' supplies Pete, anticipating Mary's own speculations and elucidating a logic he's obviously explained a thousand times before to eager descendants trying to trace their roots. 'Either they've moved, or they're away for some reason – or they're dead.

'If someone's dead,' he continues, 'that's quite easy to check. Now we've got a surname and an address, we can just look at the BMD website for the previous ten years – that's the Register of Births, Marriages and Deaths. But if they've moved it's a bit clever, especially if you're looking for a female. See, if your Anne got married, she'd be on the census in her married name. If she married in North Shields we'd find her on the Marriage Register no bother, but if she's moved out of the area you could search for years and never find the right Anne from North Shields.'

'And if she's away?'

'That's even cleverer. You can check relatives' houses if you know their names and addresses. Then there's hospitals and prisons. Inns and hotels. Though if you're after a casual labourer or domestic, they could be lodging in a private house, which could be any one of a thousand addresses. Or the poor house – there was a big poor house in Tynemouth at that time with over seven hundred folk living there.'

'I need a cigarette,' says Mary.

'No, please!' cries Ben in anguish, unable to bear another delay. He apologizes immediately, of course, sweet boy that he is, but Mary slides the pack back into her cardigan pocket and resolves to invest in a carton of Nicorettes as soon as she gets a chance.

On the Death Registry part of the BMD website, they find the unfortunate Dorothy almost immediately. It seems she died on 24 September 1898, aged thirty-four. Cause of death: Post-partum haemorrhage. Scrolling down the list for the name 'Milburn', Mary finds another entry. 'Oh dear,' she says quietly. 'I think this must be the baby she was carrying. Samuel Henry Milburn, aged thirty days.'

There's no sign of Annie on the death register, at least not under her maiden name. But they find her younger brother Richard there, too, six months after his mother died.

'One of the little bairns,' says Ben, sounding shaken. 'So that's Annie disappeared, her mam and brother dead, and the baby – what's happened to them all?'

It seems the only way to find out is to track down their death certificates at the Registry Office. To Mary's relief, this is just down the road, in the elegant old Stag Line building overlooking the river. She'd no idea what went on inside until now, but it explains the windswept brides and bridesmaids she's vaguely noticed outside on summer afternoons having their photographs taken.

Inside, a portly man in a bow tie charges her £7 each for copies of the three death certificates, then disappears through a heavy door to retrieve them from some invisible archive. Mary takes the photocopies outside and she and Ben sit down to read the swirly copperplate writing.

'What's a post-partum – that thing?' Ben asks, examining Dorothy Milburn's death certificate.

'Post-partum haemorrhage,' says Mary. 'That's when the mother bleeds to death after giving birth – usually because the placenta doesn't separate properly from the womb and keeps leaking blood until the mother dies.'

'Phew,' says Ben, blenching a little. 'What did the baby die of?'

'Gastrointestinal disease – diarrhoea to you and me. How awful. The poor little mite died just a month after his mother. Inevitable really, if you think about it. Mother dead, big sister missing, father and brothers off at sea most of the time. They'd have had to leave the baby with the grandmother, probably, or a neighbour, who'd have fed him something unsanitary from a bottle.'

'I feel a bit sick,' says Ben, looking green.

'Put your head between your knees. That's right. Good. Breathe slowly.'

'Sorry,' he says, his voice muffled. 'It's when you said about Annie's mam bleeding to death. It was like hearing my own mam had died.'

'Oh, Ben. I am sorry. I didn't think.'

'They were really close, her and Annie,' he says shakily, straightening up, 'what with doing all the cooking and that together. And she was really nice, sort of quiet and welcoming, like she always had a pot of tea on the go and some old biddy in the corner by the fire, nattering on and ponging a bit, but that was fine by Mam because she always—'

He breaks off and starts to cry softly. Mary ferrets in her pocket for a hanky and lays it on his thigh. She'd hoped this more objective method of research might have spared him some of the trauma of these recollections. But how could she have predicted this?

'Do you miss your own mother?' she asks, intuiting that the death might be resonating with events in the boy's current life.

'She keeps saying she'll have me over for a holiday, but she never does anything about it. I think she's really stressed out with the two little ones, so she can't face it.' He raises a tearful face. 'But I could help her with them, couldn't I? I'm quite good at that stuff. Cooking and that. But it's like she's frozen me in time as a whingey five-year-old.'

Mary smiles. 'I'm sure you were never whingey.'

He blows his nose and holds out the wadded hanky, then smiles with embarrassment and shoves it into his jeans pocket. 'I'm all right now,' he says, squaring his narrow shoulders. 'What did Ricky die of?'

Mary leafs through to the older boy's certificate. 'Tabes mesenterica,' she says. 'Whatever that is.'

Back in the library, Ben taps it in to Google and tracks down a website with a big table listing all the main causes of death in England and Wales over the years. 'Look at this,' says Mary. 'Over 100,000 under-fives died of measles between 1891 and 1900. Right, here it is: tabes mesenterica: 52,948 deaths. It seems to be a kind of tuberculosis, because it's listed with phthisis, which is the old name for TB of the lung. Poor little mite probably just wasted away. Fascinating. I'd no idea TB was so common among children.'

Ben scrolls further down the table. 'I can't find post-partum haemorrhage anywhere,' he says.

'That'll be included in the women who died in childbirth,' Mary says, pointing. 'Twenty-five thousand of them. That's outrageous – worse than the Third World today. And look at this: a further twenty thousand women died of puerperal fever.'

'What's that?'

'Are you sure you want to know? It's not very pleasant. I don't want you keeling over again.'

He grins at her. 'Go on. That was just the shock of Annie's mam dying. I'm fine now.'

'Well, it's a kind of septicaemia of the reproductive organs that sets in after a woman's given birth, sometimes combined with gangrene, and accompanied by foul-smelling discharges.'

'Yeuch,' Ben comments with relish.

'It was spread by doctors not washing their hands, so it was limited almost entirely to women giving birth in hospital.'

Laura sashays over, flouncing her peasant skirt. 'Hospitals? Tell me about it. I've just been reading about the Boer War. It's amazing following history, day by day, as it was happening. Anyway, this report said that men were dying in their hundreds from the thigh wounds they got from the shell casings sort of pinging backwards from their guns. The wounds would get infected and without antibiotics they'd end up dying of gangrene.' She shudders melodramatically. 'What a way to go, eh?'

'If they didn't have antibiotics, what did they do?' Ben asks.

'Amputation was usually the only option,' Mary says. 'Followed, you'll be interested to hear, by cauterization with hot tar.'

'Ouch!' Ben pulls a face, clearly both appalled and delighted.

'I thought you'd like that,' Mary grins. Then, addressing Laura: 'We've found Annie on the census, so we know she was nine in 1891. If she was sixteen or seventeen when she disappeared, that would narrow your search down to 1897, 98, 99, around then.'

'Now she tells me! I've just started on 1900. Some local worthy's just stumped up for a millennium knees-up at the Tynemouth Poor House. Bless.'

'I thought you were going to focus on the summer months?' Mary chides, not in the least bit surprised. 'That's when Ben's recollections appear to stop.'

'I know, but this stuff is just so fascinating. Ben, you'd love the fashion column. Hilarious discussions about how "unbecoming" the new flounced skirt shape is for "ladies of wider girth".'

'I'm going outside for a cigarette,' says Mary firmly. 'Then I'm planning to embark on something rather painstaking, time-consuming and boring, which none the less appeals to the obsessional side of my personality and will, I hope, prove invaluable to our investigation.'

Laura rolls her eyes at Ben. 'Which is?' she prompts.

'Well, I've made a list of all the people Annie's ever mentioned, and I want to see if I can find out their surnames and work out where they all lived and who they were related to. Who knows, I might even find out where Annie moved to – if indeed she did move. I plan to start with Flo, the best friend, and Sam, the boyfriend, and that other boy, Tom. Hopefully they'll all live within a few streets of one another.'

She turns to Ben. 'Do you want to help? Or would you rather look at the Police Court reports with Laura for those years I mentioned? See if anything jogs your memory – someone's name, maybe, or a particular incident.'

Intercepting a conspiratorial look passing between them, Mary sighs. 'I suppose it's too much to hope that you might delay your tour of fashion history until after the research is done?' she asks.

CHAPTER SIXTEEN

2007

The little research team has convened at Mary's house to compare notes. They're sitting on the bench, leaning back against the wall in the last of the afternoon sunshine: Laura and Ben are drinking tea and dunking shortbread fingers; Mary's sipping a double espresso.

Mr Skipper has already disposed of his ferocious bottom-of-the-pot-with-three-sugars concoction and is hunkered down on his Coca Cola crate, breaking the filter off one of Mary's Gitanes and peeling away the paper, prior to dividing the tobacco into three equal heaps on his thigh and rerolling it into a trio of emaciated bidis.

Mary lights up her own intact cigarette and exhales vertically, to avoid blowing smoke into Laura's eyes. 'I had rather a successful afternoon,' she reports. 'I found Flo and Sam – though the predatory Tom eludes me for the time being.' She feels energized; all this factual confirmation is like a shot in the arm. There's no way a schoolboy like Ben could possibly have picked up this kind of detail; some kind of transfer of memories would appear to be the only logical explanation.

'Hey, that's brilliant!' applauds Ben. 'We were total crap, weren't we, Laura? We went through the Police Court reports for the years you said but there wasn't anything about Annie.'

'That's because they only report cases where there's a prosecution,' Laura chimes in. 'Or if a body's found. Anyone going AWOL wouldn't be mentioned unless they'd kicked someone's head in first.'

'We found five suicides, though,' Ben says. 'People used to slit their throats instead of their wrists in them days. How gross is that?'

'Imagine how sharp the knife would have to be for that,' Mary comments with a little shudder.

'Pete reckons it was to avoid going into the workhouse,' adds Laura.

'We found loads of men lost at sea – mostly when a boat went down in a collision, but there was one young lad who got caught up in a trawl winch and another who just vanished overboard in the middle of the night.'

'So how did you find Flo and Sam?' Laura asks.

'Flo was quite straightforward, actually,' says Mary. 'There was only one Florence of the appropriate age in the vicinity without brothers and sisters. Her surname's Sheraton, by the way, and the family lived halfway up Tulley's Bank. Tom was much harder to identify, because we know less about his family situation and it was such a common name. The redoubtable Pete explained that it was traditional for parents to name children after their grandparents, so names were recycled over and over. I came across twenty Thomases in five streets before I gave up. Maybe I'll have more luck with that boat registry he mentioned.'

'What about Sam?' Ben interrupts.

'He was a challenge too, but assuming he was a year or two older than Annie, he'd have been eighteen or nineteen in 1898, which would make him about eleven in 1891 when he was on the *Wellesley* training ship, or borstal as we would have called it.'

'Did you find him?'

'I think so. There were five Samuels on the *Wellesley* at the time of the census, but only one of the right age – a Samuel Heron. Does that surname ring a bell?' Ben shrugs, so Mary continues: 'Anyway, the majority were in the twelve to fourteen age-range, so our Sam would have been one of the youngest aboard. Which might account for his rather reticent and resilient personality when we meet him.'

'Because of being bullied?' asks Ben. 'Is that what you mean?'

'I'd have thought that was rather likely, wouldn't you? Unless he was particularly burly or pugnacious – neither of which he appears to have been.'

The sun sinks lower and Mary shivers and stubs out her cigarette. From where she's sitting, she can see the place on the river where the *Wellesley* was moored over a century ago, and fancies she can still hear the voices of the boys incarcerated there, echoing across the water.

'I keep thinking about Sam on that ship,' says Ben quietly, as if reading her thoughts. 'Locked in with all them big rough lads.'

'It wasn't for long,' Mary tries to reassure him. 'I read some of the reports in the *Wellesley* file. The boys were only there for a year or two and the majority went straight into jobs in the fishing industry or on the collier ships. The Board of Trustees implied they were rather sought after once they'd had their corners knocked off.'

'Where was he living after Annie disappeared?' he asks. 'Did you find him on the 1901 census?'

'There was no Samuel Heron living in North Shields on that date, though I didn't search any further afield.'

'So Sam disappeared too,' says Ben.

'However, I did find his mother living at, let me see—' Mary consults her notebook – 'number 8 Dipper's Landing,' she announces with a flourish. 'What a fascinating process this is.' She beams around at them. 'I'd identified her earlier, you see, from the 1881 census. I found an Elizabeth Heron living with a toddler called Samuel of the right age and married to yet another Thomas – Thomas Heron.'

'Maybe Sam went off to look for Annie,' Ben suggests.

'He probably just hopped on another boat,' says Laura, examining a chipped cerise fingernail. 'There were ships from all over docking at Shields back then. Cargo ships, steam packets, trawlers, tugs, you name it. It would have been a doddle for a skilled lad to find a job.'

The phone rings inside the house.

'I suppose I should get that,' Mary says, closing her eyes and enjoying the warm sun's rays on her eyelids.

'Go on then.' Laura gives her a little shove.

'If it's important they'll ring back.'

'You should get an answerphone.'

'You gave me your old answerphone, don't you remember?'

'Then you should switch it on.'

'It'll just be some telesales person in Calcutta.'

The phone continues to ring. 'Shall I get it for you?' Ben asks.

'No, no.' Mary gets up with a sigh. 'Let's see what the idiot wants.' She walks inside. 'Dr Charlton speaking,' she says.

'So you are there!' exclaims a male voice. 'I was about to give up, then I remembered how you always hated the phone.'

'Who is this?' But she knows straight away.

'Och, now you've hurt my feelings.' Those brusque Scottish vowels; the teasing intonation.

'Hello, Ian,' she says. So he's turned up – again. Every time she moves house, she thinks she's put him behind her. But every time she eventually discovers she's wrong.

'I'm checking into the Grand in Tynemouth tomorrow afternoon,' he's saying. 'So I was thinking I'd pop over for a cuppa once I've settled in.'

'Let me guess,' she says. 'You're bringing the children for a bout of buckets and spades on the Long Sands.'

'Ha, ha. For your information, I'm here on a spot of business.'

'How many are there now?'

'Six, to my shame. All doing their bit for global warming. Four with Polly, and the lovely Christina's just pupped a second.'

'I didn't know there was a lovely Christina.' Mary's annoyed to discover that she feels piqued. She'd filed him away under 'Settled' and 'Unobtainable', whereas it would appear that to the lovely Christina he'd been obtainable after all. Now she'll have to re-file him. But under what heading? Adulterous? Incorrigible? Obtainable?

'Then we've obviously got a lot of catching up to do. Look, I've got to dash now, but I'll see you tomorrow, OK? About three o'clock. I'll bring the Hobnobs.'

Mary hooks the receiver back on the wall and stares at it. Damn.

She hurries up the three flights of stairs to her bedroom; she wants to gather her thoughts before Laura starts interrogating her. Sitting on the bed, she takes out her Gitanes then puts them back in her pocket. Damn.

Ian Campbell: the only man she's ever slept with. She thinks she preferred it when he was 'Unobtainable'. While he was safely ensconced in Primrose Hill, with his alarming job and the super-fertile Polly from PR, she didn't have to ask herself how she felt about him or whether she'd made the right decision – anything physical was out of the question.

Standing up again, she tugs her old student rucksack down from the top of the wardrobe and slaps the dust off it. Then she starts piling items of clothing on the bed: a clean pair of jim-jams; three – no, four, five – pairs of plain white cotton knickers; three pairs of ordinary socks and two of thick walking socks; walking boots, dubbin and cloth; two pairs of jeans and an Arran jumper; a spare skirt and cardie; an assortment of T-shirts and gloves; a foldaway cagoule.

As she starts packing it all systematically into the rucksack, she realizes – with a slight snort of amusement – that she appears to be preparing for a hiking trip, the first she's taken in years. Excellent, she thinks. Fresh air and solitude.

By this time tomorrow she'll be in the middle of the Northumbrian National Park and he'll have to hire a sniffer dog to track her down.

As she moves to her dressing-table to pick up her hairbrush and a small stack of white handkerchiefs, she hears the front gate creak open and glances out of the window. There, manoeuvring some kind of mountain bike down her front path, is a short athletic-looking man in khaki Bermudas wearing a denim baseball cap back-to-front, like one of those elastic-limbed Black rapper types.

Damn, damn, damn. It's him.

Mary shrinks back from the window and considers her options. She could rush out pretending to be in a hurry to catch a train, or nip out through the back yard and call Laura's mobile to explain – absurdly neurotic options, both of them, as she's only too aware. But then Ian always did make her feel slightly panicky and surreal. His infuriating Hibernian confidence, all that disquieting sexual energy apparently aimed in her direction.

She can hear him through the window asking if he's come to the right address, and Laura launching into her Café Laura routine, offering him a seat and something to drink. Three storeys above, Mary sits before her dressing table mirror and conducts an irritated audit of her appearance. Her hair's done that annoying wispy thing it does when newly washed, sliding out of its plait and coiling around her face. And she's too thin, of course, but then she always was: scrawny wrists, breasts like fried eggs on a plate. At least this skirt's fairly new.

She shrugs off her cardie and drapes an embroidered shawl round her shoulders. Then, imagining Laura's raised eyebrows, throws the shawl on the bed and drags the cardie back on. Damn.

Obviously it doesn't matter a jot what she looks like. Things were over between them years ago. When she decided to take things into her own hands. Before Shenley. Before India. Before Tibet. But he has an unnerving way of looking at one with those shrewd grey eyes, of assessing one's appearance according to some criteria of – what? Success? Desirability? *Interestingness?*

She picks up the shawl again. With her latest book in limbo, she feels she needs all the support she can get.

Footsteps coming up the stairs two at a time make her whirl round.

'So this is where you're hiding,' he says.

He's smaller than she remembers – he's always smaller than she remembers – and somewhat balder, as one might expect. But otherwise little changed: the same reddish curls, the same outdoors complexion, the same fiercely bitten nails.

'You said you were coming tomorrow,' she says accusingly.

'Would you still have been here?' He picks up her walking boots, knotted together by the laces, and lets them swing from one finger.

'I was just sorting out a few things,' she says primly, quelling an urge to shove him out of her room. She doesn't want him peering at her things, her life.

He puts an experimental arm through one of the straps on her rucksack. 'God, I remember this thing. Even empty it weighed a ton. Fucking antediluvian. Didn't it belong to a long-lost uncle or something?'

'Long-lost cousin.' She takes it from him and places it back on the bed. 'No doubt you've acquired something rather more sophisticated for your sorties to remote areas.'

He grins at her. 'You know me. State of the art.'

'What are doing here, Ian?'

'Just looking up a dear old friend,' he says, still smiling.

'I've never known you do anything without an ulterior motive.'

'How about some supper? I've booked a table at the Grand, but we can go somewhere else if you'd prefer something less formal.' He wanders over to the window. 'God, this view is fantastic. You can see half way to Oslo. Place must have cost you a fortune.'

'Actually it had been languishing on the market for some years before I bought it,' she says, pressing the last of the clothes firmly into the rucksack. 'The damp put people off, I think. That, and all the boarded-up council houses. Not to mention the marauding gangs from the Meadowell estate. But as I had no car to worry about and very little worth stealing, I wasn't as deterred as some might have been.'

'It all looks pretty upmarket now.'

'Ah, yes. Well, we have Messrs Wimpey and Bryant to thank for that. And a generous committee in Brussels. Regeneration is a marvellous thing.' She moves to the door.

'You look well,' he says, crossing his arms and leaning against the window frame.

'Don't insult my intelligence, Ian. I'm fifty years old and I smoke forty a day. Now kindly vacate my bedroom and come downstairs.'

'Those things will kill you, you know,' he remarks, unabashed, following her down the stairs. 'Assuming the diet doesn't get to you first. Are you still surviving on Ryvita and boiled eggs?'

Mary steers him back outside. 'You've met Laura, I assume? And this is Ben, who's been helping me with some research.' She glances down the street. 'Though our Mr Skipper appears to have departed.'

'Cool bike,' Ben remarks as Ian settles onto the Coca Cola crate and stretches out muscular freckled legs.

'It was a birthday present to myself last week. I thought I'd bring it up north to take it through its paces. Russian titanium frame, Time carbon forks. Light as a feather. Shimano XT gears.'

'Ian's a television film maker,' Mary explains. 'At least I assume that's still how you'd describe yourself?'

'Don't tell me you haven't been following my career.'

'She's only got five channels,' Ben says pityingly. 'She misses everything.'

'What kinds of film do you make?' Laura asks, bustling out with glasses and a bottle of red wine. 'That gin was finished,' she informs Mary, 'so I took this from the rack under the stairs.'

'Popular science documentaries mostly. Brain function, drug-induced states, that sort of thing.'

'Coo-ol,' comments Ben again, clearly smitten.

'Ian and I studied PPP together at Oxford,' says Mary, picking up her glass and swallowing three quick large mouthfuls. She takes out her pack of Gitanes and places it on the bench beside her like a talisman.

'Mary was a terrible swot,' Ian says.

'She's still a terrible swot,' says Laura.

'Whereas I sold my soul to the devil and joined the Beeb.' He takes a sip of wine and turns to Mary. 'I read your paper on "The treatment of phobia via hypnotic regression in three cases suggestive of reincarnation",' he says, reciting the title with care. 'Absolutely fascinating. I thought the way you considered alternative hypotheses was quite disarming. Took the wind right out of my cynical sails.'

'I'm a clinician, Ian, not some New-Age evangelist. Just because a phenomenon appears to be paranormal doesn't mean it shouldn't be subject to scientific scrutiny.'

'So you wouldn't mind me filming one of your hypnosis sessions?' The grey eyes meet hers in a challenge, and she understands that this is the reason for his visit.

'Do me!' cries Ben. 'I used to be a herring girl called Annie,' he says, words tumbling out. 'The doc thinks she died in some horrible way, so we've been researching her on the Internet and that.'

Ian laughs. 'Would you like to be on the telly, Ben?'

'Wow! That would be so cool!'

'Ian, stop it!' Mary snaps. 'It's not fair to tease the boy like that.'

'Who says I'm teasing?' he says. 'It sounds like he'd be perfect for the pilot of my new series.'

CHAPTER SEVENTEEN

2007

'I haven't agreed, you know,' warns Mary.

They're sitting at a corner table in the ornate dining room of the Grand Hotel. Ian's tie-less, a rumpled linen jacket draped over the back of his chair; Mary's in one of the three heavy silk salwar kameez that she always wheels out on such occasions, purchased in Delhi nearly thirty years ago for a risible handful of rupees.

'You agreed to supper. That's a start.'

'Well don't go assuming it's the thin end of any wedge.'

A waiter appears and performs a brief obsequious pantomime: shaking out starched napkins, placing warm rolls on side plates with silver tongs, pouring iced water into outsized glasses.

'I'm afraid this wining and dining lark's rather wasted on me,' Mary comments when he's gone. 'My palate stopped developing at the scampi-and-chips-in-a-basket stage some time in the seventies. Though Laura's been trying to reform me in recent years, bless her.'

'Why do you keep drawing attention to your age?' Ian asks. 'Are you afraid I still fancy you?'

'Fancy? Now there's a word one doesn't hear very often these days.'

'I do, actually, for what it's worth. And you look stunning in that Indian get-up. But that's not why I came to see you.' He leans forward. 'Mary, I'm dead serious about this documentary series.'

'Obviously,' she says noncommittally, wondering when she can decently excuse herself for a Gitanes: once they've ordered, she decides, and opens a weighty leather-bound menu to move the proceedings forwards.

'I've been thinking for ages about producing a really intelligent examination of paranormal phenomena,' Ian is saying. 'Round up some decent scholars and use a few four-syllable words for a change. Address the issues properly, from all points of view. Scientific, philosophical, theological.'

'Theological? You surprise me.' In the past he'd always been scathing about what he referred to as 'God bothering'.

'Why not? There are some fascinating issues. Could Jesus really rise from the dead? Is there such a thing as the soul? Is the Dalai Lama reincarnated?' He gestures for the wine list. 'Your paper's a perfect example of the approach I want to take. Starting with an ostensibly paranormal phenomenon – a case of stigmata, for example, or a poltergeist haunting – I want to examine all possible explanations.'

His white shirt's open at the throat and the cuffs are unbuttoned, as though he'd been interrupted while getting changed, by a telephone call or an idea that demanded to be written down. When they were together she'd found his distractibility both endearing and exhausting.

'How many programmes do you have planned?' she asks.

'I've got funding for a one-hour pilot on BBC2. If that goes well, they'll put up the money for a six-part series. After that, who knows? It depends on the ratings.' He rips his roll apart and reaches for butter, white cuff trailing across the table.

'And you want this pilot thing to be about reincarnation.'

'Yes. I want to kick off with something everyone can identify with. What if we have all been here before and will be reborn again after we die?' He's leaning towards her again, radiating passion; she can imagine how effective he must be in meetings at work.

'How much research have you done?'

'Enough to know that you're the obvious protagonist. I want a professorial figure with some real academic clout, someone the viewer can trust.'

If only he knew, Mary thinks wryly. Aloud she says: 'Am I supposed to be flattered?'

'Seriously, Mary, this whole field's full of fucking charlatans and New-Agers. You should see the cable channels. So-called shamans and charismatics. Dodgy sound effects and voodoo lighting. And what's the name of that guy who wrote the book about groups of souls reincarnating together over and over like some kind of study group? Insists some medium channelled Jesus to tell him about it, for fuck's sake.'

'Robert Schwartz – yes, his claims do seem rather far-fetched. But for what it's worth, the notion that two or more souls tend to reincarnate in tandem is well established in the literature.'

'Whatever, screwballs like Schwartz do your cause a disservice.'

'I didn't realize I had a "cause",' she says.

'Don't you?'

'As I said before, I'm a clinician, not an evangelist.'

'Oh come on, Mary. Don't tell me you wouldn't jump at the chance to argue your case on the telly.'

'So it's a "case" now, is it?' She smiles; she's enjoying this sparring with him. It's just like old times. And the idea of a documentary is starting to intrigue her.

Seeing her smile, he leans back in his chair. 'It would be one in the eye for your critics,' he says and takes a bite of his roll.

She stiffens; what does he know about her critics? 'I'm not sure my critics watch much television,' she remarks mildly.

'Everybody watches television. Stephen Hawking watches television. The fucking Pope watches television.'

'I'm not agreeing—'

'But?'

She toys vaguely with her roll. 'But I'm curious as to how you're planning to structure this pilot episode. If I'm to be the protagonist, won't you need an antagonist to present the counterarguments?'

'That will be me, obviously.'

'How do you mean?'

'My dear Mary, are you honestly telling me that you don't know what I've been up to for the past five years?'

'I'm afraid not.' She's telling the truth, and is surprised to see how deflated he suddenly seems. 'I watch the news, when I can find where they've moved it. And various grisly detective things. And I've been enjoying *Dr Who* – despite its absurd take on the reincarnation theme – and that witty *Buffy* series when it was running, on the occasions I remembered to switch it on. But that's about it.'

'So you've never heard of *Mind Games*.'

'I listen to the wireless sometimes.' Now she's teasing him.

'Mary, Mary,' he sighs. 'Contrary as ever.' Then, beckoning the waiter: 'Shall I order us some wine? Red or white?'

'You choose.'

'Have you decided what you're going to eat?'

She hasn't, and the urge to smoke makes it hard to concentrate on the food on offer. She scans the menu and chooses at random: some steak or other with some kind of terrine thing to start.

A pricy bottle of red appears and is duly rotated for inspection, uncorked and tasted. For a moment Mary sees them as if from a distance: a striking couple, of indeterminate age; the russet-haired man expensively dressed, slightly dishevelled, energetic and intense; the woman – possibly Asian – reticent in head-to-toe indigo silk, with a heavy dark plait draped forward over one shoulder like a stole. We look *interesting*, she thinks. The notion amuses her so intensely that she laughs aloud.

'I'm sorry,' she says. 'This place makes me feel slightly hysterical.' She pushes her chair back. 'I am going to go outside now for a few minutes to have a cigarette.'

'Tell me about *Mind Games*,' she says, by way of apology, when she comes back. The shot of nicotine has made her feel sharper, more focused. Less giddy. She spreads her napkin demurely over her lap and picks up her glass.

He picks his up too and chinks it against hers. 'To old friends,' he says, smiling into her eyes. Then, taking a breath: 'OK. A summary. *Mind Games* was a longish-running series I fronted, ostensibly about the tricks the mind can play on us. It started out as a short run of programmes looking at the efficacy of various therapies for different types of mental illness. What made it different was the fact that I decided to try out some of the treatments myself – including the so-called therapeutic drugs.'

'Risking life and limb for the sake of your art.'

'Hardly,' he says. 'But it went down well and established me as a bit of a celeb amongst the chattering classes. So a second series was commissioned, where we diversified into other mind-altering substances. Cocaine, LSD, marijuana, heroin.' He looks at her. 'Nicotine,' he adds pointedly.

'With you still in the role of test pilot?'

'Correct. The Jeremy Clarkson of the pharmaceutical world. The idea was that I'd go into each experience with a completely open mind, then discuss the implications with a panel of experts. So your punter gets the vicarious hit of watching someone they know get off their head on ecstasy or crack, plus the intellectual thrill of debating the intricacies of endorphins, placebo effects and legalization.'

'I'm sorry I missed it,' she says. She means it; it sounds interesting.

'If I'd known, I'd have brought along a boxed set of the DVDs.'

'What's a DVD?' she deadpans.

'You are priceless.'

Their starters arrive: small artistic heaps on enormous plates dribbled with intensely pigmented sauces.

'So what's your role in the new series? You can't manufacture your own stigmata.'

'I play the agnostic, investigating on behalf of the viewer. The idea is to focus on specific case studies, get a bit more raw human interest into the series. So with Ben, I'd get to know him on screen, visit his house, di-dah-di-dah, do a bit of that library research he was talking about. Film his sessions with you, of course. Then I'd try to find out whether reincarnation's the only explanation for his knowledge of this herring girl.'

'So you'd discuss hypnotic suggestion, cryptoamnesia, subliminal perception, that sort of thing.'

'Exactly! All the issues you raised in your article.'

Mary thinks about the paper she was planning to write about Ben's case; how she'd hoped it might re-establish her credibility. How much more powerful would a documentary on BBC2 be?

'How serious are you really about this?' she asks cautiously.

'Totally and absolutely. Never been more serious in my life.'

She looks at him: so forceful and persuasive, so bent on her agreeing. And though every instinct tells her to run a mile, she can't help being tempted.

'What about its effect on Ben?' she asks.

'You heard him. He's dying to be on telly.'

'What he wants and what he needs aren't necessarily the same thing. He might well change his mind when he considers the implications – and I can pretty much guarantee that his father will refuse permission.'

'Oh, don't worry about him.' Ian waves a dismissive hand. 'I'll film him too. That usually does the trick. Everyone wants to be on telly.'

'As easy as that, is it?' Where she had been amused earlier, Mary now finds this comment slightly repellent – especially as it now appears to apply to her too.

'Come on Mary, have a heart. I really need this new series.'

'Oh?' She raises her eyebrows. There's an edge to his voice that wasn't there before.

'If you must know, my back's absolutely against the wall at the moment,' he admits. He drains his glass and reaches for the bottle. 'The ratings were pretty iffy with the last series, so the suits have cut my budget to the bone. If I don't hit pay dirt with this pilot, I'll be banished to BBC4.'

'Wherever that is.'

He pushes his plate away. 'The documentary graveyard. Where they show all the worthy stuff no one wants to watch. First step on the road to oblivion.' He rubs his eyes; he looks tired. 'Sorry,' he says. 'I'm a bit frazzled. Too many broken nights with the baby, too many rows with Christina – too many *fucking* finance meetings.'

And for a moment Mary glimpses a different Ian to the one who's breezed confidently into and out of her life over the years, with his tight schedule and his expense account, and his exotic armoury of electronic gizmos. If she didn't know him better, she'd say he seemed rather desperate.

She softens her tone. 'Look, even if I were to agree to your film – which I haven't yet, by the way – it's not my decision. It's Ben's father you'll have to convince. And Ben himself, of course.'

'Why do I sense there's something you're not telling me?' Ian's eyes narrow. 'Why did Ben come to see you?'

'You know better than to ask me that.'

'Fucking client confidentiality.' He exhales impatiently. 'OK, OK. I know the drill. I give you my card. You phone the bloody father. Then I kick my heels while he decides whether to contact me.'

'I think he's away on his boat at present – he's a deep-sea fisherman, by the way.'

'Here you are then.' He flicks a small white card onto the table. 'Have you got his number with you? No time like the present.'

At least he allows her to finish her steak before shepherding her into the foyer and handing her some kind of souped-up mobile phone apparatus he fishes out of his pocket. Apparently it's also capable of recording conversations and showing extremely small feature films. The very idea of it makes Mary feel tired.

She leaves a message and Paul calls back minutes later. Ian arranges a meeting the following day then pockets the machine with a flourish. 'See? Total pushover.'

'Surely he didn't agree?'

'Not yet, but he will. I can tell. Fucking falling over himself.' He's joking, but Mary's not amused.

'I'd like to say, "I hope you're right". But I'm not sure that I do. I'm not sure that having his private life broadcast to millions is what Ben needs at the moment.' However much she might be warming to the documentary for her own sake, she can't see how it can possibly benefit Ben.

'Do you want a dessert?'

'What I want, I'm ashamed to admit, is another Gitanes.'

'Maybe I'll join you,' he says.

Outside the hotel, the coast road snakes north to Blythe and Berwick, south to Sunderland. They cross over to a wide pavement promenade and wander northwards until they find a vacant bench overlooking the dark sea. As she's sitting down Mary gets a sudden image of a towering black wave rearing up in front of her. She shakes her head briefly to banish it.

'I trust your room has a sea view,' she remarks.

'It's "rooms", actually. When I said I was from the Beeb they gave me a suite.'

As she suspected, he's the kind of lapsed non-smoker who pretends not to be by never buying cigarettes. She proffers one of her Gitanes and they light up and exhale in unison. 'When did you take it up again?' she asks.

'It was that fucking programme on nicotine. Did you realize tobacco's more addictive than heroin?'

'It's not just the nicotine, I find. It's all the comforting rituals one comes to associate with the habit. Even if I gave up – which, for your information, I'm not even considering – I'd probably still need to sit outside on a bench in the freezing wind forty or so times a day.'

'I came here once as a kid. Did I ever tell you? Nineteen sixty-six, sixty-seven, around then. The weather was boiling but the sea was fucking freezing.'

'That's because of the Arctic currents. The water barely warms up at all in the summer.'

'We stayed in a B and B in Cullercoats, the whole family in one room. Place was heaving with Scots. They're all in Corfu now of course, getting skin cancer, but back then all the factories would close down for two weeks and the whole populace would hop on the first train headed for a decent beach.'

He blows a series of inexpert smoke rings. She'd forgotten what a restless smoker he was, continually playing with his cigarette, rolling it around the ashtray, making patterns in the ash. What must it be like to operate continually on such a level of adrenaline?

'How's the thalassaphobia?' he asks.

'Acute as ever, but I fear Laura and Ben may have embarked on a doomed campaign to cure me.'

'I wonder if I could sustain a whole telly series on arcane phobias.'

'I used to dread the summer,' she remarks. 'Coming home from boarding school to find my old gaggle of chums heading off to the beach every day. It was a like a continual party that I wasn't invited to.'

'1967. It's all coming back now. That was the year I learnt to surf. I blew all my paper-round money on a pukkah surfboard and stayed in the water until I was blue round the gills.'

She shudders. 'Mad. Inexplicable. My worst nightmare,' she says, crossing her arms across her chest. 'I think that was the summer my parents hired a – well, a sort of governess I suppose she was. To keep an eye on me while they were doctoring. Nice lady, very prim and proper, hated the beach nearly as much as I did. But unfortunately for us both they'd issued strict instructions that she was to encourage me into the sea. So every day she'd pack a picnic and bring me here to the Long Sands, and walk me up and down along the water's edge like a frightened filly.'

He laughs. 'Poor Mimi,' he says, using his old nickname for her. 'I wish I'd known you then.'

'You wouldn't have been interested in me.'

'I bet you were pretty.'

'I was bookish and scrawny, as I always have been.'

They sit for a while, inhaling, flicking ash, each lost in their own memories.

'Her name was Miss Turnbull,' muses Mary. 'How strange. I haven't thought of her for years. She'd carry the picnic and I'd carry the windbreak and a spade. It was my job to make the table. She refused to sprawl on the sand – far too unladylike – so I had to dig two neat little trenches and create a cubic mound of sand between, then flatten the top to form a table on which she'd spread a chintz tablecloth.'

He barks with laughter. 'You're kidding me.'

'Then we'd sit either side, on folded towels, with our feet in the trenches, like in a banquette at a cafe. It was surprisingly effective.'

'I wish I'd seen you.'

'You almost certainly did.'

'Ah, yes. Subliminally, you mean.'

'Assuming you were surfing with your eyes open, you probably stared straight at me a hundred times a day.'

'Then you'd have seen me too.'

'Indeed. What colour were your swimming trunks?'

He laughs again. 'God knows.'

Blue, with a white stripe down each side. She remembers him suddenly: a red-haired boy with a surfboard, utterly fearless, swimming way out of his depth. She'd gazed at him, horrified and spellbound, day after day.

'No, wait,' he says. 'Mum got me some new ones with a drawstring, because my old ones kept being pulled down by the waves. They were blue with a white stripe down each side.'

Though she's encountered such coincidences before, many times, since she embarked on her research into reincarnation, they never fail to astonish her. 'Jung called it "synchronicity",' she remarks. 'Apparently coincidental events that he believed to be more than a coincidence – he referred to it as an "acausal connecting principle".'

'Obviously we were meant for each other.'

How typical of Ian to choose the most solipsistic of interpretations. 'Actually it's rather an interesting theory,' she says. 'In which he posits an intelligence in the patterning of non-corporeal events.'

'Why did you leave me?' he asks suddenly, and Mary wonders briefly how bad things are with the lovely Christina.

'You promised you wouldn't ask me again,' she says.

'Blame Jung.'

'I beg your pardon?'

'What other woman would bring synchronicity into a conversation about swimming trunks?'

'Even you can't expect me to launch into an analysis of our break-up three seconds after you waltz back into my life after nearly a decade.'

'Are you saying that I'm back in your life?'

'You are staying at the Grand Hotel in Tynemouth, Ian, and you appear determined to make a documentary about what has become my life's work. What does it look like to you?'

CHAPTER EIGHTEEN

2007

Paul steers *Wanderer* into the mouth of the Tyne and throttles back on the engine as the choppy waves of the open sea smooth out, like someone's taken an iron to them, into the silk of the river. He lets out a long breath, like he always does, as the engine quiets, and the boat stops fighting. That's how he thinks of it: like the sea's a muddy field, all rutted and claggy, and the boat has to plough a line straight through it.

It's a relief to see the familiar buildings on the bank glowing pink in the rising sun: that posh new terrace along from the Wooden Doll, the High Light and the Low Light, all the chippers and fish shops.

The lads are hoying offal over the side so the birds are screaming and diving, strafing the wheelhouse with gobs of white and green. He's wondering whether there's any of them weird innards going over too, but he's not said anything to the lads – and they've not said anything neither, so maybe it's only one or two that's like that. Still, it makes you think. What else is going weird that we don't know about?

Up ahead he can see the *Tricker* belching black diesel: filthy old rustbucket, should have been scrapped years ago. And that cut-price derv – amazing Bing's got away with it for so long. But that's what it's all about these days, keeping the overheads down.

The flat's empty when Paul gets in and the cleaners have been, so the cushions are all plumped up and there's that air-freshener smell, and hoover lines on the rugs. He dumps his gear and kicks off his boots, then prowls from room to room in his socks, sifting through a handful of junk mail. Where's the bairn, he wonders. And Nana. He texted them both he'd be back this morning.

He checks the fridge. Those lamb chops he bought are still there. And the two pizzas. All past their sell-bys. And that milk's off. What's the bairn been eating? It's like the flat's been empty the whole time he's been away.

He's just taking out his mobile to give Nana a piece of his mind, when he hears a key in the door.

'Dad!' It's Ben, out of breath and grinning ear to ear, run all the way up the stairs by the looks of it. 'I was at the library and forgot the time.'

Paul ruffles his hair and smiles down at him. 'I thought you'd skipped the country,' he says. 'The fridge is full of rotten food. Where's Nana? What have you two been up to?'

'I'm going to be on TV! This like really famous Scottish bloke wants to make a programme about the doc's therapy and he wants me to be in it.'

'Ian something, right? Yeah, he called me on the satellite phone. He's coming here this afternoon to talk it through.'

'Can I really be in it?'

The lad looks great: excited, pink cheeks, freckles, caught the sun a bit. *Happy*, that's what it is, Paul thinks with a pang. For the first time in years, the lad actually looks happy. 'I want to eyeball him first, mind,' he says. 'Make sure he's not taking the piss.'

'That's where I was just now, with him at the library. He wanted to see some of the stuff we've been finding out about Annie. Pete nearly wet himself when I told him about the film!'

'And who's Pete when he's at home?'

'This old library dude who's been helping the doc and Laura and me look up old maps and that. Dad, did you know our building used to be this really famous pub called the Jungle? With three bars and a disco and that, and belly dancers in cages hanging from the ceiling. Pete used to play the piano in the basement. He said it was so rough they had special spotlights they switched on when there was a fight, so the bouncers could see what was going on and break it up.'

'Sounds like you've been busy.' Paul feels like he's been away for a month, not just a week.

'And we found where Annie lived!' Lad's so full of it, he's practically hopping on the spot. 'Dad, did you know the whole river bank used to be covered with these slum houses, right down to the water, and there were millions of jetties going out onto the river, so when the big boats moored up their prows would poke right in through people's windows.'

'That'll be the old Low Town your great granda was always on about.' Paul swills old water out of the kettle and refills it. 'He said the rats were the size of rottweilers. Where's Nana? Has she been feeding you properly?'

Ben gets a shifty look on, that says he's covering up something. 'She texted me yesterday, but she hasn't been in much.' (*At all*, Paul thinks.) 'But I don't know. Maybe she has. I've been out a lot and I'm never hungry when I get in, because Laura's always cooked something or packed a picnic and that.'

'Laura? Who's this Laura? I don't know. I go away for a week and come back to find my son's been adopted by some strange woman.'

Ben grins. 'She's this really cool friend of the doc's, who does all the cooking because the doc's like totally useless about food. She runs a caff by Tynemouth Market.'

Sounds all right, Paul thinks. At least the lad's getting fed. 'Would I like her?' he asks.

Ben laughs suddenly, a really big belly-laugh. 'I don't think she's your type,' he giggles, then explains: 'I mean she's really old, like Nana's age. She says when I'm thirteen I can have a weekend job at the caff and she'll train me up to manage my own place.'

So, two middle-aged ladies and a piano-playing librarian. Pretty rum playmates for a lad his age. But it could be worse, Paul thinks. At least he's not twokking and necking jellies down the Meadowell with the chaver brats from his school.

As the kettle comes to the boil, there's another key in the door and it's pushed open by a fat arse in mauve trackie bottoms as Nana backs into the hall weighed down by carrier bags. 'Howay, son,' she grunts when she sees Paul. 'God, my fingers are killing me where these handles have dug in. Get me a cup of tea, will you? I'm gasping.'

She heaves the bags onto the table and starts unpacking. Two-for-one tubs of vanilla ice cream. A six-pack of low-fat yoghurts. Giant sack of crinkle-cut chips.

Here we go again, Paul thinks. 'I hope there's some proper food in there somewhere.'

'There's some shepherd's pies in that one, and some sausages on special offer,' she says, flapping the neck of her trackie top to cool down.

'I'm going to be on TV!' pipes up Ben.

'Stop talking daft and put those things away. I'm shattered. Paul, that's thirty quid you owe me.'

'It's true!' Ben goes on. 'This film bloke's coming to see the flat this afternoon. He wants to film me waking up and getting ready for school and that.'

'Paul? What's the bairn going on about?'

'It's that therapist I told you about,' says Paul. 'The film's about her really, but they want to use Ben as a case study.' He watches his mam's face change as the light slowly dawns.

'What time's he coming?' she asks.

'About two-thirty.' Paul turns to Ben. 'That gives you three hours to sort out your room, buddy.'

'Where's that tea?' says Nana. 'I've got to sit down.'

'Get some tea for your nan, Ben. I'm off for a shower,' says Paul, making a quick getaway.

Better leave her to it before he says something narky. Already he can see her getting in a lather over this TV bloke. Working out if she's got time to get to the hairdresser's – when what would really help is if she'd just take her bags of hi-carb shopping back to fucking Iceland.

He goes to his en-suite and peels off layers of rank dampish clothes. After a long trip Nessa used to say they could walk to the washer by themselves. His skin, underneath, is blotchy; his crotch itchy and matted; his armpits stink. Waiting for the shower to run hot, he steps on the scales and forces himself to look down. Fuck. Up four pounds. He sucks in his belly, then pushes it out as far as it will go and slaps it both sides. Have to have a word with Dougie about all them puddings he's been getting in. Normally he loses weight on a trip. Something called callisthenics, according to some lad down the Low Lights: all the work the muscles have to do to balance when the boat's heaving up and down.

Paul takes his time getting dressed. He can hear Nana jabbering on the phone in the living room and he doesn't want to get involved. He'll wait till she buggers off back to her place to get dolled up.

As it happens the film bloke arrives early, before Nana gets back, so Paul doesn't have to worry about her fussing about, getting in everyone's road. On the phone he sounded like a big bloke, but in the flesh he's five six, five seven at most.

'I bought the bike up in the lift,' he says. 'Hope you don't mind.'

He's wearing shorts and trainers, and there's bike grease on his hands, which is a bit embarrassing as Paul's put on his new leather jacket and smart kecks. But he's making all the right noises about the flat, so that's OK.

'I just wanted to check that you're happy for Ben to be involved in this documentary,' he says after he's had a bit look round and they're all sat down on the leather three-piece. 'And to find out if there's anything I should know before we start. Mary – Dr Charlton – is a stickler for confidentiality and I didn't think it was fair to ask Ben.'

'What do you mean?'

'Well, is there anything about Ben that you wouldn't want two million viewers to find out about?'

Shit, that sex change crap. Paul hadn't thought about that. 'I thought you just wanted to film the hypnosis sessions and a bit of daily life.'

'I think the viewers will want to know why you took him to Dr Charlton in the first place, don't you?'

'Can't you just say we were curious?' Paul sneaks a look at Ben, to see if he's caught on, but the lad's just sitting there jiggling his knees and grinning like he's won the lottery.

'Not really. Mary's going to be arguing that someone's suffering in their current life is often caused by unresolved issues from a previous life. So people are going to wonder what kind of suffering Ben's been going through recently.'

'So? Let them wonder. It's none of their business.' It comes out with more aggro than Paul intends.

The Ian bloke leans forward. 'Paul, I'm going to be honest with you,' he says, sort of charming and threatening at the same time. 'I really want Ben to be in this film. He's a great lad, very bright and photogenic, and this flat's bloody fantastic. And the Annie connection is perfect, especially given the fact that you're a fishing family, going way back. So I'm dead keen to film you on the boat, and contrast that with what it was like in 1898. From a filmic point of view it couldn't be better.'

He pauses with a 'but' hanging in the air. And in that split second, Paul can see it all: Ben wandering along the quayside, waiting for the boat to dock; himself at the helm of the *Wanderer* as she butts through the waves.

'But if I can't explain what's been worrying Ben, and how this therapy with Dr Charlton is supposed to help him, I'm afraid I'll have to see if she can suggest someone else for me to film.'

'*Dad!*' Ben grabs his sleeve.

Paul rounds on him. 'Don't you understand?' he hisses. 'He wants to tell the whole story. About the accident and everything.'

'What accident?' Ian asks and you can almost see the bloke's ears prick up.

'Ben was messing about with a knife when he was little,' Paul says vaguely, trying to play it down. 'And it slipped and cut him, so he had to go to hospital.'

'And that reminded him of some kind of knife trauma in a previous life, is that it?'

'Something like that.'

'Except it wasn't really an accident,' Ben pipes up.

'Shut it, Ben,' Paul snaps. 'Let me deal with this.'

'What, you cut yourself on purpose?' The bloke's talking directly to Ben now, all cosy and nice.

'I wanted a sex change—' Ben starts to explain.

The Ian bloke sits back and sucks air through his teeth. 'So that's what this is all about.'

'Look, I'm sorry, Ian,' Paul butts in. 'This isn't going to work.'

'I can completely understand your hesitation,' says Ian. 'But this is BBC2, not Channel Five. I'm not some sleazy tabloid hack out to make a schlock horror doc. I'm a serious documentary film-maker with a reputation to maintain.'

'*Please*, Dad!' The lad's almost in tears.

Paul puts a hand on his thigh. 'Think about it, buddy,' he says gently. 'What'll your friends say? The lads at school, in the team – they'll crucify you. Once a thing like that's out, you'll never live it down.'

The Ian bloke gets up. 'Look why don't I leave you to think it over?' he says. 'And I'll pop back tomorrow morning. As I said before, if you decide to go ahead, that would be great. Better than great.' He smiles at Ben. 'Fantastic. If you don't, no hard feelings. I'll go and look for someone else.'

CHAPTER NINETEEN

2007

After the Ian bloke's gone, Dad phones out for some pizzas and goes off to the Low Lights for a quick pint.

Ben stares out at the river from the living room window, thinking about the film. He really wants to do it, but Dad's right – he would get total grief about it at school. There's no way Gareth and his crowd would let it alone; they'd probably call him Annie for the rest of his life. Though right now, that's all Ben wants: to have the operation and be called Annie for ever.

His mobile rings; it's a number he doesn't recognize.

'Hi, Ben?' It's the Ian bloke, sounding serious. 'Listen, I've just been talking to Dr Charlton about our meeting earlier, and she's worried that you might take the wrong decision.'

'What do you mean?'

'Well this documentary's really important to her. She's run into a bit of stick recently, with people criticizing her work—'

'She never said.'

'Well, she wouldn't tell you, would she?'

'No, I suppose not.'

'Anyway, like I said, she really needs this film to repair her reputation, so she's worried she might have put some pressure on you without realizing it.'

'No—'

'Letting me go to the library with you, getting you all excited about being on telly. Anyway, she's really working herself up into a state about it. So she's asked me to make sure you don't feel under any pressure to agree. She knows it could be tough for you at school when the film comes out—'

'What kind of criticism has she been getting?'

'I'm not sure I should say. She'd hate it if you knew.'

'I won't let on. I promise.'

'Well, some people would argue that she's put all these memories about Annie into your head herself, as part of the hypnosis process.'

'But that's daft. I was going on about Annie for years before I even met the doc, and I knew loads about her.'

'See? That's exactly why you're so important for the film. That kind of evidence, coming from you, would make all the difference to her reputation.'

'Will she have to stop working?'

'I don't know. I suppose it's a possibility.'

'But she's brilliant. Laura says she's helped tons of people.'

'I don't expect it will come to that.'

'But the film will help.'

'Yes, but she says to make sure you understand that it'll be fine without you, and we can easily start again with someone else.'

Ben clicks off and stares out the window. He never thought the doc might need him to be in the film. He never thought how the film would affect her at all, until now. The sun's setting over Gateshead and the river's glinting with orange light. Is she looking out of her window too? They worked it out once, that her bedroom was probably at exactly the same height as his flat, but just around that bend in the river so they can't quite see each other. But they can both see the old Roman fort over the river in South Shields, and the street lights coming on along the far bank. He thinks of her tucking her blanket around him, and wiping his eyes with her white hanky. And holding him, when no one else ever holds him, ever. And no one's ever talked to him like she does, as though he understands, even when he doesn't all the time – but she makes him believe that he *could*.

And those funny-smelling cigarettes with the blue gypsy twirling on the packet. He's come to really like that smell; and the smell of her enormous coffee machine.

Ben stares down at the ferry, all lit up, churning across to the other side of the river. Maybe it wouldn't be so awful at school. Maybe being cool and famous on TV would sort of cancel out the wanting-a-sex-change stuff. Plus, if he's cured, he'll be really hard anyway like a proper boy, and he'll have loads of new hard friends, so Gareth and his crowd won't dare tease him about it. Except that'll never happen overnight, will it? Which means he'll have to put up with loads of grief in the meantime.

But if he's not in the film, what will happen to the doc? He sighs. Maybe if he just keeps his head down and ignores them – Like, how bad could it be?

Dad gets back just as the delivery lad's unzipping the pizzas.

'I want to be in the film,' Ben says when the lad's gone.

'Well you can't, so that's that.'

'Dad, please. Listen, I've worked it all out. The doc's supposed to cure me, right? So on the film it'll just be like I had this weird problem and now I'm cured. So all that stuff will be in the past, won't it? So there'll be nothing to tease me about.'

'Oh, they'll find something, don't you worry.'

'What I mean is, it'll be over. So they'll have to let it go, won't they? Plus I'll have been on telly, which is totally cool, so that will like cancel it out.'

'I don't know—'

'And you're always saying I should toughen up. So this will be my chance.'

Dad looks surprised – maybe even a bit impressed. 'Bit of bullying never did me any harm, I suppose,' he says thoughtfully. 'I used to get it in the neck about my packed lunches. Nana used to put in all sorts of weird stuff. And she never got the right size uniform.'

Ben laughs; he can just imagine it. 'What did you do?'

'I can't remember. Nicked money from her purse, probably, and bought my own gear.' Dad pulls off a long slice of pepperoni pizza and folds it into his mouth.

'Didn't it bother you, though? I mean, weren't you scared of going to school?'

'Of course,' Dad shrugs. 'But you just get on with it, don't you?'

Ben bites into his chicken and sweetcorn. 'What about the lads on the boat?' he asks. 'With the film and that, I mean. Won't you be embarrassed about them finding out?'

'Forget about me. It's you I'm bothered about.'

'I'll be fine.'

'I suppose I can always wade in if it gets too rough.'

'I told you, I'll be fine,'

'And you're sure you want to do this?'

Ben nods his head. He feels scared and excited all at the same time, but good too, because it would be him and Dad in it together.

'OK. Good lad. Well, I'd better get in touch with that Ian bloke.'

* * *

It's the next day and Ben's freediving off the causeway that leads to the lighthouse below the Priory. He was supposed to go proper diving with Dad, but his business mobile went just as they were getting the gear ready and he had to rush out 'to see a man about a dog', which means he's doing something he doesn't want Ben to know about.

Ben had all his kit out, his wetsuit and tank and that, all ready to go, when the call came. So he decides to go anyway, but leave the heavy gear behind. He's done this quite a few times this summer, ever since he saw a programme about a woman diving with dolphins, zooming around underwater in just a mask and fins. She said people have been swimming underwater for millions of years, diving for mother-of-pearl and oysters and that. You just have to learn how to hold your breath. The woman could hold her breath for eight minutes if she was just hanging in the water, or four and a half minutes finning along – which seemed ages when Ben timed it with his diving watch.

The amazing thing is, you can go down just as deep freediving as you can with all the gear on. But it's not nearly so dangerous, because of something called the 'dive reflex', which slows the heart down and diverts the blood to your vital organs to stop you wasting oxygen. But it only happens when you hold your breath under water; if you try it on land it doesn't work. Plus there's another thing called 'blood shift', which stops your lungs from collapsing when you go deeper. Because the air in your lungs compresses as you dive further down, so at fifty metres it's only one-seventh of its volume, which should suck your intestines into that space. But with blood shift, your blood goes in there instead to compensate for the pressure. But when you're breathing air from a gas tank none of that happens, because the tank keeps the air going in and out of your lungs like on dry land.

Ben bought a freediving book on Amazon and he's been doing breathing and relaxation exercises every day – when he remembers – to open up his ribcage and move his diaphragm to let more air in. The relaxation is to help stop you panicking when your oxygen's running out, because that makes you use it up even quicker.

When he tried it at first he couldn't do it at all. He was OK in his room at home, but soon as he was in the sea, he'd start frantically sucking in air, just like when he had his tank on. But after a while he began to get into it, just floating on his front, rocking on the surface looking down, doing his relaxation exercises and watching the kelp swaying far below.

Once he'd managed two minutes doing that, he started finning – really gently at first, so he didn't use up too much oxygen; then a bit stronger once he'd got used to it. And now he's started actually diving, which takes a bit more effort, so today he's brought along his weight-belt to keep him under. And it works brilliantly, and he can stay under that much longer because he doesn't have to fin to stay down, though obviously the weights make it harder to come up again.

Afterwards, sitting on a rock and tugging off his fins, he thinks that maybe if the doc tried freediving she'd stop being so scared. If she was actually under the water, looking around, instead of staring at it looming in the distance, maybe she'd start to feel more at home. She'd have to stop smoking first, though. Freediving's all about increasing your lung capacity and her lungs must be in a shocking state.

Shoving his wetsuit in a bag, he picks his way over the rocks to the sea wall and heads for home. Laura says the doc has never even tried to stop smoking. She reckons that if she had children she might have made the effort, but because she's on her own it doesn't matter. Ben's googled what smoking does to your lungs, and it's disgusting. It's mad that she can be scared of drowning, which is basically your lungs filling up with water, but keep on doing something that fills them up with black gunge instead.

He's googled drowning too, and what it feels like, from interviews with people who've nearly drowned and been saved at the last moment. And they say the only bad part is when you try to hold your breath at the beginning; because you go into a wild panic, and thrash around trying to get to the surface, which makes it worse, of course, because you're using up all your oxygen, which makes you even more desperate for air. But if you just give in and inhale the water instead, then the panic stops and you get a floaty peaceful feeling, which is what happens when the brain is starved of oxygen. Then you drift down to the sea bed – because it's the air in your lungs that keeps you on the surface – and just loll to and fro with the seaweed. So it's quite a good way to die really.

The flat's empty when he gets back. He locks the door to his room and, as he's leaning back against it, this thought comes into his head: that if the doc actually cures him, he won't have to lock his door any more. If he's cured, he can stop hiding Lily the Pink and all his girlie things. And it would be like just relaxing and going with the flow, like breathing in water and sinking down gently to the sea bed.

He takes Lily out and holds her on his knee. She's not as pink as she was, and her fur's flat and bobbly, but she smells the same: like old sheets, and that perfume he borrowed from Mam years ago, that's gone off now really, but still reminds him of her.

If he's cured, he thinks, he'll have to stop sleeping with Lily. If he's cured he won't even *want* to sleep with Lily – that's what being a boy is; wanting different things. So he'll probably just bundle Lily up with his nighties and take her to the Oxfam shop.

Ben stares at Lily and she stares back, with that crooked smile where her mouth stitching's a bit wonky. What he can't get his head round is how finding out about Annie will stop him loving Lily, and feeling comfy at night from just smelling her ear and rubbing it against his cheek in the dark. Maybe proper boys don't need to feel like that.

But it doesn't matter either way. Because the way Ben sees it, he can't really lose. Either he'll find out about Annie and she'll stop haunting him, and he'll turn into a proper boy. Or it won't work and Dad will have to let him get a sex change. Because after he's been on TV everyone will know about him wanting to be a girl anyway, and, like Dad said, there'll be no going back.

And if it gets too bad, and the kids at school really won't leave him alone, then he'll get Dad to move the boat to Eyemouth or Fraserborough or some other fishing port. Then Ben can start living as a proper girl, in a place where no one knows who he is, with specs as a disguise for the first year, maybe, and his hair dyed so people don't recognize him from the TV. Which has been his dream for ages anyway, though until now he'd always thought he'd have to run away and do it on his own. Because the main thing that's changed is Dad knowing about Annie – even though they haven't really talked about it, because Dad never really talks about anything. But it still makes a difference.

Later, Nana turns up to get his lunch, which she never usually does without phoning first and trying to get out of it, saying, 'Do you need me?' as if she really cares, which she does in a way, as long as it doesn't interfere with her knitting club and her Bingo. So he knows it's because she wants to find out about the film.

She's had her hair done a new colour, blonder with a sort of pink tint, and she's brought some cheese-savoury stotties, which she plonks on the table. 'You get stuck in, lad,' she goes. 'I've just got a couple of calls to make.'

Dad says he doesn't know why she bothered having the phone installed at her flat, when she uses theirs all the time. It really narks him that she's such a scrounger, but Ben thinks it's really funny and it's not as though she's phoning New Zealand, though he wishes she would sometimes, so he could talk to his mam casually, without having to make a big thing out of it every Sunday morning with Dad handing him the phone and pretending not to listen.

So Nana's bustling around the living room with the cordless, moving cushions around and peering at herself in the big mirror, nattering on to her friends, telling them where she is and how she thinks she should stick around in case she's needed, and apologizing for letting them down, and can they manage without her – which is really her way of rubbing their noses in it about the film. Then, right in the middle of eating his stottie, Ben's mobile rings and it's Dad.

'The home number's engaged,' he says, in a sort of whisper. 'Is Nana there?'

'Yes – shall I get her?'

'No!' Dad hisses. 'Don't let on it's me. Listen, that Ian bloke's just phoned and he wants to film a trial session with you and Dr Charlton this evening. Get you both used to having other people in the room. Is that OK?'

'I suppose so,' Ben says, and a little shiver of excitement goes up his back. 'What time?'

'About five. But don't tell your nana. He doesn't want a whole crowd of people there.'

'Where are you?'

'Just outside.'

'Really?' Ben goes to the window and there's Dad, far below, grinning up from the other side of the road.

'I went swimming by myself,' Ben says without thinking. 'Off those rocks by the Priory, where all those old dudes sit with their fishing rods.'

'Was it cold? Did you wear your wetsuit?' Dad asks, and swivels around to look downriver, as if Ben's still out there on the causeway.

It's weird talking to Dad on the phone when you can see him at the same time. It's easier to say things when he's small and far away. When he's in the room with you, he makes all the running and you forget what you wanted to say.

'I was freediving,' says Ben, and it just comes out, the thing he's been putting off telling Dad for weeks, though now he's said it, he can't think why. 'That's what it's called when you're just in a mask and fins. Guess how long I can stay under without taking a breath.'

'Ten minutes. Half an hour. Three and a half days.'

'Da-a-d!'

Dad laughs. 'OK, I would guess you can stay under for one whole minute.'

'Two minutes and twenty seconds!'

'Bloody hell, Ben. I'm not sure I like the sound of that.' But he's impressed; you can tell from his voice.

'It's much safer than breathing compressed air,' Ben says proudly. 'I got a book off Amazon that explained it all. There's a club you can join and everything. Come up to the flat and I'll show you.'

It's turned grey and chilly by the time they get to the doc's house, so they all crowd into her consulting room, where she's got the electric fire on. Dad makes a beeline for the Ian bloke's camcorder, which is this dinky little black number that does 'broadcast quality', he says; and they start up the usual sort of macho conversation men have when there's a new gadget to drool over, which makes Ben think maybe it wouldn't be so great to be cured after all.

The doc catches his eye with a look that makes him giggle. 'You know you can change your mind any time,' she says, meaning about the film, he guesses, not the therapy. 'If it feels too embarrassing or intrusive, let me know and I'll call a halt.'

She's standing by the fire warming her hands, looking pretty normal except for a bit of eyeshadow and mascara, and a shawl instead of her usual cardie, with a big heavy silver brooch to hold it together, and earrings to match. But in fact those few little things make her look really pretty for someone that old, and sort of foreign, or noble, like a Russian countess.

'What if I can't get hypnotized?' Ben's been worrying about this.

'Well, I thought we could start the session with just you and me in the room, then when Annie arrives, I'll let Ian and your father in to observe. How does that sound?' Ben nods, thinking that might work. 'Then if things are still running smoothly, Ian will start filming. But we've got our emergency signal, haven't we? So if anything bothers you, for any reason, and you want to stop, just make that signal.'

'Oh, he'll be alright,' says Laura, clip-clopping in with a jug of iced water and nudging aside a pile of papers on a side table to make room. 'Let me guess,' she says, turning to Paul. 'You must be Ben's father. Ben, why didn't you tell us what a handsome hunk your dad was?'

Dad straightens up, smirking a bit, even though what she said was really cheesy. 'So you're the mysterious Laura,' he says, shaking her hand, also in embarrassing goofy cheese mode. 'Ben's been telling me all about you.'

'Not everything, I hope,' says Laura, winking at Ben. 'A girl's got to keep a few secrets up her sleeve.' And now Ben's suddenly panicked that she's going to start telling him about Salon Laura and his walking lessons and that, which Ben can't handle right now on top of everything else. But it's OK, because Dad's taking out his wad of cash and going into his Big Man act, so Ben starts to relax again.

'Listen, thanks for feeding the lad,' says Dad, peeling off a couple of fifties.

'Don't you dare!' says Laura, slapping his hand away. 'It's no problem cooking for one more. Anyway, he's part of the family now, aren't you, Ben?'

'Well, whatever, thanks for looking out for the lad. He picked the short straw when he got a fisherman for a dad.'

'Ben says you know Harry the Crab.'

'Harry? Yes, he's a good mate and a great fisherman. How do you know him?'

'He's only married to my best friend,' says Laura, winking at Ben again. So now Ben's gripped by a new panic, because Harry's wife is the woman Laura used to be married to when she was a man, and he's terrified she'll start telling Dad about *that* now instead. But before it can get too awful, the Ian bloke butts in.

'Another proof of the theory of six degrees of separation,' he says. 'What you think is an amazing coincidence is really just a function of statistical probabilities.'

'You what?' goes Laura, but it's the doc who answers.

'Six degrees of separation refers to the theory that everyone on the planet is connected to everyone else via no more than six different contacts or "degrees of separation",' she explains. 'A psychologist called Stanley Milgram investigated it in his famous "small world" experiment, and found there were only four degrees of separation for people in America.'

'They tested it out on Facebook,' adds Ben, who heard about this ages ago. 'To see if the six degrees thing was true, and they found the average number of links between all the people on the site was 5.98.'

'So it's got to be less than that for folk in Shields,' says Laura.

'Indeed,' goes the doc, with a little smile. 'But that doesn't mean that's the only explanation for the uncanny connection between certain people.'

'Mary prefers to believe that souls reincarnate in groups,' says Ian. 'Isn't that right, hen?' But you can tell by the way he says it that he thinks it's a batty idea.

'This isn't the time to debate the issue,' says the doc. 'But yes, that is certainly what the research literature indicates and I see no reason to doubt it.'

Ian starts fiddling with the curtains, pulling them a bit more shut or open to let different amounts of light in, then peering into the viewfinder on the camera to check the effect. Then he starts moving piles of books behind the sofa, so the room looks a bit tidier. Ben looks at the doc to see if she's pissed off. Her lips are pressed together a bit more tightly than usual, but otherwise she seems to be coping quite well.

'He used to be her boyfriend, you know,' Laura whispers to Ben. 'That's why he's so rude to her – and why she puts up with it.' She beckons him into the kitchen. 'Come on, lad. Let's get the dinner started. Looks like they'll be ages in here.'

'Why did they split up?' Ben asks when they're in the kitchen.

'She won't talk about it. All I know is she left him a Dear John letter and scarpered off to India. If you ask me, he never got over it. Have you seen the way he looks at her?'

'Maybe they'll get back together again over this film,' Ben says.

'Wouldn't that be a turn up for the books? But I can't see it happening – she's far too set in her ways. Still, you never know.'

'I think he's married anyway,' he says. But a second later he's forgotten all about it, because Ian's finished setting up and the lighting's all organized, and the doc's sitting in her chair waiting for him, and Dad's lying on the sofa pretending to be hypnotized, and it's time for the session to start.

CHAPTER TWENTY

1898

It's Sunday dinner and I can hardly eat a thing. I'm that full of giddy about meeting Sam later, and can't stand the idea of dousing it with mutton and taties – so the smell of the roasts being carried home from the bakery is making me feel almost qualmy.

Flo's off to her mam's, and the Scots lasses have been invited onto one of the luggers where they're having a bit party. So our Jimmy's back with the weans for a visit, and it's just our family again for a few hours.

The littluns are hanging on Mam's skirts, and trying to climb onto her lap every time she sits down and Da's flicking them with the back of his hand, like they were flies, to get them to stand nice. And there's soon to be another, if I'm right – though Mam would never let on, what with the shame of it – and it's hard to tell, what with her petties and pinnie and that. But there's a way she's been walking, a kind of side-to-side rocking, and her varicoses have been paining her and her legs swollen from standing all day. Just looking at her face now, that quick creasing of pain as the weans clamber up.

Even Da's noticing, and asking, and putting a hand on her arm. But she just smiles and shakes her head, and tells him to carve the meat before it congeals.

It's grand to see our Jimmy for a proper blether, mind, and to wander back with him to Nana's after with the weans – though my feet want to skip and dance, not wander, for I've thought straight away that this is my chance to slip away to meet Sam.

He's pensive, our Jimmy, though, so I've to damp down my buzzingness and, by and by, we drift down to the little beach by the salt works, where the cobles are pulled up, and lean against an overturned hull in the sunshine while the bairns plodge around in the shallows.

'It's canny what you've done with your hair,' says he after a bit, which is our Jimmy all over, for what other lad would notice an extra few curls wisping out of a scarf? 'It's like you've changed in just the few days I've been away – or maybes it takes me going away to notice it. You're looking right bonny. Did you know that?'

So I say no, which is only half a lie, because I *am* beginning to know it but still can't hardly believe it.

But now he's poking at the sand with a bit driftwood until I want to kick him – and I do shove him a mite to try and jostle him out of being such a pensive old pudden. For I'm that jumping with the idea of seeing Sam, I can't see a glum face but I have to try and put a smile on it. So I ask what's the matter, and he starts on about how everything's changing, sighing like it's the end of the world. So I'm asking, what's changing then, and he's saying: 'All of us. You and me. Tom, Flo.' So I'm saying, what does he mean, but it's like he's gone off into a dream, and is staring across at a lad going up to another lad over by the Lifeboat House and leaning in close to share a match. Then after lighting up, instead of moving apart again, they stand facing each other for a spell, then the one leads and the other follows round the far side of the building.

So now I'm nudging Jimmy and he's jumping like I've surprised him somehow, and he's saying sorry sorry, I was miles away. And I'm saying the sooner this season's over the better, for it seems lodging with Nana's not suiting him at all.

And now he's complaining about how Nana's mythering on at him the whole time, about what he's up to and what time he's coming home. 'I'm just out walking, Annie – that house is so crammed with mouthy lasses, I think my head will burst if I don't get away. But she won't leave it alone.'

'Is there none there that you like?' I ask, teasing, and a look of such alarm comes over his face as makes me burst out laughing, for our Jimmy's never been a one for the lasses, for all his pretty ways.

So now I'm walking along the Tynemouth Road in the sunshine, with the trams and carts rumbling by full of day-trippers out from Newcastle, and lads and lasses on bicycles. And I'm trying to walk nice, like the High Town ladies out a-strolling on the arms of their men, with their pretty parasols – but I want to kick off my clogs and gather up my skirt, and run and run and run to the War Memorial, where Sam said he'd be waiting.

He's there watching for me when I round the corner into Front Street, and starts towards me, walking quickly, then running, and I forget all about being a lady so I'm running too, until what I was scared would be a slow and fumbly meeting becomes a thing of grabbing hands and swinging round and laughing instead. And before you know it, there we are, linked in and walking along the cobbles, blethering away like an old married couple.

Truly, it's that quick. One minute we're clumsy as a cart with two unbroken horses, jibbing and bumping though a narrow lane, next thing you know we're easy as a brace of matched trotters bowling along. And it's like when me and Flo have been parted for a few days, and there's all that missed blethering to do, so we've to talk extra fast – except with Sam there's our whole *lives* to catch up on.

Slow down, pet, says Sam at one point, for my feet have started speeding along with my tongue, till we're fairly cantering along. And he tugs me over to the railings above St Edward's Bay, where there's nets trailing down over the bank, and we lean there a spell, looking down at the cove where the trippers are camped out on the sand, with their wrapped pieces and jars of lemonade, and trailing up and down the steps with their weans on their hips.

It's as well he's steered me to the railings, for I swear if I hadn't those cold bars to hold on to, I would have lifted into the sky, like a seagull does just by opening its wings and stepping up, or a cat jumping up on a wall. That's the sort of lightness there is in my chest, being with Sam, like a soft moth whirring away inside the bowl of an oil lamp, or a kitten pouncing in a pile of shruff, or – oh, every sort of light and limber thing you can think of.

And what are we talking about? Well, there's no order to any of it. Serious matters, like me being out of my 'prentice time at the smokehouse and him studying for his mate's ticket, mixed up with daftness about our favourite biscuits. For all its muddle, though, it's like we're both trying on new shiftenings, and finding they fit, and suit us, and that we look – oh, we look so fine and bonny!

But it's hard, at times, to mind what he's saying, for all the gazing that's to be done while he's speaking. First at his mouth, which I've already said about, and his eyes that can be merry, like a bairn's, but that have a watchingness about them sometimes that's halfway towards grief, so that I want to kiss him and kiss him as if kisses were a salve for sadness. Though we've never kissed yet, of course. How can we, when the sun's still so high and it seems the whole world and his wife is out strolling along the sea front?

I was on about the gazing, wasn't I? About his eyes, which are a pale blue, like the sky before a summer fret's burned away. And his hair, combed down tidy under his cap, that looks like it will spring alive at the first breath of a breeze, which is my Sam all over: careful and tidy, but with a merry wild thing coiled inside just waiting to leap into life.

And it's me that can make it leap, that's the joy of it. For he's gazing on me too, through all my blether, and it's a stroking sort of a gaze, and I'm a cat meeting that stroking hand, that arches its back and stretches its neck up all a-quiver. I can't believe this feeling he's awaking in me with just a look, and am amazed that folk around are not staring – though what's to see but a herring lass leaning on a railing with her lad?

We've come for ice creams, but the queue outside Watt's is that long, he buys us cups of ginger beer from an ice cart instead, which is as sharp and tingling as you could wish. Then without him asking or me agreeing, we set off back to Shields by the coast path, that winds past the Priory and coal staithes, and over to the trysting hill, where the grass is long and the wyn makes private places that smell of salt and wyn flowers.

Being a sunny day, it's thronging with lads and lasses, cosied up in the hollows: sitting and looking at the sea, or picnicking, or kissing on top of a greatcoat – or under it, some of them that have no shame.

And without him asking or me agreeing we find a hollow of our own, and settle down in the grass, spreading my shawl and folding his jacket. So I'm sitting, and he's sitting, and the hollow's pressing us together and I have to close my eyes, because I want to keep this moment safe for ever: this sun on my face, this press of his shoulder, this smell of his shirt now his jacket's off, of leaf-lard and fish broth, and the vinegar smell of his oxters.

A decent lass shouldn't speak of such things, I know, but I can't help it. My skin's that tingling, like the ginger beer, and my heart galloping so fast I can't catch my breath. I know if I open my eyes and turn my face he'll kiss me, for what else are we here for? But these minutes of waiting and knowing are that precious I don't want to lose them. So I rest my head on his shoulder, like I would with Mam, and he shifts a little like she would, to put his arm around me, and I hear him sigh into my hair – or is it me sighing? I can't tell, for we're that melted together now, as if we've sat like this a thousand times.

Then without him asking or me agreeing, when we've had our fill of waiting, I open my eyes and turn my face and he kisses me.

Shall I tell more? Oh I must, for I can't but speak of it! For his lips on mine, and mine on his, are like our hands on the chair that time: polite and awkward, holding fast, not knowing how to let go. So we stay a long moment, with our lips pressed together, not daring to breathe – and I'm guessing that this is his first time too. And that knowing sends such a shiver through me as to make my lips soften, and open a little, and suck in a bit breath, which is spiced with the taste of him. So now he's noticing and doing the same, so our mouths are both soft now, and our lips barely touching, and we're just breathing together, and tasting the breathing.

Oh, but it's the tenderest thing in the world, this first kiss; and a holy thing too, like kneeling in church of a winter's evening, when the candles are lit and all the gold bits glinting out of the darkness. Why should there be shame in a feeling like this? For isn't this what men's and women's mouths were made for, and wasn't it God that made them so?

All we're doing is kissing, after all, though a more creature thing I can't imagine. For now we're breathing together, all it takes is a mite more opening and his tongue's meeting mine and he's kissing me *inside*, and I'm tasting him properly, which is the closest thing I've ever done with a body – even Mam when she's been bad, even the bairns when I'm bathing them. And I'm wondering, how can a lass give her mouth to any lad she doesn't love?

Flo said she'd to be alert for Tom's hands all the time, to keep them from opening her blouse and tugging up her skirt. But I can't see how I could ever find enough calmness to think of such things. For kissing Sam feels like a door unlocking, and once it's unlocked, all I want is to go into the room. And if his hands want to lead me there, well, all I want is to let them, and—

I can't confess it! Woman my age – what will he think of me? But it's only if you can't remember a sin that you don't have to confess it. 'For these and all my other sins *which I cannot now remember*.' Otherwise you're lying, aren't you?

I keep on going back to that night; what he wanted me to do. Dear Lord, forgive me, but I can't help thinking I made the wrong decision.

It's the funeral that's set me off. Seeing Mr M. laid into Your consecrated ground – after everything he's done, all his sins of the flesh. And what that new priest said, about how Jesus knows what's in our hearts, and that's what He meant when He said, 'Let those who are without sin cast the first stone'.

And all those folk at the church and at that do after – talk about Sodom and Gomorrah! I hardly knew where to put myself. But they all had something good to say about Mr M., didn't they? They showed me a side to him I never saw before, and it's really churned me up.

So I started thinking about Mary Magdalen and all her sins of fornication, and how Jesus loved her best of all his female apostles. And that other Mary, who never lifted a finger round the house when Jesus came to call, while poor Martha was rushing about making things nice. But it was Martha he chastised, wasn't it? For prioritizing the wrong thing, that's how I've always understood it. For doing her duty, when the occasion called for her duty to be set aside.

That Mary spent all their money on a pot of ointment for His feet, and washed them and dried them with her own hair. I've always thought that's not a very clever way to dry feet, that maybes the translation's gone a bit wonky there, and what she really used was her headscarf. But washing His feet, drying them – a woman doing that for a man, well, it's not decent either is it? But He said that was the right thing to do.

I keep thinking back to when Alfred went off. And he was crying, and begging me to hold him, because it might be the last time. And there was this queer feeling in me, a sort of hunger, but lower down. I'd never felt like that before and it made me feel ashamed. I thought maybes he could tell, and that's why he was pressing me so hard. I thought, this can't be right, this must be a sin; this must be how a lass falls into the sin of fornication.

So I pushed him away, didn't I? I was like Martha, when I should have been like Mary.

Right, she's come out and it's my turn.

He's been smoking, I can smell it. Father O'Brien never smoked or took a drink. Folk say we've to move with the times, but isn't that what the Bible's for? To keep us on the right path when things around us are changing?

'Hello, there,' he says. 'Jesus is listening, and He's ready to forgive.'

Why doesn't he stick to the proper words?

'Bless me Father, for I have sinned,' I'm saying. 'It's been three weeks since my last confession.' But what I want to say is: why can't you stop changing things all the time? Why did you get that guitarist for Mass last week? How can I talk about having impure thoughts when the box stinks of tab smoke?

CHAPTER TWENTY-ONE

2007

'. . . three, two, one—'

Mary reaches for Ben's hand. 'Hello, you,' she says as the blue eyes waver open. 'Are you OK? We seemed to lose Annie for a few minutes back there.'

'That was so weird,' says Ben, slowly focussing. 'I was in this sort of box thing, right, like one of those old red phone boxes, only really dark and made of wood, and that man talking to me was behind this little screen thing in another box, so I couldn't see his face. And he was Irish, least that's what he sounded like. I was kneeling on this hard cushiony sort of thing, and holding these weird beads for some reason. And my hands were all wrinkled – right old-biddy hands, with sticky-up veins and knobbly knuckles and that.' He looks up, becoming aware of Ian and his father standing just inside the door. 'Do you think that was Annie, when she was really old?' he asks.

'It's possible, I suppose,' says Mary carefully. 'But I think if Annie had lived to a such a ripe old age we might have encountered her before now.'

'So that was someone else, right? Like, from another life?'

'That would be my guess, yes. And when Ian's finished his film, it might be instructive to visit that old lady again to see what she can teach us.' She clicks off her old cassette tape-recorder and shuffles her notes together. 'Let's take a break there, shall we?' she says. 'I'll ask Laura to rustle up some tea.'

Ben turns to his father. 'When did you come in?' he asks, a bit embarrassed.

'Right in the middle of all that lovey-dovey stuff,' says Paul, grinning down at him. 'Your Annie's really hooked on that lad, isn't she?'

'You're not going to show all that love stuff on the telly, are you?' Ben asks Ian.

'Don't worry, I'll let you see the whole thing before it's broadcast,' he says blithely. 'You can even sit in on some of the edit sessions if you like. Come down to London, take a look behind the scenes. See how much we throw away.'

'Excuse me, can I borrow Ian for a moment?' Mary interrupts. She leads him outside to a bench overlooking the Fish Quay, out of earshot of the house. 'Was that all right?' she asks, proffering her Gitanes.

'Are you kidding? That was bloody fantastic.' Relief floods through her. Until this moment she hadn't realized quite how tense she was.

'So you think the format's going to work.'

'No question. You were brilliant and that boy's an absolute gift. It's quite uncanny hearing that girl's words coming out of his mouth – like watching a spirit possession.'

'Yes, that's one of the features of this work that convinces me we're looking at real phenomenon.'

'But who on earth was that old woman? Is it normal to jump about between incarnations like that?' He lights up and inhales deeply, then exhales in a series of quick puffs.

'That particular transition was somewhat more abrupt than I'm used to, but it's not unheard of for clients to visit several previous lives in a single session.'

'How on earth do you sort them all out?'

'Well, the progression is normally more orderly,' she says, lighting her own cigarette. 'If I sense a need to travel further backward – or forwards – to a different incarnation, I usually guide the client back to the "hallway", or whatever it is we're using as an imaginary conduit, and suggest pushing open a different door.'

'So the channel-hopping's under your control.'

'To some extent, though occasionally one overshoots, as it were, and the client will report that they can't see anything, or that it's gone dark – which usually means that the incarnation in question has died.'

'Like pressing the "off" button. How bizarre.'

Mary flicks ash and leans back, enjoying the hit of nicotine. She's beginning to feel quite absurdly elated. The more she considers it, the more she thinks that this documentary could be exactly what she needs.

'I suspect it might be Annie's burgeoning sexual feelings that triggered the sudden shifting of "channels" we just witnessed,' she remarks. 'Sex would appear to be quite a concern for that God-fearing old lady. She was in a Roman Catholic confessional box, had you worked that out?'

'Poor thing. Talk about repressed.'

'Sex isn't everything, you know,' she says tartly.

'Isn't it?' He grins at her.

'If you recall, Freud was of the opinion that satisfying work was equally important for the human organism's wellbeing.'

'And he ended up dying of mouth cancer.'

'Your point being?'

'That if he'd had a more satisfying sex life, he wouldn't have smoked so many cigars.' He examines the tip of his cigarette. 'He was obsessed with eels, did you know? Apparently he spent years dissecting them looking for their testicles. When he couldn't find them, he switched disciplines and discovered the unconscious instead.'

She laughs. 'And you deduce from this an unhealthy obsession with phallic symbols and, ergo, unresolved sexual issues.'

'Well, what do you think?'

'I think that testosterone is a very powerful hormone,' she says, 'and that it's rather a shame that our planet is run almost entirely by individuals under its influence.'

He slips the cellophane wrapper off her Gitanes packet and burns a series of neat holes in it. 'It must be strange to inhabit your world, Mary Charlton,' he muses. 'To believe all this stuff about past lives, and souls reincarnating in little batches for sessions in some infinite exercise in group therapy.'

'Actually I find my world view a great deal more reasonable and reassuring than the alternatives on offer.'

'That's the trouble though, isn't it? It's all a bit too reassuring. A bit too good to be true.'

'How is it that people can accept that a quantum particle can be in two places at the same time, or that two particles can influence one another without any measurable means of communication – and yet find the idea of reincarnation beyond the pale?'

'So what about us?'

'What *about* us?' she says, bracing herself.

'I mean, have we met before? Apart from glimpsing each other on the Long Sands in 1967.'

'Probably.'

'What do you mean, "probably"?' The cellophane ignites briefly and he stamps it out.

'I mean that you were very significant to me at a certain time in my life—'

'You broke my heart, Mary.'

She sighs and flicks more ash. 'I agree that there was a certain intensity to our relationship,' she says carefully. 'And that, in my experience, tends to suggest that an earlier agenda might have been being played out.'

'Ha!' he exclaims triumphantly. 'I knew it! Maybe I was a dog you were particularly fond of in the sixteenth century.'

Despite herself, she laughs. 'It doesn't work quite like that. A soul wouldn't just crop up repeatedly in another soul's life as a love object.'

'OK, so tell me. How does it work?'

'You've heard of the concept of karma?'

'What goes around comes around.'

'Yes. Well, though it's not necessary to a scientific account of reincarnation, I've found it quite useful therapeutically – which makes me suspect there may be some merit in the concept.'

'Hang on a sec,' he interrupts, getting up abruptly. 'You don't mind if I record this, do you? It might be useful later when I'm structuring our discussion for the programme. Wait here while I nip back for the DAT.'

He returns a minute later, ripping open a Velcroed pocket in a complicated black nylon backpack. Mary leans back against the bench while he fiddles with a chunky little machine, worth thousands of pounds no doubt, and places it on the slats between them.

'OK, nineteenth of August, interview with Dr Mary Charlton. Right, where were we?'

'I was talking about karma.'

'How about a proper definition for the record? Karma is punishment for acts committed in a past life, right?'

'I prefer to talk about it as "unfinished business", because that suggests the idea of personal growth, as in "these things are sent to try us", rather than crime and retribution per se as in the popular understanding of the concept.'

'So each new incarnation of the soul is like one of those army endurance courses, is it?'

She smiles. 'I see it more as a degree course with various modules, which one might have to resit if one hasn't achieved the appropriate grades. So if a person is incredibly vain in one incarnation, then they might suffer from eczema or psoriasis in a future incarnation.'

'To be taught a lesson about inner beauty, you mean.'

'Exactly. And how they respond to that challenge will determine whether they'll need to resit the "vanity course", if you like, in a subsequent incarnation.'

'So you're my specialist subject.'

She sighs again. 'One of many, I've no doubt.'

'And we have to resit one another until we've learnt our lesson?'

She can feel his eyes on her, but she stares out at the river, where a party cruiser is heading seaward blaring some brutish disco music from its loudspeakers. 'You could put it like that,' she says.

'I wonder what the lesson is.' He's teasing her, but she refuses to be drawn.

'With Ben, for example,' she says, 'there's obviously an issue about gender identification. So that would be his "specialist subject" in this incarnation. At this point in his life he's grappling with his thwarted desire to become a woman, coupled with a horror of the adult male form as it's beginning to manifest in his own body.'

'Go on.'

'Well, the logic of karma could suggest that in a previous life his soul might have been very attached to the notion of being female. Which would fit in with what we're learning about Annie: that she's an ugly duckling who's just discovered she's a swan; that she's in love for the first time, with a boy who adores her; that she's simply bursting with love and desire and excitement, and teetering on the very brink of womanhood.'

'Then something happens.'

'Yes. We don't know what yet, but all the indications are that she never lived to experience her female nature to the full.'

'Because she was cut down in her prime.'

'No, not in her prime. That's the whole point. It's quite possible that she and Sam never made love properly. You heard her yourself – so passionate but so gauche and nervous at the same time. I see Annie as a butterfly, newly emerged from her chrysalis—'

'But she never got the chance to fly. And you think that's why Ben wants to be a woman.'

'That's what I suspect, yes. But obviously this is pure speculation at this point. And as Freud was so fond of pointing out, these things are multiply determined.'

'So he could never be proved wrong – crafty old sod.'

'Annie's "unfinished business" with becoming a woman doesn't entirely explain the extent of Ben's alienation from his own anatomy. I've treated quite a few transsexuals, but this is the first time I've encountered a boy who has actually attacked his own genitalia with a knife.'

A florid rotund man walking a minuscule Chihuahua glances curiously towards Mary as she enunciates the words 'genitalia' and 'knife' loudly for the recording machine. 'Sorry, mate,' Ian chuckles. Then, turning back to Mary. 'Go on. You're doing fine.'

'Well, with some transsexuals the desire to be a woman can be as much a repudiation of masculinity as a desire for femininity per se. They feel they have been born into the wrong body – literally. In the sense of a bad body, a body that commits acts of cruelty and aggression.'

'All men are rapists, you mean.'

'Not exactly. In my admittedly limited experience, it's not a generic hatred of patriarchy that's being expressed in these cases. It's more a visceral rejection of a particularly unsavoury previous incarnation: a wife-beater, for example, or a serial rapist; a paedophile or a vicious homophobe; a soldier who's committed some appalling sexual atrocity.'

'So they're born not wanting anything to do with the apparatus that performed all those dirty deeds?'

'Yes. And that horror is often coupled with an intense identification with the female victims of their crimes. So the desire to become a woman can sometimes be accompanied by a need to experience some of the violence and ill treatment those victims experienced at their hands.' Mary pauses for a moment, reflecting on what she's just said. It crystallizes a theory of masochism she's been formulating for some time. She wonders whether there might be a paper in it.

'You changed the subject.'

'Did I?'

'We were talking about our previous incarnations – yours and mine. And you were going to speculate about the lessons we might need to learn.'

'Was I?' she says, deliberately vague.

'You mentioned the term "specialist subject".'

Really the man is incorrigible. 'I think it's time we were getting back, don't you? The others will be wondering what's happened to us.'

CHAPTER TWENTY-TWO

1898

It's Monday now, and we're at the farlane, and I'm that skittish after yesterday that Mrs G.'s had to have a word. Even Flo's been on at me to simmer down and mind my knife. Which I know I should, for fat Sally's had to have that thumb off, and there's worry about the whole hand if the poison doesn't abate.

The day's a drizzling one, that sprays our faces with wetness and coils hair into wispies. The fish are more slithery than ever and soon the damp's seeped into our shoulders like a cold shawl, so we're glad of our tea come two o'clock. Cupping my hands round the hot tin, I get to thinking of all the roadster lasses out in Potts' fields, scrumbling in the mud for wet taties, with feet bare as a bairn's and sacking for a skirt, and nowt but a dusty barn loft to lodge in. Which makes me solemn for a spell, wondering what union organizer there is to speak for *them*, but soon my mind's wandering back to the trysting hill, and here's that ginger-beer welling up again.

I've not told Flo yet, for she was back late. And there's a part of me wants to keep it secret – and not just because of Da – for it feels a private thing. I'm keeping private too about that other night, when Tom tried to kiss me, for I'm sure it means nowt – except that he's a lad not to trust. But it would pain Flo if she knew, and she'd maybe think I'd led him on. Which means that's *two* things I'm not telling, which is the first time ever I've had a thing on my mind and not blurted it soon as she's in earshot.

She's been private with me, too, mind. For she must have come on now, she *must* have, yet I've never seen her rinsing her rags. So maybes she's using the scullery, or taking water into the nettie. Which makes me sad to think of her sneaking round and too embarrassed to say.

* * *

It's a day or three later, after tea, and I've come down our stairs with Flo to linger a bit on the quayside. I've never seen Sam since Sunday, for he lives further upriver, and can't easy get away, for he says his mam can't spare him this time of the day. He's never said, but I think she frets and leans heavy on him.

I've asked to visit, but his face was such a picture at the thought, I set it aside – though I don't care what she's like, for she's his mam so I must love her, however trying.

Now here's Tom clomping down as usual with his oilies, so I'm slipping away quick as I can and Flo's giving me a puzzled look. But what else can I do? I'm that scared he'll say something that'll make Flo catch on – even though there's nowt to catch on to.

So off I go, hurrying along Clive Street, when I get a yen to look for Sam's house, or where I think it might be. He stays on them Scarp Landings, Jimmy says, where the houses are built over the river itself, and made of wood instead of brick, and every one has a shed or cree tacked on, and fast as they rot and sink into the mud, so there's another wherry of warped wood unloaded onto another tottering jetty and another mean leaning thing built.

I've seen the place from a distance, for the river curves upstream and shows it: all ladders and sagging timbers, and weans squatting over holes between the planks – folk say there's not ten netties in the whole neighbourhood.

Turning into the first alley, I can see why Sam's so chary of bringing me here, for half the weans have no clothes and the rest are bare from the waist down, and their mams – or sisters, maybes, for some are that young – are not much more decent, though you can tell it's not for want of trying. And I feel ashamed to be staring, for these poor folk have no choice but to be looked in on, for they've no windows and their only light is through an open door. And I'm thinking, what if I should find myself peering into some dingy room and find my Sam peering back – would he ever forgive me?

So I turn around and hurry back to Clive Street, vowing next time I venture into that place will be on the arm of my lad.

It's good I'm home, though, for there's a deal of work still to do before bedtime, and Mam looks to be ailing again – and won't be properly well, I think, till the baby's born. She's hanging nets to dry up the stairs, and they're that heavy from the rain she's glad of the help, for she's pale and gasping with the effort, which isn't like her.

When we're done, I put the kettle on and get her to sit a spell – and she does too, which is even more not like her. So I think to help a bit by threading up some needles, like when I was wee – with the weans off at Nana's, she's been doing them herself, and it cuts into her rhythm to be forever stopping for more yarn. This time of year, the nets need constant tending – it can be just a few spronks, or a great rent if a pack of dogfish has been at the catch.

So here I am threading away and Mam's sitting with her tea and a custard biscuit, and the Scots lasses are out back swilling splatters off their oilies in the rain – for they've been working late tonight, and every night this week. And the fire's hissing and the kettle bumbling away on the hob, and I'm thinking of Sam setting off on the boat with Da and our Jimmy, and praying to God to keep them safe.

Then out of the blue Mam's asking why I'm so quiet, is something bothering me? And I'm saying, no, just thinking about the lads out in the rain. And she's asking is there any lad in particular I'm thinking of? And when I look up she's laughing at me, for all that she's shattered, and asking who was it I was walking out with last Sunday. I should have guessed she'd catch on, for Mam's as careful of her bairns as Da is of his fishing, and there's not much she doesn't notice.

So now I'm spilling all about Sam, and about him being chary of asking Da's permission. Then saying *please*, Mam, don't let on, because I couldn't bear it if Da makes me stop at home. And she's asking is he that lad off the *Wellesley*, and if he is then she's heard good things about him – them's her very words! – that he's carrying a deal on his shoulders, what with his da drowned. Which is more than he's told me, and stirs up that buzzing I was telling about, till I'm tumbling out all this daft blether about Sam's pale eyes and wild hair, and how strange it is that he likes me instead of Flo. And now Mam's laughing again and asking have I looked in a mirror lately? 'You're a beauty, Annie,' she says – and them's her very words too.

And by and by, when Ellie and them have had their tea, and Flo's back, and we're having a last brew, Mam fetches out the carved knitting box from the old kist in the front room, and gives it me, along with a skein of gansey wool and a full set of needles. And gives me a squeeze on the arm, for I've been on at her since I was a bairn about that knitting box, asking can I have it, and why *not*, and when *can* I then. For it was Nana Milburn's, which she's been keeping for me, and I think I know now why she's kept it back so long. For it's the knitting box of a grown lass who knows the worth of a good thing – not a flibberty-jibbet just learning her stitches.

So now the Scots lasses are crowding round, going ooh and ahh at the dovetailing on the compartments and the good leather straps. Then by and by they fall to teasing me about all the ganseys I'll be knitting now for all my sweethearts, and Mam's giving me that laughing look again. And it's like the day Mrs Gibson told me I was out of my 'prentice time at the smokehouse, like Mam's telling me I'm ready for something, and it's something only a full woman knows, and now's my time to know it.

It's the next evening and I've just picked up the knitting box, and it's *warm*! Like Nana Milburn's ghost's had it in her lap, which is a comforting thing that has me sitting quiet in the corner with Jimmy's old gansey, copying the pattern for the back.

Mam's showed it me a hundred times, our family pattern, but it's not till you try it with your own needles that you catch on properly. See, every family, we each have our own way of knitting a gansey. For there's cables and chains, herringbones and bobbles, and you can pattern them a thousand different ways. You need about eight needles on the go at times to manage all the complications. Flo's a dab hand, of course, being how she is, but I've never had the patience, or maybe the womanliness, to give it the attention.

Now, though, I'm clicking away like a proper Scots quine, and the back's growing, though I'd to unpick it twice at the start. I'm saying it's for our Jimmy, for everyone knows he's a slow starter, so it will be a while before he's a sweetheart knitting for him. It'll be a bold lass that gets our Jimmy for a husband, for she'll have to do all the asking.

Flo's on to the arms of hers, which have no cabling so she can knit without looking, so I've the lamp by me. And Da's on the other side of it, with his paper, and Mam's melting leaf lard for the lasses' supper, so we're settled in ready for our beds – when here's a kafuffle and clatter at the door and in comes Ellie and them, fairly spitting about how the coopers have refused them more lamps.

What with the drizzle the light's fading by seven, they've needed them lit early. But the coopers are making them wait till eight to save oil, and only set them up at the end of each farlane, so them in the middle are gipping in the gloaming. The lasses tried taking turns, because being in the gloaming was eating into their speed. But that puts everyone in danger, for going from a light place to a dark one's even worse than stopping in the dark place all along.

'You should go on strike like them match girls,' says I. 'A heap of rotting herring will soon make the coopers see sense.' At which Da turns on me, very fierce, and says I should remember what butters the bread in this house, and to think what a strike would mean for the boat.

So now Ellie's arguing that the boats ought to back up the gippers, because it's their living too that's at risk. And Da's jabbing at her with his pipe stem, asking why the boats should favour a gaggle of gippers over the dealers and coopers they sell their fish to.

And I say, I'm a gipper too, Da. Aren't I worth favouring? Though I'd never normally talk back to my da – but it's got me all fired up, after what's happened to fat Sally, to think of all them devilish knives gipping away in the dark. So now Da turns on me again, even fiercer, and says to mind my tongue, for he knows coopers that wouldn't think twice about getting some ruffian to bundle a mouthy gipper in a tatie sack and hoy her in the river.

But now here's Mam come in and put a quieting hand on my shoulder, for she can't stand a barny. And she's asking if folk are wanting cocoa – which is her way of trying to sweeten the air, for we only ever have cocoa on a Sunday.

I simmer down a bit then, but Ellie's not to be sweetened. So now she's asking Mam what a beatster gets paid, for they're as crucial to the boats as the gippers.

Mam laughs and looks at Da. 'I beat for the love of it, don't I, pet?' she says, which makes Ellie roll her eyes.

'You wouldn't be laughing if your man was a drinker,' she grumbles, 'and your only money was what you got with your own hands.'

'Lucky for me, then, that he stays home of a night,' says Mam – and somehow her saying them few salving things has taken Da's edge off, so now he's chuckling and knocking out his pipe and telling Ellie that he stays home because he likes Mam's company better than 'an inn full of stotting Scotsmen'.

'Well, take care you don't wear her out,' says Ellie, and spreads her bread with the hot dripping, and sucks at her cocoa, and leaves off barnying. By, but she looks shattered, all them lasses do – hands just lying in their laps between mouthfuls, cheeks splattered with fish innards, for they're too tired even to wash their faces, and would have nodded off right there at the table if Mam hadn't chivvied them away up the stairs.

The next night they're back late again and all in a lather about some lass that's been taken off to the workhouse hospital on Preston Road. It seems she was shoved onto her knife when another lass slipped on a tangle of fish offal. 'It's a wonder it's never happened before now,' Ellie says, 'for the coopers have had the 'prentices gipping all week, instead of sweeping, to keep up with the catches, so the ground's all a-swill with oily innards.'

'Is she bad?' Mam asks, and Ellie says, grim like, 'About as bad as could be, and a lass still be breathing.'

I don't see Sam again till the Sunday, after dinner. Mam's sent me on an errand – to give me an excuse, bless her – and we're walking along the front to Cullercoats and on to Whitley, though it's not much of a day for walking, for the wind's that fierce and is chucking spits of sharp rain at us – not enough to need shelter, mind, which is as well, for every café and fish shop we pass is packed to the gunnels with trippers, and there's queues right along the pavements of folk waiting for a table or take-out.

Sam asks do I want chips, but I can't abide a queue, so we decide to keep walking till things quiet a bit down, if they ever do. But I don't mind one way or the other, for there's nowt I want more than to keep walking with my arm tucked into his, matching my pace to his, and the wind whipping both our faces.

I feel I could walk all the way to Blyth if I had to, and beyond, to Berwick and St Andrews. So I say as much, and Sam says let's wait till the season's over, then we can walk wherever we like. And I say, let's follow the herring to Yarmouth, and he says, daft lass, that's the other way up the coast; and I say I don't care what way it is as long as he's with me.

I know, I know – a lass shouldn't say such things so soon on a walking out, but we've so little time together, just this wee slice of a Sunday, and so much to cram into it.

So now I'm asking about his father and he's walking slower and putting my hand in his jacket pocket to warm it, and telling how his da was a mate on a trawler that was caught in a blizzard off Orkney when Sam was a bairn. It seems ice built up on the rigging too fast for the deckies to chip off, and the weight tipped the boat over. It was discovered next day lying on its side with its sails furled and solid with ice and only gulls on board.

Sam shivers, like it's him that's drowned in that freezing sea, and I want to hug him close and give him my heat, but there's folk about, so I just squeeze his hand. 'When they towed the boat back to Shields, they gave Mam his ditty box, but she couldn't even look at it. So I kept it, and got it open, and his things were dry and good as new – his bakkie tin and pipe, his shut-knife, all his photos. She would never even speak his name after he'd drowned.'

It seems that's how Sam came to be on the *Wellesley*. For his mam had the weans to look after, and another due any minute – so the church folk thought it best young Sam learnt a trade soon as possible to support them.

How did his mam manage, I'm asking. And he's not looking at me, and there's a tightness round his eyes. For it seems his mam and the weans were taken to the workhouse straight after he went on the *Wellesley*, and the baby was born there, and died there, too, a week later. So now Sam's on about how it was his fault – though how can it be, when he was naught but a bairn himself? 'I should have stayed with them,' he's saying, 'and kept us together somehow. Even if it meant thieving, it would have been better than letting them go to that place.'

Soon as he could, he got them out. 'I found a cook's job on a trawler and slept on board to save on lodgings. So I kept all my settlings, and when I'd enough I rented the cheapest room I could find and fetched them home.'

'How's your mam now?' I'm asking, for I'm mindful of what Mam's said about her being a heavy load. And he says she's nervy, and I say I'm not surprised. And he says no, she's always been nervy, and it was his da that kept her steady; so when he drowned she'd no hand on her tiller.

'Folk try to take advantage if there's a woman on her own,' he says, and his soft mouth is pressed into a hard line.

'What kind of advantage?' I ask, and he doesn't answer straight away – though I can guess well enough, for his mam takes in nets, and that's one step away from taking in washing. At least with washing it's women you're working for, but with nets – if it's not a proper loft business – it's the ransackers you've to deal with, and Mam says they're worst of all for taking advantage.

'There was this one ransacker, a few years back,' says Sam. 'Folk were talking, but Mam wouldn't be told. "Oh, he's a decent lad," she says, "doesn't mean any harm".' And he looks at me, a helpless look. 'I tried to stand up to him once. I'd been drinking to get my courage up, see? I was only fourteen and he was a great big lad. I even got my knife out – but he just laughed at me.'

* * *

By and by, without us noticing, we've reach Whitley, which is a fair walk, and we've found a chip shop just closing and a bench to sit on, so now we're hunching together with the wind on our backs and digging in to our bag of soggy chips. And I'm watching his fingers burrow in, the grease on them, and it's the most creature thing I ever saw, that makes me blush right down inside my cami, least that's what it feels like.

Now he's noticed me not eating – for what with the looking and the blushing, I've stopped digging in – and chooses a good brown chip and feeds it me, and touches my lips with his fingers, so I must lick them a bit, I can't help it, even though it seems a thing only a brassy lass would do. And this soft noise escapes him, like a groan – so soft I'm not sure I've even heard it, except now we're looking at each other, and there's a question in his eyes, though he's never said a word, and I know there's an answer in mine.

I can't remember the walk back, just the feel of his hand in his pocket gripping mine, so hard it hurts, that tells me better than words where we're headed. So now we're back in Shields, walking the alleys and stairs, and he's still never said a word, but I know fine we can't go to the trysting hill, for the wyn will be dripping and the grass sodden, and we've no parlour to go to, for our folk haven't been told.

I feel like a tramp, searching for a dark corner to rest in. But all the dark corners are full, in spite of the drizzle – and some of the lighter ones too, with folk that don't care if they can be seen. So I start to feel ashamed, and to hang back, and Sam stops straight away and says sorry, and I say sorry too. And he says he just wants to kiss me, and I say that's what I want too, but the alleys are full of folk that make kissing seem shameful.

Then from out of the shadows behind us comes a lad tugging a lass by the hand, and he's buttoning his jacket and she's smoothing her skirt, and he's winking at Sam and saying, 'All yours, lad.'

'We don't have to,' says Sam, looking down at me. And it's that hesitating look that convinces me, where a smile might turn me away. So I take his hand again, and pull him into the shadows, and find a wall that's dry, under a staircase to a loft, and old leaves crackling underfoot. And lean back against the wall, and untie my shawl, and open his jacket, and worm my hands inside and around his hard body, and hear that soft groan again, that's almost a sad sound, except here's the mouth that's made it, laughing against mine in the dark, then not laughing, then kissing.

* * *

Now it's early morning and Flo and me are clumping down to the quayside with our oilies, and it seems every door we pass is spilling out herring lasses, fresh from their day off and full of blether. The river's fair bristling with luggers speeding home and folding their sails as they come in, like red gulls skimming the water and landing so fast you wonder how they don't crash into each other.

Mrs G.'s all of a bustle when we get there, about a new order for red herring, for the inns are that busy they can't get enough. So the 'prentices are set on to clear the rousing floor and we've to gip a fresh batch quick as we can. We could of done with fat Sal on the farlane, but word is she's at the hospital. So come lunch break, Flo sets to collecting pennies for the family, for three shillings can buy a week of bread and bacon bits, which they'll be glad of with one of their earners laid up.

We go to the hospital after tea, which is my first visit, though I've heard tell of it often enough. They say there's more leave in a hearse from that place than ever walk out alive, but whether that's because of the state of them when they went in or the care they got, who can say? But I'd guess a fair few must have died from the stink alone – for all the carbolic in the world can't disguise the smell of rotting flesh.

We find Sal as glum as she might be, with a thumb missing and a hand swollen red as hot coals under its bindings. She brightens a bit when we give her the money, though I wonder what work she'll manage when she gets out, with just a flipper for a hand.

As we're leaving, there's a crowd of Scots lasses jostling at the big door, yelling at the doorman to let them in, and he's bellowing for them to simmer down. And suddenly they do, for they've seen Ellie stomping down the corridor behind us. And she doesn't have to say a word, for we can all tell from her face that the lass who cut herself on the Saturday has died.

So now Flo and me are backing away, thinking the lasses will push in right past us, but it's like the wind's gone right out of their sails, and some are crossing themselves and some're greeting, and by and by they're all turning round and heading back to the Low Town. And me and Flo are carried along with them, for we're gippers too, so it seems like our rightful place and never mind folk staring.

We march down to the Fish Quay, to the farlanes by the ice factory, where there's lasses still gipping though it's gone nine. And I see right well how it must've happened, for the hurricane lamps are so bright as to hurt your eyes, and the shadows so deep you can't see a thing; but they're jumping shadows, of lasses' heads and hands; and the fish flying into the sorting crans behind them, and the offal bins overflowing, and the ground swilling with grease.

By, but they're fast! I thought I could build up a canny speed, but it's nowt compared to what they're doing. And some are singing a bit, and some blethering on, but by and by they quiet down and the shadows go still.

And though nowt needs be said, Ellie says it anyway; which gets the shadows jumping again, and a hubbub starting. So now Ellie's calling for them to simmer down and say a prayer for Bella's soul – that's the name of the dead lass. Which we all do, and when we've said our amens, Ellie turns to one of the coopers and says, calm as you like: 'We'll have our lamps now, sir. And our sweepers back. And you'd better pray that's all that we ask for.'

And that's the end of it, and they set to gipping again – except I can tell Ellie's not satisfied, and the lasses still riled, so there's more trouble brewing.

Now here's two lasses standing aside, and one's greeting and the other's holding her and talking in an arguing way. Then by and by she leaves the greeting lass and walks over to Flo and me and asks if we're gippers. For it seems they're Bella's crew and will lose their jobs if they can't find a new lass to join them. Did I explain how the Scots lasses always work in threes? Two gippers and another lass who packs the fish in the barrels. So if you're missing a lass you can't earn, and might even forfeit your arie.

Flo's backing off, of course – like I said, she's always slow to take a leap. But I'm thinking that here's maybe a chance of better money, and I'm mindful of that daft talk I had with Sam, about us following the herring to Yarmouth. So though Flo's a face like thunder, I say I'll give it a try.

We go to their place at the farlane, and the lasses show me the different sorts of herring – the mattiefuls and the spents, all the different sizes – and which crans they're to go in, which is a deal to catch on to at the end of a long day, I can tell you.

And now Flo's tying on my bindings and having a cross word at the same time, and I'm getting out my shut knife to start – for this is still a trial, mind, to check my speed and if I can judge the sizes aright.

The place we're standing is part gloaming, part shadows, so it takes a while to adjust. And I'm that aware of the two lasses' eyes on me as I pick up the first mattieful, and slit her open, and look round for the offal bin, which is in a different place from where we have it, so that slows me down. Then there's the sorting crans behind me, which the Scots lasses never even look at, but just sling the gipped fish backwards into the right one. So that slows me down even more, for I've to judge it and remember which cran's which, then aim in the gloaming and pray it's gone in.

It pains me to be so slow, for I know the two lasses are praying I'll catch on. But there's so much to catch on *to*: the sizes, the places for everything, the flinging. And the other lasses are gipping and flinging so fast as to make me dizzy, and the shadows jumping, and the fish slippery. So now I'm grabbing a fish, but I've forgotten for a second how to hold it, but my other hand's still gipping away, and before I can stop it the knife's gone in and—

Let me go! I'll use it, I swear I will—

Oh – but I never even felt it go in—

CHAPTER TWENTY-THREE

2007

The doc's kneeling on the floor next to Ben, a gloved hand gripping each of his wrists, as though he's been trying to hit her, which he remembers vaguely doing. Not hitting her, of course, but lashing out at someone, or something. And trying to scream, but no sound coming out, like in a dream, which is sort of what being hypnotized feels like anyway.

But this time Dad's there too, hovering behind the doc, and his face is a total picture – worried and narky and loving all muddled up – which makes Ben try to pull himself together a bit. So where he'd normally collapse back on the cushions with the doc and start crying, to sort of let all the scary stuff out, Dad being there makes him blink back the tears and try for a shaky smile instead, to show he's OK. Which is what a proper boy is supposed to do, so it's probably something he needs to get used to.

When the doc lets go of his wrists, there are white marks where she was holding him that turn red straight away, so she starts rubbing them gently, which is comforting, and makes up a bit for not getting his normal cuddle.

'Is it always like that?' Dad asks, plonking down on the pouffe, which huffs at the sudden weight of him.

'I'm afraid this reaction is not atypical in Ben's case – though it's rare amongst regression clients generally.'

'So what the fuck was going on?'

'Well I can't be certain, obviously, but my hypothesis would be that Annie's knife injury occasioned a kind of "short circuit" in her unconscious mind, causing it to jump forwards, as it were – or possibly backwards – to a similar traumatic event.'

'And that brought him out of it, right? Like when you wake up in the middle of a nightmare?'

'Something like that.' She looks around and Ian's right there behind her, squatting down with his camera on his shoulder. 'Ian, turn that thing off please,' she snaps, like he's a naughty kid. 'The session's over.'

Dad rests his big hand on Ben's shoulder. 'You all right, buddy?'

Ben shrugs. 'I'm getting used to it,' he says, sounding braver than he feels, because the tears are still in there, locked in his throat making it hard to speak.

'Well done, everyone,' says Ian, lifting the camera down. 'That was bloody brilliant. Fascinating. Fantastic telly. Might even insert a bit of drama doc there if I can get the budget to stretch.' He pats his pockets, looking for a lens cap. 'Mary, we must talk about this. It raises all sorts of interesting questions. About Ben's own knife trauma, for example.'

'You think Ben's experience with a knife wound in his current incarnation might have potentiated his rather extreme reaction to Annie's cut? Well, it's possible, I suppose.' She smiles at Ben's dad. 'I must apologize, Paul – may I call you Paul? When two psychologists get together it can become rather technical, I'm afraid.'

'I hope you're not going to put Ben's accident in the film,' says Dad to Ian. 'Talking about wanting a sex change is fine – well, not exactly fine, but we can cope, can't we buddy?' he adds, looking at Ben. 'But I don't want to risk the tabloids getting hold of that other story, OK?'

'Of course not,' says Ian, rolling up a cable and stuffing it in a bag. 'You're the boss.' Ben can tell he's not really listening, but Dad seems happy enough – though the doc's still looking pretty crabby.

'And Ian,' she adds, in that same telling-off voice, 'I'd rather we didn't discuss Ben's case in front of him – at least not while his therapy's ongoing. I don't want our speculations to influence the outcome.'

'Right-o, hen,' says Ian, like water off a duck's back. 'But you have to do me a favour too. Would you mind terribly leaving this room as it is till we've finished filming? I'll take some stills, so I can put things back if they're moved, but it would save an awful lot of faffing about if you could bear to cope with it like this for the next few weeks.' He scans the room, looking for stray bits of gear.

'It's called continuity,' he explains to Ben's dad. 'It means I can splice footage from different days together if I have to, without books mysteriously appearing and disappearing from behind Mary's head.' Then he turns to Ben. 'And I meant to ask you if you'd mind wearing those same jeans and T-shirt for all the filming in this room. Is that OK?'

'Them Scots lassies were a right hard crowd, weren't they?' says Dad as they walk home along the lower bank later, full of Laura's chilli con carne and baked potatoes. 'Gutting herring till all hours in the rain.'

'What freaks me out,' says Ben, 'is that lass dying from just a knife slipping.'

'Why, because you think the same thing might have happened to Annie?'

'Sort of. In a way. It's more the thought of everyone working with knives.'

'That's the job isn't it? You should try gutting haddock on the boat in a swell. Half the old lads in Shields have got bits missing.'

They're passing a shuttered fish and chip shop; squashed chips on the pavement, screwed up paper in the gutter. A few gulls are flapping around the street lights like big white moths. After a while Dad says, 'Why didn't you tell me what was going on in them sessions?'

'You weren't here. And anyway, I was fine – plus I didn't want you to stop me going.'

'Still, it's a lot for a lad to cope with on his tod.'

Ben shrugs and looks down at their feet, sizes five and ten, walking past the cheapo Italian that always smells of burnt garlic. Then, 'Dad?' he asks, 'How dangerous is it really? On the boat, I mean.'

'Well it's much safer these days, if that's what you're worried about. The net gear's astern now, so there's less danger of being swept over the side. And you can see storms coming on the scanner, and radio if you get in trouble. And there's no furnace below deck like in the old days, with a lad shovelling coals for the engine. I mean, that must have been pretty clever on a rough day.'

'Pete says they used to have special hospital ships that went out to the fishing grounds, because there were so many injuries from knives and winches and that.'

'There's rescue helicopters now – and sonar to track the shoals. But apart from that, the job's pretty much the same as it ever was. Hands and feet fucking freezing, clothes ringing wet, salt sores round your neck and wrists, shitting in a bucket.'

'You never have to shit in a bucket!'

'Not on *Wanderer*, no. But the lads on the *Tricker* do.'

'They never!'

'They do too. All for a dozen monk and a couple boxes of baby haddock. Fucking mug's game.'

The tide's right out, so the river's low, revealing the ancient stones of the harbour walls, hung with slimy weed and rusty mooring rings, loops of old chain and frayed rope. Most of the boats are out, but there are a few bobbing down there on the dark water: *Wanderer*, *Colmanbinny*, *Kelpie*.

'So why don't they pack it in?' Ben asks.

'Why don't *I* pack it in, more like? What do you think? Sell the boat and get a proper job? Suit and tie. Company car.'

Ben laughs. He imagines his dad gift-wrapped in a striped shirt fresh from Markie's with the creases still in. It makes him think of the Incredible Hulk, swelling and going green, then bursting out of his clothes. 'Would you really sell the boat?' he asks.

'It's always a gamble, that's the trouble. I could sell up tomorrow, then the EU would change the rules and I'd be kicking myself. That's what keeps you hooked in. There's always the chance you'll strike gold – like all them prawn we got last year – or you'll haul a net full of monk, or they'll cut the factory quota and give the little lads a proper look-in for a change.'

'If you gave up, you could still do your nice little earners,' says Ben. 'And use the boat for long-distance diving trips. To Norway, or Iceland. That would be so cool.'

The more Ben thinks about it, the more he likes the idea. Anything to stop Dad from dragging that heavy twin rig along the sea bed, scraping up every living thing – sleepy codling and haddock, crustaceans and worms, weed, flatties, the lot – and leaving a wide dead motorway of bare rock and sand behind him. But he knows better than to say anything. He tried once, last year, after he'd seen some photos on the Internet, and he doesn't dare raise it again. Because Dad just lost it. '*Fuck* the environment!' he growled. 'It's not my job to protect the environment. It's for governments to make the rules, and me to try and make a living.'

Which is fair enough, Ben thinks, if the rules are good rules. But when the rules make no sense, like that quota crap that makes you throw back any fish you don't have a licence for, you can't go along with that. Because that could mean a squillion codling that will never grow up, with their swim bladders burst from being hauled aboard, just chucked over the side for the gulls.

Dad says when the quota rule first came in, the lads couldn't stand it. So they'd separate off the illegal fish and sell it on the black market – partly for the money, but mainly because it hurt them to throw a good eating fish back in the sea. But DEFRA brought in some new regulations to stop that, when what they should have done was ban twin-rig trawling altogether and outlaw all driftnets with small holes. Or organize a sort of crop rotation in the sea, like farmers do on land, leaving a third of the fields fallow for as long as it takes to recover. It would piss off the lads for a while, but at least there would be something left for them to catch. And they wouldn't get that stony look Dad gets on his face sometimes, when he knows something's wrong but feels he has no option; like when the old lads went on and on at him when he started using the twin-rig. Ben thinks that's bound to get under your skin if you're basically a decent bloke.

Next day Ian wants to meet Ben and the doc at the library, even though the sun's blazing so the library will be like an oven. He wants to go over how they found Annie's address again and get permission to film there.

The doc's wearing a different shawl, draped over a strappy top that shows the pale skin on her chest and makes her look really young. Ian gets them to pretend to look at computers and maps, so he can take some more photos; then Pete takes him through the Staff Only door for a meeting with the Chief Librarian. Five minutes later the door opens and Pete appears with his face tripping him because the Chief's whisked Ian off to lunch at the Saville Exchange, which is dead posh, and Pete obviously thinks he should have gone too.

Left at a bit of a loose end, Ben and the doc wander off to get stotties from Gregg's, and then go back into the library to wait until Ian gets back – which suits Ben just fine, because he's been itching to have another look at the *Shields Daily News* microfiches again. They're full of information about normal daily life from the time Annie was alive, which helps him make a bit more sense of his hypnosis sessions, like creating a whole 1898 Sims house when before he just had the people. So it's full of ads for weird potions no one would ever be allowed to sell now, because they're probably poisonous; and coal scuttles and mangles and the sort of cooker you have to put coal in – because everything was run on coal in them days, and there were collier boats chugging up and down the river the whole time.

When he's under hypnosis, he's only aware of what Annie is doing – trying to get the fish smell off her hands or helping Mam peel the taties for tea. But with the *Daily News* he can read the fashion column and find out that posh ladies had a special outfit just for riding their bikes. And there's a whole page near the back about what's happening on the river that day, like how many herring boats were moored up and the amounts of different fish they caught.

It turns out that 1898 was the best year ever for herring, with more than four hundred boats in the harbour, up from Yarmouth and Lowestoft, and down from Scotland, plus all the usual local boats. Which is so different compared with these days, where the fish market's just a pathetic little row of fish boxes piled up along one wall in a big echoey shed.

What really surprises Ben though, is that people were worried about over-fishing even then, and holding protest meetings about how the big new steam trawlers were taking too many fish and damaging the spawning grounds. Which means it's been going on for *years*, with big lads with their big macho boats shoving little lads out the way and grabbing all they can, and ignoring the old blokes who can see where it's all leading. Which is the collapse of the herring stocks, and cod an endangered species, and Dad doing his nice little earners.

At about half past two, when there's still no sign of Ian, the doc asks Ben whether he wants to come with her to the Discovery Museum in Newcastle. Pete says that's where the boat records are stored and she wants to find out who was on Annie's father's boat. Ben thinks she must know by now, from talking to Annie. But it's like she can't quite believe all this reincarnation stuff unless she sees it with her own eyes – which must be because of all the flack she's been getting, that Ian told him about.

So they set off on the Metro, with Ben sitting next to the doc, as though she's his mam, watching all the stations go by – Percy Main, Howdon, Walkergate, where the collieries used to be.

At the museum there's a posh new glass entrance attached to the side of a dirty old red-brick building. Going in is a bit like travelling through time, because the foyer is all pale wood and blue handrails; then you push through a door to the archives and the walls are covered with old dark wood panels and it smells like an Oxfam shop. When they get to the Search Room, the woman behind the counter brings out bundles and bundles of ancient forms, all stiff and brown, tied up with string, one for every boat registered in North Shields in 1898: all the tugs and trawlers, drifters and collier boats, each with the name of the boat, and its owner, then a list of everyone in the crew.

Ben hardly dares to touch them – because these are actual records over 100 years old, not microfiche copies, filled in by real people, with all their different curly hand-writings, with real blots and smudges. He unties a bundle and starts gingerly leafing through. 'Why have they got firemen on the boats?' he asks, then: 'Oh, right. I get it. They must be the lads who looked after the steam engines. They went on strike, you know – I just read about it in the *Daily News*. Because they were supposed to help with the nets when they got a big catch, so they'd be really hot and sweaty stoking the boiler one minute, then soaked with freezing water up on deck the next. They said it was making them sick, so they should be paid more money.'

Then, suddenly, before he's even properly started looking for it, there's the *Osprey*. 'Owner, Henry Milburn, 23 Lambs Quay Stairs, North Shields.' He tugs on the doc's shawl and budges over to let her have a look.

'Do you think he filled it in himself?' he asks, imagining Annie's father bent over this *actual* sheet of paper with a pen in his hand, writing in all the names.

'Look, there's Sam!' says the doc, and she seems really chuffed. 'And his name *is* Heron, so I was right about him being that little boy on the *Wellesley*. And there's Jimmy – and George Sheraton, the mate, so that must be Flo's father. And a man called John Hall, in a role they refer to here as "hawseman", whatever that means – and this must be Tom. Thomas Hall, aged 20.'

'There's no cook,' Ben says. 'That must be because Jimmy was doing it, but they were paying him as a deckie, though it has him down as a "mariner".'

'Thomas Hall,' says the doc again, slowly, as though tasting the name on her tongue. 'Initials T.H.' Then she gets up suddenly. 'Excuse me, Ben. I'm going outside for a cigarette.'

She's gone for ages, so Ben goes out to look for her. But she's not on any of the benches in the car park; so he wanders across the road to the newsagent, thinking she might be in there buying tabs, but there's no sign. So he goes back into the museum, but she's not there either; so he leaves a message at the front desk and sets off to catch the Metro back to North Shields. Typical doc, he thinks, stepping on to the down escalator; she's probably got so caught up with one of her theories that she's forgotten all about him.

When he gets back, he goes straight to the library, but she's not there. Ian is, though, parked at one of the computers. Peering over his shoulder, Ben sees that he's on that ancestors.com website and in the 'Find' box he's keyed in the doc's name, 'Mary Louise Charlton', and in the date box he's keyed in '1967'.

'What are you doing?' he asks, and Ian sort of jumps, then closes the window really fast, as though he's been caught on a porno site.

'Oh, just farting about,' he says, standing up so that his back is between Ben and the screen. 'Come to think of it, maybe you can help me. I need some images to set the scene. To show people what life was like for Annie in 1898.

'All I've got so far, you see, is Mary chatting away to you on the sofa. That's fine for radio, but with telly you can't just use talking heads all the time. You've got to give the viewer something else to look at.' He's speaking really fast, which is normal for him, but makes Ben feel slightly out of breath. 'That's why the news people fly reporters out to Basra or Nairobi. All they're doing is parroting info from Reuters, but it means the viewer gets an eyeful of whatever bomb damage there is, and gangs with machetes, and so on. Crass but necessary. What a fucking primitive species we are, eh?'

'There's some photos in that cabinet,' Ben says, 'but most of the good ones have been nicked.'

'I don't need that many. Let's take a shuftie, see what there is. If I need more I'll put a researcher on to it at the editing stage.'

'Does it have to be photos?' Ben's had an idea.

'What do you mean?'

'Well, there's this old artist dude that Dad knows – the doc knows him too actually. Anyway he's like an alky and loony combined, but he does these really cool paintings of the Fish Quay. Going back years, right to Annie's time and before. Dad says there's even one of the doc's house when it was practically the only building on the top bank.'

'So where does he get his information? Or does he just make it up?' The Ian bloke's got his Blackberry out, checking for messages. Ben can't work out if he's really interested in the paintings or not.

'That's the weird thing,' he explains. 'Dad says the paintings are well accurate, so there's always a load of old people crowded round his stall at the market, ooh-ing and aah-ing about things they remember, and trying to spot themselves as kids. Because he's even got the people right, so you can recognize them. I mean, how spooky is that?'

'But he'd be pretty ancient, presumably, wouldn't he? So maybe he can remember back that far.' Ian puts his Blackberry away and gets out a stick of peppermint lip balm. 'Sounds to me as though he might be some kind of autistic spectrum case. Have you seen them on the telly? People who can play a Mozart piano sonata after hearing it just once, or draw an exact image of St Pancras station after whizzing past it on the number 19 bus.'

Ben nods, but he's not convinced. He's seen those autistic people on TV and they seem really disabled to him, which is why what they *can* do is so amazing. But old Skip's sort of normal really, if you can class being an alky and a schizophrenic normal. 'The doc thinks he's painting things from his past lives,' he says.

'You don't say,' Ian laughs. 'Mary, Mary, quite contrary, running true to form as ever.'

'Dad says he's done loads of paintings of boats, because he used to be a skipper, right? In this life I mean. I don't know about before, because when the doc hypnotized him he had a loony fit, so she had to quit. But I can take you to see them if you like.'

Ian weighs this up. 'Actually, I might take you up on that,' he says. 'If those pics are any good, they might work rather well on the screen. Especially if I can get him talking a bit about the old days.' He turns round and quits all the windows on the computer, click-click-click really fast, so Ben can't see what else he was looking at. 'Do you know where he lives?'

'No, but the market's on every Saturday and Sunday, so he'll be on the stall today. If we hurry, we can catch him before he packs up.'

The market's heaving when they get there, with old ladies in flowery dresses fingering the antiques, and mams cruising the craft stalls with their midriffs and muffin-tops on show, which Ben thinks is a mistake unless they're brown and flat; and dads in combat shorts and trainers, which is also not a good look. And somewhere there must be a stall selling metallic helium balloons, because they're bobbing around everywhere, tied to buggy handles; and another stall is doing candy-floss, so half the little kids have pink caked round their mouths and are poking at things with the sticks.

Old Skip's stall is over in a corner, by the railings. Ben points him out and starts heading over, but Ian stops him. 'Hang on a sec while I take some establishing shots. It's never the same when someone knows they're being filmed.'

He gets out his camcorder and hoists it on his shoulder, then darts about among the buggies and old ladies, filming the stall from all angles while old Skip sucks on a rollie-up and nods as some beardy bloke natters on to him about something. The paintings are higgledy-piggledy everywhere, propped up along the front of the stall, and down either side, and hanging on the railings behind.

They're all in cool arty frames he's made out of driftwood: all sizes, from really tiny ones that you could hang in the bog, to huge paintings that would have to go in the living room, over a fireplace, if you had one.

Ben's eye is caught by one small image of two herring girls walking along, arm in arm, with their heads thrown back, laughing. But before he can take a closer look, Ian gives him a nudge. 'Now we know where all those photos went from the library,' he whispers, stowing the camcorder in his bag. Which is *so* out of order, because old Skip probably doesn't even know where the library is, plus Ben's seen him with his easel on the top bank with his own eyes and he wasn't copying from anything.

'These are bloody fantastic,' says Ian in his normal voice, looking at the paintings on the railings. 'Could be just the business.' He peers at a price tag and whistles. 'I wonder if he'd lend them to me in exchange for the publicity,' he says, half to Ben but really talking to himself.

Old Skip spots Ben and nods gruffly. 'Howay, Paul's lad.'

'You must have quite a memory to do all these,' says the Ian bloke.

'Ay,' says old Skip, polite enough, but as though he's heard it all before.

'Fancy a fag?' says Ian, taking out a pack of Marlboro and flipping back the lid. 'Take two,' he says. 'I'm trying to give up.'

CHAPTER TWENTY-FOUR

... You're down on the Fish Quay with the Scottish women. It's dark and the shadows from the lamps make it difficult to see what you're doing. You seem to have cut yourself, is that right? What happened?

1898

I sliced the top clean off one of my fingers. It bled like the dickens, and I was near swooning at the sight, thinking of that dead lass, but it was just a sliver of flesh and scabbed over in no time.

Ellie told me later that them two lasses are training up a 'prentice to do the work now, but she's even slower than me so their barrels are well down. They've got their lamps, though, so that's a blessing, but they're still simmering on about the night hours they're working for their day rate, for it seems there's no abating with the herring this season.

Da says he's never seen the like of the catches they're hauling. But it's not the size of the shoals that's changed, Da says, it's the size of the new luggers that's going after them, which can take a bigger net and a stronger capstan, and engines to take them out faster to the grounds on a still day, and back to port with a bigger catch without waiting on the tugs.

He's been barnying with the younger lads about it, for Tom's forever on at Da to fit a proper engine. But Da says where's the sense in hauling up more fish if they're to end up ploughed into Potts's fields? For the gippers can't work any faster, and there's only so many red herring a drunk Grimsby lad can stomach.

Da says there's a sort of madness with some of the crews, that makes them coal up the engine when there's enough wind for the sails, to get that bit more speed. And I've seen them myself mooring up, using the capstan to haul on the warp and ram between the boats tied up ahead of them, with engines belching and timbers screeching and lads yelling as they wedge in.

* * *

Now here's Flo and me off on the monkey run, with our clean tresses and light skirts, linked in and looking in all the shop windows. I've an inkling she's catching on to me and Sam, for she's starting to press me about what lad I like, and I'm saying no one, but she's insisting there must be someone, for I never took so much care of my looks before. Which is true enough: I did buy a new blouse last Saturday, and I've been trying that different way with my hair at the front, which she's been going on at me about for months but I never heeded before.

When I keep on that there's no one, she gets peevish, for I'm sure she can tell it's a lie. So I've started some daft nonsense about a liking for one lad, but I can't say his name for he's promised to someone else. So now she's on about is it Tom, all sharp like, and I'm sighing, for we're back to that again. So I'm saying, no, swear to God. But I don't know if she's convinced, for here he comes striding along to meet us, and I'm fretting and daresn't meet his eye and slip away soon as I can.

Now off she's gone with him, back to his folks' place, where she's invited for tea, so I'm calm again – or calm as I can be when I'm fair jumping at every dark-haired lad, thinking he might be my Sam.

But the time's passing, and he's nowhere to be seen, and other lads are starting to come up to me, and blether on – decent, like, for there's old folk about, but irksome just the same. And I'm starting to feel testy and to wish Sam would make his visit to Da, so's I could say to these lads I'm taken, and to Flo and Tom too, and stop sneaking around like a thieving brat. And link in with him in front of the whole world, and go for tea at his folks' place, even if it's just fish heads and bread. Is that such a big thing to ask?

I've worked myself up into quite a lather, so when at last here he is, leaning up against a postbox and just watching me, I'm straight off into a great rant about fish heads before he can say howay.

So he's canny flummoxed, isn't he? For last time he saw me, we were kissing at the foot of our stairs and he had to push me away, I was that loath to be parted. Anyway, he listens while I go on, and when I'm done he offers his arm and invites me to tea at his place. Just like that!

Which has *me* flummoxed, and asking is he sure, and what about his mam? And he's saying, no, it's time, and he's sorry, and he's been daft thinking we can keep on as we are. So now I'm running up the steps to tell Mam where I'm off to, and to make an excuse to Da for why I'm away.

And now we're back on Bell Street and sauntering along, but not linked in, for there's folk I know all about. But I don't mind, for it seems we're on our way again, and maybe tomorrow he'll talk to Da, but anyway I'm sure it will be soon. And by and by we're into his part of the Low Town, and I'm taking his arm and would be stepping out with my head held high, except these are alleys were you'd best watch where your feet are treading.

But now Sam's stopping and turning me to face him, and explaining he's not told his mam about us, so she'll be in a canny flap, but that's for the best for she'd be in an even worse flap if she *was* expecting me. So I'll have to be prepared to – now he stops, for he's not sure what I'm to do about his mam, for it seems he hardly knows what to do about her himself. And his face is such a picture of woe, that I'm brimming with tenderness all of a sudden, and a sort of fightingness that I suppose a wife feels when she's facing a trial with her husband.

'Howay,' is all I say. 'She's your mam and I need to meet her.'

The alley we turn down is one I've not entered before, and didn't know existed, for it's a dog's leg leading off what looks like the dead end for a beating loft, where there's a great cutch tank and heaps of clinker from the boiler, and the ground's rusty with cutch stain.

You've to pick your way over the clinker; then you're in a narrow lane of rough cobbles leading onto a wooden quay with sheds either side, except these sheds are folks' houses, and they're resting on staithes and quay planks that reach out over the water, as though the Low Town's slipped down the bank and into the river and taken the poorest folk with it, and tried to shake them off, but they're too stubborn, and have clung on and made their homes on the water itself.

Sam's house is the last in the row, patched with new wood, and freshly creosoted, so I see where his share's gone, and his time, bless him. There's beating hooks and nets on the wall, and a tin of tar by the door – to paint on the inside, I suppose, though I can't see how anything could fend off the wet in a place like this, that's built over the wet, and must get the winter rain head on, and winter swells splashing up under the floor.

There's two weans outside on a bench threading needles, who stop when they see us, and run inside shouting to their mam that Sam's here with a lass.

When she comes out my first thought is that she's a beauty, with Sam's wild hair and pale eyes, that are even more fitting on a woman. My second is that she's ailing, for her cheeks are that flushed, and there's not a spare ounce of flesh on her.

By, but she's that antsy I'm tired after two minutes in her company! So she's wiping her hands on her pinnie, and asking my name, and chiding Sam for not warning her and asking do we want tea, all before we can open our mouths. And Sam's trying to gentle her, and sending one of the weans off to the rain-barrel with the kettle, but she can't be gentled. For now she's on about the state of the house, how she's had a lint to finish so she's never swept up or done the pots – though it all seems neat enough – and sending the other wean off for Carnation, then running after with another threepence for butter.

She's jumpy, like a daddy-long-legs clattering around a lamp, and I keep waiting for her to settle, till I see that she never will, and that this is her way, and it's up to us to settle and let her clatter on around us. So I catch Sam's eye, and smile, and try to feel myself at home.

There's but two chairs, so I take one and Sam the other, while she clears tatie peelings off the table, worriting away all the while about what's for tea – which is broken herrings fried with mashed taties, for what else would it be with a lad on the *Osprey*? But I can see she's ashamed that it's poor folks' fare, so I say that's what my mam's cooking too, which is a lie, but calms her enough to ask my name again and listen to the answer this time.

Now here's their older lass back from selling greens door to door. She's getten them from South Shields, she says, for they're cheaper there, even with the cost of the ferry. They're chary of their mam, all the four bairns, like she's a china teacup on the edge of the mantle that might tumble and smash any minute.

They're right canny, mind. And the lass, Jessie, is sharp as a tack, and that close with her big brother I can see it's her I need to sweeten as much as her mam; for if Sam's the father of this house, that Jessie's shaping up fine to be the mother, for all that she's no more than twelve year old. So she's clearing the pots and setting up a lamp for her mam to beat by, for the dusk comes down early in these narrow alleys – and it's her that gives Sam the nod that it's time to walk me home.

He's canny quiet going back up the alley, so I ask why, and he says it's because I've seen his place, and his mam, so I've seen everything about him, and he's afeared I won't want him any more. And I say I haven't seen everything yet, for I've never seen his mattress, and how can a lass decide about a lad without seeing where he sleeps? Which is a brassy thing to say, but makes him laugh, and squeeze my hand, and see I'm the same loving Annie I ever was.

Oh, but if ever there's a time for a kiss, this is it, for he's needing one and I'm wanting to give it – but we can't, for the doors are open all along the alley, with folk sitting out, or doing the pots in the last of the light, and lighting lamps, them that has them, or candles.

But now Sam's tugging me by the hand, and hurrying me along, though I'm willing enough, and down another alley at the back of the sheds, to the very end, where the river's lapping in the fading light, and there's a cree that looks like a henhouse, or a place to keep nets. And he's pulling open a door, which is no higher than his shoulder, and squatting down with a box of matches and a candle, and I see that here's a bed of bricks and planks and a mattress inside, and crotchboots, and oilies on a hook and a bag for shiftenings, and a shelf with shoe brushes and a pack of candles and matches, all tidy, and an old blue bakkie tin – and two ditty boxes side by side, one dented and rusty and one newer.

What's going through my mind? Why, tenderness; and pity, for the place is so mean; and sadness, for the drowned father who's had that rusty old ditty box. But mostly a sort of trembling, looking at the bed and thinking of him lying there, under the blanket or on top of it, and wondering what he's wearing to sleep in, and blushing at the wondering.

'Annie?' he's whispering, worried like, for the Lord knows what's showing on my face. And I know I should try to answer, but the words won't come. All I can think to do is unbutton my blouse and take his hand and put it inside, on my heart.

Now somehow we're sitting on the bed, for there's nowhere else to be, and the sound of my heart's filling the little place and making the candle flicker. And his arm's going round me, and I'm leaning in, and we're as we were that time on the trysting hill: just waiting, and tasting the waiting.

I can hear him breathing, light and quick; and the water slapping at the staithes beneath; and Jessie chiding the bairns, for their kitchen's just the other side of the wall planks.

And by and by, we sit apart a bit, and he takes off his jacket and I take off my shawl, and we both of us take off our shoes – and lie down, facing, with our arms draped and our foreheads touching.

His breathing's still light and quick, and mine too, like there's no room for a proper breath so we must sip at the air. My skirt and pettie are bunched up under us, and his knee's touching mine; there's cool air on my throat where my blouse is unbuttoned. And oh, my skin is fairly crying out for the touch of his hand.

Is this what it's like when you love a lad? This sipping of the air, this heart that fills your throat and won't let you speak, this melting of the innards, like wax dripping from a candle, just from the touch of a forehead, of a knee? Just from the sense of the buzzing space between you?

Now we're kissing and I must be making little sounds, for he's shushing me – for if we can hear his mam wittering on, she must hear us too. So now we're kissing again, and somehow our legs are entangling, so we're pressing together, his thigh on my soft place and my hip on his hard one. And oh, it's so sweet and so easy, this tangling, as though God made a lass and lad to dovetail like this when they lie together.

Now I know, all of a sudden, how babies are made, for here I am pressing with a rhythm against him, and he's pressing back, and my mouth's opening so shameless on his, and all I can think of is wanting him, like a dog, like a billy goat, inside me. For the sweetness seems muffled with all this clothing between us, so I find I'm pulling up his vest, and my cami, so I can feel his skin against me. Oh, but it's such a mean bit of skin where we're touching, I feel like crying out, and set to undoing my skirt and his kecks, and never mind what he thinks of me.

But now he's finding my hands and stilling them, though his breathing's as ragged as mine. And I feel ashamed, and whisper sorry and I love you and he whispers back, no, that's not why he's stopped me. It's because he wants to do right by me, and not get a baby before he's even spoken to my da. And I whisper that I want his baby and I don't care about Da, for I'm that mad for the sweetness and can't abide the waiting.

And that's what we're like, wanton one minute, sensible the next. So now we're whispering about our future, here in Shields or on up to Yarmouth and beyond, and I'm saying I'm knitting a gansey for him, and he's saying he'll buy me a travelling kist, and that'll be us promised.

So now he's kissing me more quiet like, and tender, and helping me out of my blouse and cami, and just looking at me in the candlelight, with my hair tangled and my boobies showing. And kisses me there, on my booby, where I've never been kissed, until I've to clamp a hand over my mouth to smother my whimpers.

CHAPTER TWENTY-FIVE

1898

It's dark and I've just blown out the candle, and I'm wishing – oh, so wishing! – that I was on my own. But here's Flo nudging at me when all I want is to roll on my side and pretend I'm entangling again. So I swallow a sigh and wriggle nearer and ask what's the matter – for she's my sister and if she's a problem I need to know about it.

She ums and ahs for a bit, but eventually lets on what I suspected anyway, that Tom's been pressing her to go all the way. So I'm asking, does she want to? And she's saying his hands have been that busy she can't see it will make much difference. But she's worried if she does, he'll not respect her any more – but if she *doesn't* he'll be off with another lass.

'If he loves you, he'll not press you,' I say. But she says that's *why* he's pressing her: because he's mad for her and can't wait till they're wed. So now I'm asking, has he proposed? And she's saying no, for he's wanting to get his own boat before he gets married. So I'm saying, sharpish like, that the way he's going he'll be getting a baby long before he's getting a boat.

And now she's sort of laughing, but not laughing, saying that if there *is* a baby, maybe he'll stop looking at other lasses. And I'm saying that's never stopped Charlie Waring, who has eight scrawny weans at home but is forever nipping off upstairs with one of them loose lasses down the Seven Stars. And she's saying her Tom's not like that, and I'm asking hasn't she noticed it's always the bad lads that have too many weans? Because they're forever pressing their wives, and won't take no for an answer – for I can't believe poor Mrs Waring would choose to have all them brats about the place.

Now Flo's gone quiet, and I'm sorry for my harsh words, and saying don't mind me, and Tom must love her, for didn't he bring her to tea with his folks?

And she's sighing, and saying, 'Oh Annie' and 'I hope you're right', so I have to ask her again what's the matter.

'I couldn't stop him,' is what she's blurting out now – and though I can't see her face, her voice tells me there's tears on it. 'He said it was paining him to wait,' she says, which I can easy believe, for a lad like Tom'd say anything to get a lass to agree.

'Was it only the once?' I'm asking, and she's saying no, the first time was a Sunday in his folks' parlour, with her terrified in case his nana should barge in. But now he expects to do it every time, so she's worried about getting a baby.

So I'm asking, when was she last on her rags, and now she's crying properly and telling how she's kept going to the nettie, but there's no sign and now she's weeks past her time.

'I've heard there's things you can do to bring it on,' I'm saying now, almost whispering, for it seems wicked even to mention it. And Flo's whispering back, 'I know,' like she's thought of it too – and her voice is so glum that I'm reaching under the blanket and taking her hand and telling her we'll sort out whatever needs doing together. And she's making me promise not to tell, and I'm saying of course not, swear to God.

Now by and by, so she doesn't feel she's alone, I'm letting slip about Sam, and making her promise to keep it quiet, because of Da; and she's asking more, and I'm telling more, until we're properly caught up, like sisters but better than blood sisters, with no secrets, like we used to be.

It's the next day now and it's eveningtime, and the sun's doing it's honey-spilling on the stairs. I'm on the bench outside with my knitting, and Da's knocking out his pipe beside me, for it's that small slice of the day when men and women can be together, with the beatsters and gippers back from their work, and the crews sitting a bit before setting off for the night fishing.

Now here comes Tom, all jaunty in a new cap, come to fetch off Flo for a stroll. And I'm looking at him, and thinking of him pressing her, and I want to shake him, to wake him up to what's right there on his plate, this lovely sweet lass who might be having his baby.

Flo's off having a wash, so he grabs a stool from inside and sits alongside us in our pool of honey light. And Da's offering him bakkie, but he's shaking his head – for it's the older lads who buy the sticky dark stuff for their pipes; the younger lads smoke something drier and paler, that smells sharper and burns faster, that they roll into tabs. So that's what Tom's doing now, blethering away and pinching bakkie into a line on the lid of his tin; and here's Mam standing in the doorway with a brew and a biscuit for him – for he's like a son to her, always has been, in spite of his rough ways.

And though I could never love him now, I can see how tidy it would be if we were to marry, and our families knitted together, front and back of the same gansey. For he's bantering on with Da about the *Osprey*, and smiling up at Mam as cheeky as when he was a wean, and her smiling back. And I know he loves being at our place, for his da's been canny dour since his mam died, and likes his whisky. But the drink riles him, Da says, and makes him lash out, so it's been hard on Tom and the bairns.

Thinking of what it's like over at his place, what with missing his mam and his da stotting back from the pub, and his crabbit nana mythering on, makes me soften a bit towards him. So when he smiles, I have to smile back. So now he's budging over on his stool to look at my knitting, and holding it against him – for I've finished the front and back now and am working on the gussets for the sleeves.

And he's teasing me, saying it fits canny well, and don't I want to measure him for the arms? And I'm blushing and pulling it away, saying it's for Jimmy. But he won't have it, and keeps on about me knitting it for him, saying he's been needing a new gansey – as if he hasn't just getten the one Flo's been working on these last weeks. Which makes me cross all over again, for her sake, and sharp with him. So now he's changing tack, and is on about me having a secret sweetheart, which gets me blushing again and saying no, and wondering has Flo said something? Though she never would, and anyway she's never even seen Tom since I told her about Sam.

So now Da's staring at me too, with a frown that flusters me even more – but here's Flo come to save me at last, all pink cheeks and yellow tresses, with her hand tugging Tom to his feet and off away up the stairs to the High Town.

It's a day or two later and the gansey's finished! It's gone eleven and I've cast off the last wrist, and pulled all the trailing threads to the inside, and woven them in so's they can't catch. And Mam's ransacking it for me under the lamp, and finding a few or three ends I've missed; but's mostly full of praise, saying she's never seen me so diligent with a job, and going on about how I'm wasted as a gipper and should be beating instead. And I'm saying there's more money in gipping, and she's teasing that a beatster smells better at the end of the day – and I'm saying if your sweetheart's a fisherman, he'd never smell the difference, for he'd be as steeped in herring oil as you are.

But now I've said too much and I'm blushing, and she's laughing and folding the gansey, and telling me she'll have a word with Da tomorrow if I like – to smooth the way – for it won't do for Sam to be wearing the Milburn cables without the say-so of the Milburn skipper.

I should wait, of course, for Saturday to give it him. But I'm that proud of the work, and that yearning to see him, that next day I have to find him. So here I am hurrying down to Bell Street after tea with a brown paper package under my arm and a fruit loaf from Mam in a bag, for I've said about his mam, and the bairns, and she wants to give them something to cheer them.

So here's the old cutch tank and the rusty clinker, and the wooden alley leading out over the water – and there's Sam outside the last house, oiling his crotchboots. Part of me wants to run the last few yards, but another part just wants to stand and watch him, for when do I get the chance just to see him in his own life? So for once it's the slow voice I heed, not the hasty one, and lean against a rain barrel, and just love him from a distance: pushing his hair off his face with the back of his hand, dipping a rag in the dish, rubbing the oil into the dull leather to make it gleam.

By and by he feels my eyes on him, the way you do sometimes, like a tap on the shoulder – and looks up, and sees me standing here. And is on his feet and running, and would have kissed me right there with folk staring, but settles for taking my parcels, and squeezing my hand and leading me back to his house. But now I'm baulking, for I need to explain why I've come and I'll never manage at his place with his mam clattering about.

So I stop and say I've brought his gansey, but if he's to wear it he'll have to talk to Da first. So he asks, am I pressing him? And I say, yes, and stamp my foot, and tell him how tired I am of this secretness, and I want him to have tea at our place and be a proper sweetheart. I'm being fierce with him, I know, but it's a loving kind of fierceness and I think maybes it's the push-off he needs. For I know he's not the kind who rocks the boat, for it's been rocked too much already in his life.

So now I'm asking, gentle like, doesn't he love me? And he's saying, more than anything. And I'm saying, so what's to be feared? And he's saying he's more afeared of vexing me than he is of facing up to my da – which has us both laughing, and looking love at each other, and so it's settled.

Now here's the difficultest thing I ever had to do, which is walking away from my laughing lad and not looking back. For they say a lass must never wave goodbye to her sweetheart when he's off to sea, in case she's waving him off for ever. Nor sweep the house straight after he's left, lest the waves sweep him overboard; nor wash his shiftenings, lest she washes him out of her life. And every 'thou shalt not' makes our lads' leaving into a holier thing: our own Ten Commandments to sweeten God's temper, and bring them back safe and sound.

Oh, but there's such a brimming-up of happiness in me, to think he'll be settling things with Da before they set out. So that when he's back tomorrow – oh, dear Lord keep him safe! – we'll be out in the open, and can link in, and smile at folk as knows us, and they'll say, 'Why, isn't that Henry Milburn's lass walking out with the *Wellesley* lad? Him that's studying for his mate's ticket? By, don't they make a fine couple?'

I'm so liking this picture that I'm dawdling along Bell Street – with a daft grin on my face, I've no doubt – and folk are barging past with their crans and barrows, full of busy for the evening. Now here's Tom leaning in the doorway of the bakkie shop, looking at me, though I'm that dozy with dreaming I've never even seen him till just now.

'I'll walk you home,' says he, offering his arm so I can't but take it, for it would seem rude to refuse.

He smells of bakkie, for he's just nipped out a tab and stuck it behind his ear, and I'm thinking that's a smell I never noticed with Sam. Maybes because he's no money to spare for tabs – though most lads see bakkie as their due, as vital as bread and tea. See, my mind's all taken up with Sam, so it takes a while before I hear what Tom's on about, which is more daft gansey teasing, and is it finished yet and when can he come to fetch it.

So I'm saying, what about the one he's getten from Flo? And he's saying he's never asked her to knit for him, and I'm saying he's never asked *me* neither. Which is a mistake, for now he's thinking I *wanted* him to ask me, and is grinning down like he's caught me out.

Now we're at our stairs and I take the chance to let go his arm and pick up my skirts. But he's barring my way, and asking where's his kiss. And I'm saying, what kiss? Why, for walking you home, says he. And I say such a small service is not worth a whole kiss, but I'll shake hands if he likes – just to keep it light, see?

So now I'm offering my hand – all the while thinking, it's nowt, he must be teasing, for it's daylight and Flo could come running down the stairs any moment. But there's a look in his eyes says he doesn't care who sees us, and he's taking my hand and not letting it go, and tugging me towards him.

And it riles me that he's still teasing me, when there might be a *baby*, for sweet Jesus' sake. So I beg him to let me go, *please*, for it's all wrong to carry on so when he's with Flo. And I nearly blurt out about the baby too, but stop myself just in time. So now he does let me go, and I gather up my skirt and scuttle up the stairs fast as I can.

CHAPTER TWENTY-SIX

2007

'Thanks. That was brilliant, Ben, Mary,' says Ian. 'Another fantastic session.' He glances at his watch then starts hurriedly collecting up his equipment and stowing it away in various bespoke compartments in his backpack.

'Would you like an espresso?' Mary offers.

'Sorry.' He looks round distractedly and pockets a small black and chrome item he retrieves from the corner of her desk. 'Got to dash. I've set up a phone conference back at the hotel.'

'Oh?' Mary can't begin to imagine what that might involve.

'Budgets. Film crew. Research. Nothing to worry your pretty little head about.' She follows him outside, where he mounts his gleaming new bicycle and pedals off. She has a sense that all this haste has been manufactured so he doesn't have to explain his plans. But why? What is he keeping from her?

Ben's putting on his hoodie, getting ready to leave too.

'I believe I owe you an apology for yesterday afternoon,' Mary says. 'I felt nauseous all of a sudden – it was the heat in the Search Room, I suspect – so I went for a walk and—'

'You forgot all about me, didn't you?' he interrupts with a grin.

'I'm really sorry. I meant to call you when I got home, but I couldn't find your number.'

This is only partly true. In fact, she'd been so taken aback to discover that Tom's initials were T.H. that she'd ended up striding right past her house without stopping and simply continuing along the coast for miles, as far as the Whitley Bay golf course, then catching a bus home again. By which time she was so uncharacteristically famished that she grabbed a takeaway menu at random from a heap by the phone and ordered something inadvisable and orange, that purported to be a Madras prawn curry, and ate it far too fast with a nan bread the size and texture of a tennis racquet.

She watches him set off too then goes back inside the house and shuts the door behind her. Standing in the narrow hallway, she wonders what to do. Her consulting room, which doubles as a sitting room, where she'd normally relax doing the *Guardian* crossword or making spiderish notes in the margin of some book she's reviewing, is out of bounds. Not literally, obviously, but this continuity business makes her feel inhibited, worried about moving something without thinking. She'd quite like to look out her transsexual case notes, for example, to see if she has enough material for that masochism paper. But that would involve moving her desk and fossicking through box files.

She wanders through to the kitchen and sits at the table, leafing through the latest issue of *Analytical Psychology*. But she can't settle: the wooden chair's hard on her buttocks and the spotlight bulb aimed at the table has gone out. She considers going up to bed to read, but that seems ludicrous at this hour – and somehow defeatist, as though Ian has bested her in some obscure contest.

By way of displacement activity, she fills the kettle and amuses herself briefly as it boils by experimenting with her distorted reflection in its curved stainless steel side. The kitchen smells slightly swampish; even now, in the middle of summer. It makes her think of the meadows that were here once, whipped by the sea wind, with skylarks high overhead, filling the wide open sky with manic fluttering music, when the port was little more than a double row of fishing cottages or 'shiels' on the lower bank, and the rocks teemed with seafood of all kind, like berries in a hedgerow, ripe for the picking.

Stirring an unaccustomed cup of Ovaltine, Mary realizes she's exhausted. Performing for Ian's film, sparring with him, fending him off, has left her feeling wrung-out and rather besieged. The infuriating man knows exactly how to discombobulate her. Those absurd double entendres, for example. She's never known how to flirt. Even when she was in her twenties, and arguably in her prime, a flirtatious remark could render her as mute and prickly as a thistle. Now he's let slip about problems with the lovely Christina, she's finding his attention even more uncomfortable.

Then there's that disturbing business about Tom being Thomas Hall. Of course, there would have been hundreds of young men with the initials T.H. living in North Shields at that time. So there's no reason at all why the tobacco tin she remembers would necessarily have belonged to Annie's Tom. Still, it's never pleasant to contemplate the possibility that a previous incarnation might be an unsavoury character. One prefers to think of oneself as more sinned against than sinning.

The doorbell goes and she tenses, assuming it's Ian returning on some pretext. Hoping he'll think she's gone out, she flicks off the kitchen light then slips silently out into the hall to listen. The bell goes again, then the letterbox is pushed open.

'Coo-ee! It's me-ee!' comes Laura's voice. 'Can I come in, or will I catch you in flagrante on the stairs?'

Laughing with relief, Mary opens the door.

'What are you doing lurking in the dark?' Laura asks.

'I thought you were Ian back to torment me.'

'That bad, eh?'

'No, not really,' she sighs. 'Just rather relentless.'

'Do you fancy a fish supper? I was chopping a chaste onion when I got the urge for something stodgy and artery-clogging instead.'

'I hadn't even thought about food,' says Mary. The rest of the orange curry is in the fridge, congealing uninvitingly in its foil container.

'Well get your cardie on pronto, lass. They stop frying at nine.'

They make their way down the stairs and join a short queue of brawny young men with sunburnt shoulders. A woman in a white hat and overall is shovelling chips into polystyrene trays and scattering big scoops of batter bits on top. The place looks and smells yellow: warm, greasy, delicious.

They take their food to a bench by the river and unwrap it on their knees. Laura tears the corner off a sachet of ketchup and squirts it over her chips. 'How's it been going?' she asks.

'All right, I suppose – albeit complicated somewhat yesterday by a brief and rather puzzling detour into another of Ben's previous incarnations.'

'Anybody interesting?'

'A good old-fashioned spinster type—'

'Like you.'

'Indeed, though I've often felt that the connotations of the word "spinster" are well overdue for rehabilitation.' What is it about a chip that makes it so compelling as a foodstuff, Mary wonders. There must be some subtle alchemy of fat and carbohydrate that makes it especially amenable to the human digestive system.

'So how long's this filming going to last?' Laura asks.

'I honestly have no idea. To my shame, I've become rather disenfranchised. There was some talk of "the film crew", whatever that might be, arriving next week. But Ian assures me that's less alarming than it sounds.'

'You shouldn't let him bully you.'

'I don't think I do. It's more a question of standing back and seeing what happens.'

'Like a rabbit in a car's headlights, you mean.'

'Oh, dear. Is that how it seems?' Mary breaks open her slab of battered haddock and buries her fingers in glimmering white flakes of fish.

'You never told me what happened between you two,' says Laura.

'No.'

'Well?'

'It's not a chapter in my life I'm very proud of.'

'You managed to leave him, though. That must have taken some doing.'

'Actually I didn't intend to leave for good at first. I just needed to get away for a while. I was—' She stops herself. 'Let's just say there was something I needed to sort out. But one thing led to another and – well, if you must know, I had a bit of a breakdown. Anyway, by the time I'd resurfaced, it was six months later and I'd rather gone off the boil as far as love affairs were concerned. So I bought one of those overland tickets to India and Tibet. The rest, as they say, is history.'

'How exciting! What kind of a breakdown?'

'It was pretty dramatic, as these sudden attacks quite often are. I was diagnosed as suffering from acute delusional schizophrenia and confined for a while in what Ben would describe as "the loony bin". It was my first serious experience of a past incarnation intruding – though of course I had no inkling at the time.'

'What did Ian do when he found out?'

'I never told him – none of my friends knew. I swore my parents to secrecy and they were happy to oblige. I think they found the whole episode rather excruciating.' She remembers them coming to visit, sitting side by side in the hospital day room in their coats. Her mother had brought a fruit cake in a tin and a bottle of Robinson's Lemon Barley Water. 'They weren't really cut out to have children. They were rather old when I was conceived and I think I was always rather an inconvenient and perplexing presence in their lives.'

'So were you hearing voices, then?' Typical Laura, to home in on the gothic detail.

'Yes, to some extent. I was aware of an intermittent buzz of female voices discussing my moral shortcomings.' How strange to be talking about this now, after so many years; almost as though it happened to someone else. 'But my main symptom was the delusion that I was bleeding to death. Which was confirmed to an alarming degree, of course, every time I had a period. Though in between I was convinced I must be bleeding internally.'

'How awful.'

'Yes, it was rather distressing. Though completely explicable in retrospect, once I'd discovered how Peggy died.'

'Of course. That botched abortion,' says Laura through a mouthful of chips.

'I think the voices I was hearing were probably those of various uncharitable neighbours gathered outside Peggy's door when the doctor was eventually called. There was a spooky hushed quality to them, as if they knew they were talking about a dying woman.' She shudders, recalling the indistinct jabber that had filled her head for months. 'I often wonder what became of her son, Bobbie,' she says. 'She wasn't much of a mother to him, I'm afraid.'

She wraps up her left-over food and stuffs it into the waste-bin beside the bench. 'Sorry, Laura. This probably isn't the cheerful interlude you had in mind.'

'Don't be daft. You know what a nosy cow I am. Anyway, it's been yonks since I've had you to myself.'

Something in Laura's voice, a tightness, prompts Mary to ask: 'Was there something in particular you wanted to talk about?'

Laura stirs her ketchup with the stub of a chip. 'I didn't want to bother you.'

'Now *you're* being daft. That's what friendship is: two people bothering about one another.'

'It's just, well, them nightmares are back. Not every night, and not as bad as before. Well, the nightmares are just as bad, but they don't freak me out in the same way, because I know where they're coming from now.'

'I thought we'd laid your Tom to rest years ago.'

'It's funny you should put it like that. Because that's exactly what it feels like. Like he's a ghost, come back to haunt me. Though I'm not sure he ever went away completely. There was always the odd dream, now and then.'

'Why didn't you say? We could have had another few sessions and explored the issues further.'

'It was only now and then. And we were friends by then. I didn't want to go back to being doctor and patient again.'

Tom, Thomas. Was it possible? Mary had completely forgotten that Laura's previous incarnation had also been called Tom. 'So, am I right in assuming there's been a recent escalation?' she asks and Laura nods miserably. 'Can you think of anything that might have brought it on? Anything that might have set off unconscious associations.'

Laura looks at her. 'It's ever since we started on that research at the library. I had a terrible go that first night, and it's been on and off ever since.'

'What form have they been taking?'

'Oh you know, the usual. Getting into fights, having sex with drunk lasses, battering that poor wife of his.'

Mary peers at her friend in the darkness. She looks exhausted, as well she might, and rather diminished: not at all like the Laura she's used to. 'Would it help if I referred you to another therapist? It might be easier to confide in someone you don't know.'

'No. I'd rather talk to you. And another therapist wouldn't understand about Tom.'

'Shall we schedule another series of regression sessions?'

'Let's see how it goes, eh? You've too much on your plate at the moment.' Laura bundles up her remaining chips in their paper.

They sit in silence for a while, watching a rusty old fishing boat chug alongside the bank and manoeuvre into its moorings, belching black smoke.

'What about you?' Laura asks. 'Did you ever get a repeat of them nightmares you used to get? The ones on the boat?'

'No, thankfully – at least not that I've been aware of. Though of course we all enter a period of intense dreaming every night.' Mary burrows into a pocket for her Gitanes. 'I keep meaning to start a dream diary. If one makes a habit of jotting dreams down at the moment of waking, one's awareness of one's unconscious life becomes more acute.'

She lights up and inhales, drawing delicious smoke down into her lungs. Why is the first hit after food so satisfying? 'It's been dubbed Faculty X,' she goes on. 'It's possible to train oneself to access unconscious material – rather like exercising a muscle.'

Laura pulls a face. 'I'm not sure I'd like that.'

'No. Which is perhaps why I've never got around to it. I'm not sure I could cope with regular sorties into the lives of my fisherman forebears. They only broke through to consciousness on that occasion because I was so unwell. As you know, a high fever can sometimes bring about breaches, as it were, of the boundary between conscious and unconscious realms.'

'What about them flashbacks you were on about?'

'Yes, I should probably keep a record of those too. But they're just as disturbing in their way, so I try not to dwell on them. The tobacco tin clattering down the stairs – for some reason I find that utterly chilling. And the heaving dark water, of course.' She shivers suddenly, convulsively.

Laura pulls a sympathetic face. 'Do you think I'll ever be free of my Tom?' she asks after a while.

'I'm not sure we can ever be entirely free of our prior incarnations. If they continue to haunt us, then we have work to do. If they are quiescent, then our work is done for the time being, and they settle down into the core unconscious that makes each of us uniquely who we are.'

'It's dead spooky though, to think of them all, all my past lives, buried deep inside my mind somewhere.'

'Yes, I know exactly what you mean. It reminds me of that man possessed by demons in Matthew's gospel. When Jesus asked his name, he answered: "My name is Legion, for we are many".'

CHAPTER TWENTY-SEVEN

1898

I've woken early, I can tell from the sounds. Just a few lumpers rumbling their barrows down on the fish quay, and the nightsoil drays clopping up Brewery Bank and away. There's sleepy seagulls mewing from the chilly lums, and soft blue light slipping in through the window like pearly water over sand.

I can hear Mam out sweeping the yard, for she's always first up and likes to finish her dirty chores before breakfast: raking out the fire, emptying the slops, seeing to the midden. And I'm wondering, did Sam have his word with Da on the boat last night? And that unknowing has me so on tenterhooks that I've thrown off my blanket and pulled on my skirt before I've rubbed the sleep from my eyes.

Now I'm tiptoeing down the stairs barefoot, with my clogs in my hand, and here's the kettle hissing on the fire, and Mam leaning in the open doorway looking out, and a warm smell's rising off her – for she's been sweeping – that's her smell, that I think I'll remember all my life.

'Howay, pet,' she's saying. 'Are you ailing?' So I'm saying no, I couldn't sleep, and heard her sweeping and thought to help. But I'm too late, for what I've interrupted is her quiet time, when she has her brew and her sit down before waking the house and collecting the slops. So we sit together at the kitchen table with our tea, and stir sugar and she asks, how does your Sam like his gansey? And I say I never stopped to see, but I'm canny stirred up now, waiting to find out did he speak to Da, and what did Da say.

So now Mam's saying not to fret, and I'm saying I can't help it. But looking closer, I see that she's smiling, and it's the sort of smile that's trying to be wider, but she's keeping it small. So I'm saying, *what?* And she's saying, nothing. But there *is* something, and she's teasing me, and won't say – until I'm just about screaming with so much unknowing so early in the morning.

Then she tells me that she's had her own word with Da before he set sail last night. So now I'm fair dancing crazy, and asking what he said, till she holds up her hand and tells me that Da judges Sam to be a steady lad and a fine fisherman who's making something good of himself from a bad start.

'What about us walking out?' I'm asking, so she says, with a laugh in her voice: 'Your Da said to tell Annie he was minded to break the legs of any lad who came knocking, but he reckons that *Wellesley* lad's a better choice than most he can think of, so he's decided to stay his hand.'

A better choice than most! Mam says them were his very words!

Now I'm at the very top of our stairs, on the high bank, staring out to the Tyne's mouth, where the slow brown river meets the hickety sea – for it's canny breezy today, with white spume blowing off the tops of the waves. And from every direction, here come the luggers racing home, red sails bellying with the gold of the sun and their holds brimming with silver fish. And that's just how I feel: full of gold and silver and racingness.

I'm waiting for Flo to braid her hair, but I'm so bursting full after what Mam's just told me, that I can't stay still on the stairs, but must run up to the very top, and make my heart thunder and the breath burn in my chest. So here I am sucking in great gasps of this bright morning, that's heavy with sea smells and fish stink and lum smoke, and bread from the bakery and frying bacon bits and herring. I fancy I can even catch the velvet yellow smell of the wyn on the hill, and want to run there too, and watch for Sam's boat coming in.

For he's out there somewhere, on his way home. And when they've moored up and cranned out, and he's lain down for his bit sleep in the afternoon, that's where I'm going straight after work's finished. Never mind my tea, never mind folk talking, today all I'm doing is throwing off my oilies and running to my lad.

I mean to kiss him awake and I don't care who sees me opening his door. For aren't we promised now, and can't a promised lass kiss her lad awake from his bit sleep? And later – oh, later! – we'll go wandering out to where the wyn's thick and tight-knit, and the sun's warmed the long grass, and find a hollow to lay out my shawl.

How is such sweetness possible from just his mouth kissing me, or the sea-salt smell of his neck? Our little slivers of stolen time, them whisperings, them gentle burrowings of fingers that stir up such a buzzing that I can't see how a body can bear any more! But there's so much more to come – of his strong back under my hand, tracing the ladder of his bones, nudging into the damp tufts in his oxters. And all the places I've not seen, or touched, and hardly dare imagine – but can't help but imagine! – Oh, and just blethering, strolling along and not minding who sees us.

It's like here's a Yuletide cake, full of currants and glassy cherries; and I've had the lid off the cake tin and peeked in, and pressed the middle to feel how moist it is, and sneaked off a split almond or three, and tongued them till they're gone – and now at last here's a whole big slice on my plate!

Flo's ready now and shouting up to me to come down, but I'm liking it up here on the top bank, with the wind in my face and the sight of all them red sails coming in. So I'm shouting back no, I'm going by the top bank; and she waves and says she'll meet me down on the quay.

And all the while I'm checking the sails as they swoop in for the *Osprey*'s newly fitted dark mizzen. Oh, and there she is! Tacking out along the far shore, swift as a bird, for if there's a breeze Da likes to ride it in, and save on tug fees, and wave at the crews being towed home, tame as lapdogs on a lead.

She's too far off for me to make out the lads on deck or what they're about, but if she's the *Osprey* – and she is, she is! – then my Sam's aboard somewhere, feeling this same sun on his face, this same breeze that's whipping my skirt round my ankles.

Now I'm walking along the top bank, to Nater's Stairs, with my eyes fixed on that dark mizzen, watching her sails fold like a butterfly's wings as she comes about, then belly out again till she's aiming straight as a red arrow for the quay. And I'm thinking, if I run I can meet her, and watch her tie up, and who cares if I'm late to the farlane for once? For this is the first day of my life as his promised lass, and I want to taste every bit of the sweetness it brings.

So now I'm running, and my shawl's coming adrift, and my scarf loosening so my hair's fairly whipping round my face. And here's Nater's Stairs thronging with folk, so I must dodge round them, and grab at my scarf to stop it falling, and unhook my shawl where it's snagged on a cran, here, and again here, and say sorry, sorry, as I gallop past, taking one step, two steps at a time, and trying not to look down, for I'll lose my balance if I do, and stumble, and be delayed and I mustn't be delayed for I've a boat to meet.

Now I'm on the quayside, and there's a line of carts for the ice factory, so

I've to duck under a whiskery shire's head to get through, and step over a pile of fresh dung, and dodge round trundling barrows and scurrying herring lasses.

Now at last here's the river, and I'm ransacking the boats with my eyes for the *Osprey*. By, it's canny easy to find her when you're up on the top bank, but if you're looking for a boat on the quayside, there's a forest of masts and rigging to peer through. So I'm pacing along, bobbing my head side to side for a sight of the new luggers coming in.

And there's a commotion started up a bit along from where I'm standing – except it's more a quiet than a commotion, with crews throttling back their capstans, and loosing off their warps from the mooring posts – then using their poles to push apart, to open a space on the water for a new boat to come in. Which is something they never do, for a good berth by the market's like gold dust and no skipper would give it up lightly.

So I'm thinking, maybe there's a lifeboat arriving, or one of the hospital ships from the cod grounds – for there's a solemnness about the crews making space that sends a shiver right through me. They've gone so quiet, all the lads, setting down their crans and barrows. And all just staring at the boat that's nosing in to the berth. And I see straight away that it's the *Osprey*'s prow, with the carved bird's head—

CHAPTER TWENTY-EIGHT

2007

Ben opens his eyes and looks around. 'I remembered my sign,' he whispers.

'Yes, I noticed,' says the doc. 'Well done. That's excellent. Perhaps if you learn to control when you exit a scene, you might be able to tolerate staying a bit longer to find out what's going on.'

He shivers. 'Something must have happened on the boat,' he says.

'What makes you think that?'

'The other boats were all getting out of the way, which they'd never do normally. It was normally a right dodgems getting a mooring.'

Ian swings his camera down from his shoulder. 'So, a man overboard maybe? Or someone injured?'

'Ian, please!' snaps the doc, almost spitting she's so cross. 'I've warned you about this. If you can't prevent yourself from suggesting possible scenarios, I'll have to ban you from our sessions.'

Ian puts up a hand and ducks, pretending she's going to hit him, but he's obviously got the message.

Ben feels sick. 'I don't think I want to know what happened,' he says quietly. When he pictures the *Osprey* chugging into dock, and the other boats edging out of the way, it feels like there's this hole opening up in his tummy, and his heart and lungs are dropping into it.

'There's no hurry,' says the doc. 'Whenever you're ready.' She puts a gloved hand on his knee and rests it there a moment. The weight of it makes him feel a bit better.

'Remind me who's on the boat,' says Ian. 'Annie's father, Henry, is the skipper, right? Then there's her brother Jimmy, and his pal Tom. And Annie's sweetheart, Sam, from that training ship.'

'The *Wellesley*, that's right,' says Ben. 'Plus Flo's dad and Tom's dad; they're mate and third man. And an older lad to mind the capstan and that.' Ben can see where Ian's going with this; he's trying to work out who Annie cared about on the boat, who might have been injured or drowned – which could only be her father, or Jimmy or Sam.

He's still shivering so he sits up and puts on his hoodie – it's more proper boy than having the doc's blanket round him, but he misses the smell of it.

The doc turns to Ian. 'Ben tells me you've been looking at Mr Skipper's paintings,' she says, trying to change the subject.

'All right, all right,' he says, sitting down on the pouffe. 'I get the message.'

'They are quite remarkable, aren't they?'

'Uncanny, more like – assuming he hasn't got a secret doctorate in historical topography. I thought he might be autistic spectrum. What do you think? Or some kind of *idiot savant*. You know, focal brain damage after a fall or something.'

'His alcoholism would certainly predispose him to stumble.'

'But you have a far more interesting explanation.' He's being sarky because she's told him off again, but it's obvious he wants to hear what she's going to say.

'I wouldn't go so far as to claim it as an explanation,' says the doc. 'But as an hypothesis it does account for some of Mr Skipper's symptoms that are problematic for more conventional theories.'

Ben lies back down to listen. He loves it when the doc gives one of her lectures, because they're full of amazing ideas and she explains them really well, so he can understand even when she's using loads of big words – though some of this rings a bell, from when she's talked about old Skip before, so he feels he has a bit of a head start.

'I published a speculative paper on schizophrenia a few years ago in the *Journal of Scientific Exploration*, in which I suggested that a small but significant subset of schizophrenic patients may have been misdiagnosed. My hypothesis was that the auditory hallucinations typical of the illness may in fact be intrusions of past-life experiences into the consciousness of these particular patients.'

'OK,' says the Ian bloke. 'So why aren't we all schizophrenic?'

'Well, in the majority of people, the border between the conscious and unconscious is quite robust. When we wake from a dream, for instance, we have no trouble distinguishing that dream from reality. Similarly, we never mistake our waking reveries and daydreams for the truth. Indeed, so robust is the border that many artists find they must devote considerable effort to overcoming or subverting it in order to gain access to their unconscious inspirations.'

'And everyone knows that artists are nuts.'

'My hypothesis is that the strength or permeability of the border between the conscious and unconscious may vary from person to person and could possibly be genetic. So, just as with height or intelligence, any one individual's "score", as it were, would lie somewhere on the normal distribution. So though the majority of people have an IQ of between 80 and 120, there are always the odd few dullards at the lower tail of the distribution and a clutch of geniuses at the opposite extreme.'

The Ian bloke's leaning forward now, really into it. 'So, applying your "permeability" theory, people at one extreme of the normal distribution will be almost completely repressed, with no insight into their unconscious motivations.'

'Yes. While those at the opposite end of the spectrum may traverse that putative border with comparative ease – which may or may not be an advantage, depending on their circumstances.'

'Artists or madmen.'

'Indeed. And shamans, *nyangas*, mediums, intuitives of all kinds. In another culture – or another time – our Mr Skipper might have been revered as a visionary.'

'So much for the schizophrenogenic mother.'

Mary turns to Ben. 'Ian's referring to the theory that schizophrenia is caused by bad parenting,' she explains. 'But he's forgetting that my hypothesis only applies to a very small subgroup of people with schizophrenic symptoms.' That's what Ben really likes about the doc: that she always includes him in her grown-up conversations, and always assumes he knows what they're about, which he does, actually, most of the time.

Ian has taken out his Blackberry and is making notes. 'So, getting back to old Skip: you reckon his paintings are scenes he's actually remembering, from various past lives he's experienced in and around the Fish Quay, right?'

Ben sits up. 'Dad says he was the best skipper ever and could always find where the shoals were. Dad says it was like he knew every single rock on the sea bed. Maybe that's because he'd been a fisherman loads of times in his other lives and just got better and better at it.'

The doc smiles at him. 'In cases of exceptional skill or knowledge – with child prodigies, such as Mozart or Picasso, for example – that does often seem a compelling explanation. And there are many documented cases of children exhibiting spontaneous xenoglossy, that's speaking fluently in a language they've never encountered before.'

'I thought I might put him in the film,' says the Ian bloke, sort of shifty and casual at the same time. 'Use his paintings to set the scene and maybe show him working on one, with you doing a voiceover about your theory.'

'As long as you bear in mind that he's a very vulnerable individual. So please don't attempt to interview him – and make sure you give him a fair price for those paintings.'

'He's just going to borrow them,' says Ben, because he's been thinking it's really out of order of Ian not to buy them, because he's obviously loaded but Skip is just a poor old alky.

'Is he now?' goes the doc.

'It'll be good publicity for the old geezer,' says Ian, trying to brush it off. 'They'll be worth a fortune afterwards.'

'You should be ashamed of yourself. Taking advantage of a brain-damaged old man. I'd forgotten you were such a skinflint.'

Ian actually blushes at that. 'I think we may have identified another one of my specialist subjects,' he says, whatever that means, though the doc seems to understand.

'So you'll pay for the paintings?'

'Yeah, yeah. Anything to avoid another resit. And to show I'm serious, how's about I treat everyone to supper this evening, at a hostelry of your choice?'

They're at the Low Lights Tavern, which is a really ancient pub, just three dark little rooms with a bar and open fire in each, though the fires aren't lit now because it's summer. Dad says that before the new landlord took over and started serving food, this was a 'spit and sawdust' pub, which is what most pubs used to be before they allowed women and kids in. In the old days there used to be sawdust or sand on the floor, to soak up the spilt beer and the spit, which is really disgusting when Ben thinks about it, because everyone used to smoke high-tar tabs and pipes, so they all coughed up really gross thick brown phlegm. And the fishing pubs were open all hours, because they had a special licence; so there would be alkies in there all day, puffing away. Dad says when the new landlord took over, he had to ban the alkies because they were frightening away the ladies from the posh flats along by Dolphin Quays.

The Low Lights is Dad's territory, where he goes drinking with the lads after a trip, so it's weird to see Ian strutting around being the boss, getting the waitresses to push the tables together, so they can all sit on one long table, and moving all the chairs round.

Dad's doing his usual thing of getting out his wad of money and calling the waitress over to get the first round in. But Ian beats him to it: 'I've set up a tab behind the bar,' he goes, waving Dad's money away. 'Order whatever you like – it's on the Beeb.'

'Cheers,' says Dad, looking a bit spare. He shoves the wad back in his pocket and drapes his jacket over a chair.

Ian's said they can invite Nana, which is brilliant because they'd never have heard the end of it if they'd gone without her. It's all she's been talking about the last few days: film director this, BBC that. She's sitting opposite Laura, and they're nattering on like old mates – which they are, in a way, as they go to the same hairdresser in Whitley Bay, because even though Laura's got all the proper equipment at *Salon Laura*, she says you can never do a proper job on your own hair – though she always calls it your 'barnet' or 'riah', which is hair spelt backwards. She's always using weird words for normal things. She explained it to Ben once: in the old days trannies and homos had a special language so that they could talk to each other without people understanding what they were saying. It was a mixture of Italian and Spanish and backwards spellings; so the word for 'eating' is '*manjare*', 'man' is '*omee*' and 'face' is '*ecaff*', which is face backwards.

Nana's really dolled herself up in a new glittery top and push-up bra with turquoise lacy bits showing, and matching eyeshadow and kitten heels. She's knocking back her vodka lemonade and ordering a top-up, and doing that thing she always does when she's excited, asking question after question but not waiting for an answer, so whoever she's with ends up gaping like a haddock trying to get a word in. But Laura's not putting up with it, so she's reached across and put a hand on Nana's arm to slow her down a bit, which seems to be working, though it could be the vodka calming her down.

Compared to the racket everyone else is making, the doc seems rather quiet, taking it all in and sipping steadily at a big glass of red wine. She's looking really glam, in one of those long silk pyjama suits that Asian women wear, in a dark plum colour, with her bun unrolled into a long plait down her back. She's next to Dad, who's bagged the chair at the head of the table, which in his mind probably makes up for Ian paying for everything – though Ian's bagged the one at the other end, so between them they've nabbed both of the macho positions. Ben's seated opposite the doc, so he can see her and Dad together, which is sort of freaky, because it's seeing like the two halves of his life side by side, dipping into the black olives like it was totally normal.

'OK, buddy?' Dad asks and Ben nods. And he can feel this smile start up on his face, a really wide one, he can't stop it, until his cheeks start to ache from stretching so wide, because they're not used to it. And then he wants to cry for no reason at all, so he has to take some big gulps of his melon J2O until the smile and the tears go away.

In fact, when Ben comes to think about it, almost everyone important in his life is sitting round this table – apart from his mam, who's in New Zealand so obviously she couldn't be here – and old Skip, who's sitting over at the bar even though Ian's saved a place for him between Laura and Ben, but he's not really that important anyway.

Then suddenly everyone's talking all at once, so Ben can't keep track any more of how Dad's feeling about the Ian bloke taking over, or how drunk Nana's getting, or whether Laura's going to say something embarrassing, so he stops trying. And it's like it was on the beach that time, when he just closed his eyes and looked at the sun all warm and red through his eyelids, and just sort of sank down away from all the jabber and felt safe.

He's ordered the chicken and mushroom risotto, because he fancies something creamy and babyish, and he eats it slowly with a fork, letting the grown-ups' talk swirl around his head: Nana getting all excited about the big Netto they're opening in Charlotte Street; Dad telling Ian that their flat used to be part of a brothel above the Jungle bar. Then Laura's squealing and saying how she used to work at the Jungle forty years ago, at a bistro in the basement. 'And there was this mega trannie in charge, Lord Jim they used to call him. Kaftans, false eyelashes, the lot.' It was a really rough place, she's saying, with so much beer swilling around the floor that one of the barmaid's toes all went rotten and dropped off.

Which totally snaps Ben out of it. 'They never!' he says. 'What, all of them?'

'Feet like flippers, cross my heart,' laughs Laura. 'Go and see for yourself if you don't belief me. She married that Ronnie Russell, who got banged up for living off illegal earnings. Lives over on the Chirton Estate now. I'll give you her number, if you like.'

'You're never talking about Noreen Russell, are you?' goes Nana, and it's obvious the vodka's getting to her. 'Noreen Collins as was? She was in my class at school.'

'What was that thing you were saying the other day?' asks Dad. 'The six degrees or something.'

'Six degrees of separation,' says Ben.

'Or, as Mary would have us believe, yet further evidence that we've all been brought here for a purpose,' says Ian, waving at the waitress and doing a little pouring gesture with his hand to get her to give everyone a top-up. 'What do you think, Mary? Could this be one of those reincarnation therapy groups you were talking about? I mean, you couldn't imagine a more disparate set of characters, yet here we all are getting along like a house on fire.' His voice is jokey, but the way he's looking at the doc shows he's at least half serious too.

'You're being deliberately provocative, I know,' says the doc. 'But you're right: this is the kind of phenomenon I had in mind.'

'Go on then, how does it work?'

'I know it seems unlikely, but those who believe in reincarnation generally also believe that souls return in groups. And whenever serious controlled studies have been done, it does seem that a person tends to be reborn in the vicinity of a previous incarnation's death – which would automatically tend to promote a sort of grouping.' She reaches for her wine glass. 'For what it's worth, I have often wondered whether Laura and I have encountered one another before.'

'We were both fishermen,' says Laura. 'But so were almost all the lads round here, so that's nothing to go by.'

'It's not so much what we did in our past lives,' says the doc. 'It's more to do with the strength of our mutual attraction, if I can use that term in its non-sexual sense. You could have called an ambulance when you came round that day, but you moved straight in to nurse me instead – even though we'd only met in a professional capacity. And I let you, which was even more surprising, given my hermit tendencies.'

'And we've been friends ever since.' Laura raises her glass and reaches down the table so they can clink, and they grin cheesily at each other, like typical soppy grown-ups when they've had a few.

The doc sloshes another two fingers into her glass. 'It has been suggested that souls who have interacted intensely – either positively or negatively – in a previous incarnation are able to recognize one another at an unconscious level when they meet again,' she says.

Ben can tell that Laura really likes that idea. 'What, so if you get that feeling that you've met someone before, you probably have?'

'Maybe your two fishermen were on the *Osprey* with Jimmy and Sam,' suggests Ben. Then a new thought hits him and, 'Wow!' he goes, 'Maybe you actually *were* Jimmy and Sam! Or Annie's dad and that Tom, or one of those other men. How freaky would that be?'

'Is that possible?' asks Ian and the doc shrugs, but she's got her little smile on.

'Anything's *possible*,' she says.

'OK,' goes Ian. 'I'll ask a different question: Is it likely?'

'I honestly don't know. There are lots of well-documented cases of two or more souls encountering one another repeatedly in different incarnations. But I've no idea whether any of us would be candidates for that kind of association.'

'So how would you find out?' He's gone all serious suddenly.

'Well,' says the doc slowly, as though she's having to think really hard, 'I suppose I'd need to work with each person individually, documenting their past lives as fully as possible, going back to around 1880, just before Annie was born. Then I'd develop a sort of life-map for each incarnation, listing the places they lived and worked, who they loved and hated, who their children were and so on. Then see if there were any overlaps.'

'Why not just ask them if they served on the *Osprey* in 1898?' Ian asks.

'Because that would be hypnotic suggestion and would contaminate the findings, and invite all kinds of criticism,' says the doc. 'In that sense, we probably already know far too much about what may or may not have happened at that time. One would have to approach it far more subtly if one were to stand any chance of eliciting reliable data.'

'OK. That makes sense.'

'That's not to say it couldn't be done,' she says and she's looking quite excited now, with red dots on her cheeks, though that might be from the wine, because there's a bottle at each end of the table and Dad's drinking beer, so she's had nearly a whole bottle to herself down this end. 'But as far as I know nothing like this has ever been tried before. However, if someone here has encountered Annie in a past life, it could provide some fascinating insights into what happened to her.'

'Go on,' goes Ian, staring at her. And everyone at the table has stopped talking and is listening in, as if the doc and Ian are a sort of magnet sucking in everyone's attention.

'It would probably be a completely wild goose chase. There's no reason to suppose that any of us—'

'Why not? You said it yourself – you've always wondered about you and Laura being friends. What about *Ben* and Laura for fuck's sake? What are the odds against them getting together? And you and me on the Long Sands in 1967? Come on, Mary. Put your money where your mouth is. Do you believe in this stuff or don't you?'

'It's not a question of belief. It's a question of evidence, of methodology.'

'So? You're a clever girl. Devise a methodology.'

'Well, one should probably trial it with one person,' goes the doc slowly, like she's thinking aloud. 'Yes, that would be the way to do it. Start with a pilot study, to develop an interviewing technique, and see if the approach proved fruitful.' She looks around, as though she's coming out of a hypnosis session herself. 'This is not the way I would normally work, you see. Normally I start with the client's agenda, and try to find a way of guiding them through a past life trauma. But in this case I would have to try to guide them to *Annie's* trauma, which could prove more problematic.'

'Why's that?' asks Ian.

'Because the unconscious is only likely to be interested in its own past experiences. So I might have to nudge it a little to focus it elsewhere, which might be construed as—'

'Bloody fascinating idea though,' says Ian. 'Let's try it.'

'What? No, no. I was talking speculatively. I have no idea whether it's remotely feasible.' But it's obvious she wants to have a go.

'So? What have we got to lose? I'll film the sessions and if we get something I'll work it into the documentary – if not, I'll just erase the recording.'

'The trouble is, Laura's been helping with the research, so she's already "contaminated" as it were.'

'Thanks very much I'm sure,' goes Laura.

'What about me?' asks Dad in a flash. 'Ben's told me odds and sods, but I was away when you were doing all that work in the library.'

'And you wouldn't mind being filmed?' asks Ian.

Dad's pretending to think about it, but Ben can see he's really keen. 'No, no, you're all right,' he goes. 'Anything to help the bairn.'

'Great stuff. Mary?' Ian looks the doc straight in the eyes; she's blushing, sort of half drunk, half excited.

'How about tomorrow morning?' she says.

CHAPTER TWENTY-NINE

...Good, that's excellent, Paul. Keep breathing deep and slow. Now start walking slowly down the corridor and come to a halt in front of one of the doors. Have you got one? Good. Now turn the handle and push it open. Where are you?

1967

Where am I? *Quelle bona questioni* and no flies.

There's a pole by the bed, with a bottle dangling, and a tube in the back of my hand – bloomin' heck! Curtains all round. Well, they always said I'd wind up in hospital one day.

By, but them curtains are naff. I know it's the National Elf, but they might have made an effort.

Mary Magdalena, my head's like a cushion full of feathers and my throat's killing me. Have I been upchucking, then? Is that why I'm here? Maybes I've overdone it with the Tia Maria.

Right, let's try turning the head. Who's this then? Edith Lillian, the old trout, as I live and breathe. Sat by my bedside, bless her, with her hat on and her nose powdered, and her library book open on her knee.

'Hello duckie,' I croak, making her jump half out of her skin. Her book slaps onto the lino.

'How do you feel, pet?' she says.

'Like I've swallowed a handful of nails, washed down with a tankard of Tia Maria, then vommed the whole lot up again.'

'I've brought you a magazine and some apples.'

'I suppose a *Vogue*'s too much to hope for?' Knowing old vinegar tits it'll be one of her *Woman's Weekly*s. 'Famed for its knitting': I ask you – what a thing to be famed for.

'The flowers are from Mrs Russell and them two Scots lasses on the top floor. There's a load of cards too.'

Now I'm swivelling my head and there's this poky little cabinet fair bristling with gladdies and chrysanths. And cards! Scads of them, all jostled between the vases. You'd think it was my birthday, except for the throat rasping like an emery board.

'How long have I been here?'

'They've had to operate, pet. But you're fine. The surgeon says it went really well.'

'Operate on what?'

There's a look comes over her when I say that, a sort of panicky look I've never seen on her before. 'On your legs, Jimmy,' she says, and she never calls me 'Jimmy'. In all the years she's being doing for me, it's only ever been 'Mr M.'

'What's wrong with my legs?' I'm trying to move them, but they're like lead. Mind you, they always are a right bugger to shift first thing, what with the swelling and that, so I'm not that surprised. So now I'm trying to wriggle my toes, and I think I can feel them go, but I can't see past my belly to check. So I go to heave myself up on the pillows, which gets Edith Lillian in a right lather, because it's tugging on that tube, isn't it? And rocking the bottle on the pole, and giving me gyp into the bargain, where it's poking into my hand.

So now she's helping me, but it's like a twig trying to shift a boulder. And—

Christ! Buggering *shit*! Fucking Nora! The *pain*! So much pain, I can't even work out where it's coming from. Except it's like there's a whole bloomin' agony *orchestra* sawing out different types of pain all over my nethers. What the *fuck* have they done to me?

I must have yelled, for she's let go of me, hasn't she? And rushed off somewhere, while I collapse back blowing like a harpooned whale. And after a bit the chorus of pain simmers down a tad and I see there's another tube snaking out from under the covers – so that's why my dick's screaming blue murder. Which is a relief, in a way, because at least *that* seems to be working all right.

Now here comes a chubby nursey and a brace of *bona* big *omees* in green overalls. And Nursey sticks a thermometer in my oyster and paddles at my wrist with her fingers for a pulse. Then she's poking a needle into me and giving the *omees* a nod. So here they come, one each side of the bed, like I've died and gone to heaven, and lean into me, smelling of Brut, and worm an arm under each of my oxters to hoist me up on the pillows.

I'm expecting the pain this time, but – *Jesus and Mary Magdalena!* – it takes the breath away just the same. So by the time I'm settled, the three of us are all panting like we've just gone three rounds in the back slums. And a part of me's thinking, where's a molly's powder compact when she needs it? But another part's staring down the bed and thinking, what the *fuck* is going on here?

So here's my belly, right? Mount Etna of the *omee* nation. Then there's this metal cage they've put under the bedclothes – to stop the blankets weighing on my legs, I suppose – and there's the yellow tube snaking out from underneath. But where's my bloomin' *feet*, for Mary's sake? I'm wriggling my toes, but the bed's flat as a pancake.

'The doctor says the wounds are healing up nicely,' says Edith Lillian.

'What wounds?' I'm saying. But suddenly, like a heave of sour custard, it's all coming back to me and I'm thinking, Jesus and Mary Magdalena, where's my bloomin' *legs*? And I just stare at the blanket, the way it's pulled tight and tucked in all round, and not a hump or ridge to be seen. And suddenly it's like I'm panting but I can't catch my breath, my heart's going like the clappers—

Try to breathe slowly, in and out, good. You're doing really well. Now, can you go back a bit? Think back to what you were doing before you went to the hospital. Where are you?

I'm at the Jungle, aren't I? Where else would her Lordship be found on a Saturday night? Zjoushed up to the nines and getting ready for the eleven-o'clock rush.

Davy's buttering stotties like they're going out of fashion, and I've got a couple trays of chips ready, and the fryers bubbling like billy-o with a fresh lot, and the roasts on the side, juicing up ready for carving, with all the sauces, gravy and apple and curry and that. All tickety-boo – for it'll be full steam ahead once the doors open.

I've been feeling a bit off all day, but you can't miss a Saturday, can you? The left leg's been giving me gyp all week. Now the right one's joined in a cats' chorus of itching and burning. The doctor's said I should rest them, but how can you with a job like this? When you're on your feet half the night?

But tell the truth, I'd rather stand than sit – for I can't bear the sight of them. Big as balloons, all the colours of the bloomin' rainbow, covered with sores. To think I used to be such a *bona* skinnamalink.

So anyway, Ronnie's got the beefcake organized round the walls, and they're a sight for sore eyes, I can tell you: fresh from the gym, thighs big enough to split their kaffies. Don't you just *adore* an *omee* in a tux? And DJ Billy's setting up under the palm trees. The palms were Ronnie's idea. To make the place look exotique. Naff, more like, if you ask me. But when did our Ron ever consult the Lord Jim on matters of your décor? I mean, crazy paving on the walls? *Quelle horreur*! So there's palms and all sorts dotted round, rubber plants, cheese plants, vines trailing all over the shop with grapes dangling like purple udders – all plastic of course. Bamboo curtains, black ceiling, disco balls, strobe, UV, the whole bloomin' enchilada.

Ron got a red neon sign saying La Continental, but everyone calls it the Jungle – though that's more to do with the clientele than the décor. Mowglis, schwartzers and chinkies, ayrabs, yids, pakis, rastas – you name it, they all swarm off the ships and pile down the Jungle basement of a Saturday night. Trade and no-trade, *comme-ci comme-ça*, like Noah's bloomin' ark. And that's before I've even started on the lasses.

Ronnie's got a late licence, because the basement's classed as a restaurant. So Noreen can keep her hussies pulling pints till two in the morning. Noreen's queen of the basement bar, and Lord Jim here's queen of the galley.

Right, where was I?

You were talking about your legs hurting, but I'd like you to try and go back a bit further, to when you were a young—

You spend years creating the magnificent *omee* statue of the Lord Jim – and then your bloomin' plinths go and let you down. Mind you, the doctor says it's a miracle they've lasted so long. Eighty-seven years, man and queen. I can hardly believe it myself. He says a ship this size should have keeled over years ago. Only tried to get us to go on a diet, didn't he? I mean, I ask you! Do the aristocracy diet? Let us eat cake is what I say. What's a cup of tea without a McVities' slider to dunk? A molly might as well drink water.

The dessert counter was my idea. Ronnie pooh-poohed it at first, saying no one's going to *manjare* a chocolate mousse at two in the morning. But my desserts bring in more moolah than all them stotties and pies put together. It's the lasses; they love a sweet mouthful in the middle of the night, as the actress said to the right reverend.

Desserts are my absolute métier. Always have been, ever since the *Queen Mary*. Lemon meringue, spotted dick, rhubarb crumble. All whisked up from scratch by your auntie Jim – none of that bought-in nonsense. Sherry trifle, treacle tart, apple pie. I've seen lassies come to blows over the last slice of my Black Forest gateau. And your auntie needs a mouthful too, doesn't she? To keep her strength up. I mean, it takes energy to move the mountain to Mohammed, doesn't it?

When the legs first swelled up, the doctor said it was blood pressure and gave me some tablets to make me wee. What a carry on that was at half past one in the morning! Trying to find space at le pissoir with all them lads in there, stotting all over, slipping on the tiles, percies pointing any old where. Must be nigh on a thousand gallon of Red Barrel swilling down that gulley of an evening. Like paddling on the bloomin' beach. That Red Barrel's pretty much piss to start with, mind. Give me a Babycham any day.

The tablets did help a bit with the legs, though. Then when the sores started, I thought maybes I'd overdone it with the Immac. So I went back to shaving, but it didn't help. I was into the kaftans by then, luckily, so they didn't show. Thank Mary for the Maharishi, eh? But it got me down, seeing them in the shower of a morning, and it put a bit of a kybosh on the love life, I can tell you.

So anyway, the legs had been giving me gyp for a few days, itching and aching like, and there's this one big sore on the left one that's oozing. And I'm feeling sort of under the weather generally, a bit feverish, and my eyes are stinging from all the tab smoke – like being downwind of the bonfire on bloomin' Guy Fawkes. And it's 'All You Need Is Love' on the turntable and 'If You're Going to San Francisco', and I'm thinking, howay, that's a *bona idée.*

So I've decided: Sunday I'll take it a bit easy, then toddle off to the doctor first thing Monday. And I'm just bending over to get the profiteroles out the chiller when I come over all faint. Next thing I know young Davy's shoving a couple of dish-towels under my head and folk are leaning over the counter to see what's occurring.

CHAPTER THIRTY

1967

They've brought me back home from the hospital, and here's Edith Lillian hovering over me, fussing and faddling, trying to get me to 'wipe your eyes now, pet, and try to count your blessings'.

So it's a blessing my stumps are healing up so nicely, is it? Muchos gracias, I'm sure. And the new commode's set up next to the bed? Fantabulosa. I can hardly wait to try it. And at least they haven't taken your dick off, Jimmy. Ooh, goody gumdrops. So I'll be back on the razz in no time.

What fairy's going to want a romp with a mangled moll? Oh, I expect there'll always be some sicko that will get off on a vada at the stumps. Is that all I've got to look forward to? Trapped in a wheelchair in a Tyneside flat while some drooling dorcas whacks off on my scars?

I'm blubbing again; I can't help it. Just trying to get the bloomin' wheelchair into the kitchen's enough to set me off, and finding I can't even reach the counter to cut a slice of devil's food cake. I mean, it's not till you've tried slotting back into your life that it comes home to you, how it's going to be from now on.

So now Edith Lillian's plonking a box of Kleenex Mansize in my lap and patting me on the shoulder. 'I'll get us a nice cup of tea,' she says, like she must have said a dozen times since they dumped me back here this morning. 'Davy will be along later to help get you into bed.'

Because that's another total bloomin' palaver, isn't it? Getting me from pillar to post and back again. Off the wheelchair and on to the commode; off the commode and on to the wheelchair; off the wheelchair and into the bloomin' bed. Even with my arms helping, the old trout can't manage on her tod. I'm like one of those bloomin' roly-poly *omees*, except when I go over I can't bounce up again.

And the stairs! Well, she's wheeled me to the top, and we've looked down them, and the bloomin' face of your actual Eiger's a stroll in the park compared to the prospect of getting roly-palone down them stairs and back up again. So I'm trapped, aren't I? In a bloomin' three-room Tyneside flat, in a bloomin' four-wheel chair, with Miss Thin-slice-of-Hovis-and-a-scrape-of-Stork in charge of my galley.

Because the doctor's told her I've to cut back on the sweeties. He says that's how I got the diabetes in the first place, and the sugar's started the rot in the legs. So she's put the custard creams on the top shelf like a load of porno mags, and purged *la Frigidaire.* Vada in there now and you'd think it belonged to a nun in the middle of Lent.

By, that was a palaver and no flies! The old trout's managed to get me onto the sofa but it's nearly ruined the both of us. So I've reached out for the arm and have getten a grip, and she's heaved me up by the shoulder, and tried to tip me off the wheelchair, except she's forgotten to put the brakes on, hasn't she? So it's slipped out from under me and gone whizzing across the room, and we're left tumbling half on and half off the bloomin' sofa in a heap.

So now she's sat on the floor with her skirt all rucked up, sobbing her eyes out, saying, 'I'm so sorry, pet,' and 'it's all my fault,' and 'I thought I could cope.'

It's the first time I've ever seen her cry and it shakes me to the core. You see a body every day for ten years and you think you know them, don't you? So every day, on the dot of nine, rain or shine, here comes Edith Lillian, putting her key in the door and picking up the post, then hanging up her hat and coat, and trotting up the stairs in her sensible shoes.

I'm forever on at her about her sensible shoes. Saying she should let me buy her some proper high heels, and fishnets with lacy suspenders. Just to see the look on her face, bless her. But no, it's Hush Puppy lace-ups for our Edith, with forty denier American Tan, and Mary knows what bit of old tat to hold them up.

And placid! The things I've said to her over the years, and she's hardly blinked an eyelash. 'I'll pray for you, Mr M.,' is all she'll ever say. Or, 'May God forgive you.' I'm one of her good works, like her black babies and knitting her squares; doing the flowers in the church; that home for preggers lassies she goes on about. 'Judge not, lest ye be judged' is her favourite saying. I've heard her muttering it like one of them bloomin' mantra things when she's dusting my nick-nacks. Of course that makes me try even harder to get a rise out of her – asking her to help me choose the right earrings or lippie, telling her about some filly-*omee* I've taken a fancy to.

That's why it's a shock to see her sobbing into the shag pile. So now it's my turn to say, there, there, pet, and toss her the Kleenex. For she's a *bona* old trout, for all her holier-than-thou-ness, and she's stood by me through thick and thin.

Now there goes the doorbell, so she's scrambling to her feet and wiping her eyes, then giving her schnoz a quick dab-a-dab with the pancake, and scooting down the stairs to see who it is. And it's young Davy – I can hear his voice, but he's not coming up. Then, what's that? The door's closed again and the hallway's quiet. So now I'm miffed because they've gone off together, haven't they? On their two pairs of working legs, leaving me dumped on the bloomin' sofa like a pile of dirty washing.

And I'm just building up a fair old froth of pique, when there's her key in the Yale, and here they come back again, cantering up the stairs blethering away nineteen to the dozen. And Davy's got an armful of gladdies and Edith's carrying the Asti and beaming away.

'I thought a little glass wouldn't do any harm,' she says, opening the cabinet and fetching out the best crystal.

'Let me guess,' I say. 'The two of yous are getting married at last.'

'Better than that,' says Edith. 'Davy's got a new job.'

And straight away I'm thinking, Ronnie's got rid of me and promoted Davy in my place. Then I'm thinking, no, moll, don't be so daft. The lad's only just learnt how to work the Breville.

'Congratulations, I'm sure,' says I, still in a bit of a miff. 'Doing what?'

'Oh, lifting mainly,' says young Davy. 'A bit washing, a bit cooking. It depends on the boss.'

'What about moolah?'

Now Davy's looking at Edith – as if it's up to her what he's paid.

'Oh, don't worry about that,' she says, quite back to her bossy old self. 'He can afford it. He's no option anyway. It's either you or a nursing home, and I'm not having him in one of them places.'

The trouble is, I can still feel them. The bunions on my big toe, where I've squashed them into my stilettos, nipping sharp as ever, The scaly rash on my calves, where I raked away so hard it opened into sores: still crusty, so I want to reach for that Moroccan back-scratcher and have a good old scritch. Them creases behind my knees; I can feel the jock rot starting in again, that sticky itch, so it's all I can do not to dredge on the powder. But it's all in the mind, isn't it? The itch is real enough, but when I go to scratch, there's nowt there but thin air. But they're still aching, still stinging, still nipping and oozing away. And it's that bloomin' *vexatious* I feel like chewing on the cushions.

They try to comfort me: Davy helping with my frocks and that, getting the sewing machine going to make them hang canny in the wheelchair; Edith doling out my ration of custard creams. But when your knees ache and you need to stretch them out, and put your feet up on your Egyptian leather pouffe, but there's no knees to stretch out, and no feet to lift, well you start to wonder what's the bloomin' point.

CHAPTER THIRTY-ONE

2007

Paul opens his eyes, and for a second he just lies there on that grotty old red sofa, that should have been taken to the dump years ago – and he can't move his legs. Or rather he's forgotten he's fucking even *got* legs, because that Lord Jim bloke's had his cut off, hasn't he? So he's just lying there *thinking* he can't move his legs, which has to one of the worst things he's ever experienced.

Christ. He can still feel the pain in his stumps. He touches his thighs to reassure himself they're still there. And his belt, which is too tight, fair enough, but still cinched in to thirty-four inches, which is a lot better than it was.

Jesus, the bloke was grotesque – and once his legs were off he was even worse. Before the op he could at least see his fucking knees, more or less, when he was sat down; but afterwards, it was pure lard oozing all over the show, so you couldn't even see his crotch, and it looked like he ended at the waist, if he'd had a waist.

Paul feels sick. His heart's going nineteen to the dozen and his hands are shaking. He looks up and Ben's there, leaning forwards on the pouffe, eyes round as saucers. And Dr fucking Charlton, smiling like the cat that got the cream. And that Ian bloke squatting down at the far end of the sofa, with the camcorder on his shoulder, pointing it straight at him with its red light flashing to show he's still recording.

'Turn that fucking thing off,' says Paul.

'OK. Sorry, mate,' says the Ian bloke. 'That was bloody amazing, though. Nothing to do with Annie, but bloody brilliant all the same.'

'I knew him!' goes that Laura woman, because she's there too, isn't she? Getting a fucking eyeful. 'That was Lord Jim from the Jungle!' she's going, half hysterical with excitement. 'And that Edith – I knew her too! It was me she hired to look after him before he died.' She grins at Paul, like they're old friends. 'Even with his legs off he was a right old flirt.'

Paul rounds on the doc. 'This is your fault,' he says. 'You've put things into my head.'

'I'm sorry you think that, Paul,' she goes, not sounding sorry at all. 'But anyone here will attest that your recollections took you straight to that hospital bed without any prompting from me. On the contrary, I was attempting to lead you back to an earlier period in Jim's life. But he was so traumatized by the amputations it was difficult to shift his attention anywhere else.'

'You want me to believe I was a big fat poofter, is that it?'

'As I say, it's not what I want. It's where your own unconscious recollections led you. All I did was put you into a trance—'

'Well it's fucking ridiculous. And *you*—' he points a finger at the Ian bloke —'get rid of that film, right? Press erase or whatever you have to do. Go on, do it now, while I'm watching. I don't want any of this getting out. I'll be a fucking laughing stock.'

'You can't be held responsible for something that happened before you were born,' says the doc, in one of those calm-down therapy voices that just makes him want to puke. 'But from what I could gather from our brief meeting, Lord Jim wasn't an evil man. It could have been a lot worse. With some clients—'

'Are you joking? He was a fucking poofter, for fuck's sake! A disgusting obese biscuit-guzzling nancy boy.'

'Oy, you mind your language,' goes Laura. 'That Lord Jim had a heart of gold. Wouldn't harm a fly, the old softie. A bit of a rogue for the lads, but they all knew what they were getting into and no one ever complained that I know of.' As if the bloke really existed. As if he was something to do with Paul.

'This is all rubbish,' he says. 'She's made it up because she was getting nowhere with Ben.' Yeah, that makes sense, he thinks. 'She's probably in cahoots with Mr Camera over there, so he can get something juicy for his stupid programme.'

The Ian bloke laughs. 'What, a camp diabetic amputee with a sweet tooth, spouting Polari? If I could make up stuff like that I'd give up documentaries and take up fiction instead.'

'If you think it would help,' goes the doc, 'I could arrange a couple of private sessions to help you come to terms—'

'There's nothing to come to terms with, because it didn't fucking happen, right? And, no, thank you very much,' he says, standing up. 'I don't want any more fucking sessions. And neither does Ben.'

'Dad! No—' The lad goes to grab his arm, but Paul shakes him off and feels in his back pocket. 'There, this should square us up,' he says, peeling off a couple of fifties and throwing them on the carpet. 'Come on, lad. We're out of here.'

Paul can't get away from the place fast enough, as though just putting distance between himself and that fucking sofa will get the disgusting old geezer out of his head. He's got the lad by his wrist, dragging him along so he's half tripping half running.

'Dad, please! You're hurting me.'

Paul loosens his hand and slows down a bit, but he's still striding along. He can feel the sweat sticking his shirt to his back under his leather jacket. 'Fucking quack. Who knows how many people she's done that to? Made up some crap and passed it off as a past fucking life story. I should have checked her out before I let her loose on you.'

'Dad, slow down!' Ben stumbles and Paul yanks him up by his arm.

'There must be someone I can complain to. I'll get her struck off. And that film bloke. The BBC ought to know the kind of rubbish they're spending our licence fees on.'

'But what if it's true?'

Paul stops suddenly and glares down at the lad. 'It's. Not. Fucking. True. Do you hear me? There's no such thing as past lives. And even if there was, there's no way that creep has anything to do with me.'

'It wasn't his fault he had to have his legs off.'

'It was his fault he was so fat, wasn't it? Necking sweeties all day.' He gets a sudden flash of the biscuits coming towards his mouth, two chocolate digestives dunked in tea, choc sides together like a soggy brown sandwich. 'God, I can't believe I've just spent half an hour, an hour, whatever, inside the head of that freak.'

'If he's a freak, what am I then?' The lad's facing up to him, and there's tears on his cheeks.

'And that's enough of that Annie crap too. You're a boy, and the sooner you come to terms with it the better.'

'I thought you were starting to understand.'

'She was supposed to turn you into a proper lad, not lead you down the crazy paving to la-la land.'

'But Annie's real! We found where she lived.'

'Oh that doctor's good, I'll give her that. Even had me convinced for a while. And she's obviously got Mr Camera eating out her hand.'

'It was working, Dad,' goes the lad, chin up, standing his ground. 'The therapy and that. I mean, before I went to the doc, it was really scary and confusing, not knowing where all that Annie stuff was coming from. But now I know she existed, it's like I can separate away from her a bit and start working out who I am.'

They're walking more slowly now and Paul's let go of the lad's wrist. 'You were fine before that fucking woman starting putting ideas into your head.'

'She was *helping* me, Dad. And it's not just me. Laura was cracking up before she went to the doc. She says after her sex-change—'

'You *what?*'

'Laura, Dad, remember?' says the lad, all sarky, as if Paul's some kind of idiot. 'Don't you get it? Before her sex change, she was that young Davy bloke who was with Lord Jim in the ambulance.'

'Laura? I don't believe this.'

'Yes, Laura. That nice lady you liked so much, who's been looking after me while you've been off on the boat. Well, she had a sex change, years ago. She's got a website that says all about it. It was through her that I found the doc.'

'Right, that's it,' says Paul. 'You are never going near that woman – that man – that fucking *creature* – again. Christ, that is way out of order – I mean, she was practically flirting with me.'

'Don't worry, Dad,' Ben says in a dull, bored voice. 'She likes women, not men.'

'I don't care if she likes bleeding Labradors. If I find out you've been in contact with her again I'll take a load of lads round to that bloody caff of hers and do the place over.'

They walk along in silence. Paul's clenching and unclenching his fists. Yeah, trash the caff, that would be the thing. He imagines chucking chintzy cups and saucers all over the show, smashing them against the walls. Getting a can and splashing petrol over her frilly pink tablecloths. She'd suspect him, of course, but if he torched it, she couldn't prove a thing. Of course he'd never actually do it, but the idea calms him down and he starts to breathe more like normal, not like he's running a marathon.

'You know what, Dad?' says Ben when they get home and they're waiting for the lift to take them up to the flat. 'In the Low Lights with everyone yesterday, I was really happy.'

Paul looks down at him. 'You'll be happy again.'

'I won't,' he says quietly, almost in a whisper.

'Of course you will. Once this all blows over and we're back to normal.'

'Normal's not the same as happy, Dad.'

At the flat, Ben goes straight to his room and locks the door. He doesn't slam it or anything, which Paul's half expecting. He just pushes it shut, sort of carefully, as if it's the end of something. Like he really means it.

Paul puts on the kettle and drops a teabag in his Captain Birdseye mug, then gets a cold KitKat out the fridge and starts peeling off the wrapper. It's like a reflex with him when he's narked: make a cuppa, get out a four-stick double-K to dunk, then lick off the melting chocolate and nibble the warm crisp wafery bit until it's all gone.

Then he thinks of Lord Jim and his digestives and he chucks the Kit Kat in the bin. And a surge of hot fury, like a red tide, sweeps through him, making his jaw jut and his fists clench again. Is this what it's going to be like from now on, every time he goes to eat something he fancies? Is he going to see those fat dimpled fingers crumbling custard creams into a saucer, see all those rings, those fucking fake diamonds and sapphires for God's sake, sinking into the sausage flesh so deep you can hardly see them? His arms, thick and pale as pork joints, and the smell of the athlete's foot powder he has to sprinkle into all his creases to stop the jock-rot. Creases at his *wrists*, for fuck's sake, and his elbows, let alone his stinking crotch and all those rolls on his belly.

He tips the unmade tea down the sink and pours himself three fingers of Bell's instead. The hit settles him a bit, and he realizes he's starving.

'Ben!' he shouts, taking out his mobile and scrolling down to the number for the curry place. 'D'you fancy an Indian?'

When there's no answer, he marches down the corridor and bangs the door with the flat of his hand. 'Oy, sulky boy. Open up. I said I was getting a curry. What d'you want?' More silence. Maybe he's in the en-suite, on the bog or washing his hair or something. 'Right, I'll order for you. OK?'

A chicky tikka should tempt him out. How long can a hungry twelve-year-old keep up a sulk? Paul puts in the order then wanders back to the lounge.

The restaurant bloke said it'd be forty minutes, which is probably an hour in real money.

'Ben!' he shouts again, shrugging on his jacket, 'I'm just off down the Low Lights for a quickie. I should be back before the curry man, but I've left a twenty on the hall table just in case.'

What's freaking him out, right, nearly as much as the fat homo on the sofa, is that Laura creature. It's like everyone knew except him – the doctor, Ben, even Mr Camera most likely – and they were probably all sniggering about it behind his back. There should be a fucking government health warning on people like that, a tattoo or something, like you get on tyre retreads. She wasn't bad-looking either, that's the freaky part. If he'd been ten years older, he might even have asked her out. Christ, it doesn't bear thinking about.

Paul's that antsy he takes the stairs down instead of the lift and almost runs along the road past the ice factory. In fact, maybe he should take up running again; he's still got all the gear somewhere. Run along the sea wall to Tynemouth every morning, like he used to with Nessa when she was on that fitness kick, which turned out to be her getting toned up for her fancy man, which put Paul off the whole idea when he found out. Still, it would be good to do something like that, something to tire him out, like, and stop him going bananas and wanting to smash things up. Because that's what he really wants to do right now: kick the driver's door in on that smart new Beemer, except it's probably built to withstand that kind of thing. But that pansy little red Punto would buckle no problem. He could do them all, that whole row of little superminis parked along the front by the Italian place. Bish, bash, bosh. Crappy tinny girlie cars the lot of them.

When he was a lad, he got in with a gang who went out vandalizing every weekend. Nothing too serious, just empty buildings and that. He's not sure why he stopped. It got boring after a while, he supposes. Then the lads started nicking things, and one of them got done, and he started to see where it was all leading: to a criminal record and a crappy council flat, and some mouthy chav with a double buggy on his case the whole time. So he started on the boat with his dad, and used the dosh to join the gym. Which was how he met Nessa, a few years down the line, so that was the end of that.

Well, the end of that chapter anyway, and the beginning of a whole other chapter. The his'n'hers chapter. The B&Q, nicey-nice, barley-white chapter. God, pretty much the whole of his twenties it was like living on two different planets: on the boat with the lads, with the nets full of fucking gurnards and dabs, and quotas doing his head in and the price of diesel going through the roof – then back to Nessa with her leotards and chilled Chardonnay.

Then Ben came and it all started to make sense. Striding down the Fish Quay with the bairn on his shoulders and the lads going 'howay'. Showing him the boat, letting him have a go at the wheel, doing the whole 'one day, son, all this will be yours' bit. One of the things about fishing, that makes you stick at it, is the idea of handing it down to your son – the boat, the charts, the moorings; your good will with the dealers; everything you've picked up in thirty-odd years in the business.

Just walking past the Gut now and seeing the *Wanderer* bobbing there, with her ropes coiled and her nets sorted, gives him a thrill; makes him want to grab someone out the queue for the chipper and go, 'See that one with the fresh paint job? She's mine.'

He can see the Low Lights from here, with the doors open and the lads sat outside in the setting sun, with their tabs and straight glasses, or propped against the wall. And he's already reaching round to his back pocket for his wad, practically tasting his first mouthful of Snecklifter – when he realizes he can't face going over.

Because Nana's told the whole fucking world about the film, hasn't she? So they'll be just full of it: the BBC man, what's he like then, blah blah blah. When's it going to be on, will they be filming down the Fish Quay, is he taking them out on the boat. And that makes Paul so fucking mad, because this has always been *his place*, where he could always go if he wanted a natter or a bevvy, or just a sit in the corner by himself with the *Chronicle*. But now he can't face it. And it's all that doctor's fault.

So he turns round before the lads can spot him, and heads for Union Quay Stairs. And sprints up them, way too fast, so he's puffed before he's half way up; but he makes himself keep going, gritting his teeth, even though the blood's pounding in his head fit to burst a vessel, and his thighs feel like sacks of concrete so he can hardly lift them, and his heart's galloping like he's heading for a heart attack. But at least it's getting it out of his system.

At the top, his legs are like jelly and he flops down at one of the tables outside the Wooden Doll, which he could go into instead of the Low Lights, except it's those two dozy kids behind the bar these days, whose dad set them up in the business, more money than sense, and it's always full of their mates getting freebies, which irritates Paul, because the Doll could be a perfectly good pub, but they're running it into the ground. Which brings him back to the boat, and the business, and Ben, and what the fuck to do about the lad.

Then out of the blue he gets a flash of the bairn's face after he'd run up the stairs to the flat that time, so full of all this stuff they were finding out at the library, about Annie and that, just jabbering away like any normal kid and looking so fucking *happy*.

CHAPTER THIRTY-TWO

2007

Paul's left the front door swinging wide open behind him, a gesture far more aggressive and contemptuous than if he had slammed it.

Laura gets up to close it. 'Oh dear,' she says.

Mary sighs. 'As you so aptly comment, oh dear.'

'Oh, he'll be OK,' says Ian breezily. 'I'll go and have a word later.'

'I'm not sure even your Caledonian charm will persuade Ben's father to lie on that couch again.'

'You'd be surprised what people will do to see their faces on the wee screen.'

'It will take more than the promise of fifteen minutes' fame to get a man's man like that to accept a flamboyant forebear like Lord Jim. Paul's a member of one of the most masculine subcultures in the country,' Mary reminds him. 'Women are not allowed to go out on a fishing trip, did you know that? Even in this day and age, it's an absolute taboo.'

'Shall I go after them?' Laura peers through the curtains.

'I think that would probably do more harm than good.'

'But we can't just let him drag the lad away like that. Did you see him, Mary? He was totally gutted.'

'At least give his father time to calm down a bit.'

Laura sits down again. Then gets up again straight away. 'It's no good, I'm too churned up. You haven't got any chocolate have you?'

Mary laughs. 'No. Sorry.'

'What about ice cream?'

'I'm afraid not.'

'Right, that's me off then,' Laura announces, grabbing a turquoise handbag. 'People to go, places to see. See you kids later.'

'So what happens to Ben's therapy?' asks Ian when she's gone. He's monopolized the sofa, sitting in the middle surrounded by small pieces of expensive-looking electronic equipment, which he appears to be attaching to one another with black wires.

Mary shrugs. 'We'll have to see. Once Paul's calmed down, I may be able to persuade him to let me continue seeing Ben. But it might be the end of your film, I'm afraid.'

'Shit. What a fucking mess.'

'I think it's quite interesting actually,' comments Mary, leaning back in her analyst's chair. 'Setting aside the obvious torment of the poor man, you couldn't hope to witness a better example of karma in the making. I'd say he'll have at least one module to resit next time around, wouldn't you?'

Ian laughs. 'Homophobia 101, you mean? I don't think he's even signed up for the course in his current life.'

'What will you do about the film?'

'I'll cancel the film crew for now, but all is not yet lost,' he says, irrepressible as ever. 'I'll have a look at the footage I've got of Ben so far. There's lots of good stuff in there. With a spot of clever editing, it might be enough – though I might have to pad it out with something else.'

'Provided Paul agrees to you using it.'

'He's signed the consent form.'

Mary sits up. 'You'd hold him to that?'

Ian shrugs. 'What do you think those things are for? To deal with precisely this kind of eventuality, when someone gives permission then changes their mind at the last minute.'

The man's ruthlessness still has the power to shock her. She wonders nervously what unpleasant surprises he might have in store for her later on in this process. Still, she sets that concern aside as something far more intriguing snags her attention. She opens her notebook, checks back through her notes and makes a few calculations. Then:

'One good thing came out of that session,' she remarks casually.

'What's that then?'

'Well, I've just been looking at the dates, and it's entirely possible that Lord Jim of the Jungle and Annie's somewhat effeminate brother Jimmy are one and the same man.'

'Good grief. How do you work that out?'

'I can't be sure – James was an incredibly common name at that time, so this is pure speculation. But we can calculate Jimmy's date of birth from the 1891 census, and we know that Lord Jim was eighty-seven when we met him, because he kindly reminded us. Assuming that was in the mid-sixties—'

'He was on about that music in the basement, wasn't he? All that flower power stuff. Everyone in bare feet. 'All You Need Is Love'. 'If You're Going to San Francisco'. Which would make it the Summer of Love – which, as everyone knows, was 1967.'

'So how old would young Jimmy have been in 1967 if he was eighteen in 1898?'

'OK. Hang on a sec.' He closes his eyes, doing the calculation in his head. 'Eighty-seven. Fucking hell. So Little Jimmy Osmond grows up to be Big Jim of the Jungle. That's quite a transformation. Who would have thought it?'

'Wait,' says Mary, though her heart's thudding with excitement. 'I haven't finished. We still have to make the link to Ben's father. How old do you think he is? Thirty-nine? Forty? That would give him a date of birth somewhere in the late sixties – which is around the time Lord Jim died, according to Laura.'

'Do you realize what you're saying?'

'I hope so.' She beams at him.

'No. I mean, think about that date. 1967. It might have been the Summer of Love for them, but it was the summer of the Long Sands for us.' He grabs her hand. 'When we met for the first time.'

'We didn't actually meet, remember,' Mary says mildly, squeezing his hand then disengaging herself. 'I merely noticed you on your surfboard.'

'But we were both *there*, that's the important thing. So was Paul, Lord Jim I mean – and Davy, aka Laura, had just been hired to nurse him. What's the betting everyone else was there too? Ben and his granny, maybe even old Skip, for fuck's sake. Christ, Mary. No wonder you're so hooked on this stuff. You can talk about degrees of separation till you're blue in the face, but when you're faced with coincidences like this, it gives you the frigging goosebumps.'

Mary feels an uncharacteristic surge of triumph, which she attempts to contain. 'I don't think we should get too distracted by 1967 at the moment,' she says carefully. 'All the date coincidence suggests is that certain groups of souls may indeed meet – or seek one another out – repeatedly down the ages. What we need to work on right now is who else might have been present in 1898, when Annie disappeared.'

'Go on, then.' He picks up his multitasking phone contraption and looks at her expectantly, presumably poised, by some technological means, to take notes.

'Well,' she says, 'if I'm right about Lord Jim, we now know the current incarnations of both Annie and her brother Jimmy. Unfortunately it doesn't look as though we'll get any more information from either of them for the time being. So what we need to do now is find out whether it's possible to identify the current incarnation of anyone else close to Annie – her mother, for example, or her boyfriend – and interrogate them about what happened to her.'

'So hypnotize me.' He slips off his shoes, shoves the equipment to one side and prostrates himself on the sofa, opening his arms in a parody of submission.

'What on earth makes you think you have anything to do with this? You'd never met Ben or Paul before this week.'

'Excuse me!' he objects indignantly. 'I was the mysterious red-headed boy who so engaged you in 1967. Here, in North Shields. I was the lapdog you adored as an Elizabethan lady in the sixteenth century. I was the love of your life for a few ecstatic months in 1976. And I'm here right *now*, for fuck's sake, at exactly the same time as Ben turns up on your doorstep asking for help. I would have thought that more than qualified me, wouldn't you?'

Mary laughs. 'The main thing that qualifies you is the fact that you are both willing and available, indeed some would say "gagging for it". Whereas Laura is off goodness knows where, Mr Skipper is in a perpetually vulnerable state, and Ben's grandmother must be classed, for the time being at least, as in the enemy camp.'

'You've forgotten to include yourself.'

'Skilled though I am, I have yet to master the art of self-hypnosis.'

'So it's got to be me then,' he says, grinning smugly.

'Annoyingly, you seem to have achieved exactly what you want.'

'Which is lying helpless on your couch, completely at your mercy.'

Naturally Ian wants to go ahead straight away, but Mary insists on taking a break first; she needs time to collect her thoughts and plan what she's going to do. In terms of methodology, the session with Paul was a failure; there was no mention of his early life at all. So she's worried she'll be unable to direct Ian's recollections away from his personal traumas – even assuming he knew Annie in a past life, which seems unlikely to say the least. Taking refuge in an age-old ritual, she sets out her mismatched willow-pattern tea set and fills the kettle.

'Laura said you were both fishermen,' says Ian, sitting at the kitchen table and leafing through a heap of her unopened post.

'Yes,' she says. 'But I don't have any evidence that we even knew each other.' She wraps her hands around her cup and sips thoughtfully while he rips open a little pack of oatmeal biscuits purloined from the hotel.

'You suspect you did though,' he prompts, crunching up two biscuits in quick succession, cascading crumbs.

'It's possible, but I've never tried to cross-check past lives like this before. Theoretically it could get rather complicated. With Paul, for example, we were lucky in that there appear to have been no intervening incarnations. Lord Jim died in 1967 and Paul was born shortly afterwards. Assuming we're right, of course.'

Ian positions his recording device in front of her and switches it on. 'Mary C, twenty-first of August. Talking about reincarnation. Right.' He nods to her to continue. 'So, is it always like that? Someone dies and the soul's reincarnated immediately?'

Mary shakes her head. 'As I said before, it's complicated. From documented cases it would seem that a soul may hang around, as it were, without a body, for as many as six years. Buddhists call this state *bardo*, by the way.'

'But?'

'Well, much of the published data is from Asia and the Middle East, where prenatal and perinatal mortality can be extremely high.'

'Which makes for rather a lot of false starts.'

'Exactly. Some practitioners claim to have interviewed souls who recall dying in infancy. Some even claim to have made contact with souls who have been aborted or miscarried – but I think it's highly unlikely that a foetus would be able to articulate his or her experiences in a form that could be understood by a subsequent incarnation. However, I do think it's possible that a soul might have to inhabit quite a number of potential bodies before lodging in a viable one.'

'I see what you mean.'

'Things were pretty tough in nineteenth-century Britain too, especially in North Shields. Take my case for example.'

'If only you'd let me.'

She glares at him. 'Yes, well, immediately prior to my current incarnation it seems I was someone called Peggy, a bright girl who worked in a canning factory, gutting herring and white fish – until she got pregnant following a brief but ill-advised liaison with an itinerant builder from Aberdeen. The man buggered off and her family disowned her—'

'That seems a bit hard.'

'Bearing an illegitimate child was considered deeply shameful in those days, even in poor communities.'

'But it must have happened all the time.'

'Indeed. And if he'd been a local boy, their respective families would probably have got together and forced him to marry her – and turned a blind eye when an infant appeared somewhat less than the requisite nine months later. As it was, he simply shouldered his bag and headed off into the night.'

'Poor Peggy. What did she do?'

'Well, I'm afraid her life took a somewhat different path from then on. She lost her job and took to cleaning houses and taking in washing – for a pittance, as you can imagine. And, as a "fallen woman", she was subject to continual sexual harassment and several vicious sexual assaults from men who considered her fair game. So when one day a man offered her money for what I believe is still referred to as a "knee-trembler", she took it.'

Mary shakes her head briefly to banish the memory. 'Later she used to say that if she was going to have her bum grabbed and her tits tweaked, she might as well get paid for it.'

'What happened to the baby?'

'Robert – Bobby she called him – was a timid little boy. Clingy, always under her feet – or so she thought. I'm afraid she was rather impatient with him. I often wonder whether he's still alive. He didn't have much of a start in life, living in one room with a prostitute for a mother. She'd send him to sit on the stairs when she had a customer, but he must have known what was going on.' She can see the boy's face: his sandy freckles, the cap pulled down low on his forehead, his nervous ingratiating smile.

'What about her other kids? With no contraception, pregnancy must have been a bit of an occupational hazard.'

'She aborted at least four babies that I know of, but there may have been more.'

Ian whistles through his teeth. 'Talk about false starts.'

'I often wonder whether that's why I ended up in one of the so-called "caring professions" – to correct a mothering deficit incurred during Peggy's lifetime.'

'You could have had children instead,' Ian says pointedly, and a familiar little stab of anguish flashes through her.

She sets her cup down, avoiding his eyes. 'I suspect I make a better therapist than I would a mother,' she comments dryly. 'I was somewhat lacking the relevant role-model while I was growing up. My mother didn't really know what to do with me unless I was ill.'

'So Peggy died – when?'

'Shortly before I was born in 1956. But I can't see how—'

'But before Peggy, you were a fisherman, right?'

'It would seem so, yes,' she says noncommittally. She doesn't want to discuss this with Ian. She hasn't thought through the implications of being identified as the predatory Tom Hall – if that's who the T.H. on her tobacco tin refers to. She wants to mull it over on her own: look out the tapes of her original hypnosis sessions and try to find out a bit more about him first.

'But he might have known Annie. He might have been one of the men on her dad's boat.'

'In principle, yes. But you can't just—'

'Come on, Mary. Humour me. We might be getting somewhere here.'

'All right,' she sighs. 'I've never tried to check the exact date, but Peggy was probably born in the mid-1920s, so you'd be looking for a fisherman who died near that time, though as I said before, there could have been any number of "false starts", as you put it, between the death of someone on the *Osprey* and the day Peggy was born.'

'OK, point taken. But we could at least rule out anyone who was still alive when Peggy was born. That would narrow the field a bit, wouldn't it?'

'I suppose so,' she concedes.

'So we'd start by going to the Births, Marriages and Deaths website. You've got that list of names, haven't you?' He chuckles. 'I'll bet you were Annie's father, the fearsome skipper. What was his name? Henry. He'd have been about sixty-five when Peggy was born, right? So that would fit.'

'Following that logic, any of the older men would fit,' she points out.

'I know – but I like the idea of you being skipper on a herring boat. It's almost as far from your current incarnation as you could imagine.'

'Unfortunately, any one of the younger men would fit equally well.'

'Well obviously, assuming one of them died in his forties—'

'If he died in his teens he could *still* fit,' she interrupts impatiently. 'Don't you see? There could have been another intervening incarnation, who also died in his thirties. Or he could have died in his thirties, and the intervening incarnation could have died in his teens. The permutations are limitless! I'm sorry, Ian,' she says crossly. 'I can't see any point in this.'

'OK, OK. Keep your hair on.'

Mary takes a deep breath. 'Look, what I went through with my supervisor was a therapeutic training process, not an historical investigation. So she was concerned with exploring issues that were relevant to my personal development at the time, which happened to focus on Peggy's short but tragic life. We touched on previous incarnations, too, of course – and it does seem likely that at least one was a fisherman, perhaps even two or more. But it was only in passing, and certainly not in enough detail to determine whether they included someone who served on the *Osprey*.'

'Are you still in touch?'

'What?'

'With your old supervisor.'

'We exchange Christmas cards and bump into one another at conferences occasionally,' she says cautiously. 'The last time I saw her was at that big Mapping the Mind shindig in Glasgow last year.'

'I wonder if I should get her up here for a day or two.'

'No! Absolutely not!' It comes out much more vehemently than she intends.

Ian raises his eyebrows. 'Why not? Kill two birds with one stone. You get to fit a few more pieces into your psychic jigsaw and I get to find out if your fisherman was on that boat.'

Damn. Now she's piqued his interest, he'll never let it go. 'She's an old lady, Ian.'

'If she can schlep all the way up to Glasgow, North Shields should be a piece of piss. Where does she live? I'll send a car to take her to her nearest airport, station, whatever, and meet her at this end. Door-to-door service. Room with a view at the Grand. It'll be a nice little outing for her.'

'I don't want her here.'

'Why on earth not?'

'I finished with regression therapy a long time ago. It was a painful and enlightening experience, and it did me a great deal of good, but it's not something I want to repeat – particularly not with you filming me.'

'What's her name?'

'No.'

'Aren't you curious about your fisherman?'

'I thought you were the one who wanted to be hypnotized.'

'Does this woman even exist?'

'The issue is closed, Ian.'

He peers at her. 'What are you scared of, Mary Charlton?'

'I'm going outside for a Gitanes. If you're serious about being regressed, I'll do it when I get back.'

CHAPTER THIRTY-THREE

...Excellent. Keep breathing slowly and deeply. Keep walking along that road. There's a row of houses in front of you. Can you see them? Good. Each house has a front door, which opens onto a year of your life. Look for the one that opens onto 1898. Good. Now open that door and you'll find yourself in a hallway with some more doors. Now walk through the one that will take you to the summer of 1898.

1898

They're saying there's never been a summer like it for the herring. The quay's that crammed with craft, some of the crews are coming to blows over moorings. And the catches! Overflowing the holds, Henry says, so they've to bring the pound boards up on deck to contain them.

And here's me full to overflowing too, seems like, waddling about like a seal cow, puffing and panting up and down all the stairs of this town.

I tell you, this heat doesn't suit me one bit. So right now I'm plodding up the stairs to the loft, and poking my head out the window, trying to catch a breath of freshness. I'm hoping for a sniff of the cool sea, an updraught to dry the sweat off my face, and ruffle up the hair that's glued to my forehead. But the air's thick as pea soup, even this high, and all I can smell is rotten fish innards and the sour puffs of doused cooking fires.

I don't remember being this bad with our Emily. But it was winter when she came, so I'd have been out flither-picking, or sitting in with Mam baiting the long lines – not standing all hours in a loft like an oven, beating driftnets.

I swear you could fry a flounder out on them roof tiles today. If Ricky were here, I'd get him to fan me with the *Daily News* – but he's off at Mam's with Em and the big lads. It's that quiet without them, I can hear myself think for a change – which is not such a good thing now I'm coming up to my time; not when my legs are throbbing and I can't catch my breath. I keep pondering on what the doctor said when Em came – but it's too late now to worry about that.

And when you see them all, all the bairns, the jump and the joy of them, how can you not want another? Even though your ankles are puffy as pigs' bladders and your legs look like there's blue porridge dripped down the back. Just a few more weeks and I'll be back to myself, with another wee grunter sucking away.

By, but I'm that tired it's like a hunger; the sight of Annie and Flo's mattresses, set out so neat and welcoming, fairly makes my mouth water. I could lie down and gobble up a dish of sleep easy as mashed taties and butter.

Beating in a home loft's a lonely business without the weans here to help. They're right canny with their fingers, so there's always a row of needles threaded. It's a bind doing them myself: you lose your place on the net when you set it aside to thread up. So, now I've cut the lengths, and threaded them ready – enough for a good two hours' beating – and I'm lumbering to my feet and unhooking the net and stretching it out. By, but I'm breathless again from just lifting down a skein of lint and unfolding it in the light. The Lord knows what I'll be like in a few weeks when I'm due.

This net's not too bad; mainly spronks and crows' feet. They could use it as it is, except Henry's a stickler for his lints and would rather I spent an hour or three now, tidying up, than risk losing half a haul next week through a big tear. If I went blind, I swear my fingers would still be able to find their way around a fouled net, and light on the holes, and mend them, and tie them off neat. There's been times when Henry's climbed up to find me beating in the dark almost, when the light's faded and I've been trying to finish a big rent before going for the lamp.

I've finished this lint, but it could do with a cutching. So I've folded it and I'm bending down to hoy it up on the pulleys by the window – next thing I know I'm lying on the floor with the net beside me. I've fainted, I suppose, though I can't remember falling. And I'm yawning, and the room seems dark, though the sun's bright as ever.

Oh, but it's such a comfort to be off my feet. I could lie here cuddling the net for an hour, never mind that the boards are all crusty with fish scales and twists of creosote twine. But Henry's had his bit sleep now, and needs waking. So I'd better see if I can stand up – and I can – and grab the handrail, and go carefully down the stairs to our room.

I always take a moment to sit quiet on the edge of the bed and watch him sleep: my big fierce lad as only I ever see him, soft and loving as a fireside moggie. He likes to take his clothes off for his bit sleep – even if it's only a few hours. He says it's his way of knowing he's home: even in his sleep, he can feel the blanket on his bare skin and tell he's not on the boat. His forehead's pale, where his cap's been pulled on; and his neck, where he's tied his wrapper; and his arms down to the wrists, where his gansey's been.

'Time to wake up, pet,' I'm saying, leaning over. And he rolls towards me with his eyes shut, and reaches for my hand, and finds it straight away – like mending a crow's foot in the dark.

It's evening now and I'm just finishing my round, and there's a pound or so left, so I should try up Dockwray again. But I can't face climbing back up to the top bank in this heat, and Mam's place is nearby, so I think I'll drop in on her and take the weight off instead.

And there it is, the house I grew up in – and there's our Ricky and Emily settling down on the front step with pots and crans, to scrape taties and shell peas for their nana. Oh, and just look at our Ricky helping Em with the cran in her lap, bless him, and popping the first pod to tip them into her little mouth!

Now Emmy's looking up, and she's spotted me – so she's trying to smile, but she's a mouthful of peas, and that has to be the sweetest, funniest face in the world, all brimming with life and bonny dimples. And Ricky's seen me too, and's dropping his tatie knife and running to meet me. And here's their nana popping out to see why they've left the pots; and I can feel my legs start to sag under me, just knowing she's coming to help me off with the fish board, and bustle me into a chair with a cup of tea.

They say you never really grow up till your mam passes on, for there's always a part of you that wants tending, and a part of her that wants to do it. So here she is, peering over at me with a worried frown, and Ricky's coughing again, so that's never eased for weeks now; and Emmy's clambering onto my lap – but there's no lap because of the baby, so she's sliding off, and whingeing, so I'm hugging her best I can, and reaching out for Ricky too. And Mam's asking what's the matter? And I'm saying, just tired, Mam, this heat's getting to me. So she says, not long now, pet – meaning the Scots lasses and the nets as well as the baby coming – and promises soon as her lodgers have gone, she'll be round our place to help out.

So now I'm asking after our Jimmy and Frank, for I miss my big lads too and want to see them. And she says Frank's along by the ferry landing with his didall net, catching the herring that fall off the crans as they're hoisted ashore. And Jimmy's gone off somewhere, he didn't say where, without stopping for his tea. And the way Mam's telling it, I can see she's not best pleased.

'There's something got into that lad,' she says. 'He's out all hours, just rushes back for his oilies when the boat's setting off. And this last Sunday morning I caught him sneaking in as I was raking out the grate – so he's never been home all night.'

'Is he sleeping on the boat?' I'm asking.

'Said he forgot the time. What sort of answer's that?'

He's off his food too, Mam says, which is not like our Jimmy at all – he's normally right in there with a spoon while you're still cooking, tasting and blethering on, adding this and that. So now I'm worrying there's something troubling him: a lass maybes, or a barny with one of the lads – though Henry's never said there's been strife on the boat. And I'm starting to fret, but what's the use of that? When your bairns get older, you have to let them go and just pray they'll keep safe.

Next morning this bairn's come pounding on the door to bring word that a lad's been lost off the *Osprey*. Of course my first thought is it's Henry or our Jimmy, and I'm off running down to the quayside, with my heart thundering fit to burst, thinking – well, I'm that beside myself I hardly know what to think.

Then I see them, my precious lads – and not a mark on them – and I'm sobbing with shock and relief, the way you do, I'm that thankful to see them. And Jimmy comes over to explain that the *Wellesley* lad's gone overboard in the night, and our Annie's taking it hard.

And there she is, crouching by a stack of crans, clutching a ditty tin, with tears pouring down her face. And I'm remembering how I felt just now, running onto the quayside, thinking one of my lads were drowned – then trying to imagine what Annie's going through. For she was deep in love with that Sam, no doubt about that. I never saw a lass shine the way she's been shining these past weeks, ever since they've been walking out.

'Oh, Annie, pet,' I'm saying. 'I'm so sorry.' And I try to raise her up, but she's stiff as wood, whispering, 'No, no,' over and over.

'Come up to the house,' I say. But she doesn't want to leave the quay, and I can understand that, for I'd be the same. To turn your back and walk away – well that's admitting he's really gone, isn't it? So I sit down beside her on the cold cobbles with my legs throbbing under me, and put an arm around her, and wait till she's ready to come home.

By and by her head sags onto my shoulder and we watch the Harbourmaster arrive and take Henry aside for a word; then two police officers to talk to the crew. And all the while the capstan's chugging away, winching off the crans; and luggers are mooring up and unloading, with the odd herrings dropping like silver rain into the bairns' didall nets.

Life goes on, that's the terrible truth. A lad drowns, but there's still a haul to get to market. That's what's so hard to take: that the boats can push apart to let the *Osprey* moor up, and the crews stop work for maybes half an hour out of respect for a lost lad, but then life goes on again like the cold waves closing over his head.

CHAPTER THIRTY-FOUR

1898

When you're a mother and your bairn's ailing you feel it right along with them. So here's my poor Annie up in the loft, and she can't be still. She's done a load of needles for me, and brewed another pot of tea, though she's never touched her first cup yet, and she's swept up again, though there's nowt to sweep up.

She keeps forgetting, that's the trouble. So she'll be busy cutting off the twine, and her mouth will go soft and her shoulders loosen – then it'll come to her again, and her head will come up and her eyes will widen and stare at me, and see the pity on my face and know that it's true. And then we'll both be crying again – her for Sam's sake, and me for hers.

I'm sending her back to the smokehouse tomorrow, for she's better keeping busy. She's not the type to sit; that's never been her way. But the light's gone out of her, that's the truth of it. She had the brightest eyes, our Annie; merry brown dancing eyes. Now they're that dull, it's as if the lass that looked out through them has drawn the curtains.

I'm sitting in the kitchen and Flo's back, and had her cocoa and gone to bed, and the Scots lasses have gone up too, but Annie's still out.

I sent her off for bacon, just for something to occupy her really, but Flo's checked with the butcher and he's never seen her. She'll be walking – that's where she's been these last two nights. Says she's too het up to sleep; says she's trying to tire herself out. I can't stop her and I can't help her. All I can do is wait up till she comes home, and take her into the bed, and hold her while she sobs her heart out.

It's gone midnight and I've been to the door again, but all that's out there is fog rolling down the stairs, and the clang of boats' bells on the river. Two colliers crashed into each other in the fog last month and went down; the lifeboat was out night and day in the murk searching for survivors. They says there's more lives lost at sea in one year than in a decade down the coal mines. But it's in ones and twos that we lose them – a lad gone overboard, another crushed by a winch, an iced-up trawler capsized – and there's nowt to see: no smoke, no explosion, no charred pithead. Just the cold sea going about its business.

I must have nodded off, right here at the table with my head on my arms. It's three o'clock and I feel a bit dizzy climbing the stairs to check Annie's bed, but there's still no sign. So now I'm lighting a lamp to go look for her.

Henry says she was fighting to get on the *Osprey* that day, so I'm trying the quayside first. Because that's where I'd go if he was lost: to the last place he was, to touch the mooring posts and crans, and think of him being there. The boats are all out, of course, but here's the watchman asking what I'm doing this time of night, then saying he's seen a dark-haired lass walking out in the direction of the trysting hill.

So that's where I'm headed now, leaving the lights of the harbour behind, with my eyes on the track and the chilly fog pressing in all round. I can hear the river, though I can't see it, and bells clanging far out in the darkness like a tolling for dead souls.

My feet are squelching in my clogs from the wet grass, and my skirt's sodden and heavy at the hem. And here's that bit dizziness again, and my legs are paining that much I'm wondering how I'll ever walk home. I call out, 'Annie! Annie pet, are you there?' But there's no reply; just the bells tolling, and the water's slip-slap on the rocks below.

Now all of a sudden I'm thinking, is that where she is? Has she filled her pockets with stones and gone in to the water to join her lost lad? And the thought's like a jolt of lightning going through me, that makes me hurry over to the water's edge, and call again, and scramble over the rocks, and call again, and again – 'Annie! Annie pet, it's your mam. Oh, Annie love, please answer. I've come to bring you home.'

Then what's this? Did I dream it? A little sound that's half a sob, half a cry. And there she is, huddled in a wet hollow, shivering, with her hair dripping and tears on her face, and a heap of big stones in her lap.

* * *

I let her sleep in this morning, then send her off to Scarp Landings, to the Heron place to check on Sam's mother. Henry's given them money, of course, and paid his respects, but word is the woman's been bad since they found the lad's body. So I was thinking – well, let his lass and his mam be bad together, like, and maybes comfort each other, and find a way through to the other side.

But it's gone eleven and she's never come home. Flo's off out with Tom and Henry's in bed – he wanted to wait up, but it's his one night for a proper sleep and he was stotting with tiredness. After last night, that's how I'm feeling too. The legs are a bit easier now I'm sitting, but there's a sort of fogginess you get inside when you're dog-weary, that's as thick as the fog outside – that's never lifted for two days now – a sort of bluntness, that makes you slow and stupid.

I've been darning, but I can't stick with it. I keep thinking of Annie tending to that grieving family, and maybes too kind to leave, or wandering out on the hill in the mist collecting stones. It's no good – I have to find her.

By, but it's miserable out: the stairs all greasy with damp, and fog muffling the lamplight. I'm going to the Heron place first, then if Annie's left I'll follow in her footsteps from there.

It's Saturday night, so going down the wet stairs to Bell Street's like wading into a river of light and noise, with folk piling into the inns to escape the clammy cold, and yellow light spilling out, and tab smoke, and craik – and God knows what slime underfoot. It'll take more than a blanket of fog to douse this lot, for they're blazing with whisky and navy rum, half of them, and some are that red-eyed they can hardly see.

I was planning to walk the Scarp lanes by myself, but seeing this lot's made me wary, so I'm heading off to Mam's to fetch our Jimmy. The lamp's lit and she's up, of course – what Shields wife goes to bed before midnight in the herring season? But Jimmy's out – he came home for a quick bath and change of shiftenings, then donned his go-ashores and set off after tea.

'At least he had his tea,' I say with a sigh.

'Ay, but that's the best you can say.'

'But he's no trouble, is he?'

And now it's her turn to sigh, for Jim's her first grandson and she loves him like a mother. 'It's not him that's the trouble,' she says. 'It's other folk I worry about.'

We've to knock at a few houses before we find the Heron place. There's a faint light under the door, and a young lass opens it a crack, and slips out and whispers, sorry, sorry, but Mam's asleep, and it's the first time since Sam was drowned, so she doesn't want to disturb her.

I've seen through the crack before she pulled the door to; at the candles round the coffin; at the mother slumped forward on the table.

'Was Annie here?' I whisper. And the lass says yes, but she left after tea, at eight, eight-thirty maybes, with the new kist. So I'm asking, 'What kist?' and the lass says it was something Sam bought her, something to show they're promised.

'Was she going away?' Mam asks, but the lass says, no, nowt like that; she just hoisted the kist on her head to take it home.

'Maybe she's gone off with the Scots lasses,' says Mam as we leave. 'The first crews started packing up this morning and it would be a fresh start for her.'

'Without her boots and her oilies? Without saying a word?'

But we climb the stairs to the top bank anyway, and walk along to Shields Station to check if she's been there. The place is shut up and there's no one on duty: just a tramp snoring under a bit canvas. So we go home to mine, and I check the loft, but Annie's still not back – and Flo's still out, though it's a miserable night for canoodling.

Henry says I'm being daft; she'd never kill herself. But he wasn't there, was he? He never saw her bedraggled and keening, with a lapful of stones. He never held her while she sobbed herself to sleep, or saw her wake up in tears before she's even remembered why she's crying.

We went back to the hill and searched every hollow, but she wasn't there. Then when dawn came, and the fog lifted, we went again. And back to Shields Station, but no one remembered a lass with a green kist. I was fair nithered by then and I couldn't stop shivering, so Henry made me go home, and lay down a spell while he went to the police station.

So that was five days ago: five nights of sitting up waiting for her, five mornings when I've woken in this chair and she's still not been home.

I should never have sent her off to Mrs Heron. A bonny lass in that rough place, with a new kist in the fog – anyone could have taken a fancy to her. Or mistooken her for an uppity Scots gipper and thought to teach her a lesson. Soon as I saw her with them stones in her lap, I should never have let her out of my sight.

Henry called up the crew and they searched all over, and asked around up and down all the lanes and stairs. It meant missing a day's share, but they never said a word – that's the kind of lads they are.

He says the police never even wrote down her name. They were that run off their feet, what with drunks and brawlers, and folk that's been robbed, and the cells still flooded from that storm. They said lasses go off all the time, and turn up again a week later none the worse; and maybes she was with a lad and forgot the time, or been shamed and gone away to sort herself out – which is something I never thought of, but when it gets to be this long, you start thinking anything, don't you?

I've been bad, so Flo's been helping out. She says she's stopping at ours long as I need her and I've not the heart to send her away – though I can't help thinking if she'd spent less time chasing after that Tom Hall, and more time tending to our Annie – well, maybes she wouldn't have taken Sam's death quite so hard. And maybes that's what Flo's thinking too, for far as I can tell she's never seen Tom these last few days and has been that quiet I'm wondering if she's ailing.

I've had to knock the round on the head: I daresn't leave the house in case Annie comes home and needs me – though I'm not much use to anyone the state I'm in. My head aches all the time, and it's been hurting me to breathe. Henry wants to go for the doctor, but what's the point? He'll only tell me to rest, but how can I? There'll be time enough to rest when I'm lying in. There'll be time enough to rest when our Annie's home.

Oh, Annie! I keep looking up and expecting her to be there: across the kitchen, where she'd be tending the fire, outside swilling down her oilies in the yard. I keep expecting her bright face to appear at the door, saying howay Mam and what's for tea?

They say a wife should never sweep the house the day her husband sets off on a voyage, or she'll sweep him out of her life. So I've kept her things where she left them. There's her knitting box on the dresser; her work scarf's hanging behind the door; her boots are stood in the scullery waiting to be oiled.

The season's finished now and the town's emptied of Scots lasses. The luggers have all set sail for Yarmouth and Grimsby, where the herring's just started. And we're left to sweep up the mattress straw from our lodging rooms, and the wet sawdust from our pubs, and count our shillings till next year.

The bairns'll be back tomorrow and needing their room, so I've tonight to get the place ready. Ellie's crew packed up two days back, but I've not had the heart to do the room out till now. Tell the truth, I've not had the heart for anything much since Annie – well, since Annie what? Flitted off to Yarmouth with just the clothes on her back? Boarded a steam packet to London? But she'd write, that's what I keep thinking. If she's alive, and in her right mind, she'd find a way to send word.

I keep circling back to them stones in her lap; that terrible dull look in her eyes.

It's hard clambering up the stairs with the bucket and broom and that; I've had to go up and down three times with different things. By the end I'm hanging on to the handrail gasping for breath, with my heart hammering and my head pounding. So anyway, now I'm shifting the bedsteads, to sweep under them, and—

Oh dear Lord, no! Here's a hot trickle down my leg, and it's my waters going. So I'm sighing and thinking, well at least the bucket's up here and the cloth, so I can mop up. But now here comes a birthing pain, like a fist twisting; and it's a big un, so I think it can't be long – it was that quick with Emily, she was out and washed and latched on before the doctor could get here.

There's that heap of brown paper I've unpinned from the walls, so I'm scrunching it into a sort of nest to catch the baby, but I'm having to squat down each time a pain hits us, so it's slow going. Oh and here's another one, and another fast after, so I get ahold of the bedstead. And I can feel the head – oh, oh, and here it comes, the hot slither of arms and legs, my little red spider!

Oh come here and let me see you, wee daftie. No, don't cry, Mammy's here. There now, here now. And you're a little man, oh precious poppet. Howay, let's wipe your face. That's right, now wait and I'll get my blouse open. See, now, you came so fast I never even had a chance to change my shiftenins.

And just look at this place, all dust balls and herring scales. What sort of room is this to bring a new lad into, eh? But I'll clear it up later. Now, where's my beating knife? First thing is to get the cord cut – there – and wait for the afterbirth, then we can get settled.

Oh, but I'm so tired, let's just rest here awhile on our paper nest, and you can have a bit suck and I'll lean back against the bedstead and close my eyes.

* * *

It's getting dark – I must have dropped off. Or maybes I fainted? I can't tell. The baby's sleeping, and oh if only Mam was here to tend me, and help me into the bed and get rid of this minging paper. And wash my poor little mite, who's as smeary as offal in a butcher's window.

I wonder if I can get up. Is the afterbirth out? Let's have a feel, and – what's this? Why's everything so wet? My skirt's wringing, and the floor's flooded. Did I knock the bucket over? No, here it is. Maybes the baby's messed on us, except my blouse is dry.

Oh God no, is it blood? Please sweet Jesus, don't let it be blood.

I remember now, the doctor pressed my belly that last time with our Emily. He said it was to make the afterbirth come out. Howay, pet, Mammy's got to put you down for a bit. There now, let's take off my blouse to wrap round you. And kneel up over the paper – dear sweet Jesus, there's so much blood! – and press down like he did, and again, like this and try not to think of the hot splashes that are spurting out each time. And again, and harder, and pray to God to save us.

The baby's sleeping, bless him. I must get this blood cleared up before the bairns get home – can't have them coming in to find the place like a slaughter-house. And Henry, he'll be beside himself if he finds me in this state.

I should call for help, but I'm so tired, and the room's so dark now. I'm shivering, I can't stop. Let's just lie down next to my little man for a while, and rest a bit, then I'll call someone. There, just close my eyes…

CHAPTER THIRTY-FIVE

2007

Ian's lying on his back, eyes open, staring up at the ceiling. His chest is heaving; tears are streaming unheeded down the sides of his face and into his ears, his hair. Mary sits on the pouffe and mops his face gently with a clean hanky quelling an impulse to smooth his wet curls with her fingers.

His hands are clenched by his sides in the effort to stop sobbing. She takes one and unfolds the tense fingers. It's so familiar, this hand: the broad palm and stubby fingers: a worker's hand. She turns it over, looks at the bitten nails, the skin around them gnawed and bloody; the freckles; the gold wedding ring – a new one, presumably; it wouldn't be something one would recycle. And the tangle of raised veins, like a tree's roots: those are new too. An ageing hand, like hers. How time passes. She presses the hanky into his palm and closes the fingers back around it.

'Sorry,' he says eventually, shaking it open and blowing his nose. 'I didn't realize I would be – I mean, for fuck's sake Mary, I was fucking *there*...'

'Don't try to get up yet.'

He wipes his eyes. 'All that *blood*,' he says brokenly. 'The smell of it, like a butcher's shop. You never think about that, do you? When you see it on telly. That it's sticky, what it smells like. That we're just fucking animals walking around on our hind legs.'

'There was a problem with the placenta,' she explains. 'So she kept on bleeding.'

'But the baby was OK, right?' He looks at her, almost pleading. 'I mean, he seemed OK when I – when *she*...' He breaks off, shaken by a fresh storm of sobbing. 'His wee pink monkey feet – God, he was so fucking *tiny*. I looked into his eyes, Mary.'

'I'm afraid the baby died too, a few weeks later.' She reaches for his hand again. 'And the little boy with the cough.'

'Not Ricky? But he was never that bad. I mean, he was always poorly, but I thought—'

'I'm sorry.'

He blows his nose again, then levers himself up until he's sitting on the edge of the sofa. 'That was Annie's mother, wasn't it?' he says.

'It would appear so, yes.'

'Dory. Her husband called her Dory.' He closes his eyes, apparently trying to recapture the fading scenes. 'They were all over her, you know. The little kids, Henry. She'd be mashing taties and he'd come up behind and sort of press up against her. Or she'd sit down for a cup of tea and Emily would squirm into her lap. Even Annie. Whenever the boat was out, she'd be there in the bed, come for a giggle and a chat. Then, after Sam died, crying for hours.

'Oh Jesus,' he says as the tears come again. 'She really loved Annie. When she disappeared, it was like—' His face distorts, crumpling and reddening in that agonized manner of all men's faces when they cry, as though the emotion must force itself out; which is presumably exactly what's happening, Mary supposes, given the strictures of masculinity. Was he like this thirty years ago, when she left?

'She loved them so much,' he's saying. 'That's what gets me. God, the woman was just overflowing with it. When they were all sitting round that wobbly table she'd feel so proud, looking at them all tucking in to the food she'd cooked. And she'd go round every night, you know, checking them all, tidying their arms and legs. Not because it needed doing, but because she just wanted to see them again.'

'Ben said she was a lovely lady.'

'She'd pour Henry a cup of tea and watch him stirring in his sugar. That's all. She just really liked watching him do that one thing. She thought his wrists were sexy – can you believe that? And she loved the fact he had to have exactly one and a half spoonfuls, no more and no less, and she could never get it right.

'But they had *nothing*. That old table, chairs, dresser, a few dishes. It's not until you're there that you realize how poor people were.'

'And presumably they were relatively well off, compared with most families in the Low Town,' Mary says.

'She knew she was dying, you know. With that much blood, it was obvious. But all she could think of was, how will Henry manage with the baby? Who'll comfort wee Emily if she wakes in the middle of the night? What if Annie comes back and I'm not here? They were like a shawl she couldn't bear to take off.'

'I've always thought that it takes a special gift to love well,' she remarks. He's more shaken than she'd expected by his hour inside the mind of a dying fishwife. It's been a long time since she's seen this more vulnerable side of him. She likes it, she realizes. She likes *him*.

He reaches for his jacket and Mary clicks off her tape recorder. 'I didn't get around to buying more wine, I'm afraid,' she says. 'I don't think there's any milk either. Would you like an espresso? Herbal tea?'

He pulls a face. 'Cigarette?'

Outside, it's chilly after the warmth of the room. The sun's gone and it's windy, spotting with rain. Mary arranges the blue towel on the bench and they light up, inhaling companionably.

'This reminds me of the time we met,' he says. 'Outside that awful New Year's party in Warwick Street, when I spilt wine on your dress.'

It was a long mauve-sprigged Laura Ashley garment, she remembers: typically demure – and totally unsuitable for the time of year. The stain never came out. 'You lent me your coat, I recall,' she says. 'A big creaky thing that smelt like the interior of my father's car, that combination of petrol, cigarette smoke and warm leather.' She smiles at him. 'I suspect that's what first attracted me to you.'

'There was I thinking it was my devilish good looks.'

'Not the coat, but you just standing there in your T-shirt as though it was the middle of summer, not even noticing the cold – when my hands were completely numb. It was the same quality that drew my attention to the red-haired boy on the surfboard. I was such a timid little thing, always shivering.'

'Isn't there some drug you can take for that? Your hands I mean?'

She stubs out her cigarette. 'Certain blood pressure medications are said to help by relaxing the blood vessels.'

'But you don't take them.'

'Apparently one can now buy special "Raynaud's gloves" that can be heated in a microwave oven, should one possess such a thing. Failing that, a doctor on the BBC suggests donning oven-gloves for rummaging in the refrigerator, and carrying a hot baked potato in each pocket whenever one leaves the house.'

He laughs his big open laugh, and a gust of his familiar smell engulfs her briefly: peppery, salty, warm. She used to wear his T-shirt to bed to keep his smell with her when he was away.

'I have an interesting selection of bobble hats for the winter,' she continues. 'But I can't quite bring myself to wear them at this time of year. I persuade myself that my hair will suffice.'

'I've always loved your hair,' he says. 'I'm glad you never cut it.'

She lights up again then offers him the packet. 'Of course smoking exacerbates the condition,' she says, exhaling and leaning back, enjoying the discomfort of the bench slats against her spine. The spots of rain on her face are curiously invigorating.

'Ben thinks the Raynaud's is because your hands and feet got so cold on the boat in a previous life. He's got it all worked out. He reckons you inherited your nicotine addiction from your fisherman too, and that your sea phobia is because he drowned.'

'Yes, he told me.'

'Is that what happens?' Ian asks. 'A sort of karmic Lamarckism?'

'I'd been telling him about the concept of karmic scarring,' she explains. 'That's the theory that very intense psychological and physical experiences can leave a scar, as it were, that persists from one incarnation to the next. Unusual birthmarks, for example, can often be traced to a past-life trauma on the same part of the body – you might like to investigate that hypothesis when you do your programme on stigmata,' she suggests. 'Anyway, it's thought that unusually powerful likes and dislikes may have a similar provenance – though the karmic connection is more obvious.'

'So if you can't kick the habit in one life, you have to try again in the next?'

'I'm not doing very well with this one, am I?' she says ruefully, examining the glowing tip of her cigarette.

They stare out at the river, at the terraces of South Shields on the opposite bank glowing in the setting sun. 'Did you notice Paul with those free mints by the till in the pub last night?' Mary asks. 'Every time he passed, he couldn't resist taking one, yet he manfully refrained from ordering a dessert. I'd be prepared to wager that he's on a diet. Then lo and behold, we discover the obese biscuit-eating Lord Jim: the epitome of everything Paul's now struggling to combat.'

Ian looks sceptical. 'That's a bit *post hoc*, isn't it?' he says. 'If you'd discovered Lord Jim was a beggar starving in the gutter, you could argue the exact opposite: that Paul's sweet tooth was caused by his hunger in a past life.'

Mary nods, acknowledging the point. 'That's the trouble with karma as an explanatory principle. You can adapt it to explain almost any outcome. It's the same problem Freud encountered with his analysis of dreams. It doesn't mean it's not relevant, but I usually prefer to focus on a post-traumatic stress approach instead.'

'OK. Remind me how that would work.'

'Well, when someone experiences a trauma – a violent attack, for example, or a sudden accident – the shock can sometimes be too great to be absorbed entirely by the conscious mind. So it recurs in flashbacks and nightmares, in hysterical symptoms, in phobias.'

'And you think that's carried over from one incarnation to another?'

'Yes. When you think about it, post-traumatic stress disorder is the epitome of "unfinished business".' She sits back, waiting for him to put two and two together. She doesn't have to wait long.

'My thing about blood!' he exclaims.

'What thing about blood?' she teases.

'You know exactly what I mean. I practically pass out if I nick myself shaving. So you think that's because of what happened to Dory?'

Mary shrugs. 'It's just a theory,' she says modestly, but she's gratified by how excited he seems. 'But between fifty and sixty percent of recalled past lives end in some kind of trauma, compared to around five percent of deaths generally.'

'I wonder if I can shoehorn that into the programme somehow,' he muses, grinding out his cigarette and reaching for another. Then: 'Damn! Why didn't I record that session on the DAT? But you've got it on tape, right? It'll be crap quality, but we can probably get round that—'

It's fascinating watching his brain work, but Mary's remembered something else about the session with Dory. 'Can we get back to Annie for a moment?' she asks. 'I'd like to focus on what her mother said about the night she disappeared.'

'God – yes! I'd forgotten about that. They were all out that evening, weren't they? Flo and the priapic Tom. And young Jimmy skulking off – what was that all about?'

'Perhaps he was out exploring his sexuality,' she suggests. 'Now we know how the rest of his life panned out, that would have to be a possibility. Or perhaps he was just wandering around feeling miserable. But it's also possible that he was with Annie.'

'No, our Jimmy would never hurt his little sister,' Ian blurts out, then laughs aloud. 'Jesus, just listen to me! That's Dory talking. But she was really worried about him, wasn't she?'

'I imagine there were some pretty unsavoury characters roaming around on the lookout for a pretty young boy. He could have been involved in all sorts of clandestine or dangerous situations.' Mary takes a last drag of her cigarette and buries the butt in the flower pot.

'Maybe he saw Annie with someone.'

'It's a shame we can't ask him,' says Mary, picturing Paul storming out earlier that afternoon, the disgust and anger on his face, and poor Ben dragged along behind. The boy had looked at her, stricken, obviously expecting her to intervene. She'll remember that look for a long time, the trust it conveyed – and the look of shock and hurt that followed when she did nothing.

Ian breaks into her thoughts. 'I hate thinking of Annie wandering those streets,' he says. 'You should have seen the place, Mimi. Fucking teeming with people, and half of them drunk or on the pull.' He shakes his head.

'Dory seemed to think she'd committed suicide.'

'Or gone off travelling with that kist thing. But I'm not sure anyone really believed that. It was too out of character.'

'So we're not really any further forward.'

'Are you kidding? Surely this is just the confirmation we need for your group souls hypothesis? If I was Dory, and Paul was Jimmy, who else could we match up? This could be dynamite, Mary – riveting telly. Plus it means we can carry on with the film without Ben. I'd call that a result, wouldn't you?'

Mary smiles; his enthusiasm is infectious. 'You seem to have recovered remarkably well from your upset earlier,' she observes drily.

He grins. 'I'll feel even better if you'd walk me back to the hotel.'

They set off, Ian hoisting his new bicycle effortlessly onto his shoulder by the crossbar to carry it down the stairs to the Fish Quay. Mary smiles: he wouldn't be able to lift her bicycle that easily.

'I've still got Belinda, you know,' she remarks as they reach the bottom, picturing her old bone-shaker, with its cracked leather saddle and crooked handlebars.

'What? That old dinosaur?'

When she lived with her parents it was kept in the old coal shed; she can still conjure the tickle of coal dust up her nose as she propped it against the wall. Later it accompanied her on the train up to Oxford. 'She's shackled in the yard,' she says. 'Though I can't imagine anyone wanting to steal her.'

He laughs and, before she can stop him, tugs her forwards and plants a swift kiss on her forehead. 'Oh, I do love you, Mimi!'

'Don't be ridiculous,' she says briskly, pushing him away and setting off quickly along the sea wall towards Tynemouth.

'Why won't you believe me?' he complains, catching her up.

'One, you're married,' she says. 'Two, you're the father of an indecent number of children. Three, you're *married*.'

'Doesn't stop me loving you, I'm afraid.'

'Well it should,' she says tartly. It seems bizarre that he has so little insight into his obsession with her, when it's obvious that piqued pride is the only reason he keeps bouncing back into her life.

They walk on in silence beside the dark water. Out towards the mouth of the river a little fishing boat is chugging in to port, skirting the line of light buoys down the centre of the channel. Mary shivers and pulls her shawl across her chest, wondering why on earth she's agreed to this absurd outing.

After a while, he says: 'I came across this crazy New-Age book about soulmates when I was doing my research for this film. About a man and woman who kept reincarnating together over the centuries.'

Mary knows the book he means. '*Only Love is Real* by Brian Weiss.' She snorts derisively. 'That's the sort of thing that gives my work a bad name.'

'Total schlock, I know. But it must be based on something, surely?'

'It has been suggested that the reason some pairs of souls meet repeatedly in successive incarnations,' she says, 'is to allow them to continue where they left off, as it were, and help one another make progress.'

'Like doing their homework together.'

'I can see that I may come to regret my course module analogy,' she says. 'But if such a phenomenon did exist, it would be just a particularly potent subset of the group souls idea.'

A burly young man towed by a wheezing bulldog overtakes them.

'Would Dory and Henry qualify, do you think?' Ian asks. 'How long would they have been married at that point? Twenty years? But he still made her go weak at the knees.'

'Perhaps,' Mary says guardedly. Where's he going with this? 'They were lucky to have found one another. Annie and Sam, too. Whether you believe in soulmates or not, I think it must be rather rare to encounter one's ideal partner at a time when you are both fertile and free. There must be so many near misses down the millennia, with people marrying the wrong person, or dying too early, or being born too late; the wrong age, or the wrong sex; in the wrong place at the wrong time.' She wonders sometimes how many near misses she's had over the years. Or if perhaps Peggy's unfortunate experiences with men have rendered her too prickly and cautious even to notice when an opportunity arises.

They're approaching the end of the sea wall, where the river starts to open out into the alarming agitated mass of the North Sea. Mary backs away from the railings with a shudder and sits down on a graffitied bench. There's a grassy headland between the mouth of the river and the ruins of the Priory. 'I think this must have been the hill Dory was talking about,' she says. 'Where she went searching for Annie after Sam died. Does it seem familiar?'

Ian props his bicycle against the railings and sits beside her. 'Sort of, I suppose. But everything looks so different with all this concrete. I mean, the grass used to come right down to the rocks where the sea wall is now, and there were great heaps of seaweed piled up on the bank to dry – for fuel, I suppose.' He pauses, looking back along the sea wall, then back at the hill and out to sea. 'There was a muddy track she walked along, just wide enough for a horse and cart. And a little path off it, leading uphill to a sort of gorsy area. The gorse has gone, but you're right. This must have been the place. All the courting couples used to come here.'

'Poor Annie,' sighs Mary. 'Imagine losing the love of your life just when you've vowed to be together for ever.'

She thinks of the young girl, chilled to the bone and exhausted, numb with grief, staring out to sea. And the mother, picking her way over the rocks with a blanket in her arms, and the two of them weeping and rocking together, waiting for the sun to rise.

'You remember earlier, when I suggested you might have been Annie's father?' Ian asks.

'And I pointed out that I could have been any one of the men on that boat – or none of them.'

'What if Dory and Henry really were soulmates?' Ian puts his hand on her shoulder and turns her to face him. 'Mimi, isn't it possible that we walked here together when we were courting, before Annie was born? That we loved each other over a hundred years ago?'

It's getting dark. He's leaning towards her. She can smell his breath; sweet and smoky. He smells the same as he did when they were students, when all he had to do was kiss the corner of her mouth and she would inhale his breath like a narcotic and let him tug her into the bedroom.

'Please,' she says weakly. 'This is silly.'

His lips touch hers and her mouth opens without her volition, letting his tongue in, which is as hot and insistent as he is. She feels an answering heat spreading through her, a sudden sharp ache in parts that have been quiescent for years. How long has it been since she's let a man get this close? For a wild moment she imagines herself sinking down in the wet grass behind them, and letting him pull up her skirt and damn the consequences. Then a visceral reluctance floods through her, a reluctance she recognizes, and she shoves him away.

'Let me go. This is ridiculous.'

'But we're supposed to be together,' he insists. 'Don't tell me you don't feel it too. Give me that woman's phone number. Let's get her up here to hypnotize you again.'

'No, Ian. Please, stop this.'

'We could find out about us.'

'There is no "us",' she says. 'What about what's-her-name, your wife? Christina. Women aren't like coats. You can't just put them on and take them off again when you feel like it.'

'I never took you off, Mimi.'

'But I'm not even your type,' she says helplessly. 'I was never your type. You needed someone sparky and curvy. Someone who went to the hairdresser and cooked decent meals. You'd have grown tired of me in no time.'

'Is that why you went?' he asks. 'Because you thought I was going to dump you?'

'It would never have worked.'

'But you loved me,' he insists. 'I know you did.'

She looks at his face, so full of energy and passion, and she feels something hard and cold and sad start to melt inside her. 'You're right,' she confesses with a rueful smile. 'I did love you. I was utterly crazy about you.'

'So why the *fuck* did you leave?'

Mary takes a deep breath. 'I was pregnant,' she says. 'And I had an abortion.'

'*What?*'

'There was no other option. We'd only known each other a few months. You were going off on that BBC training. We were too young. *I* was too young. It was impossible.'

'Why didn't you tell me?'

'What would you have done? Married me? Got a "proper" job? I couldn't make you do that.'

'I could have come with you to the clinic at least.'

She shrugs. 'Then you'd have carried the guilt too. What purpose would that have served?'

'Oh, Mimi.' He takes her hand and gently peels her glove off, then presses her bare palm to his lips. The tenderness of the gesture is nearly her undoing.

'There's more, I'm afraid,' she says, closing her throat on her tears. 'There were complications with the procedure. It made me unable to have children.'

'No—' He raises a stricken face to hers.

'That's why I left. I was distraught. I felt I was being punished. I felt I didn't have anything to offer you. So I thought if I went to India, you'd forget about me.' She smiles sadly. 'I was right, wasn't I?'

'No, Mimi. You couldn't be more wrong. There's never been anyone like you.'

'Then when I came back, everything was different. You were a rising star in the BBC, I was an aesthete training to be a Jungian analyst. It was hard, but I think it was probably the right decision.'

CHAPTER THIRTY-SIX

2007

Ian's offered to call her a taxi from the hotel, but Mary wants to walk back on her own. Adrenaline's surging in her veins, and God knows what else – oestrogen? oxytocin? testosterone? – whatever combination of hormones it is that gets what's crudely referred to as "the juices" flowing. All in all, she thinks it would be wise to take herself as far away from Ian as possible for the rest of the evening.

Striding back along the sea wall, she relives that one kiss and laughs aloud at its dramatic effect on her body – out of all proportion to the brief act itself. How very strange to discover her sexual apparatus is in working order after all these years of disuse. Strange and embarrassing. And disquieting. And wonderfully, outrageously, ridiculously exciting.

The sea air is cold on her face, her throat. She throws her head back and breathes in a huge exhilarating lungful. Is she going to have an affair? No – the idea's unthinkable. It would upset the entire edifice of her quiet life. But when he put her ungloved palm to his lips, it was one of the most shockingly erotic sensations she'd ever experienced. It's as though his kiss, his removal of her glove, his big-hearted forgiveness for what she did to him, to their unborn child, to their future, has opened a new chapter in her life.

Why did she never tell him before? She knows why. Because she couldn't bear his pity. He was so successful, so busy, so *fecund*, so apparently happy without her. When she was she so – what? So solitary, so studious, so old-fashioned. So barren.

It's started to spit with rain: sharp cold needles that sting her cheeks. She pulls her shawl across her chest and walks faster. Could Ian be right about them being soulmates? If so, why has she felt compelled to reject him over and over? What if she was indeed Annie's father once, and they had loved one another – deeply, hungrily, happily – as Henry and Dory, over a century ago? What would that mean for their relationship now?

What if there were indeed two fishermen in her past, as she's always suspected: one who owned a tobacco tin with the initials T.H. scratched on the side – and the other a respected skipper named Henry Milburn, whose wife gazed at him with desire as he stirred sugar into his tea?

Well, tomorrow she'll go to the library to see if she can find out.

Next morning finds her striding along the top bank, cardigan flapping in the wind. She put some bread in the toaster before she left, but forgot to eat it, so buys an old-fashioned iced bun from Gregg's and munches dutifully through it, waiting for the library to open.

Pete's upstairs as usual, tidying maps away. 'Lost your research assistants?' he asks.

'Ben's off somewhere with his father,' she explains. 'I've no idea where Laura is.'

He guides her through the now-familiar rigmarole of logging on to the Births, Marriages and Deaths website and keying in Henry's name and approximate date of birth, and his address in North Shields – and there he is, with his death registered in 1933.

So, poor Henry lived on for a further thirty-five years after his beloved Dory died. Mary wonders how they managed, that depleted little household: Henry, Jimmy and young Frank. Did things degenerate without Dory there to keep the range going and the clothes clean? How did Henry survive without her eyes following him, teasing him out of his dourness; without her arms opening to him in their narrow bed?

Pete breaks into her thoughts. 'Tell that BBC man I've found what he was looking for, will you? He's been in a few times – seems to have caught the bug off you lot.' Then: 'Was that all you wanted?'

'There's one other person I need to track down, if that's OK. A woman who rented a room above the Push and Pull Inn on Church Stairs. I'm not quite sure of her surname or her dates, so can we start with the 1941 census and work backwards or forwards from there?'

'Well we could, if there was a 1941 census. But the war rather put the kibosh on that sort of thing – but even if it hadn't, we couldn't look at it, because census data's not available to the general public until 100 years after it's collected.'

'Oh,' says Mary, rather crestfallen. 'So what can I do?'

'You'll have to look at the voting registers – they're on that stack over there. But that just gives the names of people eligible to vote at a particular address. If you want to find out about their children, you'll have to go back to the BMD website.'

Mary takes down the tome for 1941 and leafs through, searching for Church Stairs. There's the Push and Pull Inn, but no mention of a young woman named Margaret. Then she realizes: of course, Peggy wouldn't appear on the electoral roll until she was twenty-one, the age women got the vote in those days, so she'll have to look at a later volume and pray she's still at the same address. Working systematically forwards through the Forties, she eventually finds a Margaret Louise Simpson in 1945.

Armed with a full name and address, she goes back to the BMD website – and there she is again, Margaret Louise Simpson, born 1924, died 1956 at the age of thirty-two.

So Peggy was born nine years before Henry died – which means Henry couldn't possibly be one of Mary's past lives.

Mary wanders down the library stairs in a bit of a daze. So that's that. The link Ian was convinced must have existed between the two of them had never been there – at least not in the form he supposed. The revelation leaves her feeling oddly bereft, as though a cable that electrified a part of her life has been abruptly disconnected.

Damn.

With wry amusement, she realizes she'd rather liked the idea of having a soulmate. If she wasn't to find a proper partner in this life, at least let her have had one in a previous incarnation. Poor Peggy never found lasting love, that's for sure. One certainly couldn't count that brief liaison with Bobby's father, who breezed into her life for a few sweet weeks, then was gone before she could tell him she was pregnant. What was his name? Stuart something, some Scottish name. Would he have married her? She never found out. But the fact that he left without a backward glance, without even saying goodbye, made Peggy determined not to go after him.

There's one of those drinks machines in the library's foyer, that sells execrable brown liquids in various guises, with and without milk powder and sugar; along with ostensible chicken soup, from an adjacent spigot, which gives everything a slight stock-cube flavour. Mary presses the 'black coffee' button and takes a cup of muddy liquid outside.

What now? She lights a Gitanes and takes a gulp of scalding coffee. Or is it tea? She peers at the thin brown foam that's formed around the rim. Is it possible she's pressed the wrong button?

The sun sails out from behind a cloud and warms the top of her head. If her fisherman wasn't Henry, who was he? She closes her eyes and conjures the familiar image of the tobacco tin, scuffed and scratched, with a fisherman in a sou'wester on the lid. The initials are on the side, rusty brown lines scored into the turquoise paint: T.H. The lines are roughly scratched: by an impatient man, perhaps, or a clumsy one.

Then suddenly, out of the blue, comes another image: of wet cobbles and boots clumping unsteadily along them in the dark; of putting out a hand against a damp wall, of concentrating on lifting the feet, one by one.

He's drunk, she realizes, the person in the boots. The wall feels as though it's tipping. Now his footsteps sound hollow; there's wooden boards under his feet; they seem to be tipping too. There's a door ahead, a flicker of yellow light through the crack under it: a candle. He can hear a woman laughing: a high breathy giggle, a nervous placatory sort of sound. Who's she with? Why is she laughing like that?

He stumbles back against the wall and his tobacco tin's dislodged from his pocket and clatters down the wooden stairs.

The nervous giggling stops. They've heard him.

Now he's reaching up to the brim of his hat, where he keeps his filleting knife.

And then? Nothing.

Mary opens her eyes. Her heart's thudding. The outside of the library has that greenish underwater appearance things acquire when one has closed one's eyes in the sunshine. She takes a mouthful of coffee/tea. Was that a fragment of a past life, or a scene she's simply imagined? She can't tell, but she recognizes murderous rage when she feels it.

Taking out her notebook, she attempts to marshal her thoughts. Is it possible that her recurrent image of the tobacco tin is a screen memory she's conjured to conceal the memory of a traumatic confrontation with the woman behind the door? It certainly has all the hallmarks of that Freudian phenomenon: an innocent yet cinematically vivid image, which contains elements of the memory it 'screens'. In this case, the tobacco tin appears in both scenes, whereas the knife – which the image of the tin conceals – appears only by implication in the 'screening' image: as the clumsy, impatient scratches of the T.H. on the side of the tin.

A leaden lump settles in the pit of her stomach, making her feel rather nauseous. Oh dear, she thinks in dismay. T.H. Tom Hall. A knife. And she realizes, with a pang of dismay, that she'll have to read back through all her old tape transcripts to try and determine whether Tom Hall is a part of her prehistory.

Mary's storeroom is right at the top of the house: a dusty room with cracked plaster and bare floorboards, and panoramic views downriver to the sea and upriver to Gateshead and beyond. A heap of wood along one wall is destined for shelving; she had it delivered nearly a decade ago, but never got around to perusing the *Yellow Pages* for someone suitable to complete the job. Rolls of spare linoleum are stacked against another wall, along with the remains of that grey cord carpeting her estate agent gave her when he refurbished his office. The rest of the floor space is occupied by the usual detritus one inevitably accumulates if one stays in the same house for any length of time. There's a defunct television, for example, and the old aerial from the roof; two large buff-coloured computers of different vintages plus accompanying paraphernalia.

And boxes of box files, going back thirty years, crammed with yellowing notebooks, cassette tapes, and slippery sheaves of those old grey photocopies that left a bitter taste on the fingers when you handled them. The boxes are dated – at least she achieved that – but have been moved so often that they are now in a random configuration of dusty teetering heaps.

The date she's looking for is 1983: when she was living in Brighton after her Jungian training, practising as a clinical psychologist in the NHS and seeing private clients in the evenings. Along with the town's energetic criminal and homosexual subcultures, there was a thriving ashram, which had rekindled Mary's interest in Buddhism, that had been ignited during her brief sojourn in Tibet – and introduced her to Karleen, who was lecturing at the university at the time.

She'd noticed the small sturdy woman with her straight grey hair in meditation sessions, but they hadn't spoken until they'd encountered one another at the women's peace camp that materialized briefly on the Level that year, in support of the Greenham women's trial. It was Ash Wednesday, Mary recalls, with sub-zero temperatures, and her hands had gone numb inside her thermal gloves; so they'd abandoned the fight against patriarchy and had sneaked off guiltily to a wholefood café to discuss past life regression therapy. The rest, as they say, is history.

Kneeling on the bare boards, Mary finds one 1983 box almost immediately, but it's full of client records. Inevitably, the box she's after is one of the last she opens – but there, finally, are the tapes, transcripts and notes she took during her training with Karleen: her detailed hypnotically retrieved memories of Peggy's life – and some fragmentary flashes from the life of a fisherman with the initials T.H.

She's just begun leafing through the transcripts when she hears a voice at the bottom of the stairs.

'Howay! Anyone there?'

It's Mr Skipper. Now what on earth might he want?

'Coming!' she calls, bundling everything back into the box and hoisting it into her arms.

'Where's that Laura and the lad?' he asks suspiciously as she reaches the ground floor.

'No one's here except me,' she says, shouldering the consulting room door open and plumping the box on the floor beside her chair. 'It feels a bit strange, actually, to have my house back to myself for a while.'

She offers him a Gitanes and they go outside.

'What about that BBC man then?' he asks, settling down on the Coca Cola crate and taking out his Rizlas. 'Where's he?'

'At his hotel. I don't know when he's coming back.'

'He says he wants to film me. With you, like. In that room where you talk to people.'

She frowns; this is outrageous. 'I told him not to bother you.'

'It's no bother. He's going to buy them paintings he was looking at.'

'That doesn't mean you have to let him film you,' she says. How dare Ian set this up without consulting her? 'Don't take any notice of him. He can't film you unless you're willing.'

'Only last time I was in your talking room, it wasn't very clever.'

'No,' she says, remembering. 'You became rather upset.'

'So I thought maybes we could try it again first. If you're agreeable, like. You know, just you and me. See how it goes.'

She sighs with annoyance. 'There's really no need for this,' she says.

'I told him I would.' The papery end of his roll-up flares briefly as he lights it.

'But he shouldn't have asked you.' Just when she was starting to trust Ian, he does something crass like this.

'He said I'd be on the telly.'

'Do you *want* to be on the telly?' It's a stupid question. As Ian has so often pointed out, everyone wants to be on the telly. That's what makes his approach to Mr Skipper so unacceptable.

'He said loads of people will want to buy my paintings.'

She briefly considers making a complaint to the BBC, arguing that in her opinion the old man's not fit to be on television. But he seems so determined, and has obviously thought it through carefully. Looking closer, she sees that he's shaved, too, and had a bath – or at least washed his hair. With the grease gone and the nicotine stain faded, it's a rather lustrous creamy grey.

'I'm not sure about this,' she demurs. In place of his usual blue anorak and cap, he's wearing a saggy tweed jacket: from Oxfam presumably, or the back of an unfrequented wardrobe in wherever it is that he lives.

'You can wake me up if I start hollering,' he offers.

'But it took you hours to get over it last time. I thought we might have to call an ambulance.'

One of the past lives she'd unearthed was a woman who'd been killed in a bombing raid during the war – at least that was what it seemed like. She'd been sheltering in a factory when it took a direct hit and the carnage was appalling. It seemed like three of her daughters were killed too. But it was difficult to separate those memories from scenes from what appeared to be a violent abusive relationship with a man – or perhaps a series of abusive relationships. No wonder he'd been so distressed.

'I was all right in the end though, wasn't I?' he argues, reasonably enough. 'So no harm done.'

She smiles. 'No.' With his cap off, she spies what looks like a port wine stain birthmark on his forehead, on the left side under his hair. How odd that she's never noticed it before.

They've finished their cigarettes. It might be all right, she tell herself; if she asks him about Annie and tries to steer clear of his own past life traumas. She can always interrupt the session if he gets too upset. In fact it might be rather an interesting exercise to see if the date prompt she tried with Ian will work again. She wants to do it, she realizes. She wants to see if he knew Annie in a previous life too.

'Last time it was rather confusing and frightening,' she says. 'If you remember, you kept jumping from one memory to another and it was hard to work out what was happening.'

'Maybe that's because I was on the Stella,' he suggests. 'So I was probably a bit out of it.'

'That's possible, I suppose,' she says doubtfully.

'Well I've only had tea today, down the Mission.'

It's this last detail that sways her. He's planned this, even to the extent of foregoing his precious Stella. Mary feels herself relenting.

CHAPTER THIRTY-SEVEN

...Can you see the corridor? Good. Remember you can use your sign at any point if you want to stop. Now walk very slowly along the corridor and look at the doors. Each one opens on to a different year in your life. Try to find one that opens on to a time when you were young, can you do that? It's 1898, in the middle of the herring season, and the town's full of people. Have you opened a door? Good. What can you see?

1898

The luggers are in, and the capstans are winching off the full crans, chugging away and belching puffs of blue smoke. And all along the quayside bairns are leaning out with their didall nets for the herring that's dropping out of them.

Very good. Stay in that time. Now think carefully, do you know a girl called Annie Milburn?

Of course I know Annie! We're always linking in and nattering away. But then everyone knows Annie – she's always howaying and stopping for a blether, so she's always hurrying, with her shawl loose and trailing. Spuggie, we used to call her, for she was skinny as a bird when she was wee. I was worried she'd be a fat straw in a skirt for ever, but she's filling out canny now.

I'm stopping at her place for the season and I've a notion to help with her looks, to see can we find her a sweetheart – I feel bad walking out with my Tom when she's on her own.

It's our half day, and we're washing our hair in the scullery at her place. But the water's barely warm, for we've had to wait our turn behind the Scots lasses, and they've left suds all over the floor. Annie says don't fuss, and let's clear up after, but I want to mop up and make it nice before we start, and riddle the boiler, and hoy a bit extra coal on.

She's not as shy as me, and takes off her blouse no bother to bend over the basin. So I'm helping lift that great mass of curls she's got, that's full of fish scales and sawdust, and bundle it forwards and into the water. It wants to float, but we push it down so I can work in the soap. I shouldn't look, I know, but the water's splashing and making her cami stick to her, so her boobies are showing through, and it's a shock to see them, all shameless somehow with the teats standing up—

Now we're off on the monkey run and I'm that antsy to meet Tom, and see him looking at me in that bold way he's got – though I think maybes he's too bold sometimes, like he's a horse that wants to gallop and I've got the reins and I'm worried I won't be able to keep him from going where he wants.

It's sunny, but the breeze is fierce, rocking the boats at their moorings and making the masts creak. The lads have their caps pulled well down, to keep them on, but we can't fix our shawls and scarves so easy – and Annie looks like a gypsy with her scarf undone and curls flying all over. I'm trying to keep her nice, but she's not helping, and keeps laughing at the old nanas trying to hold their skirts down, and the wind puffing them up like black balloons.

There's Tom's now – outside the bakkie shop on Bell Street, leaning against the wall with a tab, and his eyes screwed up against the smoke. He's seen us, but he's not shifting; just watching us walk towards him, with our wild hair and flapping shawls, and grinning his cheeky grin. I'm starting to smile back when I see that it's Annie he's grinning at – and not just grinning neither. And I know that look, for it's been on me often enough, and it jolts me to see him looking at Annie in that way.

She's never noticed, of course, but just takes herself off so we can link in. But I'm quiet after – a bit jarred, I suppose, to see his eyes lingering on Annie like that. I can't think how that's happened, how she's got so bonny and I've never noticed.

I've been home to fetch my shiftenings, and Mam's said she'll be checking with Mrs Milburn what time I'm coming in – as if I'm more likely to get up to mischief after ten, when my Tom's a danger any time of the day!

Da knows him from the boat, and has already had a word with Mam about him. And she's had a word with *me*, though it's the same word she has every day of the week, seems like. That it's in a lad's nature to try, blah, blah, blah, so it's a lass's duty to stop him, and that's the only way to keep his respect. Why can't she see that if he loves me, he won't go off suddenly just because we've been all the way?

Anyway, I've told her I'm invited to his folk for tea Saturday, so she's backed off a bit, and says I can bring him for Sunday lunch if I like.

It's Da knowing him that's the problem – even though he's visited, all proper like, soon as I turned sixteen, to say we're walking out. But Tom says there's always rough talk about lasses on the boat, so Da will have heard him going on, and taken it the wrong way, even though it means nowt.

Oh – so that's it. Tom's just got off me and it's done.

I thought there'd be more stages, a longer walk, like, before the end of the pier. Then suddenly my skirt and pettie's rucked up and here's my bare knees, all white and indecent. And Tom pumping away like a mongrel between them, with his nana's statue of the Lord Jesus looking down from the mantle.

Now here's a knock on the door and his nana's calling out, do we want some cocoa? And Tom's calling back, thanks Nana, that'd be champion, and we'll come through in a minute, buttoning his kecks as if butter wouldn't melt. And I'm feeling all sticky and smeary and want to run to the scullery and have a wash, for I'm thinking it'll be safer, maybes, if I swill it out, and—

It's splashed on my skirt. Oh sweet Jesus – how can there be so much?

What if she notices? What if there's a trail of slime I've missed on my skirt, and the lamp catches on the glisten? Has he left a mark where he was biting my neck? I pull my hair forwards just in case, and button my blouse, then look in the mirror.

I look just the same as before – that's the shocking thing. Not spoiled nor brassy nor anything. And I'm glad, and thinking that's me promised, and he'll be mad for me now – and never look at Annie Milburn again.

You forget how soft a body is, then you see a girder falling, and a body folding the way no body should fold, then breaking open like a red egg.

* * *

The siren's gone off and they've lit the smokescreen, so we're all running to the shelter, coughing and pulling on our masks. Mr Wilkinson's unlocked the door himself, bless him, with little Billy handing out lamps and matches. And the lasses crowding in, with the bairns all het up, bundled in their blankets.

Now here come the bombs, thuds you can feel in your chest, and we're all crouched on our mattresses, trying to guess how far, and are they coming this way, and how soon, like Tom clomping down the hall all them years ago.

Oh! Here's a bang, loud as a fist whacking against my ear, and over there, where primus was, it's just bricks and girders and the air thick with dust. And wires hanging, and broken planks, and glass crunching under my feet.

Now what's this? A roar above my head, the rattle of bottles, and something sliding. So I'm looking up and the boards are splintering and girders popping out the walls like ginger-beer corks. The whole factory's collapsing, slowly, slowly, crumpling like newspaper, creaking and groaning and buckling.

Ah! Something's hit me on the side of the head, hard as a wooden ball at a coconut shy. I reach my hand up to my hairnet, and it's a mash of hair and bone and hot blood. And I want to shout, but my voice is locked up, somehow, like in a dream when the sound won't come out—

Hello Flo? Flo? Calm down, now. Listen to me for a moment. Now you're going to leave this room, OK? Can you see a door behind you? Good girl. Now I want you to turn around slowly, and walk back though that door into the corridor. Have you done that? Good. You're safe now. So let's stay here a while, shall we? Breathe slowly, good.

Now, when you're ready, let's walk back along the corridor. There's another door there with the date 1898 on it. Can you see it? Can you see the handle? Good, now I want you to turn the handle and see what's inside.

I'm at Tom's place, helping his nana set the table for tea. And I'm looking round, and thinking how I'll change this room when we're married, to make it more homely: set them plates out nice on the sideboard, maybes, and crochet a runner for the mantle.

Mr Hall's here this time, smoking his pipe, and he never puts it down once! Even with a guest at the table and a dish of fried liver in front of him – lucky Mam's not here to see it. He's needing the barber and I think he's had a bevvy, for I can smell something and his cheeks are canny red. They say he's a mean drunk, and used to wallop the bairns, but he seems tame enough to me, blethering away jolly as you like about the Klondyking, and how the big lads are raking it in.

The door to the parlour's closed, so I'm thinking maybes I shouldn't let Tom do it again till we're wed, because I'm more than a week past my time and starting to fret about falling pregnant. And the fretting's got my innards in a twist, all of a sudden, so I can hardly look at the liver.

Now we're finished and I'm saying to Tom, let's take a walk along the top bank. And his face is tripping him, for he's wanting to go in the parlour, isn't he? But I'd feel queer doing it with Mr Hall in the next room, even if we didn't go all the way. It was bad enough with his nana there that time.

'I'd have locked the door, daftie,' says Tom later, linking in. And I say, that's as maybe, but I'd still feel queer. So he says, let's go to the hill then, and I say fine, but we'll have to watch we don't trip over Annie and her lad.

And I feel his arm stiffening in mine and he says, sharp like, 'What do you mean?' So I say, 'Nowt, I was only joking.' But it's too late; I've let it slip. So now he's stopping and facing me, so folk are having to dodge round us in the lane.

'Who's she with?' he asks. 'Just some deckie,' I say. So he says, 'What deckie?' and I say I promised not to tell, and why's he so interested anyway? Is he jealous?

And he laughs and says of course not, he's just curious. But I know he's lying, and there's a qualmy feeling in my belly, that's maybes a baby catching hold or maybes the shock of seeing how he is about Annie having a lad.

So I blurt out that it's that new lad on the boat, that *Wellesley* lad. And I'm thinking – oh, I don't know what I'm thinking. To make mischief for Annie with her da. To make Tom leave off looking at her because she's taken.

Can you make a bad thing happen just by wishing it? There was I wishing Annie wasn't so bonny – and now her Sam's gone and drowned and she's like a wooden doll, that sits stiff and quiet till she's told to tie on her bindings for work, or swill her oilies, or rinse her smalls and pin them out to dry.

It's one of them foggy evenings, when we can't see across the river, and our clothes are damp and our skin cold and clammy. I've been to Tom's place for tea and he's just walked me back, and come in for a cup of cocoa and a bit blether with Mrs Milburn.

And I've been to the nettie again, and pressed my belly, in the hopes of bringing something on. And I was wishing Annie were here to talk to, then remembering she's in no fit state to talk to about anything, so if there is a baby it's Tom I've to talk to about it.

I'm only half listening when Mrs Milburn says she's sent Annie off on an errand. But suddenly Tom's getting up and flicking his tab on the fire, and saying that's reminded him he's forgotten to padlock the hatch on the boat, and he'll do it now. And he's off out the door, just like that – not even stopping to finish his cocoa.

So we're left sitting, Mrs Milburn and me, staring at the closed door. And she gets out her darning and rests her feet on a stool. But I can't settle. The way he's rushed off has got me antsy, thinking he's maybes gone looking for Annie, to walk her home safe. And a shudder's gone through me at the thought that he's wanting to start on with her instead of me – because she's on her own again, isn't she, now Sam's passed? So I catch up my shawl and tell Mrs Milburn I'm going after him.

The fog's so thick, I can't see him at first, and stand breathing the clammy air, looking all round – then I spot him, under a lamp post at the bottom of the stairs rolling a tab. So I hang back a bit, then when he's struck his match and set off again, I follow him.

He's headed to the quayside, where the luggers are moored so close you couldn't pass a piece of paper between them, and three, four deep, so you could walk halfway to South Shields without getting your feet wet. Not that you can see that far, just hear the rigging thrumming and dripping in the mist.

Now he's stopped and pulled a bunch of keys from his pocket and's heaving on the warp of a boat and climbing aboard. It's the *Osprey* – what other boat would it be? And I chide myself being such a daftie, for it seems all he's doing is locking the hatch after all.

So now I'm thinking I'll climb on board too and surprise him, and we can have a bit cuddle in the fo'c'sle. And maybes then I'll let on about the baby. For it's been weeks now since I was due, so it's time we got things settled and told our folks and set a date for the wedding.

But what's this? Here's a brand new kist by the mooring post – what's that doing here? So I'm guessing he must be meeting some brassy Scots lass on the boat, and that's why he was in such a hurry. Sure enough, here he comes jumping onto the quayside, and hoists the kist on his shoulder and hoys it aboard.

I'm feeling fair qualmy now, and shivering, with the shock of it I suppose. For wasn't he sitting with me at his Da's table less than an hour ago? So I'm drawing nearer, wanting and not wanting to hear what they're about – except it's obvious, isn't it? For why else would a lass be alone with a lad on a boat on a foggy night?

I can hear their voices now. And the qualmy feeling's getting worse, for that's a lass's voice I'm hearing – though I can't hear what she's saying. And Tom's laughing, teasing like; laughing like it's the most natural thing in the world. So now I'm half crying and half retching at the same time, and thinking I'm going to throw up, so I find a heap of crans to hide behind.

It's splashed on my skirt. How can there be so much?

See, he was laughing, like he did with me, like it was the most natural thing in the world. That's what got to me.

I can't go home like this – Mrs Milburn's bound to notice. Is there a pail somewhere? I need a pail, and a cloth, and water to rinse it out.

I feel like screaming, but my voice is locked up, somehow, like in a dream when the sound won't come—

Flo? Can you hear me? It's all right. Just breathe slowly, in and out, in and out. Good. Concentrate on your breathing. Now let's go forward a bit. Look around you. What's happening now?

They say you should be careful what you wish for. So here's the fiddle band's playing and the old folk sitting round the wall, nodding and clapping away. Now Da's leading me into the middle of the floor to start the dancing off, and he's whisking me round so my skirt billows out, and all my new lace petties, like the dress of a princess. And I feel like crying, for this should be the best day of my life – but how can it be after what's happened with Annie?

The room's rushing past, all smiles and clapping hands and roses and dahlias – all the pale colours, pink and yellow and white, for I couldn't bear the look of them red roses and threw them out, which made Mam's mouth go all small. So now I'm thinking how her mouth will be when I tell her about the baby, and she adds up the months. But she'll not be able to say a word, will she? For I'll be married.

I'm looking round for Tom, for it's him that should be dancing with me really, so folk can see us smiling together on our wedding day and never think there's owt wrong.

There he is, over by the barrel with his mates, filling up. I wish he'd look up and see me whirling round with my hair loose and my cheeks rosy, and love me again, and be like we were before, and forget about Annie.

But it's his da who butts in next, and breathes whisky on me, and is so blattered he can hardly dance at all. But I can't refuse him, can I? For we're related now. So I try to smile and be nice, as he lumbers around leaning on me. Maybes he'll be different when I'm settled in at their place, keeping things nice. And folks'll say, that lass has made all the difference to that rough family.

Freddie Fenwick butts in next, and teases me saying he's gutted that I'm taken now. So I tease back, though my heart's not in it, saying there's scores of lasses here who'd be happy to have him, and he's saying but none's half so bonny, and I'm saying don't be daft—

Now here's Tom at last, and he's shoving Fred a bit, saying 'get your hands off my wife', joking like. And I'm glad, for it's him I want to be with – except he's dragging me over to the door, laughing and making a big show of 'having a word with the missus in private', as though we're off canoodling. But his hand's that hard on my arm, and his fingers digging in, so I nearly cry out, and trip over my petties, and try to slow him down.

Outside it's chilly and rain's spitting down. I'm looking up, thinking he's wanting a kiss, but oh! He's slapped me instead – a sharp blow to the side of my head, that fair breaks my neck with the force of it, 'for behaving like a slut'.

I stare at him – this lad who's just promised to love and to cherish – and for a moment I hardly recognize the face that's staring back. For there's no love in it at all, just a sort of disgust, like he's stepped in something minging in the lane.

It's the beer's got to him, probably, and the worry of these past weeks, and the baby coming and all. So though my head's ringing with pain, I take a breath and force a smile instead, and say howay, pet, let's go back in for they'll be missing us.

Then what's this? A hot trickle from my nose, that I dab at and find my hanky's bright with blood, which makes me qualmy for a moment, so I lean against the wall. And I'm thinking, where can I rinse it out, for it's a good lace hanky, brought new for the wedding, but I can't let folk see the blood or they'll know something's amiss—

* * *

When he hits me, it's like when a coconut's whacked by a wooden ball at the fair, and one falls and the other bounces away, and neither one cracks. Every time it happens, it takes me back to that first time, when I'm looking as bonny as I ever will, in the dress of a princess, with folk clapping and smiling.

Then he drags me away to knock some sense into me – that's what he always calls it, 'knocking some sense into you' – saying he could have had any lass in Shields, and he's never loved me, and I've trapped him, and I deserve everything I get.

Some mornings I can hardly bear to look, but just pull on my clothes quick as I can, then tie my hair back and wash my face. Then check in the mirror to see if anything shows, and fix my scarf and hair so it doesn't.

He's canny with his fists, for all that he's half stotting when he hits me. He knows folk'll talk if they see any bruises. The bairns know, though – Kath and Winnie anyway, though I try to hide it from the littluns – and the big lasses help by keeping the littluns out of his road. So we're all hiding and lying, and never at peace except when he's off on a voyage.

I'm in the nettie, staring at that splintered hole where he kicked the door in last winter, and broke the lock, then fixed a new bolt but never patched the place where he kicked it. And I'm sitting and sitting, and the blood just keeps coming, so I know I'm losing this baby. Which is just as well, I suppose.

How long have I been here – two hours, three? The littluns came knocking but I sent them away to use the pail instead. Now here's Kath, my brave lass, knocking again, gentle like, asking should she send for the doctor. But I can't have the doctor here, for he'd see the bruises.

So I say, howay, pet, it's just a belly-ache, and not to worry, I'll be right as rain soon, and can she bring more paper, and a pail of water and a cloth, for there's blood all down my skirt and I need to wet it before it sets.

If you get water on a blood stain before it dries, it will always come out. All those days running to the nettie before we were married – and pressing my belly and praying for blood on the paper. They say you should be careful what you wish for.

CHAPTER THIRTY-EIGHT

2007

Next morning there's still no sign of Ben. Paul puts his ear to the door, but there's no sound. But at least he's eating – he's checked and the foil containers from the Indian are in the bin, and there's a dirty spoon and fork in the dishwasher. While he was at it, he checked the knife rack too, then told himself off for being so daft.

He bangs on the door with the flat of his hand. 'Oy! Sleepy head! Fancy going out later? Maybe go to the travel agents, see if there's any last-minute offers – what do you think?'

Nothing. He tries the handle, but it's locked of course.

'I'm making a cup of tea if you fancy one,' he says, wondering how long the lad's going to keep this up.

He wanders through to the kitchen and fills the kettle. If he doesn't bring the lad any food, he'll have to come out. Then maybes they can go down the Mission for breakfast and have a bit of a natter and that will get them back on a more even keel.

The buzzer for the door goes just as he's settling on the sofa with a cup of tea and reaching for the remote. It'll be the postie, he guesses, buzzing whoever it is in and hearing the lift trundling down to the ground floor. He leaves the door open and goes back to turn the telly on.

'Hello! Anyone home?' A woman's voice at the door.

Paul turns round in surprise. But it's not a woman's voice. It's that Laura creature. What the *fuck* is she – he, *it.* What the fuck is *it* doing here?

'You're not seeing Ben, if that's what you're after,' he says.

'Actually it was you I wanted to see.'

'Well I don't want to see you, so you can just turn round and fuck off back where you came from. You're lucky I don't report you to the police – for corrupting a minor. In fact why don't I just do that right now?'

He opens the drawer and takes out the *Yellow Pages* and that DNA letter's right there, underneath, grinning up at him.

'Don't be daft,' Laura says. 'There's no need for that. I'm not stopping long.'

'Too right.'

'This isn't about the film, by the way.'

'I don't care what it's about.'

'It's about Ben's therapy.'

Paul snorts. 'Funny sort of therapy, hypnotizing people and putting weird ideas in their heads.'

'Ben needs help, whether you like it or not.' Laura comes right into the room and sits down on the sofa. 'How's he coping?'

Paul stands by the door, glaring at her. 'Coping with what?'

'With you kicking away all his supports, of course. Banning him from seeing his therapist slap bang in the middle of the healing process.'

Healing process my arse, Paul thinks. Stirring up process more like. 'He'll be fine,' he says. 'I'll take him on holiday and he'll forget all about it.'

She leans back and crosses her legs; she's got ankle boots and shocking pink tights on for fuck's sake. 'Wanting a sex change isn't something you can just switch off, Paul. I tried for years – even got married to a lass. But it was hopeless. "I yam what I yam," as Popeye used to say.'

'Well Ben's not like you, thank God.'

'How do you know? Have you asked him? Have you ever sat down with him and actually asked how he feels about being a lad?' Paul crosses his arms and stares her down. If she's expecting an answer, she's not getting one. She sighs. 'Children have been known to top themselves when they've been refused the operation, did you know that?

'Yeah. The doc threatened me with that when she convinced me to go along with her so-called therapy in the first place. I should probably report her too, for blackmail or something. Threatening behaviour.'

'Well,' she says, getting up. 'I've said my piece so I'll be off. You mind you look after that lad of yours.'

After he's closed the door – well, there's no way he can just sit calmly watching the telly waiting for Ben to show his face. So he grabs his jacket and heads down the Fish Quay for breakfast.

* * *

Them marine biology students are in the Seamen's Mission when he goes in, sat by themselves eating beans on toast, for fuck's sake. Must be vegetarian, something pansy like that. Macrobiotic.

Seeing them reminds him about dropping in on that Dove Marine Laboratory to find out what's going on with the flatties. All that business with the filming's put it right out of his head. So when he's finished his fry up, he drives out along the coast road to Cullercoats.

The Dove place is an old red-brick building, like an old-fashioned school-house, nestled under the cliff just above the beach; weird little building, been there for yonks. He presses an entryphone thingie and says he's come about the research on the flat fish. Inside, once he's buzzed in, a studenty-looking lass in jeans appears at the top of a wooden staircase and clatters down to meet him.

'Have you got an appointment?' she asks, all smiles and big teeth.

'I'm a skipper from Shields harbour,' says Paul brusquely – because there's no way he's going along with any appointment crap. 'I want to know what this research is all about.'

Her smile fades and you can see her shifting gears. 'I'll see if Dr Markham can see you,' she says stiffly. 'Only she's a bit busy at the moment.'

She's expecting him to stay down in the hall, like a good doggie, but he follows her up the stairs to a lab room kitted out in white melamine. An old biddy in a white coat is sorting through a cool box full of plaice, sluicing them down in the sink then laying them out, overlapping, on the draining board like plates.

'So what's happening with them plaice?' Paul asks when she looks up. 'That's my livelihood you're poking into.'

Credit where it's due: once she's found out who he is, she's very civil; shakes his hand, offers him a seat, sends toothy off to make him a cuppa. Then she talks him through what she's doing – which is basically looking at the bollocks of male flatfish to see if they're turning into females.

She cuts one open to show him: decent male plaice, good colour, nice and plump. 'These are the testes,' she says, spreading out the contents of the gut cavity and separating out a pair of palish pink blobs. 'See how swollen and lumpy they are? They should be elongated and smooth, a quarter that size. It's one manifestation of a process called "feminization",' she explains. 'When we examine the blood of these creatures, we find traces of a substance known as vitellogenin, which is a yolk protein that's normally only found in female fish.'

Paul suppresses a shudder. 'So what's causing it?' he asks.

'People used to blame the contraceptive pill – women excrete the oestrogens and they end up in the sea. But we now know that pollution from paint and plastics manufacture is far more damaging. You probably remember when TBT was banned a few years ago – that was why.'

Paul nods. TBT was the paint they used to keep barnacles off the hull. Bloody brilliant stuff. He and the lads stockpiled it for months when they heard it was going to be banned.

'This feminization,' he says, 'does it stop the fish breeding?' He's staring at the pink blobs and even he can see they're not right.

'They still produce some milt, but we're seeing a lot of abnormal sperm – as you might expect – with huge misshapen heads, two tails instead of one, that sort of thing. And cell growth around the tails that prevents them swimming.'

Which freaks Paul out a bit, actually. Because he's heard the odd rumour on the news, but this is a bit too close to home. Is it the stuff they've been painting on the boats that's caused the problem with his sperm?

When Paul gets back to the flat, there's still no sign of Ben, but his wetsuit's gone from the spare room, so it looks like he's gone for a swim. More of that freediving nonsense, most likely. But he can't get into much trouble just holding his breath, can he? It's not like being twenty metres down with a tank and your air line getting blocked.

He changes into his tracksuit, thinking he might go for a jog to clear his head, but after that breakfast he's not sure he can face it. Might be better to sort out a proper exercise routine, he thinks, lacing up his trainers: every morning first thing, maybe, whenever he's not on the boat. Start like you mean to go on.

Truth is, that plaice business is really getting to him – like it's a curse or a punishment or something. Least that's what the old lads down the Mission would say. Though what it's a punishment for, he's no idea. But that's typical of some of the old blokes. Now they're out of it, it's easy to myther on about what everyone else is up to.

God, the fuss they made when the twin-rigs started coming in! Well they were right, in a way, considering what happened with the prawn grounds last year – those Scots and Irish twin-riggers hammered them to death. Still, the old lads are stuck in the Dark Ages, with all their superstitions. Can't set off if a woman says goodbye; can't carry your boots with the toes pointing up; can't wear anything green. It's a wonder they ever got to sea at all. Can't even mention the word 'pig', for fuck's sake. What's that about?

Still, when you look at those plaice with their weird innards, it gives you the fucking heebie-jeebies.

CHAPTER THIRTY-NINE

2007

Mary lies in bed. She doesn't often lie in bed in the morning; she's one of those people whose eyes pop open as if the lids are fixed to a spring, already seeking out the window to see what the weather has in store. But this morning she's rather achy, with that peppery feeling at the back of the throat that presages a cold. Damn.

She rolls over and hunches the duvet around her shoulders. Caffeine, nicotine, Lemsip, in that order, she prescribes for herself. Slice of wholemeal toast, maybe.

Then telephone Ian to tell him about her fascinating session with Mr Skipper. Except she doesn't have his number; he's always been the one to contact her. In fact it's rather odd that she didn't hear from him yesterday, considering he's been practically camping in her consulting room for the past week.

She could telephone the hotel, she supposes, and ask to speak to him. Or leave a message. Saying what? 'Please call Mary'? It just seems rather undignified. She's never called him before and she doesn't see why she should start now.

Damn. She smiles ruefully. Is this what a single kiss has reduced her to? Waiting powerless by a silent telephone for some man to call? Surely this can't be why she's a bit under the weather?

Going down the stairs, she's aware of something else nagging at the back of her mind. And there, just inside the open door to her consulting room, is that box of old tapes and transcripts she dumped there yesterday. Aha, she thinks, as the penny drops. So that's why she's woken with a cold. It's because she doesn't want to open that box and investigate the evidence it may contain about the identity of T.H. Double damn.

She measures out coffee for a double espresso and switches on the Gaggia.

Mary is of the opinion that disease rarely strikes at random in the developed world; it is usually invited in, as it were, by a body whose immune system has been weakened by stress or depression or – in this case – by a reluctance to perform a potentially upsetting task.

The rattle of the letterbox signals the arrival of the postperson – she uses the politically correct term with affectionate irony, even in her thoughts – and she wanders back out into the hall, to find a single hand-addressed envelope lying on the mat. Feeling in her pocket for her Gitanes, she unlocks the front door and takes the letter outside to her bench.

It's from an old client, someone she worked with quite intensively shortly after moving to North Shields. He'd been impotent, she recalls, and afraid of the dark, conditions she'd traced to a previous incarnation as a young girl who had been abused nightly by an uncle who'd moved into the family home when her father died. Lighting up and taking her first delicious drag of the day, she reads:

Dear Dr Charlton,

I have been meaning to write for ages to express my gratitude for the help you gave me all those years ago. I've been a different man, and it's all thanks to you. You might be interested to know that I did ask that lady out eventually, and we were married six months later! The reason I'm writing now is to tell you that a nice girl from the BBC got in touch this morning, to tell me about the film they are making about you. I gave her as much information as I could, including some research I did a few years back trying to trace little Helen's details. I meant to contact you then, but it slipped my mind. I can't tell you what a thrill it was to find her family in 1930, living above that butcher's shop in Hexham, exactly where I remembered! The BBC girl couldn't say when they would be showing the film, so I'll have to make sure to look out for it. I am so glad your work is at last getting the recognition it deserves.

Yours sincerely,

Geoffrey Johnstone

Mary rereads the letter, then folds it and slides it back in its envelope. She sucks strongly on her cigarette and exhales, sucks in and exhales, four times in quick succession, until she fancies she can actually feel the nicotine fizzing in her blood. She always chain-smokes her first two Gitanes of the day; she needs the double dose to top up the drug to its usual circulating level and combat her night-time withdrawal. Three minutes later, having stubbed out the second, she leans back to consider the implications of the letter.

What does Ian think he's playing at, contacting her past clients without her permission? He only had to mention it and she'd have written to Mr Johnstone herself. Typical Ian, she thinks crossly: too gung-ho to bother with the niceties; too impatient to wait for – what is it they call it? – snail mail.

She comes inside and heaves the *Yellow Pages* onto the hall table, fully intending to call the hotel and give him a piece of her mind, but she stops herself mid-dial – calm down, Mary – and telephones Laura's mobile instead.

'*Bongiorno* ducky!' trills her friend's voice in her ear. 'I'm just turning into Beacon Street on my way to see you.'

'Are you? How perfectly delightful.' Mary feels her eyes prick with tears. A dose of Laura is exactly what she needs. 'Shall I put the kettle on, or would you like a latte?'

'Have you got any milk?'

'Damn. I am sorry—'

'Just as well I've brought some with me then, isn't it? And some fresh bread, so break out the Lurpak, lassie.'

Mary walks out into the street to watch Laura clip-clopping towards her in mauve culottes and high-heeled ankle boots.

'I've just been round to see that Paul,' Laura reports once they're settled at the kitchen table with butter melting into hunks of warm bread. 'I tried to reason with him, but he's still spitting feathers.'

'Was Ben there?'

'No sign, but Paul seemed to think he was OK.'

Mary sighs. 'What a mess. I'll go round myself in a few days.'

'So?' Laura fixes her with a scurrilous smile. 'Fill me in. What's happening with Ian?'

'He seems to think he can go on with the film without Ben,' says Mary, deliberately misunderstanding her. 'He's become quite excited about that group souls theory we were talking about. Having discovered that Lord Jim was Annie's brother Jimmy—'

'*What*?'

Mary laughs at the expression of total amazement that comes over her friend's face. 'I was forgetting you weren't around when we worked that out. The dates matched, and the – er – homosexual leanings.'

'Homosexual fallings over and rolling around in it, more like, in the case of Lord Jim.' Laura unscrews a miniature jar of blackcurrant jam Mary recycled from the last conference she attended and spreads it on her bread.

'Anyway, that appeared to support a group souls approach, so Ian then persuaded me to regress him.'

'Why am I not surprised?'

'And he turned out to be – you'll love this, Laura – he turned out to be Annie's mother.'

'Holy Mary Magdalena, as the lovely Lord Jim would have said. What did he make of that?'

Mary takes a bracing sip of her coffee. 'It was quite upsetting for him actually. She ended up dying in childbirth, on her own. It was awful.'

'And there was I thinking I was having all the fun.' Laura clicks two sweeteners into her latte and agitates the liquid with her spoon. 'Have I missed anything else?'

'Then yesterday Mr Skipper asked me to regress him again.'

'But I thought, after that other time—'

'I know, I know. But he was so insistent, I hadn't the heart to refuse. And I was incredibly careful to take him into a shallower trance whenever I thought he was getting too upset. It was a rather interesting process actually, trying to keep him focussed on memories of Annie. I might write it up later.'

'So he knew Annie too, is that what you're saying?'

'Remember all those traumatic experiences from that other session we had, years ago? Well, it turns out they were from the latter years of Flo's life, when she was married to Tom.'

'Old Skip used to be the lovely Flo? There's a turn up for the sailor's trousers, and no flies. It's like a cast list from a play. So who's left to match up?'

'Well assuming there's any validity whatsoever in this group souls idea, there are still three significant characters in 1898 that we haven't matched up with their 2007 incarnations. Annie's father, Henry; her boyfriend, Sam – and the priapic young man who looks increasingly likely to be her murderer.'

'Tom.'

'It seems Flo followed him the night Annie disappeared and overheard him with a woman. His relationship with her seemed to go downhill after that.'

'He married her, though. Wasn't that what you said?'

'She was pregnant, so he had no option. And I suppose it gave her a motive to keep quiet about what he might have been doing that night.' Mary's musing aloud, but it makes sense. Flo was pregnant and besotted with Tom; she was clearly desperate to get married.

'What, marry me or I'll tell everyone what you did to Annie?'

'It was hard to get a clear picture – despite my interventions it was still a pretty fragmented account. But that would seem a reasonable hypothesis.' Mary rips off a crust and dips it in a tiny jar of clear honey. 'He gave her a terrible time once they were married, though. Terrorized the entire family.'

Laura's animated face subsides suddenly, like a balloon when the air's been let out. 'That was my Tom, wasn't it?' she says. 'Tom the rapist and wife beater. Tom the all-round total utter bastard. He killed Annie too, didn't he?' She pushes her plate away as if the very sight of it makes her feel nauseous. 'That's why I've been getting them nightmares again. It's him come back to haunt me.'

Mary puts a gloved hand on her friend's arm. 'I know it might look like that, but please don't jump to conclusions quite yet. You remember how many Toms I found when we were doing that research in the library. Even Sam's father was called Tom. There could have been any number of wife-beaters in that little lot.'

'But what about your group souls thing? If we were all there in 1898, one of us has got to be Tom.' Laura fishes a pack of Nicorettes out of her bag and presses a little square of gum out of its foil compartment. Her hands are shaking.

'I agree that is a possibility. But don't you think something as serious as a murder would have come up in one of your sessions with me?'

'Maybe I was avoiding it – like Ben.'

'But there was absolutely no indication in our sessions that you were avoiding anything – and why would you remember all the other violent things he did and omit that one significant act?'

'Sweet Mary Magdalena,' says Laura, chewing furiously. 'What will Ben do when he finds out? I was his pal—'

'Laura!' Mary slaps her hand on the table. 'Just listen for a moment, will you? I think it could very well be me who murdered Annie in a previous life.'

At last, she's got her friend's attention. 'You know those flashbacks I told you about?' she asks. 'Well, do you remember me telling you about a tobacco tin with some initials scratched on the side? Well, the initials were T.H., Tom's initials. Then yesterday I got another flashback, involving a knife.'

Laura stops chewing and stares at her. 'You saw a knife?'

'Yes. It was most disquieting.'

'I never saw a knife, did I? My Tom always used his fists.'

'That's certainly what I recall of our sessions.'

'Hard to kill a lass with your fists.'

'Yes.' Mary sighs. She's dying for a cigarette. 'I've just looked out my old training notes to see if there's anything from my original regression sessions that will cast a light on what happened.'

Laura laughs suddenly. 'It's lucky you can't hypnotize yourself, isn't it? How would that look on telly? The therapist who murdered her own client.'

'Oh God!' Mary buries her face in her hands. 'I hadn't thought about that. How excruciating.' Now she really needs a cigarette.

'Better keep schtum with that Ian then. I wouldn't trust him as far as I could throw him.'

Mary eyes the Nicorettes packet. 'He told Mr Skipper he wanted to film a session with him – without consulting me first. That's why the old boy turned up here yesterday. He wanted to have a trial run. Then I find out this morning that he's been contacting old clients of mine without my knowledge.'

'Have you asked him about it?' Laura reaches for the bread; she seems to have regained her appetite.

'That's another thing. Having taken over my entire life for the past week, he hasn't been in touch for days.'

'That's the meeja for you, though, isn't it? Use people up then throw them away like paper tissues.'

'Thank you for that analogy, Laura.' Mary feels in her pocket for her Gitanes and curves her hand comfortingly around them. 'To tell you the truth, I find I'm rather hurt. I was beginning to think he might have changed. Mellowed, perhaps; become a little more vulnerable, a little less self-centred. Then the night before last—'

'You've never let him seduce you?' Laura admonishes her with delight. 'I don't know. Leave you alone for a second and look what happens.'

'It was only a kiss, but I was beginning to think—'

'You've been out of it too long, that's the trouble. You've forgotten the rules. You should try a spot of Internet dating. Get back into the swing of it.'

Mary shudders with distaste. 'I don't think I ever was in "the swing of it", as you put it. And I'm certainly not going to start now. But perhaps I have become too reclusive.' She takes out her cigarettes and puts them on the table. 'I've been thinking of getting a lodger,' she announces, quite surprising herself. But now she's voiced the idea, she realizes it's something she's been considering vaguely for several weeks. 'And now, if you don't mind, I have to go outside for a cigarette.'

CHAPTER FORTY

2007

When Laura's gone, Mary stands in the hall and glares at the silent phone, the letter from Geoffrey Johnstone on the hall table, the *Yellow Pages* still open at Grand Hotel. She picks up the phone and starts to dial, then hangs up with a sigh.

In her consulting room – where the velvet curtains remain annoyingly half-drawn, to accommodate the lighting requirements of Ian's damn camera – the sun slants in like an accusing finger, spotlighting the box of old files she carried down from the attic.

She picks up the box and humps it over to her desk, only to remember that Ian moved her anglepoise over to the other side of the room because it 'cluttered the view of the bookshelves'. Damn. Restless and irritable, she dumps the box back where she found it, then decides to put her agitation to good use by getting on with 'this lodger business', as she has already begun to think of it. After all, she tells herself bracingly, she can put a stop to it at any time if no one suitable turns up.

Extracting a biro from her cardigan pocket, she starts to draft an advert on the back of Mr Johnstone's envelope.

SINGLE ROOM IN NORTH SHIELDS WITH SEA AND RIVER VIEWS. AVAILABLE IMMEDIATELY. SHARE KITCHEN, BATHROOM, SITTING ROOM, GARDEN.

She hesitates, wondering what else to write. All mod cons? That might be stretching the truth a bit. And which room should it be? Whichever it is, she'll have to organize some furniture before showing anyone around.

She plods up the stairs to survey her spare rooms, starting with the one on the first floor, which is jam-packed with furniture from her parents' old house. She'll have to convert this into a sitting room, she realizes, because she can't have the lodger lolling about in her consulting room, can she? Mary sighs. This is turning out to be rather more complicated than she'd envisaged.

She continues up the stairs to the second floor, to the room she's always thought of as 'the spare bedroom', though all it contains is an ironing board and a wardrobe of old clothes. How would she feel having the lodger sleeping here, just one floor below her own bedroom? Would she disturb whoever it was when she tiptoed downstairs to the loo in the middle of the night? And what about *vice versa*? Computer games and Radio One, or, worse still, Radio Two; or one of those dreadful local stations, where the presenters shout about carpet sales and traffic jams the whole time. Would it be unreasonable to impose a sound curfew?

Then there's the thorny issue of significant others. Mary sighs again. She's not sure how she'd cope with a lodger with a sex life. Some kind of *cordon sanitaire* would definitely help, she muses, reaching her own little sanctuary on the next floor up and sitting down on the bed. Perhaps she should move into the attic? It would mean a longer excursion to the loo, but that might be worth it for the sense of separation she'd get from any youth culture and carnal activity on the second floor. She gets up and wanders over to the window.

Looking down at the Fish Quay, at a view that resonates to her very bones, she wonders whether she's ready to move on from this room yet. Perhaps it's time to contact Karleen after all, to see if she can help explain the hold it has over her.

Pressing on to the attic, Mary pauses at the threshold and tries to imagine it transformed into a bedroom. It would need painting, of course, and carpeting; and she'd have to find a new home for her 'archive'. But because the staircase terminates here, it's significantly larger than the rooms below and the view, of course, is magnificent. But what's that? She crosses to the far side where there's a spreading brown stain on the bare boards beneath the radiator. Damn. That explains an equivalent spreading brown stain on the ceiling in her bedroom, that she keeps vaguely noticing, then forgetting to investigate.

The leaky radiator rather takes the wind out of her sails and leaves her feeling thwarted and oddly forlorn. It seems she has a choice of two irksome tasks: organize some plumbing person to fix her leaking radiator, or embark on a possibly disturbing examination of the tape transcripts of her hypnosis sessions with Karleen. Call the plumber or open the box? After traipsing back downstairs and flicking through the *Yellow Pages* to 'P', she opts to call the plumber.

But before she's even started trying to decide among the hundreds of contractors listed, the phone rings.

'Hello? Dr Charlton speaking.'

'My darling girl, it's grand to hear your voice.'

'Karleen? How very strange. I was just thinking of you.'

'Isn't that so often the way of it? There now, and I've even got my coat on to go to the Post Office, but my hand reached for the phone instead of the doorknob.'

'I was about to phone the plumber,' says Mary, smiling into the mouthpiece. She pictures Karleen in her red duffle coat, propping her walking stick against the wall.

'You know why I'm calling, I suppose?'

'Actually, no. I've no idea. But I was going to ask whether you'd mind conducting another series of sessions with me. A couple of issues have come up recently that I think need exploring.'

'Well, now you've got me confused. I'd be delighted, of course – it would be a joy to work with you again. But that BBC man said you'd probably need some convincing.'

Mary tenses. 'Ian called you?'

'Didn't you know? I assumed that was how he got my number.'

'What did he say?' Really, the man is incorrigible. How dare he contact Karleen when she'd expressly asked him not to?

'Only that he was making a documentary about past life regression and wanted to rope me in – as a witness for the defence sort of thing. He was on about getting me to regress you again too, though I couldn't follow his logic there. The film's about some little boy you're treating, am I right?'

'Ian Campbell has his own agenda,' says Mary grimly. 'And he doesn't always tell me what that might be.'

'Ian Campbell. Now why does that name ring a bell?'

'He's quite a celebrity, I'm told. Hard to avoid, apparently, if you're a fan of BBC2.'

'Isn't that the name of that boy you had a fling with way back? The one that started all the trouble with Peggy?'

'How on earth do you remember that?'

'My hips may have seized up, but I still have a full set of marbles.'

'I told him not to contact you.'

'I suppose I might come over as rather doddery on the telly,' says Karleen without rancour.

'Don't be silly. That's not what I meant at all. I would just prefer not to be hypnotized for this documentary. Anyway, how are you keeping?'

'Oh, creaking along as usual. Still seeing a few clients. Trying to balance the painkillers with the side-effects. But what about you? What are these mysterious "issues" you want to explore?'

Mary settles down on the bottom stair and pulls her cardigan across her chest with her spare hand. 'I am beginning to suspect that I may have been involved with the boy they're filming, in his previous incarnation as a herring girl.'

'Ah,' says Karleen. 'And you fear the involvement might have ended in tears.'

'It looks like she was murdered.'

'I see. Which might prove embarrassing if it was revealed in the course of this film?'

'Yes – which is why I'd prefer not to be hypnotized. But what's really worrying me is not knowing. Having something like that in my unconscious and being completely unaware of it.'

'So what makes you think you were the murderer of this girl?'

'Images, flashbacks, that sort of thing. The fact that I'm thalassaphobic and the girl's killer was almost certainly a fisherman. The fact that I feel so protective of Ben now. I'm getting such a strong sense of karma with this case.'

'Would it matter? Surely Peggy suffered enough to have worked through several lifetimes of bad karma?'

'It makes me feel as though I've lost my way. I thought I was on one path – you know, working through all those issues around infertility and solitude, my dislike of being touched; beginning to make some progress. Then I discover there might be a whole other journey I've yet to embark on.'

'As the wise women say, these things are sent to try us.'

'But I'm worried, Karleen. If I was the man I suspect, there's a depth of violence there that I never encountered in my sessions with you.'

'I'd have thought something like that would have made itself felt at some point. But I suppose we never really got around to exploring your other incarnations, did we?'

'Then yesterday I remembered a knife. Fishermen used to carry their filleting knives in their caps, to avoid accidents at sea. I had a flashback of reaching up to my cap and then seeing the knife in my hand.' Mary shivers.

'What else do you remember?'

'Just fragments. A tobacco tin, for some reason. A woman laughing nervously, as if she's afraid – or guilty, perhaps. I don't know.'

'Do you remember stabbing her?'

'No – but that doesn't mean I didn't do it.' She closes her eyes for a moment. 'What will Ben think if he finds out I'm the one who killed his herring girl?'

'Oh, Mary, I'm so sorry. I wish I could help.'

'You are. I mean, it's helping already, just talking to you like this.' In the silence that follows, Mary hears her friend grunt softly, either with pain or effort, and pictures her pulling out a chair and easing herself down on it.

'What makes you think the woman laughing was this herring girl?' she asks.

'I don't know. I don't know who she was. I don't even know it was a true flashback. All I remember is him wanting to slit someone's throat – it might not even have been her throat he wanted to slit.'

'And that's all you remember.'

'Pretty much. That's why I wanted to see you.'

'So you have no idea what might have led up to that point, or what happened afterwards?'

'He'd been drinking. The knife was in his hand. It's obvious, isn't it?'

'You don't know. Perhaps it was the man he was after. Perhaps he was provoked.'

Karleen's right, of course. A single flashback of a drunken fisherman with a knife doesn't mean she was Tom Hall in a previous incarnation. She needs to keep an open mind until she's worked systematically through all the information she has. And then, if it starts looking likely, she'll set off to Lyme Regis with her rucksack and ask Karleen to regress her.

'Is there a good B and B near your house?' she asks.

'My darling Mary, you'll stay with me and I won't hear a word of an argument. I have a young girl that helps me these days, so it's no trouble. And there's a bottle of Bushmill's in the cupboard with your name on it.'

'It will have to be next month, if that's all right with you. I can't see Ian agreeing to me absenting myself for a week in the middle of filming.'

'So how will you manage in the meantime?'

'I'm going to look through all my old transcripts now, to see if there are any clues there. With any luck I'll find something to disprove my suspicions. And it's possible that some more evidence will emerge from regression sessions with Ben and various other people who were a part of Annie's life.'

'What other people?' Karleen asks sharply, and Mary can just imagine her friend sitting forward with interest.

'I'll explain when I see you. I've been trying something completely new with this case. Time will tell whether it will prove fruitful.' Then: 'I can't believe Ian phoned you! He offered to fly you up here, I suppose.'

'He can be very persuasive, your Ian.'

'He's not "my Ian".'

'But I said I'd have to discuss it with you first.'

'Oh, Karleen. I would so love to see you. It's just—'

'You'd rather I had nothing to do with this film. Look, I'll call him now and tell him no. I'll play the sweet old lady and say my back's giving me gyp.'

Mary lets out a long sigh of relief. 'Don't you want to be on the telly? According to Ian, it's all that seems to motivate people these days.'

'I won't grace that with a reply. And I'm sure you're more than capable of holding your own against Hester without my help. It's a shame, though. I was rather looking forward to the chauffeur-driven car.'

Mary stiffens. 'What's that about Hester?'

'Oh, this documentary's all her idea according to her. She says it's a pilot for a series about paranormal phenomena she's cooked up with some BBC producer – your Ian presumably. That's why I was so pleased to be invited to take part. I thought you could do with someone batting for your side.'

'He never mentioned Hester was involved.' She grips the phone tight.

'In retrospect it occurred to me that might have been why she wrote such a stinging review of your paper. To impress the BBC and set out her stall, as it were, as an opponent. For what it's worth, I didn't get the impression that your Ian was trying to set you up. On the contrary, he seemed genuinely concerned to give you a fair crack of the whip.'

'I'm not sure that "fair" or "genuine" are appropriate adjectives in this case,' Mary says tiredly. 'And for heaven's sake stop calling him "my Ian".'

CHAPTER FORTY-ONE

2007

Ben's phoning New Zealand. His mum's on speed dial on the landline phone in the flat. All he has to do is press three and the tinny jingle of her overseas code trickles into his ear. It's lunchtime here, but four in the morning where she is. He imagines the handsets trilling in the dark in his mum's bungalow on the other side of the world – there's one in the kitchen, she's told him, and one in the lounge – and his mum grunting and rolling onto her back in the double bed, waiting for the answerphone to kick in. He always dials 141 before pressing the speed-dial button, so she doesn't know it's him, though she probably guesses.

After she left she kept a phone by the bed to begin with, and always used to pick up when Ben rang her in the middle of the night. But her new bloke complained, so she unplugged it and arranged a regular time for Ben to call, which is embarrassing because Dad's usually there listening in, plus Ben doesn't always feel like talking to her at his regular time.

Calling her answerphone is like a bad habit that he can't break, like playing Sims 2 at night when he's supposed to have his light out, or eating a whole pack of Doritos. It's totally pathetic, and it doesn't even make him feel better, which is usually the reason he's phoning her in the first place. It just buries him deeper into being miserable: because it makes him think of her big new bungalow, with the sandpit and swing in the garden, and her big new life with the kids and her big new bloke: a proper family, when all he's got is Dad, who's never there, and Nana, who's useless.

'Hi there!' goes Mum in her jolly answerphone voice, and she's got a kiwi accent now, so she doesn't even sound the same any more. 'You've reached the Taylor residence. Nessa and Callum and the girls can't take your call right now, but we want to hear from you, so please leave a message before you hang up. Bye-ee!' It's that 'Bye-ee!' that always gets him, like she's just running out of the door, like she can't wait, off to somewhere sunny and exciting, back to her new life, when he's stuck at home on the fifth floor by himself, heating up some crappy pasta ready meal in the microwave.

She sent a photo at Christmas, showing her new blonde hairdo, and a letter which was all about her job, and the weather – which she goes on about every Christmas – and about how weird it is sunbathing and having a barbeque on Christmas Day, which she also goes on about every year.

The microwave pings as he hangs up the phone. Then Nana's at the door too, with an armful of chicken and chips. And suddenly he can't face it, all that crap food coming at him from all angles, so he grabs his diving gear and says he's got to rush. Which is a stupid lie, because now he has to carry his diving bag, and he's still hungry, but it must be better than staying cooped up with Nana and talking about why he's not doing the film any more.

He ends up at the caff in Tynemouth without meaning to, because if he'd been concentrating he'd have avoided it like the plague, because if Dad finds out he'll be livid. But he wasn't concentrating, at least not on that. He was just trudging along, staring at the pavement, pretending his diving bag was a Dick Whittington sack, and he was running away to seek his fortune. So when he finds himself at the caff he can hardly believe it. But his shoulders are so tired by then, from lugging the bag, and his tummy's so totally rumbling, that he goes in anyway and sits down.

He's such a regular by now that Molly, the waitress, gives him a wave and 'howay', and all the old ladies swivel their cauliflower heads to see who she's waving at. 'Hot chocolate, right?' Molly calls out, grinning away. 'With cream and sprinkles?'

'And a ham roll, please, and a glass of water.' He's blushing, but it's nice to be recognized.

'If you're after Laura, she's not in,' says Molly when she brings over his tray. 'Pay at the till, OK, pet? I'm up to my eyes with her off.'

Ben spoons whipped cream and sprinkles, wondering what the doc's doing, and if that's where Laura is, and if the Ian bloke's found someone else for the film. It's only two days since the bust-up with Dad and already it feels like everything's going on without him. Like he's stuck in the middle of the Billy Mill roundabout, with cars whizzing round him, carrying all the people he knows then heading off in all directions leaving him behind.

* * *

After lunch, he wanders down to St Edward's Bay. Now he's lugged the gear this far, he thinks he might as well use it. It's a sticky grey day, so the beach is almost deserted. Just an old bloke with a spaniel, and a couple of mams huddled on a towel in their hoodies and smoking, while their kids sleep in their buggies.

He sits on the bottom step to change, wriggling quickly into his wetsuit, which is really hot and clammy in this weather, so he feels like a boil-in-the-bag meal when he's ready. But the sea's perfect when he gets in: flat as a grey mirror, so you can see everything, every ripple in the sand, every little strand of seaweed.

He goes in along by the rocks and swims slowly round the headland beneath the old Priory, where he's never been before, because the Deep Blue lads normally take them out towards Whitley Bay, where the wrecks of the *Wansworth* and *Ethel Taylor* are. For a while he just snorkels, checking out the marine life – though it's more like checking out the litter in some places, with old drinks cans and plastic bottles dotted about and carrier bags caught on the rocks and drifting like weird-coloured seaweed. Which makes him even more depressed than he was when he started. He's read on Google that they've found used condoms and plastic bottles in the remotest parts of the Antarctic, because the different seas are all joined together, so whatever crap you chuck in at North Shields could end up anywhere in the world.

After a while he decides to practise freediving, holding his breath on the surface to start with, then actually diving with his snorkel flapping against his cheek, compensating his mask and ears carefully as he goes down, then finning along close to the sea bed. It feels like he's down for ages, but when he checks his watch it's only two minutes – though that's not bad for dynamic apnoea.

Next he tries a bit of hyperventilation before he goes down, though he knows he shouldn't really, because it prevents you wanting to breathe out by lowering the CO_2 in your blood. Because it's too much CO_2 that makes you want to breathe out and rush to the surface, not lack of oxygen like most people think. So you can trick your body into not breathing for longer, even though you've run out of oxygen in your blood, by getting rid of the CO_2.

So he hyperventilates for a bit, then goes down again, and fins along like before, and it's true: he can stay under for much longer – thirty seconds longer, in fact, which is loads more. He hyperventilates again and when he goes down this time he spots a pipefish bustling along, all businesslike, and follows it for ages, thinking about how impressed Dad will be when he tells him how long he's held his breath – then remembering, with a little stab of anguish, that he's not talking to Dad any more. He's not talking to anyone any more.

Sitting on the rocks tugging off his fins afterwards, he notices a small dinghy chuntering away at anchor a bit further out, and some old dude bent over a couple of crab pots. This is the kind of fishing Ben approves of, where it's a battle of wits between the fisherman and the crab, and you only catch what you're looking for. It reminds him of tribes in the Amazon and Borneo, where hunters really understand the animals they hunt, and set snares in places they know the animal will be; so the ones who pay the most attention always catch the most food.

Ben thinks that makes it fairer, but with some kinds of fishing it seems the less you know the more you catch. Dad says that in some countries people set off explosives in the water, which kill every living thing, and they all come floating up to the surface, so all you have to do is pick out the big ones. But all the tiddlers are killed too, plus everything else, so the water's coated with a scum of dead creatures for the gulls to eat, and no fry to grow into adults the next year. How stupid would you have to be to do that? It's the same with the big factory boats, because they have state-of-the-art computers to track the shoals, and trawl rigs to drag along the bottom, and machines to gut the catch. Anyone who can press a few buttons could do that job.

The old dude straightens up and Ben sees that it's Skip, which is a bit of a shock, because he didn't realize he still had a boat, but not that surprising really. Then he sees that Skip's calling him over, and waving a flask of tea, so before he knows it Ben's pulling on his fins again and swimming out to the dinghy.

Skip's busy stowing a long line of hooks when he gets there, pulling off the uneaten baits of mussel meat and chucking them over the side. He looks different somehow; Ben can't quite work out why – then realizes it's because he's had a shave and washed his hair.

In a bucket by his feet is a small heap of fair-sized plaice. 'Wow!' Ben whistles in admiration. 'Where did you catch those?'

'Up south aways,' says Skip, nodding gruffly in the direction of Sunderland. 'Not far. You use the motor to get away from the shore, then let the current take you. I reckon it takes the fish along too.'

'Are they all for you?'

'One or two of the littluns maybes. I'll sell the rest to Turnbull's. Lad there gives us a fair price and no questions asked.'

'What does he do with them? I mean, he can't sell them, can he?' Dad's told Ben all about this; about how everything has to be on the books these days or you get done by DEFRA.

Skip shrugs. 'I don't ask so he don't tell. Gives them to his mates for all I know.' He leans over the side to swill out the lid of his flask, then pours a fresh cup for Ben.

Ben takes a wary sip. He's not keen on tea usually, but this is dark brown and sweet as toffee, with a hint of salt from the water round the rim; not like normal tea at all. 'Dad says you were the best skipper in Shields,' he says.

'Does he now?' If the old bloke's pleased, he's not showing it.

'Why did you give up, then?'

'Ach, my heart wasn't in it anymore.' He coughs, then spits neatly into the water. 'First *she* went – then the fish. Mind you, the fish had been going for years before that. Time was they were landing that many herring they were just hoying them on the land as fertilizer. Then they just disappeared. One year the catches were spotty, next they were gone. Just like that.'

'So what happened?'

'Bigger boats, bigger engines, bigger nets. Once they started on with the seine purses, the herring never stood a chance. Ten year on, there was nowt left.'

'Like with the cod.'

'Ay. You'd think they'd have learnt wouldn't you?'

'Dad says the flatties are going the same way. He says DEFRA should stop giving so much quota to the factory ships.'

Skip sighs and lights a rollie-up. 'You don't need a trawl to catch a plaice. See, your plaice isn't too canny as a swimmer. So she uses the tides to move along the coast. All you have to do is wait for the tide to run, then you run with it.'

'And you'd just catch plaice and nothing else?'

'Ay, pretty much. If you timed it right.'

'So why doesn't Dad do that?'

'You've got to know your fish, that's the trick. And your tides, and that. How the currents move over the sea bed. It's not something your sonar can help you with.'

'I'll ask him to try.'

'Ay, lad. You do that.'

But they both know it's pointless. If you've got a powerful engine and a heavy twin-rig you go trawling and that's that. You don't go drifting along quietly following the tide with a long line.

'Can I come out with you some time?' Ben asks shyly, after a while.

'Don't see why not.'

'Really? Wow! Can I bring my diving gear? I've never seen a plaice swimming.'

'If Paul says it's OK.'

'Will you show me where you put the lobster pots? And the crab creels?'

'I'm going out Sunday if the weather holds. Bring a proper gansey, mind. It can be chilly when the wind gets up.'

'I've only got a puffa jacket,' says Ben, 'but it's got two zips.' He's staring at the old man's gansey; it looks like there's some writing knitted into the pattern. 'RS,' he reads aloud. 'What does that mean?'

'Robert Simpson. Them's my initials. *She* knitted it for me, didn't she? Had it over thirty year. Look after a good gansey and it'll last for ever. She knitted the patches an' all. See, it's made so you can turn it front to back when the elbows go. It'll see me out, I reckon.'

Nana's gone by the time Ben gets back to the flat. She's left the chicken supper for him, wrapped up by the microwave, and the whole place smells of vinegar. He chucks it in the bin then wanders down the hall to his room and unlocks the door.

There are some days when he doesn't even see his room; it's just the place he goes when he wants to be on his own. But other times he can't ignore the decor, it's so in his face, and he feels like he's been forced to share with a macho brother or cousin. The thing that offends him the most is the black-and-white striped Newcastle United wallpaper. Until now he's just put up with it – because Dad chose it and he hasn't wanted to upset him. But after what happened with the doc and the film, he doesn't care about Dad's feelings any more. So he starts picking at a loose bit with his thumbnail and soon there's a big raggedy hole where he's scraped the paper away, and loads of little black and white curly bits on the carpet.

He stands back and looks at the mess he's made. It's more difficult than he expected; he thought it would peel off in big satisfying strips, but you have to scratch at each little bit and it takes ages.

'You want a steam gun for that,' says Dad, who's suddenly materialized in the open doorway. 'And a proper scraper.'

'I sort of started, then I couldn't stop,' Ben explains.

He'd expected Dad to be cross, but he seems to be OK with it. 'It's your room, buddy. Do what you like with it.'

'I want to get rid of the paper,' says Ben, but what he means is, I want to get rid of *your* paper.

Dad comes into the room and looks round. 'So what do you fancy instead? Another paper, or some kind of paint job?'

Ben shrugs. 'Paint probably. I don't know.'

'Howay, then. I'll take you to B&Q before they close. We can grab the stripping gear and some colour charts at the same time.' He picks up a hoodie from the bed and chucks it at Ben to put on.

Ben makes a show of draping the hoodie over his chair. Does his dad think he won't see through all this, that he's being all nicey-nice to make up for ruining the film?

'Do you want to do it yourself,' Dad asks. 'Or will I give Norm a ring? See if he can fit it in next week – it shouldn't take long. Or we could do it together. What do you think?'

Ben doesn't answer. He just shoves his hands in his pockets and walks out of the room.

At B&Q Dad fills a trolley with everything they need: dust sheet, two sorts of scraper, steam gun, sponge. Then they come home and shift all the furniture into the middle of the room and Dad starts demonstrating how to use the steam gun – because there's a knack, apparently – which ends up with Dad doing most of it himself, and Ben sitting on the dust sheet just watching, and getting up now and then to shove all the wet peely bits into a bin liner.

The whole thing puts Dad in a good mood, because he thinks they've done this father–son bonding thing, which always cheers him up, so he starts talking about booking a holiday – 'having a break' he calls it – and 'getting away'. Which really means getting Ben away from Laura and the doc and Annie, and getting back to 'normal'.

Ben doesn't say much. All he wants is for Dad to get bored with his new toy and leave him alone.

'What about Barbados?' Dad says. 'I could take you shark-fishing on one of those big boats. Or reef diving somewhere. Hawaii or somewhere. Thailand – have they got reefs there? Get you some proper hot-weather gear.'

'What about New Zealand?' says Ben, more to piss Dad off than anything else. But it works, because Dad's mouth goes sort of tight and thin, and ten minutes later he's handed over the steam gun and gone off to the Low Lights.

CHAPTER FORTY-TWO

2007

With the black-and-white wallpaper off, Ben's room looks completely different. Underneath the paper it's just plain plaster, pale pinkish and dusty, which makes the room seem much bigger; and the furniture's still shoved into the middle, so his bed's facing a different way, which Ben quite likes, because lying there makes him feel different too. Which is exactly what he wants, because the idea of his life being back to 'normal' makes him want to scream – literally, until his head aches – or smash his fist against the wall.

He's found a feng shui website that says if you sleep with your feet facing the door, it's bad feng shui because that's how you'll be carried out when you're dead. But if you align your body north-to-south that's good for the cells because of electro-magnetic fields. And if you lie with your bed in the north-east that means a fresh start. So that's where he's going to put his bed once he's painted the walls, which is opposite to how it has been, which was in the south-west. Because the south-west means harmony, which to Ben means giving in to Dad, which he is never going to do again.

Dad's been nagging at him to get started on the painting, probably because he fancies having a go with the roller before he goes off on the boat. But Ben hasn't decided on a colour yet; plus he quite likes making Dad wait, and pissing him off, and watching him trying not to show that he's pissed off. And he's enjoying the in-between feel of the room at the moment, and the idea that it could go in any direction; because now the paper's off, it's his room, properly his, instead of Dad and his perfect imaginary son's.

Ben's still not really talking to Dad, just saying 'please' and 'thank you' and 'OK'. It's not that he's in a sulk; it's more that he can't be bothered. He used to make an effort with Dad, but now he just thinks, what's the point? And Dad's either trying not to notice, or being really chummy-chummy, which makes Ben really angry when he thinks about it, so he's trying not to think about it – which basically means staying in his room and going on the computer all the time.

Today Ben's been on Sims 2 for nearly nine hours and he's beginning to feel a bit weird, sort of dizzy and tired at the same time, and like he might throw up. He's been applying the principles of feng shui to a new Sims house, which means looking at loads of feng shui sites, which are a mixture of sensible advice, like making sure you can see who's arriving at the front door, and bonkers instructions like hanging bamboo flutes from the ceiling or putting a green ceramic frog in the west quadrant of your garden.

Nana knocked at one point to say there was half a lasagne in the microwave if he wanted it, which he didn't. And Dad banged a bit later to say he was heading off to the boat.

Ben hasn't even got around to getting dressed yet, or brushing his teeth. And the curtains are still closed, because where the computer is now the sun shines directly onto the screen so he can't see properly. So it's like being in a pinky sort of cave, that pongs a bit of sweat and damp plaster – plus there's a slight whiff of spunk from his pjs, which must mean something, except Ben really doesn't want to think about it, because whenever he thinks about what's going on inside his body he just can't bear it.

Ben reckons that as long as he's not actually *talking* to the doc and Laura, he can still do some research and Dad can't complain – and he won't know anyway, because he's off on the boat. So he's come to the library to look up Lord Jim. He's not sure what he's going to discover, but he's vaguely hoping there might be something that will make Dad feel a bit less spooked about being the reincarnation of a fat old gay dude with no legs. Maybe he won a medal for bravery in the war or something, or wrote books, or gave all his money to charity. Anyway, it's something to do. And if he bumps into Laura or the doc there it won't be because he's gone to see them on purpose, so maybe he'll get away with it.

On the way in, he thinks he spots Ian taking the steps two at a time up to the local history section, but by the time he gets up there himself, there's no sign of him and it's just Pete on his own helping an old lady work the computer.

Ben logs on to the BMD site and starts looking for a James from North Shields who died just before Dad was born in 1968. Which is hopeless, of course, because James was one of the most common names in those days, so there's squillions of them. So then he narrows it down to just blokes over eighty, because he has a vague memory of Lord Jim saying he was eighty-something, and he must have been pretty decrepit to have his legs off like that. Now there's just twenty-six names on the list, which is still loads, but at least now he can face going through them one by one and seeing if any of them seems right.

So he's just scrolling vaguely down when one jumps right out at him: James Harold Milburn. Annie's brother! It must be! So Annie disappeared, but her brother stuck around and grew up into Lord Jim. Which means that Ben and his dad were once sister and brother. How totally weird is that?

He borrows a pen from Pete to jot down the address: 59 Seymour Street, North Shields, NE29 6SN.

The house, when he gets there, is in the middle of one of those old terraces of Tyneside flats that stretch all the way down the street, with front doors opening right onto the pavement, two by two, with one front door leading to a staircase to the upper flat, and one opening into the hall of the downstairs flat. Number 59 is an upper flat, which is annoying because it means Ben can't peer in, which would have been pointless anyway, as it's nearly forty years since Lord Jim died. Still, it would have been cool to have a peek and try to imagine what it was like in 1967.

Now it has replacement windows and those beigey vertical blinds that old ladies go in for, that swivel open on chains of little ball bearings. Squatting down, Ben pushes open the letterbox to see the stairs, which are covered in a dark red flowery carpet. There's a sprinkling of grey gravel stuff in the hall that a cat's kicked out of a litter tray, which needs emptying by the niff of it.

Ben remembers Lord Jim going on about the stairs, how being stuck in the flat in 'this bloomin' wheelchair' was like being in prison. He can understand what he meant now; because it must have been quite a performance hoying a big bloke like that up and down them narrow stairs.

He considers ringing the bell, but chickens out, so wanders along to the end of the terrace instead, then down the back alley behind the houses, past all the yards, with broken glass and razor wire along the tops of the walls. He's looking for the rear of Number 59, but there aren't any numbers on the rear gates. Then at the far end of the alley, he spots a familiar figure and there's old Skip, trundling towards him with a supermarket trolley full of paintings, back from his stall in the market probably.

'Howay, Paul's lad. What you doing round here?'

'I was looking for someone's house, but I think I've got the wrong address.'

'What street you after?'

'It doesn't matter.'

'This here's my place, if you fancy a cuppa.' He unlocks a hefty padlock on a yard gate then pulls back a butch-looking bolt.

Ben follows him into a yard that's completely covered by transparent corrugated roofing; like a creaky sort of conservatory, with the doors and windows of the house looking out into it. The whole yard's kitted out as an artist's studio and carpentry workshop for making picture-frames, but there's a load of fishing gear in there too. So there's jam-jars of brushes and easels and paints and that, plus a Black and Decker workmate and stacks of old wood and doors propped up against one wall, plus nets hanging on another wall, and a heap of pots and creels. But even though there's so much stuff in there, it's really tidy and everything has its proper place, like a sideways bookcase for stacking the paintings, and hooks for the broom and the mop; so it's really quite cool considering it's an old bloke's place.

Inside the flat it's a bit dark and dismal, because the conservatory dims the light from the windows. Ben sits on a wooden stool with a padded plastic seat and watches the old bloke fill a dented old kettle and light one of those little camping gas gizmos – even though there's a proper gas cooker in the kitchen and an electric kettle. Has he been cut off or something?

'Carnation milk all right?' Skip asks. 'Real goes off in a blink on the boat, so I got out of the habit.'

Ben nods. 'Can I use the bog?' he asks. He doesn't really need to go, but he wants to nose around a bit.

It's a typical lower Tyneside flat, with the bathroom tacked on the end of the kitchen. Dad says people used to put planks over the bath and keep coal underneath, but old Skip has sheets and towels soaking in his.

Ben does his business and dries his hands on a threadbare pink towel. There's frilly nets over the window and a china Jesus at one end of the windowsill, with a matching Mary at the other, and a little vase of plastic roses on a lace doily in between. He sneaks a look in the medicine cabinet. There's loads of weird old stuff in there – he doesn't know what half of it's for – like a flat tin with a grinning picture of teeth on it, and a chubby brown bottle of Senokot pills, whatever they are, and a little bottle of olive oil, for some reason; and that ointment for your bum Dad used when he got constipated on that Atkins diet; and some Yardley's lily-of-the-valley talc, and aspirins and multivits; all grey with dust and looking like they've been there for years.

The tea's ready when he comes out, in tin mugs on the kitchen table, and there's some custard creams on a chipped plate, even though there's a little tray right there on the worktop, set for tea, with a pot and milk jug and everything; and loads of thin flowery china cups on hooks, and matching saucers on a shelf above.

Ben bites into a custard cream. 'What's through there?' he asks, pointing to another door.

'Oh, that's her lounge. It's a mucky job, on the boat, so I always tried to keep a bit separate.' He sucks up a mouthful of scalding tea. 'So I'd come in the back, like just now, through the yard. And she'd come in the front, so's she could have her lounge and her bedroom to herself. Then when I'd cleaned up, we'd meet in the kitchen for tea.'

'Who's she, then? Your wife?'

'Ha!' He laughs. 'She were old enough to be my nana, never mind my wife. I was her lodger, like, from when I was sixteen. She took me in after Mam died. Said if I'd see to all her odd jobs I'd be doing her a favour. She never married, see? So it worked out fine all round.'

'What happened to her?'

'Passed away years ago, God bless her.' He slurps the rest of his tea. 'I like to fancy she's in there still, knitting away and listening to her hymns.'

'So who lives there now?'

'I go in sometimes to have a bit of a hoover round, to keep it nice for her.'

The idea of the old lady knitting away behind the closed door makes Ben want to go and look. 'Can I see?' he asks.

'Help yourself. It's not locked.'

Ben pushes open the door to the lounge, which is typical old lady decor, with flowery wallpaper and a swirly carpet. There's one of those tall old-fashioned armchairs by the empty fireplace, and he goes to sit in it, and turns the radio on, except it's all crackles and he can't find the station. There's a dusty old copy of the *Radio Times* on the side table and he looks at the date: 22–28 January 1994. So it's probably been there ever since she died.

It's peaceful sitting in her chair, but sort of sad. The arms have special covers on, to stop them getting dirty, and there's a white lacy cloth over the back, that looks like she's crocheted the edges herself. Leaning back with his head against the crochet, he rests his wrists on the arms of the chair.

'You all right, lad?'

'There's an old copy of the *Radio Times* here with that Joanna Lumley on the cover.'

Skip hovers in the doorway, like he's scared to come in.

'I never liked to interfere with her things.'

'Oh. Sorry.' Ben jumps up, feeling guilty.

'No, you're all right. She's gone now. I'm just being daft. The front hall's through that door and then her bedroom's on the left.'

There's a heap of mail on the front doormat and Ben scoops it up. 'Miss Edith Lillian Turnbull, was that her? There's loads of mail here for her.'

'Just give me my stuff and put the rest on that shelf,' says old Skip from the doorway.

'Isn't there someone you should send her stuff to? Like a sister or a cousin or something?' Ben's leafing through the heap of envelopes, taking out the obvious junk mail.

'Leave it be, lad. If there's something important, they can knock on the door, can't they?'

'This one looks important,' Ben says, fishing out a white envelope with National Savings & Investments printed on the front. 'Shall I open it?'

Old Skip sighs. 'Go on then.'

'It's about her Post Office account. They say they're "discontinuing the savings account option", whatever that means.' He reads on down the page. 'It says she's got to open a new account and put her money in that instead.'

'Ay, she was always on about her savings. In her will, she said I could have the lot, but I never found her pass book. Not that I ever looked, mind.'

'I could look for it if you like,' Ben offers. He quite fancies a bit of a rootle through the old lady's things. It will be like continuing his research, he thinks, into how people lived in the old days.

'I don't know,' Skip says.

'Only if you want.'

'It's just I don't like going in her rooms. She liked to be private, did Miss Turnbull. And I always tried to respect that.'

'I'll be really careful not to disturb anything.'

The old bloke sighs again. 'Go on then. I don't suppose it will hurt.'

Ben pushes open the door to the old lady's bedroom. It smells musty, like the air's been there a long time. There's a saggy single bed in the corner with a padded nylon cover stitched all over into little diamond shapes. And a plain brown rug beside the bed, with a pair of old-lady slippers on it, and a nightie folded on the pillow, with a brown handbag laid tidily on top. He looks behind the door, and there's her fleecy dressing-gown, and one of those nylon housecoat things old ladies wear over their clothes when they're doing the cleaning.

Ben picks up the handbag.

'It's not in there,' says Skip from the hall. 'I had to look inside for the nurses when she was taken in. They were after her reading glasses. Then – later, like – I put her watch and her glasses back in there for safe-keeping.'

'What about in the drawers?' Ben asks. There's an antiquey-looking wardrobe and a matching chest of drawers with another Jesus statue on it, and a hairbrush with a comb stuck in it, and a few white hairs wound round the bristles.

'I told you, I never touched her things.'

It's spooky seeing the hairs there; it makes the old lady more real. Ben can imagine her brushing her hair, or in the bathroom patting some of that lily-of-the-valley talc under her saggy old arms. He opens one of the top drawers and this smell sort of wafts out at him, the way some people have their own special smell. Hers is soapy and biscuity. He's a bit embarrassed to rummage around in there, because it's all big white knickers and vests, like from the oldies corner of Markie's, and flat little lacy bras, and a pile of embroidered hankies. So he just pushes the things sideways to check if there's anything underneath, which there isn't. He tries the other drawers, with her nighties and tights, and piles of cardies and scarves – but no pass book.

'There's nothing in here,' he says, pushing the last drawer shut and looking round the room again. Old Skip's lurking in the doorway now, as though he feels he's got to keep an eye on things.

There's another armchair by the window. Next to it is a round table with a tasselly lamp on it, and a tatty black bible; and on the floor beside it there's a sort of tapestry bag hanging from a wooden stand, with knitting needles poking out, which must be where she kept her crochet and knitting stuff.

'I bet it's in here,' says Ben, lifting the bag onto the bed and easing it open. Shoving his hand down to the bottom, past balls of wool and reels of cotton, he feels a wad of papers and booklets held together by an elastic band. 'Bingo!' he cries, pulling it out.

He goes to hand the package to Skip, but the old bloke backs away. 'Nay, Paul's lad. You do it.'

When he takes off the elastic band, it's so rotten it snaps in his fingers.

'That's her pension book,' says Skip.

'And here's the savings book. Wow! There's thousands of pounds in here. Look!'

He thrusts the book at old Skip, who takes it gingerly. 'Six thousand four hundred and sixty three pounds,' he reads the numbers slowly. 'Bloody hell.' He sits down on the chair and stares at the book.

Ben leafs through the rest of the papers. 'Here's another fifty quid,' he says, discovering a fifty-pound note folded inside a book of second-class stamps. There's a battered little address book, with crackly brown Sellotape holding the cover on, and a notebook with a cardboard cover.

'What you got there, lad?'

'Some kind of notebook.' He flips open the cover. 'Wow! Look at this. I think it's her diary. She's dated all the pages.'

He turns to the first entry: '"14 November 1993",' he reads out. 'It just starts in the middle of the month, so she must've just gone on writing till she finished a notebook, then started a new one. "Lord, thank you for last night." Who's Lord? Oh, right, I get it. It's like she's writing to God. How weird.'

'Ay, she was very godly, was Miss Turnbull.'

'Sorry. Is it OK for me to read it?'

'I doubt there'll be owt to be ashamed of, knowing her.'

'Here – you'd better have it.'

'No, you're all right. There comes a time for everything and I guess this is probably it.'

'"The arm was a little easier today, thanks to your grace, so I slept better than I have for weeks. The lad is away, so I had a simple breakfast, just Hovis and a boiled egg." Who's the lad?'

'That's me. I was always "the lad" to her.'

'I wonder where the others are.'

'Eh?'

'The other diaries.' Without thinking, Ben kneels down and pulls a dusty plastic suitcase out from under the bed. Inside, when he pops the catches, it's packed with cardboard shoe-boxes tied with string. Ben opens one, but he doesn't need to. It's obvious what's inside.

'Wow! Her whole life must be in here,' he says, sitting back on his heels. Then, remembering why he'd come to Seymour Street in the first place, 'I wonder if she knew Lord Jim.'

Old Skip looks up. 'Lord Jim from the Jungle? Oh ay, she knew him right enough. She used to do for him. He had the flat upstairs, see. Gave her a fair run-around, too.'

Ben stares at him. 'Did you know him?'

'Not to speak to, as such. Well, she wouldn't let me speak to him, would she? He was a queer, see. And I think she were scared I'd be turned, like, just being in the same room. But everyone knew him.' He chuckles. 'I mean, you couldn't miss him, could you? The size he was, togged out in them frocks and wigs and that.'

'He was nice though, right?'

'Oh ay. Do anything for you, they said. She couldn't cope with it, though, him going with the lads. Only tried to get him along to see Father O'Brien, didn't she?' He chuckles again. 'But he was having none of it. She took it hard when he passed, mind. She was up at his place all hours when he was poorly at the end. Then they fell out about something – I was off on the boat, so I don't know the whole story.' He nods at the shoe boxes. 'It'll all be in there somewhere most likely,' he says.

CHAPTER FORTY-THREE

2007

Ben flips through the notebooks, looking for 1967. There are four – she's written the dates down the cloth spines in blue biro. Still kneeling on the floor, he picks one up and opens it at random.

31 May 1967

A blowy day. The sheets had twisted themselves round the line, so will need ironing. I was worried for the lad and said a prayer for his safe return.

Mr M. was still in bed when I went up and he'd left the bedroom door open, so I couldn't help seeing in. Clothes strewn everywhere and that blonde wig draped over his bedside lamp. It's always a shock to see him with his wig off and to remember that underneath all that make-up he's just a fat old man with a few wisps of white hair. At least he was on his own!

I gave the bathroom a proper do. Ran the sink full and rinsed the powder off all his perfumes and lotions and that. It gets everywhere, that stuff.

At 10.30 I got out the hoover. It woke him up, but I couldn't just leave it. That dark brown shows every bit of fluff, but at least there's not that cat to worry about any more. He turned up in the kitchen in his nightie and told me off for "ruining his beauty sleep".

He said there was a brawl at the Jungle last night and they had to call in the police. Usually the bouncers can manage, but he said a gang of young tearaways from Sunderland came in at 2 looking for trouble.

His legs looked worse, what I could see of them, and he couldn't get his slippers on. He's been using some ointment, but it doesn't seem to be having much effect. He saw me looking and said he'll have to go barefoot now, like a proper flower child, and paint his toenails and wear bangles round his ankles. What is he like?

When I'd finished in the upstairs flat and had my lunch (the rest of the cream of mushroom), I offered up a decat of the rosary for him. Mrs Jessop says I should stop doing for him, but I think you have to keep the door open. You never know what drives people, and it's never too late to repent. When I think back to what the lad's mother had to put up with, and how she ended up, poor lass. Well, it's easy to judge, isn't it?

The lad came in around six and I made us a nice cottage pie. He went out to the Mariner's Arms afterwards, but was back before the news (thank you, Lord), and went straight off to bed.

1 June 1967

When I left to go up to Mr M.'s, the lad still hadn't stirred, bless him. It was a hard trip, he said, with heavy seas, and they'd had to go further than usual looking for fish.

Mr M. was having breakfast when I arrived. He had that waffle thing out and was trying different toppings for work. I tasted a few for him, but liked the simple lemon juice and caster sugar one best.

He's started taking some pills, to "rev up his system" he said, and help him get some of the weight off. One of the dancers gave them to him. They are supposed to stop you feeling hungry, but he still got through six of them waffles. They stop you sleeping too, he said, so he was up half the night.

He came over a bit poorly when I was washing up. His heart was going nineteen to the dozen, he said, but he was right as rain by the time I left.

I hate to think what's in them pills, mind. I'm sure Dr Fraser wouldn't approve. I don't know what the police are playing at these days. Young folk seem to be able to get anything they want without a prescription, just by stopping someone in the street. Mr M. says there's booths at the Jungle that are like a chemist's shop some nights and the cleaner's always fishing needles out of the toilets.

He was drinking glasses and glasses of water, which is not like him.

In the afternoon I went to play Scrabble with Mrs J., then popped in to the church to do the flowers. The water in the vases was green, so I scrubbed them out in the vestry. I looked on the rota to see who was on last week and it was Mrs Cooper, so what can you expect?

The lad had brought a load of cod cheeks back, so we had fish pie for tea. He showed me a drawing he'd done of landing a catch, with the waves towering over the boat and the lads all togged up in their oilies. It gave me the willies to see it. When you queue up for a fish supper, you don't think what them lads have to go through to get it, do you? It made me think about my Alfie and his boat going over.

I never thought it at the time, but looking back it was probably for the best that we split up. I don't know how I would have coped if we'd been married. So thank you, Lord, for sparing me that pain.

2 June 1967

Mr M. was in a right state when I arrived this morning, lying on the sofa in his nightie, gasping for breath with his hand on his chest. I thought he was having a heart attack, but he said it was just them pills. I wanted to dial 999, but he said don't be daft, he'd be fine. So I made us both a cup of tea, then did the hoovering and scoured the oven with that new stuff. You have to spray on some pink foam and wait for it to dissolve all the muck. I decided if he wasn't better by the time I cleaned it off, I'd call Dr Fraser.

He'd got dressed by then, and put on his make-up, but he wasn't right. So I went down to fetch my crochet and sat with him till the doctor arrived.

He wanted to go in to work, but Dr F. said he should take it easy until them pills had worn off. They're very dangerous, apparently, so Dr F. said it's a good thing I called him. Anyway, he's left a diet sheet and a load of prescriptions, so I popped straight out to the chemist before they closed and brought back a whole carrier bag full of stuff: cream for his legs, water pills, and two more pills I didn't recognize the names of.

The lad's got an old bootlace and has tied his hair in a ponytail so he looks like a tinker. I don't know what the world's coming to…

So the old bloke's not well, thinks Ben. Hardly surprising, given how he ended up. Still, it's really weird seeing it all from the old lady's point of view. Ben flicks forward a few pages to see where this is going.

15 June 1967

The nurses asked me to take in some pyjamas, but all I could find were those baggy silk trousers he wears sometimes, which would just draw attention to the problem.

I didn't like to go through his things, but what could I do? I found a few cotton nighties that weren't too frilly, and a couple of long smocky tops, so I took them in instead. I don't think they understand at the hospital what he's like.

I popped into Markie's on the way to get him some plain cotton panties, because none of his were suitable. All nylon and lace, most of them. I didn't like to look too closely. It's amazing what you can get in his size.

He looked so pathetic lying there, with his wig off and his stubble growing back. Normally, you hardly notice his age. The fat sort of pads out the wrinkles, so with the make-up on, he could be anything from 50 to 150.

They said he came round for a bit last night, but not enough to realize what's happened.

I was sitting by the bed saying the rosary when he woke up again. He had forgotten why he was there, so we had to explain. It took a while for it to sink in. I'll never forget the look on his face, poor dab.

I asked did he want me to fetch the priest, but he dried his eyes and said he'd rather I fetched a manicurist. Typical Mr M.! I'd brought in a load of cards from his flat, which got him worrying about visitors, so I went back later with his shaver and make-up and a couple of wigs, and a negligee thing he wanted to put over his nightie.

The lad was away, so I had cheese on toast and half a tin of tomato soup.

16 June 1967

I gave Mr M.'s a quick going over. Even when a place is empty, there's always dust. There were four more cards, so I took them in with me. Those two Scots lasses were in visiting when I arrived, so I nipped off for a cup of tea. It's a disgrace the way some folk dress, and in the daytime too! I'm sure that red-haired one wasn't wearing a bra.

I came back later and it was only Noreen Russell there, so I came in. She'd brought him a huge box of Black Magic, which he's not supposed to have because it's the sugar that did for his legs in the first place. But it's hopeless talking to him. He went through all the layers looking for the strawberry creams and ate them all. Then he started offering the box around. There were two big lads in green overalls wheeling a trolley down the corridor and he had them in eating up all his hard centres. I had a couple of montelimars.

From the looks of it, he's not changed at all. I did hope that the shock of losing his legs and coming so close to death would make him see life differently. But if anything he's worse than ever, propped up on his pillows like Lady Muck, receiving visitors, surrounded by cards and flowers. It made me feel so cross, I had to leave.

I popped in to St Cuthbert's and lit a candle, then I did a whole Stations of the Cross. I offered it up for Your guidance, Lord, and it calmed me down. I thought about Your agony in the garden, and how Your apostles couldn't stay awake, and about Simon of Cyrene, who carried Your cross for a while. It made me realize that what you have to do when someone is suffering is just stay with them and do whatever they ask. So it's not what I want for Mr M. that matters, it's what he needs of me.

So I went back to the hospital and the nurse let me in, even though visiting time was over. They'd pulled the screens round his bed because he was crying. Poor dab, what a sight he was, sobbing away with his make-up streaked all down his cheeks. I got some of that Pond's Cream and some tissues and cleaned him up, then sat with him until he fell asleep.

3 July 1967

I spent the morning in the upstairs flat having a bit of a dust round and moving the furniture ready for the wheelchair. I sorted through his towels and put a pile ready in the bathroom, and a couple of flannels. I'm not sure how he's going to manage with washing and that, but I thought they might come in handy.

At about eleven I had to sit down for a bit because it was starting to get to me. How on earth is he going to cope in this flat in a wheelchair? It takes two orderlies to get him on to the toilet in the hospital. I don't know how I'll manage him on my own. And what if he needs to get up in the night? Then there's my rotas to do, and my visits. I can't be with him all the time. And the lass will be back from boarding school next week, and I can't let them down, so that'll be me taken care of from 10 till 4. So that leaves poor old Mr M. on his own up here for six hours.

After a bit I said a prayer and the Lord gave me the strength to pull myself together and go into town. I bought a tall Tupperware container for if he needs to go in the night, and a rubber sheet just in case. I thought about getting nappies, but they'd never go round him. But I did get a pack of nappy pins, to pin a bath towel round him if need be.

I popped in to see Mrs J. and she told me about her aunt who was in a wheelchair, and what they had to do for her. It's the stairs I worry about. He's given me a blank cheque to cash, to cover me until he's sorted, but it didn't seem right so I left it in that silver teapot on the mantelpiece. Going round the shops buying them things made me want to cry.

The lad's still away, so I just had a tin of pilchards on toast.

4 July 1967

Davy rang my bell this morning, asking after Mr M. He thought it was today he was coming out, so looked in to see if he needed anything. I told him it was tomorrow, but I was just getting some rock buns out of the oven, so he stayed for a cup of tea.

He says Mr Russell is holding Mr M.'s job open, but no one is really expecting him back at work, because he'll never reach the counter now. They've got some bakery delivering cakes and that, and a new lass on the till, so they're managing fine at the moment.

He wants to ask Mr M. to teach him how to make his desserts, but I said he should wait a bit until we see how he is. He might not have the heart.

Davy's planning to start his own caff one day, so he wants to learn the trade. I asked why doesn't he get a job in a decent place, like Binns in Newcastle, nice-looking lad like him, but he thinks he'll pick up more at the Jungle. I can't see it myself, but I suppose he knows what he's doing.

He's coming round tomorrow to help me get Mr M. to bed, so that's a blessing (thanks be to You, Lord Jesus). I couldn't sleep last night worrying how I was going to manage.

I took a bag of rock buns over to Mrs Cooper, for the Christian Aid coffee morning tomorrow. She's said she'll set everything up, as I'll have to wait in for the ambulance. I said to be sure and buy enough milk, but I don't think she was listening. I hate to think what sort of a mess she'll make of it.

5 July 1967

Thank You, Lord, for Your mercy in sending me that Davy. I feel like a weight's been lifted off me, which it has in more ways than one! And it's all thanks to You. Sitting here in my armchair writing this, I feel very blessed.

Mr M. came home today, and he did try to be brave, poor dab. But it must have been so embarrassing needing them three big lads to get him up the stairs. I made them a cup of tea, and they polished off a whole plate of Battenberg. Mr M. was his old self when they were there, 'being mother' with the teapot as usual. But when they'd gone, he went quiet, which isn't like him at all. I said will I wheel him round the flat, but he said no, he'd got to learn to do it himself.

These flats aren't made for wheelchairs, mind. But then I don't know anywhere that is. He kept getting stuck in the doorways, then having to reverse and try again, because the chair only goes through if you face it straight on. There's probably a knack to it.

He managed going to the toilet on his own, by pushing up on the edge of the bath. But we got in a right old muddle trying to get him onto the sofa and I'm afraid I got a bit upset. Then Davy came round and sorted everything out. He's not a big lad, but a man's always stronger than a woman, so it made all the difference.

He's trying to save up, so he's offered to look after Mr M. for a month or so until he's settled. I was worried about the money, if Mr M.'s not working, but he says he's got a little nest egg put away, so that's all right.

8 July 1967

Dr C. telephoned this afternoon to ask would I fetch young Mary home from Newcastle station. She had been called out on an emergency, and the other doctor had his rounds to see to. I wonder why some people have children if they don't have time to look after them. She insisted on paying double as it was two days before I was supposed to start and such short notice.

I waited under the clock and the lass seemed pleased to see me, but it must have been a disappointment not to have her mother there. She had found a porter to bring her trunk. I gave him sixpence, but he made a face so it probably wasn't enough.

The lass comes up to my chin now, but still looks like she needs feeding up. She was shy at first, but was soon chattering away. She seems so grown up these days, asking how I am and what I've been doing, just like a proper lady. To hear her, you'd never know she was from Shields. It makes me wonder how much longer they'll be needing me.

She had a front door key with her, which was a blessing as the doctor had forgotten to leave one for me. But the fridge was practically empty and I couldn't see anything suitable in the larder for the lass's tea. So we went out to the Co-op for fish fingers and a tin of baked beans. I brought some proper tea too, and a pint of milk. I don't know how people drink that dusty tea-bag rubbish.

After tea I helped the lass unpack, then got out the Scrabble and she beat me! I realized later she would probably have preferred to watch the television, but I didn't think and she never mentioned it, bless her. She's such a polite lass. It can't be much fun being looked after by an old lady, but she never complains.

Dr C. (Mr) came in around 6 and went straight out again, and Dr C. (Mrs) didn't get back till 7.30. She looked all in (she'd been trying to get some poor mad lady into a mental hospital), but she gave the lass a hug, which is more than her husband did!

CHAPTER FORTY-FOUR

29 July 1967

The lad's started going out on two-nighters, but he says the herring have disappeared. Last year they could still find a few, if they cast about a bit. But this year he says it's spooky how empty the fishing grounds are. I said I would pray for him, but he said it's too late for that. The time to do something was when the smaller fish started to go a few years back, because then you knew there'd be no full-size ones coming through.

It's sad to see the Fish Quay these days. When I was a girl you could walk from one side of the Gut to the other on the decks of herring boats, and the town was full of herring girls and crews up from Aberdeen and Peterhead.

I was talking about it to Mr M. this morning. He used to be a cook on a drifter, he says, and minds when the holds were so full, they had to heap the fish up on the decks. He said the old lads warned about taking too many, but nobody listened. "Klondyking", he said they called it, as if the fish were gold. It's an ugly thing, Lord, the sin of greed.

I wonder sometimes whether Mr M. losing his legs is a punishment from You, Lord, to teach him self-restraint in this life, so that he has a chance of being reunited with You in heaven when he dies. I tried to talk to him about it today, saying he could look on the operation as a chance to change his ways.

But he just laughed and threw the paper at me, where there was a headline saying the government have just passed a law to make it legal for men to have relations with each other! "So even the Prime Minister approves of b——," said Mr M. The paper was calling it "the queer's law". I don't know what the world is coming to. They'll be allowing homosexual priests next. At least if it's illegal, people will try to stop themselves doing it. Pope Pius had the right idea. He knew that if you allow women to have sex without getting pregnant, soon everyone will be doing it whether they're married or not. Then where would we be? It's already starting to happen, with the pill and that, if them loose lasses down the Jungle are anything to go by.

Mr M. was on about it all the time I was there, but Davy could see I was upset. He's such a sensitive lad. I worry about him, working in that place, and spending so much time with Mr M. What if it rubs off on him?

He calls Mr M. "Lord Jim", of course, because that's what they call him at work, or 'your majesty', which is a sort of joke between them. And Mr M. calls him "Laura", which I can't understand at all, but the lad doesn't seem to mind.

I did ask Mr M. today if he still needed me, what with Davy coming in, but he said let's see how it goes.

30 July 1967

I went to the 8 o'clock Mass today, because I can't stand what he's done to the High Mass. Mrs J. was there too, and Mrs C. – so that's all the Flower Ladies going to the 8 o'clock now. I wonder if he's noticed?

They started on Davy's cookery lessons upstairs this morning, which is good in a way, as it gives Mr M. something to do, but it means that diet's gone straight out the window. I asked Davy to pop in to see me on his way out and had a word about it.

He says he hasn't the heart to stop Mr M. eating, because it's one of the only pleasures he's got left. He says Mr M. knows it's bad for his diabetes, but he'd rather die fat and happy than "live on in misery gnawing on a lettuce leaf" as he puts it. So I suppose it's only a matter of time before he goes bad again.

Davy's got some big lads from the Jungle coming round every Friday and Saturday now to help him carry the wheelchair down the stairs. Then they all go off to the Jungle for the evening, and wheel him back home at some ungodly hour. Mr M. calls the big lads "my babysitters", because they look out for him while Davy's working in the kitchen. He's got the chair all decked out with ribbons and velvet cushions these days, and has one of those sequinned embroidered bedspreads over his stumps so you'd never know.

Yesterday I noticed that Davy was wearing a bit make-up too, when they set off, so I had a word with him about that today as well. It's partly my doing that he's working for Mr M., so I don't want him being turned.

He said lots of young men these days are "rebelling against the macho image". That's what he called it. That's why lads are growing their hair and wearing flowery shirts. The make-up's all part of it, he says. It doesn't mean he's turned homosexual. Still, it bothers me, seeing such a handsome young lad in eyeshadow and mascara, so I think I'll have to have a word with Mr M. about it too.

The lad was home when I got in. He's jacked it in on that herring boat and is going back on the trawlers. He's got a place on a boat going to Iceland tomorrow night, so he was getting all his stuff ready. He was seeing to his own washing, bless him. I hope it will be dry in time.

31 July 1967

I went up ten minutes early this morning, to be sure of catching Mr M. on his own. I said my piece about corrupting the lad but he just laughed and called me a "silly old trout". Usually I'd just let it go, thinking I've done my bit and now it's up to You, Lord. But this time I just couldn't let him laugh it off. I thought, that Davy deserves better, so I kept on about it, telling him that the lad really wants to make a go of his caff business, but there's a risk he'll go off the rails with all them bad influences at the Jungle. So I don't want Mr M. encouraging him in immoral behaviour.

I told him I'd seen Davy in make-up on Saturday and I was worried he was heading down the wrong path.

"What if that's the path he's chosen?" said Mr M. So I said that it's our duty to help him resist temptation, because he's only young still, and he's got a chance to make something of his life. And Mr M. says, "What you mean is, you don't want him turning out like me." So I said yes, I was sorry, but even if the Government allowed it, I didn't think wearing women's clothes and going with men was how God intended a man to live.

So Mr M. says, "What about love thy neighbour as thyself? What do you think God meant by that?" (Except he always says "Goddess" instead of "God", which is a sort of blasphemy I suppose, but I don't think he means any harm by it.) He was trying to be smart, but I wasn't having any. So I made him promise not to encourage the lad in any of that 'gay' business.

Davy arrived then, so we had to leave off, and I sent them out of the kitchen so I could do the floor. When I was done I had a quick cup of coffee and went round the lass's house.

It was a nice sunny day, so we took a picnic to the beach. Her mother's keen to get her in the water this year, but I can't see it myself. She's brought her a copy of The Observer Book of Sea Life, *so we took that along and spent a while peering into rock pools.*

It reminded me of going flither-picking for the long lines as a lass. We'd tuck our skirts into our drawers and clamber all over the Black Middens, looking for mussels and limpets and that.

The lad left after tea. I always want to wave him off, but he says it's bad luck, so I've to pretend I never even heard the door closing behind him. I'll say a special prayer for him later.

11 August 1967

My hands are shaking as I write this. Dear Lord, please have mercy on Your servant. I am so upset I hardly know what to do with myself, so I thought I'd try writing to see if it would calm me, even though it's only 4 in the afternoon.

I popped upstairs to give Mr M. his change at about 1. He'd paid me too much, and said to keep the rest, but I wasn't comfortable with that, so when I had the right coins I thought I'd take them up. I wish now that I hadn't bothered.

I never ring the bell, because I've got my key and anyway he can't get to the door any more. So I let myself in and I could hear him and Davy having a gay old time in the bedroom, laughing away. I didn't think anything of it, because they always have a good laugh together, chatting away in that jokey language they use.

So I came upstairs as usual, and the bedroom door's open and there they are. Lord, I can hardly bear to write what I saw. Mr M. was in his wheelchair and he was dressed, if you can call it that, in his underwear (not the panties I brought from Markie's) and that negligee. It was like he had started getting ready to go out, but hadn't decided what to wear.

The wardrobe was wide open and there were clothes hanging on the doors and lying all over the bed, scarves, kaftans, blouses, all sorts.

But it was Davy that upset me. I thought at first I'd made a mistake and there was a lass in the room, but then I saw that it was Davy in one of Mr M.'s wigs (the long auburn one). He was wearing that purple silk kaftan, with a load of different beads, but from the state of the room, I'd say he'd had on half the clothes there.

*He was walking up and down in front of Mr M., just like one of the lasses on that Miss World contest, and Mr M. was clapping his hands and saying, "*Fortuni! Fortuni!*", some nonsense like that, and, "Give me a twirl, heartface."*

So Davy twirled around, sort of tossing his head to shake the wig hair back over his shoulders, then he must have seen my face, because he rushed straight past me to the bathroom and slammed the door.

Anyway the upshot of all that is that I've left the job. Twenty-six years and it's come to this! I said to Mr M. that he'd broken his promise, so I didn't want to do for him anymore. I said he should be ashamed of himself corrupting a nice young lad like Davy. I said I couldn't carry on knowing that sort of thing was going on as soon as my back was turned.

Of course leaving won't stop it from going on, but at least I won't have to think about it now.

I never saw Davy. He stayed in that bathroom the whole time I was there.

Mr M. doesn't really need me now anyway, so it's not like I'm letting him down.

I didn't feel like eating, so I just had a bit of buttered toast for tea, then sat and tried to do my crochet. But I couldn't settle, so I walked to St Cuthbert's and lit a candle, and sat for a while praying to You for comfort. Then Father Gregory came in to lock up and asked if I wanted a word. But I just shook my head and left.

At least I've got the lass on Monday to take my mind off it.

CHAPTER FORTY-FIVE

2007

The following morning finds Mary sitting on her bench in the sunshine with a sheaf of typescript in her lap. She remembers typing it on her old Olivetti. Typing was so physical in those days, she reflects; one had to punch the keys really hard to make an impression; so different from those sensitive little flat squares on today's computer keyboards. She's on her third espresso and her umpteenth cigarette, toiling through Peggy's unfortunate life – but here, at last, is one of the episodes she recalls from a different life story.

She sees that she's inserted a heading that reads: *NOT PEGGY. WHO?*

K: … What can you see? etc.

M: The boards are lurching. That lamp needs trimming, the glass is covered with soot. Why won't he leave it be? Can't he see she's not interested? Oh—

K: … Alarm sign used, then session resumed, subject asked to re-enter same life at an earlier time

M: I'm feeling qualmy, like the beer's sloshing around in my belly. And the taste of that bakkie's making it worse. I'm looking down, trying to walk straight, but my feet feel heavy, somehow, and the boards like they're tipping. And for a moment I've forgotten what I'm about, where I am, what I've come to do. Then I hear her voice saying something from inside, and it comes back to me, this great whoosh of anger and I reach up to check my knife's there.

Then I feel a chill and find my flies are unbuttoned – when did that happen? I can't even remember going to the pisser – so I fumble a bit and get them done up, and I'm cursing myself, and her, and him. And now my jacket's come undone, so I've to fix that too, but I've got the buttons out of order somehow, so I must be worse gone than I thought.

So I'm trying to sort the buttons, but I'm so spitting angry my fingers won't work, and I'm just ripping them open, and his tin's come out of my pocket and's clattering down onto the boards.

K: *... Alarm sign used again. Session terminated. Poss. return to this life when Peggy finished?*

Aha, Mary thinks. So there's the tobacco tin that's been haunting her. She flicks forwards another few pages; she thinks there were several more episodes like this, from Peggy's predecessors' lives. Right, here's another one: *NOT PEGGY. WHO?*

K: *... What can you see? etc.*

M: *She's gone down to the kitchen with the bairns to find out what's happening about tea, if she's supposed to make it or if they do and what time and that. So I take my chance to look in his ditty box again. I wrapped ticking round it, so it wouldn't rattle and draw attention, so now I unwrap it. And there's that photo where she's looking like an angel, sat still for the camera. How'd they ever get her to sit that still?*

Now I've got his bakkie tin out and it's popped open just like that, easy as blinking. And there's his roll of Sweet Virginia and his papers, and his box of matches, little scattered wisps of dry bakkie. The smell's that sweet, like toffee almost. And all the while I'm listening out for Mam coming back up the stairs, because I don't want her seeing and getting upset. Maybe I'll try smoking something myself, later when she's not around, and it will remind me of him.

So I shove it in the pocket of my jacket, so that's him kept safe, like, even though she's not bothered. And I'm going to the window and looking out, at all the lums belching smoke, and the seagulls paddling along the ridges of the roofs. I never realized how high we were, and I'm thinking I'm glad we've got the slops pot, for it's a fair tramp down all them stairs for the nettie in the middle of the night—

'Howay, Doctor. You alright?'

Mary sets the pages aside and looks up. 'Mr Skipper! Come and join me.'

'Is that Mr Ian here yet, then?'

'No, was he supposed to be?'

'He said ten o'clock, so I'm a bit early.'

Mary takes a breath, trying to control herself. This is getting beyond a joke. 'This is the first I've heard of it,' she says carefully. 'What's the plan, then? Did he say?'

'Only that we were going to do another of them memory sessions and he was going to film it. You're not going out, are you?' he asks anxiously. 'Only I'm sure he said it was today.'

'I'll call him, shall I? Maybe there's been a misunderstanding.' She goes inside and dials the number for the hotel. Ian's not in his room, apparently, but the girl thinks she saw him going into the lounge. After a lengthy pause while she despatches some minion to locate him, Ian appears on the line.

'Ian? It's Mary. I've got Mr Skipper here saying you arranged—'

'Shit, shit, shit! God, I'm so sorry. I completely forgot.'

'What shall I tell him?'

'I don't know. Make up something. Look, I can't talk now. Things are going crazy. There's been all kinds of hassles with the film crew.'

'When were you planning to inform me about this regression session?'

'I tried to phone you.'

'No you didn't,' she says crossly.

'Yes I did. Check your answerphone.'

'Well you didn't try very hard. You just assumed you could waltz in here this morning and—'

'Sorry, sorry. Look, I've really got to sort this. I'll call you later, OK? Lots of love.'

'No, it's not OK. What's going on, Ian? Why are you contacting all my old clients?' But he's hung up.

Skip looks up expectantly when she comes back outside.

'I'm afraid Mr Campbell's been detained,' she explains wearily. 'Some crisis with the film crew apparently.' Lots of love? What does he mean, lots of love?

'Ah.'

'I'm sorry.'

'It doesn't matter,' he says, though it obviously does matter. His hair's freshly washed, she notices, and his tweed jacket looks like it's been to the cleaners.

She hands him a couple of cigarettes and they sit in silence while he goes through the familiar intricate rigmarole of creating a handful of bidis.

'How are you, anyway?' she asks. 'No after-effects from the other day, I hope.'

'Right as rain, thank you, Doctor. Bit of a headache is all. But that's to be expected if you're off the Stella, isn't it?'

'Have you stopped drinking completely then?' Mary keeps her voice neutral, trying to hide her amazement.

'Just for a few days. See how it goes. It's all this remembering, see. I want to be sharp, like.' He looks across at the far bank. 'When you're on the Stella, you're always losing things.'

'I can let you borrow that tape, if you need to jog your memory.'

'No, you're all right. It's fresh in my mind still, most of it. In fact I been getting more, the more I think about it. To fill in the gaps like.'

'Some people might prefer to forget some of those things,' she prompts gently.

He looks at her. 'That Tom, you mean? Oh ay. I won't forget him again in a hurry.' He rubs his chin thoughtfully, as if surprised to find it clean-shaven. 'You hear about them battered wives, don't you? And you think, why does she put up with it? But she thought she deserved it.'

'Did he ever love her, do you think?'

'He loved that other lass, didn't he? That Annie. That was the trouble. It was there between them the whole time. So she was always trying to please him, to make up for not being her. Then he'd want to thump her – because you do, don't you? When a dog's all over you, you just want to slap it down. So then she'd try harder, which made him even madder.'

'Then once the baby was born, they were both trapped,' Mary says. 'You can see how such a situation might escalate, can't you?'

The old man stares into the distance. 'It drags you down, loving someone that can't stand the sight of you. It makes you feel like nothing. Worse than nothing. You forget there's any good in you.' He blows smoke.

'She must have felt so guilty about not telling anyone what happened that night.'

'It ruined her, I reckon. Her whole life was a sort of lie from then on. Funny, isn't it? How one wrong thing can turn everything bad?'

'Guilt is a more powerful force than most people are aware,' Mary muses. 'We tend to assume it's merely a reaction to some ill one has committed, but I think it's actually an urge in itself that can motivate all kinds of self-destructive behaviour.'

'He was always saying he wanted to teach her a lesson. He blamed her for everything.' He pushes the hair off his forehead to reveal the edge of his port wine stain. 'See this?' he says. 'I got this off her, I reckon. Because that's where he'd always hit her, on the side of her head where the bruises wouldn't show. He liked to get her kneeling, didn't he? And make her say sorry. Then he'd hit her to teach her a lesson.'

She lights another Gitanes and they smoke quietly for a minute of two. Then: 'I reckon Paul's lad will be along later,' he says casually. 'Got something to show you.'

'Oh?' Mary wonders if Paul knows about this visit. 'Any idea what?'

A knowing smile: 'I'll let him tell you himself.'

'What have you two been up to?' she asks, vaguely considering whether she should be concerned. A vulnerable young boy spending time alone with an alcoholic schizophrenic, albeit one temporarily on the wagon.

'I been doing a bit painting,' he remarks, changing the subject. 'Not them old scenes, from Flo's time and that. I been doing things from my today life instead, from back when I were a nipper. To anchor me, like.'

'Has it been successful?'

'I been trying for a likeness of my mam. It's just the beginnings, mind. I don't know if it will come to something.' Then, raising his hand in a wave: 'Here comes the lad now.'

Ben breaks into a run when he spots them, then stands there grinning.

'What's all this about?' she asks, taken aback by how very *very* pleased she is to see him. As he charged in through her gate it's only by sheer effort of will that she prevented her arms gathering him into a hug.

'I found out where Lord Jim lived – and it's right over old Skip's place! His landlady used to look after him before he died. And look! She wrote all these diaries, like going back to the year dot. So there's tons of stuff about Lord Jim and what he was like, what he said and that.'

'I'm not sure you should be talking to me about this,' Mary cautions.

'They're sort of private, but Skip said it was all right to read them.'

'I mean, I'm not sure your father would approve of you being here.'

'I don't care what he thinks,' he says, jutting his chin mutinously. 'Anyway, he's not here. He's off on the boat till tomorrow night.'

'Nevertheless, I think I really ought to inform him that we've been in contact, don't you? It could be tricky for me professionally otherwise, if he were to find out.'

'Do you have to?' He looks pleadingly at her.

'Unfortunately, it appears I've mislaid the number of his satellite phone,' she says, smiling. 'So how about if I just leave a message on his landline?'

'So he won't get it till he gets back – which means we've got nearly two whole days!' He beams at her, and there it is again, an almost physical impulse to reach out and hold him.

'Look, here's one of the 1967 diaries. It's got all about him having his legs off, just like Dad remembered.'

He hands it to Mary: it's one of those hard-backed exercise books with a cloth spine. It's the kind she uses herself, actually, though they're difficult to find nowadays.

'She knew him for ages, Skip says, like thirty years or something, ever since he moved into the flat. So I thought there might be something about Annie. I mean if she knew him for that long, maybe he talked about her disappearing and that.'

Mary opens the diary at random. The writing is neat and old-fashioned; the unhurried hand of someone who likes things nice and tidy. '"Another terrible day,"' she reads, then looks up.

They're both watching her, waiting for her to react. Seeing their expectant faces, she bursts into laughter.

'Come on,' she says, getting up. 'If we're going to read them together, let's find somewhere a bit more comfortable, shall we? What about the Seamen's Mission? I'll treat us all to bacon sandwiches.'

CHAPTER FORTY-SIX

25 August 1967

Another terrible day. My cold was a bit better, and that Vaseline helped with the chapped nose, but I still felt very low. I can't remember being this bad last year when the lass went off on holiday. But I was still doing for Mr M. then, so I was keeping busy, and the lad was in and out with the herring boats so I wasn't on my own so much.

Mrs J. popped in with half a dozen eggs and some Lemsip, but she had to get back for her grandchildren. I keep thinking of Alfie, I don't know why. I keep thinking, what if I'd said yes and we'd ended up with a baby? Would it really have been the end of the world?

After she'd gone, I had a little cry, then put the radio on for Woman's Hour, *and slept for a bit in the chair. Mr M. had his music on all afternoon, and folk up and down the stairs, so I kept the radio on.*

Davy rang the bell later. I didn't feel like talking, but he insisted, so I asked him in for a cup of tea.

I must say he looked very well, with a nice tan and his hair blonde from the sun. It was too long, of course, but that's the fashion now, isn't it? At least he wasn't wearing make-up, so that's something.

He told me that Mr M.'s been taken bad these last few days and has been asking for me. I said it doesn't sound like he's bad, what with the music blaring out. (That wasn't very charitable, Lord, I know, but I was feeling so poorly.) Davy said it was the visitors who put the music on and he was sorry if it disturbed me.

I asked why Mr M. wanted to see me and Davy said he thought he "wanted forgiveness". I said that didn't sound much like Mr M., and Davy said no, but he hasn't been much like himself lately, so maybe that's why.

He said he's still eating those custard creams like they're going out of fashion, and he's never stuck to that diet, so the weight's not come off. And he's been on antibiotics for weeks because the sugar diabetes means he's been getting one bug after another. But every time he gets better, he goes down with something else. He's got pneumonia now, and the doctor's talking about putting him back in the hospital.

I couldn't face going up to see him this evening, so I said I'd think about it.

After Davy left, they turned the music off.

Maybe I'll pop in tomorrow if I'm feeling a bit brighter.

26 August 1967

I managed a boiled egg for breakfast. The milk's been piling up while I've been bad. I had to pour a whole pint away because it had gone sour. That got me started on clearing out the fridge, so I finished that off before I went up.

But I wish now that I'd gone up yesterday, when he was asking for me, because he'd taken a turn for the worse by the time I got there. Davy had stayed the night (there was one of them rubber lilo things propped up behind the sofa) and said he hardly slept at all, because Mr M. was talking in his sleep. I felt his forehead and he was red hot, so I think the fever had probably made him delirious.

I thought I'd still be cross, but when I saw him lying there, sweating in one of his frilly nighties, I just felt ashamed that I'd not been more forgiving.

He was asleep, and his make-up was off. He had a scarf tied round his head like a sort of turban, instead of the wig I suppose, so he looked for all the world like a fat old fishwife snoring by the fire. Davy looked all in so I sent him off to take a nap, while I pottered round tidying up a bit. It was almost like old times, with Davy and me working together.

The phone rang at about 11.30 and I answered it. It was someone asking after Mr M., so I said he was asleep and left the receiver off.

I woke Mr M. at 12 for his pills. He's still on the antibiotics, but I don't know what good they're doing. He hardly recognized me, and fell back asleep straight away. Davy came back at about 4, so he was asleep for nearly 6 hours, poor dab! He called Dr Fraser, and he came round at about 5.30 and said he didn't think it was worth disturbing Mr M. to take him to the hospital. He never said, but it was obvious what he meant.

After he left we had a cup of tea and Davy set out a plate of custard creams, which made us both laugh and cry for a bit. Then Davy went off home to pick up a change of clothes, so I got my knitting and my rosary and sat with Mr M.

He was snoring away, propped up on the pillows (Dr F. said he'd be more comfortable like that), then he sort of spluttered a bit so I looked up, and he was staring straight at me.

"Is that Edith Lillian?" he said, so I said yes, and he said, "Silly old trout," and closed his eyes again. I thought he'd gone back to sleep, but a bit later he reached out his hand and said, "Are you still there?" I caught hold of it and said I was. Then he said, "I did a bad thing, Edith. A long time ago. I should have said something, but I never did."

So I asked did he want me to call Father Gregory, and he said no, he'd rather talk to me. Then he said, "He was lugging something heavy." So I said, "Who?" And he said, "Tom." And then he said, "It must have been her." So I said, "Who do you mean?" But he'd closed his eyes again.

I kept a hold of his hand, and stroked it a bit to let him know I was there, and a bit later he opened his eyes again and said, "I knew it was Annie." I didn't know what he was talking about, but there were tears pouring down his cheeks. Then he said, "We looked everywhere for her. I kept hoping I was wrong."

I got a Kleenex and wiped his eyes for him, but he kept crying and saying, "I'm so sorry," and, "I should have said something." So whatever it was had obviously been on his conscience for years. I tried to comfort him by telling him that God is merciful, and will always forgive a sinner who truly repents, but I don't think he could hear me.

27 August 1967

He's gone and everything's settled. Davy called the Co-op and they took him away this afternoon. They didn't have a coffin big enough, so they had to wrap him up and tie him onto a stretcher. It was quite a business getting him down them stairs, but they managed it with care and respect, so I suppose they're used to that sort of thing.

Davy said he talked once about wanting a proper funeral, with lots of flowers and black lace, so he's going to have a word with that new vicar at Holy Trinity about it tomorrow. Davy says he's quite 'trendy', so Lord knows what the service will be like. There's still quite a lot of money in his bank account, so that's all right.

Once I put the phone back on, it never stopped ringing all day.

I can't believe he's gone. When I popped downstairs to have a quick bath and change, I kept thinking I could hear his wheelchair trundling around upstairs. It was an extra large one they had to get in specially. I wonder if they'll come to collect it, or if I'm supposed to take it back. How do they know when someone passes and doesn't need their wheelchair anymore?

Davy went home, but came back later and knocked on my door saying he couldn't settle. I made us cheese on toast and hot chocolate and we watched that Terry and June *programme to take our minds off it for a bit. Then I said a prayer, and Davy joined in, and I said he could fetch down the lilo and sleep here if he wanted. So that's where he is now. He went out like a light, bless him.*

Dear God, in Your mercy, forgive us our sins now and at the hour of our end, amen.

CHAPTER FORTY-SEVEN

2007

Ben's sitting with the doc and old Skip down the Mission with the remains of their stotties on thick plates. Old fishing blokes keep trundling in and out, going howay to Skip and getting their teas and fried eggs and that, scraping chair legs on the floor and lighting up.

The doc started off reading Miss Turnbull's diary between mouthfuls, to catch up to where he'd got to, but now it's open between them on the table, and they're reading it together. They've just got to the bit where Lord Jim's on his death bed and Ben can hardly believe it: there in Miss Turnbull's old-lady handwriting, with all its careful loops, is this tiny little glimpse into Annie's life.

'He saw Tom!' he says. 'He was carrying Annie's body!'

'It certainly looks like that, doesn't it? And it preyed on his mind ever since.'

'So why didn't he tell someone before?'

'I don't know, Ben. Perhaps he was frightened. Or ashamed. Perhaps he was somewhere he shouldn't have been. It can't have been easy for a young man with his proclivities at that time. It's hard enough these days for people to admit to being homosexual.'

'Oh,' says Ben. 'Right. I'd forgotten about that. So he kept quiet to protect himself.'

'Possibly. Without asking him, we can't know for sure.'

'So Dad's got to be hypnotized again.'

'After his last experience, I doubt there's much hope of that,' says the doc, getting out her tabs and looking around – at the big new No Smoking signs on the wall and all the old blokes puffing away.

'But he's our only witness!'

'To continue with your detective analogy, this is certainly a very good lead. But it's not the only one.' She leans back and blows smoke up into the blue cloud hanging over the tables. 'Did Mr Skipper tell you about our interesting time together yesterday?' she asks.

'No. What happened?' Ben's eyes have started stinging, but he doesn't mind.

The doc glances at old Skip across the table, as though asking for permission.

'Go on,' he says. 'You'll tell it better than me.'

So she tells Ben all about how old Skip used to be Flo in a previous life, which is really weird, and how that Ian bloke used to be Annie's mam, which is even *weirder.* Which starts Ben going through everyone he knows in his mind, trying to match them all up, like in a game of Cluedo, which leaves him with Laura and Nana and the doc in this life, and Sam and Tom and Annie's dad in 1898 – which makes him feel sort of sick and excited at the same time.

'Did they say what happened to Annie?' he asks after a bit.

'I think perhaps it's better if we don't talk too much about that,' says the doc. 'It might influence our future sessions – in the unlikely event that your father relents and allows me to hypnotize you again.' She raises her eyebrows at him. 'No advance on that front, I assume?'

He shakes his head and she squeezes his arm with a gloved hand. 'I'll have a word with him when he gets back, shall I?' she says. 'You never know, perhaps a bit of sea air will make him see things differently. Meanwhile, I think we ought to let Ian know about these diaries. Do you have his number?'

'It's under BBC,' Ben says, handing her his mobile – then taking it back again when it's obvious she has no idea what to do with it. 'Here you are. It's ringing,' he says, handing it back.

'Do I need to press something?'

'Just talk into it like a normal phone when he answers.'

She holds it nervously to her ear, like she's afraid it's going to irradiate her brain.

'Hello, Ian? It's Mary – yes, he lent it to me – yes, well that's because I *was* angry. You can't just – well, don't you think I deserve an explanation? Thank you, yes. I would appreciate that. But in the meantime something's happened with Ben – no, he's fine. But there's something I think you ought to see.'

Why is she being so narky with him, Ben wonders. Have they had a row or something?

'He's found some old diaries at Mr Skipper's house,' she goes on. 'They appear to have been written by Lord Jim's housekeeper, if you can believe that – yes, I know, amazing coincidence – though naturally I'd have a somewhat different perspective on it. Anyway, it seems young Jimmy witnessed something the night Annie disappeared, but neglected to report it at the time – I've got the relevant volume here, but there are lots of other volumes, Ben says. Yes, at Mr Skipper's house – here, I'll pass you to Mr Skipper. He'll give you directions.'

She hands over the phone like she can't wait to get shot of it. Ben sort of hovers to see if the old bloke needs help too, but he's into it straight away.

The doc looks jittery. She digs into her cardie for her tabs, then shoves them back again. Then she says she's going up to the house to get her notebook and rushes off without finishing her bap. When she comes back down ten minutes later, all pink and out of breath, she's got one of her shawls on instead of her cardie, and has done that thing with her eyeshadow.

Ian's waiting outside 59 Seymour Street when they get there, pacing up and down, jabbering into his Blackberry and smoking furiously. His bike's chained to a streetlamp with a chain as thick as Ben's wrist. It's probably got one of those sat nav homing gizmos fitted too, that give off a signal when they're stolen so the police can track it down.

When he sees them, he high-fives Ben. 'Hey, Ben, my man!' he says in a mock American accent. 'I thought we'd lost you.'

'You have. I mean, Dad doesn't know I'm here.'

'So where's these diaries then?' Ian goes. Ben had been vaguely hoping that Ian would try persuading Dad to change his mind, but it doesn't look like he's going to. In fact it looks like they've all being getting on fine without him, which makes him feel really sad, plus it seems so unfair because it was him that started everything off in the first place.

Old Skip fishes out his bunch of keys and sorts through till he finds a little gold Yale, which he hands to Ben. 'You do it, lad,' he says and Ben understands that it's because he doesn't want to be the one leading the way in through 'her' front door.

They all crowd into the musty little hall and Ben pushes open the door to Miss Turnbull's bedroom. And now he knows exactly what the old bloke feels like, because it seems wrong, all of a sudden, to have these strangers tramping into her private space, stirring up her still air with their busy bodies. But it's too late to stop now, so he pulls the plastic suitcase out from under the bed and snaps the clasps open.

The Ian bloke's in there straight away, like you'd expect, squatting down in his khaki shorts and going wow and fantastic, clicking away with his stills camera. The doc's standing back a bit, as though he's a kid opening a pressie she's given him, which is pretty much how he's behaving actually. As if the diaries belong to him now. Which makes Ben want to push him away and close the case and shove it back under the bed.

He catches old Skip's eye and the old bloke shrugs. 'Leave it, lad,' he says quietly. 'Like I said, it's time.'

'I've got one of the 1967 ones,' Ben says, handing it over. 'The bit we found where it says about Annie is marked with that Metro ticket.'

Ian plonks himself on the bed with his knees apart, like it's just any old bed. And Ben wants to say, 'Look, this is the bed she slept in, right, the old lady who wrote that diary you're so interested in.'

They all watch him flicking through the notebook, reading bits to himself here and there, and he's so wired there's practically steam coming out of his ears. 'So this is that old woman Lord Jim was talking about, right? The one who was always praying for his immortal soul. Fucking hell! This is like the bloody Missing Link.'

'I'm glad you think so,' says the doc, but she doesn't look it. She looks sort of nervous and narked at the same time.

'I mean this will be fucking fantastic telly. What with the link to old Skip's paintings. Right, mate?' he says to Skip. 'Your studio's down there, I assume? The place where you keep your paintings. So I can do a pan from your studio down the hall to this room, can't I? Fucking A. Couldn't be better.' Then, 'You couldn't rustle us up a cup of tea, could you, Skip mate? With all this excitement, I'm as parched as the bottom of a parrot's cage.' As though old Skip's his servant, thinks Ben, and we're all just here to give him what he needs.

But even though Ian is totally bossy and selfish, Ben can't help admiring the way he just goes for what he wants. Like now, where someone else might be chatting away politely while the tea's being made, he's just ignoring everyone and reading the diary.

He's read the confession bit, where Lord Jim dies, and now he's working backwards to see if Annie's mentioned again, which she isn't, as Ben's already checked. But maybe he didn't look hard enough, because it seems like Ian's found something, because he's gone all stiff, like a dog on a lead when it sees a cat up ahead; and he's turning the pages really slowly, reading every word, then flicking back again just to make sure. Then, after a bit, he holds the diary out to the doc.

'Here's a section you ought to look at,' he says. And there's a look on his face Ben doesn't quite get, as if all the excitement's drained out of it and he's really worried about something.

The doc reads out the bit he's pointing to: 'Davy arrived then, so we had to leave off and I sent them out of the kitchen so I could do the floor. When I was done I had a quick cup of coffee and went round the lass's house.

'It was a nice sunny day, so we took a picnic to the beach. Her mother's keen to get her in the water this year, but I can't see it myself. She's brought her a copy of *The Observer Book of Sea Life*, so we took that along and spent a while peering into rock pools.'

Ian's peering at her face. 'Does that ring any bells?' he asks.

'It depends,' says the doc. 'Let me check.' And she zooms off down the hall with Ian hot on her tail. What on earth are they on about, Ben wonders, following them into the kitchen, where old Skip's squeezing out teabags and lobbing them into a black bin liner overflowing with crumpled Stella tins.

'What was the name of your landlady, Mr Skipper?' the doc asks. 'Only I've a feeling I might have known her when I was a little girl.'

'Miss Edith Lillian Turnbull she was called, but I always called her Miss Turnbull. Like a mother to me, she was.'

'Miss Turnbull,' goes the doc; and for some reason she looks really shaken.

Anyway it turns out that old Miss Turnbull used to be the doc's childminder or nanny or something, because her parents were GPs, so they had to work during the summer holidays. So they paid the old lady to look after her. Which is totally amazing, because that means that old Skip and Dad and Laura and the doc are all associated with this one house in Seymour Street, if you count the upper and lower flats as one house.

'Do you remember coming here?' Ian asks, and the doc shakes her head.

'I didn't even know where she lived. She just used to turn up on the front doorstep at ten every morning and hang up her coat in the hall. She could have dropped from the sky like Mary Poppins for all I knew. I remember she always used a hanger instead of a hook and draped her scarf around it as though the hanger was a very thin neck. Then at four o'clock on the dot, she'd take her coat off the hanger and off she'd go.'

'And you never followed her?'

'No. Why would I?' But she looks really worried, as if she can't trust her own memory – though Ben can't see why on earth it's such a big deal.

She turns to old Skip. 'You don't recall a little girl visiting the house that summer, do you?' she asks. 'She'd have been about ten, but probably looked younger. Small and skinny. Long dark hair held back with a hair band.'

The old bloke shakes his head. 'I knew she'd got the job, like, but I never clapped eyes on the bairn. But then again, I'd have been off out on the boat most the time.'

'So she could have come here without you knowing it.' Ian looks at the doc, as though he's asking her a question. And it's suddenly like they're the only two people in the room, and they're having this secret conversation.

She shakes her head. 'All I can say is that I have absolutely no recollection of being in this house,' she says, like she's apologizing for something.

'You know what this means, don't you?' says Ian, and he seems really rattled, even more than the doc, which is saying something.

'If I never came here, I don't see how I could possibly have known—'

'I mean it's fucking Bridey Murphy all over again, isn't it?'

'That case was never properly resolved. You do realize that, don't you? They blew that new evidence up out of all proportion. The fact that she had Irish neighbours as a child didn't disprove anything.'

'Look, I need time to think about this. Let me have a proper look at the diaries, then we'll talk, right?' Ian crams a custard cream in his mouth and stands up. 'All right if I borrow these for a few days?' he asks, though he's telling really, not asking, because he's already slipped all the 1967 diaries into his backpack.

It seems very quiet with him gone – like when the TV's been blaring and you hit the mute button.

'What was all that about?' Ben asks.

The doc sort of slumps back in her chair. 'Ian's worried that I might have been putting ideas into your head,' she says. 'And into your father's head, and Mr Skipper's. He thinks I read all these diaries when I was a little girl and made everything up.'

'But I was going on about Annie for years before I met you.'

'I know, Ben. But that's what this documentary's about. To find out whether reincarnation exists. Unfortunately all the evidence is hearsay. That's when you have to rely on what people heard other people say.'

'What, so me talking as Annie and Dad being Jimmy, that could all be made up?' Ben tries to digest this. 'But that's nuts! Why would we make all that up?'

The doc sighs. 'It's complicated, Ben.'

This must be what Ian was telling him about, Ben realizes suddenly. The kind of thing all the doc's critics have been going on about. 'So you need some proper proof,' he says. 'Like a knife or a body or something.'

The doc smiles, but it's a sad sort of smile. 'That would be ideal, yes. But these events happened well over a century ago. And our last living witness died out in 1967 with Lord Jim.'

'But we've got his diaries!'

'They're Miss Turnbull's diaries, Ben, not Lord Jim's,' she reminds him. 'So we've only got her word for what he told her.'

'Well I believe her,' Ben says stoutly. 'And I believe Annie and Flo and Jimmy and all them.'

'So do I, Ben,' says the doc. Then she sort of pulls herself together and turns to old Skip, who's started clearing away the tea things. 'How very strange and delightful to discover that you knew Miss Turnbull,' she says. 'She was an important role model for me. At a time when I was feeling somewhat alienated and lost, I think she rather saved me.' She smiles, remembering. 'She taught me that one didn't always have to do what people expect of one.'

'Ay,' says old Skip, 'she was a one-off, was Miss Turnbull.'

'I think she became rather fond of me,' says the doc.

'When you went back to that boarding school, she was really sad for a few days,' says Ben, recalling what he read in the diary.

The doc gets up and wanders into the old biddy's lounge, with its swirly carpet and shag-pile hearthrug, then back into the bedroom. 'You know, none of this is in the least bit familiar,' she says. 'But I suppose it's just possible that she brought me here – if she'd left something behind, perhaps, or if Lord Jim needed something during the day.'

'Did she ever talk about him?' Ben asks.

'Never – at least not that I recall. But from what we know about her, that's not surprising, is it? She'd have done her utmost to prevent me from ever crossing paths with him.'

'We could check by looking at the diaries.'

'Indeed. Unfortunately Ian's snaffled the relevant volumes – which I should have predicted really.'

They wander back down the hall to Skip's bit of the flat. Closing the door to Miss Turnbull's lounge, Ben feels like apologizing for disturbing her.

'I still can't believe Ian was Annie's mam,' he says. 'Because she was always, like, thinking of other people's needs and he never does, does he? And he's got all those kids, right? But he never says a word about them. I mean, normal grown-ups, right, if they've got kids, they're always comparing you with them, telling you what year they're in at school and what their hobbies are and that.'

'Reincarnation's not like genetic inheritance, Ben,' says the doc. 'The resemblances between generations operate according to different rules. Take your father, for example.'

'Dad's nothing like Lord Jim.'

'Exactly. But they are on the same spiritual path. And you and Annie are different too, but you're walking together, in some sense, through the same landscape.'

'Like holding hands.'

'Yes, that's a very good analogy.'

Ben has a think. 'I've got to make Dad agree to be hypnotized again,' he says.

CHAPTER FORTY-EIGHT

2007

Paul's been off on the boat, but he didn't dare go far – not with Ben still in a huff with him. He thought he'd try them prawn beds again, that got hammered a few year back, and got a canny haul; nothing to shout about, but enough to keep the lads happy and cover his costs. He kept calling the lad's mobile, but he never answered. So he got on to Nana and nagged her into going round twice a day, and to keep banging on his door till she gets an answer – and to call him straight away if she doesn't.

He keeps thinking about what that Laura creature said – about kids topping themselves – and wondering if he's been too hasty, hauling Ben away like that. He's thinking maybes one last session might be alright, to let the lad say goodbye and that, draw a proper line under the whole thing, before they go off on holiday. So that's what he's decided.

When he comes in, Ben's in the kitchen mixing a strawberry Nesquik, and he actually says 'howay', which is a relief compared to the silent treatment he got before he went away. Maybe absence makes the heart grow fonder or something.

'Howay, lad,' Paul says, slinging a load of late sun brochures on the coffee table. 'See if there's anything there you fancy.'

Ben sort of shuffles them around for a bit, even opens a few, so at least he's making an effort. So now Paul's thinking that maybe they can start painting his room tomorrow, do something together before he has to go off again.

'What do you want for supper?' he asks.

'I don't know. Anything.'

Paul opens the fridge, hoping Nana might have got in something they can eat, but it's hopeless as usual. Would it kill her to get in a steak and salad once in a while? Couple of decent lamb chops; maybe a pack of broccoli and new potatoes?

'What about Chinese?' he calls over his shoulder.

'All right. If you want.'

Popping a couple of Diet Cokes, they sit on the sofa together and look through the menus. Ben's got a yellow highlighter to mark the dishes they want – which is pretty much what they always have, give or take a tub of crispy seaweed.

'There you go,' says Paul, handing Ben the remote. 'Check out the viewing options while I call this in.'

After he's put in the order, he listens to the messages on the land line. There's two from old Bing, on about some crab pots he wants shot of – then that doc comes on the line saying something about an 'accidental meeting' with Ben and Mr Skipper.

'Accidental my arse,' he growls as he hangs up. 'Ben! What's all this about? I thought I said to stay away from that witchdoctor and her hangers-on.'

'I went to the library to look up where Lord Jim lived,' says the lad, looking a bit sheepish. 'I thought if I could find out a bit more about him, maybe you wouldn't be so, I don't know, like upset and angry and stuff.'

So that's why he's being so friendly all of a sudden. 'You've no business checking him out. I told you before, that pervert's got nothing to do with me.'

'But I just wanted to—'

'I don't care what you "just wanted" to do. You're not doing it any more, right?'

'But we found some diaries.'

'Oy! Read my lips. The subject's closed.'

Ben opens his mouth like he's going to give him some lip, then shuts it again and walks out the room. Just like that. One minute they're side by side on the sofa, chatting about holidays and Chinky chow, next thing you know he's back in his burrow again. Hearing the key turn, Paul wishes the lad *had* given him an earful. At least they'd be talking. The way it is now, they could be living on different planets.

He wanders over to the window to stare out at the river, at the ferry over the far side setting out from South Shields. Maybe he should get a proper girlfriend, instead of just a Saturday night casual; someone to, like, be there in the room with him and the lad, nattering on the way lassies do. So it's not always just the two of them, in each others' faces all the time. Someone who'd do a bit of decent shopping for when he gets back, maybe even cook a Sunday lunch now and then. Say what you like, Nessa was always good at that sort of thing. 'Catering', she called it. Weird the things you remember.

Sprawling back on the sofa, he scrolls down and clicks on to some cable channel where they're showing three old episodes of *Top Gear* back to back. Even Paul reckons that might be a bit too much of a good thing.

When the Chinese arrives, he puts Ben's on a tray with his pop and a fork and bangs on the door to say it's on the floor outside. Like a fucking prisoner, he thinks, except the key's on the wrong side.

He's just got his all spread out in front of the TV, with the Kikkoman and a couple of cold Stellas, and a length of kitchen roll on his lap, when the bell goes again. Probably the delivery lad realizing he's given him too much change, he thinks, getting up and opening the door. But it's that BBC bloke.

'What are you doing here?' Paul says.

'Look, I'll only be a minute.'

'You've got a fucking cheek.'

'I completely understand how you feel – and I agree. If it's any consolation, she had me totally convinced too.'

'You what?' This isn't what Paul's expecting at all.

'I feel I owe you an apology.'

'Too right.'

'Look, can I come in for a sec? I promise I won't keep you long.'

Somehow he's in through the door before Paul can stop him, and is parking his bum on the sofa, cosy as you like.

'Hey, this looks a good spread,' he comments, helping himself to a prawn cracker. 'You don't mind, do you? I haven't stopped since breakfast.'

Paul feels a bit of a prat, with the TV on and the cartons all open, like he's been caught pigging out in his pyjamas. 'Help yourself,' he says. 'I'll never get through it all. I always order too much.'

'Well, if you're sure you don't mind.' Ian picks up Paul's fork and digs into the chow mein. 'Hey this is great. Thanks, mate. You've saved my life.'

'Do you want a beer?' Paul finds himself asking as he walks through to the kitchen for another fork. 'There's more cans in the fridge. Do you need a glass?'

'Yeah, thanks, great,' says the Ian bloke, swigging from Paul's tin of Stella. 'Is it OK if I slosh some soy on the rice?' he asks, and reaches for the Kikkoman.

'Ben's in his room,' Paul says, sitting down and forking into the special fried.

'Good,' says Ian with his mouth full. 'It's probably better that he doesn't hear this.'

'Hear what? What's all this about?'

'Sorry, mate. You know how it is when you're really hungry? Low blood sugar and all that. I'll be human again in a minute.'

They tuck in in silence for a while, while Clarkson rabbits on about the Fantasy Car of the Year, a Ferrari 430 Scuderia.

'They cost an arm and a leg, those fucking things,' Ian comments, scooping up a slurp of sweet and sour with a prawn cracker and cramming it into his mouth. 'And where do you find a mechanic when it goes wrong? Right. Yes, where was I?'

'Something about Dr Charlton.' Paul's trying to hang on to his indignation, but all this chummy eating is taking the wind out of his sails.

'Yes. Right. Sorry. Bear with me a sec. I want to show you something.'

He wipes his hands on a piece kitchen roll and pulls a *North Tyneside A–Z* out of his backpack. One of the North Shields pages is marked with a yellow Post-it. 'Right, this red blob marks the house in Seymour Street where Lord Jim of the Jungle lived in 1967. And this other red blob is where a little girl called Mary Charlton lived at the same time. Not a million miles away, right?'

Paul shrugs, wondering where the bloke's going with this.

'Now little Mary had a child-minder in the summer of 1967, and that child-minder turns out to have been Lord Jim's housekeeper, the lovely Miss Edith Turnbull – a lady you might remember from your brief sojourn on the good doctor's sofa the other day.'

'The silly old trout? Fucking hell!' Paul has to admit that's a weird coincidence.

The Ian bloke looks pleased. 'I couldn't have put it better myself.'

'So? Why should I be interested in this?'

Ian crunches up some more prawn crackers. 'Because, my friend, this means that Dr Mary Charlton might actually be pulling the wool over our eyes.'

'Go on.'

Ian wipes his hands again and pulls one of those old-fashioned cardboard-bound notebooks out of the backpack. 'It's all in here, mate,' he says, slapping the notebook on the table. 'The personal diary of Miss Edith Lillian Turnbull aged, oh, I don't know, sixty-five and three-quarters, give or take.' He jabs his fork into the chow mein and slurps up a massive dripping mouthful. 'Look, do you mind turning the sound down on the telly?' he says. 'I can't hear myself think.'

'Sorry,' says Paul, a bit shamefaced, burrowing down between the leather cushions for the remote. He'd forgotten that posh people have a thing about talking with the TV on.

'OK, here's what I think's been happening,' says Ian. 'I think that this whole mystery has been cooked up by Dr Charlton from information she saw, or read, or overheard, about a missing herring girl called Annie, when she was being looked after by Miss Turnbull forty years ago. And it's been reignited, catalysed, whatever, by Ben turning up and telling her about his secret friend, who was also – coincidentally – called Annie.'

'I don't get it.' Paul drains his glass and pops another can.

'Hang on,' says Ian, raising his fork like the conductor of some orchestra. 'I haven't finished. I've been looking into a few of these cases of reincarnation and there's been quite a lot of research – as you might expect – by people trying to prove or disprove the phenomenon. Well, in some of the cases they've investigated, the child who's supposedly been reincarnated turns out to have had access to information about the person they claim to have been in a past life.

'So there was this really famous case back in 1952 of an American woman – Virginia Tighe – who was hypnotized by a man called Morey Bernstein. What is it with American names? Anyway, under hypnosis, this Virginia woman started jabbering away in a broad Irish accent and said her name was Bridey Murphy, who was born in Cork in 1798, then married and moved to Belfast, where she died in 1864.

'Bernstein was convinced he'd stumbled on a case of reincarnation, because Virginia was born in the Midwest, had been brought up by her Norwegian uncle in Colorado, and had never been out of the country. Yet there she was nattering on about the minutiae of life in nineteenth-century Ireland.

'Well, it turned out that before she went to live with her uncle at the age of three, baby Virginia lived with her natural parents, who were both – you guessed it – part Irish. What's more, an Irish immigrant called Bridey Murphy Corkell lived across the road from her uncle's parents' house in Chicago, which the family visited when Virginia was a kid.'

Paul's beginning to catch on. 'So, she made up all this stuff about Bridey Murphy from things she'd picked up as a nipper?'

'All totally innocent, of course.'

'And you're saying that this is what happened with the doc too, right? When she was a bairn.'

'Got it in one. I think that Mary must have overheard Miss Turnbull talking about Lord Jim to one of her cronies, and sneaked a read of her diary. Maybe she even met the great man himself one day, and asked him about his long-lost sister. Who knows? The point is, she had every opportunity: she lived practically round the corner and was seeing Miss Turnbull almost every day that summer.'

'What does the doc say about all this?'

'Claims she never saw any diary and never went to the house. But I reckon that little Mary realized that there was a bit of a mystery about what happened to this Annie. So she let her childish imagination run riot until she'd created a whole drama about knives and boyfriends.'

'That doesn't explain how she got all that stuff about Lord Jim into my head, though. Christ, I can still see him sitting in that wheelchair.' Paul shudders.

'That could have been simple hypnotic suggestion. All she had to do was get you to, in quotes, "remember" what she'd read in the diaries as a kid, about the amputations and the Jungle and so on. It's all in there,' he says, flicking through the closely written pages. 'You can check for yourself if you like.' He picks up a spare rib and rips a length of sticky meat off it with his teeth. 'Who knows, she might even have seen the poor old queen, being wheeled through the streets in all his finery after the op. That's not a sight you'd forget in a hurry!'

He drops the stripped rib onto the table, then picks up another and rips into it. 'She did exactly the same thing with me,' he remarks with his mouth full. 'That's how I know how you feel. It was after you stormed out, and she was talking about how she needed to track down someone else close to Annie – like her mother, for example. So I volunteer, like a muppet, and find myself living through the last agonizing minutes of Dory Milburn's post-partum haemorrhage.'

'And you reckon it was the doc who put that into your head too.'

'How else would it get there? But this time the information must have come from all that research she's been doing at the library. You should see what it's like up there, Paul. She's got that librarian at her beck and call, getting out maps and photos, checking out all the old census data. She'd researched Dory's cause of death just days before she hypnotized me.

'Anyway I got all excited – I mean, it all seems so fucking *real*, doesn't it, when you're under? And I mentioned it to an expert in the field – someone who's been advising me about the programme – and she practically chewed my ear off. Didn't I think it was suspicious that I just happened to, in quotes, "remember" being Annie's mother barely an hour after saying how useful it would be for the film? Once she'd pointed it out, it seemed so obvious. Tell you the truth, I felt rather embarrassed. So I went off and started asking a few questions about Mary's childhood.'

'I still don't see how the doc can make you remember things that didn't happen.'

'Don't get me wrong. I'm not saying these things didn't happen. The historical record proves that at least some of them did. All I'm saying is maybe they didn't happen to you and me in a previous fucking life.' He takes another swig of Stella. 'Hypnotic suggestion's a very powerful phenomenon, Paul. In fact you don't even have to be hypnotized for someone to plant an idea in your mind. You must have seen those magic shows on the telly, where a punter draws a picture and seals it in an envelope and Derren Brown or whoever knows exactly what they've drawn?'

Yes, Paul nods. He's seen them – bloody uncanny.

'So you know it's all done with suggestion. At some time earlier in the show he'll have planted the idea for the picture in the punter's mind – and lo and behold that's exactly what gets drawn.'

'So you think the doc's been doing something like that with me?'

'How else would you come up with all that crazy stuff about Lord Jim of the Jungle?'

'So can't you do something? She can't be allowed to get away with this. Put it in the film without her knowing, like they do with those *Rogue Trader* programmes. I don't know, get hold of some old photos of the doc as a nipper with the old trout to prove the link; show the bits of the diary where she's mentioned.'

'I'm not sure we need to go that far,' Ian says. 'All we need to do is carry on filming with Ben, but investigate Mary at the same time to see whether she might have been putting all those ideas into his head. Then we'll wheel on some experts to explain what I've just told you.'

'And put an end to all this reincarnation nonsense once and for all.' Paul can see how it would work.

'Assuming that's what's happening – yes, that's the general idea.'

'Sounds all right to me,' says Paul.

'So you're OK with Ben being back in the film?' says Ian, getting out his Blackberry and making a note.

'Sure. I'll get back on that couch again myself too, if it will help.'

Ian looks up in surprise. 'Seriously? That would be bloody brilliant, mate. The doc's itching to get you regressed to when Lord Jim was a young man.'

'Anything to expose her game and stop her ruining any more lives.'

'That's a deal then.'

They clink glasses.

'Do you think she's doing it on purpose?' Paul asks.

'That's the sixty-four thousand dollar question, isn't it? Mary's work is very important to her, so she'd have a strong motive for fabricating support for her theories. But that doesn't necessarily mean she's aware of what she's doing. Everything we've been talking about could have been going on at an unconscious level.'

'What, so she wants to believe in reincarnation so much she's put those things into our heads to convince herself too? Talk about weird.'

'Have you ever heard of Clever Hans?'

Paul shakes his head and pops another can. Now what?

'OK, Clever Hans was a famous German horse who could do arithmetic. His owner used to hold up a problem on a card and Hans would paw the ground with his front hoof until he'd counted up to the correct number for the answer. For years he had everyone convinced – and made his owner a tidy packet on the show circuit. Until some sharp-eyed observer noticed that people watching the show would sort of tense their bodies as the correct number approached, then relax almost imperceptibly when it was reached. Well it turns out the horse had noticed that too, and that's what he was responding to.'

'Still pretty clever for a horse,' comments Paul.

'The point is, neither the owner nor the audience was aware of how they were influencing the horse.'

'So the doc might be doing it without realizing.'

'It makes you wonder, doesn't it? Look, thanks for all this. That beer really hit the spot.'

'Do you fancy another?' says Paul getting up.

'Cheers, mate. But not a word to Ben, right? We don't want him spilling the beans to the doc before the film's finished.'

CHAPTER FORTY-NINE

. . . Am I talking to Annie? Good, now I'm going to take you back to the summer of 1898. Do you remember that day? It's windy and your skirt's blowing around your ankles. You're walking along the top bank, looking out to sea for the Osprey, *and when you see her, you decide you're going to surprise Sam by meeting him as he steps off the boat. So you run down the steps to the quayside, but there's something wrong. Tell me again what happens.*

1898

There's Da's boat coming in, and all the others are pushing apart to make space for her. And it's that quiet, all the shouting's stopped. Lads all round are shushing each other, like they're in church. So I'm ransacking the deck with my eyes, to find out what's happened, and there's Jimmy's hoying the warp ashore to tie up; and Da's at the tiller, and Tom's reefing the mainsail.

Sam must be below, I'm guessing, for I can't see him up top; or maybe he's down in the hold filling crans.

Why are the older lads not helping him? Why are they just standing about on the deck? Why's nobody fired up the capstan to haul the crans ashore?

I push closer, and see Jimmy's face, which is set as a stone; and Da's, which is shattered as I've ever seen it, like he's never slept for a fortnight. And Da must feel my eyes on him for he's looking up, and reaching out a hand – for all that he's a half furlong away still – and passes the tiller to Tom, and clambers over the cluttered deck towards the quay.

Next thing I know, his big hand's on my shoulder and he's leading me away and telling me to be strong, for there's been an accident and Sam's gone overboard.

But he's wrong! Sam's just gone below to get his sea-bag, I'm sure of it. Or he'll be cranning herring in the hold. So I'm shaking Da off and running back to the quay, and pushing past the gawping crowds that have gathered, and hitching my skirt to climb onto the *Osprey* and find him myself.

Now folk are shouting and Jimmy's grabbed me, but I've fought him off, for I need to get to the hatch to look inside, but Tom's pinned me from behind – and right in front of me, barring the way, is his da, Big John Hall. And my heart stops dead to see him, for there's tears streaming down his face.

If he'd been shouting like the rest, trying to stop me, I'd have fought on. But tears? Oh sweet Jesus, Big John Hall crying? Why's he crying?

Now somehow I'm back on the quayside, sitting on a stool someone's fetched from somewhere, God knows, and looking at a broken herring between the toes of my boots, that's been stood on, then dried out, and pecked at by seagulls, and will soon be nowt but white bones, flat as a nit comb.

Jimmy's putting a ditty box in my lap and says it's Sam's. I try to open it, but it's locked. There's a wee key on a bit string in Sam's pocket; I felt it when he was warming my hand that time. I remember thinking, here's the key for his ditty box. I remember fingering it, marvelling how warm it was.

I shake the box, and hear the mumble and tattle of his few things, and I can't even think what they might be, I've known him such a short time. Sweeties, maybes? A bit soap, a bit money? A photo of his mam on her wedding day?

And here's Da squatting down beside me, and he's saying that crotchboots are heavy as rocks, so Sam would have sunk in a moment; and the water's that cold, even in summer, it knocks the breath out of a body. 'So it were quick,' he's saying. And I'm saying, 'You don't know.' And he's saying, 'Oh, Annie, pet. I'm so sorry. He was a grand lad.'

So now I'm looking up at them all, at all the crew standing round, and asking didn't anybody see anything, hear anything? And Tom's telling how he got up to take a piss, and found the boat bucking in a heavy sea, and the tiller loose and the boom swinging and no one on deck.

'Did you check in the water?' I ask, and I know I must have asked it afore, but I never liked the answer, so I have to ask again, and again, until someone says something different.

'We held the lamps over the water,' says Jimmy, in a slow voice that says he's told me this already. 'But we couldn't see him. So we shouted, then we listened. But it was pitch black, Annie, and the sea was so wild. What with the planks creaking and the sails flapping, even if he was shouting we'd never have heard him.'

'But he wasn't shouting, pet,' says Da softly. 'By that time he was long gone.'

'But he can swim!' I'm saying. 'All the lads from the *Wellesley* can swim. He could be out there right now—'

'We found his oily jacket,' says Da. 'One of the other crews hooked it out of the water.'

'He must've taken it off so's he could float better.' I can see him flailing in the black water, shrugging it off, then taking a breath and reaching under to yank off his crotchboots. I can hear him yelling for help—

'No, pet. I've seen lads go overboard and float, and I've seen them go overboard and sink, and I'm telling you no one could float in that sea.'

'Why aren't you still out there looking for him? He'll be freezing out there—'

'We did look, for hours. And the other crews. But it's no good, pet, he's gone.'

Now he's straightening up, and taking off his cap, and the other lads are all turning and taking their caps off too – for here's Sam's mam coming, half running, with her eyes wild and her shawl untied and trailing on the ground.

But there's that much fury welling up inside me at the sight of her that I can't stand up to greet her. For she's had him for years, *years* – when all I ever had was a few wee slivers of his time, and could have had so much more if she'd been less of a burden. It's my time with him that she's stolen, time that's mine by rights. I thought there'd be so much of it, days and days, our whole lifetimes stretching out, my hand warm in his pocket—

It's been rough weather these past days, with a wind that's got the windows clattering and smoke belching down into the kitchen from the lum. The river's full of flotsam and a stinking brown rug's spread over the harbour water, with branches matted with strips of sacking, and rotting cran spronks and barrel staves, and poisoned rats and drowned puppies, and gulls squabbling and flies buzzing in a mucky black cloud.

And all along the Scarp when the water's low, and on the beaches and rocks beyond the salt works, tramps and travellers are sorting through the minging rubbish, for stuff they can sell, or burn, or eat – God preserve them.

Flo wrinkles her nose to see them, but I'm thinking: how would it be to stop being a nice lass and just live as a wild thing? All I'd need is a blanket and a gipping knife, and I could live on flither from the Black Middens and curl up in a wyn hollow and make believe Sam's with me. I'd not need to talk to folk, nor see them looking at me, nor worry am I crying again? See, I can't tell any more if my eyes are wet or dry, for they brim over without warning; and it might be the smoke tearing them, or the grieving, or maybes they've been weeping so long they don't know how to stop.

I'm at the farlane now, and gipping, and there's nowt to do but catch up a herring and hold it, cut and flip out the innards and toss it into the cran. I'm like a wooden shuttle that rattles to and fro on the loom and feels nowt. They leave me alone mostly, the other lasses, and talk over and around me; my lips are stiff and can't form words anymore, so it's like I'm down in the farlane with the herring, cold and dumb as they are.

They're speaking of the strike that's planned for next week, about the rate of pay for the night barrels, and how the Scots lasses are wanting support from Shields gippers, to stop the coopers taking on local lasses in place of the strikers. And someone's saying how two of the Scots lasses got beat up yesterday, as a lesson to the others to simmer down.

And I'm thinking, I can't care anymore what's happening with the Scots lasses, or Flo's baby, whether it's staying or not, because all I can manage is to keep my wooden hands going, and the air going in and out of my chest, and my eyes dry enough to see through.

But now the blethering's quieted and the lasses have slowed their gipping, and some have stopped, so I rest my knife and look up – and there's a policeman talking to Mrs Gibson. And she's coming over, and telling me to fold my knife and wash up, for the constable's wanting a word.

He's brought me to a place they call Dead Men's Dene: a miserable sour beach up the coast from South Shields, one of a stretch of miserable sour beaches, where the sea dumps its rubbish after a storm. A clutch of poor folk have set up shelters by the road, made of bits of timber and patched sail canvas and tatie sacks; and live by gleaning, I suppose, for there's fields all about, and ransacking the reeking flotsam thrown up by the tides.

The wind's bellying the shelters, and whipping up the sand. It stings my cheeks as we take the steps down to the soft sand, and plod through it to the high-water mark, where there's a line of flotsam deep as my knees, and dogs burrowing and scabby weans digging in with their hands.

I've been told why I'm here, and there's a part of me that's taken it on board. And it's that part that's walking along beside this ridge of stinking tangles to where another constable's waiting, with a whispering cluster of folk, by a tarpaulin weighted with driftwood and rocks.

But there's another part of me that's stayed rooted to the road above, and cannot go a step further, and is watching a thin lass in a black scarf fall to her knees as the tarpaulin's lifted, and she sees the new gansey crusted with salt, and nods yes, that's the gansey she's knitted for her lad.

And she's making this high mewing sound, this poor lass, like a seagull crying for its mate, thinking of the day she gave it him, the loving look in his eyes that said they were promised. She never saw him wear it. She never looked back to say goodbye.

Now I'm kneeling, and reaching out a hand to tend his hair, which is matted with sand, and the sand fleas are jumping, and the constable's touching my shoulder, saying, 'Come away now, pet. Don't upset yourself. The face is a bit of a mess.' But it's too late, and I've seen them, the places where the sea lice have started, and been driven off by the waves, and started again, and the gulls – and who can blame them, for wasn't he just the sweetest lad as ever lived?

Oh, and here's his feet, white and clean, with the toenails cut nice, like he's just stepped out of the bath on a Saturday night.

'Some tinker's stolen his boots,' says the constable, and I'm thinking, how strange a lad's feet are, so bony and long, like they're off a creature that's hardly human.

The constable's brought me home, and I'm remembering I've left my oily down the smokehouse, and worrying will Flo bring it back or should I go fetch it? Except I'm not sure I can walk down those stairs, or any stairs, ever again, for fear of what might be waiting for me at the bottom.

The house is empty and the fire's out, so I poke it a bit but haven't the heart to riddle it properly, and wander into the yard, where I've hung out my smalls, and feel if they're dry, but can't make my arms lift to gather them in. So I sit at the table and listen to the clock tick, and look at flies landing on a few spilt sugar grains, and rubbing their hands. And let them land on my bare arm, and scuttle over it, and probe at my skin with their black tongues, and feel the dry and wet of them scuttling and tasting me, and think of the flies landing on my sweetheart on that heap of minging flotsam.

When does a soul leave a body? At the moment of death? Or does it stay for three days, as Jesus' did, till the funeral's done and the body buried? And what if the funeral's delayed, and the body can't be found, what then? Does it stay tossing and turning on the cold sea bed?

My eyes are leaking again, and dripping on the table, and that mewing sound's coming from of my mouth, that seems the only sound I can make, or will ever make.

Now what's this? Someone's knocking at the door, and turning the handle – and here's Tom in the kitchen, taking his cap off and pulling up a chair opposite. And I'm wondering, why's he here? Has he a message from Da? And for a mad moment I think he's come to tell me it was some other lad went overboard. Then I'm remembering, oh sweet Jesus, Sam's drowned – and wondering when will this knowing lie still in my heart, and not be forgotten, and remembered, with the shock of that remembering, over and over again?

So I'm wiping my eyes on my shawl, which is already dark with tears, and saying sorry the fire's out so I can't get a brew on, and he's saying he just wants to find out how I am. And I say, you can see how I am, and laugh a bit, for I must be a pitiful sight, with my raw eyes and wild hair. And he says, you've always looked beautiful to me, which is a lie, for he hardly noticed me before this summer. But I'm too weary to say so, and too teary to send him away, or ask after Flo, and just sigh and sit quiet and wait for him to finish what he's come for.

He's gone to the window now to look out at the back yard, where my bit washing is, and I know I should jump up to draw the curtains, but I can't make my legs move, nor can I care what he's seeing. And by and by he sits down again, and says it wasn't till he saw me with Sam that he realized what he felt about me, and how he's never loved Flo that way, and he'll end it with her the minute I say.

He's waiting for me to speak, but all I can do is stare at him, at the gansey Flo's knitted him and the silk wrapper she's bought him tied round his throat; at the handsome brown face and the smiling white teeth. And by and by, he stops smiling, and picks up his cap, and straightens his gipping knife in the binding, and says, 'I just wanted to tell you how things stand.'

Then, when I've still not answered, he scrapes his chair back and takes my hands in his, and tugs me round to face him, and says, 'Oh, Annie,' and pulls me up and into his arms.

And a part of me wants to shove him away, but another part is so weary with weeping, and trying not to weep, and just living one minute after the next, that I can't find the strength, and just stand there like a raggy-doll, with my eyes shut and my arms by my side, and wait for him to let me go.

But he's not noticing, or not caring, and is nuzzling into my neck, like a kitten burrowing for the teat, and grasping my bum through my skirt.

Then it's like it was on the beach, and I'm stood by the mantle watching this big lad fumbling at the buttons of this sad lass's blouse, and pressing his hard thing against her thigh. Now he's got her blouse open and her cami undone, and one broad hand's on her booby, kneading it like bread, and the other's rubbing at the front of her skirt.

And she's just standing there, limp as boiled cabbage, with her head turned away so's he can't kiss her, and her face wet with tears and her arms just hanging. And by and by he leaves off grabbing and licking and calms himself and says sorry, and you're upset, and there's no hurry; and takes his cap and leaves.

CHAPTER FIFTY

2007

Looking at Ben lying there after the session, it strikes Mary that he looks thinner, or perhaps taller; etiolated, she thinks the term is, like a plant that's been grown in the dark. She wonders if he's been eating properly; she rather fears he may have been depressed.

'As that's the first session we've had for a while, I thought maybe we'd end it there,' she says. His blonde fringe has flopped down over one eye; her hand itches to smooth it back from his forehead and rest there, as it's done in the past, letting his young heat seep into her cold palm.

'I could have taken it a bit further,' she explains, 'but I thought we should save any possible revelations for when Ian's here with his equipment.'

'I'm starving!' Ben announces suddenly, sitting up and shrugging off her Indian blanket. 'Shall I run down the Mission for some of them bacon baps?'

She smiles: nothing wrong with his appetite then. Handing him some coins, she's glad he's simply assumed they'd eat together. After all that's happened with his father, she would have hesitated to propose such a thing herself. However, the idea of losing him again – she's intrigued to find that this is how she's phrasing it in her mind, 'losing him again' – fills her with unaccustomed dismay. Something about this case, about this boy, has dissolved her armour and left her vulnerable as a hermit crab without its shell. This business with Ian, for example. Telling him about the abortion – letting him kiss her, for God's sake. What was she *thinking*? When every instinct should have warned her he couldn't be trusted.

But that's what happens when you let yourself unbend a little, love a little. Some people reward you with a wide grin and a bacon bap – and others by scheming behind your back. The choice couldn't be starker: open your door and risk a kick in the teeth, or stay safely locked in your tower for ever.

Smiling wryly, she goes outside for a cigarette. It's sunny and clear; the bench slats are hot against her back and there's a smell of chips wafting up from the Seamen's Mission. She exhales and closes her eyes briefly, picturing Ben squirting ketchup from the plastic tomato on the counter, then carefully re-wrapping the baps and trudging back up High Beacon Stairs. Resting her cigarette on the rim of the geranium pot, Mary peels off her gloves and flexes her fingers in the sun; then tilts her face upwards slightly so she can feel its rays on her throat. Is this what happiness feels like, she wonders? Warm hands and a boy you're fond of bringing you something to eat? And is it worth the risk of letting someone like Ian undermine her entire career? She closes her eyes again, surprised to find them stinging with tears. Because she realizes that the answer is 'yes'.

A moment later Ben appears, breathless and pink-cheeked. 'I've been thinking,' he says, laying a puffy, red-smeared paper bag in her lap. 'Do you think Tom killed Annie? Because he thought she was going to just fall into his arms, didn't he? He never expected her to say no.'

Mary sits up and marshals her thoughts back to the issue at hand. 'He does appear to be rather an arrogant character, doesn't he? But that doesn't mean he's capable of murder. And it's still entirely possible that she simply left town when those herring girls moved on, in an attempt to put Sam's death behind her.'

'And left her mam and da, and Jimmy and the bairns?'

'I just don't want you to jump to any hasty conclusions about Tom. The unconscious can't always tell the difference between a dream and reality. If you offer it an idea, it has a tendency to take it at face value.'

'So you're worried that if I start thinking of Tom as a murderer then I'll start making up memories to fit in with that idea.'

'I couldn't have put it better myself.' She smiles grimly.

'And then people will start to criticize you, right? And say there's no such thing as reincarnation.'

Mary sighs. 'There will always be people who say there's no such thing as reincarnation, Ben. It just doesn't fit in with our society's view of the world. Let's just say that I'd rather not furnish them with any additional ammunition.'

They're quiet for a bit, munching away, then something strikes her. 'Do you remember that time Jimmy and Annie were sitting together on the beach? Do you think he was trying to tell her something?'

'About being gay, you mean? I don't know. She wasn't really paying much attention, was she?' He bites into his bap again and a splat of ketchup drops onto his jeans. He wipes it up with a finger. 'I keep thinking of how Jimmy grew up into Lord Jim. I mean he used to be so skinny and sort of twitchy, always trying to keep in the background.'

'What you find with many gay men is that they leave home at an early age to explore their sexuality in private, as it were. Jimmy's transformation probably took place when he was in the merchant navy, where social norms were somewhat more lenient.'

'I think he was probably happier as Lord Jim, don't you? Before he got amputated, I mean. At least he was being true to himself.'

'He certainly seems to have found the ideal niche at the Jungle.'

'Then me and Dad ended up living on the top floor of the same building – I mean, how cool is that?'

'Has your father ever spoken about how that happened? Was he drawn to the place in some way do you know?'

'He says it was Mam's idea. She liked the idea of a penthouse.'

'I've often wondered how it is I ended up in this old building. It's far too big for one person and it's a devil to heat because the walls soak up moisture like a sponge. And you might have noticed that it's far closer to the sea than I'm comfortable with.' A wry smile.

'Do you think you lived here before, then? When you were one of them fishermen?'

'It's possible, I suppose. After 1808, when the building was taken out of commission as a lighthouse, it was used to house the families of men lost at sea. But the tower section, with my room in it, was constructed in 1727, which broadens the possibilities quite significantly.' She bites into her bap and chews on a salty red mouthful. 'It was an odd feeling, though. As soon as I walked in through the door, I felt at home. I even knew which bedroom was mine.'

'I felt like that at old Skip's place. Like, I really wanted to go into Miss Turnbull's half of the flat. Then when I got there I just wanted to sit in her chair and look out the window. And I found her Post Office book straight away, pretty much. I just had this hunch that it would be in her knitting bag and that the diaries would be under the bed.'

'That's how I'm so certain I never went there as a child. I had absolutely no sense of familiarity whatsoever. Though I am concerned that I might have read her diaries at some point – perhaps dipped into her handbag when she was otherwise occupied. Though it would have been entirely out of character and, again, I have absolutely no recollection of having done so.'

'If you never went to the flat, you couldn't have read the diaries.' He seems very sure about this.

'How do you work that out?'

'Because she kept the up-to-date one at the bottom of her knitting bag.'

'Perhaps she brought her knitting bag to my house one day.'

'No – it's really big and heavy. Didn't you see it? Plus it was the place she kept all her valuables, so she wouldn't just carry it around with her, would she?'

'I suppose not,' Mary says, deliberately noncommittal; but something small and tense, like a fist, deep inside her chest, relaxes and opens when she considers what Ben's just said.

She takes a deep breath and blows it out again slowly, feeling her ribs open and her shoulders sag with relief. Until this moment she hadn't realized quite how much that small possibility had been gnawing away at the back of her mind – that she'd read the diaries as a child and had somehow constructed this whole mystery out of her own imagination. Now it's resolved, she's able to focus more closely on what Ben's just revealed about feeling so at home in Miss Turnbull's rooms.

'Have you heard of a phenomenon called déjà vu?' she asks, wrapping up the uneaten half of her bap. A fresh hypothesis is taking shape in her mind, chasing away all possibility of eating.

Still chewing, he shakes his head.

'The term means "already seen" and it refers to the sense one occasionally has of having experienced something before.'

'Like sitting in Miss Turnbull's chair.'

'Exactly. Or in my case, gazing down at the Fish Quay from my bedroom window.' She takes out her Gitanes and lighter and holds them on her lap, waiting until he's finished his bap. 'In the past, of course, the phenomenon was simply taken as evidence of reincarnation – that one had actually lived through the experience in question before. But these days people prefer to believe that it's due to a temporary mismatch between perception and consciousness, whereby an event is perceived a fraction of a second before it's consciously experienced, so that one experiences both the event and an apparent "memory" of the event at the same time.'

'Is that what you think happened to me at Miss Turnbull's place?'

'I don't know, Ben. Scientists have come up with many explanations for the phenomenon over the years, but have never been able to prove anything – mainly because it's been so difficult to replicate such a rare and transient experience in the laboratory.' Ben's watching her intently. She wonders to what extent he's understanding all this. She really should get out of the habit of voicing her theoretical musings aloud. 'However, one team of researchers did have some success by using post-hypnotic amnesia – that's when a hypnotized person is shown something then instructed to forget it. When their test subjects were brought out of their trances and presented with the, in quotes, "forgotten" material again, the majority did indeed insist that they had never seen it before. But around thirty percent reported a sensation of déjà vu.'

'So they'd all seen it before, but only a few of them remembered it.'

'Yes.'

'So I really did sit in Miss Turnbull's chair.'

'Or you experienced a temporary glitch in your perceptual processing. There could be any number of explanations.'

Mary watches Ben picking the last of the bacon from his bap and eating it, then screwing up the ketchup-sodden bread in the paper bag. She's waiting for him to put the information together.

'There was a *Radio Times* from 1994 in her room, with Joanna Lumley on the cover,' he says eventually. 'That was just before she died.'

'And when were you born?'

'November the twenty-third, 1994.'

'And when was she born, do you think?' Mary asks.

He looks at her. 'I don't know. Skip says she was really old, like all doddery and sort of shrunken and bent like you get with old people. So there was this really little old walking stick on the bed, like something a midget would use.'

'She was already pretty old in 1967, when she was looking after me. Though I suppose anyone over forty seems ancient to a ten-year-old schoolgirl.'

'You know that old biddy with the spooky hands I got that time? The one who was talking to that man in the box?'

Mary nods and smiles.

'That was Miss Turnbull, wasn't it?

'That would seem to be a distinct possibility.'

He mulls this over for a moment. 'So we've met before, then. You and me, I mean. When you were a little girl.'

'Again, that would appear to be a distinct possibility.'

He's grinning at her. 'She really really liked you.'

'I really really liked her too.' She finds herself grinning back, ridiculously pleased, then leans over and kisses him swiftly on the top of his warm, apple-scented, blond-streaked, glossy boy's head.

'I was thinking of getting a lodger,' she remarks abruptly, changing the subject – she's not used to managing affection; she's out of the habit. 'A student, perhaps,' she adds. 'Someone who can introduce me to the worldwide web, or whatever it's called, and won't mind a bit of damp in the kitchen.'

Ben eyes her sceptically. 'You'd have to get broadband fitted first,' he says. 'And a proper telly. No one'll put up with your gear unless the rent's like ten quid or something.'

'There must be some young people who aren't addicted to technology. An anthropology postgraduate, perhaps. Someone who's spent some time in the Third World.'

'No offence, doc, but your place is sort of like being in the Stone Age.'

'Laura's always talking about broadband.'

'Plus there's no dishwasher or microwave. That kitchen needs a total makeover.'

'Perhaps I'll just give up on that idea, then.'

'Wouldn't it be annoying having someone around all the time?' he asks.

'Undoubtedly, but I'm not sure living on one's own is an entirely healthy state for a human being either. We are quintessentially social animals, with the most highly developed communication skills of any species.'

'Do you get lonely, then?'

'Not lonely, as such, no. Lazy is probably a better term for it. When one lives alone, there are certain spheres of interpersonal endeavour that one doesn't have to bother with any more.' Like love, she adds to herself; like jealousy and insecurity; like hurt, pain, bereavement.

'I wonder why Miss Turnbull never got married.'

'After Annie's experience of losing Sam, perhaps she never quite dared to commit herself.'

'Like a scar, you mean? Like your fear of the sea?'

'Yes. Or perhaps she simply never found the right man.'

'What about me? If Annie and Miss Turnbull never got married, maybe I won't either.'

'Well, that's why we're doing this therapy, Ben. To help you make conscious choices in your life, as opposed to being driven by past agendas.'

'I wonder why it's always Annie I remember, and not Miss Turnbull.'

'I can't answer that definitively. But from what we know, it seems your Miss Turnbull lived a relatively uneventful life, rather on the outskirts of other people's dramas. So perhaps there's not very much there to, as it were, catch the attention of your subconscious.'

'Maybe her soul just needed a rest after Annie.'

Mary smiles. 'I wouldn't be at all surprised.'

The sound of a car tooting its horn and drawing up outside the house interrupts them.

'Guess who I've brought to see you,' says Ian, shoving the gate open.

'Dad!' cries Ben, beaming. 'Are you going to be hypnotized again?'

'Can't let you have all the fun, can I?'

'Is this true, Mr Dixon?' asks Mary in surprise. 'I'm delighted, of course, but after last time, I assumed—'

'Blame your friend Ian,' says Paul, winking at Ian. 'He twisted my arm. Said it would make all the difference to the film. So here I am, raring to go.'

CHAPTER FIFTY-ONE

... Think back to the summer of 1898. It's the start of the herring season. Where are you? What are you doing?

1898

I'm down in the rope room coiling the warp. It's dark and there's a swell, so the boat's heaving and creaking. The lads are hauling, up on deck above me. I can hear them giving it, one, two, three, shake; and the herring thudding out of the net. Now here comes another length of dripping warp through the hatch for me to stow.

And I'm thinking: Sam's gone overboard, but we're carrying on like nothing's happened. I mean, he could be out there right now, hanging on to a buff in the dark, with his gansey wet through, freezing to death. But we can't even start searching properly till we've got the nets out of the water.

Da's face when he gave the order – well, I never thought I'd see him like that; he was in tears almost. He said there's no point in us shouting and waving the lamps; if we're to look for him, we have to haul the nets first. Because there's a chance Sam's got caught in them, isn't there? And even if he's not, we can't search with nigh on two miles of driftnet tugging at us, and we can't cut them free or we'd get caught foul of them ourselves. So we have to haul, even though it's eating up time when we could be looking.

So here I am below deck, blind to what's happening up top, reaching up to grab another length of wet warp, that's thick as my arm and rough as shark-skin, and my palms burning, and freezing water running down to my oxters. The floor's sloshing with water and the lamp's smoking and lurching side to side, so the place is black with paraffin grease and spattered with spits of seaweed and herring scales.

How could he have gone over? I mean it does happen, it's something you hear about. But not in the summer, not in the middle of a drift. Tom was on about the deck being slippy – but it's always slippy; that's part of the job.

When we're done hauling, I climb back up on deck, and part of me's expecting Sam to be there as usual, scraping gildeds over the side for our breakfast. But it's dark still, just a glimmer of grey on the horizon, and there's no sign of him; just the lamps swinging and the lads clearing up, mucking the nets and shooting the last of the herring in the hold. And the way they are, quiet and grim, brings it home to me again that he's gone.

Da's for'ard sounding the bell again, to tell the other luggers there's a lad gone over. I can see them in the distance, the few crews that's out tonight, their lamps moving as they check in the water.

And I'm looking at Tom now, unhooking one of our lamps and leaning over the side – and I'm wondering, why didn't he wake us when he found the deck empty and Sam gone? Why was he just standing there smoking when I came up? Why wasn't he unhooking the lamp then and searching overboard?

And I keep thinking, and I keep pushing the thought away – but it keeps coming back at me, like another length of warp through the hatch: that maybes they've had a barny, the two of them, and Tom's shoved Sam and that's how he's gone over the side.

Can you remember what happened earlier that night? What did you see? Let's start when the boat set out that evening.

It's right blowy and we're on the boat getting ready, and Mickey's mythering on because he thinks it's too hickety to go out. The port's full of flotsam the river's brought down after the rain, twigs and branches and that, like a solid raft, with rats scampering all over. And the wind's making the water heave under its coat of rubbish, and the rigging's clattering against the masts, and there's scuts of white out in the river.

Now here comes Da walking down the quayside with Sam, and they're keeping time with their feet and walking slow, so you can tell they're having a word. And I'm thinking it'll be something about the fishing, for Sam's dead keen and Da can talk fishing till the cows come home. Then I see him clap Sam on the back, and the lad's grinning fit to split his face apart. I mean, you should've seen him – like he'd been handed a thousand gold sovereigns.

And he swings up on board while Da stops off to howay the skipper from the *Sanderling*.

Then I see Sam's putting on that gansey our Annie's been knitting; least I think it must be the one, for she was on to the cuff last time I looked and it's the same pattern Mam uses.

So Sam's walking out with our Annie, and I never knew! Never even suspected, though there was bound to be somebody someday, wasn't there? It gives me a jolt, mind. For it shows how far I've slipped away from my folk. Not so long ago I'd have known what Annie was about before she even knew it herself. But since I've been stopping at Nana's, and off out every evening – well, I've not been taking heed of hardly anything else.

'Howay, Wellesley,' says a voice behind me, and it's Tom and Big John climbing on board. 'Stow this, will you,' says Tom, and hoys over his sea-bag so it dunts Sam on the shoulder – which is typical Tom, to keep a stew on the stir. See, there's nowt wrong with asking a lad to stow your sea-bag, specially if he's new. But Tom has to take it that bit further, doesn't he? And chuck it so Sam's no chance of catching it before it dunts him.

Tom can go too far sometimes, see? Always poking at something with a stick to see what will happen. Like with that poor nancy lad, on the beach by the Priory. One of the old 'longshoremen had to row out to untie him in the end and they'd to take him to the hospital. Down the Seven Stars after, Tom was boasting how him and the others had trussed him up and tied him to a mooring post for the tide to finish off, saying that'll teach him, dirty little nonce – so I nipped outside: I didn't want to hear, did I? But maybes I should have stayed, because now I keep wondering what they did to him first. If I'd stayed at least I'd have known.

The poliss came and lifted Tom later and done him for aggravated or grievous bodily or something, and that's not the first time he's been hoyed into them cells for being free with his fists.

So anyway, now Tom's spotted Sam's new gansey and he's saying, 'Hey, Wellesley, who's knitted that for you?' So Sam's saying just a lass he knows, and Tom's saying, 'What lass is that then?' And, 'Let's take a look.' But Sam just smiles and pays no heed, and drops down into the fo'c'sle with the bags.

Tom must have seen the pattern on the gansey, though, for it's like mine and Da's: runs of herringbones between rows of cables and net-mesh diamonds; the same pattern Nana knitted for Granda, the same one Mam makes for us now without thinking, year on year, natural as the bones in her fingers.

Over by the capstan, Big John's joined Mickey in whingeing to Da about going out tonight; for the wind's never letten up all day. But Da says it's a full moon, so the herring'll be on the rise, even in this swell. He reckons it's worth a trip, for we'll get there in no time on this wind, and shoot and haul quickly and get twice the price for the haul – because most the boats will be stopping home. He's got it all worked out, see? Where to go where the swell will be softer, how to ride the wind, how long to drift. If I tried for ten year I'd never get to be the way Da is with his fishing.

Da asked me once where I was headed. He was hoping I'd take on the boat, see? But he knows I'm not up to it. I mean, you've only to hear him shouting to the deckies, telling them to reef up, and come about and that. I'm never doing that in a million years.

So anyway, we've gone out, and shot the nets, and now we're on the drift – except there's no sitting out on the deck tonight, for it's blowy and spitting rain. Sam's taking the watch and I'm in my berth, listening to Tom settling down. See, the way the berths are made, mine goes across the way, and the others run for'ard to aft either side. So Tom's head's right next to mine, just the other side of the partition. I like to think of him lying there in the dark, with his hand on his dick maybes, having a quiet pull.

Tonight, though, he can't settle. Over the groaning of the timbers and Mickey and Big John's snoring, I can hear his straw crunch as he rolls over, then back again. Now he's found a bite to scratch at, sounds like. Now he's sighing and rolling over again, and though I can't see him I can tell there's not a morsel of sleep in him, even though it's hard graft sailing the boat in a swell, pulling on the ropes, reefing and unreefing, going about, so he must be weary.

I'm just dozing off, when I hear him roll over sudden like and clamber out of his berth. Off up to the deck for a piss, I suppose, so I lie awake for a while with that picture in my head: of Tom getting his dick out and pissing into the black waves. It makes me hard, so I turn to my side and start on a bit of a wank, but then I think I'll wait till he's back for a proper go.

So I'm waiting for him – but he's never come back. And I think I can hear voices up on deck, but it's hard to tell for the creaking of the boat. Is he spelling Sam, maybes? Or having a barny? But I'm wide awake now, and I need a piss too. So I climb down out of my berth and go up the ladder.

* * *

The wind hits me as soon as I put my head up, and a hiss of spray whips me across the face. The sails are reefed and the boat's leaning to starboard, bucking on the waves, with the water slapping at her side. I check around and there's Tom by the port lamp having a smoke, so I have my piss, then go over.

What with the slapping of the water and the wind, and the chattering of the rigging, he doesn't hear me coming – then jumps out of his skin when he sees me and flicks his tab into the sea.

'Where's Sam?' I ask, looking around.

'God knows. Down the fish room? Deck was empty when I came up.'

'Why'd he go down there?' The hatch is battened down, but I open it to take a look anyway. Because there's something about the way Tom's talking, sort of shifty like, that's got me worried. It's pitch black in the fish room, of course, so I light the lamp and crouch down and sort of swing it around inside. Then I try in the rope room, though Lord knows why he'd be in there.

'Did you see him?' I ask.

'I told you, no. I came up for a piss and found it like this.'

'Do you think he's gone overboard?'

'Don't be daft. He'll be somewhere.'

'I've checked everywhere.'

'So, try the berths. Maybes he's having a kip.'

I know he's not there, for I'd have heard him coming down the ladder – but I look anyway. And now I'm thinking he must have gone overboard, but at the same time I can't quite believe it.

So I check the deck again – though there's nowhere there he could be – and Tom's unhooked the starboard lamp and is leaning over the side to check the water. Because that's the only place we haven't looked, though there's nowt to see in this weather, except black waves rearing up, on and on, slope-slap-and-gully, slope-slap-and-gully.

Come daybreak, one of the other crews hooked Sam's oily jacket out the water. There's something cold and terrible about hauling fish when there's a lad overboard – even though it's the right thing, the only thing, to do. Sailing home later, you can see the pain of it on Da's face. That's a skipper's burden for you, summed up right there.

So when we dock, it's Da who calls the Harbourmaster. And later, when the police come, it's Da they talk to first. But then they call us all in, one by one. And by now there's a great crowd of bairns and old folk round the Harbourmaster's office where they've set up, all jostling and giving it what's happened and who's died, like seagulls squabbling over a cod's head.

Tom goes in first and comes out pulling his cap on, so I can't see his face. Then I go in, and there's this burly policeman with a red-porridge nose sat behind the desk, and a younger lad with a notebook on a stool. And their helmets side by side on a cabinet like blue plum duffs.

So I tell them about coming up for a piss and finding Sam gone, and how I searched for him and that. And they say, what was Tom doing when I came up? So I say, looking in the water – which is true, in a way. But I never said how long he was on deck before I came up; I never said I heard voices. If they'd asked, I would have said. But they never asked, did they?

When I come out, and push through the crowd, Tom's waiting for me, sucking on a tab.

'What did you tell them?' He's picking bakkie off his lip, not looking at me.

'Just that he was gone when I came up.'

'Is that all?'

'That's all I said – but, Tom, I was awake when you went up. I thought I heard voices.'

'What?' Now he's looking straight at me, and he's rattled.

'I didn't tell the poliss, because I wasn't sure. And it would have looked bad.'

'I told you, the deck was empty when I went up.'

'So why didn't you wake us straight off?'

'I don't know. I thought he'd be somewhere. Then by the time I realized, it was too late.' The tab's only half smoked, but he drops it and grinds it out with his boot. 'I never saw him, right? You couldn't have heard us, because he wasn't there when I went up. Anyway it was that blowy last night, you couldn't have heard anything. It must have been the timbers creaking.' He stops, like he knows he's blethering, and takes out his tin to roll up again.

Then after a bit, like he's been mulling it over, he says: 'It was raining, wasn't it? Do you remember? He probably slipped on the deck.' As if Sam was some green 'prentice who'd never been on a boat before. And I just wish he'd keep his mouth shut, because the more he goes on about it, the harder it is to believe him.

And I feel qualmy, all of a sudden; like I've swallowed something rotten. So I move away a bit and retch into the gutter, but nowt comes; so I spit instead and the gob lands on a smashed crab's claw.

When I straighten up, there's something different about him. He's stopped blethering on, and there's this hard look round his eyes. 'It's funny how some things make you qualmy, isn't it, Jimmy?' he says now. 'Like that other night when I saw you coming out of that alley and you were wiping your mouth.'

'I was throwing up,' I say – and you know what they say about blood running cold? Well that's what it feels like, seeing that look on his face.

'First this big nonce comes out buttoning his kecks, then here comes our Jimmy wiping his mouth.'

'I was scared. I thought he was going to rob me, but he was just having a piss.'

'I believe you, Jimmy. But it's not something you'd want your da hearing about, is it?'

Then he walks away. Just like that.

After he's gone, Da's come over for a word, but I can't speak for shivering. Because the thought of Tom telling Da what I'm about – well, I might as well pack up and leave right now. He thinks I'm just upset about Sam, so he tells me to leave the making up for now and to go back to Nana's for a lay down. 'He was a grand lad,' he says. 'Would have made a good skipper.'

Him saying that makes me want to blub, because I'll never be the man he wants. I'll always be 'young Jimmy the cook', sneaking round the alleys for some lad to wank off with. And now Tom's on to me, I'll have to watch my back even more. What sort of life's that?

I've wandered away from the quay and along towards the Tyne's mouth, to the little pebble beach by the salt works where the cobles are pulled up. It looks so normal in daylight; you can hardly believe the goings on come nightfall: that long wall where Danny kissed me; that dip in the pebbles between the cobles where he give it me the first time, the feel of him edging it in, and the pebbles digging up through my coat, that knot of dry tangles by my head, the smell of sea salt and tangles.

I knew that young lad Tom battered and tied up. He was in the class below me at school: skinny fair lad with blue eyes, bonny as a lass; lives over by Ropery Bank. Thing is, I really liked him. He was quiet, just got on with things. I like that. Since then I've been looking out for him. I don't know why – to say sorry, something like that, give him a smile to say I understand – but I've never seen him. He's run away, I suppose, with that story nipping at his heels like a dog, off to somewhere nobody knows him.

* * *

After Sam went overboard, I couldn't face going back to our house. I know, I should have been there for Annie's sake. But I felt dirty, like I'd rolled in something and didn't want her to smell it on me. I even tried keeping away from Nana's – because the bairns are there, aren't they? Little Emma and Rickie. And our Frank in the loft with me, for God's sake, waiting up and wanting a blether about what's happened.

See, it's got all mixed up – Sam and Tom and Danny, all them other lads I've been with – into a big mucky tangle. And if any bit of it comes unravelled, if I say about Tom, the whole lot will get dragged into the open. I keep thinking, what if Da finds out?

So I'm not stopping home, and I daresn't go down the lanes any more, and everywhere I turn, there's Tom scowling at me like I'm something the cat's sicked up.

Mam's come to find me. I've been half expecting her for days now – because Nana must have said, mustn't she? About me not eating, and being out all hours? So here she is, sat on a mounting block with her fish plank propped against a wall, waiting for me. How she guessed this is the way I'd come, Lord knows. But that's Mam for you, isn't it?

When I see her, by Jesus it's a shock. She looks that shattered, her face sagging like a candle that's melted in the sun – and the size of her now! Annie'd said there was a baby on the way, but the way she's swelled up these past few weeks it looks like it could come any minute. Her eyes are closed and she's swaying a bit, so I think she's maybes dropped off – and I'm just thinking of sneaking away when she opens her eyes.

'Jimmy?' she says with a soft smile, like she's coming out of a dream. 'Is that you? Thank God. I was just about to give up.' And the way she says it, that load of weariness in her voice, I know she's meaning more than just waiting for me today.

I think she's come to have a word about me stopping out, but it's Annie she's worried about; how hard she's taken it since they found the body. 'Before, see, she could tell herself he'd swum ashore. Now she's seen him with her own eyes, it's like a light's gone out in her, Jimmy. And she can't settle. Every night she's out walking, and I haven't the heart to keep her in. But I'm that feared for her, wandering all hours. You know how rough it gets, this town, this time of year. So look out for her, will you? And tell the other lads, if they see her, to please bring her home to her mam.'

So I say, of course I'll keep an eye out. Fact I'll go out tonight specially. And all the time she's talking I'm fizzing with it, aren't I? Thinking it's an excuse to go round the alleys again, and down the lifeboat shed, and the salt works, and if Tom sees me I can tell him I'm looking for Annie. That's how I am, see? No better than a horny dog humping a sea-bag.

That night I go round the pubs by the Bullring, and a Grimsby lad buys me a top-up and wanks me off, quick, quick, down the side of a cutch tank. Then I do him, and by the end of that I'm hard again, and wanting to shove it up. I've never done that, see, it's always been the other way round. But this lad seems like he's up for it, but not here – there's too many folk. With a wank, see, you can leave off any second and face the wall like you're having a piss.

So I say to follow me to the Lifeboat House, and he says not now, for he's to get back to his boat. So I say, tomorrow, then – it's Saturday, we'll have more time. And he says, right you are – so that's sorted.

After, I go looking for Annie – along the quayside, then back along Bell Street and Liddell Street, where folk are stotting out of the pubs into the fog, like bairns playing blind-man's-buff. And I'm thinking, maybe she's safer walking in the fog, for it's easier to slip away if someone starts on at you. But then it strikes me that maybe that's worse, because if someone does want to try it on, you'd never know you were being followed till it was too late.

Da's said we've to go out to the herring grounds tonight, even though the water's flat as a mirror. He's booked a tug to pull us out to where he thinks there'll be a breath of wind. That's Da all over: always planning how to get a haul to market at a good price, whatever the weather, and beat the other crews to it. So once I've checked the alleys and lanes by the Scarp where Sam lived, I nip along to Nana's to pick up my oilies and head off back to the boat.

Da says Annie was still out when he left, and Mam's fretting. So I tell him I've been looking, and he says, good lad. Then he rubs his face with his dry hands, which is something he does sometimes, like trying to wash away what's worrying him. And all the time I'm tipping tea in the gorger, I'm thinking of tomorrow night, and meeting that Grimsby lad, and if he'll still be up for it.

It was one of those trips you're glad when it's over. We found a breeze, if you can call it that, and the haul was goodish. But coming back was a nightmare – we even had the oars out at one point. And Tom got in a barny with Da again about getting an engine fitted, so Da's back at him straight away asking how many times we're becalmed in a year – for he knows you can count them on the fingers of one hand – and is that reason enough to pay out for a total refit and new engine? And coal to fire it, and the extra fireman to tend it?

He would have left it at that, except Tom's turned away, hasn't he? And started mythering on under his breath. So now Da's riled, saying if Tom paid more mind, they could have made more use of what wind there was, and if he's not careful he'll be stuck as a deckie the rest of his life. And though he's never said, I can tell that he's comparing Tom with Sam – and Tom knows it too.

Anyway, we get home eventually, and moor up and cran out – though the fog's so thick the lumpers seem like they're barrowing into a white wall. And Tom slopes off early, with a face like thunder, straight after Da, leaving me to swill down. And he's taken the padlock with him, hasn't he? So I have to wedge the main hatch closed best I can and hope no one notices the hasp hanging. Day like this, it would be easy for some toe-rag to slip aboard and help themselves.

What with the fog, I'm worried the Grimsby lad will stop in. But he's waiting round the side of the Lifeboat House when I get there later, looming out of the gloaming in a big coat with the collar up. I've got my coat on too, so we're well set. There's a couple of lads about, so we walk along the beach, chatting a bit and chucking pebbles into the fog, with the moon a faint blur on the horizon.

He says he's working as a nightman, but was down the Seamen's Waiting Room today about a berth on a cargo ship. So I say, what's the pay like? And he says fair, but not as good as a share with a decent skipper – but it's a way to get away from folk that know you.

Now we've reached the place where the cobles are pulled up, and I scout around a bit to check if we're on our own, and take my coat off and lay it down on the pebbles, and he takes his off and sits beside us. And I don't know who's started it, but now we're kissing, and wriggling down with his coat over us, and the bells of 'longshoremen tolling out over the river.

Then – oh God, oh God – we're doing it, aren't we? Side by side like spoons in a drawer. And he's whispering to take it easy, and I'm trying – but he's so hot, and so *tight*, I can hardly bear it.

'Stop moving,' he whispers, 'and breathe slowly.' So I do, and relax against him, and he sighs, then I sigh, and then we laugh a bit. But that makes him clench even tighter, so I'm on the brink of spurting again. So I have to try and relax again, but this time it's easier and I can reach round and hold his dick, and lick his neck, and wank him slowly till I can tell he's ready to spurt too. And that's how we are, moving and not moving, waiting to spurt, under the fog, under his greatcoat, the two of us, right *there*—

Now here's footsteps on the pebbles and the sound of someone panting, like his chest's fit to burst, like he's been running, or carrying something heavy.

I try to stop and pull out, but it's too late, for he's started clenching me tight, in a rhythm, again and again, clamping his hand over mine on his dick, and pumping it, until I can't stand it and we spurt together.

The footsteps are nearer now, and there's a thud, then something big being dragged over the pebbles right past our heads – just some old 'longshoreman off on his coble, most likely. We're panting away, but I've pulled the coat right up over us, so we're hidden. So I'm thinking, if he spots us he'll think we're just a normal couple of sweethearts.

I can hear him dragging whatever it is over to one of the cobles and hoying it in, least that's what it sounds like. Now he's fixing the oars and setting off, towing the coble down to the water. I pull out, and wait a bit to give him time to wade in and push off, then I put on my coat on and stand up.

He's still there over by the water, and I was wrong – he's a young lad, not an old codger. And he's got a box or something open on the boat, and's hoying stones inside. What's he up to? The stones are clanging in, like into a tin bath, so I'm thinking it must be a metal box.

'Looks like he's going to dump something,' says the Grimsby lad, buttoning up his kecks.

And I'm just thinking there's something familiar about the lad hoying the stones when he straightens up and looks straight at me. And even in the fog, in the dark, I can see that it's Tom – and he can see that it's me. We stare at each other for a long moment, then he pushes the coble into the water and wades in after it – and he's gone, rowing off into the fog.

CHAPTER FIFTY-TWO

2007

Paul lies still for a while with his eyes closed. He can hear Ian's camera running, the seagulls mewing and chuckling outside. The doctor's saying something, but he pretends he's still under, or whatever it's called. He doesn't want to look at her, at that do-goody therapy face she'll have pasted on, the face that says she knows how he's *feeling*, that she *understands*. When he's just been having it off with some nonce, for fuck's sake.

Was he hypnotized? It didn't feel like it. It was more like just thinking about something, like watching a film – except you're *in* the frigging film and some of it's hard porn. It was the same last time. He was expecting to feel woozy and disoriented afterwards, like waking up from a dream, but it was actually sort of normal – apart from it being so fucking traumatic, obviously, what with the obesity and the amputations and that. But the process itself felt normal, like his mind had been wandering and just sort of noticing things, and then getting caught up; like when he thinks about Nessa and her new bloke, then starts imagining what they're doing, and it sort of escalates until he feels like smashing their smug faces in.

That's what makes it so fucking creepy – the idea that all this pansy stuff is just under the surface, like a part of him, just waiting to come out. Even if the doc's put it there, it's still fucking creepy. Seeing inside the mind of that twitchy little nonce, sneaking around, bundle of horny nerves. Talk about pathetic.

Mind you, that Tom would put the fear of God into anyone. You wouldn't want to get on his wrong side. Because it's obvious it was Annie's body he was lugging down to that coble.

That's what Paul can't understand: how Jimmy could have seen all those things and not said a fucking word. She was his *sister*, for Chrissake. Didn't he owe her that much? Being a nonce is bad enough, but being a coward's even worse in Paul's book.

Was he hoping Tom would be grateful? Is that it? And whisk him down one of them alleys for a spot of fishy rumpy-pumpy? Paul shudders, remembering: the stink of that other lad – his tabs, his piss, the sharp smell of his sweat – the rough hand yanking at his trouser buttons.

Then his eyes fly open. Ben! Was he listening to all that?

He stares round the room, blinking in the light, trying to focus. And there's Ben, crouched down on the pouffe just like last time – and grinning like a frigging Cheshire cat.

'Howay, Dad,' he goes. 'You all right?'

'What's he doing here still?' Paul asks angrily, sitting up. 'That was way past the watershed stuff.'

'I'm twelve, Dad. I know what gays get up to.'

He's still grinning, like it's the best thing since sliced bread, to have his dad getting it on with some lad on TV.

'That was bloody brilliant, mate,' says Ian. 'Fascinating. Just what the doctor ordered.' Then, to the doc: 'Looks like we've located the villain of the piece.'

'We still have to establish that it was a body in the box he was carrying. But I agree it does seem likely. It's intriguing that Tom's implicated in Sam's death too.' She turns to Paul. 'Thank you. I know how difficult it must have been to subject yourself to this disturbing process a second time. But I hope you can see now how very valuable your contribution has been to unravelling the mystery. If it wasn't for you, we'd never have suspected that Sam was murdered.'

Paul looks sideways at Ian. He keeps having to remind himself that the doctor's made all this up – because he can still feel the rasp of that warp on his hands down in the rope room, still feel the pebbles digging in through his great coat on the beach. If it's all just hypnotic suggestion, he's got to hand it to her, she's canny good at it.

Ian lifts the camcorder down from his shoulder and turns to the doc. 'What would you say if someone suggested that was a bit too much of a coincidence?' he asks. 'That Jimmy just *happened* to be awake when Tom went on deck, and just *happened* to be on the beach when he was getting rid of the body?'

Paul checks out the doc, to see how she reacts. But Ben pipes up before she can answer: 'But that's what it's like when you're living a secret life,' he says.

'You're always awake when other people are asleep, or in weird places where nobody knows you. It's not fair to says it's just a coincidence.'

The doctor smiles. 'Very eloquently put, Ben.' She turns back to Ian: 'Does that answer your question?'

'I'm just saying that *some* people might say it's rather convenient that's all.'

'Poor Jimmy,' says Ben quietly. 'He was really on his own, wasn't he?'

'That's no excuse,' says Paul, getting caught up despite himself. 'He should have gone straight to the police soon as he realized Annie was missing. If they'd looked through Tom's things they might have found something, I don't know, some blood on his kecks, or a locket or something.'

'He couldn't!' says Ben. 'They'd have asked why he was there. And Tom would've landed him well in it. It would be all over the Low Town in five minutes.'

'So? Serve him right.'

'Dad! How can you say that? You were *there*. You know what it was like for him. He never chose to be born that way.'

'He chose to go with them lads, dirty little nonce.'

'He wasn't hurting anyone.'

'He hurt Annie, didn't he? By staying quiet. He let his mam and dad keep on looking for her. He let Tom get away with it.'

'He was *scared*!' shouts Ben. 'Don't you get it? What if his dad found out about him being gay? And the lads on the boat? You know what happened to that other lad. You know what they'd have done to him.' His cheeks are flushed with anger, his hands closed in fists.

Paul becomes aware of the camera humming again and looks round. Ian's crouching behind his shoulder, lens focussed squarely on Ben's face. And Paul understands suddenly how this must look from the outside: the lad who wants a sex change standing up for the lad who's gay, and the whole world against the both of them. And an ache starts up at the base of his throat, like his collar's too tight or something. After a while he recognizes the feeling as sobs caught down there, like a purse-seine full of mackerel, drawn in so tight they can't move.

'Turn that fucking camera off,' he says gruffly, embarrassed at getting so caught up in this farce, that's basically just that doctor's warped imagination.

'Right-o mate. Sorry about that,' says Ian, looking not sorry at all – more like the cat that got the cream. 'It's second nature, I'm afraid. I see a spot of argy-bargy, and the camera seems to turn on its own.'

'You'll clear everything with me before you use it, right?'

'Dinna fash, mate. Ninety percent of what we shoot gets binned anyway. That's the trouble with digital. It's too easy to keep turning. With film there's always a cost implication. In the old days you'd have a budget and a box of stock and that was you. You had to make it last. But with this little beauty, the world's your lobster.'

He hands it over, and Paul weighs it in one hand. 'So what's the memory like?' he asks, wondering if there's an underwater equivalent. If it's not too pricy he might look into an upgrade before their next trip abroad.

'Two point eight mega-pixels – but with the 16-gig memory stick duo you can keep going for ages. Five hours HDV recording time, 1080 resolution. Got it in March and never looked back.'

The doctor's scribbling something in a notebook. 'I wonder if this is why Jimmy became so obese later in life,' she says in a vague sort of voice, like she's talking to herself. 'To counteract that rather shrinking and apologetic persona he seems to have cultivated as a young man.'

'It certainly got him noticed,' comments Ian, taking back the camera and stowing it in a padded pouch in his backpack.

'It's as though he was trying to make up for not revealing himself earlier – by courting public opprobrium with his rather gothic lifestyle.'

'"Kick me, I'm a poofter" you mean?'

'Have I mentioned before the idea that guilt can be an actual motive for self-harm, as opposed to simply a reaction to sins committed? I'm wondering if perhaps Jimmy actively sought out punishment for not speaking out about Tom.'

'So he buys a wardrobe full of sequins and eats himself to death.'

'Great,' comments Paul bitterly.

'I liked Lord Jim,' says Ben stubbornly. 'He was kind and funny. And him being big and sort of obvious must've made it easier for other lads to, like, be what they wanted. Like Laura when she was that Davy, before she had the op.'

'It's a shame he never seems to have had a lasting relationship,' says the doctor. 'Perhaps that was another way of punishing himself.'

'Oh please,' Paul objects. 'Now you're making him out to be some kind of tragic hero. When in fact he was just a nervy little nancy who grew up to be a big fat OTT poofter.'

'Maybe he was in love with Tom,' Ben suggests, ignoring him. 'And couldn't bear to think he was a murderer. I mean, you didn't actually see him kill anyone, did you, Dad? So it could have been an accident with Sam. With Annie too – maybe it was a mistake he was trying to cover up. Maybe he got drunk or something and tried to kiss her and it got out of hand.'

'No,' says Paul, thinking back. 'Jimmy knew there was something dodgy going on. He was just too much of a scaredy-cat to say anything.' And he realizes he's doing it again, isn't he? Getting all caught up in something that never happened.

'Maybe he didn't *want* to believe it,' Ben argues, 'and was hoping he'd be proved wrong. That's what I'd do if I found out something really evil about your nice little earners.'

'Perhaps that's Jimmy's legacy to you, Paul,' says the doc quietly.

'You what?' Now what's she on about?

'Well, it hasn't escaped my notice that you are rather a forthright person.'

'Call a spade a spade, you mean? So?'

'And that you appear to have garnered a great deal of power and respect in your community. I imagine they call you "Big Paul" – am I right?'

'How did you know that?'

'Yet you're not particularly "big" in the literal sense of the word. So what they're referring to in your case is the power of your personality, your influence – your masculinity if you like – something you probably take for granted as your birthright, but which I sense young Jimmy Milburn longed for but never truly attained. Remember how he talked about his father? His fear that he might be a disappointment to him?'

'Fascinating,' says Ian, tapping notes into his Blackberry. 'So you'd trace back every aspect of a personality to some unfinished business in a previous incarnation.'

'Not *every* aspect, no.' The doc sighs and looks exhausted for a moment, like her mask's slipped sideways. Watching Ian sparring with her, Paul finds himself feeling quite sorry for her. The poor dab's got no idea what's in store.

'Which ones then?' Ian asks.

'Don't try to bait me, Ian. I'm not in the mood.' She rubs her hands across her eyes, smudging her eyeshadow – probably forgotten she's even got it on. 'Past life regression is not an exact science, any more than psychoanalysis is. You can't apply the same simple formula to every case. Things are—'

'I know, multiply determined – as in "unprovable".'

'Yes. But in my experience, any particularly unusual or dominant personality trait does often turn out to be the expression – or resolution – of a conflict in a previous life. Talking of which—' she sits up a bit and fixes Ian with one of her stern looks – 'I have a series of rather large bones to pick with you.'

Paul gets up. He's had enough of all this psychobabble. 'Right,' he says. 'I need a bit of fresh air. If it's all right with yous two, me and Ben have got a bedroom to paint tomorrow. Right, buddy? Ian, you can get me on my mobile if there's anything else.'

The next day, after dithering over a sort of dark maroon at the paint-mixing station in B&Q (same as the doc's got on her skirtings, come to think of it), Ben's decided on one of those nothing white colours. He says it's because he doesn't know who he is at the moment, so he doesn't know what colour he wants. Then he goes and loads four giant cork boards on to the trolley, 'so I can try out some art things', plus a big candystriped rug, which is not especially girlie, thank goodness, but not proper lads' gear either.

Back at the flat, they get on their new overalls, spread out the dust sheets and set to work. Paul's done this before, when he and Nessa got their starter flat, so he goes round the edges with a paintbrush, while Ben slurps what looks like melted icecream into the tray for the roller. He's expecting the lad to slop it all over the shop, but he gets the knack dead fast, and in an hour the first coat's on.

Standing in the middle of the room with their Kit Kats and mugs of tea, they survey what they've done.

'It looks loads bigger,' says Ben, rubbing dried spatters of paint from his forearm. 'And really really light.'

'Be even better when the top coat's on.'

'I'll do the boring bits next time if you want a go with the roller.'

'No, you're all right. I'd probably slop it and make a mess.' Then, rubbing the lad's cheek with his thumb: 'Look at you, daftie. Covered in white freckles.'

Ben grins up at him. 'How long before we can put the top coat on?'

'This weather, we could probably start on that first wall straight away. You'll have to sleep in with me the next few nights, mind. Even with the window open, I'm not having you breathing in all them fumes.'

'Can we order pizzas and have them in bed with a DVD like when I was little?' What he means is, after Mam buggered off.

Those first weeks after Nessa left, Ben wouldn't let Paul out of his sight; to be fair, Paul felt pretty much the same. So they sort of stuck together, night and day, until Paul thought he ought to put a stop to it. Which was the only time he ever raised his hand to the lad, which still makes him feel sick thinking back. Because it did the trick, right enough, but he never wants to see a look like that on the bairn's face again.

'What made you change your mind about the film and the doc and Laura and that?' Ben asks.

'What, apart from you giving me the silent treatment and going on hunger strike and locking yourself in your room? And Nana giving me GBH of the bloody earhole every time I saw her?'

Ben grins. 'Well, I think it's well wicked.'

'What? Letting the world and his wife sort through our dirty washing on TV?'

'I mean, everything's so cool now, after being so totally crap. Like my new room, and you being in the film, and investigating Annie and that. Then finding out I was Miss Turnbull – that was so *weird*! Reading her diaries and sitting in her chair and that.'

'You don't think it's a bit neat, how all that came together?' Paul says carefully. He doesn't want to give anything away, but he thinks he ought to prepare Ben for what's in store.

'When I worked out the dates, I was like *wow*! Though it is a bit spooky thinking about being an old biddy in another life.'

Paul tries again. 'You do know that Ian's job is to investigate all that, don't you? It might not all pan out the way you expect.'

'But the really mint thing is it's nearly sorted now, isn't it? Like what really happened to Annie. I can hardly believe it. In a few days we'll know everything, and it will all be over, and I can start my new life.'

Ian's arranged to meet Paul in the Maggie Bank, just up the hill from the flat. It's a noisy, busy pub, with quizzes and live music and that, because Billy Neville makes a proper effort, unlike some landlords Paul could name; plus there's always a decent load of bar snacks and a proper restaurant tacked on the back.

Ian's sat in a corner booth with a glass of red wine. 'Let me get this one,' he says, waving a twenty at the chav behind the bar. 'Pint of Snecklifter, right? Or shall I order up a bottle of this Merlot?' Like there's a posh wine cellar or something, instead of a load of cheapo crates out back, driven up the A1 from Calais in the back of Billy's old transit.

'Yeah, thanks,' Paul says. 'Wine would be great.'

'Thanks for coming along to Mary's yesterday. It made all the difference.'

'No problem.'

'Amazing, isn't it, the detail she got out of you? Anyone seeing that would be totally convinced you were the reincarnation of that lad.'

'It felt so real, man. Afterwards I kept having to remind myself that the doc was doing it, like making me come out with that stuff.'

'I thought you might have been putting some of it on, you know, hamming it up a bit for the camera.'

'No way. I was right there, least that's what it felt like.'

Ian sits forward, his eyes narrowing a bit. 'So you had absolutely no sense she was leading you in any way, or putting words into your mouth? The experience was utterly genuine as far as you're concerned.'

'Too right.' Paul pulls a face, remembering. 'She knows what she's doing, that doctor.'

'You're still OK with that permission though, right mate? Not too traumatized? Not rethinking your sexuality or anything?'

'You are joking, I hope.'

The chav brings a bottle over, plus another couple of glasses. 'I spent the afternoon on the phone to my researcher,' says Ian, pouring the wine. 'She's been tracking down some of Mary's old cases, then following them up to see if their past incarnations really existed. You'd be amazed what people will let slip when you say it's the Beeb on the blower.'

'How does the doc feel about that? You checking up on her old cases?'

'Put it this way, she's not exactly over the moon. But she's a big girl. She's known all along this is a proper investigation, not some happy-clappy cable crap.'

'What sort of thing are you looking for?'

'Anything really. Cases where the past-life regression details are contradicted by the historical record. Blatant confabulations—'

'What, where the patient just makes up stuff? Like being Joan of Arc or Napoleon or something?'

'Actually I'm expecting something a bit more mundane. A miner dying in a disaster that never happened, or a nurse at a hospital that never existed. That sort of thing – where there are some really concrete "memories" we can check up on.'

'So you think Ben's case is a fluke?'

'I don't know. It's too early to say. But Mary can't have read the diaries of every old biddy in the country, can she?'

Paul sips his wine. 'I'm going to have to tell Ben some time, you realize. So he's not too upset when the film comes out. He's pretty keen on the doc, you know.'

'As long as you wait till I've finished the shooting. I want to be sure all the hypnosis sessions are in the can before the shit hits the proverbial.' He sloshes more wine into his glass. 'And it's early days yet. Who knows? We might find that all her past cases check out. Got to keep an open mind, eh?' And he crams a handful of dry roasted into his mouth.

Ben's asleep when Paul gets back, slumped down in a nest of pillows on the double bed, with the lights off and the TV on. It's some rom-com with that Hugh Grant bloke, the one they caught with a hooker's head in his lap, silly twat. Doesn't seem to have damaged his career, mind.

Easing the remote from the lad's fingers, Paul turns the sound down, not wanting to wake him by turning it off suddenly. The pizza box is open on the floor, just the crusts left. Paul takes it into the kitchen and pours himself a Bell's, then shoves his own pizza in the oven. While he's waiting for it to heat up, he wanders into the hall and catches sight of his reflection in the mirror.

He looks knackered, he thinks, and his hair needs cutting. And his eyes are doing that puffy thing they do when he's drinking too much. He peers closer, checking out the broken veins on his cheeks – occupational hazard on the boat, but the booze can't help. Better cut down before his nose starts to go, like the alky lads on the top bank. He checks out his profile. At least he's got a proper nose – not like Nessa's little button, like a piece of putty someone's just stuck on, like the bairn's nose when he was a nipper.

He used to worry the lad would be stuck with her putty nose, but lately it seems to be straightening out just fine. They do say you can tell a family resemblance from the nose, but Paul's that close he can't see it. He feels like asking folk, sometimes, if they can see it, but he's worried they'd guess why he was asking. What gets to him sometimes, if he thinks about it, is that folk might already have clocked something Paul's missed, the shape of the lad's ears, maybe, or his eyes, that's the spit of Nessa's new bloke.

Daft to dwell on it, really, when all he has to do is open that fucking envelope and get the matter settled for good. He opens the drawer. The letter's there, of course, where it always is.

He never told Nessa about doing the test. It's never seemed anything to do with her. In his mind it's always been between him and the lad.

He takes the letter out and holds it up to the light for a moment, then puts it back and closes the drawer again.

Truth is, he's scared to find out. But maybe now's the time. Sink or swim, sort of thing. So if Ben is his, then he's got to stand by him, hasn't he? Thick and thin. And if he isn't? Well, then maybe the lad would be better off in New Zealand with his mam – he's been going on about it enough.

Come to think of it, that would make sense all round. Get him out of the way before the film comes out. Let Nessa deal with all the Annie crap for a change. Then if the worst comes to the worst, and the bairn really can't settle in his boy's body, then at least she'd be able to help him with his clothes and make-up and that. Be a role model.

'Ha!' Paul laughs aloud briefly. Let her bloke put *that* in his pipe and smoke it!

Later, slipping into the bed beside the lad and easing the extra pillows out from under his head, Paul pauses a moment and looks down at him. His mouth's open and he's snoring a bit, and his breath smells of onion from that extra topping; and his cheeks are pink and creased, from being bundled up in all them pillows, and there's sweat on his upper lip. He could be six, worn out from footie practice, back when Paul used to dunk him in the Jacuzzi, then wrap him in a bath sheet and chuck him in the bed while he watched *Match of the Day*.

Bless him, the bairn always tried to stay awake, but within minutes his little head would be nodding. And he'd sleep though it all: Paul swearing and whooping, punching the duvet, knocking back the Stella. That was before the accident, of course, when things were more normal. Before it all went a bit pear-shaped.

CHAPTER FIFTY-THREE

2007

It's just gone nine and Ben's on his way to the salon. He's not actually asked Dad if it's OK to see Laura, but he's never told him he can't either, so he reckons that counts as permission, in a way. Plus, after giving Dad the silent treatment last week and standing up to him for a change, Ben feels it's time he started doing what he wants a bit more.

She's dead chuffed to see him, which he's relieved about, because it's been ages and he was wondering if maybe she'd got someone else to sweep up and do the cossies and that. But they slot back into it straight away and it's like old times – her tea and his hot choc, plate of bourbons in the caff with the sign turned to 'closed' – before heading upstairs to the salon to see what needs doing.

When he tells her about Dad being hypnotized again she nearly falls off her chair. 'What on earth did that Ian Campbell say to change his mind? I never thought we'd see Big Paul within three miles of that couch.'

'I don't know,' says Ben. Actually, he'd assumed it was because he was giving Dad a hard time, but now he comes to think of it, it wasn't until Ian came round and necked all the Chinky chow that Dad started to come round.

'Go on then,' says Laura. 'Don't leave me all agog. What happened in the session?'

So he tells her about how Jimmy had been leading this secret life as a gay and that's how he came to be on the beach that night and saw Tom hoying something heavy into a coble.

And Laura just sits there, with her mouth literally hanging open – just like people say, but Ben's never seen it before – with her bourbon stuck in the air half way into it. 'So it *was* Tom that killed Annie,' she says. 'I knew it.'

'We think he killed Sam too,' Ben says. And explains what Jimmy saw on the boat the night Sam went overboard.

'Stone me sideways and leave me out for the crows!' goes Laura. 'I don't know, leave you lot alone for a few days and all hell breaks loose. What else have I missed by ironing frocks and waxing toes and serving up a few pots of Earl Grey?'

'Right, you remember, that old biddy who looked after Lord Jim, that Miss Turnbull?'

'Don't tell me, she's turned out to be a raving lezzer on the quiet.'

Ben giggles, because that is just so out of order. 'No – she was me! I mean I was her – between being Annie and being me now. And I found her diaries, which was how we found out about Jimmy and Tom.'

Laura's finished her bourbon, but now it's her tea cup that's frozen in the air. She puts it back in the saucer and stares at him. 'Jesus and Mary Magdalena. So you were old Miss T., eh? Well there's a turn up and no flies. I knew her really well, did you realize? At one time I was in and out of that flat like a fiddler's elbow.'

'I know! How weird is that? There's loads of stuff about you in the diaries, about how you helped out with Lord Jim and that, when he was in that wheelchair, and how he encouraged you to come out as a trannie.'

'Ay, one in a million that Lord Jim – though I'm not sure Miss T. saw it that way.'

'Plus it turns out that Miss Turnbull used to babysit for Mary when she was little.'

'So Mary was "the lass" she were always on about. Well, well. Funny I never met her – well, not so funny really, when you come to think about it. I mean, Miss T. would never have let her near the place with Lord Jim just upstairs. She was forever on about how he was going to "turn" me, like I was a jug of milk or something.'

Ben sits up straight. 'Are you sure the doc was never there? Only she's really stressed out about it.'

'Why?'

'Because of the diaries. Ian says if Mary read the diaries when she was little, then she could have read the bit about Tom being on the beach that night.'

'So?'

'Well, Ian thinks the doc might have put that whole story into all our heads by hypnosis. But she couldn't have seen the diaries, could she? You were there the whole time when Lord Jim came out of hospital and you never saw her.'

'Never clapped eyes on the lass. Plus it was October by the time he died, so she'd have gone back to that boarding school long since.'

'You've got to tell Ian!' Ben's excited: this is just the sort of evidence the doc needs. 'You've got to go on telly and testify that the doc never saw them diaries.'

'Hang on a bit, that doesn't mean she never saw them. After Jim died, Miss T. could have brought her to the flat any time.'

Ben slumps in his chair. 'So she could have seen them later.'

'You're really worried about this aren't you?'

'It's that Ian bloke. I don't know why, but I don't trust him. I keep thinking he's going to do the dirty on the doc. I mean, you should have seen him with the diaries at old Skip's place. Ordering everyone about, like he didn't care what happened to anyone as long as he got his film done.'

Laura nods, like she knows what he means, which makes Ben even more worried for the doc.

'You know the other thing Mary's stressed out about?' asks Laura. 'She thinks that Tom might be one of her fishermen. You know, one of her past lives. How would that look on the telly, eh?' She pours more tea and clicks in a couple of sweeteners. 'Which means she's between a rock and a hard place, isn't she? Either she's making it all up and her career's down the khazi, or she's the reincarnation of a lad who murdered her favourite client.'

'Bloody hell,' says Ben. Then he remembers something. 'Wasn't your fisherman called Tom too?'

Laura nods. 'According to Mary half the bloomin' population of Shields back then was called Tom.'

'So it could have been either of you.'

'Quite right, or some other poor dorcas altogether. But it's been rather preying on my mind. In fact if you hadn't dinged my dinger this morning, I'd be sat in that library right now with Pete checking out the Births, Marriages and Deaths again.'

Pete's sorting old photos when they get there: a load of pictures of cranes from that old Swan Hunter shipyard that closed down. 'Well, if it isn't the BBC research team,' he says, closing a tattered folder and shoving it into a crammed filing cabinet. 'Is that Ian Campbell coming along later? Only I've got that info he asked for, all printed out and collated, all them searches you and the doctor's been doing.'

'Fantabulosa,' goes Laura winking at Ben. 'We might need to vada that little lot later, if that's OK. But we've got something else to investigate first, haven't we Ben? On that BMD website.'

Pete sits down at a nearby computer and boots up. 'We're interested in a lad called Thomas Hall,' says Laura. 'He was born around 1880 and we need to find out when he died. His address should be in them other searches you did with Mary, though I suppose he might have shifted a few times since then.'

'He's one of the lads on that boat, right? The *Osprey*, wasn't it? Hang on a sec,' he says, and gets up to leaf through a heap of photocopies on his desk. 'You never know. If he inherited the house from his da, he could have stayed put till he died.' He clicks through a series of windows, then: 'Bingo! There he is: Thomas John Hall, born 1880, died 1948. Will that do you?' He beams around at them. 'Right, was there anything else?'

Ben waits for Laura to say something, but she's staring at the screen in a sort of a daze. He gives her a bit of a nudge. 'What's the name of that woman Mary was always talking about?' he asks. But before she can answer, he remembers: 'Peggy, that's it.'

'You'll be talking about Margaret Simpson, I expect,' says Pete. 'The doctor was in here a week or so back looking up her dates for some reason. Let me check – it'll be in here somewhere.' He sorts though the photocopies again and pulls out a single sheet. 'OK, here we are: Margaret Simpson, born 1925, died 1956. How's that for service?'

Ben does the sum in his head. 'That means Peggy was born twenty-three years before Tom died,' he says. 'So Tom couldn't have been Mary's fisherman after all!' He turns to Laura, but she's gone pale under her tan and her mouth's gone sort of quivery and thin. Then he twigs. 'When were you born?' he asks.

'Thirtieth of November 1948.'

'It doesn't mean that Tom was your Tom.'

'No, but it looks pretty likely, doesn't it?'

'Maybe he's my nana. You're about the same age, aren't you?'

'No, I've been expecting this from the start.' Laura sighs. 'And just think how you'd feel if it was your nana murdered you in a previous life?'

Ben stares at her as the information sinks in. And he's remembering what it felt like that time at Annie's house, when Tom came to visit, and she was totally sad and numb from seeing Sam washed up on that minging beach – but Tom tried it on anyway. How gross and macho was that?

'I think I'd rather it was her than you,' he says in a small voice.

'Right,' says Pete, pushing his chair back. 'If there's nothing else, I reckon I'll leave you to it – whatever "it" is. Though if you ask me, I think the lot of yous are all off your rockers.'

CHAPTER FIFTY-FOUR

2007

It's nine o'clock in the morning and Mary's striding along the sea wall to the Grand Hotel to confront Ian. She did consider phoning first to tell him she's coming, but she doesn't want him evading her again. As soon as she'd mentioned she wanted to talk to him yesterday, he'd become unaccountably distracted by an urgent 'crisis with the film crew' and whizzed off on his bicycle.

The sun's hot already and the sea's glittering and reassuringly flat. With her gloves off and her hair freshly washed, she feels both militant and slightly agitated at the idea of being alone with him in his hotel room. The combination is rather exhilarating, albeit somewhat tiring.

At reception the woman gives out his room number without hesitation – 'top floor, turn right when you come out of the lift' – as though Mary is the latest of many overwrought women to have requested it, which, she reflects grimly, she probably is.

She listens briefly outside before knocking. He's on the phone to someone, talking loudly, and the television's on – and is that the radio, too, burbling away in the background?

He flings open the door with his mobile gizmo still clamped to his ear. 'Good grief!' he exclaims when he sees her. Then, into the phone: 'Viv? Look, we'll finish this later, OK? Something's come up.' He presses a tiny button and drops it into his pocket. 'Come in, come in. Is anything wrong?'

'You tell me,' she says tartly.

'What do you mean?'

'I mean I have been on the receiving end of several pieces of disquieting information in the last few days, about your research activities for this documentary – not to mention poor old Mr Skipper turning up unannounced expecting you to be filming a session with me. And you haven't had the decency to contact me once. And if I hadn't come here myself, you *still* wouldn't have contacted me, am I right?'

He opens his mouth to object, but she's into her stride now. 'What's more, when I tried to talk to you yesterday, you scuttled off before I could say anything. Now I'd like you to switch off that infernal mobile contraption, and all the other bits of distracting media equipment in this room, and tell me what's going on.'

He grins at her. 'You look gorgeous when you're angry, do you know that?'

'And don't think you can get around me with absurd compliments.'

'You do, though. Your hair's coming loose and there's freckles on your nose. And that scarf's always suited you – I assume it's the same one? The one I bought you on that camping trip in Totnes?'

'Ian,' she says severely. 'I want some answers.'

'Have you had breakfast yet?' He's still grinning. It's utterly infuriating.

'Stop trying to deflect me. This is serious.'

'So is breakfast,' he says. 'I was just nipping down to catch the last service. Would you care to join me?'

'Surprisingly, I find I don't feel very much like eating at the moment.'

'Mind if I get them to send something up then?'

She sighs with impatience. 'You are impossible.'

Picking up the hotel phone, Ian reels off a list of instructions about varieties of coffee and fruit, types of egg dishes and various bakery goods with French names. Through an arch Mary can see an enormous unmade bed: white sheets tangled, pillows askew. The coverlet's in a heap at the foot of the bed. An array of those ridiculous 'bed cushions' has been slung into a corner. What she'd assumed was the radio burbling away turns out to be a second enormous flat-screen television in the bedroom, tuned to a different channel to the matching one blaring in the lounge.

'Right, where were we?' he asks.

'You were trying to variously charm, undermine and distract me from my quest, which is to find out exactly what you've been doing behind my back.'

'Are you planning to sit down ever?'

Mary looks around. There's a three-piece suite in this room, and a small circular table over by the window, with two upright chairs either side, as well as a full-sized desk against the far wall embellished with his usual slew of black wires and obscure black electronic attachments. Propped against it, astonishingly, is his bicycle – how on earth did he persuade them to allow that?

She opts for one of the upright chairs by the table and sits down primly with her hands in her lap, while he roams the suite obediently, retrieving handsets and switching off the televisions.

When he's finished, and sitting opposite her, she says: 'We'll start with Karleen, shall we? I expressly asked you not to contact her – but you went ahead anyway. Did you think I wouldn't find out?'

'She called you, I assume.' He seems unabashed.

'She's one of my dearest friends, Ian – of course she called me! And she told me something very interesting about who else is involved in this series of yours. Are you aware that Hester Griffin is one of my fiercest critics?'

'I was going to tell you, but I wanted to get everything straight in my own mind first.' At least he has the grace to look slightly sheepish.

'So how long has Hester been involved? According to Karleen the whole series was her idea.'

'No, that's total bollocks. Typical Hester blowing her own trumpet. She heard I was nosing around, doing some preliminary research into paranormal phenomena, so she called me up and suggested a meeting. I think she was angling for a presenting gig actually, and when she saw that was out of the question she presumably thought the next best thing was appearing as chief prosecutor in the case against reincarnation.'

'So it was her idea to do the programme about me.'

'No, I'd already decided I was going to get in touch. But having her on board helped tip the balance with the suits. You have to admit she's a bit of a looker. Ideal telly fodder.'

'I can imagine,' Mary comments drily.

'Come on, Mary. You must have known I'd consult her.'

'Yes, but I expected you to consult *me* first! What if she'd contacted me out of the blue and I hadn't known about her involvement? Imagine how humiliating that would have been.'

'I was just trying to protect—'

'I don't need protecting, Ian. I've been facing this kind of criticism for the last twenty-five years. The only thing that's different about now is that I've just written a book that I would very much like to have published.'

'Now who's not telling the truth? I saw your face when you realized your Miss T. was the author of those diaries. You were really rattled, admit it.'

'Of course I was rattled! Because this time I'm not going to be grappling with Hester in some obscure academic journal, am I? This time it's going to be on prime-time television. Is it surprising I'm getting somewhat hot under the collar?'

Realizing that her hands have closed into fists, Mary opens them slowly and takes a deep breath. 'I am only too aware that the theory of reincarnation seems utterly outlandish in this day and age; and that the idea of groups of souls reincarnating together seems even more preposterous – even to me. Hardly a day goes by when I don't wonder what on earth I'm doing, delving into people's past lives, when I don't come up with a hundred alternative explanations for the phenomena I'm seeing.'

'But?'

She shrugs helplessly. 'But the alternative explanations are so *elaborate* and involve such bizarre feats of memory and perception – not to mention coincidence – that in the end they just seem even more preposterous.'

'Are you sure about that?' Ian leans forwards in his chair. 'Mary, when I told Hester about what happened when you hypnotized me, she practically wet herself. According to her, that was absolutely textbook hypnotic suggestion. Because it was just after you'd been doing all that research in the library, and Paul had just dragged Ben away, so we needed something else for the film.'

'So she thinks the details of Dory's death were all conjured up by me in an attempt to salvage my career.'

'You have to admit it looks pretty iffy. So I thought I'd ferret around, do a bit of research to see if I could get together some supportive evidence, to shift the argument back in the other direction. That's why Viv's been following up some of your past cases, to see if your published accounts match the historical record. And why I got in touch with Karleen to interview her for the film.'

'But why didn't you *tell* me?'

'I didn't want to worry you unnecessarily. Hester had let slip that your new book was running into trouble—'

Mary snorts. 'It was doing fine before she put her oar in.'

'So I thought I'd rustle up a decent case for the defence before I said anything. Then Ben found those fucking diaries and it all went frigging tits up.'

'Ah yes,' Mary says. 'The diaries.'

'Yes, the diaries. The ones you might have read as a girl. Are you refuting the Bridey Murphy interpretation now?'

'Yes, totally – though you're right, I was pretty discombobulated at the time. But I've since discovered that Miss Turnbull never took the diaries out of her flat, and would never have allowed me near the place in case I encountered Lord Jim. I know, I know,' she says as he opens his mouth to object, 'it wouldn't stand up in court, as it were – but it's enough to convince me, which is all that matters to *me*.'

'Do you think it's enough to convince three million BBC2 viewers?'

Mary shrugs. 'They'll have to make up their own minds.'

A heavy square machine she hadn't noticed earlier whirs and beeps suddenly then starts churning out a series of typewritten pages that look disturbingly like one of her own academic papers.

'So what happened when you investigated my old cases?' she asks.

'Most of them check out with the historical record – which is pretty bloody amazing, actually – but I'm afraid there were one or two striking anomalies.'

'You do realize they could be due to cryptoamnesia too,' says Mary. 'Hester probably neglected to mention that it can work in two directions – both to create a false memory and to adulterate or otherwise distort a true one.'

There's a knock at the door and, when he opens it, a uniformed waitress wheels in a loaded trolley. The scents of fresh coffee and warm brioche fill the room and Mary discovers she has an appetite after all. When the waitress has gone, she pours herself an unaccustomed bath-sized bowl of latte and dunks the corner of a similarly outsized croissant.

'You were telling me about cryptoamnesia,' says Ian, lifting the silver cover off a plate of smoked salmon and scrambled eggs and reaching for the pepper-grinder.

'Well, when people encounter a gap in their memories they tend to fill it in with whatever seems to fit with the surrounding information – which is not always what actually happened. In the purest case you get a completely fabricated memory, in which every detail is untrue. But what more often results is a patchwork of remembered and imagined events as the conscious mind attempts to paper over the cracks, as it were.'

She takes another bite of croissant, then cradles her cup in two hands. Any moment now, she'll start wanting a Gitanes, but there's a discreet 'no smoking' sign on the table and a smoke alarm in the ceiling immediately above. She wonders what would happen if she opened the window.

'Hester thinks I should call in a second hypnotherapist,' remarks Ian casually. 'To find out from Ben how much of this Annie story he was picking up from you. Apparently this was never tried in the Bridey Murphy case – though God knows why; it's the obvious thing to do – hypnotize that Virginia woman again and find out if she really did meet the real Bridey Murphy when she was wee.'

Mary stiffens. 'Why not just hypnotize me?' she suggests sarcastically. 'Find out if I did read that diary. Find out how much I knew in advance about all the *hundreds* of cases I've treated in this way since I started practising.'

'I want to believe you—'

'I don't need your *belief*, Ian,' she snaps, pushing her plate away. 'When I agreed to this film, I knew there was a chance I'd be blown out of the water. And of course if that happens, it will be enormously difficult for me on a whole series of levels. But that doesn't mean I want to be cosseted and protected. I want to find out about this phenomenon just as much as you do – even if it means I'm proved wrong.'

'Oh, I do love you.'

'For heaven's sake! Can't you be serious for a minute?'

'I am being serious, Mimi. You're clever and passionate, utterly original, sexy as hell—'

'Please don't start that all again.'

'When you kissed me the other night—'

'As I recall, it was actually you who kissed me,' she objects.

'But you kissed me back – don't try to deny it.'

'What about Hester?' she asks, then regrets it immediately.

'Hester? What's she got to do with it?' Then his face clears. 'You think I'm having an affair with Hester, don't you?'

She blushes. 'It did cross my mind,' she says. 'After all your comments about how bad it was with the lovely Christina.'

'Hah! So you've been considering it then.' He shoots her a triumphant look. 'After all these years of playing hard to get, you're finally considering having an affair with me.'

She opens her mouth to deny it, then closes it again. What would be the point? He wouldn't believe her – and he's right, in a way. A part of her has been toying with the idea ever since she walked him back to his hotel that night.

'Come on then,' he says. 'Kiss me again.'

'What?'

'Take off your ridiculous boots, Mary Charlton, and let down your hair and come to bed with me.

Before she can object, he's fallen to his knees in front of her and has started to unlace one of her Doc Marten's. She knows she should stop him, that this is ridiculous, that she's being irresponsible – but she seems to have lost the power of speech, and the sun's warm on her hair, and her legs have gone weak, literally—

He's just easing the boot off when there's a loud knock on the door. 'It'll just be the waitress for the trolley,' he says, getting to his feet. 'Sorry, I should have put up a do not disturb notice.'

But when he opens the door, Laura and Ben are standing there.

'Howay, lad,' says Laura. 'Get your gear together. It's time to put your Auntie Laura on the witness stand.'

CHAPTER FIFTY-FIVE

... Can you see the hallway? Good. And the doors? Now I want you to open one of the doors and step through. Where are you? What's happening?

1919

It's a Sunday and I've just wakened up. The curtains are drawn so God knows what time it is. My head's splitting and I want to spew up. I roll over and there's the slops bucket by the bed, and the smell tips me over the edge, so I'm retching, puking up, and it stinks of whisky. And each time I retch, it's like my head's going to crack open and my eyeballs pop out of their bloody sockets. And I'm thinking: what a fucking stupid waste of a day off.

Now here comes Flo with a cloth and a bowl of water, and kneels by the bed and wipes my face for me, and takes the bucket off down the stairs to empty in the nettie. So I'm flopped back on the pillow, feeling like shit, when she comes in again with a fresh bucket and a cup of tea, then opens the curtains a bit – enough to see by, but not so much as to make me wince – and she's just pulling the door closed behind her when I call her back.

'Thanks, pet,' I say. 'That was some night.'

'Ay, seems like.'

And I reach out a hand and she takes it and comes to sit on the bed. And I'm trying to dredge up a morsel of tenderness for her, for she's bonny enough still, and does her best, I suppose. I can see a fresh bruise on her arm, where she's rolled her sleeve up. It's a funny shape: long and narrow. Further up, I can see the edge of an older one peeping out: greenish, fading.

Last night's and last week's, I'm thinking. I can't remember doing them, but how else would she get them? And that red one under her hair on the one side that never fades, that makes me ashamed to look at. Talking to her now, man to wife on the bed of a Sunday morning, I can't think what gets into me.

Half the time I don't know my own strength, see? With the bairns, right, I forget they're only little; so I go to give them a bit slap, for cheeking me, giving me a look, and they go over like bloomin' skittles. Thing is, you need that sort of force when you're dealing with a mouthy deckie, or some snooty Scot down the Low Lights.

Then after, I'll catch her staring at me with that sorrowful look on her face, and it makes me want to give her one too. Not that she'd ever say anything – oh no, not her. I'd like it better if she'd have a proper barny with me. But she thinks if she plays nicey-nice, and smiles, and puts on her lacy pinny, that'll sweeten me. Well it might work with her mam and da, but it's not working with me.

So here's me lying in bed, drinking the tea, and I'm thinking, how did this happen to me? When did I go from being a young lad with all the lasses chasing me, to a husband with a wife he can't stand and a houseful of bairns he never asked for? Because she's trapped me, hasn't she? Florence butter-wouldn't-melt Sheraton. What with that Annie business and getting herself pregnant, well I had to marry her, didn't I? It was either that or bugger off somewhere like nancy Jimmy did.

Bugger off! That's a laugh, isn't it?

Looking back, though, that's exactly what I should of done, and never mind how it looked. Packed a bag and hopped on a trawler bound for Iceland or somewhere. Shetland. Norway. But you don't think, do you, when you're young? You can't see into the future. You can't see that if you keep doing what you're doing, you'll keep heading where you're heading, and you'll get there in the end – but it'll not be where you want to be.

So now I'm thinking: I'll make it up to them, her and the bairns. I'll stop boozing. Because that's the problem, isn't it? You come ashore and go straight down the boozer with the lads. Thing is, when you're back off a ten-day trip, and you've cranned out and collected your share, well you've got to let off a bit steam, haven't you?

Then you come home and you've a different kind of steam to let off, but the bairns are there, and she's got the tea ready and her careful welcome-home-pet face on, when all you want to do is pull her skirt up and bung her one. But you can't, can you? Not with the bairns there. So then you want to bung her something else, for trying to make it better when it was broke a long long time ago.

* * *

It's nowt to do with the money. The money's great. Even if I piss half it down the drain, I'm still raking it in. I told skipper Milburn, didn't I? The otter trawl's the gear to go for. But he'd never listen. It's got these canny tickler chains at the front, see, that tickle up the long stuff from the bottom while you're pulling the net along, so there's nowhere else for them to go but inside.

Amazing what gets scooped up with the cod, mind. Stuff I never knew was down there. Fry all shapes and sizes, penny stamps, shrimp, crab, weed. Most of it rubbish, but still.

By, but there's nowt like the sight of a bulging cod end coming to the surface when you're hauling a trawl catch, with the warps straining and the capstan screaming at full steam. And you're hauling and hauling, bracing your legs – then here it comes, this great mass of fish, and the boat's listing right over with the weight of it, and the gulls going crazy. Then there's that beautiful moment, when the cod end's clear of the waves and you've swivelled the crane to bring it over the boat, and it's just hanging there dripping water and small stuff, then you pull the warps and let it spill onto the deck like a great whoosh of silver spunk.

With the long lines, see, it's all winding, winding, winding; then every few feet or so there'll be a cod or haddock to unhook and chuck in the hold. Fair enough, it's only the biguns that take the bait down – the littluns just nibble it off, don't they? So you've a cleaner catch, and you can sort them as you're unhooking. But I can't be getting on with that faff any more.

With the herring it was the same malarkey with the old lints. So you'd shoot the nets and they'd hang there like a curtain while you drifted, and the littluns would swim straight through, and the biguns would get stuck and try to back out, but they can't because their gills are caught. So when you haul you've got a net stuck full of flapping fish that you've to shake out, yard by yard, one-two-three-shake, one-two-three-shake, for three, four, five hours, spell and spell about, which really takes it out of you.

Looking back I can hardly believe we did it like that. I mean, the seine nets make it so easy, with small holes so the fish don't have to be shaken off, and two drifters either side, so you wrap it round the shoals, and pull the lower warps tight, till you've made your purse. So it comes up like a cod end, doesn't it? All in one go: a purse of silver darlings, all sizes. And the deckies sort them – seven inch and over for the market, and the tiddlers shovelled on to the farm trucks for fertilizer. What could be simpler?

Anyway, like I say, we're raking it in.

I see skipper Milburn sometimes, down the quayside: still on the *Osprey*, still mooring up along by Clifford's Fort. He's stuck with the long-lining – though God knows who he's got picking flither for him these days, and setting the hooks and mucking, since Mrs Milburn's gone.

Da says he's never got over it – the two of them going, one after another, so quick.

... Good, very good, Tom. Now I want you to go back to when you were a younger man. It's the summer of 1898, the middle of the herring season. Where are you? What are you doing?

1898

I've got Da's matches. He's thinks he keeps losing them, leaving them in the pub and that. But I've nicked them, haven't I? So he can't have his bakkie till he's brought some more. I like to see him casting about for them, then cussing and stamping out the house down to old Ma Burdon's shop. Stupid bastard.

I tried smoking his pipe once. When he was passed out in bed one night. I tipped the spit out and wiped the end, then tamped in a bit of fresh bakkie and tried to light it, sucking on it like I'd seen him do, to make the flame go in. I must have been about ten, eleven – coughed so hard I nearly puked up! It's like anything though, isn't it? Hauling, coiling, splicing, gipping. You get the hang in the end.

That night, though, trying to get the pipe lit, I burnt my fingers on the match. You've to keep the match going, see, sucking and sucking on the flame till it catches. And it takes bloody ages because pipe bakkie's sticky as treacle.

God knows where Mam was. Out in the scullery most likely, sorting herself out; having a bit cry.

Anyway, the matches kept burning down, so I'd drop them just before the bakkie caught. It was driving me nuts, so this one time I held on to it instead of flinging it away; I was that mad to get the thing lit. And this time I did it! Fingers stung worse than with bloomin' jellies, but I got that pipe lit.

After that I kept on with it, didn't I? Striking a match, then keeping a hold till it burnt down. It got so's I could hardly feel it any more. I mean, I could still feel it, sharp as ever, but it never broke through to me any more. I could look at the flame burning lower, and the wood going black, and just squeeze tight and breathe slow till it went past.

The night Mam died I went out and bought three boxes. I wanted to kill my da that night. If he'd not been blubbing and clinging on to me, I would have done too. I mean, it's a bit late to myther on now about how he loves her, when she's popped her clogs. I wanted to kill her too, for leaving us with him. But that was Mam, wasn't it? Always leaving us with him. One slap too many and off she'd slope to Nana's till he sobered up. Never gave a thought to what would happen to us, did she? Load of quivering mice locked in with a spitting cat.

I kept thinking, one day I'll stand up to him. If I do enough matches, it'll make me hard. But by the time I was hard enough, she'd pegged it, hadn't she? It was her heart, the doc said. I felt like saying, what heart? That got kicked out of her a long time ago.

Thing is, soon as I faced up to him – you know, gave him a proper thump – he keeled over, didn't he? It was pathetic. One minute he's roaring, stotting, lashing out at me. Next thing you know, he's out in the scullery wiping the blood from his nose. And when he comes back in, he's never said a word. Just sat down to his tea as if nowt happened – and never tried it on with me again.

I look at him now, great lump of lard, and wonder how I was ever so scared of him. It's like anything, see? You've just got to show who's the boss.

Good, now stay in that time. You're still a young man. Do you know a girl called Annie?

Annie Milburn? I can't remember a time when I didn't know spuggie Annie. She was always tagging along with us, wasn't she? Me and the lads: Jimmy, Collie and Hylton. We were a gang, see? And she wanted to join in.

Then later, after Mam died and Da was put in jail after that barny down the Bullring – well they shared us out, didn't they? The lads off the boat. Took a bairn each till Da had done his time. And I went to the skipper's place, and berthed in with Jimmy and Frank.

Right up to that point I was fine: burning my matches, keeping it going – even at the funeral – and later, seeing Da getting lifted and carted off. But lodging at the skipper's place really did for me. The way Mrs Milburn was with those bairns – it made me want to blub like a wean. Watching them tugging at her, asking for a cuddle, and getting one – it made me feel it all, see? About Mam dying and that.

Anyway, spuggie Annie's there too, isn't she? And I remember thinking, that's what she'll be like when she's married, all hugs and dimples like her mam. And then I got to thinking, if we were wed, she'd be like that with me, and I'd be part of her family stead of mine. I mean, it was daft really. I was only eleven, twelve, something like that. So she'd have been nine, ten still, flat as a pancake up top. But I asked her to marry me, didn't I? I'll never forget the look on her face: lit up like a hurricane lamp, she was that chuffed. She thought the sun shone out of my arse in them days.

That's why it's such a shock to see her with another lad. See, at the back of my mind I always think she's still promised to me.

Anyway I'm with Flo now – that's Annie's friend – and we've been walking out a good few months. So I've been to her folks for tea and she's been to mine, all that malarkey, and it's trundling along tickety-boo. And I've been thinking: this'll do you, Tom. Because the lads are all after Flo, aren't they? They call her 'the princess' because she's that far ahead of the others, with her looks and her book learning.

By, but there's nowt like a decent lass for driving a lad crazy. It's like you're playing cards, and you're winning, undoing her buttons, pulling up her skirt, but the game stops before you've laid down your hand. Then next time, it's a new deal, and a new hand and you've to start playing all over again.

So anyway, here I am on Bell Street, rolling a tab and waiting for Flo. And I look up and here she is, strolling along with Annie. I mean, Flo's always with Annie, isn't she? Since they were weans they've been in each others' pockets. But today something's different, and it's like I'm seeing Annie as a grown lass all of a sudden, instead of just Jimmy's skinnamalink sister.

You know when you're tacking and come about? And there's that muddle of loose halliards, and the boom swinging and the sail slack; then the wind catches again, and the sail bellies out and you tighten the halliards and that's your boat tight, skimming along in a fresh direction? Well that's what Annie's like now. I mean, one minute she's all sixes and sevens, bony and flat-chested, hair all anyhow, giggling, blethering away – next time I look she's filled out, glossy as a mattieful, with her boobies bursting out of her blouse and that great mass of shining curls. And them wicked dimples and dark eyes! How come I never noticed her eyes before?

So Flo's linked in with me, like she always does, and Annie's moved away to give us a bit time together. And I'm thinking, fuck me, there's my little Annie all grown up.

See, I can't quite believe it. Here's Flo hanging on to my arm, soft and sweet as you like. And suddenly here's spuggie Annie in the picture. To tell the truth, it's knocked me sideways.

Two minutes later, she's off blethering away with that *Wellesley* lad – *Wellesley* gutter-scrote, more like. Lives with the dregs down the Scarp, mam's a bit of a push-over. Anyway, it seems he's everywhere I turn these days. Fetched up as a nightman last winter when I was off with my chest and now the skipper's taken him on permanent.

He's one of those polite lads. You know, quiet, careful what he says. So it's all ay sir and right you are skipper. Makes me want to swear for the sake of it, just to add a bit spice to the air. Da says to let him alone and what's wrong with wanting to make a good impression with the boss? But this new lad's following him round like a puppy, hanging on his every word. And the skip's lapping it up, isn't he? He's even got his chart book out, to show the lad what's in it, how to fill it in and that. And there's George Sheraton looking over his shoulder. Because he's the mate, isn't he? So what's in the skipper's book's his business too.

The skipper showed it me too, when I first started, and I tried to catch on. I couldn't read his writing, that was the trouble. The charts were fine, I could follow them no bother. But that load of scribbles! I don't see how anyone could read them.

Folk say a decent don skipper's book is worth its weight in gold. If it's filled in right, it shows exactly where the fish are, different times of the year, different weathers, different tides; how to find them using what landmarks and that, and what's on the bottom, rocks and wrecks, sand and shale. Da remembers when the skipper got it. They're handed down, see, from skipper to skipper, and sometimes money changes hands, but usually it's more like an inheritance. So when one skipper retires, he'll pass his book on to his son, if he's got one, or his mate. And it's a big thing, like a king handing over his crown.

There was a bit of a barny, because it was Da's uncle who was skipper at the time, so Da thought he should get the book. But you could never trust my da with something like that. He'd get hammered the next Saturday and sell it for thrippence ha'penny. Third man in a three-man race, that's my da for you. Big John Hall, third man. Pathetic.

Now I'm down the Low Lights with a load of trawler lads, having a jar or two before going back on the boat. The sand's sodden with beer slops and the air's blue with bakkie smoke, so you can hardly see to the bar.

They're on about how all the big new custom-built trawlers are being brought by businessmen instead of skippers, because the skippers can't afford them, and once they've taken their cut there's damn all left for the crew. So the only way to get a decent share is for the crew to club together on a new steam trawler. And they're asking am I interested, and I'm thinking, that's not a bad idea.

Then blow me, here's the *Wellesley* lad breezing in, and Jimmy's ordering him a half at the bar on the skipper's strap. He's come to try and get in with us, most likely – though he'll not get far unless he stumps up for a round. Jim says the lad's short of cash, but them's new crotchboots he's got on, so he can find it when he has to. Anyway, it turns out he knows some of the trawler lads from working as nightman, so they're all howaying and trying to stand him a top-up, and he's shaking his head but they'll not take no for an answer.

I've gone out the back alley for a piss, because it's starting to get to me, him being in with them too. And there's two lads out here, stuffing their dicks back in their kecks – but the trouble they're having buttoning up and the way they scuttle off, you can tell they've not been pissing. Bleeding nonces. As if there's not enough lasses to go round. Town's fairly crawling with slags up for the season. And not just slags: Irish, gypsies, tramps. Even Da's getting it free these days.

Ought to truss them up, like they did down the boatyard last year to that other pair of nonces they caught at it: hang them from the purlins like pendulums and swing them into each other till their bones crack. Or kick them till they piss blood, like we did with that little nancy by the Priory. He'll not be pumping anything for a while.

So anyway, I do the old one-two-three-shake and come back out, and Wellesley's sat down at our table, hasn't he? Cool as you please, with a fresh half in front of him and Jimmy blethering away. So first it's Annie, then Jimmy. Like I say, it's starting to get to me.

So I have to wedge in my chair, don't I? And Jimmy's giving it, 'Budge up, budge up for Tom', which makes me feel daft, like he's doing me a favour, when everything was just fine before Wellesley decided to barge in.

Anyway there's a fresh pint there waiting for me, so I drink it straight off and bang the tankard down by Wellesley's elbow, to make him jump. Then I get out my tin for a rollie, and do a few matches, with the lads watching, and it calms me down a bit. So now I'm lighting up, and sucking the smoke down. And that calms me too, what with the matches and the tab and that load of beer sloshing round in my belly.

The craik's about gippers and nurses, daft lads' talk about which one's the best bet. So I'm saying it's six and two threes in the dark, for they both smell of herring, which cracks all the lads up – except Wellesley, sipping away at his half like he's never even heard me.

'What's the matter, Wellesley?' I say. 'Never smelt a lassie's minge?' And he still doesn't look up. So I lean towards him and blow a cloud of tab smoke right in his face, so he can't ignore it; but he just wafts it away with his hand like I'm a fly or something.

So now I'm set on getting a rise out of him, aren't I? And I've remembered that talk about his mam, how she was going with one of the ransackers a few year back. 'So how come you're out on the piss? Your mam entertaining again, is she?'

And he gets up and says, cool as you like: 'Sorry lads, got to go. Thanks for the drink.' And walks out – just like that.

After he's gone, the lads go quiet, like he's taken all the craik with him and left us staring at a mucky table loaded with empty glasses and brimming ashtrays. And two lads drink up and leave straight away. And another lad starts laying into me for rubbing Wellesley's nose in it. 'He's got a lot on his plate, that lad,' he says. 'So he could do without your nonsense.'

So now they're all going on about him, aren't they? How he's having to look out for his mam all the time, blah blah blah. And how he caught her at it when he was maybes fourteen, fifteen, and downed a few bevvies to get up the courage; then went at this big bruiser with a knife, the lad who was doing her. Never got near enough to hurt him, mind, just waved it around a bit, then puked up on his shoes.

And I feel like puking up myself, don't I? Because the whole thing's made me look like a mean bastard when all I was doing was trying to get a bit respect.

Later Flo tells me Wellesley's been going up the trysting hill with Annie, and that's really gypped me off. Like he's in my pub with the lads, he's on my boat sucking up to my skipper, and now he's walking out with my lass.

Because I've started making a few moves on her, haven't I? When Flo's not around, I've seen her home a few times, had her in a bit clinch. Not that she's easy, mind, and I wouldn't expect it. How can she be, when I'm going with her best friend? So I've been biding my time, waiting till I've had enough of Flo. I mean, it seems daft to stop now, when I'm getting what I wanted.

She'll kick off when I say I'm with Annie, so I'd best keep out of gipping distance till she's calmed down. And her da will spit feathers. But it's not him I've to answer to on the boat, is it? It's the skipper. And if I'm with Annie and she loves me, well, he can't argue with that.

CHAPTER FIFTY-SIX

1898

It's that gansey that's finished me. See, I really thought Annie was knitting it for me. As a sign, see? To let me know she's waiting for me to finish with Flo.

Flo's already done me one, of course. She started it as soon as I visited with her da about us walking out together. I'll say one thing for Flo, she's a dab hand with her needles. Takes after her mam, I expect. No wonder there's so much lace and that round at theirs.

So anyway, there's me teasing Annie about this damn gansey one day, next thing I know here's Wellesley on the boat wearing it! And the skipper grinning away like he's known all along. And it's like they're laughing at me, him and Wellesley, though how could they know what's been going on in my head? Still—

And I can see it all slipping away: Annie, the boat, sitting round the Milburns' table for Sunday dinner. There's nowt I can do about it, see? Because he's already *there*, isn't he? Somehow when I've not been looking, he's gone and wormed his way into my berth.

So anyway, we've set out to the herring grounds, and all trip it's eating away at me: how Wellesley's grabbed what should be mine by rights, so when it's time to turn in for the drift I'm so antsy I can't sleep. And everything's getting to me – the bugs biting, Da and Mickey snoring, the creaking of the timbers – till I feel like I've been buried alive in a bloody coffin and need to punch my way out before I go crazy.

I keep wondering has he done her yet; I can't get it out of my head. See, there's a bit of me thinking, if he's not gone the whole way, then it's not too late. I can go round her place soon as we get back and tell her I've finished with Flo, and we can be together.

But this picture keeps coming into my head, of him laying with her in one of them hollows on the trysting hill, or pressing up against her down some alley. All the while I've been supping tea in the Sheratons' bloomin' parlour, he's been kissing my Annie's mouth, putting his tongue in, undoing her buttons.

I'm hard as fucking wood just thinking of it! Bastard! Now he's even got me whacking off to his gropings!

I'm that churned up, I don't know whether to spit or spurt. So I clamber out of the berth and head up on deck.

By, but it's blowy up here, with a spray off the bow as the boat leans into the swell. Wellesley's up reefing the mizzen so she won't tip over so much, then unhooking the lamp to check the buffs. And for a minute he's just any deckie going about his work – till he turns to put the lamp back, and his oily flaps open and I see that new gansey again. And it all comes flooding back, the shock of seeing him wearing it, and the skipper grinning away.

'Howay, Wellesley,' I say, coming over. 'Canny gansey.'

And he says, 'Just in time, eh? That other one was on its last legs.'

So I say, 'What did you give her in return, then?' Because I've got to know, haven't I? It's driving me nuts.

'What?' He turns to me, with a halliard trailing from his hand, like he can hardly believe what I'm saying.

'You know what I mean.'

'That's none of your business.'

'That's where you're wrong. It is my business what you've been up to with my lass.'

He laughs a bit at that, and goes back to tying the halliard. 'If she's your lass, why don't you ask her yourself?'

It really riles me, that he's not taking me seriously. 'So have you done her yet?' I ask, flat out like that, and he straightens up to face me.

'Look, can't we stop this?' he says, in the sort of tired voice you'd use with a whingeing bairn. 'You've had it in for me the second I stepped on to this boat and I'm sick of it. If you're after Annie, I'm sorry. But she's with me now and that's that.'

And he sounds so sure and four-square, it's got me rattled. 'It's not serious, though, is it? I mean, how long's it been? Three, four weeks?'

'We're promised to each other. That's serious enough for me.'

And he's turning away again, like that's it done and dusted. Which makes me want to smash his bloody face in.

'So have you had her yet?' I say, giving him a bit shove to show I mean business. 'Have you picked her cherry?'

'I'm not talking about this any more.'

'How does she like it? A bit rough and ready, I expect. She was always a bit of a one for wrestling with the lads.'

He's trimming the port lamp now, not looking at me.

'Hey, Wellesley. I'm talking to you.'

'Well I've finished talking to you,' he says, and never even looks up.

'I said, how does she like it?'

And he's just ignoring me, isn't he? Hanging the lamp back up, then going past me over to the other side for the starboard lamp.

So I grab him by the shoulder, and when he tries to shake me off, I slap him – a good hard one, round the head. And that's felled him, hasn't it? And I'm thinking, now he's got to answer me. But he just picks himself up and carries on, like he's just tripped over something.

So I shove him harder, to make him stumble a bit, but he just grabs onto the boom and goes on with what he's doing. So I shove him again from behind, thinking, that'll teach you to turn your back on me, Wellesley. He's so surprised, he never even shouts till he hits the water.

Afterwards, it's like when Mam died. This thing's occurred that I can't think about, so I light my matches and make my mind go blank and just get on with it. So by the time we've moored up and someone's called the poliss, it's like it never happened almost.

I've told them the deck was empty when I went up to take a piss, and they've just swallowed it, haven't they? The skipper, the crew, the poliss. So there's part of me thinks it's true too. Except Jimmy's come up to me after, and says he reckons he's heard voices on deck. But that's all right, because it's Jimmy, isn't it? He'll never dare to dob me in. He knows fine what will happen to him if he does. Ever since I saw him coming out of that alley down by the Push and Pull – I mean, it was bloody obvious what he'd been up to with that big nonce. If he wasn't the skipper's lad, I'd have done him over weeks ago.

* * *

So now it's Wednesday, I think. I've been biding my time with Annie, thinking I'll wait a bit till she's got over it. Because she was in a right state on the quayside when the skipper told her about Wellesley going overboard.

Tell the truth, it surprised me to see her like that. I mean, they'd only been walking out a few weeks. So anyway, that's why I'm thinking I should take it easy.

Meanwhile Flo's driving me nuts being all lovey-dovey and making me go out walking with her, and look in shop windows at things she can't afford. That was fine when we were courting and that, pussyfooting about. But now I can't be bothered with it – can't be bothered with *her* really, except when she's on her back on the parlour rug with her skirt up.

Anyway, I've given it a few days, and I've heard Annie's got off work early because she's had to go and identify the body. So I'm thinking, she'll be needing a bit comfort after that, and I can tell her where things stand with me and Flo and maybes that'll make her feel better.

She's at the kitchen table when I get there, in a patch of milky sunlight. Her scarf's off and her hair's coming out of it's ribbon, and she's just sat there, like someone's propped her up in the chair and she's never moved since. And that's shaken me too, because it's not like my Annie to sit still. And when I lift her up, to give her a bit cuddle and a feel, she's like a dead weight in my arms, like she's fainted or something – except when I check, her eyes are open and there's tears pouring down her cheeks.

It's the shock of seeing the drowned body, I expect. God knows what sort of state it would have been in by then. It would be enough to upset anyone. Give her time and she'll be right as rain.

This waiting's really getting to me. I thought things would be different, see? With Wellesley out of the way. I thought I'd get back in with the skipper, and walk out with Annie, and be right back on course – except it would be a better course because I'd know where I was heading.

But the skipper's been a right bastard since Wellesley's gone, picking holes in everything. This sail's reefed wrong. Why's that halliard tied like that? Da says it must be preying on him, to lose a lad – but still. There's no need to take it out on the rest of us. It's like we can't put a foot right. And when someone expects you to mess up, well that's what you do, isn't it?

And it's all landing on me, because that nightman he's taken on is worse than useless. So I've to do half his work as well as mine. So the skip will give me an order, like slacken off the jib, and I'll do it – and he'll just sigh, like I've not done it properly, not tucked the fucking end in or something, God knows. Which would have been fine before Wellesley came along with his Navy training and that.

By the end of the week, I've had a bellyful so I grab my sea-bag and head off home soon as the skipper's gone ashore. Then later, when I'm sat all nice and cosy drinking cocoa round the Milburns' place with Flo and Mrs M., I realize I've brought the boat's padlock with me, so the lads can't lock up. Which gets me riled all over again, so I rush off to do it before the skipper cottons on. And all the way there, I've got the key in my hand and I'm squeezing it so it really digs in, and I keep squeezing, digging it in, thinking stupid, stupid, stupid.

By, but this fog's so thick you could slice it with a knife and the cobbles are that slimy underfoot, I nearly go over a few times. The boats are all in, moored that tight you can't see the water, just a long row of prows poking out of the mist, and mooring ropes criss-crossed like cats' cradles.

Now I've got to the end of the quay where we're tied up, and what's this? Brand new kist sitting by the mooring post – big green metal one – and no one around. So straight away I'm thinking, some scrote's ransacking the boat and brought a kist along to stow the stuff in. So I look on the boat, and sure enough, there's someone crouched over by the hatch.

I swing on board quietly, gearing up for a scrap – but it's Annie! She's come to find me, hasn't she? She'll have been wandering around in the fog with that kist, and it's got too heavy, so she's come looking for me to walk her home.

I can't see her face clearly in the gloaming, but I can hear from her voice that she's crying – and no wonder, for it's a filthy night for a lass to be out on her own. Anyway, she says she was wanting to see inside the fo'c'sle, so I open the hatch and get the lamp lit, and help her down.

Oh, but it's so *good* to be close to her, so close I can smell her hair and hear her breathing—

I've got my hands round her waist to lift her down the ladder and my fingers meet almost, she's that slender. Like a flower, I'm thinking, and at that moment I just want her so much there's an ache comes to my throat, so I pull her closer, to smell her some more, her neck, her ear—

Now she's pushing me away, the daftie, but there's nowhere to push me. Still, she's shoving at me anyway – and she's that strong! I'd forgotten that about her. If you got in a scrap with Annie as a bairn, you'd soon know about it! So

I'm thinking, right, if that's how she wants to play it, that's fine by me – and it makes a change from Flo, I can tell you.

So we're scrapping, and she's panting, trying to wriggle away, and I'm hard as a bloody truncheon, and we're kissing – and suddenly she's bitten me on the tongue! And Jesus it hurts, and my mouth's full of blood, so I'm spitting it out. And now she's gone for my gipping knife and's slashing at me – and gets me too, on the arm, before I catch on to what she's about.

So anyway, I get the knife off her no bother and cut her blouse open. And I'm even hotter for her now, aren't I? Seeing her standing there with her boobies showing and her eyes flashing, her cami splattered with blood where the knife's nicked her – and looking so bloomin' gorgeous I have to laugh right out loud. And I know I've got to have her.

So now I've pinned her arms and I'm on her, and I've got the knife at her throat, just to spice it up, like. And after a bit she stops fighting and goes quiet. And Jesus, it's the sweetest feeling in the world, to know I've got her at last, soft and quiet in my arms.

Then I'm pushing in with my cock, feeling it stopping, then forcing it through. And I'm thinking: that's it! That's her cherry gone! And then I'm laughing again and thinking: fuck you, Wellesley, I've had her first and now she's mine, mine, mine.

Let's stop there for a moment, Tom. Good, you're doing fine. Now I want you to keep your eyes closed and relax, and wait there until you hear me call your name and ask you to continue.

'What on earth's the matter?' Mary whispers, glaring at Ian, who's been gesticulating wildly at her, completely ruining her concentration.

'Find out what he did with the body!' he hisses.

'What? Look, if you must interrupt, let's at least have this discussion in the hall.'

As soon as she closes the door, Ian's rounds on her. 'It's the perfect opportunity to prove your case!'

'What on earth are you talking about?' She's been so caught up with Tom's drama, she's finding it difficult to focus on what he's saying.

'If you get him to tell you where the body is, and we can find it – that's the most powerful proof of reincarnation that I can think of.'

'Assuming he's the only person who knows where he dumped it.'

'Why would he tell anyone? He's raped and murdered the poor girl. He's not going to go broadcasting that around now, is he?'

'But it's been in the sea for over a hundred years. There'll be nothing left to find.'

'You've forgotten, haven't you? Remember the kist? The body was in a bloody steel box!'

Mary stares at him as the logic sinks in. If Tom tells her where Annie's body is, and it turns up exactly where he said it would – well, publishers would be falling over each other for her book.

Hello, Tom? Are you still there? Good. Now listen very carefully. I want you to go back to that night in August 1898. You're down in the fo'c'sle of the Osprey *and Annie's dead. What are you doing?*

I'm getting the kist down the ladder, thinking I'll put her in that, and it will be like a sort of coffin. But when I try to put her in, she looks indecent somehow, folded up in her bloody clothes, with her knees to her chin – and I can't bear to leave her like that. So I take her out again, and strip her down to her shift, trying not to look at the gashes, and wash the blood off her – and she's so *white* underneath all them layers.

Then I get out that new topsail from the locker, and unfold it, and curl her up on it like a wean sleeping, and wrap it round her and tie it with a length of rope. And it's still not right, but it's better, and at least I can't see her face. So I put her into the kist again and close the lid.

Think carefully now, Tom. What did you do with the kist?

There's a load of cobles pulled up on the pebbles over by Clifford's Fort, just up from the Lifeboat House. The old lads use them for crabbing and that. So I haul the kist over, and hoy it into one, and open the lid and pack her round with pebbles, then wade into the water and push off. I don't want it shifting, see? Once it's dumped, it needs to be heavy enough to stay put. Because if someone opens it and sees she's cut, and finds out I'm cut too – well, they could put two and two together.

So I'm rowing out to the Tyne's mouth in the mist, and I've not got a bell or a lamp, so I'm rowing blind almost, with just a grey blur where the moon should be and the fog pressing in, and the smell of the sea to guide me, and the sound of the 'longshoremen clanging their bells.

All the time I'm rowing, I'm trying not to think. I'm just leaning forward to hoy the oars into the water, and back to pull them through it, forward and back, forward and back, feeling my arm stinging where she's cut me, and my kecks clinging from wading in to push off. But I don't mind the wet and the cold, and the nip of the gashes, because they're something to fix on, aren't they? Like burning my matches, to stop me getting lost in what's happened.

And by and by I decide on a place to take her, a place all fishermen steer clear of, because it'll foul every net and line within spitting distance.

Does it have a name, this place?

They call it White Lady Reef, God knows why. The Devil's Reef, the skipper calls it. A ridge of rocky ledges and gulleys stretching right out into the bay round by where they're building that new lighthouse in Whitley. The skipper says there's gulleys there that are more than a furlong deep and more.

So anyway, that's where I'm taking her, rowing close in to be sure I've got the right place. It's a clever job to hoy it over the side, mind, with all them stones weighing it down. So I upend it and sort of grapple it overboard, and end up going over with it, and capsizing the coble, and thrashing round for ages righting it and finding the oars then climbing back in.

Are you absolutely sure of the place? White Lady Reef?

Sure as I can be. The fog had lifted a bit by the time I got there, and it was getting light. And the skipper's had the landmarks drummed well into me, so all I'd to do was get a fix on St George's church, and that new lighthouse and row a course between them.

CHAPTER FIFTY-SEVEN

2007

'Three, two, one,' goes the doc, and Laura collapses back against the cushions, because she's been all tense, leaning forwards, like she was actually in that boat, soaking wet, rowing off into the night.

Ben feels like collapsing back too, except he's on the pouffe, so there's nothing to collapse back on to. He feels sick, and a bit faint, like it was him being hypnotized instead of Laura. Because he could see it all, like he was really there – and he was, in a way, some of the time, except he can't remember it. But he can almost see Tom's face, all the hurt and hate and sex on it, sort of showing through Laura's make-up and wrinkles. And it's really freaking him out, because this is *Laura.*

So anyway, there she is on the sofa, opening her eyes and blinking; and she's trying to smile, but it's coming out a bit crooked because she's sort of crying too, and holding out her hand towards him. And part of him wants to take it, and let her pull him into a cuddle, but another part is thinking, 'That was *rape*! And you didn't even fucking *realize*'. Because that's what gets him, that Tom was so caught up in his own twisted little macho world, he really thought Annie would want to go with him.

And now here's Laura with her mascara running and her arm reaching out, with its charm bracelet quivering – and even though he knows it's her really, and not Tom, he just can't bring himself to touch her. And his arms are crossing and folding by themselves, and sort of pressing tight into his chest – he can't help it – and he's staring down at the carpet, at what looks like a tab burn on the patterned rug and the grey cord carpet showing through.

He's shivering, he realizes, but the doc's wrapping her Indian rug round Laura instead of him, and is sitting next to her on the sofa, trying to comfort her. Which is understandable, but it wasn't Laura who was murdered, was it? It wasn't her who was raped and knifed and probably bled to death on that boat.

And all the time that Ian bloke's jabbering away on his Blackberry, walking up and down with an unlit tab in his hand, like he wants to smoke but can't even spare the time to light up.

After a bit, Ben realizes Ian's talking to Dad – he must have called him on the satellite phone – asking how soon he can get back, because he wants to use the boat to go looking for Annie's body and film the whole thing. Then Dad must be asking what's happened, because the Ian bloke's telling him that it's turned out that Laura was Tom, and he killed Annie and put the body in that kist Jimmy was talking about, and they've just found out where he's dumped it.

Then Dad must be asking about diving gear, because the Ian bloke's saying he's going to try and get this ace wildlife photographer to do the filming, with underwater cameras and that. And they go into a great long macho discussion about sound recording and metal detectors and that – which sort of freaks Ben out, because it's *Annie's body* they're talking about searching for. In fact the whole situation is totally doing his head in: Laura snivelling on the sofa with the doc, and Tom slashing at Annie with that gipping knife and bundling her into that kist thing, and her body mouldering away inside it for over a hundred years.

'Are you OK about that?' asks the doc, and Ben realizes she's talking to him.

'What?'

'Are you OK about them going to look for the body? I mean, it's all rather sudden, isn't it? It would be understandable if you felt you needed a bit of time to get used to the idea.'

Ben stares at her and his eyes fill with tears. Because that is exactly what he needs. Because he hasn't had a chance to talk to her about it properly yet, like on his own; but there's Dad and Ian going on about magnetometers and what you can pick up on a sonar scanner. And it's too late to stop them now, because he can hear Ian talking to this whizzy wildlife bloke and getting the film crew all organized, so there doesn't seem much point in making a fuss.

'No—' he begins, 'I mean, yes, I'm all right.'

And because he just can't stand it any more – looking at Laura, and trying not to cry, and wanting a cuddle off the doc, and hearing that Ian bloke really in his element bossing people about – he gets up and charges out of the house.

* * *

As soon as he's outside he stops running, and just walks very fast along the top bank with his head bent, butting into the wind, and his hands stuffed in his pockets. And after a bit the tears sort of sink back into his chest and he slows down; and when he looks up, there's Skip up ahead, painting away at his easel, so he slows down even more and wanders over to take a look.

There's not much to see yet, just a sort of wet brownish sketch of a woman leaning in the doorway of a pub in an alley at the top of some steps.

'Howay, Paul's lad,' says old Skip, like he always does – it's a sort of joke with them now, to pretend he's forgotten Ben's name. 'How's that TV thing going? You had any more of them talking sessions with the doctor?'

Ben shakes his head. 'They've been filming Laura,' he says. 'It turns out she was that Tom in her past life. So the doc hypnotized her and she told them where Annie's body is. Dad's taking them out on *Wanderer* to look for it.'

'Where is it then? I knew he'd got rid of it like, but he never said where.'

Ben repeats what Tom said, as though it's tattooed on his brain: 'You've to get a fix on the big church – St George's, I think – and St Mary's Lighthouse and row a course in between. White Lady Reef, the place is called.'

'White Lady, eh? They'll never get a great bugger like *Wanderer* in there. She'll foul up in two seconds.'

'They're going to use the sonar. Dad seemed to think it would be all right.'

'Then he's dafter than I thought. Them rocks are evil round there and the currents are all over the shop, specially this close to full moon. With a dinghy, you'd stand a chance, if you tilted up the outboard and took the oars with you. Even then, I wouldn't like to try it.'

'I'd better tell them,' says Ben. 'They should probably anchor further out.'

Old Skip shrugs and turns back to his painting. 'That Ian won't be happy with that,' he says. 'So let's hope Paul's still got the sense he was born with.'

Then, remembering something else: 'When you see the doctor next, can you tell her I was wanting a word – only I don't like to disturb her now, not if she's still with that Ian.'

Ben always gets a shock these days when he opens the door to his room. He keeps expecting the Newcastle black-and-white on the wall, and his bed in its usual place, but instead there's all this brilliant cream paint everywhere, and the new stripy rug that almost completely covers his old blue carpet, and the new cork boards just waiting for him to start pinning things up.

He lies down on his back on the rug and stretches his arms and legs out sideways like a starfish. It's very quiet. The room smells of fresh paint and warm wool and sunshine; and it's as though his whole life's been stripped away, like the old wallpaper, and he doesn't know how it's going to turn out. His mobile beeps in his pocket but he ignores it; it'll just be Laura again with another message and he's not ready to deal with her yet.

The doorbell goes and he gets up, thinking it'll be Nana forgotten her key. He's just about to buzz her up when he hears the lift opening and men's voices.

'Look who I found outside,' says Dad, shoving open the front door.

'Thought you'd got rid of me, eh?' says the Ian bloke, shrugging off his natty black nylon backpack.

Dad's still in his big boots and gansey; sea-bag on his shoulder, load of creaky yellow oilskins under his arm. Next to the Ian bloke he looks really massive and rough: stubble, sunburnt face, oil-stained hands.

'Do you fancy a beer?' Dad asks, dumping the gear in the hall. 'Coffee? Tea? Ben – you sort Ian out while I get washed.'

'Just water, thanks. I've OD-ed on caffeine today.' Ian plonks himself down on the sofa and fishes out his Blackberry.

'Viv? Listen, can you track down that harbourmaster again? Tell him we can't wait till next week. We've got to do the interview tomorrow – I know, I know. Try to sweet-talk him – No, not yet. But she'll be fine. I'll call her later – About ten? Nine? Whatever. We've got to get it done before we set off on the boat – What? – Oh I don't know. Camp outside his door. Use your initiative. Call me later, right? Bye.'

He winks at Ben. 'I don't know. Can't get the staff these days.'

'Was that the film crew?'

'Viv, my PA. Fantastic girl really. I should probably be nicer to her.'

'Are you going to interview Laura?'

'Later maybe, when she's recovered a bit. No – I'm trying to set up an interview with Mary, down on the quayside. I want to get her reaction to all these revelations before we set off on your dad's boat to look for the body.'

'Why?' Ben wants to know.

'Well, this is a crucial test of Mary's reincarnation theory. Assuming Tom really did murder Annie that night – and this whole thing isn't some strange product of Mary's imagination – and assuming he never told anyone where he dumped the body, then he's the only person who could possibly know where it is.'

'So if you find it where Laura said, then that proves Laura used to be Tom?'

'That's right. And if we don't, Mary will have to explain why. That's why I want her spelling out the logic, on the record, before we set off – so we can get her reaction on film when we've finished the search.'

Ben's not sure he likes the sound of that; it sounds like Ian's trying to set a trap. But before he can say anything, here's Dad back from the shower after about six nanoseconds, in clean jeans and bare feet, freshly shaven and ponging of CK One.

'What if we actually find something?' says Dad. 'Wouldn't that be a turn up for the books?' As though he thinks the expedition is a waste of time from the start. 'Though that Laura stuff you told me about fits in exactly with what Jimmy said about hearing someone lugging something down to that coble.'

'And Laura wasn't there when you were hypnotized that time, was she?' says Ben. 'So that's a sort of proof, isn't it?'

'Not if it all originates with Mary,' says Ian. 'In that case, the more neatly it all fits together, the more suspicious it starts to look – though I'm keeping an open mind, of course, as befits a BBC producer.' And he winks at Dad, like they're sharing some secret joke, which makes Ben really sit up, because it means there's something they don't want him to know about. So he sort of wanders off into the kitchen and opens the fridge as though he's getting himself a drink, but it's really to make them forget he's there.

'Did you have any luck with the doc's old clients?' Dad's asking, like it's something they've talked about before – which makes Ben even more suspicious.

'Nah, but it's early days yet. It takes ages to wade through all that confidentiality bollocks. I'll put another researcher on to it when I get back. I can layer all that stuff in later, at the edit stage.'

'So this is all cosmetic, right? This trip, the diver, all the gear?'

'You might say that – I couldn't possibly comment.'

'You're not seriously expecting to find anything, are you?'

'I'd say the odds are around a squillion to one, but I feel I owe it to Mary to give it a go – and the viewing public deserves a bit of a spectacle. Plus it gives us a chance to film you on the boat.'

'It could be tricky getting up close, you know,' Dad says doubtfully. 'That reef's notorious.'

'But you've got sonar, right? State-of-the-art, you said. And I'll have the magnetometer beeping away, sweeping the sea bed for lumps of metal. It looks like a torpedo, apparently. Measures distortions in the earth's magnetic field. Should be brilliant telly.'

'There's probably some old anchors down there.'

'So we'll have a few false alarms – so what? It all adds to the excitement.'

'And I've got the Aquapulse if we want to home in on something,' says Dad, starting to get into it.

'Jeff says he's got his own gear, so don't worry about that.'

Ben wanders back with a glass of orange juice and sits down. 'Skip says you should go in with a dinghy,' he says, though he doesn't know why he's bothering.

'Can't fit a film crew in a dinghy, mate,' says Ian, as if Ben's an imbecile or something.

'Don't worry, buddy,' says Dad. '*Wanderer* can turn on a sixpence. I'll drop anchor and keep the chain short. We'll be fine.'

After Ian's gone, Dad sort of bustles round for a bit, tidying up, then he comes to sit down next to Ben on the sofa.

'What's up?' he says.

'What?'

'Your face is tripping you and you've not said a word for half an hour.'

'I don't trust that Ian bloke,' says Ben. 'I don't think he wants to find Annie's body.'

'What if it's not there?'

'I don't think he's even going to try properly.'

'But if the doc's having everyone on, don't you think we need to know?'

Ben rounds on him angrily. 'See? You're in on it too. This is all a plot to make her look stupid.'

Paul puts a big hand on Ben's knee. 'Listen, buddy. Isn't it time you faced up to the possibility that there's no kist and no body down there?'

'There is! You weren't there. You never heard Laura. That was Tom talking, I know it was.' He can still picture the coble; Tom grappling with the heavy kist.

'So we'll go out with some decent equipment and have a proper look. Can't say fairer than that. And if we find the body, all well and good. And if we don't, well hopefully that will put an end to this Annie business once and for all.'

The phone goes and Dad picks it up. 'Paul Dixon here – Oh, hi, Ian. What's up? – Oh, right. I mean, I'm sure they know what they're doing, but still – What about *Wanderer*, then? Do you still...? – OK. Right you are. Bye.'

'What's going on?' Ben asks, because Dad's face has sort of closed up, like he's cross about something but doesn't want to show it.

'Ian's chartering a boat to do a recce before they start filming. This wildlife diver's a bit nervous, apparently – he's been talking to some of the lads over at Deep Blue. He thinks they might need something a bit smaller, a bit more film-friendly, so they're off down the Royal Quays tomorrow to check out some other options.'

'So they might not use *Wanderer* at all?' Ben asks.

Dad shrugs. 'Says he won't know till they've looked at what else is available.'

Now Ben's getting worried. 'But you're still going, right?'

'At the moment it's just Ian and the diver bloke, I think. Plus the skipper of the other boat, of course.'

'*Dad!* You've got to go! What if they find something, then pretend that they haven't?' That's exactly the sort of thing that Ian bloke would do, Ben thinks, just to make things difficult for the doc.

Dad laughs and sort of half clips him round the ear. 'Now you're talking daft. Why on earth would they do that?'

Then Ben gets an idea. 'Why don't *we* go, Dad? Just you and me. We could borrow old Skip's dinghy and row right up to the reef like Tom did. Then go down with the Aquapulse and sort of mosey about. It would be really cool.'

'What, without that magnetometer? We wouldn't know where to start. It would be like looking for a needle in a haystack.'

'*Please*, Dad,' Ben says.

'Look, tell you what I'll do,' says Dad, and he gets up to put an end to the discussion. 'I'll go down the Royal Quays tomorrow and ask to go along with them, OK? Will that satisfy you?'

Ben nods, but he's not convinced. He saw that wink that passed between them. He reckons Dad would say anything to get Annie out of his life.

CHAPTER FIFTY-EIGHT

2007

Laura's fiddling with her new mobile phone, peering at a screen the size of a postage stamp and pressing tiny pink buttons. The phone itself appears to be mother-of-pearl, with a lid that pops open like a powder compact. Watching her friend bent over it, red nails frantically clacking, Mary doesn't know whether to be impressed or appalled. She feels sometimes as if she's the only person in the country who doesn't feel the need to carry some intrusive warbling gizmo about their person at all times.

'Come on,' she says bracingly. 'Let's go for a walk.'

'Ben's not answering my texts.' Laura raises a stricken face.

'Give him time. He's had a shock.'

'But we should be with him. Talking him through it.' She jabs at another button and presses the thing to her ear again, then stares at it in frustration when there's no answer.

'Have you left a message?' Mary asks. 'Then there's nothing else you can do. When he's ready, he'll get in touch. Meanwhile I think we need a change of scene.'

'But I've texted him we're at your house,' she objects.

'So text him again! For heaven's sake, Laura.'

'Where are we going, then?'

'Out! Anywhere! I don't know. Yes I do. Take me to that shop in Tynemouth you're always nagging me about, where they sell the sort of garments you think I ought to be wearing.'

'Raspberry Bazaar? Are you serious?'

'If I'm going to be a media superstar, I can't keep wheeling out the same old outfits all the time, can I?'

Laura taps one final message into her powder compact then snaps it shut and drops it into her handbag. 'Right, got your chequebook? I'm holding you to this, Dr Charlton. And I don't want a repeat of that Ikea fiasco.'

Mary smiles ruefully as her friend reapplies her lipstick and fluffs up her hair in the hall mirror. 'Retail therapy' – isn't that what they call it? Sometimes it seems a good deal more effective than the talking variety she normally dispenses.

The shop, when they get there, is not nearly as dreadful as Mary had been fearing – Tynemouth is littered with expensive emporia, full of cashmere and linen, and coiffured shop assistants who look like they'd faint at the sight of a pair of Doc Martens. This shop's more like the cluttered boutiques she remembers from the seventies: poorly lit, crammed with beads and scarves, joss-sticks and dream-catchers, and racks of roomy, oddly shaped separates in the rich muddy colours she favours – all products of Asian child labour, no doubt.

'See? Trust Auntie Laura,' says Laura smugly, watching Mary leaf gingerly through a rack of floor-length silk culottes. 'Just your kind of schmutter. I bet they've even got those bedspreads with little mirrors on.'

'What do I do? Is there a changing booth or something?' Mary's idea of shopping is scooping up three identical size 10 woollen cardigans in various dark shades and taking them to the checkout at Marks and Spencer.

'Through that door. You go in and strip off and I'll bring you some cats and camisas to try on.'

Mary starts to object, then stops herself. Would it hurt to give Laura free rein? This outing is about distraction, after all, not about seriously equipping herself with a suitable new wardrobe. But after two hours in her undies, trapped in a back room festooned with paper flowers and swathes of fabric Laura refers to as 'throws', she discovers she has purchased an alarmingly large heap of assorted garments wrapped in cerise tissue paper. Surrendering her credit card, she can't even remember what half of them are. Laura won't let her look at the total. 'It costs what it costs,' she says firmly. 'That's a decade's worth of *bona* clobber you've got there.'

Later, sitting outside in the sunshine, over cappuccinos at a nearby café, surrounded by her purchases, Mary lights up a well-earned Gitanes. 'Not quite how I'd planned to spend my afternoon,' she remarks, still somewhat bemused. 'Still, I hope you're satisfied.'

'I would be if one of these dowry messages was from Ben.' Laura's bending over the mother-of-pearl compact again, jabbing at buttons.

Mary waits until she's finished. 'That single session doesn't mean it's all over with Tom, you know,' she warns. 'There's obviously quite a bit more work we need to do before we can put him back to sleep in your unconscious.'

'Not today though, duckie, if it's all the same to you,' Laura says, clicking sweeteners onto a raft of froth and cocoa dust. 'I've had my fill of rape and knives for the time being.'

'We obviously terminated your therapy too early – and that was my fault. I'm so sorry – I could kick myself.' Mary gives her head a little shake of annoyance.

'Don't be daft.'

'No, I should have insisted we carry on with the sessions after my illness. But I was so pleased to have you as a friend, I let you convince me there was no need to continue.' She smiles sheepishly.

'So we're both to blame,' concludes Laura. Then, after a bit: 'I never cottoned on before that the lad was abused – Tom, I mean.'

'It sounded as though he was dyslexic, too. Did you notice? So that was another humiliation to bear.'

'Poor little sod.'

Mary regards her thoughtfully. 'Are you ready to forgive him yet, do you think?'

'I don't know. I mean, there's always a choice, isn't there? There's plenty of abused kids that don't end up raping and murdering, battering their wives. No one's ever totally out of control – there's always that moment when you're on the brink and you can tip either way.'

'Whatever he did, though, you've been making up for it practically every day of your life. Nursing Lord Jim, setting up Salon Laura, helping Ben and God knows how many others. Tom's given you a quest.'

Laura snorts. 'I don't think Ben would see it like that.'

'Yet you've changed his life. Don't lose sight of that. Remember how lost he seemed when we first met him?'

'Soon as I spotted him at the caff, I knew. There was something about him.' She smiles fondly, spooning foam.

'Strange, isn't it, that instant connection? At the risk of labouring a point, I can't help thinking there must be some unconscious recognition that takes place at moments like that. What some might call a meeting of souls.'

'Did I ever tell you that I clocked you too, years before I came to you as a patient? There was this mad zelda in some ethnic knitted hat with ear flaps wandering round the Co-op first thing every Monday morning, muttering away in a world of her own.'

Mary grimaces in dismay; she hadn't realized how odd she must seem sometimes. 'Where were you?' she asks.

'In that Post Office bit in the corner, depositing the takings from the caff.'

'How embarrassing.'

'When you opened your door as Dr Charlton, you could have knocked me down with a feather.'

Later, weighed down by rustling carrier bags, they walk home the long way round, beside the sunny river, tracing the route Annie and Sam took on their first date over a hundred years earlier.

Mary keeps stopping to rub her hands and flex her fingers to keep the circulation going. 'Did you check your mobile again?' she asks as they reach the bottom of High Beacon Stairs and pause to contemplate the long climb to her house on the top bank.

'*Zilcho, nada, nanti*,' says Laura, snapping the lid closed.

'Did I mention I've advertised for a lodger?' Mary remarks a few minutes later, somewhat out of breath, around a third of the way up. 'I thought it was probably time I stopped living on my own. If I'm less of a hermit, perhaps I won't be so prone to kissing unsuitable ex-boyfriends. What do you think?'

'*Bona idée*,' Laura comments, puffing along beside her. 'Though I hope you're not expecting me to apply. There's many a good deed I'm prepared to do for a friend, but that avocado suite's more than a girl of my taste and discernment can abide.'

Mary laughs. 'I was thinking more of a student, someone poor and needy who'll head off somewhere cheap and dangerous for long holidays on a regular basis and leave me in peace to contemplate the vagaries of the unconscious mind.'

They reach the top of the steps and collapse on a bench to get their breath back. A massive container ship of some kind – carrying double-decker buses, perhaps, or combine harvesters – is trundling up the river in front of them.

'Talking of unsuitable ex-boyfriends,' says Laura, 'did we interrupt a bit of clinch this morning by any chance?'

Mary feels herself blushing and Laura's eyes widen. 'We did, didn't we? Mary Magdalena! How long's this been going on?'

'Nothing's going on.'

'But you'd like it to, right?'

Mary reaches in her pocket for her Gitanes. 'If you'd asked me a month ago, I'd have said that no force on this earth would persuade me to get involved with a ruthlessly ambitious twice-married film director with six children.'

'But now?'

'Now it's just as bad an idea as it ever was. Suffice it to say, you and Ben saved me from committing what would undoubtedly have turned out to be a disastrous error of judgement.'

Mary lights up and blows smoke, staring at the vast flank of the container ship as it churns past. 'When Ian found out he was Dory in a past life, he became obsessed with the idea that I was Henry and that we'd been soulmates for millennia.'

Laura chuckles. 'As chat-up lines go, that takes some beating,' she comments.

'So I went to the library out of curiosity and discovered the dates didn't work. Henry was still alive when Peggy was born.'

'So if you weren't Henry and you weren't Tom in a previous life, that only leaves—'

'Sam. Yes, it does rather look like that.'

'No wonder you're so scared of the sea.'

'Anyway, deep in the throes of my anxieties about being Tom, I decided to check through all my old transcripts. Come to think of it, that was only four days ago – how extraordinary! It feels like a lifetime away. Anyway, I was searching for those glimpses into other lives that I told you about.'

'Your fishermen, yes, go on.'

'And they included a puzzling little vignette of myself as a boy gazing out of a very high window.'

'And you think that might have been Sam seeing the view from your bedroom!'

'As you know, the place used to be an alms-house for the families of fishermen lost at sea. It occurs to me that Sam's family might have been billeted here for a time after his father was drowned. Which might explain why I decided to buy my house – and why I felt compelled to choose that particular bedroom.'

'So who was that T.H. *omee* you were going on about then? And what about all that business with tobacco tins? Because that Sam never smoked, did he? My Tom was forever giving him a hard time about it.'

Mary stubs out her cigarette and collects up her carrier bags. 'Come on,' she says briskly. 'Let's go and have another look.'

'I did find something about a tobacco tin,' Mary says, squatting by the box in her consulting room and leafing through papers. 'It's in here somewhere. I marked the places where I went off-piste with Post-its.' Then she straightens up: 'There! See what you make of that.'

Laura takes the sheaf of typescript and starts to read: '"She's gone down to the kitchen with the bairns to find out what's happening about tea, if she's supposed to make it or if they do and what time and that."

'You're right – that could easily be when they first arrived here and they're not quite sure how things are organized.' She reads on: '"So I take my chance to look in his ditty box again. I wrapped ticking round it to quiet the rattle and not draw attention, so now I unwrap it and open it up. And there's that photo where she's looking like an angel, sat still for the camera. How'd they ever get her to sit that still?

'"Now I've got his bakkie tin out and it's popped open just like that, easy as blinking. And there's his roll of Sweet Virginia and his papers, and his box of matches, little scattered wisps of dry bakkie. The smell's that sweet, like toffee almost. And all the while I'm listening out for Mam coming back up the stairs, because I don't want her seeing and getting upset."

'He keeps saying "his tin", doesn't he? And why is he trying to hide it from his mother?'

And all at once Mary understands. 'T.H.! Thomas Heron. The letters scratched on the tin – they must be the initials of Sam's father. Don't you remember, that day in the library? All those Thomases?' She beams at Laura. 'It all fits in: Sam told Annie that his mother was being pestered by the man who checked her nets. That's what those lads in the pub were talking about that evening with Tom. About how one day Sam decided to confront him.'

She snatches back the transcript and leafs back to a previous page. 'They said he'd had a few drinks to give himself some Dutch courage, didn't they? Right, now listen to this: "I'm feeling qualmy, like the beer's sloshing around in my belly."

'Then he says: "I hear her voice saying something from inside, and it comes back to me, this great whoosh of anger and I reach up to check my knife's there."

'That must be the knife I remembered! And now this: "So I'm trying to sort the buttons, but I'm so spitting angry my fingers won't work, and I'm just ripping them open, and his tin's come out of my pocket and's clattering onto the boards."'

She holds out the typescript and stares at it, as though she can't quite believe it. 'That's the bit I kept seeing, the tin clattering to the floor.'

'So you were Sam, and Ben was Annie. No wonder you're so fond of the lad.'

'Then Sam came back as Miss Turnbull and we met again.' Mary sinks down onto the pouffe as the information settles in her mind. Then: 'I wonder who I was between Sam dying and Peggy being born.'

'Maybe Miss T. had a secret sweetheart we don't know about,' says Laura. 'And it's you and Ben who've been the real soulmates all along.'

The phone rings suddenly, deafeningly, in the little hallway. It's Ian, slightly peeved that Mary hasn't called. 'Don't you ever check your answerphone?' he asks. He wants to film an interview about her findings so far – 'uncontaminated', as he puts it, by the results of the expedition to search for Annie's remains.

'It will be our first formal interview,' he says. 'The crew's arriving this evening. So you'll be on camera, talking to me. Are you OK with that?' He wants her down on the Fish Quay – 'to give a bit of atmos' he says, whatever that is – first thing tomorrow morning.

'Will Hester be there?' Mary asks nervously, as an uncomfortable jolt of adrenaline surges through her.

'Not at this stage, no – though I'll send her the transcript and no doubt she'll have some comments to make.' At least that's something less to worry about, she thinks. 'You won't be facing her until all the location stuff's in the can. Once I've done a rough edit, I'll get you up to London for a proper studio session.'

'What do you want me to wear?' she asks. 'Shall I fish that top out of the washing basket again?'

'Don't worry about that. There won't be any continuity issues if we're not in your consulting room.'

When she replaces the receiver she notices that there is indeed a red light blinking on her answerphone. 'I seem to have a message,' she says, gesturing helplessly at the machine. 'Laura, help me. Do you remember how it works?'

'See that button where it says "Review Messages"? Press it. Go on, it won't bite.'

There are three messages: the two from Ian that she already knows about – and one from Mr Skipper, sounding typically polite and hesitant.

'Hello, Doctor? Sorry to bother you, only I need to have another one of them remembering sessions. I been thinking about that Flo and how it was a bit muddled, like. Only it's coming a bit clearer now, so I wanted to talk to you, if that's all right. Anyway, you know where I am. When you can spare the time, like.'

'How strange. I wonder what that's all about,' Mary says vaguely. Then, turning back to Laura. 'So, which of my wonderful new outfits do you think I should wear to be on the television?'

CHAPTER FIFTY-NINE

2007

Ben rolls over and opens his eyes. The rising sun's sneaking into his room, a thin pink stripe high up on his cream wall – Dad's ordered some new maroon blinds, but they haven't come in yet.

He closes his eyes again; he's had a terrible night. He kept sort of half waking up, then lying there not knowing where he was, and staring round his room, trying to get used to it: the big orangey squares on the walls from the street lights down below, bleached out by the moon's pale blue squares trundling slowly across them.

Now it's light and here's that bright pink stripe of sun, getting wider and yellower, until he can see it through his closed eyelids and he knows he'll never get back to sleep. And now he's hungry too, but Dad won't be up for ages, so he decides to nip out on his own and go down the Seamen's Mission for a sausage bap.

It's weird going down the Fish Quay these days, since all those sessions with the doc. He keeps half expecting it to be like it used to be: totally buzzing, with towers of herring barrels everywhere – but it's just a few old blokes drinking Stella on a bench and nine or ten boats moored up. The Mission's open, though, and they're buttering a squillion baps, but the sausages aren't ready yet, so he has bacon again instead.

He wanders along the river past Clifford's Fort, munching and chucking bits of bread for the gulls. This is the beach where the cobles used to be, but it's all smashed up old polystyrene fish boxes now, washed up by the tide, and car tyres and that; Q tips and crisp packets all mixed in with the seaweed. And where the roads are now is different too, plus there's the car park and public loos, so he can't work out how it used to be. Chucking his bag in the bin, he starts to walk back home, but when he gets there, instead of pressing the entry code, he keeps on walking and, after a bit, he finds he's got to Seymour Street.

It's still only six-thirty, and there's no one around, so he peers through the letter box of number 59, to see if the old lady who lives there now has cleared up that litter tray, which she has. So then he pushes open the letterbox of number 60, where old Skip lives, but there's a bristly thing there that stops him seeing in. And he's just going to walk away, when he hears the whistle of Skip's battered old kettle, so he knows he's awake.

'I didn't know if you'd be up,' Ben fibs, watching old Skip pour out ready-mixed tea and Carnation milk into two chipped enamel mugs.

'I can never stop in bed,' he says, 'and this early light's good for my painting.'

The Push and Pull pub picture's leaning against the wall, unfinished. On the easel now is a painting of a woman's face. Ben stands in front of it; the face looks sort of familiar, like maybe he's seen her in a dream or something. 'Who's that?' he asks.

'That's me mam, just before she died.'

He's painted a gash of bright red lipstick on her face, and her head's tilted up and sort of sideways, as though she's just about to say something angry. Except there's half a smile there too, somewhere, maybe around the eyes, so it looks like maybe she's teasing, but means it at the same time.

'Did you talk to your father about that White Lady Reef, then?' asks old Skip. 'Only I've looked out my old books if he wants them – if he can make any sense of them, that is.'

'Can I see?' asks Ben.

'Ooh, I don't know about that.' The old bloke sucks his teeth doubtfully, but Ben knows he's joking. 'Go on, then. They're out on that bench there. Ought to lock them up probably.'

'Dad's got his on a load of DVDs,' Ben offers. 'He got a safe put in Nana's flat for them, but he won't tell her the combination.' He giggles. 'She's really narked about it.'

'Skippers used to keep them in a big walk-in safe down the fish cannery in the old days. Massive combination lock, night watchman, the lot. Paid a monthly fee. I always gave mine to Miss Turnbull; told her to hide them for me.'

There's a page marked with a squashed Rizla packet. 'That's the reef, on the right there,' says old Skip when Ben opens it to have a look. 'See, there's branches coming off of it, and gaps through. Them's what makes the currents so clever.' He points a yellow-stained finger. 'I reckon Tom would've rowed to here, see? Then drifted up along here,' he says. 'You tell your da.'

'Can you take me?' Ben asks suddenly. Why didn't he think of this in the first place? Because there's no way Dad would be seen dead puttering about in a dinghy. 'I want to go down with the metal detector.'

'What about that BBC man?'

'I want to go down first.'

'Why's that then, Paul's lad?'

'I don't think he's going to look properly,' Ben says. 'But it's not just that.' There's a silence while he wonders how to explain. 'You know when Ian was here,' he begins, 'and we were reading Miss Turnbull's diaries? And he just plonked down on her bed, so her handbag slipped onto the floor, and kicked her slippers out the way? Then he just sort of grabbed all the 1967 diaries and went off with them without even asking?'

Old Skip nods. 'So you don't want him doing that with your Annie.'

Nana's at the flat when Ben gets back, and she's all excited because they're filming down on the Fish Quay, and she's going on and on at Dad to take her down with him because he's 'a friend of the director'. And Dad's going, OK, OK, though you can see he doesn't want to.

Then in the middle of all that, the phone goes and it's Ian again. Which totally freaks Nana out when she realizes, so she starts doing that annoying mime thing that people do when you're talking on the phone and they want to talk to you at the same time. Then when Dad turns away, so he can't see her, she starts whispering, really loud – 'Paul! Paul! Ask him if I can come and watch!' – so Dad has to flap his hand backwards to try and shut her up.

Ben hangs around for a while, to see whether Dad is going out on that film recce after all. But it sounds like they're talking about some other filming in a few days, because Dad's saying, OK and are you sure and see you on Monday then, and he'll make sure the lads are all there. Which means Dad's not going to look for Annie, and the Ian bloke's fobbed him off by promising to film *Wanderer* pretending to go off fishing instead. Which means Ben has to go by himself.

He slips into the spare room where they keep all their diving gear – the wet suits hanging up in the en-suite shower like hollow black people, the air tanks in the bath. The Aquapulse's on a shelf in the wardrobe. He shoves it in his diving bag with his fins and that, his torch and spare batteries, his diving knife and mask, his suit and weight belt. At the last minute he remembers the thirty-metre line – just in case, though he doesn't think he'll have to go that deep.

'I'm just off swimming, OK?' he announces from the hall when he's ready.

Dad's scrolling through names on his mobile. 'OK, buddy,' he says without looking up. 'See you later.'

'Have you had any breakfast?' calls Nana, like she always does. Then, not waiting for an answer: 'Paul? When are we going down the Fish Quay?'

'Did you bring your book?' Ben shouts to old Skip over the noise of the outboard as they head out past the Priory and turn north towards Whitley Bay. The sun's high and there's a little breeze flicking the surface of the water, so it's all fresh and glittery, like tinsel.

'Don't you worry, Paul's lad,' he shouts back. 'I had a good look before I came out.'

It's too noisy to bother talking, so Ben just sits trailing his hands in the water and practising his breathing exercises. He's excited, that's the trouble, because it'll use up too much oxygen; so he's making himself calm down by doing that colour-meditation exercise, that katabasis, where you go through all the rainbow colours, really trying to concentrate, and relax a bit more with each colour. So you start with red, which is an exciting buzzy colour, which is how he feels right now; then you go to orange, then yellow; and each time you switch colours the excitement calms down a bit more until you get to blue and violet, which are the most relaxing. His freediving book called the bluey shades 'the colours of the unconscious' and says katabasis is like going down into the underworld.

The weird thing is that's exactly what happens in real life when you're diving. So at the surface you can see all the colours, but as you start going down the reds and yellows start to go and everything looks greeny, even the orange stripe on your fins. So even that deep – which is hardly deep at all – you have to use a torch to see what colour things really are. Then when you go deeper, the green starts to go too, and things start turning blue, which is why the sky looks blue, because it's deep into space.

So anyway, he's doing his katabasis exercises, and by the time he's finished, they've arrived. Well, not exactly arrived, but old Skip's cutting the outboard and pulling it up out of the water so it won't snag on the rocks, and is getting the oars ready. Ben peers over the side, trying to see the reef, but the sun's bouncing off the ripples, dazzling him, so it's impossible.

'How do you know where we are?' he asks.

'I look at the church, the dome, the lighthouse. The lamp-posts help a bit, I think. The trees. You have to tell your mind where you want to be, then let it work it out by itself.'

Turning down Ben's offer of help, the old bloke rows silently for a while, then lets the boat drift – then, at some sign Ben can't see, drops the anchor over the side. 'There you go,' he says, looking pleased with himself. 'Time for a cuppa before you start?'

'OK.' Ben doesn't really want one, but it seems rude to say no.

'They were good friends, them two lasses, weren't they?' says old Skip, handing over the first cup. 'That Annie and Flo. Always linking in, nattering away.'

Ben takes a scalding sweet gulp. 'Until Tom started messing around,' he says.

'Ay, he came between them right enough.' The old bloke extracts a packet of squashed fly biscuits from his anorak. 'That Flo never had another friend like Annie, you know. She had her bairns, of course, but it's never the same, is it?'

Ben hands back the cup and Skip unscrews the thermos for a top-up. 'She chose wrong, I reckon, choosing him,' says the old bloke.

'But Annie should've said something,' says Ben. 'I mean, Tom was trying it on with her all the time. If she'd said something, maybe Flo would have chucked him.'

'Ay, well, maybes it were too late by then. Maybes she were already pregnant.' The old bloke coughs and spits over the side. 'I reckon she weren't properly in her right mind back then, what with the baby on the way, and how he was getting about Annie. I reckon a part of her hated Annie for that.' He stares off out towards the horizon as though in a kind of dream, then sort of wakes up. 'Anyways,' he goes, looking back at Ben. 'If she were here now, I reckon she'd have wanted you to know she were sorry.'

Ben nods. 'They were always linking in, weren't they?' he says, remembering.

'Ay, nattering away.'

'What's that then?' Skip asks, watching Ben strap on his weight belt.

'It helps me stay under,' Ben explains. 'If you're not weighted, you have to keep finning and expending energy to stop yourself floating to the surface.'

He's nearly ready; just the Aquapulse to sort out. He's used it loads of times before, but always with Dad there to help put it on. There's an earpiece and a strap in case you drop it. He switches it on and a slow *bleep-bleep* starts up behind his left ear.

'Don't forget your line,' says old Skip. He's tied one end to the boat; Ben's supposed to clip the other to his belt, and tug on it if he gets into trouble. He's planning to tie it around the kist if he finds it, then fin to the surface and help Skip haul it onto the dinghy.

As soon as he's in the water, he can feel his heart going, so he snorkels for a bit doing his relaxation exercises until it slows down. Then he unclips his torch and dives.

Once he's down to five metres there's kelp all around, like being in a jungle with the wind in the trees, only in slow motion; or one of those shampoo adverts with swirly brown hair filling the screen in slippery waves. He keeps putting his hand out behind to feel for the line, because actually it's quite scary, being totally surrounded by the weed and walls of rock, so it's nice to think of old Skip up in the dinghy in the sunshine, sipping tea and lighting a rollie-up.

He checks his watch and he's been down for two minutes, and he really wants to take a breath – probably because feeling scared has used up his oxygen. So even though he hasn't really started searching, he fins up to the surface.

Next time he goes down, he pays more attention to the Aquapulse, finning gently along trying to hear when the beeps quicken up. He's decided it's better to stay near to the surface, so he doesn't have to hold his breath for too long. Then if he gets a good signal, he'll go down properly.

The first time it happens, he gets so excited he has to float for ages getting his breathing under control. But it's just an old anchor, wedged in a crevasse: all gnarled and rusted up, covered with weed. Next time it's a bucket, one of those old-fashioned metal ones, except there's only half of it left, like rusty lace held together by kelp and mussels.

After half an hour he's beginning to get the hang of it: finning along, listening, diving when he hears something, then coming up to check where the boat is, so he doesn't keep searching the same bit of reef. He even thinks he's beginning to hear the difference between a big object, like an anchor, and a piddly little bit of chain or something. Which means he doesn't have to check every single little *bleep-bleep-bleep* any more, though he's getting a bit fed up of anchors – how many are there down here?

Skip calls him over next time he surfaces and insists he gets out for a cup of tea. 'I don't want you freezing to death on me,' he says, making Ben take off his gloves and fins so he can check his hands and feet, and touching Ben's cheeks with the back of his freckly old hand. The hand smells of tabs; it reminds him of the doc.

Next time the Aquapulse speeds up it sounds different. He dives down and fins around for ages, but he can't see anything, even though the beeping is really loud, so there must be something there. He comes up for a breath, then goes down again and this time he gets his knife out and starts hacking at the weed, where he thinks the object must be, which uses up his oxygen really fast, so he has to come up for air.

But next time he goes down, he knows what he's doing, which is scraping away at this one flat bit of rock; except now he's cleared away some of the weed and coral and that, he can see that it's not a rock. So now he's really focused – *really* focused – because he's found an edge, and it's straight, with a bit of a ridge along it, like you'd find on a lid. So he's certain this must be the kist. What else could it be?

It's driving him bananas, going up and down all the time. So next time he comes up, he does a bit of overbreathing so he can stay down longer – and it's brilliant; he gets another twenty seconds and manages to clear away another load of weed. It freaks Skip out a bit, though, and he's waving and shouting when he comes to the surface. So Ben shouts out that he's found something, that's why he's staying down, and he's going to try and tie the line around it.

He overbreathes again, a bit more this time, and scrapes at the weed until he can reach an arm right under the kist – though even with the weed hacked away it looks nothing like a metal trunk, more like a mossy old rock. When he checks his watch he's been down ages, much longer than he realized, so he fins up for more air and floats on the surface a bit longer this time before overbreathing and going down again.

This time he unhooks the line from his belt and passes it under the kist, and again at a slightly different angle, so the kist's tied up like a Christmas parcel. It's tricky work, holding the torch and tying the rope at the same time, and he starts wanting to take a breath, but he goes through his colours, trying to relax, and it works – though by the end the water's started looking murky, as though the rope's scraped lots of little floaty bits off the kist making it so he can't see properly.

So anyway, he tugs on the line, to let old Skip know he's tied on the rope, and looks at his watch to see how long he's been down. But he can't see the numbers because of the fog, so he thinks he'd better go up anyway, because now everything looks grey, probably because his torch battery's low.

He tries to move his legs, to fin to the surface, but it's like his fins are caught on something, and his legs feel really heavy, so he decides to unclip his weight belt, but it's so murky and dark it's as though the fog's inside his head and he can't remember what to do with his fingers, and now the torch has gone out and everything's so blue, so blue and foggy…

CHAPTER SIXTY

1898

A fog's been lying on the river these past two days. The skippers curse it, for a fog means a flat sea and a tug all the way to the herring grounds. But I like the blunt dank greyness of these days, when you can't see the river, or the boats coming home without him; and lose sight of the bottom of any stairs and what might lie down there.

On days like this your life shrinks in to what's close by, and your plans to setting one foot down after another, and not caring where you're going, for where's the place that's worth going to if he's not with you?

Still, my feet have been walking without me telling them, walking because I can't be still, for to be still is to know that he's gone and never coming back. So though the days find me gipping where I should be, come the evening when our tea's eaten and the pots done, and Flo and Mam are on at me to please, pet, take the chair by the grate, and I can't bear their kind eyes a minute longer, I have to snatch up my shawl and run out the house into the fog and let my feet take me where they will.

It's the muddy lane to the trysting hill that calls them, and the rabbit trails winding between the wyn banks, where spiders' webs cling in the misty gloaming, loaded with fog dew. There's a hollow I've found, that sweethearts shun, for it's too small to lie down in, and too perilous, being perched on the edge of a sheer drop above the river's mouth. And it's here I wait for night to come, and listen to the night's noises: the wet grazing of rabbits, the little squeaks of their kittens; the quiet lapping of the river's tongue on the rocks below. And further out, the warning bells of 'longshore cobles back from checking their pots, the growls and coughs of the old lads, the plash of oars in the darkness.

If Mam hadn't come to fetch me last night, I'd be there still. I was thinking of the wet earth under me, of worms swimming slowly though it; of the cold black river, and how easy it would be to fill my pockets with stones, and let my feet carry me down into the water.

Mam took me home, and filled the hot bottle, and wrapped her arms round me till my shivering quietened, and my weeping started, then quietened too, and I was yawning – then sleeping, I suppose, for next thing I know it's morning and she's bringing me a cup of tea and saying I'm to stay back from work today because there's a task I've to do.

I've been keeping Sam's ditty box by my pillow, and hug it close, and fancy I catch the ghost of the scent of him; but it's vain really, for it's just a cold little tin, and its only smell is of rust and herring oil. So today Mam says I've to take it to his mam, for it's hers by rights, and might hold something she needs.

By, but it pains me to walk these poor lanes again and linger with tears in my eyes to see the row of mean wooden houses, with the fresh-creosoted one at the end.

I hear his mam's keening before I get there: that same seagull mew that comes from my mouth, that's sometimes the only sound a body can make on account of the wringing of its innards and the strangling of its soul.

Jessie's outside with the bairns, sat with hunks of bread and a bowl of broth. When she sees me her glad smile fairly breaks my heart – I've been so caught up with my own grief I never thought of this poor brave lass and the load she'd be carrying.

'I've bought his box,' I'm saying. 'From the boat. I think the key might still be in the pocket of his kecks.'

And she's saying, 'Thank you,' and, 'His body's inside, but Mam won't let anyone get him ready, and I'm that afraid of him turning—' She looks at me, a pleading look that says she's at the end of her tether. 'We've got him on ice. She did let me do that. But fast as we can bring it, so it's melting. The room's awash.'

I ask, is there a coffin, and Jess says the church folk are bringing one today, for of course they've no savings. 'But we can't put him in the ground the state he's in.'

And while we're speaking, a group of giggling bairns gathers near and asks to see 'the drowned lad', and all at once here's Sam's mam roaring out through the doorway with a broom and her hair all loose, and screams at them to be gone.

'They keep coming,' says Jess. 'Every hour, different bairns. Mam can't stand it.'

And before I can think what I'm doing, I'm following his mam back into that dim room, and taking her two hands in the two of mine, to hold her steady like – for didn't Sam tell me that's what his mam was always needing: a steady hand on her tiller? And I'm staring into her wild eyes, that are the exact same shape and colour as his, and telling her I loved him, and we were going to be wed, and I'm sorry. Then, when her wild look abates a bit, saying: howay, let's prepare him together.

I know what to do, for it's not long since I helped Mam lay out my other nana. So I send the bairns off for cotton wool, and Jessie sets out his go-ashores – for she's washed and ironed them all ready, bless her – and braids up her mam's hair to be more decent, and ties on her pinny. Then, when we're set, Jess sends the bairns outside and lights the lamp and I push the door closed.

They've laid him in the tarpaulin from the beach, with its edges flapped over to cover him, in a nest of melting ice, on planks resting on stools. There's a tin bath beneath to catch most of the melt; and a puddle for the rest, seeping out over the oilcloth, with a line of rags to contain it, and a pail to wring them into. And there's a smell – Oh sweet Jesus, keep me strong! But how could there not be, after so many days?

So we kneel on the wet oilcloth, the three of us, and say a prayer; then I lift the flaps and there he is, my lovely lad, greyer and duller than before, and sunken somehow, as a fish goes when it loses its freshness. And I look at Jess and we both look at her mam, who's staring and staring at the body, and shaking her head; and I know what she's thinking, for it's what I'm thinking too – that it's not Sam any more, that's he's gone, and all that's left is the flesh and bones his soul wore.

And that knowing makes it easier, somehow, to lift him onto the table and take his clothes off and comb out his hair; then wash his body – oh, all the tender parts I've never seen, that are greenish now, like a body under water; and cold, oh so cold, cold as a fish in a farlane.

I've two pennies in my pocket, which I lay over the place where his eyes were, and make plugs of cotton wool for the mouth and nose. But the other parts that need cleaning, his mam cleans, with the tenderness of a mother with her baby, and pushes in the plug, and rests her bony hands on his flat belly a moment, then pulls on his good kecks.

Now we're finishing, tying up the black silk to hold his jaws closed, settling his dark curls around the sad mess that's his face. And I would hold his hand and kiss him goodbye, except he's already long gone.

Now I'm opening the door, and the bairns are pushing in and whingeing for their tea – for the light's going and it's late. The fog's thickened, and billows in with them, stinking of brown river sludge and coal smoke. Plunging out into it, I tug my shawl up over my nose, and step carefully on the greasy boards, from one seep of mean candlelight to another, for there's no street lamps in these poor alleys.

Now what's this? Quick footsteps behind me, and Jessie calling me to wait and saying to come with her round the back to Sam's room. 'I didn't want to say in front of Mam, for she'd fuss,' she says. But it seems the day before he drowned Sam gave Jess a guinea to buy 'a travelling kist for Annie'.

'He said I was to choose it,' says Jessie, 'for I'd know better what a lass would like. He said it was his promise that you'd be together.'

I can't see her face clearly, the light's that thin, but I can hear from her voice that she's crying. And I want to say thank you, but I can't trust my voice neither; so I let her take my hand and lead me to Sam's low door, and unlock it, and duck down to feel for the candle.

The sight of his little room, flickering before me, is nearly more than I can bear – though it's as empty of him now as his body is, with the bricks stacked and the planks gone, to the kitchen I suppose, and his ticking emptied and hanging on a hook.

'The shop was cram full of Scots lasses,' Jessie's saying, 'so I asked them which one to pick. I was going to get one of them wooden ones with metal bars, like they all have, but they said the new steel ones are lighter and never rust nor get worm and last a lifetime. A lifetime, Annie, that's what they were saying. So I knew that's the one he'd want for you.'

It's painted green, with black handles and a brass padlock on the hasp. It's the nicest kist I ever saw, and I tell her so, and give her a hug, which is something folk round here hardly ever do – except she's so small and good and brave, and must be needing one so much, for her arms are round me in a trice and cling so hard I've not the heart to push her away. I can feel her little shoulders shaking with sobs, and hot tears soaking into my blouse. And through my tears I'm making a secret promise: that I'll be a sister to Jess, just as I would be if Sam were alive; and it will please him, and make his soul smile, and keep him with me.

Now she's pulling away and saying sorry, sorry, and wiping her eyes and asking, will I go to Yarmouth with the Scots lasses when they leave? And I'm saying no, not this year, for there's folk here that need me, and I can't think of leaving them yet. And I never say, and she never asks, but she knows the folk I'm speaking about.

I should go home, I know, for Mam will be worriting, but my feet want to wander, taking me along Clive Street and Liddell Street into Bell Street, where the fog's thicker than ever, blurring the street lamps, though I can't tell if it's the fog causing the blurring or my tears, which keep welling up and will not be staunched.

It must be Saturday, for the streets are packed with folk in their good clothes: the lads striding out and the lasses swaying, all full of life and laughingness, and that ginger-beer fizzing I felt once and can't believe I will ever feel again. And sneaking into the dark alleys, with quick glances back to see if they're noticed, there go the sweethearts – and them that's not so sweet, but still want a wide coat and a dark doorway. And here are the drunks stotting along the walls with their kecks unbuttoned, pissing in the gutters and not caring who sees.

Now here's one swaying towards me with a wet stain down his leg, and he's lunging out to touch me, for my arms are up holding the kist on my head and cannot push him off, so I have to kick out – so I do, and hard, and catch him where it hurts, and see him fall to his knees, and am glad, oh suddenly so very glad, to see him go down. And would kick them all if I could, Tom and the all rest of them, and see them buckle, and kick them again: for all the ugly manliness in them, the mucky graspingness that has no respect, and can't see when a lass is grieving, or can see it but doesn't care, and wants her anyway. Then kick them again, for their stinking breath and minging sweat, for their hot blood and beating hearts, for being so *alive* when my Sam is so dead.

So I'm walking faster now and fair spitting at any lad who'd stop me for a stupid blether – for they've all had a skinful – or make a grab for my shawl, or my boobies.

Now here I am down on Union Quay, where the fog swirls thick as a blanket, with drunken ghosts stumbling through it with their arms out. The boats are moored three deep, but I can barely see past the first, only the odd few deck lamps glimmering like pale halos in the fog, only hear the flat river slapping at their hulls.

Now this looks like the *Osprey*'s warp, tied to a mooring post, with its red and black bindings, so I set down the kist and look closer. But it's not; the patterning's wrong. But the sight makes me want to search her out, and go aboard and look for Sam.

I know, I know I won't find him, but maybes I can find the place he slept? And lie down there and close my eyes and feel close to him.

It's like skirting the edge of a wild wood, with the masts creaking and the hulls scraping together all along Union Quay, and wet fog tangled in the rigging, a forest of saplings clustered together, dripping and swaying on the water.

I find the *Osprey*'s out at the end of the fish quay, past Clifford's Fort, so I set down the kist and kick off my clogs and I've clambered aboard in a minute. The fo'c'sle hatch is closed, of course, and won't yield when I pull on the handle, but the hasp's hanging so it can't be locked. So I pull again, and again another way, and then again, then harder; then punch it and curse my lass's weakness, for it seems this is all I have left of Sam, this chance to touch the place he lay before he died, but I can't get to it.

I suppose I'm weeping again, but quietly, though it's hard to know, for my cheeks are damp with the fog and the rigging's dripping all around. But here's someone swinging aboard, calling, 'Who's there?' then, 'Annie, is that you?', for I suppose he's heard me sobbing.

'What are you doing?' It's Tom, squatting down beside me, trying to see my face.

'I can't get the hatch open,' I say. So he asks why I want to, and I say, oh just to see where the lads sleep. And he asks, is it my kist on the quay, and should he hoy it aboard, for anyone might take it – then goes off before I can answer and brings it back.

Now he's tugging the hatch open, and climbing down to light the lamp – then reaching up a hand to guide me down. But I don't want to go down any more, not with him there, but can't refuse now I've said. So I'm stepping on the ladder and jumping down, and he's catching me, which is something else I don't want. So I try to push him away, but there's nowhere to push him, for the place is that narrow I can't see how seven big lads could ever fit in here.

Now Tom's smiling, showing me the berths and telling how the lads top and tail it like bairns to fit in, and how there's some, like our Jimmy, who sleep tidy, but others are the very devil, with snoring and thrashing about.

Which is Sam's? I ask, seeing the mattresses all wedged together on the bunks. And Tom laughs and points out one, and slaps it with his hand and says it's Big John's now, and I can see the grease of his hair on the ticking, and feel sick that my Sam's been blotted out so soon.

'That's a canny kist,' says Tom. 'Are you going away?' And I tell him Sam bought it me, for I always wanted one, and dreamed of following the herring to Yarmouth and Ireland and Shetland one day; and I must be crying again, for Tom's pulled out the end of my shawl and is wiping my eyes with it, and telling me not to be sad, and to forget Sam, for he was never good enough for me.

Now he's pulling me close and saying he'll look after me now. So I've to heave him off again, sharpish, and tell him it's Flo that needs him, not me. And he's saying I liked it fine yesterday in the kitchen, and asking is that why I keep pushing him away, because of Flo? And goes to kiss me, pressing me back against the ladder, so I can feel him against me, his belly and his thighs, the hard shape in his kecks.

And I'm thinking, why's he doing this? And ducking my head away from his mouth and begging him to stop, please, he's hurting me. And he's asking, did I tell Sam to stop too? And I say, that's none of his business. Then he says it *is* his business, for he loves me and wants us to be together.

So now he's asking again, did I stop him, and what did we do, and starts to list all the things, pressing up against me all the while. And the listing – Did he suck your boobies? Did he pull up your skirt? Did he get his fingers inside? – is getting him roused, so he's pumping at me in time with his talking, but riled too, when I won't say.

Now all of a sudden he's staring at me and saying, 'He's had you, hasn't he?' with a look of such fury that I have to cry, 'No! But we were good as married, so what does it matter?'

And now a sort of cold smile, that's halfway to a snarl, comes on his face. 'There's an easy way to find out,' he says, and yanks my skirt up to my waist.

So now I'm begging, 'Tom, please, no! He's never touched me there!', feeling his rough hand grappling with my pettie, the cold air on my legs. I can't hardly believe what he's doing, this lad I've known since we were bairns. I can't believe he's jabbing with his fingers when I've never even let him kiss me. And that rush of anger that rose up in Bell Street comes over me again, and I slap his cheek hard as I can, and see him backing away and laughing like we're playing a game.

'I like a lass who fights,' he says, rubbing his cheek. 'Flo's so easy, it's no fun any more.'

And here he comes at me again, smiling and reaching for my skirt. So now I'm turning to scramble away up the ladder, kicking out backwards best I can, but it's no good and he's tugged me back down, and around, and is ripping off my shawl and yanking at the neck of my blouse – and kissing me, on my neck, my throat, all the while I'm fighting, as though he's used to a lass fighting, and likes it, and thinks it natural.

Now he's got me pinned against the ladder again, and he's twisting my head round with his hand, to kiss me on the mouth, and his breath smells of tabs and red herring, and his tongue's mashed against my lips, and pushing at them, hot and hard until I can't bear it, and open up and bite down on his tongue, and taste his blood in my mouth and hear him scream down my throat.

But it stops him for a moment, and gets him off me; so we're both standing and panting and spitting blood.

'I won't give up, Annie,' he says, wiping his mouth with the back of his hand. 'And I always get what I want in the end. Your *Wellesley* lad soon found that out.'

And I say, 'What do you mean?'

'He thought he could take everything, didn't he? My boat, my lass. Getting into the skipper's good books, going after his mate's ticket, going after everything that should be coming to me.'

'What did you do to him?' I'm listening, but I can't understand what he's saying.

'He wouldn't tell me if he'd had you, see? And it was driving me nuts. So I hit him, then I shoved him – then I watched him go under.'

'You killed Sam?' I stare at him and I can't believe it.

'I had to stop him. He was spoiling everything. It was like he'd put some kind of spell on you, on the skipper. Don't you see?' He reaches a hand out, pleading like, but I brush it away. 'I had to, Annie. I love you. I couldn't bear to see him with you.'

While he's talking something shifts inside me, and I find I've stopped flapping and flailing like a chicken in a coop, and trying to save my stupid virtue – and I've started thinking of my Sam, shoved overboard into the cold sea for the sin of simply loving and wanting to make a living. And that thinking makes me more cunning, and to notice Tom's gipping knife in the band round his cap.

So I grab for it, and flick it open – all in a moment – and stab at his heart, but quick as lightning his arm's there, and I'm stabbing into his gansey instead, and he's grabbing my wrist and twisting the knife away so it clatters on the floor.

Now he's laughing at me again, and picking up the knife, then slashing at the front of my blouse, and my cami too, until my boobies spill out. So I'm trying to pull the sides together to cover them, but he's snatched my hands away and is staring at my chest, and laughing at the sight of my bare boobies.

I try to kick him again, but he's too close, and he's got the knife at my throat, and's unbuttoning his kecks. And he's forcing me back on Sam's mattress and pulling up my skirt, his hard knees pressing my thighs open, the buckle of his belt digging in; his mouth sucking me, his hips grinding against me – and oh, here's the hot pain of his thing jabbing inside me, the rasp and drag of it deep in my innards.

Now the licking's stopped, and my skin's chill where he's wet me, and here's his face staring down at me, but not seeing, or just seeing what he wants to, or seeing and not caring. And I'm whispering, Tom, please, no, but now his hand's clamping over my mouth so I can't catch my breath, and I try to heave him off, but my arms have no strength, so I'm telling him, please no, with my eyes.

Oh, and the noises he's making, the grunt as he whacks into me, the slurping noises as he sucks on my booby and neck, his smell of sweat and beer and tab smoke, his whispering that it's so good and he loves me.

Then he's bucking and roaring with some kind of pain, it seems like, and poking his hard thing to the very heart of me.

Then it's all over, and he's collapsed on top of me, panting and laughing into my hair, as though it's nowt but a race he's run and won. And I'm thinking, is this what love's like for a lad? This fighting with a lass and liking it, and getting riled and roused at the same time, as though it's the same hot blood driving them both? So he can hurt a lass and say he loves her in the same breath, then laugh and think she'll love him back?

Now what's this I'm seeing over his shoulder? A lass's foot on the ladder, a lass's skirt coming down through the hatch. Flo? Oh sweet Jesus, Flo!

And I want to scream out that Tom's forced me, but all she's seeing is him laughing and heaving up off me, as if this was the most natural thing in the world. Now he's standing up and buttoning his kecks, and I'm wrenching my skirt down and scrubbing at the wetness. And I can tell what she's thinking, for her face says it all.

Next thing I know, she's got a knife from somewhere and is lunging towards me, slashing at my face, my boobies, any part she can reach, and Tom's grabbing at her and wrenching the knife away, then shoving her against the ladder and slapping her around the head until she sinks sobbing to the floor.

And I'm buttoning my blouse, to be decent again, but it's soaked with blood – so I'm wondering, where's it coming from? My hands are red too, but I can't see any cuts, so I touch my face and can't find any there neither. So now I'm thinking it's maybes my chest that's been nicked, and move my hand down, and find here's warm blood pumping from a gash on my neck.

Why can't I feel the pain of it? For there's that much blood it's started dripping on the floor. And I'm thinking, maybes I should wrap my scarf round and twist it tight, but then how would I breathe? But I have to try and stop the blood somehow, so I press my hand on to it, to try and keep the edges together, but it's slithery as a herring so I can't—

Now Tom's lowering me onto the floor somehow, and he's ripped my blouse off and is wadding it onto my neck. And he's sobbing – or is it Flo sobbing? I can't tell, for the light's fading, like there's a dark blanket covering me, or a fog seeped in from outside. And it's so cold, I can't feel my hands any more, or the boards under me, and it's like I'm floating, floating, and I'm thinking of my Sam sinking under the cold water and wondering if this is what it's like to drown—

CHAPTER SIXTY-ONE

2007

Mary's down on the Quayside, perched on a flimsy metal chair at a flimsy metal table, as directed by Ian. She's watching him 'set up' for the interview, which seems to involve striding around pursued by a retinue of gorgeous young things clasping clipboards, and with various items of electronic equipment strapped to their torsos. They're all wearing faux military trousers, she notes with amusement – even the girls – and overlapping layers of torn T-shirt, which they appear to have put on inside out.

When she had donned her own new outfit – a casually draped sage-green tunic and matching trousers, with self-coloured embroidery at the neck and hem – Mary had felt rather fetching: understated and elegant. But surveying all these muscular tanned limbs in energetic combat clothing, she feels puny and overdressed. And *freezing*, of course – don't the young feel the cold? Despite the sun, there's a chilly wind ruffling the surface of the river.

A stunning young redhead comes over and introduces herself as, 'Viv, Ian's PA'. 'Are you all right sitting here by yourself?' she asks kindly, as if Mary's an aged relative. 'Can I get you anything? It won't be much longer.' And she's off, before Mary can reply.

Ian breezes over. 'Ah, there you are – good,' he says, as if he hadn't just asked her to sit exactly there. 'We're nearly ready to start.' Then: 'If it's OK with you, I thought we'd carry the table a tad closer to the river so we can get Paul's boat in shot.' Mary shrugs, hiding a smile – as if it matters what she thinks.

Eventually they're ready and she's sitting primly with her legs crossed, chafing her bare hands together, with a heap of lobster pots and fishing nets behind her. Ian perches on the chair opposite and two of the gorgeous young things squat nearby, poised and alert, aiming various items of alarming equipment at her.

'OK – quiet, everyone!' Ian shouts. 'And – turn over!'

'Try to ignore them,' he says, leaning towards Mary. 'This is just you and me talking, so just relax and answer my questions. Remember, we can do this as many times as you like, so don't worry if you get in a muddle.'

'What makes you think I'm going to get into a muddle?' she enquires archly, but in fact that's exactly what she's afraid of: that she'll lose her train of thought or go off at some theoretical tangent. Feeling a sudden acute need for a cigarette, she takes a sip of water. The table's equipped with a carafe of water and two glasses – furnished presumably by the lovely Viv – along with, for some reason, five large empty whelk shells. But no ashtray, Mary notes with regret.

Looking up, she spies Paul in the distance, outside that Italian restaurant, and his mother (what on earth is the woman wearing?) in a small crowd of people being held back – 'out of shot', Mary supposes – by one of the gorgeous young things. There's a matching small crowd, similarly restrained, gathering on the pavement along the quayside in the opposite direction. Mary takes a deep breath and turns back to Ian.

'So Dr Charlton – Mary – this has been quite an intense couple of weeks.'

'Yes, it's not every day you discover two unsolved murders committed over a century ago.'

'Later today, we're going out with a specialist diver to search for the remains of one of those murder victims. The body we're looking for is that of Annie Milburn, the herring girl you believe to be a past incarnation of Ben Dixon, the young boy whose case we've been following in this programme. If we find Annie's body, what will that tell us?'

Seeing his earnest, sincere, made-for-TV expression, Mary feels a giggle welling up. She forces herself to concentrate.

'As far as we know, no one except Annie's murderer knew what happened to the body,' she says. 'Tom was alone in that little boat and he probably never told anyone where he went – why would he? It would open him up to a criminal investigation. So if we find Annie's body where he said it was, I'd say that was strong support for reincarnation.'

'And if we don't find anything?'

'That would be disappointing, obviously. But there are any number of reasons why the kist might not be where Tom said it was. It was a foggy night, so perhaps he was mistaken about where he dumped it. Perhaps it was shifted by currents and storms, or broken up and its contents dispersed. I'm told that once they're exposed to sea water, human remains don't last very long.' Mary shrugs in what she hopes is a disinterested manner. 'It would be nice to have a definitive answer, but I'm afraid that not finding Annie's body in 2007 doesn't prove it wasn't there in 1898.'

'Isn't that rather convenient for your theory?' Ian asks smoothly, and there's a glint in his eye that she recognizes.

'It's a matter of logic, not convenience,' she says tartly. 'I'm only pointing out the obvious.'

'Are you saying that one can never prove that reincarnation *doesn't* exist; one can only ever prove that it does.'

'Yes – though that doesn't imply, of course, that one shouldn't subject the phenomenon to rigorous scientific scrutiny. However, in this case, if we fail to find Annie's body, we would have to invoke your Scottish verdict of "unproven".' She leans back in her chair; she's beginning to enjoy herself.

'There is one thing that's been puzzling me,' he says. 'We have, in quotes, "witness statements", from both Tom and Jimmy about Tom's guilt, but so far we've heard nothing from Annie about what happened that night. Why didn't any of this come out in your sessions with Ben?'

'I believe that Ben was blocked,' Mary explains. 'In almost every session, there came a point beyond which he couldn't progress. It was as though he didn't want to remember what happened that night.'

'Is that normal?'

'No. In fact, it's rather unusual. Though some very repressed individuals may take a few sessions to open up, as it were, the vast majority of my clients are eventually able to explore past traumas.'

'So why is Ben different?'

'To be perfectly honest, I don't have an answer to that. I can only suppose that something happened that night that shocked Annie very deeply, so deeply that her own consciousness found it difficult to encompass.'

'What, even more shocking than being raped and murdered?'

'Yes, though I know that seems hard to believe. But rape and violence were endemic in North Shields at that time, so would have been things Annie was, to some extent, prepared for.'

'Because Tom had already assaulted her, is that what you mean?'

'Yes. So I'm wondering what else happened – if perhaps he said something, or did something, or if someone else was involved.'

Ian leans in. 'Isn't it possible that the reason Ben found it so difficult to remember Annie's murder was because it never happened?'

'Of course it's possible,' Mary acknowledges. Where's Ian going with this? 'But as you yourself reminded us, we now have independent testimony from Annie's brother Jimmy that Tom pretty much confessed to disposing of a body that night. And of course we have Tom's own testimony from Laura that you filmed yesterday.

'For what it's worth,' she adds, 'Laura wasn't present at the session where I questioned Annie's brother Jimmy. Yet her "witness statement", as you call it, corroborates everything Jimmy told us.'

'So how does all this relate to Ben's desire for a sex change?'

'In his regression sessions, Ben described Annie as being deeply in love and blissfully happy. Her boyfriend had asked her to marry him, her father and mother had approved the match. That windy morning, running along the top bank to meet him, she was just brimming with excitement and joy. You filmed that session, so you heard what she was like. I think you'd have to agree that was probably the happiest moment of her life.

'Excuse me—' Mary stops for a moment to control a slight quaver in her voice. Seeing these scenes again, from Sam's perspective, as it were, is affecting her more than she'd anticipated.

'From what we now know,' she continues, 'that was the last moment of happiness young Annie Milburn ever had. The boat she was meeting came back without her beloved Sam. And the life she was so joyfully embracing – well, that life ended the moment she reached the quayside, and saw the boats pushing ominously apart to let the *Osprey* tie up—'

She breaks off again, tears welling up, and Ian waits for her to collect herself. Then: 'So she discovers that Sam's lost overboard,' he prompts.

'This is the essence of karma,' Mary explains in a steadier voice. 'Annie was on the brink of her life as a woman, but she never experienced it properly. From the moment she saw those boats making way for the *Osprey*, all she knew was loss and violence. First Sam drowned, then she was herself raped and murdered. It's my belief that this karma, this "unfinished business", is what explains Ben's desire to be a girl. He wants the female existence Annie was denied all those years ago – and he wants to repudiate the violent masculinity that stole it from her.'

'Are you suggesting that all sex change cases can be explained by traumatic events in a past life?'

Mary uncrosses her legs; her feet are beginning to go numb. Damn. 'Every case is different, obviously,' she says. 'With Laura, for example, the "karmic causality" – if I can call it that – is rather more straightforward.'

'Sorry, Dr Charlton,' Ian breaks in, 'excuse me interrupting. I just want to remind our viewers that Laura was born a man but had a sex change about fifteen years ago. Am I right?'

'Yes. Having committed multiple atrocities in her incarnation as Tom, Laura didn't want anything to do with her masculine persona and embarked on a series of gender reassignment procedures in 1992. Since then she's devoted her life to helping other men realize their ambitions to pass as women.'

'What about hormonal influences? Isn't it now thought that gender dysphoria – the sense that one has been born into the wrong body – is caused by an insensitivity to testosterone in the womb? So the baby's born with a male body and a female brain?'

'Indeed,' Mary acknowledges. 'And in the majority of male-to-female cases that's probably the only explanation one needs. But as you know –' she smiles at him – 'these things are multiply determined. And there's ample evidence to suggest that past life experiences can affect the body as well as the mind.'

'Surely you're not implying that karmic influences can cause a hormonal imbalance in the mother of an unborn baby, as way of furthering a karmic agenda?'

She sighs. Why does he always take things to their most absurd extreme? 'No, that's not what I'm implying – though I wouldn't necessarily rule it out. All I'm suggesting is that certain foetuses may be unusually sensitive to hormonal anomalies, and that such sensitivity might – and I stress might – have its roots in a karmic process.'

'But what about—'

'I'm sorry, Ian,' Mary says suddenly. 'My feet have gone completely numb. Would you mind awfully if I walked around a bit to try to get the blood moving again?'

Ian frowns briefly, then waves a dismissive hand. 'Sure, no problem,' he says, then yells, 'Cut, everyone! We're taking a break. Be back here ready to start in ten.' Then: 'Can I bum a surreptitious fag?' he asks, sidling up to Mary as she lights up. 'My team disapproves – and quite rightly.'

'I'm sorry about having to break off like that,' she repeats, stamping her feet from side to side. 'I should have put on some thermal long johns or something. But once it's got that bad, I have to do something or I'll end up in hospital.'

'No bother. Listen, I should probably go and pay my respects to Old Ma Dixon over there. Come with me, will you? People like that terrify me.' He pulls a face to demonstrate.

'I'd have thought you'd be used to it by now,' Mary comments mildly, proffering her lighter. '"People like that", as you put it, are your bread and butter, aren't they? People who'd do anything to be on television, regardless of how they're portrayed?'

'So why do I feel like a lamb chop in a piranha pool?'

Mary laughs. Surely he's not expecting her to feel sorry for him? 'You're offering something everyone craves: recognition, acknowledgement. You've seen what neglected children are like – they'll do practically anything for a bit of parental attention, even if it's just a clip round the ear. Adults are the same; they just express it differently.' And you exploit them, she adds silently.

'Well thank God you didn't suggest regressing her,' he says exhaling smoke in three quick puffs. 'Why didn't you, by the way?'

'I have absolutely no idea,' Mary admits. 'It was an obvious thing to do. But it honestly never occurred to me that she had anything to do with our configuration of souls – if I can call it that. It's entirely possible that I'm wrong, however. And it's not too late.' She pauses. 'Perhaps she was Henry,' she suggests slyly, 'and she's that soulmate you were looking for.'

He shudders. 'Now you're really scaring me,' he says.

She watches him stub out his cigarette and switch on the charm. 'Hey, Paul, mate! Sorry to cordon you off like this. How are you, Mrs Dixon?'

'OK, quiet please! Now, *turn*!' shouts Ian as he sits down again. 'Dr Charlton, can you tell us something about your theory of group reincarnation?'

Mary blinks. It really is quite amazing the way Ian transforms himself in a split second from irascible director to patient attentive interviewer.

'It's not my theory,' she says. 'It's something a number of reputable observers have noted over the years. Group reincarnation is the idea that certain communities of souls may seek one another out repeatedly, over and over, at different times. So you might find a mother reincarnated as her daughter's son, for example; or a grandfather as his colleague's nephew.' She smiles as something occurs to her. 'There is a famous Buddhist story about a man who goes fishing with his dog—'

But Ian doesn't let her finish. 'When you hypnotized Ben's father,' he says, 'and discovered that he had been Annie's brother Jimmy in his previous life, did that surprise you?'

'Yes, of course it did. I'd come across such apparent coincidences before, in passing, but this was the first time I'd investigated the phenomenon of group reincarnation directly.'

'There have been quite a few "coincidences" with this case, haven't there?'

'A further three that we know of so far. You've just filmed Laura reliving her past life as Annie's killer – Laura is the person who introduced Ben to me. I've also recorded sessions with a retired local fisherman, an associate of Ben's father, whose previous incarnation appears to be Annie's best friend, Flo.' Mary smiles. 'Then there's you, of course.'

Ian laughs and turns confidingly to the camera. 'I should probably explain here that Dr Charlton regressed me a couple of weeks ago – at my insistence, I should add – and discovered that I also had a part to play in Annie's short and troubled life. I've got the session on tape and I'll be playing an extract later in the programme.'

'This will probably seem very strange to your viewers,' Mary says.

'What, that I should turn up out of the blue to make a documentary about reincarnation, only to discover that I was caught up in the very same drama as Ben in a previous life? You have to admit it does seem unlikely.'

Mary shrugs. 'I think it was Sherlock Holmes who remarked that when one has eliminated all the likely explanations, the remaining logical possibility – however unlikely – has to be true.'

'But I was born and raised in Aberdeen, for God's sake. Apart from a fortnight's summer holiday in the sixties, I've never spent any time in North Shields.'

'I'm glad you've mentioned your place of birth,' Mary says – and she is: this discussion has explained something that's been at the back of her mind ever since she regressed him. 'What evidence there is on the subject suggests that souls tend to reincarnate in the general vicinity of the place where their prior "host body" died. So Annie was murdered here in North Shields, and Ben was born in North Tyneside General – not a million miles away. In between there was another incarnation, another woman, who died in that same hospital about four months before Ben was born.'

'So how did my soul end up in Aberdeen?'

'Without regressing you again I can't be sure, but I would hypothesize that at some point in your soul's journey, you had an incarnation that travelled between North Shields and Aberdeen.' She looks at Ian, waiting for him to come to the conclusion she's just reached.

'The herring fleet, of course!' he says. 'They sailed down from Scotland every year, following the shoals south.' Forgetting the cameras, they grin delightedly at each other for a moment. 'OK, let's say for the moment you've convinced me,' he says. 'Surely by telling me that, you've contaminated the evidence? If you hypnotize me now and I remember a life aboard some herring boat, how can I be sure it's not because you've put the idea in my head?'

Mary sighs inwardly. Here we go, she thinks, mentally squaring her shoulders. Gloves off – and just when she was starting to relax too.

'You're right, of course,' she admits. 'Suggestion – hypnotic and otherwise – is a very powerful influence and incredibly difficult to eliminate from an investigation of this kind. In the end it often comes down to a balance of probabilities. In your case, for example, once I'd put you in a trance, I could ask you the name of the boat you were on – assuming we discovered that you were indeed a fisherman at some point – and who you married and when. Then we could check the various archives to see whether what you recall is supported by the historical record. As the circumstantial evidence builds up and up, it begins to seem almost perverse to question it. As I said before, once you've eliminated the likely, the unlikely has to be true.'

CHAPTER SIXTY-TWO

2007

Paul's beginning to feel a bit of a twat, gawping at the filming. They've got them cordoned off so far away he can't hear anything, just see Ian and that doctor sat either side of a little table they've brought onto the Fish Quay, like it's the Costa Brava or something. It's a bit like watching TV with the sound off, and bloody boring, frankly. Nana's drinking it all in, mind, waving at some crony of hers in the crowd down the other end.

Then suddenly it's all over, and everyone's milling around and switching on their mobiles to take photos of the film crew, and tell all their mates – because they've had to turn them all off, haven't they? So they don't interrupt the filming.

So anyway, Paul switches his phones on too, and one of them beeps straight away to say he's got a message. And it's Ben, except it's not Ben talking, it's Skip on Ben's phone saying the lad's been diving and he hasn't come up.

Paul stares at the phone. He wants to find out when Skip left the message but he can't remember what button to press. How long has he had his phones off? Half an hour, an hour? He calls Ben's number and listens to it ring. Nana's saying something to him, about going over to say hello.

'Shut up!' he snaps as it goes onto voicemail, and there's Ben's voice saying to leave a message.

'Don't you talk to your mam like that,' says Nana.

'Shut up! Shut *up*!' he yells, and strides away from her. He's got to think. Where's the lad been diving? Then it comes to him: White Lady Reef. Of course, he'll have gone looking for the kist.

Once he's on *Wanderer*, it all comes into focus, cold and clear so he knows exactly what he's got to do. He gets on the satellite phone and maydays the

Coastguard, then he gets the engine ticking over and jumps ashore to find Ian. It'll take too long to go back to the flat for his diving gear, so he's after that nature bloke's stuff.

Five minutes later he's pushing off and gunning the *Wanderer*'s engine. Ian's saying something, but he's not listening. He's just concentrating on edging out past the *Tricker* and the rest, and heading out to sea. He checks the fuel gauge; half full, thank God. What was Skip thinking of going out with the lad on his own?

The Coastguard radios back. They're scrambling a Sea King. Can he tell them what happened. 'I don't know. I just got this voicemail. My lad was diving round the reef and he never came up. When I phoned back I couldn't get an answer.'

The engine's screaming at full throttle like a speedboat, the rev needle's hovering as near to the red as Paul dares. He's trying to think back to his diving training, how long it takes for someone to drown. It's not knowing that's the trouble. Maybe Skip's jumped in and dragged the lad up to the surface but can't get back on the boat to reach the phone. Maybe they're just clinging on to the side, shivering.

He relaxes his shoulders a bit and tries to breathe normally. The helicopter's on its way, the boat's going as fast as she can. What about the diving gear? He checks over his shoulder and the nature bloke's nearly finished getting togged up – which isn't what Paul had planned at all. He thought it would be him going down. But now he comes to think about it, how can he? He's the only one who can work the radar and get the boat in close enough.

Ian's there with his camcorder out, filming away. Bastard. Has he got no sense of decency? And the doc's there too, huddled in an old gansey it looks like; must have found it in the cabin.

Paul feels a surge of anger building in his chest. If it wasn't for bloody Ian, if he hadn't been so dead set on going with that other boat, Ben wouldn't have needed to go looking for the body. And the doc too, digging her oar in, messing with everyone's heads.

How long will the Sea King take to get there from – where is it? – RAF Boulmer? How long does it take someone to drown? He keeps going back to that, trying to remember. It's longer than he thought, and longer in cold water for some reason. But it is ten minutes? Twenty? Half an hour?

A picture flashes into his mind of driving Ben to hospital that time, lad bundled up in the duvet on the front seat, face pale as death, blood soaking right through. How long had he been passed out on the kitchen floor before Paul found him? Because he'd left the lad on his own that time too, hadn't he? Nessa had called and they'd had some stupid barny about something, God knows what, so he'd nipped out for a jar to take his mind off it.

He hears the helicopter before he sees it, a sort of throbbing buzz that could be coming from anywhere. Then he spots it, smaller than a bumble bee, heading out to sea from the north – and the speed its going, it's obvious it's going to get there first.

Now Paul thinks he can see old Skip's dinghy, a flash of blue bobbing on a blue sea. 'There she is!' he yells, and Ian and the diving bloke start going, where? where? And it's like watching the filming on the Fish Quay, except this film's called 'Sea Rescue' or something, like one of those action documentaries they're always showing on Channel Five. Because the helicopter's reached the dinghy and is hovering above it, and even at this distance you can see the power of the bloody thing, the great dent it makes in the water, the spray it's kicking up.

Now there's something dangling: a man. They're winching someone down to the dinghy. Paul squints, trying to see. He's got binoculars down below somewhere but he daresn't leave the wheelhouse to get them. Is that someone in the water? Fucking hell, the turbulence that propeller's creating!

He blinks and tries again to focus. Yes! There's someone hanging onto the side of the boat, just like he thought, pale hair plastered to his head. He can't see who it is. The guy on the winch is in diving gear, thank God. He's landed on the dinghy, and he's fiddling about with something. Now he's going in, he's going in…

'He's going in!' someone shouts behind him. It's Ian pointing the camera at the helicopter.

'Has that thing got a zoom?' Paul yells – but of course it has. 'Who's hanging on to the side?' he shouts. 'Can you see?'

Keeping his eye on the viewfinder, Ian shouts something to Mary and she makes her way towards Paul, clinging to the rig, the pulleys, the wires. 'Sorry, Paul. The man clinging to the boat is Mr Skipper. It seems Ben's still in the water.'

Paul looks at his watch, but the numbers don't make any sense. He's no idea how long it's been, how long since he got the message, how long it's taken him to get this far. Nearer now, he can see that of course it's old Skip clinging to the boat – and he's in a bad way by the looks of it.

His satellite phone rings and he clicks on, and it's some bloke on the helicopter telling him to keep away.

'But it's my lad down there!'

'I know you must be concerned, sir, but it's in our hands now. You have to trust that we know what we're doing.'

Paul throttles back and lets the *Wanderer* surge forwards on her own momentum for a while, then stabilizes her on the spot, his eyes fixed on the water where the diver went in, at the winch line loosely swaying in the air.

'What the fuck are you playing at?' yells Ian. 'Can't you get any closer?'

The line straightens and tightens; seconds later the diver breaks the surface with Ben in his arms and is winched up into the helicopter.

'Ben!' Paul shouts.

Was he moving? Was that his feet kicking?

The phone rings again. 'Is he alive?'

'We're administering CPR, sir, but I'm afraid it doesn't look good. Lad's been in the water a long time. We're going to winch the old man on board then take them both to North Tyneside General.'

On the way to the hospital, all Paul can think about is the sight of Ben dangling from that harness, fins trailing, like a fish on a line. And he looks so small, just a tiddler, too young to be caught.

At the A&E it's fucking chaos, of course. People all over the shop: drunk blokes, stupid old ladies, kids. He barges past them at Reception and shouts at the woman there asking where they've taken Ben, but she won't say. Tells him to take a seat, for fuck's sake. Take a bloody seat!

So then Ian has a go and waves his BBC ID at her, and she smiles and asks him to wait while she picks up the phone to call someone. But Paul's seen where she looked first, how her eyes flicked towards some double doors – so he charges off through them. And he's in a wide corridor, with trolleys and that all down it, covered with medical stuff, and drip stands and wheelchairs, and cubicles either side.

He zigzags down the corridor, half running, looking in each cubicle. A nurse tries to talk to him, but he ignores her. Everyone's trying to keep him away from his son and he's fucking not having it.

Then he's reached the end of the corridor, and there's an RAF bloke taking off his jacket, and he's really sweating – why is he sweating? Great dark stains under his arms and down his back – and some bloke in a white coat's bending over Ben and punching his chest with both hands, then counting, then punching his chest again. And someone's sliced into Ben's wetsuit, to get it open, so it's peeled away like a black skin, and inside it there's Ben's narrow flat chest, and his chicken ribs, which look so fragile Paul's worried that doctor bloke's going to crack them.

And Ben's face – the doctor's pinching his little nose now and angling his head back, and blowing into his mouth, and his throat's so pale, the skin seems transparent. And his eyes; you can see the blue veins on his eyelids, and his hair's all matted into salty curls on his forehead.

He looks like a child that's been cut from the belly of a fish. He looks like he's asleep and they're trying to wake him. He looks—

He looks— Sobs crowd into Paul's chest until he can't breathe—

He looks like a girl.

The nurse who tried to stop him before catches Paul by the arm. 'Come away now, sir, let the doctors do their work.'

He lets her pull him back outside the room, but he can't leave. He's fucking not leaving.

They do that thing with wires and clamps he's seen on TV, holding them against Ben's little chicken ribs, and shouting, 'Clear!', making his skinny little body jerk like a baby Frankenstein's monster; and again, 'Clear!'; and again, 'Clear!'.

Then it all stops: the punching, the shouting. The doctor looks at his watch. Why is he looking at his watch?

In the silence Paul can hear a whirring sound behind him. He spins round and there's Ian with his fucking camera: pointing it at Ben, at the doctor looking at his watch – then slowly up to focus on Paul's face.

CHAPTER SIXTY-THREE

2007

Mary watches helplessly as Ian rushes through the swing doors after Paul, ripping open the Velcro on his backpack. She turns to the startled receptionist. 'I'm sorry—' she begins, then wonders why on earth she's apologizing. As Miss Turnbull so aptly pointed out, there's a time to be Mary, and there's a time to be Martha – and if ever there was a time to be Martha, this was surely it.

Hurtling after the two men, she spies Ian standing in an open doorway near the end of a long corridor with his camera on his shoulder. As she comes to a halt behind him, a terrible slow-motion tableau comes into view: Ben lying pale and motionless on a trolley, a doctor turning away from him – and Paul, his face a mask of anguish, lunging at Ian and punching him in the stomach.

Ian crumples to his knees, shielding his damn camera with his body. Paul stands over him, fists clenched, tears pouring down his face, obviously straining every sinew to prevent himself from kicking him. Mary feels like kicking him too.

Then he turns back to Ben and starts to gather the boy into his arms.

'I'm sorry, sir. We can't let you take him,' says a uniformed man Mary hadn't noticed before.

'But we've just finished his room,' Paul says brokenly. 'The blinds are being fitted tomorrow.'

'I'm very sorry, sir. There will have to be a post-mortem.'

Mary leans against the door and takes a long shuddering breath. Ben's dead. She can't take it in. He can't be dead. Not Ben, not her Ben; with his jiggling knees and bony shoulders, his apple-scented hair.

But they're talking about a post-mortem, so he must be.

Eyes burning with tears, Mary stares at the body – 'the body', when does it become 'the body'? She sidles into the room, past Ian scrambling to his feet and backing into the corridor, past the doctor filling in some kind of form. Her need is sudden, desperate, visceral. She has to get closer; she has to touch the boy one last time.

Stealthy and quick as a pick-pocket, she slips around to the far side of the trolley and picks up one of Ben's hands. It's colder than her hand; even through her gloves she can sense that. So she peels them off and chafes his cold hand between her warmer ones.

'Get away from him,' growls Paul. 'Haven't you done enough?'

She replaces Ben's hand and looks up. 'I'm sorry,' she says. 'I was only trying to—'

'Just get out, OK? You and your fucking BBC man. Just leave my lad alone.'

Touching Ben's hand once more – a quick tap, a quick goodbye – Mary turns to leave. And there's Ian again in the doorway, with his camera whirring.

'Turn that *fucking* thing off!' she screams through her tears. And this time she does kick him: on his shin, where it really hurts, as hard as she can.

The adrenaline from her assault on Ian propels her back into the reception area. She glances around wildly at the quiet rows of waiting patients, aware suddenly how she must appear: windswept, tear-stained, distraught. Not knowing what to do next, she blunders into the disabled toilet and locks herself in, then sits down and surrenders to a storm of sobbing so violent it has her retching into the hand basin.

As it abates, and she splashes cold water on her face – marvelling with a numb kind of detachment at how the mind rations the ebbing and flowing of strong emotion – she suddenly remembers poor old Mr Skipper.

'Excuse me,' she says to the bemused receptionist when she emerges, 'I'd like to enquire about the old gentleman that was brought in by the helicopter with Ben Dixon.'

'Can you tell me his name?'

Mary thinks for a moment. 'Everyone refers to him as old Skip, so I've always assumed his name was Mr Skipper.'

The receptionist peers at a computer screen. 'You're not next of kin, then.'

'I'm his doctor – well more of a friend than a doctor. I don't think he has any relatives.'

'There's no Mr Skipper here. You must mean Mr Simpson. Funny sort of friend if you don't know his name.'

'Is he all right?'

'Do you know who his next of kin might be?'

Mary squares her shoulders. 'I'm his therapist,' she says firmly. 'Can I see him?'

'I suppose it's OK. He's been admitted to the medical ward for observation. It says here that he's suffering from hypothermia and it looks like he might have had a slight stroke. They're going to give him a scan.'

The old man's sitting up in bed in a hospital gown. He looks thin and frail without his usual bulky layers of vest, shirt, jumper, anorak; his arms are pale and sinewy, slightly freckled; there are straggly grey hairs at the base of his throat.

'Howay, Doctor,' he says in a slurred voice – the effects of the stroke? 'How's the lad? They won't tell me.'

Mary pulls up a chair. 'He's dead, Mr Skipper.' She hears herself saying the words, but she still can't believe it. 'I'm sorry. I'm sure you did what you could.'

'Oh,' he says, and his whole body seems to sag, like a puppet with its strings cut. 'I went in after him, but I can't swim, see? I never learnt.' He raises a hand in a helpless gesture, then looks down at the other, lying motionless in his lap. 'My arm's not working,' he says, seeming confused. 'And my tongue, or something. I can't get my words out properly.'

Oh dear, Mary thinks: left-sided paralysis as well as dysarthria. All the signs of a right hemisphere stroke. 'Have you had your scan yet?' she asks.

'They just gave me some pills and left me in here,' he says. 'They've put my clothes in a bag in that cupboard. They're all wet.'

'Are those your keys?' Mary asks, though they obviously are. 'Do you want me to fetch you something dry? And some pyjamas, perhaps?'

'How's the patient?' Ian asks, materializing at the foot of the bed. He drags a chair over from beside the startled-looking young man in the next bed. 'You don't mind, mate, do you?' he asks.

'Mr Skipper's had a serious shock,' says Mary heavily, scowling at Ian. 'The doctors are going to give him a scan.'

'Has he told you what happened?'

'I'm not sure that's relevant at the moment.'

'No, you're all right,' slurs the old man. He tries to heave himself up on the pillows, but collapses sideways onto his useless left arm. 'Bloody arm's stopped working,' he says apologetically.

'Are you OK for me to film this?' Ian asks. 'We need to know what Ben was—'

'*Ian!*' Mary rounds on him. This really is the limit.

'It's OK, doctor. If it's about the lad, I don't mind. What do you want to know?'

'Just tell me the whole story in your own words.'

'Well, we'd gone to look for that lass's body. The lad was worried you wouldn't— um— I mean—' He breaks off uncomfortably. 'He thought it would be better to go in with the dinghy. He was doing that breathing thing so he could stay down longer, so I wasn't that bothered to begin with. Then when he didn't come up, I started hauling on the line. But he'd tied it to that kist he was after, hadn't he? I thought it was him I was hauling up, but it was the kist with that lass's body in.'

'So what did you do?'

'Well, soon as I saw it weren't him, I went to drop it back down. But then I thought, what if it lands on the lad? So I hauled it on the boat – damn near killed me, it were that heavy, all crusted with weed and what have you. Then I took off my boots and jumped in after him.

'I didn't know what to do.' He looks pleadingly at Mary. 'I never learnt to swim, see, and I didn't have them goggle things, so I couldn't see properly, and my clothes were dragging me down. So I sort of dived, best I could, and felt around a bit. But it was hopeless, so I came up again and grabbed a hold of the boat and pulled Ben's bag over and got out his phone to call Paul.'

'What happened then?'

'I was going to dial 999 for the Coastguard, but I dropped the phone in the bottom of the boat and I couldn't reach it. I tried and tried.' He starts crying then: rough, ragged sobs, shaking his old body like a fit of coughing. He grabs Mary's arm with his good hand. 'Tell Paul, will you, Doctor? Tell him I was only trying to look out for the lad.'

At this point a solidly built senior nurse bustles over and ushers Ian and his camera out of the ward, explaining firmly that, BBC or not, he will have to speak to the Trust Manager. Mary shakes out a clean handkerchief and hands it to the old man.

'If I hadn't taken him, he'd have gone on his own, see?' he says in his strange new slurred voice. 'Only I couldn't have that, could I? Not after what she done to that Annie.'

Mary tries to focus on what he's saying. 'What do you mean?' she asks gently.

'*She* done it, didn't she? That Flo. That's what I wanted to tell you. It was Annie's blood on her skirt she were trying to clean off. That's what I were seeing that time.'

'Where are you going now?' Ian asks as they make their way out of the hospital.

'I said I'd fetch him some dry clothes.' She shakes the bunch of keys at him. She feels wrung out and numb, slightly nauseous, slightly faint. When was the last time she had a cigarette?

'Let me call a taxi. I'll come with you.'

'Don't be silly.'

'You shouldn't be on your own.'

I'm fine on my own, Mary starts to say, then stops herself. Of course she's 'fine' on her own. But that's not the point, is it? She's been 'fine on her own' for the last thirty-odd years and where has it got her? 'Thank you,' she says instead.

In the taxi he gets out his black phone thingie and makes a series of curt calls about boat charters and coastguards and permissions – to retrieve Mr Skipper's dinghy, presumably, and gain possession of the kist and its contents. As though it's just another logistical problem for him to deal with. As though Ben's death—

Ben's death – the words don't make sense. How can he be dead? She thinks of his guileless blue eyes squinting in the sunlight that first time she hypnotized him; of his breathless pink-cheeked grin as he plonked a bacon roll in her lap; of the poignant narrowness of his shoulders as she wrapped her Indian rug around him. When the taxi windows seem to mist, she realizes she's welling up again. She gets out a fresh hanky to wipe her eyes, but the tears keep on coming: she can't stop them. She blows her nose and Ian looks up.

'Sorry, got to go,' he barks into his phone, then: 'Poor, poor, little Mimi,' he says in a softer voice. 'Come here.' And he gathers her into his arms.

Mary subsides against him and tries to let herself cry properly, but she's too inhibited – or maybe it's too late. And she realizes that the moment has passed – if there ever was a moment – and that she can't possibly consider opening herself up to a man who's prepared to point his camera at a father grieving over his newly dead son. So after a while she disentangles herself and sits up.

Immediately his phone rings; he puts it to his ear without thinking. 'Hold on, I'll pass you over,' he says and hands the phone to Mary.

'Who is this?' she asks.

'I thought you'd be with Ian.' It's Laura.

'How did you get this number?'

'He phoned me once and my phone remembered his number,' says Laura. 'Amazing, these modern contraptions n'est ce pas? Have you heard from Ben? He's still not returning my calls and—'

'Laura, listen. Something terrible's happened. There's been an accident. Ben's dead.'

'What?'

'He went diving for Annie's kist and he drowned. Mr Skipper was with him and he's had a stroke, but I gather the doctors think he might recover.'

'Say that again. I'm not sure I heard you. Did you say that Ben's dead?'

'They couldn't revive him. We've just come from the hospital.'

'Oh God.'

'I know. I still can't believe it.'

'But it's my fault. If I hadn't said where the body was—'

'Assigning blame isn't helpful, Laura,' Mary cuts her off impatiently. 'If anything, it's my fault for letting him witness the session, then allowing him to run off afterwards. You were right; we should have gone after him.'

'Where are you?'

'On the way to Mr Skipper's place to pick up some clothes.'

'I'll meet you there.'

'We'll only be a few minutes.'

'Where then?'

'I'll call you when I know.'

The taxi comes to a halt outside 60 Seymour Street and they get out. Ian pulls out his wallet while Mary sorts through Mr Skipper's bunch of keys for likely candidates. Trying them one by one, she succeeds on her third attempt and pushes the door open over the inevitable heap of special offers and takeaway menus.

They walk through to Mr Skipper's part of the flat. It's very quiet, very still. Feeling like an intruder, Mary goes into his bedroom and starts going through the old man's meagre possessions: a drawer of neatly balled, carefully darned socks – had he darned them himself? – greyish threadbare Y-fronts, string vests, long johns. As she starts laying out a few things on the bed, a wave of sadness sweeps over her so suddenly and powerfully that she falls to her knees and starts sobbing and keening, clutching a striped pyjama top to her chest.

After a while she looks up, and finds Ian standing in the doorway watching her. 'You're right not to trust me,' he says.

'Let's just get these things, shall we?' she says, pulling out her hanky again.

'I did go to bed with Hester.'

'Ben's *dead*, Ian,' she says tiredly, blowing her nose again. 'Can't we talk about this another time?' But she knows they won't, because it doesn't matter any more. Hester doesn't matter any more. Ian doesn't matter any more. Ben's was the soul she really cared for all along.

Later, when she's packed the clothes into a plastic bag and is en route to the bathroom on a quest for toiletries, Ian calls Mary into the conservatory.

'Hey, come and look at this,' he says. 'It's quite extraordinary.'

He's staring at the easel with an unfinished portrait of a young woman on it. Looking into the woman's eyes, Mary gets the strongest sense of déjà vu she has ever experienced.

'It's Peggy,' she whispers, drawing closer. 'Peggy Simpson. That's her scarf. And that lipstick, and the way she's plucked her eyebrows. Every detail – how could he possibly know?'

'So who's Peggy Simpson when she's at home?' Ian asks, then: 'Oh, right. I remember. One of your previous incarnations. And old Skip just happens to have caught her exact likeness, without nicking any photos from those open access filing cabinets at the local library.'

Mary stands back and looks at the painting from a distance. Is it possible she's mistaken? But how can she be, when she's seen that face so many times in the mirror, applying that red lipstick again and again – three, four, five times a day – every time some strange mouth wiped it off? No, it's definitely Peggy – how very peculiar. She resolves to ask Mr Skipper about it. But first things first: she has to find where he keeps his razor and toothbrush.

'Can you call a taxi on that magic gizmo of yours?' she asks, coming out of the bathroom a few minutes later. Then: 'What on earth are you doing now?' She sighs with exasperation as Ian points his camera at the painting. Really the man is incorrigible.

'You know what? I honestly have no idea,' he says quietly, lowering the camera and switching it off. 'But there's something about her, isn't there? She looks so familiar. If I didn't know better I could swear I've seen that face before somewhere.'

'Presumably we've all stolen her photo from the library,' Mary says drily.

* * *

After they've dropped off Mr Skipper's clothes at the hospital, Ian instructs the taxi to take them to the Fish Quay. 'Viv says the Coastguard won't let us fetch the dinghy,' he explains. 'It's a potential crime scene, apparently, so they're impounding it until after the post-mortem.'

'What about the kist?' Mary asks.

'That's where we're going now,' he says. 'We're going to film them towing it in. Then I'll see if I can persuade the Coastguard to delay opening it until we can get a proper forensic archaeologist involved.'

'Can I borrow your phone to call Laura?' Mary asks as they turn off Tynemouth Road, heading down the hill to the harbour. It goes straight to voicemail, so she leaves another message. 'We're heading to the Fish Quay,' she says. 'There's been a change of plan. Why don't you meet us there?'

Mary stands alone on the quayside with the wind in her face and her shawl wrapped around her. Ian wants to film her gazing out to sea as the Coastguard vessel comes into view, towing Mr Skipper's little blue dinghy behind it.

Her first impulse was to refuse, but she can't muster the energy for the requisite amount of indignation. What does it matter anyway? What does anything matter now? Tears stinging her cheeks, she allowed him to position her, like some overwrought book-cover illustration, as the Coastguard boat chunters slowly in to the Gut. There are only three fishing boats moored up, so it's a straightforward manoeuvre. How different from the jostling and pushing apart Annie described when the *Osprey* docked in 1898 to report that Sam had been lost overboard.

In the dinghy, lashed to the seat, is a large vaguely box-shaped object covered with deep-sea detritus. It looks like a rock at low tide, bristling with peculiar algae and calciferous forms of life. It looks like what it has become: a part of the sea bed.

CHAPTER SIXTY-FOUR

2007

Paul doesn't remember exactly how he got back to the flat. He's got a vague image of some social worker type, trying to get him to sit somewhere, sign something, phone someone. It was fucking doing his head in, so he barged out and grabbed a taxi, chucked a twenty at the driver. But now he's home he wishes he was back at the hospital. At least he'd be near Ben, what's left of him.

What do other people do? Drink fucking tea. Sit around mythering. Fuck that.

His phone beeps with another message from Nana asking why they rushed off. He chucks it on the sofa. What good would she be? Wailing and flapping about, wanting to know every detail, filling the flat with her fucking cronies.

He paces around the flat, one room after another, like he's looking for something. The cupboard's open in the spare room; the Aquapulse's missing from its box. Ben's wetsuit's gone from its hanger in the shower. If Paul had bothered to check in here he'd have known what the lad was planning.

He wanders down the corridor to Ben's bedroom and tries the door. Locked, of course; always fucking locked. He bangs on it with the flat of his hand, like he's always done when he wants to go in; then bangs with the other hand; then rests his forehead on the door, eyes stinging with tears, trying to imagine that Ben's still inside – on the computer maybe, playing that weird house-building game with that fake family. Sims, that was it; cost a fortune, all the bloody updates and expansion packs: Sims go on holiday, Sims garden makeover, Sims shopping mall.

He slaps the door again, with both hands, then he does what he's stopped himself from doing ever since the lad started locking it: he kicks it open.

Ben's smell wafts out to meet him; that posh shampoo he always uses. Paul hesitates; it feels wrong to step over the threshold without being invited, like he's a vampire or something and the lad's put a spell on the room. Especially now it's all painted, like it's really his space.

The window's open still, to let the paint smell out, and the sun's blazing in. Ben's duvet's crumpled, where he's sat to put his trainers on; there's a little bum-shaped dent there. And his old PE bag's sticking out from under the bed, like he's been looking for something and not shoved it back properly.

Paul tugs it out. Why's the zip half open? He thought this old bag had gone to Oxfam years ago. Inside is something pale and flowery. What the *fuck*?

Pulling it out, Paul sees that it's a nightdress: flimsy pretty little thing; size 10, 100 percent cotton. Marks and Spencer. And underneath is that fucking stupid cuddly toy – what did Ben call it? – Lily the Pink. Lad saw it in Fenwick's one Christmas and Nessa got it for him. They had a right bust-up about it, too, with Paul trying to get her to take it back, or at least get the lad something that wasn't fucking *pink*, for God's sake.

What else has he got stashed in here? Paul empties the bag out on the floor: knickers, must be about twenty fucking pairs; polka dots, little hearts, lacy edges, all colours. When's he been wearing them, then? Hasn't been putting them in his washing basket, that's for sure. Another nightie; couple of lacy vest things and matching pyjama bottoms. An unopened packet of 'almost bare' tights, for fuck's sake.

He pulls open a drawer and it's full of navy and blue Y-fronts and socks; normal boy's stuff, thank God. The next one's T-shirts and jeans. So he's got one set of proper clothes in their proper places, and another secret stash of girlie gear.

Now Paul's started, he can't stop. It's like when he found out about Nessa and her bloke: he had to go through everything – dirty knickers, credit card statements, the lot – to see how bad it was.

In the lad's en-suite, behind the loo rolls in the cupboard, he finds a couple of innocent-looking toilet bags. But inside they're crammed with make-up and that: foundation, blusher, eyeshadow in those little palette things Nessa used to go in for. And loads of other gear he doesn't even recognize. Remover this, moisturizer that. Nail varnish, eyeliners, lipsticks.

Half an hour later the room's a right tip, but he's satisfied he's searched everywhere: under the bed, under the mattress, inside the pillow cases, back of the wardrobe. He's had all the drawers out to see if there's anything taped to the back; been though all the lad's pockets. There's just one thing left, and that's the computer.

While he's waiting for it to boot up and sort itself out, he starts putting stuff away again. He feels disgusted with himself, like when he's been on some naff porn site or eaten four Kit Kats in a row. It's like he had to find out, but now he has, there's a part of him wishes he'd left it all alone.

The computer gives a little chirp to say it's ready and he sits down at Ben's chair and clicks on 'bookmarks' and 'history'. And there it is, the lad's secret life, all mapped out. Support for transsexual kids, hormones to delay puberty, causes of gender dysphoria, legal aid for underage children, plastic surgery. The list goes on and on. Sites about decommissioning fishing boats and emigration to New Zealand, sites about sustainable fishing, about diving off Norway and Iceland.

Why didn't the lad say anything? But Paul knows why; it's bleeding obvious why. Because his father wouldn't listen, that's why. The lock on that door – it's not Ben who's locked him out, it's him who's refused to come in.

Turning the computer off, Paul surveys the room. Everything's back where it was; the drawers and cupboards are closed; the old PE bag's back under the bed; the duvet's fluffed up and straightened.

He stares at the bed and his breath catches in his throat: because the dent's gone now, of course, hasn't it? He's gone and fluffed it up out of existence. That little hollow where Ben sat this morning putting his shoes on, the last sign he had left of the lad – and he's gone and destroyed it.

Desperate for something else, Paul grabs the lad's pillow and buries his face in it, breathing in over and over, trying to catch the smell of Ben's neck, his scalp, his hair. Then he drags the PE bag back out and hugs Lily the Pink to his chest, and thinks of Ben secretly cuddling her at night, and lies down on the bed and sobs and sobs until he can't breathe; then gets up and stumbles to the en-suite for loo roll, and blows his nose and swipes at his face; then simply staggers around the room, half blinded by tears. He doesn't know what to do, where to put himself; like when you're stotting drunk and throwing up, flailing out of control. Or like the boat in a squall, flung around by the waves.

At one point, in a fit of fury, he flings the damn cuddly toy across the room as hard as he can, then stares shocked at the pathetic way it looks splayed face-down on the carpet. And picks her up, and lays her on Ben's pillow, and lies down beside her.

* * *

Hours later he gets up and goes into the sitting room. He's got to tell Nana; he can't put it off for ever. And the lads, to cancel the next trip. And Dougie, to get started on the funeral arrangements. Reaching for the phone, he realizes he's carrying Lily the Pink, so he sets her down carefully in Ben's place on the sofa.

Sitting down beside her, he tries to remember the last time he sat here with the lad. Last night, wasn't it? Lad was trying to get him to come on that diving trip with him. He can almost hear him: 'Please, Dad, just you and me. It would be really cool.' And he'd turned the lad down.

And sent him off to dive by himself, with an old alky for a buddy – a mad old alky who can't even swim.

What's the bairn doing hanging out with old Skip in the first place? What kind of mate's that for a lad of twelve? A mad old alky, a trannie and a shrink. What a way to spend your summer hols. Except he claimed he was happy, didn't he? That evening with that weird crowd at the Low Lights, or charging up the stairs just full of that research they were doing at the library – lad was practically glowing. And what did his loving bloody father do? Tried to put a stop to it. Tried to get him to forget all about it, made him shove it back under the bed.

Paul picks up Lily. He'd tried to make Ben get shot of her too, hadn't he? Now he'd do anything to have the lad back as he was, frilly nighties and all.

The phone goes and it's Nana again. He clicks it off without answering and wanders back into Ben's room. He tucks Lily under the duvet, then changes his mind and brings her back into the sitting room. He goes to the fridge and pops a can of Stella, then upends it in the sink after two gulps.

Wandering back out into the hall, he finds himself by the little table and pulls the drawer open. There's the letter with Ben's DNA results, under the *Yellow Pages*. He takes it out, like he's done a dozen times before. He could open it now, couldn't he? Find out if the lad's his own flesh and blood. Put an end to it once and for all.

He takes the letter into the sitting room and places it in the middle of the coffee table. Then he sits down and looks at it. All he has to do is rip it open and he'll know for sure. Without thinking, he reaches for Lily and holds her in his lap, then presses his nose between her ears, breathing in her Ben-smell. And it occurs to him that it doesn't matter what the fucking letter says. Ben was his son; Ben will always be his son. It's just taken him till now to find out.

* * *

It's dark by the time he gets to the doctor's house, and the lights seem to be off, but he bangs on the door anyway, then finds a bell and rings it. He doesn't care if she's in bed. He's got to speak to her.

Pressing his face against a glass panel, he sees a shaft of light down the end of the hall, a door opening. He rings the bell again, for good measure, then stands back as more lights come on and first the inner door, then the porch door opens.

She's fully dressed still, with a dressing-gown over her clothes, and sheepskin slippers. And she's been crying. In fact she looks a complete mess: puffy eyes, blotchy cheeks, smudgy mouth; and that chapped red nose you get when you've been blowing it a lot. What's she so upset about? Then it comes to him: of course, Ben. He's spent half the summer at her place. She's crying about Ben.

'Mr Dixon,' she says, like she's been expecting him. Or maybe she's just too upset to care. 'Come in, please.' She seems dazed, really out if it. 'Can I offer you a whisky?' she asks, gesturing vaguely, obviously just going through the motions. 'Ian kindly furnished me with a bottle before he left. His idea was that I should make a hot toddy. He provided a lemon, too. But I haven't the slightest idea how to go about it.'

She leads the way into her so-called consulting room and switches on the light, then winces and switches it off again. 'This small light's a bit kinder, I think,' she says. 'And the fire. Please—' pointing towards the sofa. 'Sit down while I fetch us some glasses.'

Paul parks himself on the edge of the sofa, then gets up again and roams around the little room. He picks up a wooden elephant, then puts it back in its place.

She returns with a bottle of Glenmorangie and two unmatched crystal glasses on a tray. 'Do you want water? I'm told a little splash brings out the flavour. I prefer the raw hit myself.' She pours out two triples and hands him one.

Paul takes a big gulp; it burns the back of his throat. 'Tell me about Ben,' he says.

'What do you want to know?'

'Anything. Everything.'

'I can let you have the tapes from his sessions if you like. They'll fill you in about Annie and perhaps help you understand something of his desire for a sex change.'

'But it wasn't just the sessions, was it? He's been practically living here all summer. Either here or at that caff place.'

'He was – he became – almost a part of the family.' Her eyes fill with tears and she pulls a soggy hanky from her dressing-gown pocket. Taking a mouthful of her drink, she tries to pull herself together. 'I think it was important to Ben to be amongst people who knew his secret and accepted him regardless,' she says in a steadier voice.

Paul stares into the fake flames on the fire. 'I thought if we never talked about it, it would go away.'

'He loved you very much, Mr Dixon, I do know that. And he admired you tremendously. For years he tried to be the son you wanted him to be.'

'I let him down.'

'Don't be too hard on yourself.'

'No, I should have been with him. It's the first thing they teach you when you learn to dive: never go down without your buddy. First fucking rule.' He starts crying again, knocking the tears away with the back of his arm.

She takes out a fresh white hanky from somewhere and shakes it open, then lays it on his knee like a waiter in a posh restaurant. Picking it up, Paul suddenly feels like laughing. Talk about the Dark Ages. Hasn't the woman heard of Kleenex?

'I found all this stuff he was hiding in his room,' he says. 'And I realized there's this whole side of him I never knew.'

She opens her hands in her lap. 'There's nothing I'd like more than to talk about Ben, Paul. He became very important to me—'

The phone rings suddenly in the hall, one of those old-fashioning *dring-drings* that go right through you.

'Sorry about this,' she says. 'It'll stop soon, I expect.' But it doesn't, and there's no sign of an answerphone kicking in either. So after about twenty rings, she goes out into the hall to answer it. 'Hello? Dr Charlton speaking,' she says. Then, 'Hello? Hello? Is there anyone there?'

'How very strange,' she says, hanging up. 'It sounded like there was someone crying, but they wouldn't speak to me.'

'Try dialling 1471,' Paul suggests.

'What?'

Is she joking? 'Last number recall. Haven't you read *Bridget Jones*? It's a number you can dial to find out who's just phoned you.'

'How amazing. Will it work on my phone? What was it again?'

'One-four-seven-one,' he repeats slowly, while she presses the buttons. 'Right, now just listen.'

'It's Laura's mobile number,' she says, looking worried. 'I hope she's all right. Excuse me, Mr Dixon. Please bear with me. I think I ought to call her back.'

She dials the number. 'Laura, is that you? It's Mary here. Are you all right?' She listens intently, then: 'OK, well you'd better go and be sick then – yes, yes. I'll wait here – yes, off you go then.'

With the phone still clamped to her ear, she turns to Paul. 'She's rather the worse for wear, I'm afraid,' she says. 'In fact I've never known her like this before – she's normally rather an abstemious drinker. I wonder how much she's had.'

She listens intently for a few minutes, then: 'This is ridiculous. I can't hear a thing. She might have passed out for all I know.' She hangs up the phone, looking distracted for a moment. Then: 'I'm so sorry about this, Mr Dixon, but I think I'll have to go to her. If she's passed out in that state she could inhale vomit and suffocate.' Shrugging off her dressing gown, she goes charging up the stairs and clomps down again a minute later all togged up in boots and a duffle coat.

'Oh dear, this is terrible,' she says, dithering in the hall. 'I can't leave you like this. Can I call someone? What about your mother?'

'She doesn't know yet. I couldn't face telling her – she'd just go on and on.'

'You're more than welcome to stay—'

'No, I'll give you a lift. Come on, the car's just outside.'

He doesn't know why he's offered to drive her. He doesn't even know why he's come to see her, not really. He just wants to understand as much as he can of Ben's life – he owes him that much at least. To make up for – well, anyway it's what the lad would have wanted, what he deserves.

'I'm so grateful for this,' says the doc, fumbling with her seat belt as they set off. 'She's probably fine, but there's a real danger of alcohol poisoning too, if someone's not used to drinking.'

'What's set her off then?' Paul asks. He's trying to sound sympathetic, but it's sticking in his craw a bit.

'I expect she's blaming herself for what happened to Ben.'

'How's the fuck's Laura to blame for Ben?'

'Oh, a host of reasons. For telling us where the body was for a start. If it hadn't been for her, he'd never have gone diving on that reef. And it was Laura who set the ball rolling in the first place, by introducing Ben to me, then taking him on at the salon.'

Paul hardly dares ask. 'What salon's that then?'

'Salon Laura – above the café. I'm sorry, Paul. I assumed you knew. It's a beauty salon for transvestites. Ben used to go there to help with the clothes. I don't know the details – that was between the two of them – but I think Laura was teaching him deportment, how to put on make-up, that sort of thing. She's something of a specialist.'

He takes a deep breath. 'Go on.'

'There's nothing more to say, really. Laura was Ben's friend, that's all – probably one of the few really close friends he had.'

When he pulls up in front of the house, the curtains are drawn but there's a light on upstairs. The doctor rings the doorbell, then pushes opens the letterbox to listen. Paul edges between a collection of overflowing plant pots to see if he can find a crack between the curtains – but all he can see is folds of red velvet.

'I'll nip round the back,' he says. 'See if the kitchen door's unlocked.'

He takes a note of the number and trots along to the end of the terrace, then counts the houses back, like he used to when he was breaking and entering with the lads. Then he hoists himself up on a wheelie bin, and vaults over the wall down into the yard on the other side. Thirty seconds later he's in. He turns the light on in the hall, then checks the lounge – red velvet all over the show, flowery this, lacy that, like a posh brothel – before letting the doc in through the front door.

'There's no one downstairs,' he says. 'Shall I look upstairs, or do you want to go first?'

'Let's go together, shall we?'

The whole of the upstairs stinks of alcohol and puke. Paul pushes open the door to the front bedroom. 'She's in here,' he says.

The bedside lamp's been knocked over and there's spilt wine on the carpet. Laura's on the floor, spread-eagled in a pink negligee. There's a puddle of vom by her head.

'Looks like she's had a right skinful,' he says, wrinkling his nose.

The doc kneels down and feels for a pulse. 'She's still alive, thank God. Laura? Laura, please try to wake up.' She looks at him. 'I think she's unconscious.'

'Do you want me to call an ambulance?

'No, wait. I think she's coming round. Laura? It's me, Mary.'

'Is that *Dr* Mary?'

'Yes, Laura. Let's get you sitting up, shall we? Mr Dixon, can you pass me that dressing-gown?'

'Dr Mary, you've got to help me.'

'That's what I'm here for, darling.'

'You've got to phone a ghost man for me.'

'What ghost man?'

'I need a ghost man to get him out of me.'

'Get who out of you, Laura? What are you talking about?'

'Evil spirit. In here.' Laura thumps her own chest with her fist. 'Tom's evil spirit.' She claws at herself, as if trying to rip her skin apart.

The doc turns to Paul. 'I think she's asking for an exorcist,' she explains. 'She seems to believe she's possessed.' Then, 'Oh dear,' she comments in dismay as Laura voms up another load on the carpet.

Rinsing out the cloth again and tipping the contents of another bucket down the bog, Paul wonders how he's ended up in a trannie's house in the middle of the night mopping up puke and talking about exorcists. They've got Laura washed and huddled on a chair in the red velvet sitting room, with a bowl handy in case she feels like hurling again. The doc's got the coffee-maker going and he's sorting out the upstairs. The doc tried to stop him, but he said he was used to it, with the 'prentice lads on the boat – there's forever one of them seasick or pissed or something. And it's something to do, isn't it? Scrubbing at that pink carpet. Something to fill his head, fill his hands, stop him thinking for a few minutes. Stop it hurting so much; stop him blubbing; stop him fucking *smashing* something.

'Mr Dixon!' calls the doc from the bottom of the stairs. 'Coffee's ready if you want it.'

He looks at his watch: three o-fucking-clock in the morning. Twelve hours since he put in that mayday call. He swills out the bucket and comes downstairs. It looks like Laura's perking up a bit; she's got her hands round a flowery mug, sipping away – is everything pink in this bloody place? But the doc looks completely washed out.

He slumps on the other armchair and leans back, closing his eyes.

'Do you believe in evil spirits?' Laura's asking the doc.

'You know I don't,' says the doc. 'I think that cases of so-called "spirit possession" are better understood as the intrusions of past-life personalities into a current incarnation.'

'It's just that I keep thinking that Tom's in *here* somewhere.' Laura thumps her chest again.

'He *is* in there, Laura. But not like that, not as an alien entity that has to be punished or exorcized. You can't exorcize him – he's a part of you.'

Now Laura starts crying, he can hear her with his eyes closed, weird little gasping sobs, then the sound of her blowing into another of the doc's hankies. 'Would it help to know that it now seems likely that Tom wasn't the one who killed Annie after all?' asks the doc. 'According to Mr Skipper, it was Flo who stabbed her.'

Paul opens his eyes a slit. Now what's she on about? He'd almost forgotten about all that past-life crap.

'Tom still shoved that poor lad overboard though, didn't he?' says Laura. 'And raped Annie and got rid of the body. It's still my fault that Ben's dead.'

Suddenly Paul's had enough. 'Look, shut up about it being your fault, OK? How can it possibly be your fault? Ben's known you for what? Four, five weeks? That's fucking *nothing. Nothing.* I've known him his whole *life*!' And now the tears are coming again, hot on his cheeks. 'If anyone's to blame for his death, it's me. He asked me to go diving with him and I turned him down. It's my fault he was down there on his own, not yours. It's my fault he drowned.'

The doc's pulled back the curtains and it's fucking *light* outside. And when she nips out for a tab this great wave of birdsong comes crashing in through the front door to rub his nose in it. Paul feels like he's been trapped in this frilly little overstuffed room for days; but every time he thinks about leaving, he pictures Ben helping out at the caff, Ben hiding his flowery knickers, Ben trying out all those different eyeshadows and wiping them off again before anyone can see. And he makes himself sit there with it – with him – for a bit longer.

'So what kind of stroke was it?' he asks when the doc comes back in. She's been filling him in about old Skip.

'He's paralysed down his left side, but I think it's probably temporary. He wanted me to let you know how sorry he is for taking Ben to the reef.'

'Seems like everyone thinks it's their fault,' Paul comments. Then he gets up and puts on his jacket. 'I'd better go and see him then, hadn't I? Set the poor old sod straight about a few things.'

CHAPTER SIXTY-FIVE

2007

On the way to the Preston Road cemetery, Mary stares out of the taxi window. The children have gone back to school. There they are, trailing along the streets in their uniforms, scuffing through the first of the autumn leaves, everything about them proclaiming their reluctance to return to captivity.

Ian's gone on ahead; Paul's given him permission to film the service, provided it's just him in the chapel, 'not that whole fucking circus'. Strange how we've all cohered since Ben's death, Mary reflects, as though our connection, as long as it lasts, will somehow keep the boy with us – though perhaps it's not so strange when one comes to think about it.

The cemetery comes into view, a long wall she'd somehow never noticed before, and behind it: acres and acres of the dead of North Shields. Is Peggy buried here? How could she not be? And Tom and Lord Jim; Miss Turnbull, Dory and Henry; and Flo, pulled from the ruins of that terrible bombed factory with her daughters. And Sam. If she searched, would she find a gravestone for him too? Is there a pauper's corner in this graveyard?

The taxi turns in through the entrance and drives slowly through the grounds, past roses, clipped box hedges, great trees towering over the graves, their roots creeping gently between ribs and into skull cavities, binding the living to the dead.

The chapel's tiny – as a kindness to those with fewer mourners, perhaps – so it's quite a squash to get everyone inside. And that's a good thing, Mary thinks, watching fishermen shuffling along to make room for waitresses from Café Laura and boys from Ben's football team at school.

Ian's stationed himself at the end of the centre aisle, at the back with his camera. There's music playing, some slow pop ballad Mary doesn't recognize. When did that become acceptable, she wonders. Don't people play hymns any more? Laura nudges her and whispers, 'I chose this one. He used to have it on all the time at the salon.'

The vicar – Mary presumes it's the vicar – starts to speak, then invites Paul to say a few words. Mary forces herself to gaze at the coffin: small and smothered with flowers, its size alone brings an ache to her throat. Swallowing hard, she closes her eyes and pictures the bodies inside: Ben's stitched up after the post-mortem's Y incision; Annie's an untidy bundle of powdery bones in a new linen bag. Tears seep out between her eyelids and she reaches into her pocket for a clean hanky.

How would Ben have reacted, she wonders, if he'd been there the day they opened the kist. And seen those crumbling rags of old canvas, the fragments of skirt and shawl, that gossamer web of dark hair that dissolved almost as soon as they looked at it. If he'd seen Annie's remains, would he still have insisted on a sex change? How might his journey have ended? Except the journey of a soul never ends, she knows that. He could be reincarnating again at this very moment.

Paul's finished speaking now and is beckoning Laura to the front of the chapel. 'I've told you all about the Ben that I knew, the Ben who made us proud. But there was another side to the lad that I never knew about – not until after he died, really. As soon as he could speak, Ben wanted to be a girl. He kept his feelings secret, but they never went away. And this summer, for the first time, he found someone to talk to about them. Laura, can you say something about the Ben that you knew?'

Mary exchanges a smile with Mr Skipper, beside her in his wheelchair – she can't get used to calling him Mr Simpson – as Laura launches into a typically exaggerated account of her early encounters with Ben and their vain attempts to get Mary into the sea.

Then it's Mary's turn. She can feel Ian's camera behind her as she squeezes out into the aisle and makes her way to the front of the chapel.

'Most of you have probably heard that Ben's is not the only death we're mourning today, and his is not the only body in this coffin.' She places a hand on the coffin; the blonde wood is warm to the touch. 'Ben drowned trying to recover the remains of a young woman he believed he shared a soul with. Her name was Annie Milburn, and she died in 1898 at the age of sixteen.

'Ben's father has been kind enough – and open-minded enough – to allow Annie's bones to be cremated with Ben's body, and their ashes scattered together on the White Lady Reef, where her body was found.

'Annie was a beautiful, ebullient young woman, who embraced life with unusual vigour and enthusiasm. It was almost as if she knew that it would be taken away from her. I believe it was Annie's sheer love of life that charmed and ensnared Ben's soul and made him want to be a girl. Ben once described himself as holding hands with Annie in his life, so it seems appropriate that they should be together again today.'

The post-funeral party was still in full swing at Paul's flat when Mary slipped out. The combination of Laura's food and Paul's drink, and Ian darting around with his camera whirring, ensured that no one wanted to leave. Mr Skipper, still resolutely teetotal, was clutching a Diet Coke with his good hand and explaining the vagaries of lobster-trapping to a rapt audience of young footballers. Ben's grandmother had backed Ian's PA into a corner and was insisting drunkenly on the merits of a documentary about the knitting of traditional ganseys. Ian himself was being almost insufferably cock-a-hoop following the news that 'the suits' – whoever they are – had approved 'the rushes' – whatever *they* are – and had decided to commission the whole series.

And Paul and Laura – well, what can she say? Against all the odds, Paul and Laura would appear to have become – No, not friends. Not quite, not yet. But definitely on a road heading in that direction. Mary smiles. Amazing what cleaning up a bit of vomit will do to create a bonding experience.

If only Ben could have seen the two of them bumping into one another in the kitchen, jostling amiably over access to the oven, the sink, the fridge. If only he could have been there too. She can picture him arranging hot crostini and sausage rolls on plates, all pink cheeks and greasy fingers; then handing them round – that solemn determined expression he'd get on his face when he was concentrating. A familiar surge of grief washes through her. A few precious weeks, that's all she'd had with him. A crash course in – what? Tenderness? Motherhood? Love?

Walking along the top bank to her house, Mary supposes she should have stayed to help with the clearing up. But once she'd said her piece at the cemetery, all she wanted to do was escape back to her quiet familiar world of books and clients and Italian coffee. And her thoughts about Ben. He had softened her somehow: made her less twiggish and snappy. More open; more hungry for experience.

She quickens her pace, energized suddenly. Her consulting room is waiting. At last, at last, she's been allowed to open her curtains and reclaim her comfortable cluttered territory. Striding along in the sunshine, she makes a list in her mind of all the diverting activities she's been denied these last few months: that intriguing new heap of books she has to review, the masochism paper she wants to write, that long-postponed visit to Karleen to explore Sam's life and that of her other fisherman forebear.

In the distance a flotilla of little yachts is setting out from the sailing club at South Shields and scattering like confetti on the water. Perhaps I'll join a sailing club, she thinks – and the idea amuses her so much that she laughs aloud. So Ben forced her to conquer her thalassaphobia after all, though not in the way he'd intended.

Her house hoves into view, a seagull perched on the cupola, and she quickens her pace. Yes: a double espresso and a pristine pad of lined A4, that's what she wants. And solitude: precious, luxurious solitude.

The woman gets to her feet as Mary opens the gate. She's pregnant, Mary notices at once. Probably not that far gone, but on such a slender frame the hard high bump is unmistakable.

'Can I help you?' Mary asks, only mildly irritated.

'I am coming here for the room. There was advertisement in the paper.'

Damn, Mary thinks. She'd intended to cancel that advert. 'How did you know where to come?' she asks.

'I am sorry?' The woman looks confused.

'The address. Who gave you my address?'

'I telephoned the number and a lady told it to me.'

Damn, damn. Mary sighs with annoyance: this must be Laura's doing.

'I am sorry. This is a bad time, yes?' The woman turns to go.

'No, no. Please – sit down. Would you like a cup of something? Coffee? Tea?'

The woman sits down on the edge of the bench. She looks Asian – Indian, perhaps? 'I was thinking I will walk to see the house. Then I like it so much! So

I am waiting here until you come home.' She spreads her slim hands in apology. She reminds Mary of one of the housekeepers at that Ashram in Chennai. 'I like the sea very much,' the woman adds shyly. 'I think the sea will be very good for my baby.'

Oh dear, Mary thinks. A baby. A lodger and a baby.

She sits down beside the woman and takes out her Gitanes. Then she puts them away again.

Damn.

FURTHER READING

REINCARNATION

For latest research in this field, see recent editions of the *Journal of the American Society for Psychical Research* and the *Journal of Scientific Exploration.*

12 Real Life Reincarnation Stories in the News: global evidence of reincarnation and past lives, ed. Richard Bullivant, Kindle edition, 2012

'A critique of arguments offered against reincarnation', by Robert Almeder, *Journal of Scientific Exploration*, vol. 11, 1997

An Introduction to Jungian Psychology, by Frieda Fordham, London: Penguin, 1953

Introduction to Buddhism: an explanation of the Buddhist way of life, by Geshe Kelsang Gyatso, London: Tharpa, 1992

Life Before Life: a scientific investigation of children's memories of previous lives, by Jim B. Tucker, London: Piatkus, 2006

Many Lives, Many Masters, by Brian L. Weiss, London: Piatkus, 1994

Mindsight: near death and out-of-body experiences in the blind, by Kenneth Ring and Sharon Cooper, New York: iUniverse, 2008

Old Souls: the scientific evidence for past lives, by Tom Shrouder, London: Simon and Schuster, 1999

On Life After Death, by Elisabeth Kübler-Ross, Berkeley, CA: Celestial Arts, 2008

Only Love is Real: the story of soulmates reunited, by Brian Weiss, London: Piatkus, 1996

Other Lives, Other Selves: a Jungian psychotherapist discovers past lives, by Roger J. Woolger, London: Thorsons, 1999

Proof of Heaven: a neurosurgeon's journey into the afterlife, by Eben Alexander, London: Piatkus, 2012

Reincarnation: a critical examination, by Paul Edwards, Amherst, NY: Prometheus Books, 1996

Synchronicity: an acausal connecting principle, by C.G. Jung, tr. R.F.C. Hull, London: Routledge and Kegan Paul, 1955

The Tibetan Book of the Dead, tr. Gyurme Dorje, ed. Graham Coleman with Thuuten Jinpa, London: Penguin, 2005

Twenty Cases Suggestive of Reincarnation, by Ian Stevenson, Charlottesville, VA: University of Virginia Press, 1974

Wisdom of Near-Death Experiences: how understanding NDEs can help us to live more fully, by Penny Sartori, London: Watkins Publishing, 2014

LANGUAGE

A Dictionary of North East Dialect, by Bill Griffiths, Newcastle upon Tyne, Northumbria University Press, 2004

Fantabulosa: a dictionary of Polari and gay slang, by Paul Baker, London: Continuum, 2002

Fishing and Folk: life and dialect on the North Sea coast, compiled by Bill Griffiths, Newcastle upon Tyne, Northumbrian University Press, 2008

The Newcastle Electronic Corpus of Tyneside English (NECTE), Newcastle University, www.ncl.ac.uk/necte

Northumberland Words: a glossary of words used in the county of Northumberland and on Tyneside, vols. 1 and 1i, by Richard Oliver Heslop, London: published for the English Dialect Society by Kegan Paul, Trench, Trübner & Co., 1892–4

VICTORIAN LIFE

A Woman's Place: an oral history of working-class women 1890–1940, by Elizabeth Roberts, Oxford: Basil Blackwell, 1984

Late Victorian Britain 1875–1901, by J.F.C. Harrison, London: Fontana, 1990

The Classic Slum: Salford life in the first quarter of the century, by Robert Roberts, London: Penguin, 1973

The Dillen: memories of a man of Stratford-upon-Avon, ed. Angela Hewins, London: Elm Tree Books, 1981

LOCAL HISTORY

Cullercoats, by Ron White, The People's History Ltd, 2002

Images of England: North Shields, by Eric Hollerton, Stroud: Tempus, 1997

Images of England: Tynemouth and Cullercoats, by John Alexander, Stroud: Tempus, 1999

Inns and Taverns of North Shields, by Charlie Steel, Stroud: Tempus, 2007

North Shields: living with industrial change, by North Tyneside Community Development Project (CDP), vol. 2, London: Home Office, 1978

North Shields: women's work, by North Tyneside CDP, vol. 5, London: Home Office, 1978

Ordinary Lives a Hundred Years Ago, by Carol Adams, London: Virago, 1982

The Life and Times of Francie Nichol of South Shields, Francie Nichol, as told to Joe Robinson, London: Allen and Unwin, 1975

FISHING AND DIVING

A Brief History of Royal National Mission to Deep Sea Fishermen, North Shields, 1899–2001

A Drifterman's Diary: an account of herring fishing in Norfolk in the days of sail and steam, by J.E. Holmes, Yarmouth: 1994

Beyond the Piers, by Ron White, The People's History Ltd, 2002

Deep Sea Voices: recollections of women in our fishing communities, by Craig and Jenny Lazenby, Stroud: Tempus, 1999

Dive the North East Coast, by Peter Collings, Deep Lens Publishing, 1986

Following the Fishing: the days when bands of Scots fisher girls followed the herring fleets round Britain and scores of trades depended on the harvest of the sea, by David Butcher, Newton Abbot: Tops'l books, 1987

Hello Sailor!: the hidden history of gay life at sea, by Paul Baker and Jo Stanley, London: Longman, 2003

Herring Girls and Hiring Fairs: memories of Northumberland coast and countryside, by Maureen Brook, Newcastle upon Tyne: Tyne Bridge, 2005

Living from the Sea: memories of shoreside life in the days when fishermen's nets were often full, but their pockets usually empty, by David Butcher, Sulhampstead: Tops'l Books, 1982

Manual of Freediving: underwater on a single breath, by Umberto Pelizzari and Stefano Tovaglieri, Crystal River, FL: Idelson Gnocchi, 2004

North Shields: memories of fish 'n' ships, by Ron White, The People's History Ltd, 2002

Patterns for Guernseys and Jerseys, by Gladys Thompson, London: Batsford, 1969
The Bonny Fisher Lad, edited by Katrina Porteous, The People's History Ltd, 2002
The Driftermen: life in the tough days of Britain's vanished herring fleets, recalled by the men who manned them, by David Butcher, Reading: Tops'l Books, 1979
The Last of the Hunters: life with the fishermen of North Shields, by Peter Mortimer, Nottingham: Five Leaves, 2007
The Long Line: three plays by Tom Hadaway, North Shields: Iron Press, 1994
The Trawlermen: memories of the men who manned Britain's trawler fleets through the great days of sail and steam, by David Butcher, Reading: Tops'l books, 1980

ACKNOWLEDGEMENTS

Researching and writing *Herring Girl* has taken a very long time. My first notes, in September 2006, begin: 'A character investigating past lives – plus a sceptic. How can thoughts be transmitted? Time is not necessarily linear.' The person who accompanied me throughout this journey, who has been my first reader for over fifteen years, is playwright and creative writing tutor Margaret Wilkinson of Newcastle University. As well as commenting tirelessly on the structure and drafts of the novel, Margaret also guided me through Buddhist approaches to reincarnation and karma. She has been, and continues to be, the best possible writing companion.

I am also grateful to uber editorial consultant Lisanne Radice, who briskly intervened to renew my faith in the novel when my motivation was at a low ebb.

Hypnotherapist David Holmes conducted me though a past-life regression session, and introduced me to the character that would become Edith in *Herring Girl* – thank you so much. Thanks, too, to everyone who shared their past-life regression experiences with me, particularly the writer Amanda Scholes.

My fishing informants include ex-skipper Paul Dowse of Moir Seafoods in North Shields, Neil Robinson of the Port of Tyne Harbour Master's Office in North Shields, and the ever-intrepid Peter Mortimer, who chronicled the contemporary fishing experience in his book *Last of the Hunters*. I also want to thank Margaret Gill of the Dove Marine Laboratory of Newcastle University for information about local research into the feminization of fish.

Deep Blue in Whitley Bay taught me to dive, so thanks are due to them; and to Mark Hussman, for descriptions of his many North Sea dives – as well as guidance on Asian English syntax. Also to the Newcastle Electronic Corpus of Tyneside English (NECTE) at Newcastle University for archive recordings of Geordie dialect, which helped me 'hear' the historical conversations I was writing.

Like Mary, Laura and Ben in the novel, I spent many illuminating hours in the local history section of the library in North Shields, where the librarians – particularly Alan Senior – were incredibly knowledgeable, patient and helpful both to me and the many others trying to fathom the process of tracing the dead via census, microfiche, parish records, photography and website sources. I'm also grateful to librarians at the Tyne and Wear Archives at the Discovery Museum in Newcastle upon Tyne, who helped my research into the ownership and crew members of fishing vessels in the 1890s; to staff at the General Registry Office in North Shields, for advice on tracing people via birth, marriage and death records; and to John Crawford of the Buckie and District Heritage Centre, for a long discussion about sleeping (and other) arrangements aboard herring boats at the turn of the century.

Thanks are also due to the many people who responded to my advert in the local paper for reminiscences of La Continental Bar (aka 'The Jungle') in North Shields in the 1960s – especially Lillian Burn, Alan Fidler, and an elderly man who preferred not to give his name but who spoke to me for well over an hour about his experiences as a young gay merchant seaman.

I'm grateful too to Justin Dix, Senior Lecturer in Marine Geophysics and Geoarchaeology at the University of Southampton, who answered my many questions about what happens to the human body when immersed in the sea after death, and about circumstances that might help delay or prevent decomposition; and to Bob Williams of Aquapulse International Limited, for information about using ultrasound devices to search for items underwater.

None of these very obliging and generous informants should be held responsible if I have misunderstood, misinterpreted or misrepresented anything they have told me.

Finally, a huge thank you to my agent, Charlotte Robertson, for her intelligence, tenacity and energy, as well as for insights that helped shape the final manuscript; and to my editors, Rosalind Porter and Charlotte Van Wijk, and copy editor, Caroline Knight, for those last few crucial tweaks that an author simply can't see for herself, but which make all the difference.

Debbie Taylor
The Old High Light, North Shields

TYNEMOUTH WARD EAST
EMOUTH
D WEST
NORTH
HIELDS
ARD
RIVER TYNE
Sunday School
Brandling Ter.
Terrace
Hudson Street
Corporation Yard
Borough Saw Mills
Timber Yard
School
Dene Saw Mill
Low Lights Chemical Wks.
Chy.
Northumberland Street
East Percy Street
Saw Mill
School
Mission Church
Pearson Street
Church Street
Charlotte Street
Inn
Dockwray Square
High Lighthouse
Toll Square
Union Quay
Lighthouse
P.O.
Fish Quay
M.Ps
Peggy's Hole
Harbour Engine Wks.
Dolphins
Maitland's Quay
Dolphin
Low Dock
Ward Bdy.
Und.
C.C. at L.W.
Parly. & Mual. Boro. & Union Bdy.
Co. & Parly. Boro. Bdy.
G.P.O.
Town Hall
Market
Bank
East Popery Banks
Landing Stage
Ferry Station
Market Place
Direct Ferry
High Brewery
Bull Ring
Engine Works
Tyne Boiler Building Works (Disused)
Trinity Buoy House
Shipbuilding Yard
Lifeboat House
Slip
Salmon's Quay
Engineering Works
Corporation Staith
Grace's Home
Grave Yard
Mission Ho.
St. Stephen's Church
Marine Engine Works
Kirton's Quay
Boatbuilding Yards
Well
Brick Works
Clay Pit
Palatine Street